To Free a Soul

Duskwalker Beginnings

Book Two

Opal Reyne

ISBN: 978-1-7643370-0-7

Cover art: Sam Griffin
Editor/proofreader: Messenger's Memos

Author's note on language

I'm from AUSTRALIA.

My English is not the same as American English.
I love my American English spoken readers to bits. You're cute, you all make me giggle, and I just wanna give you a big ol' hug. However, there are many of you who don't seem to realise that your English was born from British English, which is what I use (although a bastardised version since Australians like to take all language and strangle it until it's a ruined carcass of slang, missing letters, and randomly added o's).

We don't seem to like the letter z.

We write colour instead of color. Recognise instead of recognize. Travelling instead of traveling. Skilful instead of skillfull. Mum instead of mom. Smelt is a past participle of smell. We omit the full-stop in Mr. Name, so it's Mr Name. Aussies cradle the word cunt like it's a sweet little puppy, rather than an insult to be launched at your face.

Anyway, happy reading.

<u>*Trigger Warning*</u>
Major spoiler below

Please only read further if you have triggers, otherwise you will seriously spoil the book for yourself.

Firstly, I will list what triggers **AREN'T** in the book so you can stop reading in order not to spoil it: No rape, non-con, purposeful harm done to the FMC by the MMC, torture, suicide/self-harm, ow/om drama, abortion, mental/emotional abuse, incest, or drug/alcohol abuse.

Please consider stopping here if your trigger has been detailed above as the rest are spoilers.

This duet (2 books) contains a wide range of triggers. Most of these have been detailed in the Duskwalker Brides series, but we see them from Lindiwe's and Weldir's perspectives.

Trigger warnings relating to book two:

Seizures and mental wellbeing revolving around Nathair's memory fragments.

There is death, grieving over death, and child loss. Faunus nearly dies, and Aleron does die. We know this from the main series, but the scenes revolving around this may be upsetting for many. There are also the issues revolving around Lindiwe and Merikh, as detailed in the main series.

There is A LOT of pregnancy. There are also scenes of childbirth and child rearing. These are all of our lovable Duskwalkers.

There are depictions of depression and mental health. Loneliness. Loss of identity.

Weldir is a god who eats souls, and Nathair is a serpent. There are vorarephobia triggers due to this.

Ophidiophobia trigger due to being bitten by a venomous snake.

Animal deaths, due to our Duskwalkers eating them and Lindiwe hunting them.

I'm going to put this here even though I don't really want to, but... the dreaded miscommunication trope. This series will be riddled with it, but please understand that almost all of their problems can't be fixed with a simple conversation. There are deeply rooted issues, and much learning has to happen before any healing can be done. This is a **slow burn.**

As always, my books have gore.

To all the MonsterFuckers out there who love a shadowy daddy,

this book is for you.

Weldir proves himself to be the ultimate dad by the end, but what becomes of his new form? It'll sparkle, it'll glint, and he'll do very naughty things to his mate with it.

I hope you're prepared for the surprise, the possessiveness, and all the spice we lacked in book one.

I would like to give a big shoutout to the wonderful **sensitivity readers** who helped to make this book a safe place for those I am trying to positively represent. As you all know, representation is a big part of what I want to do, but I want to do so in a way that isn't harmful.

Thank you to Diamond, Erin, and Anica for your contribution towards BIPOC sensitivity.

I would also like to give a special thank you to Ruthie for your contribution towards BIPOC and overall sensitivity.

I appreciate all the time and effort you put into helping me with this book. You will forever have a place in my heart.

PROLOGUE

A time unknown, but near the beginning

With a world-rumbling, desolate roar, Weldir threw himself against the confines of his enclosure. The obstacle, the very hindrance to his escape, thumped from the impact and then undulated outwards like rippling water.

He rushed to the other side of the fortification and crashed into the barricade there. The confines that kept him here, seething and storming, rippled again, and no matter how hard he shoved and shoved, they wouldn't relent.

With another roar, the sound beastly and inhuman even to him, he darted down through the ether of nothingness to find a weak point. He had no idea of the shape that kept him in – whether it was round, enneagon, or even rhombus. He'd never been able to find a corner, no matter how he tried.

"Let me out!" his impalpable, incomprehensible, discarnate essence bellowed. **"I tire of being in my prison!"**

He tired of being stuck here with nothing but himself and his disjointed thoughts!

"Hushhh, little one," a weak, feminine voice cooed at him, and a set of brown hands touched the outside of his prison. *"Shh. Shh."*

She spun it, brought it closer to her face, and the darkness gave way to dim light on one side. He did not feel his world shift or rotate in her space. Like the movement evaporated more of the darkness, a section below him glowed with life, revealing some kind of bed of thick, leafy vermillion-coloured vines.

The soft mound of a bosom pressed against his prison, as if she brought him closer to cuddle whatever shape he was in. Only then did a hard edge – revealing he wasn't in some kind of sphere – show itself. No matter how thoroughly he felt along that edge, he couldn't perceive it.

Weldir held back a growl, hating how she'd once stated it sounded like a cute, mousy squeak, due to their differing sizes. She was huge in comparison to his *prism*, as she was able to gather it in her arms like it was precious.

Her palm rubbed the edge of his prism, momentarily obstructing his view of her haggard face as she attempted to soothe him without ever touching his very form. He often wondered if she truly did it for herself, pacifying her guilt and regret in a falsehood of trying to ease him.

Nothing would ease him, not in here.

Once the shield of her palm was gone, he peered into her eyes. They lacked pupils, making her golden irises appear like discs that flickered over his crystal entrapment, unable to see him.

Although her eyes were utterly mesmerising, the rest of her features were drained and worn. Like every bit of liquid and fat had been sucked from her very body, her brown face was gaunt and her skin loose, wrinkled, and ashen. It made her nose, cheeks, and arching brows more prominent in an unhealthy way, showing just how sickly she'd become since he'd been trapped here.

This wasn't the face of his *mother* that he remembered.

Her youthfulness was still apparent, but her skin had once been plump and vibrant.

Her lips had been full, and so ample that just the minutest flick of her tongue against the seam had them dipping as though unbelievably malleable. Now, they were thin, dehydrated, and cracked, surrounded by wrinkled lines that made her mouth droop.

Her hair had once been a magnificent cloud of springy, corkscrew golden curls, so tight they haloed her head. Now they were white, brittle, and lacking in volume, as if the very health of them had been sucked away – just like their golden colour.

Behind her, iridescent wings unattached to her back flickered before quickly sagging upon the vermillion vines and the silver bedding. They once glowed a glittering gold, much like the crown that still floated above her head like an angelic halo, but both had dulled immensely.

The whites of her eyes reddened and her bottom lip shook. *"You just need to control your form, and then I can free you."*

Weldir, unable to hold it back any longer, let his growl reverberate all around him.

"I know I've been saying that for so long," she croaked, then glittering water brimmed her eyes. She pressed her forehead to his prism and gave a shuddering sob.

His growl ceased when one of her tears, clear like water, fell upon the bed below her. It met a dried pool of flaking gold – the evidence of other tears she'd long ago shed.

Her eyes no longer leak gold, he thought, observing the fresh tears she shed. *Crying is sapping away the little mana she has left in her reserves...*

Well, other than keeping him here.

His prism, the prison that kept him in this darkness, was all she could muster. Her mana was dependent upon her life force, and as her eyes drooped, she continued to waste a little more in crying... for *him*.

It wasn't enough to pacify his fury, but it was enough to keep him quiet about it.

"I'm so sorry I did this to you," she cried into the glasslike barrier keeping him in. A few of her tresses snagged on the vines, straightening their lengths before releasing and springing back into curls. *"I'm so sorry that I can't help you."*

Her tears, pity, and apologies did much to soothe him further, and he grumbled as he brought himself closer.

"I know you did not mean to do this," he stated, pressing himself against the barrier right where her cheek was.

Although she couldn't hear him, his bashing against the inside of his prism had managed to stir her from her deep, regenerative slumber.

"Weldir... my sweet little pool of darkness. I'm so sorry I didn't protect you as I was supposed to, and needed you to save me."

He pulled away from the barrier and stared at her.

I wish she would stop blaming herself. No one had known this would happen. *She was only trying to protect the mortals, as is her duty.*

It's not her fault that I am merely a floating consciousness.

Weldir, in his prism, entirely lacked a form. He *was* the darkness within it, the empty vastness of nothing. A being whose shroud of consciousness ate all the light. He couldn't touch himself, see himself. He could be heard, but his voice was too quiet, like the echoing in the back of someone's mind.

In reality, his prism of whatever fucking shape was made of a crystal so pure it looked like glass. Inside it should have been penetrable to the eye, and had it been anyone else, they would have been seated inside it and able to wave to the outside world.

No. He filled it like a storm of clouds, and his roars and growls were merely a squeaky thunder she could *just* perceive.

It'd been that way for *Elven* decades.

From the very moment he'd been born and his consciousness had tried to absorb anything and everything. From the Elven world she rested inside of, to the other deities he'd consumed until not even a fragment of them survived. His cloud had eaten his many fathers, his brothers, his sisters, and even one of the three pinnacle deities – an uncle, one of the triplets.

All that remained was her, one of his potential fathers, and Rökul – an uncle. His grandparents, long forgotten, no longer existed within this plane of life and hadn't for a long time. The god in charge of death had made her own realm to be with the many dead, but she was a recluse and preferred the quiet.

They all doubted she knew what had happened to her fellow deities, or it was possible she cared so little that she still hadn't returned. Mayhap it was even fear that Weldir would break from his prism and consume her as well that kept her at bay all these decades.

She must know, he often thought. *Those eaten by the Daekura will have told her.*

And the Daekura were the very reason as to why Weldir was the way he was. When he looked up at the Gilded Maiden, who no longer shed ethereal golden tears, the Daekura were also the reason for her frail state.

He couldn't ignore his hand in all this, despite the fact that he'd been prematurely born, disorientated, and incapable of controlling his mist. He'd just greeted the world, malformed and too soon.

He remembered nothing of when she tried to aid the Daekura by giving them fully evolved forms. He'd been told the tale of how she'd taken the darkness that housed their bodies and caused their hunger, so they could live normal Elven lives like she could sense they were supposed to.

She wanted to love them and bring them into her heart, like all the Elysian Elves who lived within Nyl'theria.

His mother, the Gilded Maiden, could never have known how chaotic that darkness was. She was supposed to be immortal, with nearly infinite mana to offer, with power so strong and magnificent that no other could compare.

Yet it infected her. It festered within the well of her mana pool and drained it away from her very bloodstream.

Within the heartbeat it'd taken for it to reach Weldir, his unborn body had nurtured her in return as a means of survival. He took that darkness, consumed it himself until *he* became the void, the death, the *evil* that it was, and made it his own.

But Almethrandra, his mother, couldn't hold that kind of chaotic energy. She couldn't heal through it, siphon it out, or fix it. Her body gave up, vomiting black goop from the pit of her immortal soul. Golden tears had run black, and anything they touched melted and sickened.

Her womb couldn't hold him as he roiled and toiled under the broken power he'd absorbed. He had left the safety she provided *violently*.

What followed was him reaching out to anything and everything for stability in an attempt to find a physical form when his own transcended space and reality. It wanted to house something or be the centre of something, and yet nothing he touched offered salvation.

When the crystal cage surrounding him had locked in tight, and he'd stared down at his uncle Rökul, the god's lavender skin had paled, the blue of his hair dull as he'd writhed on the ground, gaunt, thin, with his mana and lifeblood half eaten. Just a few seconds longer, and he, too, may have been consumed in Weldir's birthing frenzy.

The first thing he remembered afterwards was Almethrandra's shaking hands holding his prism as she limped around, only to collapse. Weldir had bounced – he didn't know how far – into a corner of the room and underneath something. It'd been an exceptionally long time before he'd been retrieved and placed within Leyfr's vermillion mending vines alongside his mother.

Silence had been his life from then on.

Until memories played around him. A life he didn't know nor understand, singing, dancing, and movement all around him.

It took him too long to realise they were Almethrandra's, and even longer to understand that it was knowledge about her, their realm, and sometimes even the lives of Elysians in their parallel mortal world.

When she'd had very little to give, she'd played them for him when he'd bashed against his prison, and had wept as she did – just as she did now. But her lucidity was infrequent and short, and already he could see her eyelids waning against the tiredness.

"Hurry up and collect your essence, so that I may hold you

one day," she whispered with an exhausted sniffle.

He growled at that.

He had no idea how to do such a thing! *Do you think I have not tried? My efforts are for naught!* Yet rather than focusing on escaping once more, he turned his endeavours inwards.

He pulled at the cloudy, fraying edges of his conscience. He sucked, he yanked, he pushed and pushed to no avail, as he'd done the years before and would continue to do for the years to come.

He ate at himself, and coughed himself up. He eclipsed himself, and shadowed what he could. He bubbled, boiled, and frothed in the darkness of his own vastly empty self.

All the while, she slept peacefully and shared dreams that always sat at the very edge of his periphery. He chased those sounds, those images, as much as himself, his mist and cloud circling and circling, *rumbling* and *rolling,* until...

He didn't know whether it was yesterday or tomorrow that it happened.

Much like the Daekura, with their glossy void-black bodies, something formed. It was transparent, ghostly, and gave the impression that nothing else was inside him except essence.

After so long, Weldir couldn't help staring in awe at the only part of him he'd ever created.

A spectral, shadowy, pitch-black right hand.

In that same moment, he realised his stomach held another place, a realm somewhere outside of himself – and just as trapped within his prism.

ONE

October 9th, 1830

The soft candlelight illuminated a well-polished Blackbutt desk scattered with an array of thickly bound leather books. Its orange radiance shone along the thin nib of a feathered quill pen, and the glass vial of ink refracted just enough to cast an orb of muted light against the pages of an open journal.

Bookshelves situated against every wall gave the room a musty aroma. The scent tingled her sinuses, occasionally making her nose wiggle as she tried to ignore the irritation mixing with the pleasant frankincense that wafted from every nook and cranny of this temple. The wooden floor was cold, allowing a draft to creep underneath the skirt of her long robes, ensuring she shivered.

Lindiwe straightened and sat back from the book to glance at the dying fireplace safely tucked away from all the flammable material. With just a twitch of her face, a shadowy tentacle glittering with sand formed.

The magical limb curled around a log of dried firewood and gently placed it atop the smouldering embers. New flames licked at its fibres, and before long, the chill in the air subsided.

She was able to concentrate on her studies peacefully.

Autumn cooled this part of the world. Snow collected upon the windowsill in front of her, partially obscuring the view from the tower in which she sat. The creeping shadows of late night made it even harder to ascertain the outside world, but the strategic sprinkling of firelight glowed a path to a stronghold opposing this temple.

Guild members trained well into the evening tonight, and she only watched in pensive thought or to relax her tiring eyes. They were there, and she was here in a different stronghold, but it often seemed like her current life swayed and pulled between both.

It'd been that way for eighteen years.

The length of time passing may have been long and strenuous for humans, with their finite number of years, but for her... it was merely a time which she spent in the northwest of Unerica, a country so large it only outsized Austrális by a fraction. Although she'd been staying in this city for that long, she'd been living in Unerica for over twice that. She could be here for another eighteen years, and it wouldn't matter to her as someone undying.

She'd given birth in Unerica two times already and had let her monstrous children roam free to hunt Demons. After spending a year or so with each of them, guiding them to make sure they didn't drown before they knew better, or helping them against predators, there was no reason to visit them when they were mindless and easy to enrage.

Once they understood life, she returned to hole up in this large city, studying and training as if the minutes ticking by didn't matter. It had long become a hobby she threw herself into with tenacity and unbending will.

Slipping the shaft of the quill from its ink, she waited for the excess to drip back into the bottle before scribbling down a note in her journal. Lindiwe copied the words from the temple book, so she had the knowledge for her own safekeeping.

This journal was one of many she owned, which were scattered between her room within this stronghold, and the world she'd only visited fleetingly in the past eighteen years to create life. A place of beautiful nothingness, of comforting weightlessness; somewhere so vast it could hold all the knowledge she wished to retain without the evidence of time withering it away.

Somewhere in the ether, she had her own library. Most of it was filled with books she'd scribbled her notes into, many taken from dilapidated buildings before they could be fully destroyed.

Her haven. And her home, considering she still lacked one in the real, living world.

After slipping her quill back into the ink jar, she raised her arms above her head and stretched to relieve the tension from slouching over the table like a prawn. She tilted her head to the left until the muscles in her neck screamed in protest, then moved it the opposite way before arching over the book in front of her once more.

"Hello, Lindiwe," a familiar, depravedly decadent voice rumbled in the back of her mind.

Her youthful features, still twenty-two and unageing, twitched in surprise before falling into a nondescript, unbothered expression.

"Hello, spirit of the void," she answered.

"Ughhh," he groaned out. She could almost imagine those chalky, dark lips pulling back in disgust to reveal glossy black fangs. *"I've always hated being called that."*

A laugh almost slipped out, but she skilfully twisted it into a hum. "You only hate it because *he* gave you that name."

He, being Jabez, someone who Weldir had never hidden his dislike of.

"Sure, but why must it be spirit?" he argued. *"I'm more than that. Could it not be god of darkness, or god of the void?"*

"Demi-god," she corrected, unable to quell the small, playful smile that curled her lips.

"A god is a god, no matter their status. The only reason I'm not a fully fledged deity is due to my lack of a form."

Lindiwe pouted. "It's only a title."

"An unbefitting one. It's equivalent to me saying, 'The human that sits in that chair.' It has little meaning."

"If it has little meaning, it should mean little to you."

A soft growl enveloped her, one that had her insides quivering with delight. *"You, raven, are starting to become irksome in your teasing."*

An outright laugh escaped her, and she leaned back in her chair. "What else would you have me do? I can't say your name freely, and I do love the way you pout at being called 'spirit of the void.'" She surveyed the cosy library and its bright and flaming fireplace. "You shouldn't have given away how much it vexes you."

"Perhaps not," he grumbled.

She leaned her elbow on the table and placed her chin in her awaiting palm. Her smile of humour softened. *He complains that I'm not forthcoming, and then still complains when I tease him.* Over the many years, she'd learned it was rather easy to ruffle Weldir's mist.

And of course she took every ample opportunity to do so.

They'd found a comfortable push and pull between them. He'd become her friend in the longevity of her life, and she often leaned on the rare and infrequent moments their disjointed relationship shared.

She needed that light, as her life was often shrouded in darkness. Weldir was Weldir; his ability to share deep emotions was as stilted as ever. He was capable of understanding, but he lacked the ability to share in anything real or truly empathise.

It didn't help that they were worlds apart.

He was there, Lindiwe here, and no love had ever blossomed between them. Just a fondness in the quiet foreverness. She was still his servant, and he her master. She was still a human, and he a god from another fantastical realm.

It was doubtful their hearts would ever align.

Least of all, from his side. And without true nurturing, *never* from hers.

"You have yet to tell me why you're bothering me on this fine evening," she stated playfully.

"All you do is study your little spellbooks. I hardly believe I

can 'bother' you during such a task."

"They're not spellbooks, and you know it." She picked up a round spectacle and hovered it over the lines within the book. Words of another language shifted to English under the glass, while the surrounding lettering remained foreign. "I'm grateful the Anzúli are allowing me to study their work."

"Pertaining to spells. Hence, spellbooks."

Lindiwe rolled her eyes. "And alchemy, history, and all the other tidbits of knowledge I've discovered in this library."

Her lips pursed, and she narrowed her eyes at the line she needed to read twice. Although she understood Anzúlean, the language of the Anzúli, there were a few words that still escaped her.

They often blended together to create a conglomerate of confusing adverbs for Anzúlean, with little added stars and swishes that required context to understand. She'd learned most of them, but having her translation spectacle, which resembled a magnifying glass with a chain instead of a handle, made it comfortable sitting in this library for long periods of time.

By the will of her mind, she could shape the words to translate into English. And with just a little more thought, she could also shift the translation to any Earthly language. The translation spectacle was a much needed and very beloved tool.

"You could always steal these books and study them in my realm," he offered, his deep voice devoid of any emotion that *should* have accompanied such words.

"I'd rather not steal from these kind people. And secondly, Earth is where I belong. I can't live in your realm." She almost ended her words with 'Weldir' to ensure her point was well made, but she couldn't say his name here. "Must I point out that you have yet to tell me what you need of me?"

When there was a small pause, she pulled away from viewing through her spectacle to wait patiently.

"It has been many years, Lindiwe. The land you currently reside in is vast, and I would like more of our offspring there. Especially north of your location."

The delightful shiver tore down her spine and collected as a heating pool between her thighs, making her squeeze them together. More offspring meant more *sex*, and Lindiwe found that titillating and body-thrumming at just the mere mention.

It had been sixty-nine years since Leonidas was brought into the world, and the procreation begetting him had been the beginning of passion between them. They'd brought six other Duskwalkers into the world since then, although none in Austrális. Two more in Zafrikaan, one in Pyrssia, then one in Siran. She even did her duty while she was here in Unerica, in this city, leaving for a few months to a year to grow them, spend time with them, and then gift them their adulthood with their skulls and horns to wander Unerica as Weldir's unwitting servants.

Each bout of intimacy was hotter and wilder than the last.

She'd come to long for those moments. For lust to swirl inside her like a destructive cyclone, abrading her down to her very core and leaving behind a trembling, wet woman floating in ethereal darkness.

Even now, it had her skin flaring with heat, and the pool between her thighs dampened further.

She wanted to claw into his chalky body or his physical barriers with need, bliss, and mind-bending euphoria. Her nipples pebbled under her thick robes, scraping against the material, but they wanted to graze against whatever solid patches of his torso he could manage with his lacking form. Her thighs pleaded for the same pleasurable torture around his narrow hips.

Oh, but there had been wormy tendrils there too. They clung to her breasts, pinching her nipples as they circled, or glided between her sensitive thighs and the lips of her throbbing folds. Minor additions that didn't last long when he finally made his way inside her and broke Lindiwe apart little by little until she became a needy mess – or a satisfied puddle – for him.

Despite her physical reaction, her tone was heavy with disappointment. "If that's what you want."

"You can always return, as you have before."

I know that, but... my time here is ending. I'm almost done reading all of their texts, so why return for those few when I can just do so now? Especially if I stay away for a few years and... Although it was doubtful the Anzúli would let this stronghold and its close neighbour fall, it still worried her. *Their magic isn't as strong as it started out.*

Generations had already passed. The Anzúli had been on Earth for almost a hundred and fifty years, and many had lost their lives when they first came here. Their numbers dwindled and then flourished as they found lovers within their sector or in others, only to grow stagnant once more.

Many were young. Most of those living in this temple stronghold were under the age of twenty, and over half of those were under the age of thirteen. The adults were spread out between taking care of their children and helping the humans outside the borders of this large city.

It was even harder for those who didn't have a newly built Demon slaying stronghold attached to them, like this one. The western sector of the Unerica guild was lucky in this regard, but no other temple had such additional protection.

She opened her mouth to respond, but her desk candle flickered in a gust from the door behind her as it opened. She greeted the interrupter of her conversation and thoughts with an inquisitive brow furrow.

"Evening, Lindiwe," Kyrah muttered, storming into the library and immediately moving along the wall of shelves in a wild search.

"Come to join me, have you?" Lindiwe prodded with a mischievous grin.

The brunette woman paused, turned to Lindiwe, and sneered over her glasses. "You know I would never. You can stay buried beneath these boring pages, and I'll be right where I belong: not here."

Ignoring Weldir, who was likely waiting for an answer and watching them, she lowered her translation tool and placed her chin in her hand once more. "Come on, surely you can't detest reading *that* much."

"I wouldn't say I detest it. The act of reading just isn't one I find enthralling."

"Then why are you here?" Waving with her free hand, Lindiwe gestured towards the book in front of her. "I was enjoying myself before you came stomping in here like a trist."

"A trist! Ha!" Kyrah exclaimed with a false laugh. "How absurd." Then she narrowed her inhuman lime-green eyes at Lindiwe, all three of them. Her pursed lips softened, only for her to chew the bottom one and reveal the youth in her nineteen-year-old gaze. "I don't really stomp around like a trist, do I?"

The laugh that burst from Lindiwe was raw and loud, and she bounced in her chair slightly. "You're asking the wrong person, Kyrah. I've never seen any of your creatures."

Kyrah stamped her foot, and the floor gave a resounding thud beneath her boot. "But you're *how* old?" The young woman threw her hands up. "If you've really lived almost two hundred Earth years, surely you've been to Anzúla and seen one."

Lindiwe had stopped hiding her immortality from the Anzúli. She'd also stopped pretending that she was touched by Uxos' – their great goddess of shadows – magic.

They knew all that she was willing to share, except what she wasn't – *who* her power came from and was forever tied to.

Lindiwe waved to the book in front of her, which had no relation to what she was about to say, but would highlight her point. "I only know what I've read. If you picked up a book every once in a while, maybe you could have answered that yourself."

She'd dived into the world of Anzúla – home realm of Kyrah's people – through the knowledge of pages. A trist resembled an ogre, if an ogre and a moth had a baby. They were fuzzy, large beings, thick of muscle and gut, with moth-like wings and antennae, and an oddly human face. Yet, despite their nine-foot height and heavy frames, they could be quite agile in flight.

Delicate in the sky, loud on the ground.

"And I would say two hundred years is a bit of a stretch. I believe I look more like my age, a hundred and seventy."

"You look barely twenty-four, and you know it," Kyrah argued, pushing her glasses up her thin nose.

Due to the thickness of the glass, and the fact that there were three pieces required for the woman's three eyes, their heaviness caused them to slip back down the bridge of her nose. The two lower frames were octagonal, with the top one diamond-shaped to fit on the bridge of her spectacles.

Kyrah spun away, her white robes fluttering around her lean calves as she continued her search. "I'll get out of your hair shortly. One of the Unerica sectors would like a certain spell, and apparently we have it."

I should have guessed, considering the hour and her primary skill. Kyrah was best with scrying, which had been tested and confirmed to be her primary skill.

Choosing to leave the woman be, Lindiwe peered outside. The Demon Hunter Incorporation's stronghold was still bright. With all those torches, it was hard to believe the hour was late. Those who weren't protecting the city that surrounded both their stronghold and the Anzúli temple would soon be crawling to their hard beds.

"Is it okay if I return to you by the end of the year?" Lindiwe stated, tapping her index finger against the table. "I think I can finish everything I need to by then."

"Talking to *him* again, are you?" Kyrah commented dully.

"Then I shall see you shortly," Weldir stated through their bond, his voice echoing around in her mind. *"I'm intrigued to see how many souls you have collected with the Demon Hunters."*

Her lips curled at that. *You have no idea.* She had quite the surprise for him.

"Yes, I speak with the spirit of the void," she answered Kyrah.

A groan forced its way through the bond, and her lips curled further, but with humour. She picked up her translation tool and inspected the spell she'd been engrossed in earlier.

A way to create illusions of creatures through blood magic. They would do little but frighten someone or give the impression that the wielder didn't travel alone. She wondered if she could give the illusion of having bears, cougars, or even wolves as companions in her travels to frighten off the Demons.

Tracing the inscription with her fingertips, she read the notes. *I don't even need a body. Just the blood and the incantation will do to recreate the animal.* The only visual indication that the illusion wasn't real would be the presence of flickering flames coming off its flesh, fur, or feathers.

Her elbow came out from underneath her when Kyrah rudely stole the book she was reading. She'd been so light on her feet, likely after Lindiwe's earlier teasing, that she'd snuck up on her.

"*You,*" Kyrah sneered, with a playful glint in her lime eyes. Her delicate dark brows narrowed as her pale cheeks puffed out. "You had the book I wanted all along!"

Without another word, Kyrah spun on her heels, wafting a cascade of vanilla and something else otherworldly over Lindiwe before stomping out.

"Hey! I was reading that!" Lindiwe yelled, throwing her arm over the chair's backrest towards the door that was already slamming shut.

With a sigh, she slipped back into her chair properly. "Gosh. That girl has no manners." Another smile spread across her face. "She reminds me of myself when I lived with my parents."

The yearning in her heart panged, but it was merely an echo of nostalgia. Of long ago – a time not forgotten but very much a healed wound.

I guess tomorrow I should train with the Demon Hunter Incorporation. She groaned, already imagining the aches and pains. Just as she'd been training with the Anzúli in their temple, she'd also been learning how to wield weapons, so she could fight using those she could conjure with magic.

She leaned forward and blew out her candle, and let the shadows she was familiar with guide her.

Someone else would come to put out the fireplace. Her gaze flicked over the wooden protection charm above its mantle, etched with the Anzúli symbol. At the fireplace's mouth, a translucent sphere held back the smoke and flames licking against the spell.

The Anzúli had magic for everything; even something as simple as stopping this library from burning down when there was no one monitoring the flames.

TWO

Black feathers tickled up and down the edge of Lindiwe's jaw as the high altitude billowed around her. She pulled her raven cloak of feathers tighter over her shoulders, adjusting the material so it sat more comfortably.

More snow was expected to fall for a minimum of another month, but at least it would begin to taper off in the coming weeks as the world in the northern hemisphere warmed. The southern hemisphere would only grow colder now.

Her white dress robes did little to keep out the wind, but she couldn't feel the cold with the Anzúli talisman tied to the inside of her cloak. To her, the snow cushioning her seat upon the tallest tower of the Demon Hunter Incorporation was nothing but a soft place to rest.

She couldn't say the same for those below.

"They really do look like Demons from up here," Lindiwe mused, as she watched those waking up to begin their morning routine of exercise and training.

Each member wore their uniform, including the mouth covering and hood. Many shrouded themselves temporarily in thick black cloaks, while others had donned white ones to match the snow as camouflage. That was the only spot of colour for now, although in the warmer seasons, they often shrouded themselves in thin brown or green cloaks to match their environment.

She swept her gaze over the many collecting in the courtyards or outdoor training areas, some of them weary-eyed and bleak as they rubbed their tired faces. Once their overseer of training yelled, many of them promptly stiffened in alertness.

"I've told you before that they appear like Demons," Weldir responded, his voice distant as always, but no less husky and inviting.

"Yeah, I know. I just keep forgetting until I see them from afar," she stated. "If I wasn't well familiar with their uniforms, I wouldn't be able to decipher the difference."

She'd trained with them many times over the past two decades, to the vexation of most guildmembers. Being an honorary Demon Hunter, not in name or rank, ruffled a lot of pride-hurt feathers.

She'd been an outlier; someone who'd trained with them but lacked a position within the guild.

It still amazes me how often humankind will evolve similar ideas, even when they're worlds apart. The Demon Hunter Inc., Knights of Shadow, Night Stalkers, and Demonslayers, were all names of different organisations that were created to hunt Demons.

Most wore very similar black outfits, choosing to fade into the shadows like their enemies by wearing tight-fitting, quiet material. *Then again, I think the Anzúli* – who all spoke to each other through scrying tools – *have been guiding them.*

Their outfits resembled each other's just a little too closely for coincidence, as did their ranking system. Even their strongholds were similar no matter what part of the world she travelled to, although this could be due to history having a hand in it.

Since she was from Austrális, she considered them all Demonslayers, but in this country, they were controlled by the Demon Hunter Incorporation.

I don't like how they force trade here for protection, though.

In most other places across the world, their assistance was free or trade was appreciated, but Unerica still had a rather unfair bartering system. The Knights of Shadow – or Shadow Knights – were more like religious templars. Their god of worship? Somehow, they'd taken Uxos' partner, Yavol, as their leader. Then again, Yavol was the god of war and destruction, so Lindiwe found that to be rather fitting.

Just further proof the Anzúli are guiding them...

She searched the soft pinks and lilacs of the dawning sky.

Fluffy clouds glowed with orange, like the very edges of their minuscule droplets had caught fire. She'd flown through many clouds and had come to discover they were nothing but puffs of water, each time leaving her feathers damp. When she'd flown for too long, she often tried to gulp at the clouds for refreshment.

Maybe it's time I change my feathers, she thought, wondering if the horizon could give her an answer on that matter. *It's been over a hundred years since my cloak was first created.*

She often pondered on whether or not her monstrous children would react to her differently if she didn't appear like the very creatures they fought against.

But I love my raven form, my cloak. She had a deep attachment to them, as they offered a sense of freedom. *And I wouldn't know what other kind of bird to pick.*

An eagle? If so, she'd rather choose the wedge-tailed eagle, as it was larger than the one in Unerica, and much more ferocious. *Most of their feathers are brown.* Which, for Lindiwe, was just too close to a raven's dark plumage and could easily be mistaken.

I could choose a rainbow lorikeet or a parrot. Then again, she wasn't inclined to be too colourful either.

There are many species of owls... And she did like their meaning: wisdom. Many cultures considered them a warning, while others saw them as spiritual protection. *I guess an owl would be a good choice.*

"Hey, Weldir," she started, pulling her satchel closer to her lap. "I'm ready to leave now."

"I was wondering why you had that thoughtful look upon your face."

Her brows furrowed deeper. "I didn't have a look on my face. This is how my face always is."

"Then you must always look thoughtful."

She'd spent nearly eighteen years here, and it was the longest she'd spent anywhere. It was understandable that she was forlorn. But it couldn't compare to the yearning in her heart to find that home in Austrális, the place in which she was born.

"Are you going to say goodbye this time?" he asked, with a hint of curiosity in that rough voice of his.

She *almost* shivered in delight at it, knowing what would come after she left this place.

"No. I've never been great at goodbyes, and I told the Anzúli when I first arrived that I may just up and disappear. The elders will explain it to the others."

It was time to withdraw from society and life, and be Weldir's semi-obedient servant once more. Wholeheartedly.

"Before you take me to your realm, I want to thank you for allowing me to stay here for as long as I saw fit. I obtained a lot of useful knowledge that will help us, and it was nice immersing myself amongst people again after so long."

"Of course, Lindiwe. I trust your judgement."

She smiled. His trust was not unfounded, and she'd long ago begun to tentatively trust him in return.

Even after all this time, astonishment always filled Lindiwe when she materialised in Weldir's realm. It wasn't Tenebris, as she'd never been fully eaten by him, but it was his world, his place, his empty darkness.

For over a hundred and fifty years, it remained unchanged.

As did its owner – mostly.

He was still just swirling fragments, as if all the souls he consumed never truly added to his lacking solidness.

His growing mist stops him from obtaining any semblance of a real form. Over the decades, she'd seen those tiny black granules reach further and further, swiping through forests, mountains, and meadows. *Sometimes it feels like a waste to give him souls when it does little to grow him.*

For once, just once, she'd like to see him in completion, rather than as ribbons of chalky, globby outlines, or like layers of black see-through frayed cloth – like now. It depended on how his tangible parts were made up that day.

"Hello, little raven," he greeted, his voice louder and no longer echoing now that he was before her.

The urge to needle him and call him spirit of the void pestered her, but she kept that to herself.

"Hello, Weldir." Lindiwe shifted into her Phantom form, the one that was tangible to a deity of spirit, and dug into one of her side satchels. "I have much to give you today."

"I can sense that."

Tiny flames hovering and twirling inside a vial began to empty before she'd even retrieved it. As if the glass itself was meaningless, the white flames exited through the very sides. What were barely the size of her thumb now sparked to life and grew to the size of her palm as they floated towards his outreaching hand.

Multiple souls rotated around his upward-pointing claws, and enough of his face coalesced to reveal a proud smile.

"You've brought me eleven this time."

Lindiwe rolled her eyes as she pushed the magically re-enforced vial to the side to obtain other items. *Of course that's all he truly cares about.*

Yet, the moment she pulled out one of her many journals, the blunt end of a black glittering tendril tipped back the spine like how one might pull it from a shelf. It brought it to him, and he folded his legs as the pages quickly flickered open.

He was reading them, committing them to memory, even as

the pages turned so quickly it was nearly indiscernible to the human eye. A pattern followed with the seven others he took, and each one furrowed his brows, until his head completely disappeared to reveal his thinly muscled shoulders and chest.

"So many spells. Most of these look unhelpful," he muttered. "How does magic detection assist you? Or changing your eye colour?"

Lindiwe shrugged as she pulled out her final journal. "I thought they were good to memorise at the time. I may need to detect magic in the future, and learning how to change my eye colour is the first lesson they teach children to produce a glamour."

"Why would you want to produce a glamour?" His headless torso moved as if he looked up at her pointedly, not that she could bloody well see his expression. "You're lovely as you are."

Her cheeks warmed due to the unprovoked compliment, and her eyes shied away. He didn't often offer them, as he could be rather rough around the edges.

She took them at face value, rather than assuming anything substantial. Weldir probably found beauty in her, in the same way he'd see it in a tree or a precious rock. Just something that was pleasing to his eye, but in the grand scheme of his heart – nothing.

"It doesn't matter anyway. Your magic doesn't allow me to glamour myself, so some of the spells I've written down are a tad pointless."

She pulled pouches of seeds from her bag, some crystals, and then a bag with a grainy powder. Tendrils collected all of them and dragged them through the ether. He opened each item, noting the contents with curiosity, only to pause at the final one.

"Why do you have a bag of salt?" he asked, pinching a few pieces.

"Hey! Be careful with that."

Swaying her hands to push herself forward, she closed the distance between them as though they were floating on the surface of water. She cupped what solid parts of his hand she could, making him drop what he'd pinched back into the small satin bag.

"That salt is blessed," she stated, pulling the drawstrings shut. "Just a pinch is enough to bless a five-kilo bag. I can't replicate the protection spell, so I'd rather not waste a single bit of it."

He absentmindedly tossed it behind him into the ether of his world using a tiny tendril wrapped around the neck of the pink bag.

"There are more important things I can focus on." Hands formed, and they brushed over the feathers of her cloak covering her biceps. "You've come over to me, which is very unlike you."

The tips of her ears heated. He was right; she'd put herself almost against him. Her heart betrayed her and picked up its rhythm, stammering in her chest because she *knew* what was coming next. It also fluttered shyly because Weldir, somehow, had learned to be rather sultry and teasing with his words.

It was surely a fabrication, all designed to entice her for sex, and Lindiwe was unashamedly drawn to it. She didn't care if it was fake and forced, not when she found it arousing all the same. His husky, rich, and sinful voice was perfect, and it added a layer to his words that could easily soften her into needy putty in his barely existent hands.

"First, though, you did bring me a meal." He lifted his chalky left hand, and the eleven souls of deceased humans came from seemingly nowhere and twirled above it.

Then they shrank for ease of consumption.

Lindiwe once thought she'd be unnerved by watching him eat souls. Turned out she wasn't.

He leaned back, so she wasn't in his way, and placed one in his mouth. Weldir didn't chew, his fangs likely capable of destroying them to pieces, but merely swallowed it whole. His face, neck, and chest seared with white light before it dissipated into darkness where his stomach was – Tenebris.

With each one he ate, he gained a mere *millimetre* of growth to his form, but it would still allow him to better touch her and vice versa. Her body thrummed in preparation, and with the anticipation she'd come to cherish in his presence.

It was the only reason she ever came here.

"*Now* I'm ready," Weldir playfully rumbled, wrapping his arms around her waist.

He pulled her flush against him, but much of her sunk through where his body should be. What was solid allowed her to not fully meld into him.

A mischievous smile curled her lips as she pulled on the tie of her feathered cloak. It floated off her shoulders, and she wrapped her arms around his neck.

I want to try something different.

Her body thrummed with excitement at her plan.

THREE

February 28th, 1831

Lindiwe no longer flinched whenever Weldir leaned in for a kiss. After the last few successful times, she'd garnered faith that he could be gentle... and it wouldn't feel as though she'd been punched in the mouth with a brick.

She met him halfway, her heart leaping for the feel of his soft lips, and the way hers would eventually swell.

Her eyelids lowered, and she wrapped her arms further around his neck to deepen the kiss. The hardness under her forearms was a barrier over his shoulders to support her, as he still lacked enough of a physical body for her to rest upon.

She didn't mind. He was trying, had proven that many times, and that's what she appreciated.

In the past, the beginning of sex had been a little stilted. She'd held onto this awkwardness around him, and she'd been able to sense a small amount of nervousness from him. There had always been a pause where they assessed each other, both trying to get closer yet fumbling their way to the first touch.

She adored that this might be the start where none of that was needed. For once, it felt natural.

They knew why she was here, as she only ever came to his realm for this reason – to create children for him. Well, that's why *he* wanted her here, whereas Lindiwe had long ago begun to crave the creation.

The years in between allowed her mind and body to build up the anticipation. Now her nails dug into the barriers over his shoulders as she tilted her head for more and moaned when he deepened the kiss himself.

The press of his long canines occasionally nipping on her bottom lip by accident felt wrong – a reminder that he wasn't human. That's what made it feel naughtier. The wetness of her own saliva, as Weldir didn't have any, mingled between them, and she braved sucking on his lower lip. She then bit down on it and tugged, catching him off-guard.

He broke the kiss. His mouth darted to the sensitive spot on her throat, and her pulse thumped against his lips when he bit down on it in retaliation.

She didn't know whether to giggle or moan, but the latter won out when he sucked on it. His nose traced the side of her neck as if with purpose, and a cascade of goosebumps prickled down her body. He gripped her backside, and his big palms kneaded roughly, pushing her more against the parts of him that were tangible.

Her nipples hardened against the silky white Anzúli robes, and as the prickles descended further, they collected in a hot, needy coil low in her belly. Arousal pooled between her thighs, and she tilted her head back while biting her bottom lip.

Weldir's hands – the palms of them tangible while the backs of them weren't – caressed up her curves. His fingers dug into the seams of the material around her shoulders, and his claws lightly nicked her heating skin. He drew open the neckline of the garment and pulled it down as he licked across her neck, another wonderful shiver cascading over her.

By the time she was unclothed, her body thrummed for the next step, when so long ago she'd been utterly terrified about it.

His soft lips, more malleable than usual, lowered to suck across her left collarbone.

"Weldir, wait," she whispered, reaching up to grab his left horn since it was more visible, and therefore tangible.

He paused just as he placed his mouth against the flat part of her chest, and Lindiwe knew where his next destination would have been. Especially as he'd been 'expertly' caressing a hand up the inside of one of her thighs.

He was starting this how he always did: by placing his lips around her nipple and touching her clit.

She leaned forward to look down at him, and with his lips still against her chest, his head dipped back slightly to greet her gaze.

Licking her lips nervously, she almost told him it was fine to continue. Especially as his expression appeared more heated than usual, and she wondered if he'd been practising it – she knew it didn't come naturally to him.

Palming down his shoulders and chest, knowing she touched some of the solid streaks of his swirling torso, she said, "I want to try something different."

She'd been wanting to give rather than just take from the very beginning.

"What did you have in mind?" he asked, lifting to tower over her due to their differing heights. He placed his hands on her curved hips, resting them there – but she knew his grip was to keep her near.

Drawing in a calming breath, Lindiwe strove for sensual and confident, rather than letting the anxious, bashful clamouring in her heart win. She traced the pad of her index finger down his leanly muscular chest until she reached his navel. She didn't know how she managed to keep her gaze on the pitch-black wells of his eyes, but she did.

"Umm, I was thinking I could go down on you," she murmured playfully.

I've heard men love this. Now that they were being touchy with each other, her mouth wanted to do more than nip with her words and kisses.

Weldir opened his mouth and then immediately shut it. Then, for a long while, he remained still, his expression unchanging. His chest, always lacking in breath, never moved, and she could never perceive a heartbeat under her palm no matter how hard she tried.

He stared down at her silently, thinking *very deeply*.

The sultry smile she'd been wearing began to crack. *He doesn't want that?*

He finally lifted a hand and cupped her cheek, then parted her lips by pulling down on the fuller bottom one with the pad of his thumb. "I think I would like to see you use that pesky mouth of yours on me, rather than against me."

Her smile renewed, and a spark of nervous giddiness coiled in her belly and chest.

Her fingers skimmed down his body, tracing what she could while the pads of them occasionally dipped into nothingness. Lindiwe just pretended he was completely there, so the motion didn't falter or feel odd. Then she reached his groin, and the plane that led to where his cock was.

Or, rather, should have been.

When she looked down, there was nothing.

"Uh, do you mind?" she asked, really wishing she hadn't needed to.

Don't most men get erect by now? Actually, that brought on a load of questions. *I've never seen his penis just dangling.* She should have, right? Considering he never wore clothing.

She loathed to admit that she'd never been comfortable peeking at his groin, and did so fleetingly. Just enough to know nothing was there when there should be. *I guess it's like... inside him?*

That question was answered when right where a cock would be, a bulge formed, and then something pushed forward from within him. It was all one colour: chalky black like the rest of him, with the slightest outer glow of grey that silhouetted his entire body.

At least it looks like the paintings and sculptures I've seen.

The girth was impressive, but Lindiwe had already surmised that after having it inside her. It was long, but not enough to make her clench her legs together in concern. The head, more bulbous than the rest of it, had a small slitted line connecting to the frenulum.

She was relieved that at least something about it was like a human man's.

Keeping her eyes on it, her gaze a little more excited than she truly wanted it to be, she knelt. She gasped when she swayed back in the lack of gravity and reached out for something to anchor her, only to grab his dick. She let it go with her cheeks heating.

"Could I have something to lean on?"

In an instant, her legs, which had been swaying beneath her, were propped up as if she knelt on a floor. Her body relaxed into it, like her weight had become something of substance. Even her breasts felt a little heavier, and her hair didn't float up around her head as much, only the tips waving as if they were just too light to be weighed down.

Placing her left hand on one of her spread knees for balance, she swallowed when her hungry gaze landed on the cock right before her. She shifted her focus higher to meet his eyes and noticed how he towered over her.

This is the first time I've ever been on my knees for him. She'd never needed to bow to him and pretend he was better because he was a god. This would be much more fun anyway, and so she confidently wrapped her hand around his cock.

An inch gap separated her fingertips from her thumb, and a tentative stroke downwards against his glittering, chalky girth revealed the base was slightly thicker.

Lindiwe licked the seam of her lips, wondering what she wanted to do first.

Leaning forward, she parted her lips, and her heart pounded heavier, bashing against her ribcage while arousal pooled at her core. She drew her tongue underneath it, starting from just behind the flared head and going to the slitted tip.

Weldir tasted like nothing. He always had. His kisses were tasteless, as was his 'skin' from the few times she'd trailed her mouth across it. As she held his gaze while swirling her tongue around the broad tip, there was no seed. She wet him with her tongue, making the matte hue of his flesh shine, and her skin flushed with heat as she took in the path her tongue had drawn.

Yet the moment she placed her lips around him and slid him inside, everything else about him felt just right. He was as hard as stone in the centre, yet the outside of him was soft and giving against her tongue, her lips, and even her teeth. She had to part her jaw a little wider than was truly comfortable, but the strain reminded her she was really sucking his cock and *that* felt nice.

She even gave a little moan of satisfaction as she slipped further down him.

Weldir was quiet; he always was.

But the more of him she took in, the darker his expression got until he hit the back of her throat, her lips halfway down his shadowy cock. His eyes grew slitted, narrowing down at her, and for just a moment, his lips drew back as he gave a soft growl of approval.

She hoped her fist at the root of him, slipping back and forth in time with her mouth, felt nice, like she was working his entire length. She made sure her teeth didn't scrape him too much with blunt hardness, and she slipped her tongue all around to give additional sensation.

She could feel her lips swelling more than usual, hot and tingling from her ministrations. Adoring it, and how her body dipped back and forth and put tension on her clit, had her going faster.

She eventually pulled back far enough to release the head, then kissed the side of his tip before gliding her lips and tongue down the side of his length. She kept her gaze on it so she could see where she was going, kissing her way back up to the tip and then swirling her tongue against it.

It didn't swell like she'd read it would, nor did he produce any precum. She frowned when she thought it was a bad sign.

"Is this okay?" she asked, hoping she was doing well.

Both of them knew neither had done this before, and she just wanted to know if it felt good, since he was so quiet.

"It is lovely," he said, one of his clawed fingers tucking a stray curl behind her ear. "I'm enjoying watching you down there." He traced his finger along the length of her jaw until he reached her chin and then tilted it up roughly. "But I prefer it when you're looking up at me."

Her thighs tightened and her pussy walls clenched as he forced her gaze to his. Her confidence rebounded tenfold, and she locked eyes with him as she went faster. Her mouth was messier as she lathered his cock in kisses, pulling it to the left and then the right to make sure she left them on both sides. Then she drew her tongue from the very base of him to the tip in a slow line before encompassing the head with the damp warmth of her mouth once more.

She played with it there, swirling her tongue repeatedly. When she went to pull away, Weldir held the back of her head and very gently pushed down so that she'd swallow him halfway again.

I guess he wants me to just suck him. Although she'd been enjoying teasing him, she was relieved that he'd taken some of the control and initiative.

He tilted his head to the left, as if watching her more intently when she pulled back and went down as far as she could.

Lindiwe paused when something narrow, about the thickness of a thumb, dipped between the dampness of her folds and grazed her clit. When she pulled back to look down, Weldir's hand stopped his cock from leaving her mouth, just as the thing speared her pussy deeply.

Releasing his cock from her fist, she gasped around his girth as she slapped her hand against his hip. Then she moaned, her legs spread wider, and she ground on what she thought might be one of his tendrils. Her thighs shook when it thrust inside her, and the precision of it pushing forward and rubbing against a sensitive spot had her sight blurring.

"I didn't tell you to stop," he rumbled above. More than usual, his voice had her belly fluttering and her insides quivering.

Renewing her sucking, she anchored herself by gripping the base as she undulated on his tendril and pumped her mouth around him. Both felt wonderful, both crept her closer to release, and she ceased mapping her path when her thoughts bled out. She just slipped her mouth and tongue up and down him mindlessly as she moaned around his girth, going harder, faster, and *deeper* when she clenched around his tendril, trying to match its pace.

And when a second one joined the first, but curled in a way that its length could rub against her throbbing and aching clit, Lindiwe trembled.

Her eyelids slid shut as she let out a muffled cry, her orgasm soon to wash over her in a ravenous, thundering wave. She tried to keep going, to keep pleasuring him, but her hips twitched and shuddered in need, constantly breaking her rhythm. She had to pause around his cock to breathe through her nose and gave him her swirling tongue instead of true movement.

Oh god. I'm about to come. The words even sounded like a moan in her mind.

"I told you to look at me," Weldir snarled out, as he gripped her jaw and shoved her face up once more.

She could barely open her eyes to give him an agonised wince, while her sight grew hazy and her back bowed. The blissful cry she let out around him was muffled, broken, and loud as her inner walls clamped down on both thick tendrils. She held onto the base of him for support as her body uncontrollably moved to heighten her orgasm, uncaring of the squelching sounds it made.

Wetness dripped from her, and the tickle of it only aided her. She came hard, and his thrusting tendrils ensured it continued on.

When it finally ceased, she was thankful he let her pull her mouth free. She fell forward with her hand on his hip and panted as she came back down from bliss.

Except Lindiwe wasn't given more than a moment of reprieve.

Whether Weldir threw her higher with his magic, or he lowered himself, it didn't matter. One moment she was on her knees, and the next they were on both sides of his head as he buried his face against her pussy.

"Wait! I just came–" Her words cut out on a desperate moan when his tongue speared her lips and roughly grazed her clit.

He was fast, his tongue doing circles with just the right amount of hard pressure, and she disintegrated into a wanton puddle. Both her hands reached for his horns, but only her right palm was able to curl around one. The other dived into the wisps of his short hair and grabbed what strands she could as she bucked against his face.

His hands at her thighs, keeping them spread for himself, somehow moved to her breasts within an instant. The feel of them was unnatural, like he shouldn't be able to palm and knead them so well with how far down he was. When her watering eyes focused on her chest, she was given her answer.

He'd separated them from his body, and she had no clue he could do that. Never in her imagination had she thought he could detach his limbs.

Rather than being freaked out, she grabbed the back of one and made it grip her breast harder. The other pinched her nipple right as he speared her entrance with his tongue, and she bit down on her swollen bottom lip to stifle her moan.

Locking her legs around his head, she used her grip on his horn and hair to grind against his face. Weldir didn't need to breathe, so she didn't have to worry about him suffocating. It allowed her to unabashedly keep him down there until she was happy and her spirit soared out of her body.

Still riding the high of her first orgasm, the second soon crashed through her due to the oversensitivity. The sound that should have exploded out of her was cut short by her seizing lungs and caught in her throat instead. Her legs trembled with each spasm of her insides, and flashes of light dotted behind her clenched eyelids.

Only when her pussy stopped clamping did her body unlock,

and she was finally able to take in a sweet, although false, breath.

Her thighs, biceps, and even her abdominal muscles twitched as she lay there floating for a few seconds, trying to collect her thoughts. It was an ill omen when Weldir kissed and *nipped* with his sharp fangs up her body, leaving wetness behind in his wake – all of it her orgasm.

She shivered when he did it over one nipple before he worked his way to her neck.

"You have a very lustful body, Lindiwe," he muttered next to her ear in a tone so rough her shiver deepened. "It very much likes being touched."

The rasp that left her was one of pleasurable pain as the tip of his middle finger pressed down on her clit. He moved around her until his chest was against her back, and the streaks of it brushing across her skin had her bowing into his palm when he grasped her left breast.

A tendril wrapped around her thigh and lifted, spreading her once more. She was given no warning when he pinched both her nipple and clit as his cock speared her pussy from behind.

Lindiwe locked up, and she reached back to grab his hair or horn – she didn't care which one – when he buried his face, covered in her climax, against her nape. Even his nose was wet, and she vaguely remembered grinding her clit against it while his tongue was swirling inside her.

"Wait!" she pleaded through shallow huffs. "Please wait."

She'd just had two intense orgasms. She needed a fucking moment to not feel like she was vibrating and aching. *Just let a woman breathe for a second!*

"Why?" he asked against her skin, his lips ticklish and sending goosebumps down her limbs. "I can tell you're enjoying this."

His cock felt so big inside her swollen and hot pussy that it clung to him fervently when he pulled back. Before she could even get a word out, he thrust in again, and all she could do was weakly moan when the flared head rubbed against the tender ridge inside her, the one that sparked delightful pleasure in her muscles and veins.

"See? You asked me to wait, yet your body keeps screaming for more."

Lindiwe whimpered. She couldn't deny it.

Not when her head lolled to the side and her eyelids flickered as he began to pump fast inside her, and she did nothing but pant, moan, and bounce in the fragments of his shadowy arms. His fingers petted her clit constantly, causing her legs to shake and kick, and all she could do was hold the back of his hand like an anchor and hope he'd press more firmly.

She never closed her legs, instead spreading them further as if that would somehow get him to reach deeper. Like her body needed more of the length she knew she couldn't take.

And this was what she had begun anticipating all these years. The passion, the lust, the way her body craved the pleasure until she'd shed every drop she had to give. Lindiwe would rather be fucked to within an inch of her life than ask him to stop, knowing she'd likely go just as long until the next time. She intended to savour this moment when it was so rare and special, with the hope it would hold her over until he summoned her again.

Even when it started to hurt, even when her poor clit throbbed and ached, and her breasts felt overstimulated, she didn't ask him to stop. Instead, she gave herself over to the part of her that needed more, until she obliterated and became dust that would collect in his mist.

"Harder," she pleaded between chaotic breaths. "Please, Weldir."

Everything got faster, his hips hit deeper, and Lindiwe's hips refused to cease moving to greet him. She clawed her nails into the back of his hand, tugging his hair until her back arched and her toes curled, and she let out a lustful scream as she came.

And even then, her body didn't wish to stop clinging to his.

FOUR

March 8th, 1831

Eyes homing in on her target, Lindiwe pulled taut the string of her conjured bow, and took in a steadying breath. The weapon's shadowy upper limb and grip glittered black in the sunlight, highlighting its magical origins.

Travelling lightly worked to her advantage, as did having the ability to create any weapon at her disposal. Daggers, bows with an infinite number of arrows, spears, and even swords could be made from nothing but her imagination. After spending nearly two decades training with every kind of tool she could possibly need at the Demon Hunter fortress, she was lethal out in the wild forests.

Closing one eye to better her sight, she waited for the wind to settle. Then, releasing her breath as she slipped her fingers from the bow's string, her black glittering arrow shot through the air. She made sure it'd hit true and deliver a quick and merciful death.

The snowy owl, resting its tired wings on a boulder jutting out from the snow, didn't have the chance to escape before it was pierced in the heart.

Like with most creatures killed by Weldir's magic, its white flaming soul floated out from its chest. Retrieving her glass vial from her satchel, Lindiwe opened the top of it, and the soul was sucked inside by a spell Weldir had woven into the material of the container itself. Afterwards, she picked up the bird by its feet as her arrow finally disintegrated like drying sand.

This is the third one, she thought, and she lifted it high in the air to inspect its pure-white feathers.

She lowered it so it would dangle as she walked through a snow-covered forest of Kanata. The country was situated above Unerica, a little larger in size, and its beauty was just as riveting as everywhere else she'd been in the world.

Its landscapes were breathtaking. It had some of the most majestic mountains she'd ever seen, all of them covered in icy white powder in the winter, while crystal-blue, pristine lakes appeared in the summer. Forests were scattered all over, and the trees were diverse with fir, pine, birch, oak, and maple – many of which changed colour with the evolving seasons.

All of this butted up against coastlines that were just as mesmerising as the rest of the country.

She'd visited Kanata a few times during her near-fifty-year stint in Unerica. Both were wondrous countries with landscapes that showcased the power of nature, and how it could be shaped in ways the human mind could barely comprehend.

She'd even left one of her children along the border, letting them choose where they wanted to venture. They often visited both, roaming back and forth between each country, from what Weldir had informed her.

Lindiwe intended to leave the one currently growing in her womb much further north.

It was early days, which meant she would have been at least a few months into her pregnancy had they been a human. But, like all her children, this one grew just as quickly and seemed to be on track to be born in a five-week gestation period.

A little exercise is good for me, she thought, placing her hand over her swelling belly. *And I'm actually pretty excited to make a new cloak.*

With her scent-masking spell activated, the blood of the creature in her hand and her own smell didn't lure any devilish monsters to her. She couldn't hide the crunching of her feet in the snow, but the talisman at her waist was warm and ensured the cold didn't creep into her toes.

Although shifting into a Phantom would have alleviated the tiredness in her aching limbs, she refused to do it unless absolutely necessary. It slowed the process of her pregnancy and delayed it by the amount of time she was in that form.

Thankfully she didn't need to walk far, perhaps an hour, before the very voice she longed to hear trickled through her consciousness.

"You've brought me another," Weldir stated, informing her that she'd reached the edge of his mist.

It was so thin, she couldn't see it like usual. Surely in a few more decades it would span all the way through this mountain range's forest. The portal to Nyl'theria, the Elven realm, was at the centre and a few kilometres away, proving just how far his reach was.

She shifted into her Phantom form so that the owl in her fist would fade. He took it from her through his mist, but she *swore* he appeared before her in a glimpse of the murkiest and lightest outline of his body.

Or maybe she was just hoping he was there.

Lindiwe tucked a curl behind her ear after she shifted back to a human. "Do you think you have enough now to make me a white cloak?"

"I won't know until I try."

"I guess we'll have to do that in a few months, though. They're a rather large bird in comparison to ravens, but I'll find more just in case," Lindiwe said, looking around the dense brush. The expanse of spruce trees held up thick blankets of snow, ensuring the world around her was vibrant and teeming with life. Her breaths came out as puffs, and despite the chill in the air, her cheeks warmed. "I don't want to be without my current cloak until this child has their skull and horns anyway."

"I'd rather you not be without your ability to shift while you, and they, are delicate."

She hardly considered herself delicate, even when pregnant. His magic meant she was formidable, and only the ease of quick travel was why she wished to keep her feathered shroud.

But she appreciated his care.

It also reminded her of their last bout of intimacy, and she fidgeted because she might have been a little greedier than usual. She couldn't remember how many times she'd come, but she'd passed out almost immediately afterwards while thrumming with satisfaction.

She'd woken up bare... and not alone.

As much as she should have been mortified that he'd been watching her while she slept naked, without even a blanket to shield her, she just couldn't muster up the emotion. Weldir had always been watching her, would forever watch her, and her sore and tender body had *tingled* in reaction to it for once.

She also couldn't remember the last time she'd woken up that well rested. She'd turned shy due to being naked and at the recollection of what had transpired before she fell asleep, but she hadn't felt uncomfortable.

The conversation afterwards had been awkward, but that was simply because she hadn't known what to say after being fucked so thoroughly. A lot of this was still new territory between them, and even if she lost her inhibitions while they were in the middle of sex, they still resurfaced afterwards.

So she'd grabbed her clothes and left.

But the memory of it lingered, and her belly often coiled with desire, which led to heat pooling at her core. Every time she spoke to him, she remembered.

And she wanted more, even if she didn't dare ask for it.

She knew it was best that they kept the act to merely making offspring – or rather, servants. Lindiwe worried she'd grow too attached if she allowed them to cross that line where sex was no longer a duty but something they enjoyed outside of it.

Even after all this time, and the fact that things between them had changed, she knew she had to keep her heart closed off to him.

It was doubtful he felt anything more than duty and desire towards her anyway. And she refused to fall in love with someone who was entirely incapable of giving it in return.

Still, it didn't mean she disregarded the way her belly flipped at knowing he was there, nor could she ignore how her heart stuttered when a strange yet genial and warm chuckle, deep and sensual, curled around her brain.

"What's so funny?" she grumbled, her eyes narrowing into suspicious slits at the empty space before her.

"Nothing, little female," he answered with mirth. "Nothing at all."

FIVE

Weldir made sure his chuckle wouldn't be heard this time. *I'm sure she would be angry if she knew what I've been doing.*

It didn't stop him, though; it never did.

He inspected the way her eyes narrowed into suspicious slits in his viewing disc, which was completely different from the lazy-lidded version of her before him in stone.

I really did like her on her knees for me, he thought, as he cupped her stone jaw like he did when they were last intimate.

Although her mouth should be open, he actually kept it closed since it wasn't surrounding his girth. Had he wanted to, he could have used his own body to play out that scene once more, but he refrained from doing so... again.

He tucked the one curl behind her ear that always strayed next to her temple, as if that was the way it naturally fell. Her stone eyes looked up at him with heat, with desire, and he'd long been fond of that expression cast towards him.

The real Lindiwe stepped away from his mist, intending to venture into the forest – or perhaps she was heading to find humans to momentarily insert herself amongst for easy food. Since she no longer intended to continue their conversation, he let the silence that often hung between them return.

He turned his attention to the second sculpture he'd already made, as well as the third.

I couldn't pick my favourite moment.

He liked her on her knees, but he'd also become deeply enamoured by the way she held his horn and hair and ground on his face. The moment his female was intimate, she grew bold, daring, and rather greedy when it came to her lust. He was smitten by it, and she could be as rough with him as she liked, so long as he was gifted with the song of her climax.

The last sculpture was difficult to understand what was happening unless he inserted himself into its scene. Holding her from behind as he played with her clit and breasts seemed to make her more ravenous than usual, and he made a mental note to touch those places more intensely when he fucked her in the future.

She craved all kinds of touch, and he was eager to supply it.

But what had made him chuckle was that she'd tucked her hair behind her ear while wearing a rather cute and shy expression, when the many faces before him were sultry and heated. Wanton. Some of them depicted her biting her lip, and on others, her mouth was parted midway through a moan.

Weldir's precious cave of memories... and the centre of it was full of debauchery. All her many poses during their rare moments of intimacy, each one sculpted down to the minutest detail.

Her body hides nothing.

Every twitch, every vein that popped and throbbed, every tiny hair that lifted as goosebumps rained down her skin. How the muscles of her thighs shook, her feet arched, and her toes curled.

It was those unhidden moments he enjoyed the most.

The female who, most of the time, was reserved, formal, and restrained with him, showed a different, softer facet. Like a cut and polished stone, each face was beautiful, each one perfect, even if the surfaces were differently shaped.

Now that he was done carving, which he'd been doing since she left his realm, Weldir looked up.

He'd created a new alcove a little while ago, and he often liked to visit it. Since he didn't need to worry about gravity, or which way was up or down within his own realm, he floated into the opening above.

Setting his feet down on the surface of a new nook, he took in much more sentimental memories of her.

There was one where she slept under a cover of leaves from the rain, with one of their offspring curled up in her arms. Another of her smiling up at the sunshine with her fanning eyelids closed.

But there was a new one here; one she'd accidentally shared with him.

He'd decided to place it in the middle, as it was rather special.

Lindiwe was lying on her side with her knees up, her hands cupped together under her left cheek and chin as she curled into herself. The stone was naked, like she'd been, and its eyes were closed in sleep. Her curls floated around her head, loose, glossy, and slightly tangled from where Weldir had gripped them to keep her head on his cock.

It was the second time she'd fallen asleep in his realm, but this one had not been from the exhaustion of tears from losing Nathair. No, it was peaceful, and he'd found watching her lulling and tranquil.

He'd always wanted her to find comfort in his darkness, but she'd never give either of them that.

It was nice being close to her.

To hear her heartbeat and breaths. It'd been intimate in a wholesome, tender way to witness the gentle rise and fall of her busty chest. To see her lips relaxed, parted, and supple while her eyelids flickered from whatever peaceful dreams she'd been having.

It was like his non-existent heart had yearned to cherish this memory more than the much raunchier ones.

It left him with the same feelings as before: hope and fondness.

Their relationship was still shaky, and there were delicate, gap-filled bridges he didn't yet know how to cross safely, but he hoped this was a start. That all they were doing now was the beginning of *something* more, although he couldn't quite comprehend what.

They were mated, their fate threads entangled.

Really, there was no need for them to solidify their bond when nothing they did would make a difference. She was his. Lindiwe was his mate, the mother of his offspring, and a servant.

They made a deal, a bargain, and that was being honoured.

Yet he wanted to deepen this bond as much as possible to see how far it went and what kind of end was achievable.

His tenderness came from logic, and not from a true heart. He didn't know if his lack of physical form would mean that he would forever be lacking in other ways. A deeper emotional connection, or the ability to make their intimacy more meaningful, might just be entirely out of his grasp. A major obstacle was his inability to see her side, to feel for her, or to appreciate her beyond what he thought was logical.

She was remarkably pretty; he didn't need a heart to see this. But their relationship was superficial at best, and non-existent at worst.

Eyeing her sleeping stone form, he sighed.

It matters little.

He dematerialised so he could enter another alcove, then brought up viewing discs of all his offspring, making sure to update their sculptures. Some remained the same, while others changed vastly.

He started with the youngest in Kanata and moved backwards from there. Each alcove belonged to a different continent they'd placed their offspring on thus far, and he made sure each one was correct up to the most minute detail.

Each alcove caused his mist to tighten against him as a sense of... longing sifted through him. He'd never greeted his living offspring as adults, and that often weighed on Weldir. That was until he arrived at the alcove closest to the exit of the cave system he'd created.

Nathair could quickly eat away at the thrum of loneliness.

I'm not truly alone. He did have one of his offspring, even if his intelligence was rather subpar compared to humans. *He's not a great conversationalist, but he is rather amusing.*

His eldest offspring was quite cheeky, even though he'd kept his promise about not eating any more of Weldir's precious souls.

Nathair was slow to learn, and the task was time consuming and gruelling. He forgot much, although simple reminders aided him. He *always* lied about forgetting, either stating he did know or that Weldir had never informed him – which was never true. He liked to be chased, and the only way to play hide-and-seek with him was to disconnect Nathair from the rest of Tenebris momentarily so he didn't accidentally harm a deceased human.

Nathair's inability to smell Weldir meant the game was unfair, so he whistled to give the Mavka a direction to follow. Weldir never cheated in their game by utilising their fate strings, as that would ruin the experience.

It was much more fun to stumble across the serpent hiding his torso in a bush, while he lacked the understanding to hide the rest of his lengthy tail. Then he'd flee with a playful yelp, and Weldir let him believe that he was actually fast enough to escape.

If Nathair turned on him to incite a battle, Weldir turned invisible until he calmed. That, or he herded him back to his lake, so he'd rest.

Even though he isn't very bright, I spend much of my time speaking with him, he thought fondly.

They spent many days watching viewing discs together, and he'd explained everything that Nathair pointed a claw at.

However... he could not bring up the disc of the one who killed him, as it often upset him. Somewhere within the bout of new humanity, he'd come to resent his brother for stealing away his life.

Nathair felt stagnant and removed from life, which often disturbed Weldir's mist with a forlorn emotion. He was partly to blame, as Nathair's life in the afterworld was entirely Weldir's fault. He hadn't been whisked away to a new life, but a dead one, where he lived in a sense of limbo.

Never progressing. Never truly experiencing anything.

His life was meaningless, and that bothered them both.

Nathair could often become inconsolable when he was reminded of this. Weldir hadn't known his offspring could cry until Nathair shed ethereal tears that floated from his sorrowful blue orbs. He'd whimper as he cuddled himself in the huddle of his own tail and ask Weldir *why* he was here, in this realm. Why it was he who had to be subjected to this boring and mundane life of stillness.

He also questioned why his own sibling had killed him, constantly forgetting that it had been an accident, and not something done maliciously.

Nathair would react in two ways whenever Weldir attempted to soothe him. He would reject the placations, as Weldir couldn't offer him a solution other than his presence. Or he'd lash out violently, asking how Weldir could torment him by keeping him here against his will, demanding to be returned. To be given life and taken from here so he could truly live.

Sometimes he was enough for his offspring, and at other times Weldir was his tormentor. It was... dispiriting.

But there is nothing I can do, he thought solemnly. *I cannot even give myself true life.*

Moving back to a different child, he didn't feel any better when he looked upon... *Merikh.* Especially when he saw him walking with Jabez through the Veil. He stood on two legs and was the first of his offspring to reveal that they could change into a more humanoid version.

The name felt wrong, foreign even, but it was Orson's newly appointed name. He didn't know what the word signified, since Jabez was the one to give it to him.

Merikh's fur was long and shaggy in some places, but it had

shrunk a little around his waist and abdomen. His quills were still long and sharp, and Weldir counted each one to make sure his sculpture was accurate.

His bones have almost disappeared entirely. He could only spot the top of his sternum and collarbones, and a few knuckles on his hands and toes. He was large, standing a few inches taller than Jabez, and slightly more muscular.

He likely sees my offspring as a tool. Something he could use to empower himself, as Merikh was stronger and faster than any Demon, and his quills made him a weapon *and* a shield. Then again, he was violent and quick to slip into a rage. He'd seen Jabez somehow skilfully evade an enraged Merikh a handful of times.

At least the halfling never lashed out at his offspring.

No, worse, he often applauded him for it. Jabez *liked* that Merikh was this way, having even taken him to a human village to destroy.

Weldir didn't know if he was furious about that or thankful for Merikh's increase in humanity as a result. Merikh was actually rather intelligent now. He stood like a human, often spoke like one – although brutishly – and wore pants as if to emulate them.

He was weirdly accepted by the Demons who surrounded Jabez, and if he wasn't, both would make them scamper off with their tails between their legs.

That easy acceptance left Weldir feeling at odds with himself.

He valued the companionship his offspring had, and that it made him... *happy.* Content even. Merikh wanted this bond and protected it fiercely. It kept him safe, even from Weldir's biggest foe. Yet Weldir's hatred of Jabez had also grown over the years. Mainly because he was in the way of Lindiwe and Merikh rekindling whatever relationship they *could* have.

She'd attempted to intervene after Jabez took Merikh to feed on the village of humans – Weldir having kept her informed. She'd grown enraged, disappointed, and... frightened. She didn't want their offspring to be the cause of such devastation and destruction, no matter that Jabez had, oddly, protected the young and vulnerable behind a ward.

Getting Merikh to listen to her was like talking to a wall, and she couldn't fully explain *why*. She didn't want to reveal that Merikh was the creation of someone Jabez hated as much as Weldir hated him in return.

She'd tried to do this without Jabez, but the two were near inseparable. So she'd given up and just confronted them both.

He still remembered the conversation as if it were happening before him. It wasn't a recent memory, but Weldir could never pinpoint where on the ravels of time it was.

All he knew was that it was years before Lindiwe left for Unerica...

"He is evil and will turn on you the moment you are no longer useful to him," she stated firmly, pointing at Jabez's grinning face.

His sharp fangs looked more prominent than usual. His crimson eyes had an arrogant edge to them that wasn't present the last time they'd faced off at the waterfall. He looked older, somewhere in his early to mid-twenties, and his hair was shoulder length.

"I don't see why you give a fuck about who he spends his time with," Jabez pointedly answered, loosening his crossed arms to shrug with exaggerated nonchalance.

Weldir noticed the way her pretty features winced, and how her eyes darted between them as she scrambled for a suitable answer.

"Because I've befriended other Duskwalkers and they aren't inherently evil." She pulled her shoulders back and lifted her pointed chin. "You took this one to a village and destroyed it."

"We did see another Mavka there as we were leaving." *Merikh sneered, his red orbs brightening to show his growing anger. He mimicked Jabez and folded his arms across his muscular chest, which caused his narrow hips to push forward.*

"You just want to get in the way of his evolution. You want

him to be stunted, like the other Mavka we saw. The feline-skulled one." Jabez cocked a brow, as if daring her to say otherwise – when he couldn't be further from the truth.

Lindiwe no longer deterred their offspring from evolving. She often wasn't there to stop it. She was always in another part of the world when they ventured near humans and had grown to accept that this was just a part of what happened when it came to their offspring.

They didn't always attack villages, towns, or cities, and were more curious than anything – depending on the Duskwalker and their level of humanity. Anzúli had scent cloaks around most villages now, so his offspring just sniffed along the borders and walls and then usually meandered away with boredom.

Merikh loosened his folded arms enough to point a claw at her. "You see us as monsters, as a danger, and want to protect the humans."

The hurt in her eyes was unmistakable. "I could never see you as a monster, Orson."

Merikh cocked his head in a lack of understanding. "That's not my name. Whoever I was to you died the moment you took the serpent one from me."

Tears instantly brimmed her doe-brown eyes, reddening the whites of them. "You did that! Don't blame me for taking his skull somewhere safe when you were the one who killed him!"

Merikh stammered as he stepped back, his orbs flashing blue, then orange. "N-no. You did. You destroyed him."

Both Weldir and Lindiwe registered that Merikh had warped memories of that time; he no longer remembered it clearly. In the same way he often forgot his name or how to speak at the time.

"It means he doesn't remember how he killed him," Weldir stated through the bond. "He cannot tell Jabez how to destroy his own kind. This is a good thing, Lindiwe."

With the way her forehead scrunched up and her eyes crinkled in anguish, she agreed, but it was obvious she didn't appreciate the silver lining in this.

"I took your brother to Weldir's realm after you destroyed him, Orson."

"That's not my name!" Merikh roared, parting his maw to flash his fangs in their Duskwalker way as he bared his claws. He then bashed a fist against his chest where his heart would be. "It is Merikh!"

She flinched and her eyes crinkled further, almost with loss. "Merikh, then," she conceded. She levelled an intense glare at Jabez like she wished the world would crumble on top of him. "He will turn on you. Exactly how he turned on me."

"Because I didn't care about you," Jabez answered, the bridge of his nose crinkling. "You're Weldir's fucking pet. You're the enemy, and in our way."

"As the protector of humans and Duskwalkers, I don't approve of this." Then she turned a beseeching expression to Merikh. "Do you remember nothing of the time we spent in Nathair's territory?"

"I barely remember you at all. Only my hatred of you and what you did."

Her hands fisted at her sides. But her anguish deepened, and she didn't have a response.

Jabez narrowed his eyes suspiciously at Lindiwe. Then he stepped forward, stalking around her and encroaching on her space. "Why do you care for Mavka so much?"

Lindiwe steeled her expression and lifted her chin once more. "Why do you care for him so much? I am deathless, and they aren't evil. I have found companions where I can. Shouldn't our time at the waterfall have made it obvious as to what I seek?"

Then she stared up at him in her incorporeal form when he towered right in front of her.

"Come near us again, and I'll be much quicker at killing you. Then you can go back to Weldir like a good pet and lick your wounds, and come back for me to do it again."

"I could end you within a heartbeat." She sneered up at him. "You have no idea the power I wield, and the only reason I have

not done so is that I could incinerate this entire forest with a black fire not even I could put out if it reaches far enough. The flames would engulf every tree, rock, Demon, and Duskwalker until they reached the shores. And even then, they would not stop."

He chuckled menacingly and arrogantly down at her. "That's doubtful."

One thing Weldir knew about his mate was that she was short-tempered when it suited her, she held grudges, and she hated being tested. She loathed her ego being prodded at and couldn't stand losing.

Jabez didn't even have the chance to react when she bounced forward while turning physical. Perhaps he hadn't expected her to become tangible and put herself in danger by doing so. Regardless, she grabbed his wrist and set it alight. Within a second, the black flames engulfed his hand, and he belted out a scream Weldir found rather satisfying.

She grabbed the edges of her raven cloak and flapped it, turning them into temporary wings to leap over an enraged Merikh, who lunged at her. Instead of attempting to put the fire out, Jabez wisely – although unfortunately for Weldir – gouged into his elbow and removed his own arm before the flames could claim him totally.

The sounds of severing a limb were drowned out by Merikh's roar as crimson blood squirted from the wound. Jabez's brown complexion grew ashen from the pain, the blood loss, and his companion turning on him.

With a furious snarl in her direction, Jabez bolted through the forest as Merikh gave chase, needing to evade the biggest threat. It gave Lindiwe the opportunity to encase the still-burning limb in a shadowy dome to protect the surrounding grass, shrubs, and forest.

"I hope my son eats you," she whispered spitefully as she knelt in front of the dome.

She placed her hands on either side of it and filled it with sand. It took a while for her to snuff out the flames that quickly spread and licked at the inside of the dome.

"I thought you said you would never do that." Weldir tried his hardest not to let humour trickle into his tone.

"It was only his hand," she murmured defensively, rolling her eyes. "You told me he's been able to heal worse wounds, especially those given to him by Ors..." She closed her eyes and took in a calming breath. "Merikh."

"What if it had spread?"

"I don't care what would have happened to him. He's creating an army, killing humans, has me hunted, and is corrupting our child. Merikh isn't evil, and I don't want Jabez making him so." Then she lowered her voice as she muttered to herself, rather than him, "But he'll never listen to me. I see that now."

"What of the forest, then? What if Merikh had tried to touch him?"

"I would have stopped him. And we've all brought you enough untainted souls to have enough magic right now that I could have encased any burning areas in a massive ward."

He gave a hum of thought. "I don't, actually. I've used most of it."

That made her head rear back, her eyes widening. "What? Already? It's only been a few days!"

"And I have spread my mist further since then."

She winced just as the black flames sputtered out, and she released the protective dome she'd cast over them. "Oops. I shouldn't have done that then."

The memory faded when the current Jabez said something, and a word caught Weldir's attention.

He paused, and his mist collected tighter to him. He threw his arm out to bring the disc of Lindiwe closer, finding she was awake as she ate at a table with many other humans. She sat in some kind of tavern and gulped down a lumpy, broth-based meal.

"Did you know the Demons have begun calling our offspring Mavka all over the world, and not just in Austrális like we thought?" he asked her.

She had no contact with Demons, so she continued to use the term Duskwalker rather than Mavka.

He'd almost forgotten he'd wanted to have the conversation surrounding it with her, but she'd either been asleep, preoccupied, or he hadn't thought about it during the times she was receptive to speaking with him.

Jabez saying it to Merikh only reminded him just now.

Her eyes squinted as she looked left and right before bringing her wooden bowl closer to herself. In the loud tavern, she whispered down into her food so as not to be overheard. "Really? How could they all come to the same word?"

Like she couldn't help herself, she placed her hand over her very round stomach in thought and for comfort. It wasn't long until she would give birth.

"It is a word for forest creature in Nyl'kira. I have heard other terms being used, like Daesrin, but Mavka is the most common."

"There's a mythological creature called that in one of our languages, although I still can't pick which one," she whispered, scooping up some of the broth with her spoon, and a pea floated in the steaming liquid. "But I do know they have no correlation."

"Languages incidentally cross all the time," he answered. "You of all people should know this."

Lindiwe pouted at her spoon before she finally opened her mouth and sucked the contents inside. She quickly swallowed and said, "I still don't like the term. I like Duskwalker. They're more than just a beast roaming a forest."

He tilted his head at that. "I actually think it's better."

Her brows twitched into a frown as she eyed the person who sat a little close to her on her bench seat. She slid down it to make room, causing the male human to grunt and pull the other way, as if he hadn't realised he'd encroached on her space.

"Why do you think it's better?"

"Because Demons are who our offspring will come into

contact with the most. It's also a Nyl'therian word." Maybe he was biased, due to his Elven nature, but he liked that a piece of his original home was given homage through his offspring.

It was better.

"I still won't use it," she bit out.

"Then we are at an impasse. I will use it," he stated firmly, leaving no room for her to attempt to change his mind.

He hummed a chuckle when she poked her tongue out, then she resumed her meal without another word.

Seeing Merikh was well, and now that Weldir had updated his sculpture, he moved onto his next offspring.

Fenrir had changed much over the years, as he often wandered aimlessly throughout Austrális before returning to the cave he'd found within the Veil's cliff wall.

Every year aided his strength and form, turning him from gaunt to just healthy enough that his muscles pushed against his protruding bones without engulfing them like Merikh. He'd had very little contact with humans, but Lindiwe had attempted many times to teach him English whenever she visited.

The lessons were slow, as he was deeply untrusting, but he wasn't needlessly violent. Fenrir was cautious, although he desired a bond with her. He could be rather obedient when he understood her words. He didn't mind her near his territory, so long as she didn't go anywhere near the opening of his cave.

Leonidas, on the other hand, had made a nest southward in the Veil's forest. Hidden well by trees and shrubbery, an opening beneath a pile of boulders was just big enough to allow him inside, but he had to squeeze his shoulders through.

His form was similar to Fenrir – strong, but thin around the waist. And he still displayed many visible bones.

Leonidas was calm, aloof, and... cheerful? It was the only word Weldir could use to label his mountain-lion-skulled offspring, as very little seemed to bother him. Moving through the world curiously, he tried far too often to play with his meals.

The Demons nearby weren't fond of him and mostly left him be.

SIX

November 21ˢᵗ, 1831

Burying her face in thick shagginess, Lindiwe nuzzled her nose into the blue-black feathers as hard as she could muster. The large, magnificent creature below her, reaching a little under eight feet, made a harsh, bird-like bawk, but the sound was muffled through their forcefully closed beak.

Autumn chilled the air, but she soaked up their near-scorching heat rather than use her talisman. She moved away from between their shoulder blades to bury her face into a nape of glossy feathers.

The deadly, frightening being struggled against the magical bonds she'd threaded around their legs, and those that strapped their arms and great wings against their body. Their caribou antlers, towering and large, brushed over her, but their head was trapped enough that they could only minutely shake it. Against her magic, she perceived them trying to open their owl beak, gaining a sliver of room before it clacked shut.

"Mmm, I'm going to miss you!" she exclaimed, hugging their back with her arms and legs.

"I think you're distressing our offspring," Weldir *rudely* told her.

"Oh, they're fine!" she yelled, planting her hands against the base of their wings and lifting up on straightened arms. "I never get to cuddle them when they're all big and scary, and I never usually get to say goodbye."

"I don't think Ookpik appreciates your goodbye hug."

Lindiwe parted her lips to say something, accidentally sucked a curl into her mouth, and quickly swatted it away. She narrowed her eyes and pouted.

"Well, I deserve to soak up a few seconds before I leave. I don't understand why you even care."

The warm, decadent, masculine chuckle that radiated throughout her skull instantly had her stomach tightening into knots. Instead of letting her shiver of delight win, she dived her arms back in Ookpik's feathery back and hugged them from behind as Weldir spoke.

"I don't. I just find enjoyment in teasing you."

With her face hidden so he couldn't see her scrunch it up, she would have poked her tongue out if it weren't for the fact that she'd taste feathers if she did.

Ookpik was face down against the ground, offering her little snarls and bird-like barks through their shut beak. Each one vibrated through their muscles into her, and as much as she knew she was distressing them, she savoured it.

They'd forget this stress within hours anyway.

The name she'd chosen was the native word in the area for snow owl, which she found fitting with the skull she'd chosen for them. They were rather... pretty, with a neck and back of long black feathers that glistened with a blue sheen in the light. The rest of them was shaggy fur like a caribou, and the combination of their animalistic features made them rather striking.

When her Duskwalker child gave a whimper, Lindiwe sighed as she let her body relax on top of them. She likely weighed absolutely nothing to them, but she conceded and let herself roll off. Then, with autumn leaves crunching below her, she jumped to her feet.

She crept behind them, ready to turn incorporeal, and released the magic keeping them bound. They were freed.

As if she were a terrible being and something to be frightened of, instead of spinning around with razor-sharp claws bared on their humanoid hands, Ookpik let out a yelp. They scrabbled in place as they struggled to gain purchase on the muddied ground, then finally bolted into the forest. She threw her arms up against the dirt, rocks, and debris they kicked up as they fled from her.

The moment was bittersweet.

Although a smile teased her lips, her eyes crinkled with the same anguish as when one of her children finished forming from a juvenile into an adult. Ookpik's scent stained her arms, and she rubbed her nose against one to try to commit it to memory.

Then she brushed her caribou-skin dress of dirt and closed her eyes while lifting her face to the rich light, letting it cascade over her to combat the chill that came from Ookpik's disappearance.

"Well?" She cocked a brow playfully. "Are you going to take me or not?"

"I didn't know if you were ready." The world came out from under her.

There's no point in me staying, she thought as her arms lifted above her head due to the inertia of falling before she slipped into the comfort of weightless darkness. *I'll return when they've achieved more humanity to teach them what I can.*

She'd stayed long enough that they understood the worst of the dangers.

"Hello, Lindiwe," Weldir greeted, floating upright – or it could have been sideways, who knew with his realm – a few metres from her.

Due to his orientation, she felt as though she was lying on her back on top of the ocean's surface. She waved her hands to change the way she floated, mimicking his upright position until their gazes could meet each other's properly.

"Hello, spirit of the void," she sang.

The right side of his face cringed and flaked off, joining his pointed ear to make that more visible. She laughed at his instantaneous dislike of the term, which was exactly why she adored using it.

"I should punish you for that," he stated with a growl.

A cruel smile pulled at her lips. "Only if you want to upset me."

He came closer, his mist lagging behind the spiralling streaks of his visible physical form. Then he circled her, much like one would when assessing someone from head to toe and front to back.

"You're lucky I find your teasing preferable to your everlasting ire." He came to her front and grinned, and it was too large to be natural as he flashed his chalky black teeth and demonic canines. If she didn't know better, it would have come across as menacing. "Any new artefacts to unload from your person?"

The crook of his elbow moved, revealing he likely had his hand out, even if she couldn't see it. She opened her satchel and offloaded a few drawstring bags and a new journal.

His hand formed when she reached out with the bags, and he wiggled his claw tip at one of their necks to peek inside. Once his curiosity was sated, tendrils attached themselves to the four small bags and disappeared with them, and he took the book from her awaiting hand. He flicked through it, and although the pages turned quicker than she could blink, she wondered if he'd committed every line she'd written to memory.

"Do you want me to change your cloak now?" he asked before he'd finished with the journal, momentarily peeking up at her with only the bottom of his left eye down to his chin visible.

She pulled at the ties at her throat and handed her black raven-feathered cloak to him. "If you could."

He took it and brushed a thumb through the weathered and damaged feathers. The way he peered down at them came across as odd, and perhaps sentimental, but her heart had already said goodbye to the garment.

She was ready for change and had been for a while.

"I'll inform you once it's ready," he said, letting it go, and a tendril attached to it kept it tangible to him while dragging it away.

Placing her hands behind her back and holding her right wrist, Lindiwe swayed back and forth on the heels of her feet – hoping it didn't look odd in the ether she floated in. "Actually, I was wondering if I could stay this time?"

His face disintegrated entirely when he reared back, his head becoming just a cloud of mist. "You want to remain here?" he asked, a frown evident in his puzzled tone.

"I was hoping I could read through my journals and check what items I've left here." She tried to muster an understanding smile. It was the first time she'd offered to remain in his presence, so it had to be strange to him that she wasn't trying to flee. "I thought I could do this while I wait."

"It might take me some time, though."

Rather than the conversation running in circles, she lowered her eyelids in annoyance and hiked her thumb over her shoulder. She'd already spelled out her desire to stay rather clearly, if she were being honest. "You can send me back to Austrális if you don't want me here."

"No," he said immediately. "I would welcome your presence here."

A grin of triumph parted her lips. *That's what I thought.*

Lindiwe didn't realise she was moving through his realm – or was the realm moving around her? – until the items scattered in the distance came closer. There was no rush of air, no rustle of hair or clothing, as if the nothingness was utterly empty of perceivable movement. Even when she swam through the ether, it felt like brushing through still air.

Her cheeks warmed in embarrassment at just how much she'd amassed.

Dozens of small pouches filled with seeds, dried herbs, interesting bone fragments, and blessed salt created a substantial pile. A neat collection of precious or beautiful crystals glittered, with a large egg-shaped fire opal in the middle. The odd pebbles that she liked the colour or shape of surrounded it in a star shape.

Her journals lined the entire space in a ring, with books placed together in sections, and upon closer inspection, they were separated into their contents. A section for all the things she'd learned at different Anzúli temples, another for the flora and fauna of every land she'd visited over the many years. Another section was of her personal diaries, which lacked any emotions and were just retellings of what she'd done during different periods of her life to help pass the time.

Folded stacks of clothes were put into piles depending on whether they were dresses she wanted to keep or special garments she collected from lands far from Austrális. There were even a few traditional items of clothing from Unerica, Kanata, Zafrikaan, and Eyropea, reflecting how she'd held onto those cultures after immersing herself in them temporarily. Even one of the interesting hats she'd taken from Pyrssia had been placed on top of the pile, along with a pair of clogs from a country close by.

An array of knick-knacks further filled the endless space, creating a vortex that started from what she believed to be the first one she'd left here and ended with the last.

Guilt slipped down her spine at the ball of white feathers – the evidence of the snowy owls she'd hunted for her new cloak – with the corpse of one hugging it. Had it not been so still, she would have thought it was merely resting.

Next to it was a much smaller ball of black feathers.

Every item had the tiniest blob of black, highlighting Weldir's magic holding onto each one to keep all of it tangible to him.

Lindiwe had never known what he'd done with her things, but she'd assumed they'd just be scattered as a messy congregation of her stuff.

Something warm and pleasant swelled in her heart at seeing this place. It felt like a... *shrine* to her and her memories.

Everything had been placed with artistry and care. Her pulse quickened, and she brought her hands together so she could pick at her nail beds, struck by a tenderness that fluttered in her stomach.

I can't believe he did all this, she thought, digging her thumbnail into the side of the other, unsure of what to say or how to show her appreciation.

It looked like he *cared*, but that didn't particularly align with how he could often come across as emotionless or emotionally false.

I thought he'd changed because he'd been emulating humans. Pretending to be one simply to placate her and make it easier to relate to. *Was I wrong?*

Why go to all this effort when it had been doubtful, until now, that she'd see it?

She peeked at him, expecting him to gauge her reaction to all this with a suave smirk. Instead, the demi-god had crossed his legs and begun plucking the black feathers from her cloak without a care in the world, unaware that she might be feeling strange.

He obviously thought nothing of it.

He was probably just bored, her mind grumbled as she kicked her legs to float closer to her belongings. *I'm looking too much into it.*

Gingerly pulling a book from the ring of them, she crossed her legs as well, flipped open the cover, and read through the very first journal she'd written of Anzúli spells. She figured starting from the beginning and familiarising herself with them would take up most of the time as she waited.

"Your handwriting has improved over the years," he commented dully, never lifting his head away from his task.

She peered at the shaky, although carefully recorded words. "Well, I didn't really know how to read or write when I met you. Most commoners, especially women, didn't have the time or means."

It was one of the first things she'd taught herself when she started hunting occultists. She'd needed to learn how to read their letters and notes that she pilfered from their corpses, as they were often leads.

"I know." He slowly pulled on a feather with a tendril while making sure he didn't damage the cloth of the actual cloak. "Memories of humans have detailed such things. Humankind has not been kind to its women in many places, and even less to those born of poorer families. I've never understood that inequality."

Lifting her gaze away from the journal entirely, she gave him her full attention. "Is it not like that in Nyl'theria?"

"No. The Elysians protect their weakest. They shelter everyone, and crime is low due to that equality. No one feels the need to fight for resources, or steal them from another, when the basic necessities for life are freely given. A home, comforts, and even grooming products are provided always, and food, water, and even many baths are often in public spaces to encourage unity and bonds."

The young Lindiwe would have been horrified to learn of public bathing, but she'd done it many times now in cultures that provided those spaces. It had allowed her to stop feeling so shy and insecure about her body, as it was just what housed her spirit – well, would have, if Weldir hadn't taken it.

She was still bashful about being *touched*, but her cheeks no longer flushed in embarrassment at her own nudity in public – so long as she was aware of the eyes upon her.

In places where she thought she was private, the appearance of others could still catch her unaware and fluster her.

"Could you tell me more about the Elven realm, then?" she asked.

"What more do you want to know of it? I've already explained what the forests are like now, due to the Demons that inhabit them. I've also explained the society itself and how it's managed by the synedrus council. Honestly, I know the basics, but the inner workings of Lezekos City are actually beyond my knowledge. I'm only aware of what my mother shared with me through my prism."

"That was the prison you were kept in?"

"Prison, shelter, haven – it really depends on how I view it. It protected me as much as it protected everyone from my destruction. I came to appreciate it as much as I hated it." Then Weldir paused and looked up at the nothingness. "Actually, we are still inside it."

Her brows came together in puzzlement. "What do you mean we're inside it?"

"My realm is me, and I still lack a true form. If I were to leave it totally, I would consume everything – unless my mist is contained fully within a physical form." He shifted his face to meet her gaze, and the spots collected together like he wore a mask. "There are different parts of me. The parts I manifest and the parts that just are. The mist on Earth is my mana. It cannot touch the world, but it can touch souls. It's partially visible to the human eye due to its makeup, but it's not tangible in any form. My essence – the parts of who I really am – is tangible, and it eats everything it touches, wanting a form to stabilise itself, without ever achieving it."

"Then why have you not consumed me?"

"Because that part of me I have forcibly housed within the realm within my stomach. Into my centre. The prism helps; it shields and provides stabilisation. Without it, without something physical containing me, I'd no longer have such control over it. Spirits are not tangible. They are not real or alive, and therefore cannot be eaten. You currently sit between Tenebris and the prism wall, in darkness I cannot control, within mist I cannot contain, but is harmless. The best way to explain is it's like you are within my mind, and I can move you anywhere within me – my heart, my lungs, the place that creates essence – but we cannot go outside of those borders."

"I'm sorry, Weldir, but I don't understand."

And she really hoped he never took her to the place where his *seed* was likely stored.

He gave a hum of thought. "The form you see before you is

the one I have chosen. It is the physical shape that feels the most right, but it is still just a manifestation of my magic. As it stands, my true form, my soul, is the shape of the prism, although I don't know what it is. There are two of me: an external physical form that reaches the edges of my prison, and then the internal physical form that you see before you. If I were to ever be given a real body, I believe it would all pull together, like the splayed-out threads of a cloth being tugged into a decipherable shape. I long ago realised I am... broken. In pieces. I doubt that will ever change, and that I'll ever leave my prism."

"Then how are you able to visit Earth?" she asked, shaking her head.

"In the same way my mist does: manifestation. My mist is a link, and I'm able to take this body there through it, just not my soul. But the makeup of this form is different to it, and as I am not *truly* there, I cannot interact with the world other than through my voice, through thought. My mist is visible due to the toxicity I push out, which momentarily allows it to be seen, and you have mentioned you can smell that toxicity. It's actually clear, invisible, like me when I am there. You see me when I consume a soul because I have taken the essence of something else, which pushes the boundaries further, but I still cannot interact with life. Without assistance, I am nothing but a soul harvester there, just like I am a danger without assistance from the prism."

Does that mean I'm technically in the Elven realm right now? The only answer she could come up with was yes.

Lindiwe thumbed the edge of her journal's back cover. "Doesn't that upset you?" she asked, wondering why there had been no deflated edge to his voice, no crack of pain or longing.

His voice had been smooth, empty of emotion, and devoid of life. Like someone telling a story.

"This is just how I am. I'm no longer bothered by things I cannot change. I've come to accept it and appreciate it, as I don't want to be a violent, all-consuming entity upon the worlds."

I guess it's like how I've come to accept my place in the world and in our marriage. Things no longer bothered her, and she looked for the positives where she could.

"At least I'm no longer truly alone," he stated, his gaze holding hers much deeper than before, until he lowered his face back to his task. Her stomach tightened in surprised tenderness, as well as pity, and the feelings grew when he added, "I have you and Nathair."

Giving him a weak smile, she nodded as she returned to her journal. She drew the side of her nail over a sentence.

He can be so confusing sometimes. Not because of the complexity of what he was, but what he said to end it. *Because of me and Nathair?* She peeked around at all her things again, floating in his ether, before darting her gaze to him still working and then back down.

He's never shown whether he's lonely or not, or if he can even really feel it. Lindiwe had. She'd proven to him time and time again, whether through words or actions, that there had been a sickly hole developing where her heart was.

But what do I know of loneliness in comparison to being locked away in a prison for nearly a millennium and a half? That was the time frame he'd estimated in Earth years when he first explained it to her. *I guess we're lonely together.*

There was a void between them that not even pleasure and touch could breach. It made it more bearable, though, and she could admit that their relationship wasn't, for the most part, strained. There was no love, only lust. Passion in their needs, but no comfort of the spirit.

But I do have some value to him other than just being his servant. This place and his words were proof of that, and it made her chest ache for him in more ways than one.

Was it enough for her to open her heart to him? Never. She needed more than this. To feel cherished, treasured, and loved. She felt appreciated in the way one would value a friend, and she couldn't fall in love with a friend who was entirely out of reach. Someone far away, not physically, but emotionally.

Someone who couldn't support any growth, when they didn't even know how to sow the seed properly.

This didn't mean she couldn't see his efforts, and it was those efforts that heartened her.

Even the fact that he was changing her cloak, despite it still being fit for purpose, was heartening. He could have told her to remain a raven, as an owl was similar in form, but he didn't.

Once she was finished reading the first book, she moved on to the next, occasionally peeking up at him through her lashes. It wasn't long before the feathers were plucked from it, and the holes and claw marks in the plain dark-grey cloth began to shut, as if he was stitching it back together with his magic. Then he brought the body of the white-feathered owl closer, and plucked and threaded the plumes through the material one by one.

He barely moved from his cross-legged position as he worked. His form constantly shifted, appearing like chalky ink moving across invisible paper.

Sometimes large sections of his bare chest and lightly muscular abdomen would be revealed by the blobs as they moved up and over his torso, neck, and the side of his jaw before breaking apart. Other times the inky spots were more spread out, revealing his lean thigh, or calf, or even a foot, while his elbow and face became visible in parts.

Her mind was able to map these movements and paint a perfect picture of what Weldir looked like entirely.

A shadowy demi-god who had pointed ears and long, twisting horns that ran from his hairline and through his two-inch-long hair. His face was chiselled to near perfection, with a broad jaw, high cheeks, pleasant brows, and a nose with a small bump in its straight descent down his face. His lips were full, but they were pushed out due to his large canine fangs hidden away behind them.

His long body gave the impression he was lithe, and his build was athletically strong, rather than bulky. That strength was a lie, of course, as he probably could have crushed anything in those godly hands of his. Hands that were big, could touch roughly as well as gently, and were tipped with claws.

His eyes had once unnerved her. The glossy pools of ethereal darkness had felt all-consuming, and she'd worried that if she stared into them for too long, she'd fall into the void and be eaten. But as the years went on, and they grew closer in the disjointed and sparse time they spent with each other, she found them to be hypnotising.

It didn't help that his lashes, often sprinkled with dust from his mist, made them lovelier to look upon.

Weldir was... attractive. She'd known that from the first time she pieced together his features in her mind in full. Actually, she often found him to be devilishly handsome, to her demise, and very few human or Anzúli men could compare to the wonder that was Weldir.

Just the simple knowledge that she'd touched him, and had been touched in return, had her insides warming in memory. How those pretty lips and sharp fangs had played across her skin, and how she'd delved her hands into the wispy strands of his hair or curled them around a hard horn. Or how his clawed fingertips had dug into her soft thighs. If he hadn't healed her after every sexual experience together, she no doubt would have been bruised or sporting little cuts.

Her legs had been wrapped around his narrow hips, or that arrogant and ignorant head of his. His hands had touched almost every inch of her, but were mainly locked on the places that felt the nicest, like her breasts, pussy, or gliding up her spine.

Only when her core clenched in want from the memories did Lindiwe realise that she'd been chewing on her bottom lip and blatantly ogling him.

Her face flared with heat as she sucked in a silent gasp of surprise and looked down once more. *Oh god, please don't tell me he noticed me staring at him.* She cringed. *I'm so glad he doesn't have the power to read my thoughts.*

Because right then they'd been wildly perverse and naughty.

Her mind radiated with a groan, but she resisted showing how uncomfortable she'd made herself. Especially since shifting her position to close her legs and fold them to the side proved just how wet she'd made herself.

It's not my fault. She pouted as she flipped a page despite not reading a word of it. *I usually don't stay here for very long... and when I do, it's usually to make another child.* To fuck, and from her side, orgasm over and over until she was breaking apart to make up for the years she'd go without.

She actually didn't like that he healed her. It meant the injuries and aches from well-deserved and passionate sex were lost when she actually wanted to hold onto those things. All she was left with was the ghost of the memory in her mind.

She was horny... *a lot.*

Now that she was receiving pleasure, she craved it.

Enough so that she squirmed because the idea of another child only deepened her ache. Not because she wanted another one, but because of what happened beforehand.

Stop it. She wanted to smack herself with her journal but refused to let Weldir know of her internal struggle.

The longer she sat here in his presence, the more she was tempted to crawl – float – over to him and see if they could be intimate *without* there ever being a result.

Once more, she didn't want to let him know just how needy her body could be. He was already too privy to that when they *were* in the moment, by how her inhibitions let go and she'd claw at him for more and more until she was disintegrating into a thrumming, satisfied puddle.

She didn't know if he'd be into the idea, and the inclination she had that he'd reject it also left her silent.

It meant her aching clit and throbbing, damp pussy bothered her every second she stayed there, and she found it difficult to keep her eyes from ogling him. Which, considering he was her husband, she *should* be allowed to do. She should be allowed to go over to him aroused and know she'd be accepted, or naughtily crook her finger at him to come closer.

But her rapidly beating heart, panicked yet full of desire, refused to let her try.

She merely pretended nothing was amiss as she moved onto a new journal.

"Is something wrong?" Weldir asked, not looking up from his task. "Your heart has accelerated."

Lindiwe wanted to crawl inside herself and expire. Her neck heated at being caught out, and her trembling fingers curled into the soft-bound book. "I just have a lot on my mind."

Lots of naughty, perverted thoughts.

Ugh, I've lived a hundred and seventy-one years and I'm acting like a callow girl. Lindiwe should be *beyond* such things. She should be mature and in control at all times, but it was like she couldn't shake that part of her.

Then again, maybe that's what it was like to be human, and it had nothing to do with one's lived age.

I've seen people in their seventies act less mature than those in their twenties. Sometimes life made people grow and harden much too fast and at an alarming and saddening rate.

She often felt like she was fumbling through life, even now. It had hardened her, but her situation was also so wildly abnormal that it was frequently puzzling.

"Is there anything I can do to put you at ease, then?" he asked, lowering the cloak now entirely covered in white feathers while looking up. "I'm enjoying having you within my realm."

There was something he could do, and it would require either his hand, tongue, or cock... or maybe all three.

"You're enjoying me here? We aren't really talking though," she mumbled to get away from her thoughts, her cheeks warming under the compliment.

"Does that matter?" He tilted his head. "It is nice to hear someone's heartbeat and breaths in a place where I do not have my own to fill it. It is... nice knowing my realm isn't empty of your life."

When she didn't say anything, just wriggled uncomfortably because his damn voice was petting her and making her wetter, his visible brow pinched inwards.

"Should I be filling the silence?" He lifted the cloak to look down at it, spreading it out with both his hands – although one was invisible to her. "It's difficult to cast magic like this and speak at the same time."

"N-no, it's fine," she answered with a false grin. "I'm enjoying going through my things and having your silent company."

He lowered the cloak to peer at her as if he wanted to decipher the very fabric of her soul. Then after a long moment he turned his gaze down and resumed his task. She was thankful he let the conversation die.

He brought the dead owl closer and cut into it with a claw. Then he appeared to draw out some of its blood with nothing but his mind. A bubbling stream moved through the air, while the light-blue mana stone attached to her cloak floated and the blood encased it.

Hovering his hands on either side of it, a bright light radiated from them. Silence rang in her ears. *Is he doing some kind of incantation in his mind?*

Then Lindiwe noticed the bright light actually had a shape. Tiny threads twirled with the blood until they were twisted tightly, and they wrapped around the mana stone and slowly began to sink inside it.

"Wait," she rasped, her eyes widening. "You can use magic that isn't of shadows?!"

Weldir grunted as his hands pushed closer towards the mana stone. He didn't answer, nor lift his head, and Lindiwe winced.

Oops. He did say he couldn't talk at the same time. She turned back to her own task – she was supposed to be reading.

But she was interested in the fact that he could use magic that was entirely colourless and wondered what else he could do. At the same time, giddiness simmered inside her at knowing her cloak was likely going to be ready soon.

Since he was distracted and wouldn't watch her strip, she took the opportunity to change into a dress that would be suitable for the warmer seasons of Austrális. She folded her sealskin garment on top of a pile she thought best fitted it.

As the many hours passed, unable to be tracked in Weldir's realm, she eventually curled up on her side. Deciding to rest in a place of utter safety while she could, surprisingly she dozed off quickly.

Only when something tickled her cheek and brushed over her temple did she flinch and fling open her eyes. Weldir was next to her, with his foreclaw close to her face, like he'd brushed a curl behind her ear.

Exhaustion continued to pester her, but her cheeks warmed because all her earlier thrumming meant her dreams hadn't been innocent. They hadn't been for a very long time, often waking her with a prevalent ache between her thighs over the years.

He handed her cloak to her. "It is done."

Blinking against the tiredness and desire battling each other, she spread it out with a wide smile curling her lips. "It's perfect. Thank you so much."

He nodded, then floated back to give her a small amount of space. Adoration filled her as she thumbed the snowy owl feathers, excited to transform into one for the first time.

I wonder if the flight will be different. If it would *feel* different, not just in the air, but in her heart, her spirit.

"Would you like me to transport you to Austrális now?"

The question caught her off-guard. Not because it was strange, as that was usually where she would start her check on her children when she'd been away for a long time, but because she hadn't expected him to offer it so readily.

Her heart sank a little at the prospect. *I've been here for hours and he hasn't wanted anything.* He didn't even ask to touch her, or for an offspring.

Maybe my expectations were a little too high.

She had no one to blame but herself for that, especially as she was complicit in perpetuating Weldir's ignorance by maintaining her silence regarding her wants. She just... the idea of being rejected so sharply like he'd done in the past still lingered as a sore spot and made her hesitant to reach for more.

It stopped her from being confident.

A small sigh flittered out of her as she threw the white-feathered cloak over her shoulders to test its fit. It hid her blue knee-high dress almost completely.

"Austrális is good. I'd like to check on Fenrir and Leonidas first."

"What of Merikh?"

She scrunched her nose. *I really hate that name.* She hated that the name she'd given him was taken from her, and even more so because the name had been special to her – a tribute to her father and his memory.

But she would use it because she respected his wants.

"I think he'll try to kill me on sight, so that's not really a good idea. I've been practising at making scrying discs like the Anzúli. Once I've perfected it, I'll be able to check up on him without him knowing."

"I don't think he'd like that."

Lindiwe averted her gaze as guilt nipped at her stomach. "I know, but I just want to be able to check that he's safe." Then she shot him a little glare as she said, "You do it all the time."

A wide grin revealed his fangs. "But I watch everyone. This is not unusual for me."

But I watch everyone, mur mur mur. She opened and closed her mouth to mock him.

"Austrális, *please*," she demanded, cutting him a playful scowl.

"Nathair does that." Weldir's tone held the mildest chuckle.

Her brows drew together. "Does what?"

"Mocks me when I speak. I find it quite humorous."

"Well, he *is* my child." She tried to laugh it off.

"That he is," he answered, as darkness rushed out of her sight and she was hurtled into bright midmorning sunlight.

A little discombobulated, she tried to get her bearings and note her surroundings while searching for danger. Cool wind swept through her hair and clothing, pushing it all around and towards the canyon below.

Getting ready to leave the cliffside of the Veil, she took a step towards the forest, only to pause. She lifted the hem of her cloak, and a smile split across her face.

"Thank you, Weldir. Truly."

"You are welcome, owlet."

Lindiwe blinked. *Did he just call me a baby owl?*

SEVEN

A time unknown, but a curious one

Lifting a hand, Weldir made three fish manifest above it, creatures he'd practised sculpting after looking into the memories of fishermen.

He cast them into the water, and a bubbling trill came from its depths as Nathair chased them. His tail shimmied side to side as he swam, going along the edges so his side fins could brush up against the rock face.

The sail fin along his back made him look like a gigantic shark lurking, and it allowed Weldir to know exactly where he went beneath the surface.

His offspring playing often brought him great joy, and he lowered himself to sit on the edge of the rock. Nathair never tired as he tried to snap his maw around each fish – never to win because Weldir wouldn't let him. He even tried to slap his hands around them, and occasionally head-butted a wall when the fish disappeared inside it and he didn't have the intelligence to stop.

Weldir sat and watched him for a little while. Now that he was comfortable, and Nathair was distracted, he was able to move onto other tasks.

Tiny dots of black, shadowy magic formed all around Weldir before expanding into viewing discs. Some were partially below his sight line, and others above it. Creating them dug into his well of mana, but he didn't mind.

Thirteen discs formed, each one showing an offspring meandering through Earth and its many forests, meadows, and mountains. None were aquatic like Nathair, and even though one had wings, the feathery appendages were too droopy and heavy upon their back to fly.

Weldir checked on all his offspring, noting most of them weren't doing anything out of the usual.

The discs spun around until he brought the one of Lindiwe and Odie to the forefront so he could watch them. They sat in the colourful hues of morning on a patch of grass within an open space between the trees. Frozen morning dew clung to leaves and branches, the season cold where she was, with piles of dirty, melted snow lingering on the ground.

It must be early spring.

A sense of ease weighed in his mist as he witnessed her trying to explain his name to him again, for what had to be the dozenth time.

"Odie," she said, as she pointed to him.

"Mavka," he answered, pointing at himself.

"Nooo." She shook her head and waved her hands back and forth. "You are a..." She narrowed her eyes, and he could almost read her thoughts by her expression alone. She didn't want to say it, didn't want to call him a Mavka, when she preferred the term Duskwalker. She yielded, likely seeing it was less confusing for him. "You are a Mavka. Mavka. Your *name* is Odie."

He pointed at her. *"Odee?"*

She slapped her hand against her face before patting her chest. "Lindiwe. My name is Lindiwe." She patted it again. "I am a *human.*"

You are a Phantom, little owlet. Weldir kept his silence.

Odie snorted a huff through the nose hole of his otter skull. "Lindiwe-human-thing. Confusing." He waved his hand at her. "Always come. Always annoying." He pointed at his chest. "Me name Mavka. It what beasts call I."

He still has his wording all jumbled up. At least he was getting the foundations down.

Odie waved his hand once more at her dismissively, his claws glinting in the light as he turned to leave her presence. She threw her hands up with her fingers taut, and he could see the scream she was holding back.

He let a chuckle trickle through their bond.

"Don't you dare laugh!" she shouted, slapping at the ground as she stomped to her feet to follow after him. "Because all the Demons have been calling them Mavka, they all think that's what their names are! It's frustrating."

All the noise she made annoyed Odie enough that, while on all fours, he bumped his hip against the trunk of a tree. Dew rained down on her, causing her to squeal softly in surprise.

A deeper chuckle escaped him, and she gritted her teeth and scrunched up her face, which he found remarkably cute. Her glossy curls, now soaking wet, showed more of their length by being weighed down. She chased after Odie, and he increased his pace to get away.

Given his bright-yellow orbs, he merely thought it was a game.

Weldir partially watched their play – although he didn't make Lindiwe aware of it – and moved on to check other discs. Ari was battling against three Demons, but it appeared as though he'd gone out of his way to hunt them. Leonidas was napping inside his cave before night came, whereas Fenrir was wandering Austrális in the region Weldir believed was the northwest. Dymphna was sniffing at the ground to find a suitable spot to sleep in the oncoming sunlight, then he plonked himself down for a morning nap.

Weldir inspected each of the discs and his offspring, occasionally pausing at a more active one as they ventured through the world. A grizzly-bear-skulled Mavka who lived in Unerica came across their sibling with a lynx skull. A fight ensued, and Weldir watched to see who the winner would be.

The lynx one eventually limped away on all fours with

reddened orbs, leaving his brother's skull discarded on the forest floor to be healed in twenty-four hours. Weldir didn't inform Lindiwe of this, as it would only upset her. The fierce grizzly would be fine; he could see that Mavka's soul was still attached to his skull, which was perfectly intact.

One thing Lindiwe informed them all of was that their skulls were precious, and not to break each other's. And to never, *ever* tell anyone of this fact.

Which brought Weldir to Merikh.

The disc was fuzzy, and no image appeared. Instead, he looked upon glittering sand like his mana searched and searched for him but couldn't find his eldest living offspring.

He's hidden behind Jabez's ward again.

He flicked his hand to the right in front of the disc and instead peered through his mist at Jabez's castle. It was a small building, but enough to look grand and gothic in an odd place like the Veil, and it was rough in its shape and finish. Those who built it weren't great architects, but it was sufficient and looked strong.

There was one tower on the right-hand side, while the rest of the castle could be called more of an elaborate, four-level manor. The top of it could be patrolled, and he'd often seen Merikh and Jabez standing up there during the night as they conversed.

Gardens of thorny bushes surrounded it completely, making it appear as though the person within the castle didn't want unwanted guests climbing their way through. They were tall and thick, their thorns sharp enough to collect dewdrops. Hedges around the side made a small labyrinth before leading to an open portal. There was a gated opening barring those who crossed over from Nyl'theria from stepping onto his lands, and clearly Jabez had his castle built close by so he could watch over it.

If Weldir knew what he'd done with the mana stone that powered it, where he'd likely buried it, he would have told Lindiwe to steal it long ago.

Despite the fact that he could note all these details, Weldir, no matter how he tried from his realm, could not see inside the building. There was a barrier in place, a mostly clear one that had an oily, rainbow sheen to it like a bubble. His mist couldn't penetrate it; therefore, his sight couldn't.

But Lindiwe can walk through it in her Phantom form.

Just as he was about to rotate his viewing discs to bring another forward, a claw pierced the one before him. A finger followed, and it wiggled up and down. He pushed the disc to the side and faced Nathair, who had clearly breached the surface of the lake with the goal of interrupting him.

"Attention," he demanded, slithering onto the land to circle Weldir within his tail.

"Maybe I'm too busy to give you attention," he answered, rotating his head around and around to follow his skull. "I believe you're also missing a 'please' somewhere in there."

Nathair stuck out his tongue and blew air with it, then proceeded to shove his body across Weldir's lap. He lay across him, the physical parts of Weldir's body keeping him up, and wriggled back and forth. With his arms folded on the ground to provide a resting spot for his chest and head, he thumped his tail on the grass in a silent demand.

Weldir gave in and scratched his back and sides, and all of Nathair's fins quivered in delight while he rumbled a near purr.

Within a short span of time, perhaps minutes, loud, contented snorting came from his serpent offspring before he fell asleep under the power of Weldir's petting.

His mist spread out from him in contentment, pleased that after so long within his realm, Nathair saw him as safe. He relied on Weldir to ease his loneliness, and Weldir did the same in return.

He continued to scratch Nathair's scales, being careful that his claws didn't harm him. Weldir avoided his gills when he moved to pet his neck, as they were rather sensitive. Nathair eventually rotated to his side while asleep and pushed more of his tail around Weldir as he subconsciously demanded stomach rubs as well.

His left hand stroked Nathair's thin, scaly abdomen as he used his right to rotate the discs, noting both Fenrir and Leonidas were on the move during the early morning. Just as he went to shift his focus and check on one of his many other offspring, he paused when a log cabin in the forest came into view.

Fenrir hid behind some bushes to watch a woman pull out vegetables from an already upturned garden. Her actions, although frantic and fast, were calculated as she picked each one carefully while leaving many others behind. She threw them into a backpack, gasping every time a twig snapped in the distance, then reached for a kitchen blade.

The woman held it to her chest protectively, shaken but with a slitted, narrowed glare.

She looked prepared to fight, as if she expected something to jump out of the bushes and attack her. The straight strands of her black hair were tangled like a nest. The dress she wore was pale pink and of poor quality from what he could tell, compared to the elaborate garments Lindiwe had stored in his realm.

Once she had everything she wanted from the garden, she yanked up her bag and headed back inside with swift steps.

That's when Fenrir stepped out of his hiding place. He lifted his bony wolf snout into the air, sniffing deeply before huffing out with his orbs shifting a dark yellow. On his hands and hind legs, he skulked over to the garden to shove his nose into where she'd knelt, then clawed at the ground like she had.

He pulled out a vegetable and took it with him as he lowered himself and headed towards the opening of her cottage. He skulked up the steps, sniffing each one, and followed the sounds of thumping, hurried footsteps and the clanking of items knocking to the ground.

This... is not going to end well, he thought, when Fenrir poked his head inside.

As he continued to rub Nathair's underbelly, he cupped his chin at something peculiar. *Fenrir hasn't rushed inside in a bloodlust.* His actions were more curious than anything. *This woman must not smell of fear.* Even if her hurried actions inferred otherwise.

She passed Fenrir, not seeing him as she turned her back towards the door while standing in a kitchen area. She checked the contents of a small ceramic jar before closing it and putting it in her backpack, then clipped a small iron skillet to it.

She's packing to leave her home.

She threw the backpack on, which joined the bulky satchel she had at her side.

When Fenrir stepped a hand through the threshold, the floorboards underneath it creaked. She checked over her shoulder, then sucked in a gasp. She brought a kitchen blade to her chest defensively, while her backpack and arse hit the counter she'd been standing at.

She moved to the side, deeper into the house, and her bag knocked items off the counter, leaving behind a mess.

"H-how did you get inside?" Her wide eyes darted from the doorway to Fenrir's wolf skull. "The sun is out. You shouldn't have been able to survive."

Fenrir's skull twisted, causing the rattle of bones from within it, and he pushed his wide shoulders through the entrance.

"Back, Demon!" Her trembling hands swiped her blade through the air to ward him off. "Y-you've had your fill! Now back off. Go back to the forest."

Weldir rotated the disc to get a different perspective, and a scene played out before him.

Claw marks littered the walls and furniture was upturned, showing that a kerfuffle had not long happened. And now that he was looking at it from a different angle, he noted the dried streak of crimson blood upon the ground that led through the doorway and down the stairs of her yard.

Fenrir gave a rumble, which could have been mistaken for a growl as he came closer to her.

"Get away from me, you vile creature!" she shouted, slashing the air again. "You've already taken my family from me, but I will not let you have one bite of me. I will use this blade. I swear it. You come closer to me at your own risk."

Her feet knocked into broken furniture, and she tripped to the side. She scrambled backwards into the corner when Fenrir, uncaring of the danger, skulked closer.

When he encroached on her space to sniff at her, she screamed and sliced her blade through the air. It connected with the crown of his skull and broke in half due to its low quality. Fenrir yelped, his orbs turning white, and sat down while covering the top of his skull from her blow.

"No hit," he whined at her.

Her blue eyes somehow managed to widen further. "Oh heavens, it spoke." She covered her mouth as she shook her head. "Did it steal Blakely's voice?"

She winced and shrunk into herself in preparation for a final strike when Fenrir reached a clawed hand towards her.

"Do it. Just kill me then. Make it fast."

Instead, he placed it against the wall next to her head to balance himself and sniffed at the top of her head. She made herself even smaller as he inhaled her hair and then moved down to her cheek.

He gave another rumble, this time with his orbs shifting to bright yellow. *"Smell nice."* His deer tail wagged against the ground. *"Pretty."*

"E-excuse me?" she rasped, opening her eyes to look at his skull.

She screamed when his large hand encompassed her thin arm and pulled her along the cabin floor. She fought against him, kicking and yanking, which caused the contents of her bags to clank against the wooden boards.

"Let me go!" She screamed louder when he took her all the way outside and hoisted her up over his shoulder. "Put me down, Demon! What more could you want?"

Fenrir ignored her shouts and her knees kicking into his chest as she punched at his back. On three limbs, he carted the woman through the forest with a wag in his deer tail. His orbs remained bright yellow; he was quite happy with himself and the new thing he'd found.

Something that, apparently, never smelt of fear as she was carried. All she showed was rage, and it didn't cease no matter how far he took her. She even buried her face in the fur of his back and tried to bite him before resuming her yells.

Nothing she did mattered, weightless and weak to something as formidable as a Duskwalker. He was able to carry her and all her bags without issue.

Although the day pushed into its highest peak, Weldir kept that viewing disc at his centre while he brought the one displaying his sleeping mate closer.

"Lindiwe," he called. When she didn't stir, he did so louder. "Lindiwe, wake up. Something is happening that may be of interest to you."

She flinched and then curled deeper into herself on her side. Burying her face in her hands, she then rubbed at her eyes before peeking them open.

"Weldir? Did you call me?" she asked, her voice sleep-laden and with a lovely rasp.

"Yes, little female. I did."

As if that was all she needed, her eyes opened wide, and she sat up within her protective dome. "What is it? What's wrong?"

She reached for the handle of her bag, pulling it closer to her from where she'd been using it to cushion her head.

"I wouldn't say anything is wrong just yet." His gaze slipped to the viewing disc of Fenrir and a still-fighting human.

Her eyes narrowed into a glare that held no fire. "There's always something wrong when you call me like this."

"I guess it would depend on your perspective. Fenrir has come across a human, but he's decided not to eat her."

Her full lips pursed in thought. "Then what's he doing?"

"From what I can tell, he might be taking her to the Veil."

"And he's not eating her?" She brought her knees up to her chest and covered her mouth as her expression grew more pensive. "Is she not afraid?"

"She seems more enraged, to be honest." Then he thought

back to the state of her home. "I'm guessing a Demon came through the night and killed, stole, and ate her family. She has mistaken our offspring as the culprit."

Lindiwe slipped her gaze to the side coyly. "In all fairness, he could have done so if he was the one to stumble upon their home. Her... assumption wouldn't be wrong."

"I was watching. It was not him. Fenrir came upon her as she was packing her artefacts to leave."

"Without someone to protect her, she must have been escaping to a nearby village then," she muttered. She looked up at the sky momentarily. "And it must only be early morning there. She was waiting for the sun."

A small silence was shared between them as he watched both his mate and his offspring. When it went on for too long, Lindiwe unmoving upon the ground as her eyes stared off into the distance, Weldir broke it.

"What do you want to do?"

Her lips drew inwards as they tightened. "I... don't know."

"It's likely that he'll eat her," he pointed out.

"Exactly. Why intervene if what he'll do is just natural for him?" Her fingers picked at the seam of her satchel. "But the question is..."

"What if he doesn't?"

Her voice was small. "Yes, exactly."

"We can wait to see what happens." Then Weldir offered a possibility that hadn't come to mind until now. "They are soul eaters. There is a possibility that if they eat the soul of a living human, they could bond with one."

She lowered her face with her lips parting on a quiet gasp. "Like what you and I have?"

"Perhaps similar."

She regarded this new information in depth, darting her eyes back and forth across the ground. But he knew her expression and what the invigoration in it meant.

Lindiwe was excited about their offspring finding mates.

"Let me know what happens if they reach his cave," she said, grabbing her bag to rifle through it in search of her writing charcoal and journal. "If she makes it there... I'll get you to bring me to your realm to watch what happens."

Lindiwe flicked through the pages of her journal until she found a blank one. At the top, she marked the date, and it orientated Weldir to how long they'd truly been bonded. A hundred and forty-nine years had passed.

March 14th, 1832, she wrote.

EIGHT

A time unknown, but of strange beginnings

Huddled in the corner of Fenrir's cave, the human never took her eyes off the Duskwalker who sat before her. His backside was on the floor, his arms straight to hold up his bowed torso, and his deer tail wagged. His orbs flickered between bright yellow for joy, and dark yellow in curiosity.

Although it was daytime, the cave was deep enough to be shaded. A dusty sunbeam cascading from the entrance and an oil lantern on the ground next to her feet brightened everything enough for her to see.

Her pale-pink skirts were dirty and leaf debris clung to her. Her brown lace-up boots were neatly placed to the side, with her socks tucked into their openings. Glaring through falling strands of her black hair, she pulled one of her satchels closer and flipped open the flap. She retrieved an uncooked carrot and crunched down on it loudly.

Her blue eyes seemed to narrow further at Fenrir as she chewed.

"She has barely moved from her spot except to relieve herself," Weldir commented as he tipped his head to the side to look at his mate. "Fenrir learned quickly of this need during their travels to the cave."

"Did a Demon not come upon them?" Lindiwe asked, her

eyes never straying from the disc.

The white feathers of her cloak lifted and swayed, as did her hair. Sitting cross-legged and similarly to Weldir, she was much more animated as she absentmindedly picked at her nails or scratched at an itch. She appeared restless.

"They managed to arrive without interference," he answered her, resuming the observation of his offspring's captive at the sound of another crunch.

"I'm worried about what will happen when a Demon does eventually come." Her voice was small, yet her furrowed expression was indecipherable. "If he tries to protect her, he could go into a bloodlust and kill her without realising what he's doing."

"Do you think that will bother him?"

"Who knows? He might not care, or maybe he won't remember."

"You seem... nervous."

She finally pulled her gaze away to where Weldir's head was, even though there was little for her to see right now.

"I am. Fenrir is sweet. He's rather obedient, and even if he's wary of me, he's never really pushed me away. I think he's... lonely... and has been since he gained much of his humanity." She bit down on her bottom lip, the corners of her eyes crinkling before she looked down at her hands. "I want him to find a friend. To find... *love*, if it's possible."

"Aren't you being too hopeful?"

She was allowing herself too much yearning for this when it was likely to fail. *I don't see the human living past a few days. Fenrir would inevitably eat her, or a Demon would. She's likely going to flee and get herself killed.*

Not only was Fenrir's cave at the fringe of the Veil's forest, but she'd also need to safely navigate up the cliffside and then escape through the infested forest above. There would be no escaping for her, and Fenrir would chase after his prey before she could get far.

Despite the way her heart was beating fast and echoing in his realm, Lindiwe offered him a strange smile. "Sometimes all you need is hope."

What a preposterous notion! Weldir didn't say that, though; he'd learned that stating his objections could upset her.

"Take me home," the human demanded, Weldir having missed her final bites of her carrot and whatever she'd done afterwards.

Fenrir tilted his head, and his impala horns cast a devilish shadow against the wall behind him. *"No. Stay."*

Then he leaned closer to sniff at her face, and she shrank into herself while bravely, albeit foolishly, pushing at his bony snout. He licked at her hands, and his purple tongue slipped between the spaces of her fingers.

She cringed in disgust.

She retracted her hands and wiped them on her dress. "You can't keep me here, Demon."

"Demon?" He tilted his head the other way as he pulled it back. *"Furnrearh not Demon. Furnrearh is Mavka."* He bashed his fist against his skeletal, protruding chest, and a hollow thud reverberated. *"Mavka."*

The female's lips twisted. "Did you just call yourself Fur and Rear?"

Fenrir shrugged. *"Is name."*

"It's stupid to call yourself something just because you're furry," she stated matter-of-factly, lifting her chin. "And mentioning your rear is impolite."

"It's only because he said it wrong," Lindiwe whined defensively, covering her eyes with one hand and shrugging with the other. "At least he finally figured out the gist of it, and that his name isn't actually Mavka. *That* was a pain to unfold in his mind." Then under her breath and laced with a sigh, she muttered, "And it's more than I can say for *most* of my children."

"Furnrearh," Fenrir stated, punching his chest again. *"Is Mavka."*

"No. Call yourself something else," the human demanded.

"I refuse to call you a furry *arse*." She whispered the last word as if she found it indecent.

"*Furnrearh,*" he said again, before pointing at her. "*Human. Little thing.*"

"I have a name, and it's not human nor little. Nor am I a *thing*." Then she grumbled, "But I honestly can't expect any etiquette from a monster."

Weldir looked at Lindiwe to see how she fared with their offspring being called such a thing. Her face was expressionless and dull, and that could only mean two things when it came to his mate. She either didn't care, or she was boiling with rage over it; there was no middle ground.

It also made it exceptionally difficult for Weldir to know if he'd truly done something wrong or not.

"*Human smell nice,*" Fenrir said, leaning in once more with his deer tail wagging.

"My name is Katerina. Stop calling me human." She braved pushing his snout to the side, and he resisted at first before letting her win. "If you're too stupid to make up a name, I'll give you a new one. It can be my gift to you for letting me go."

Obviously she spoke too fast and too complicatedly for Fenrir, and he sat there twisting his head one way and then the other in quick succession. Rattling came from him, like dry bones clacking together each time, and it likely didn't help his cause.

Katerina cupped her narrow chin and tapped against her cheek in thought. "I think I'll call you... Orpheus. I think that's fitting. If I try to run from you, I'll likely be eaten by a Demon or a snake, and if you look for me, I'll probably die anyway." She picked up the tangled ends of her hair and sneered at them before throwing the mess over her shoulder. "I'm in hell, since you brought me to the Veil – of all the idiotic places – and you're obviously already in love with me like in the tale. Even in this pathetic, disgusting state."

Clearly realising she'd rambled to a being that barely understood a word of what she said, she rolled her eyes with an exaggerated sigh.

She placed her delicate, pale hand against her chest. "Katerina. Katerina is human." Then she pointed at him. "Orpheus. Orpheus is Demon."

He patted his chest. *"Mavka. No Demon."*

"Fiiine." She pointed at him again. "Orpheus is Mavka. Orpheus is your new name."

"Orfeee... us?" He tilted his head yet again.

"Not Fur Rear. Orpheus." Then, as if she thought it would help her situation, she leaned closer and placed her hand over his chest. "Your name is Orpheus."

He nodded. *"Orfeeeus."* Then he pointed to his chest while repeating the word as if to commit it to memory. *"Katareka name Orfeeeus."*

Weldir's mist vibrated with humour at the way he said his new name, and he turned to Lindiwe to share in that with her. It stopped the moment he found her looking off into the nothingness with an angry furrow to her brows and her lips hardened into thin lines.

"Something has upset you."

Her fists clenched tighter until the skin across her knuckles was taut. "A little."

"Why? She has given him a new name. I would think this is a good sign."

"Because it's not his name. This is the third child who has renamed themselves. I've always hoped they would one day learn their names, and right as he was beginning to do so, she takes it from me, from him. It's just... it's not fair."

I see. I hadn't thought about how carefully she picks their names, often with meaning behind them.

Seeing his mate in need of consoling, he reached across while forcing the physical parts of him to his right hand. He lifted her chin and turned her face to him, gentle and coaxing.

"Fenrir has a new name, but we know what it originally was, what it meant. That is all that matters. He is still our wolf-skulled offspring, and now he has a new name to go with all that hope you have. It is a name for a new beginning."

Not that Weldir believed her faith was well placed.

Lindiwe's expression relaxed as she blinked up at him. Her full lips parted, and she held his gaze longer than he thought she would. She didn't pull away, didn't groan in dismay or glare. Actually, from what he could gather, she appeared a little dumbfounded by his words and actions.

A wounded smile lifted her lips. "I guess that's true."

She only pulled away to look into the disc when Katerina spoke.

"Okay, Orpheus. Now..." She rolled her shoulders back and lifted her chin. "Take me home. I want to leave."

"Stay, Katareka. No safe."

Katerina threw up her arms. "I want to go home!"

Orpheus snapped his fangs with a growl at her loud exclamation. She gasped, her eyes widening, and then audibly swallowed.

"Okay." She pulled one of her satchels to her chest protectively. "I'll stay. J-just don't hurt me."

Orpheus gave a pleased, wolfy chuff before reaching forward. Katerina attempted to duck her feet away, but she could only scooch them so far against her backside. He gingerly grabbed her foot, as if he wanted to be careful, only to yank it too far and high, making her slide down the wall and onto the ground.

Kicking to no avail, Katerina twisted and tried to pull away as Orpheus grabbed the toe next to her big toe and wiggled it. He played with all of them curiously, and even when she laughed because he tickled her with a stray claw, she looked nothing but panicked.

His touch was inquisitive, even when he pulled her skirt in the air to look underneath it, finding a pair of white shorts, and nothing of interest. He moved onto her hands, playing with her fingers like her toes. Each time she pulled against his hold and whined about it, telling him to let go.

Yet when he grabbed her hair to sniff it, she let out a cry, and he immediately backed off with his orbs flashing orange. He lowered submissively, realising he'd hurt her when that hadn't been his intention. Shaking, the female backed against the wall again and shoved her skirt down until it hid her feet. She brought her three bags closer to shield herself, and he tilted his head at her.

Then he tentatively inched forward. When she didn't openly reject his approach, although Weldir knew by her expression that she was wary, he curled up at her feet with his back almost on top of them. She pulled her feet out from underneath him swiftly and wrapped her arms around her knees. He was blocking an easy path to the exit, and Weldir was unsure if he did it on purpose or not.

Perhaps he just wanted to show her he was safe – although that absolutely wasn't true.

"I want to help them," Lindiwe whispered, her eyes unmoving from the pair. "There must be something we can do. Something to keep her safe. I... understand why she's so nervous, but hopefully he gains her trust."

"What do you suggest?"

Uncertain, she absentmindedly picked at the side of her thumb again. "I'm not sure. I could give them some blessed salt to stop the Demons from entering his home, but I don't know if that will suffice. If it rains, it'll wash away the protection."

Weldir considered potential options until his sight landed on her cloak. It sat around her shoulders comfortably, and she seemed to prefer the weight of it after so many years. She hadn't even shed it when she arrived here.

But what his gaze really fell on was where the mana stone would be underneath it. The stone was attached near the ties of her cape, dangling its weight against her breastbone.

"I could possibly make a protection enchantment that she could wear on her person, like how I made your cloak."

Lindiwe reached up to curl her fingers around the mana stone and turned to him. "I don't want to give up my cloak. I need it."

He called an array of items to him. Above his left hand floated the other mana stone fragments she'd mined, showing he had many he could use. Above his right hand hovered three pieces of jewellery she'd left here: a silver ring with a diamond on it, a thick golden bangle, and a silver circlet diadem that had diamonds glittering along its twining arms.

"I can fuse a stone to any one of these, if you don't mind giving one of them up."

As she regarded each one carefully, her expression grew pensive. Then she flicked her gaze to him. "The ring could be the wrong size, as could the bracelet. I think the diadem would be best."

Weldir made the ring and bangle disappear as he grasped the circlet. "Then I will make the enchantment."

"While you're doing that, I can bless one of the sacks of normal salt I left here with the pouch from the Anzúli. I'll also double-check if the spell needs an incantation or not. I know which journals to check, so I should be done by the time you're finished."

Decision made, they both drifted off to complete their respective tasks.

Weldir watched his mate approach the entrance to Orpheus' cave at midday, which allowed bright sunlight to shine over her. A subtle gust of wind pushed her cloak around her legs, while her curls bounced to the side within the confines of the ponytail she'd thrown them up in.

The dress underneath her cloak was an altered Anzúli robe, as Lindiwe had learned that the colour of her clothing impacted the hue of her feathers' stems. This hadn't been an issue when her cloak had been one of raven feathers, as the darkness hid any colour.

She cradled a burlap sack on her hip, while her satchel was crossed over her torso. Inside it was food, the diadem, and an array of other useful tools Lindiwe had spares of and thought might be of assistance. Fire-starting tools, a thin blanket, a water sack, and a few smaller items.

A growl started quiet and low – a warning for the one approaching to back away. Lindiwe didn't heed that demand, and it turned into a snarl before Orpheus skulked out of the cave on all fours. He blocked the entrance protectively, his fish fins and fur raised on their ends to show his growing aggression.

"W-what's there?" Katerina's voice echoed from within the shallow cave. "Is it another Demon?"

"Leave," Orpheus growled, his voice gruff, distorted, and beastly as he puffed himself further. *"Go away. My human."*

Lindiwe's lips tightened and her eyes crinkled. "That's unlike you. You're usually calmer upon seeing me."

"Wait..." Katerina's gasp echoed. "Is that another person?" The sound of clanking items and shuffling feet came from within before the female's wide blue eyes peeked over his shoulder. "Please save me! This beast is keeping me trapped here!"

Something glinted in Lindiwe's eyes, even when she steeled her expression and voided it of emotion. Whether it be guilt or uncertainty, she shook her head.

"I... shouldn't interfere. It's not my place to," she answered. "I came to help him."

"No help." Orpheus bashed his chest with a deep thump. *"Is strong. I protect."*

"Why would you help a Demon?! I'm the one who needs help!" Katerina pushed at Orpheus' shoulder to get him to move, but he didn't budge an inch.

"He isn't a Demon," Lindiwe stated with a sigh. "He's a Duskwalker."

The black-haired female's eyes grew impossibly wider. "What the hell is a Duskwalker?"

"It's what he is," Lindiwe answered, gesturing to him. "He is born from..." She sucked her lips into her mouth warily. "All you need to know is that he isn't a Demon. They call themselves

Mavka."

Katerina regarded him. "Is that why he has a skull head?"

"Yes. When he was first born, he was fed fish, a wolf skull, and part of an impala antelope. He gains humanity and intelligence from every human he eats. Although Demons have a similar trait, they are vastly different. He isn't... evil like them. At least, not at his core."

The female narrowed her eyes at Lindiwe. "You seem to know a lot about him."

"I raised him," Lindiwe admitted. "I know everything there is to know about Duskwalkers."

Katerina's expression paled, making the dark impressions under her tired eyes more sunken. "You raised him?!" She stepped back. "What kind of human raises a monster?"

Weldir chuckled when Lindiwe cut the female a rather lethal glare. "He isn't a monster."

"No human," Orpheus cut in, pointing at his mother. *"Is Phantom bird thing."*

Perhaps their past encounters allowed Orpheus to accept Lindiwe at a distance, but he was remarkably calm about her presence now that they were talking. Weldir wondered if this meant he would eventually welcome a proper relationship with her in the future.

Much in the same way Weldir and Nathair had grown a bond due to constant exposure to each other. He'd whittled down Nathair's aversion to his strangeness.

Lindiwe didn't have as much endless time, nor was it in her best interest to annoy their offspring too deeply or they'd attack. Weldir, on the other hand, was impervious to harm, and was much more forceful because he had the freedom to be that way.

"I don't understand what's happening," Katerina muttered lowly. "What's a Phantom bird?"

"I'm able to change forms into a snowy owl." Lindiwe cleared her throat, and it was something she only ever did when she was out of her depth with someone or something. "I was once a human, but I have bonded with a demi-god, and he has turned me into a Phantom. It allows me to turn incorporeal, like a spirit. He doesn't quite understand that I can be many things."

"That's witchcraft," the female whispered, horrified.

"Witchcraft and witches are outdated terms. I'm no different to the temple acolytes that protect towns."

"Except you're not one." Katerina levelled an untrusting glower at her. "And they're no better. Anyone who follows the temple will be condemned and will greet the gates of damnation. My family refused to live under their evil curses and spells."

She believes in the faith that Lindiwe once had. Weldir never understood this mindset about faith. There were other gods, other religions, other customs that brought goodness to the world, and yet they were so vehemently renounced.

Weldir had never met this god, who didn't even have the care nor decency to share his name, only his teachings. And his followers condemned the Anzúli when they were here to save them, leaving themselves open to Demon attacks because of it.

Apparently going to heaven by being eaten was preferable to them than the idea of allowing others of a different faith to help them.

But, like many religions across Earth, most were giving up their faiths. They prayed to the temples, not to their god, because they offered food, water, medicine, shelter, and spells that helped them. They placed their worship in tangible assistance, rather than in fears of the unknown.

This female and her family were apparently too strong-willed to falter like the rest of humankind.

"And yet here you are, in the Veil, because you chose not to be protected. Where is your god now?" Lindiwe answered, surprising Weldir.

Then again, he probably shouldn't have been shocked by her rather cold words. She belonged to him, and over the years, her ideologies regarding faith had been warped and twisted by him. She prayed to no one, sought faith in no one but herself, because she had no need for any other deity except him.

She was aware of the other Elven gods, but she cared so little about them that she likely didn't spare them a second thought.

"He is here, as he always has been. This was his will, and he's merely testing me as one of his mortal children." Katerina folded her arms and rolled her shoulders back rather self-righteously. "You're a witch, a master of a Duskwalker. You won't help me, and you can apparently gallivant through the Veil. Sounds like trickery and evil to me."

"I'm a master of no one, least of all a Duskwalker who can think for themselves. And like I said, it's not my place to interfere with his wants," Lindiwe answered in a closed-off tone. She gestured to the burlap sack on her hip. "I've brought blessed salt that can be used as a barrier to stop Demons from entering his home. I also brought some food and water, as well as an enchanted diadem that should–"

"Why should I take anything from you?" Katerina sneered, and the blue of her eyes seemed colder than before. "Anything you give me is likely cursed. I won't touch something that could be impure and taint my soul."

Lindiwe's cheek twitched and her jaw muscles pulsed. "So you would rather be eaten or starve?"

"I'd rather go home!" Katerina yelled, causing Orpheus to step forward and snarl at Lindiwe. "Either help me do so or leave!"

"I already said–"

Katerina threw her hands into the air and went deeper into the cave. "Then I refuse to speak to a vile witch. I'll figure out how to escape on my own."

Orpheus, with dark-yellow orbs, tilted his head, seeming bemused at her willingness to go into his home. It was obvious he didn't quite understand what had happened, or what had been said.

Lindiwe's lips parted in disbelief, and she shook her head, causing her ponytail to sway.

"Fine, I'll show you, Orpheus," she stated with a sigh.

"You've been watching us!" Katerina yelled from within the

cave, likely due to Lindiwe saying his new name he was gifted the day before. "You spy on us like an evil spirit!"

Lindiwe took one step closer, just one, and it snagged Orpheus' attention. He leapt forward with a roar, Lindiwe too close to him, his new female, and the entrance to his home.

She relaxed her expression, dull and unimpressed, as a shadowy dome materialised over him and the cave. Orpheus bashed into it, then swiped his claws right where her torso was.

Since he was unable to penetrate it, he paced within the barrier, snarling at her when she moved. Lindiwe placed the burlap sack on the ground and then removed her satchel to rest it next to it.

She threw her right hand to the side and a spike of shadowy magic formed. With very little effort, she knelt and stabbed it into the ground right next to the cliff face. She proceeded to draw a semi-circle around the dome, with pointed looks at Orpheus, who eventually calmed enough to watch her while snorting annoyed huffs.

"You must dig into the ground so that the wind doesn't blow away the salt line," she explained. "See? Carve. You must carve."

She picked up the burlap sack and opened it. Her hand slipped inside the bag of white grains, and she obtained a careful fistful, making sure hardly any fell out of her palm. From just an inch high, she proceeded to sprinkle a small amount into the groove she'd made to form the salt line.

"Do not waste it. Be careful. Be slow," she explained multiple times, as repetition was the best way to teach him. "Rain removes protection. You must protect your human and sprinkle more salt when dry."

Orpheus, who had backed up to the entrance of his cave, snorted a wolfish chuff. *"Rain bad?"*

"No. Rain is good. Rain is clean, but rain is bad for protecting your human." Lindiwe walked over to her satchel. "Be good. Don't hurt your human. Feed her, keep her warm."

Opening up the flap, Lindiwe retrieved the diadem from it

before tossing the satchel through her barrier. Food and the water sack partially slid out from its opening when the bag landed next to Orpheus' hand, and he leaned down to sniff it with mild interest.

"I told you, I don't want your cursed food or water," Katerina said as she peeked out from behind Orpheus.

"In the Veil, you take what you can to survive," Lindiwe answered, backing away. "You'll die otherwise."

The two females held each other's stares. Then Lindiwe flipped up the hood of her cloak, proceeded to shift into her owl form, and flew off. Katerina's eyes grew stark, her jaw fell, and a raspy near-scream escaped her.

"She really turned into an owl!"

Weldir could only imagine how horrified she would've been had Lindiwe turned into a raven, as it could have easily been mistaken for a Demon.

I'm surprised she didn't want to return to me straight away, as we discussed. Then again, his mate looked rather... jaded after the interaction. *She is likely upset and wishes to clear her mind.*

NINE

A time unknown, but of subtle truths

When his mate finally landed near the edge of a cliff, she transformed into a human with her back to the Veil's horizon.

"Do you feel better?" Weldir asked, noting her clenched fists.

Many hours had passed, enough to note the falling sun and long shadows. She stood in the light and regarded the forest with a stiff face.

"No. Not really," she eventually answered, before looking down over the cliff. "But there is no point in wasting more energy. I'm ready to return."

Pleased that she would fill his void once more, Weldir lacked any hesitancy and brought Lindiwe to his realm. She materialised in the nothingness, and her ghostly form became solid as she shifted into a tangible Phantom for him.

With one last look at the many viewing discs before him, Orpheus front and centre, he turned to greet her. It was unnecessary, as she'd already begun to swim towards him. Halting at his side to peer into the disc, she went to place her hand on his non-existent shoulder to steady herself. He made his physical self coalesce there as a piece of support.

Her expression was closed off, but her eyes glinted with rapt interest. "How are they?"

"Mostly the same. She has told him you are untrustworthy, and he doesn't understand why. He isn't adept enough with language to have such a cohesive argument just yet. It is also obvious he can't remember much of what you have done to help him, either. It's like he has an impression of you but can't remember specific memories or details."

Her lips pushed forward into a purse. "She better not turn him against me. It has taken me decades to get to the point where he trusts me, and even then... it's fragile."

"She has taken to calling you the Witch Owl."

The bridge of her cute nose scrunched. "I guess she isn't wrong, but I don't particularly like the term. 'Witches' were often just normal women who were taken to silence them. I'd consider any of our magical capabilities to be coincidences or power loaned to us by gods." Lindiwe narrowed her eyelids into a scowl. "Why are you grinning?"

Am I? Weldir thought, noting how he perceived pressure. *I didn't think my humour was so apparent.* Although it did vibrate within his cloud rather violently.

"Because you don't like it. If you call me spirit of the void, I will retaliate and call you the Witch Owl."

Her jaw fell, and she placed her hand over her heart as if he'd wounded her. "That's mean," she grumbled, before the smallest smile curled her lips.

It fell when she brought her gaze back to Orpheus, who was back outside, wasting salt as he sprinkled more into the carving Lindiwe had made. His orbs were dark yellow, and he even scratched at the groove to deepen it in places out of curiosity.

Weldir was sure he'd come to understand the significance of the magic when night and Demons came. Which brought on a question he'd had since his mate left Orpheus' home.

He regarded the item enclosed in her fist. "You took back the diadem?"

With one hand on top of the other, she opened the top one to reveal the diadem with a pale-blue mana stone. The teardrop gem dangled from the centre of the silver circlet, where there was a delicate vee that would point down to the wearer's brows.

As Lindiwe thumbed the stone, it clinked against the metal. "I don't want it to be lost because she refuses to take it. Maybe another one of our children will seek a companion and need protection from the Demons."

"The human is rather..." He trailed off, unsure of how to describe her. He thought her rejection of Lindiwe's aid had been quite foolish.

"Things didn't go as I thought they would," Lindiwe said, folding her legs to the side. "I didn't expect her to be hateful towards me. But... I understand it. She has every right to feel the way she does, to believe what she wants."

"She believes in the god of your past."

"Hmm." She brought her hands, and the diadem, into her lap. "It's why I get where she is coming from. It's hard to shake that mindset. I know I struggled with it. Even now I can still feel the foundations inside my mind and heart, can still hear my parents whispering to me the teachings. Faith that strong just doesn't disappear."

Weldir tilted his head at that, and at her fidgeting hands. "But she will let it go, as did you."

"What if she doesn't?" She looked down at her lap before curling her hands tighter around the jewellery. "Why does this feel so... wrong, Weldir? Why do I feel like we're doing the wrong thing?"

"Wrong?" Weldir asked, his tone rather perplexed. He waved his hand towards Orpheus. "I only see this as a benefit. He will have a companion, or she will gift him more humanity. She is already further expanding his vocabulary and teaching him, even if it is accidental. All I see is his growth."

Her brows pinched with an emotion he couldn't decipher. "But how is that fair on her?" She turned her face to him with a beseeching expression. "How are we any better than the occultists who sacrificed women to the Veil? She has no other choice but to stay there or die, just as I was given no other choice but to..."

She averted her gaze to the side, and her jaw clenched tight enough that the muscles in it ticked. A shadow of emotion seemed to fall over her, tensing her shoulders and back.

"Sometimes one must be sacrificed for the greater good. It is how we learn, and we can pass this knowledge and help on to our other offspring should they need it. It's selfishness at the cost of one life."

"How is this good?" She waved at the viewing disc. "Every life matters. No one should be sacrificed. It's... it's cruel."

"And yet we have allowed our offspring to cease many hearts."

"I've never been pleased about that," she grumbled curtly. "The right thing to do would be to take her home, but I think... I think he would hate me for taking away his friend. I don't want to lose his trust in a way that he may never forgive me. He needs me too much to grow hateful of my presence if no one else will be there for him." The hurt on her face worsened and tears dotted her lashes. "Even if she makes him hate me, so long as she survives and he has someone, I think that'll be okay."

Weldir leaned forward, even if it was only in her periphery. "Is this why you flew for so many hours?"

"Yes. My heart was telling me to do one thing and my mind another. I want him to be happy, but at the same time, I'm riddled with all this guilt that I just don't know how to process. I feel so out of my depth with this."

Seeing she needed comfort, Weldir tentatively slipped his fingers into a clenched fist, so he could gently hold her hand. "And you settled on not interfering, other than offering aid to our offspring."

"I picked Orpheus. I decided to pick a future in which he can be happy." She looked down and clasped his hand in return. "I'm hoping that she just needs time to accept and care for him. If Merikh's friendship with Jabez has shown me anything, it's that our offspring can form bonds. That they can emulate human affection."

"Will you be upset if he eats her?"

"Yes, but... really, it would be long overdue. He should have done so when he first met her. I'm surprised she's lasted this long. That *any* human has."

Weldir considered her words as they both stared at the viewing disc.

The little female was sparking her tinderbox so she could light her lantern before darkness truly settled upon the world. Once done, she shuffled back against the wall with a blanket and then pouted with her arms folded on top of her knees.

Orpheus was outside scouting the area to make sure it was safe, completely and blissfully unaware of her negative emotions towards him and his existence.

"Perhaps they are more like me than we considered," Weldir said quietly, inspecting his wolf-skulled offspring intently.

"What do you mean?"

"They are incomplete creatures that seek companionship, even if the means are not always fair. They are going against their nature, and they will likely stumble, as I often have. I hope that doesn't make us any less deserving of affection, even if we aren't always able to properly reciprocate it."

Joy radiated through Weldir's mist when he saw Orpheus back at the salt line, sitting at it as he twisted his head one way and then the next. *He understands, even if it doesn't seem like it.* His language capabilities were stilted, but he comprehended enough that he didn't immediately ruin Lindiwe's work.

He even brought the satchel she'd left behind inside and dumped it in front of Katerina, who sneered at it. When his back was turned, she gingerly kicked it to the side.

If Lindiwe can come to accept me, then surely this human can accept my offspring.

That had taken decades, but that was due to their inability to share real moments. They couldn't exist long term in either realm, as she had a duty to perform in hers, and his realm wasn't a life worth living. There was no possibility of him existing in her world, when he could not touch it, taste it, or even smell it.

He would merely haunt her, like a spirit.

She sought the light, and he belonged in the void.

Katerina looks upon Orpheus similarly to how Lindiwe once looked upon me. Seeing it again, a gaze that wasn't narrowed on him but on someone who was just as ignorant, formed pity in his consciousness. *Hopefully she learns to trust him long before he realises what that gaze means.*

Although Weldir's thoughts had turned forlorn, especially regarding his mate, he had this yearning to look upon her beauty. To know that her gaze had lost its ire and spite, and she now looked upon him fondly.

He hadn't expected to greet her stare, or for her brown eyes, filled with flecks of mesmerising golden amber, to appear so... tender. There was a softness to her expression as her eyes flicked side to side while she regarded him.

Her shoulders relaxed. Then a small smile curled her full lips, and it made her cheeks swell, as if with mild joy. "Do you seek affection, Weldir?"

"Don't most beings?" he asked rhetorically. "I may be a god, but I still wish to experience such things."

"Demi-god," she corrected, as her smile grew.

"Ugh." Weldir rolled his eyes, not that she could tell by the lack of whites in them. "I have told you before: a god is a god, no matter their status."

A small laugh escaped her.

The sound of her humour, so rarely shared with him, echoed in his realm. He grasped at it with his mana and tried to trap it within his mist permanently. It faded before he could find a way to do so.

"Thank you, Weldir." She continued to hold his hand – finally hers had stilled from the anxious picking.

"For what?" he asked. "Our opinions differ on the matter of what is good and what is wrong about this situation."

"Because even if you didn't mean to, you made me feel better. Thank you for letting me talk to you, and for not disregarding my feelings even if you don't agree with me."

Weldir's mist tightened against him as something pleasant

sparked through his being.

"Of course. I've... always tried to be a source of comfort for you."

He often wanted her to see things his way, not because he wanted to be right, but because it was often simpler and lacked emotional ties, or human morals and ideologies. Which in turn could alleviate her guilt or pain.

Generally, he only ever made matters worse.

"I know," she answered softly. "I think I've begun to see that."

His mist drew impossibly tighter against him, and he felt pressure across his face. He believed his own smile had formed, one that might be rather triumphant.

Only intense emotions tended to have a physical reaction that he couldn't control.

They sat together in silence, watching Orpheus until it was late into the night and the female he had in his keeping curled up underneath her blanket to have a fitful sleep. Whether it be luck or coincidence, no Demons came to disturb them, and his offspring guarded her vehemently through the night.

"Is this how you've been watching us?" Lindiwe asked, gesturing to the other discs.

Weldir followed her gaze to the view of Dymphna, who ambled alongside a stream through the forest. After so many years, his third-eldest offspring was large and muscular. He'd lost many of his bones due to eating many creatures, and had long ago gained his gender and much humanity.

Nowhere near Merikh, who had dozens of human deaths on his clawed hands, but enough to be rather intelligent.

He was one of the only Mavka who knew their name clearly.

"Yes. I spend much of my time like this," Weldir admitted, turning his sight on one of their newer offspring.

This one also had a wolf skull. Wolves had been a formidable foe against the Demons, their numbers still large due to how they hunted and defended in packs.

Freki had pronghorn antlers and had a name from the same

origins as Fenrir. Perhaps that was why the name being taken from Lindiwe bothered her so much.

Their stomach was gaunt, giving their body a sickly, starved appearance, and all their bones still protruded. They had yet to find their gender, since they hadn't stumbled upon any humans thus far.

"I find it... relaxing," Weldir continued, letting his sight roam. The edge of each viewing disc glittered with black sand and smoke, giving them all a mystical and enchanted aura. "I'm a part of your lives, even if it's only distantly. I often complete my tasks while watching you all. I witness, as that is all I can do."

"I didn't realise you cared so much."

Weldir's mist pulled in tight, only to release. He turned his face to her and found her watching Ari hunting low through the stalks of tall grass. On all fours, he slowly approached a group of Demons who were seated around a small campfire, each one more humanoid than average. These had eaten many humans – or Elves – in their time.

"I care quite deeply, Lindiwe."

How can she not know this? He'd never hidden his fondness for his offspring. *Perhaps it's because she's never seen it.*

When she craned her neck up at the view of Odie, Weldir's gaze drifted down the column of her throat, over her collarbones, and then down to her chest.

I could show her how much I care.

He had the nagging desire to reach out and brush along her jaw to see how she'd react. To caress lower until he skimmed his claws down the exposed part of her chest, and maybe even deep inside the neckline of her dress. He wondered if he'd steal a surprised gasp, if her skin would cascade in goosebumps, or if she'd give him a heated gaze – such a rare, although beautiful, thing.

There was something about Lindiwe that was mesmerising to his mind. What had started out as curious fascination had moulded into something else entirely, and he couldn't quite place what.

All he knew was that he found her alluring in all ways.

Her eyes, sparkling with so much life and personality, were akin to a tiger's-eye gemstone, the brown flecked with amber like molten crystal. They were no longer just brown to him; they were more than that – deeper, more vibrant.

Her dark lashes fanned around them, long, lush, and offering so many expressions he struggled to fathom. Her brows were arched sharply, giving her youthful face a maturity to it that he'd come to appreciate.

Her skin was soft beneath his touch, always yielding, and had little black spots dotting it here and there. One on the back of her shoulder, another on the inside of her knee, and many more. Beauty marks, he believed the humans called them, and he'd counted all seven of them and knew where they were by memory.

Although he found her deep, rich-brown skin was best highlighted in his shadows, for selfish and greedy reasons, there was something spellbinding about the way the sun shone over her. It made her glow, just as the moon washed her in pale silver light that revealed all the best parts of her – like her curved nose, her high cheekbones, and cute little round ears.

Her lips were full, two-toned, and so pliable they dipped under any kind of pressure.

Then there was her body...

What had initially disinterested Weldir, simply because *nothing* had truly interested him, had since ensnared his full attention on many occasions. The more he touched her, made her quiver and tremble, the more he wished to completely enfold her in the mist of his body.

Her breasts were modest, drooping like pretty teardrops, and were sensitive. Holding one brought him enjoyment because they were so soft they yielded in his grasp, whether that be his hand or his tendrils. Her nipples, dusted darker, could easily make her breasts jiggle in reaction if touched just right.

He never thought he'd find a waist attractive, but there was something about seeing his hands holding hers that made him want to brush over her side more.

Shapely legs held up a squishy and round arse, and putting them into any position he desired had become a game for him. The more relaxed she was, the lustier she became, and the further he could manipulate her limbs until their muscles were taut.

Her body, her face, her gaze, and curly hair weren't just beautiful; they were striking in ways that Weldir still struggled to comprehend.

But there was more that lurked beneath the surface. Things the eye could not see.

Yes, her soul was spellbinding, but so was her voice when it was gentle and welcoming. She held herself with grace, with resilience and determination, but he rather liked it when she submitted to him. When she gave over her trust in the most intimate of moments, Weldir knew she could permanently enchant him if she tried.

I want to reach out to her. To see if he could spark something more in her. *She has never stayed this long in my realm.*

Not once had she deigned to share his space for days, filling his realm with her voice, her presence, and even the echoes of her beating heart and lulling breaths.

He wanted it to mean more, that he was finally gaining something with her, but knew that was a false hope on his end.

She only seeks to make the process of conceiving offspring more enjoyable. She'd never reached out to Weldir otherwise. *She isn't here for me, but for them.*

For their Mavka offspring, and to watch over Orpheus in particular.

Surely if Weldir touched her with the intention of pleasure without the result of another growing within her, she'd reject it. She may even leave, wary of being in his prolonged presence once he made his yearning known.

He didn't want to ruin this. He wanted her to stay for as long as she permitted it, in hopes that she would do so again in the future.

Even when she drifted her gaze around as if to look at the disc next to him, and halted when she found him staring at her, Weldir said and did nothing. Not even when her eyes locked with his as he tried to find out the answer to an unasked question did he dare falter.

Her eyelashes flickered. Then her heart accelerated, thumping louder and more rapidly within his void. He thought the swelling pink of her cheeks was a mistake, or he worried he'd misinterpret what it meant.

TEN

March 23rd, 1832

Lindiwe situated herself upon a sturdy tree branch, which creaked under her weight. Settling in for comfort, she flapped her wings and lowered her feathery tail so her knee joints were bent. Then she inspected the creature below, who sniffed at the dirt and grass as he moved through the forest.

Luckily for Orpheus, the forest above the Veil was abundant in wildlife. The animals were wary of anything approaching, but less so of him, as he lacked the pungent reek of unevolved Demons.

Her children had pleasant, earthy smells to them. Orpheus in particular smelt of mahogany and pine, and she would have buried her nose in his fur many times had he let her.

He lifted his wolf snout up to her, and proceeded to release an annoyed, snorting huff. He deviated from the path he'd been making through the forest to avoid coming near her.

When he was out of sight, Lindiwe released her talons and swooped through the air to follow. She landed upon another branch to watch over him.

"Go away." He swiped his right hand backwards through the air in her direction. *"Bad Witch Owl. Evil."*

Lindiwe felt nothing regarding his words, as she knew they weren't truly his thoughts. They had to be Katerina's. The fact that he hadn't immediately attempted to climb this tree to kill her proved he still trusted her nearness.

She readjusted her grip from where a sharp knob of tree bark pushed into the middle of one of her four-taloned feet.

He halted to sit on his rump and puffed his fur in aggression with a quiet growl bubbling past his fangs.

"Smells sickly sweet. Magic?" he continued, as his claws gouged into the earth. *"You give Katerina rotten things to eat."*

That's only because everything I gave the stubborn woman spoiled after she rejected it for too many days.

"Now Orpheus leave to hunt." He gave a whiny groan. *"Orpheus want to stay, but Katerina hungry."*

With frustration bubbling in her stomach, Lindiwe lifted off once more. She swooped at Orpheus and kicked one of his impala antelope horns.

Be quiet and hunt. You're scaring off prey with your needless talking. He'd grown rather chatty now that he had someone he liked talking to.

Orpheus yelped, swiped his arm above his head, and continued on.

A hare popped its head up in the distance, and he got too excited, lunging for it with a roar. The noise he made scared it off. Within seconds of it zig-zagging through the forest, Orpheus took off to chase it in a mindless bloodlust.

His side crashed into tree trunks, and he barrelled through shrubs and bushes when it tried to use them as temporary cover. He snarled and snapped his bony wolf snout like a mad beast and then dug at the burrow it'd darted into.

He never saw it poke its head out of the ground behind him from the other side of the burrow a few seconds later. It fled while he hollowed out the hole until he could stick his head inside it.

For a little while, his orbs remained crimson with bloodlust as he searched for something else to eat and chase.

When he finally calmed, he sat down on his hind legs and lifted his right clawed hand to scratch at the top of his skull. He appeared unsure about what just happened, his dark-yellow orbs a further indication of his confusion.

Shaking it off, he pushed on in search of food for his woman. He eventually stopped talking after Lindiwe kicked one of his horns repeatedly for doing so, which sufficiently annoyed him into silence.

It didn't take him long to realise he needed to approach his prey quietly and to skulk low as he did in order to stay out of sight. Unfortunately, his size and weight were unwieldy, and he hadn't learned that even the smallest twig snapping or leaf crunching could give him away.

Each hare, deer, and bird was frightened off quickly, and their smaller, more agile bodies made it easy to escape. Any that didn't, and were eventually caught by him, were consumed in the excitement of the hunt.

After many hours, Lindiwe knew too long had passed. The sun was descending, and soon his home would be dangerously in the shade.

She flew off ahead and searched the ground with her enhanced owl vision. Her ears picked up on the slightest scratching, and she followed the sound of another hare, gliding towards her prey. It was given no warning as she snatched it from the ground.

Being careful of her sharp talons so she didn't make it bleed, she snapped its neck. Then she flew back towards Orpheus and dumped it on the ground right before his hands.

He paused with his head tilted at it before lifting his snout to her when she landed on top of a boulder. His dark-yellow orbs peered into her black eyes.

With an annoyed, head-wobbling grumble, he swiped up the hare and began his journey to return to the Veil.

He'll eventually figure out how to hunt on his own.

Until he did, Lindiwe would be there to help him provide for his human.

ELEVEN

May 19th, 1832

The tip of a pointed quill meeting cheap paper scratched in Lindiwe's ears. The glide left behind a neat stroke of ink as she held a wooden ruler to the page to ensure a perfectly straight line. As the black ink dried, the glossy sheen reflected the sunlight peeking through a beautiful bay window.

In the background, two fireplaces on either side of the spacious library were carefully maintained by multiple human attendants. The area was quiet and peaceful, and she went unnoticed as she worked.

Craning her neck to the side, she rubbed at a corded knot where her nape met her shoulder. She winced at the pain, pushed in hard to loosen it, and then tried to ignore the twinge as she curled back over the low writing desk. She double-checked the page of the book she was copying to make sure she had recorded the directions and measurements correctly.

She didn't follow everything exactly, instead simplifying the steps in a way that someone who wasn't a master craftsman could emulate easily.

Of course he'll need help reading the words and numbers. Then again, she truly thought it would be idiotic on his companion's part to not assist. *She asked for this, so she'd better be thankful.*

Well, Katerina hadn't asked Lindiwe, but demanding that Orpheus find her somewhere suitable, like a house, in the Veil was rather ridiculous. Almost as if... the woman was looking for an excuse to dislike her son by asking for something that was entirely impossible.

So here Lindiwe was, gathering all the knowledge he'd need so she could prove to the woman that her son was good. That he was of higher thought and could be taught everything, provided he had a willing teacher.

She could have stolen the book rather than meticulously copying it, but she tried not to be a thief where possible. She didn't mind doing the work, so long as it would be put to good use.

Once she was done, she flicked through the pages of furniture that could be hand built and found things like a table, chair, bed, and even a counter. She also squished onto a single page how to make a low-quality fence. Nothing needed to be fancy, only practical.

Warm shelter. It was more than Lindiwe had all these past years.

Seeing as she had a few blank pages left, she tapped the brown feather of the quill against her lips.

I guess... the only other thing I can think of is how to sow a small garden. Lindiwe had helped her father farm, so she didn't think it would be a hard task to make a fruit and vegetable patch. *I'm glad I found all those seeds now.*

Done with the library, she wiped the quill tip on a pad to clean it, pushed the cork into the ink bottle, and stood. An attendant was kind enough to take them from her so they could be placed in their correct homes.

The smell of dust pervaded her nostrils even when she left the library and escaped into the fresh late-afternoon air. She flared them, then rubbed the tip of her nose to help rid herself of the musty smell of old books.

Bright sunlight pierced her eyes, so she placed her hand above her brow to shield them as she looked down the street.

People were still walking around, and many of the stores were thankfully still open. In an hour, it would be a very different story.

Although Ashpine City was protected from the Demons by the Anzúli temple that sat on the top of a large hill, people still feared the night. They hid away in their homes and barely made a peep, as if any noise would alert the nightmarish beasts of their presence.

It likely helped, as the stone walls surrounding the large and lush city had scent-cloaking enchantments aiding them. Unless a Demon came this way out of curiosity, they were invisible by smell.

The southland border helps too. They would likely finish building it in a decade, but it was a task that'd been underway for nearly half a century. The border crossed the southernmost part of Austrális, and every log they staked into the ground was another foot the Demons couldn't easily get through.

A few citizens of Ashpine regarded Lindiwe warily as she walked past them, her snowy-coloured feathers catching people's attention. She ignored them and found the merchant who sold nails for building and repairing.

She stopped to purchase three large crates.

"Are you sure you'll be alright to carry them on your own, missy?" the man asked, raising a blond brow at her when she picked one wooden crate up.

"I'll be fine, thank you." She forced a smile on her face as she pretended it wasn't heavy. "My husband is right around the corner, and he'll take it from me."

He tipped his black hat to her. "Well, alright then. Let me know if you change your mind. I'll be waiting here for you to collect the rest."

She nodded and then proceeded to walk along one building before entering a narrow alleyway. She placed the crate upon the ground, covered it in black mist so an unsuspecting eye wouldn't notice it, and did this twice more with the other two crates.

After brushing her hands of dirt and potential splinters, she placed them on her hips. *Those slats of wood from the crates would be good to repurpose into a fence. I'll make sure to note that in the journal, so they can use them for the garden.*

She ducked out of the alleyway to find a craftsman store that sold hammers, axes, shovels, and saws. There, she also found a handheld manual drill and bought that just in case. She had to visit multiple other merchants to buy thick twine and rope, a crowbar, and a sharpening stone. The last item was a bark spud, which was much harder to find than she'd expected.

By the time she was done, sweat slicked down her temples and the nape of her neck, even in the cool autumn air. At the twinge she felt in her back, she winced but tried to ignore it. Any tenderness was soon to fade away permanently.

Kneeling in the shroud of shadows made by the two buildings, she rearranged everything in a certain way and then sat on top of the crates and items. She turned incorporeal, checked to make sure everything shifted with her, and nodded once to herself.

"Weldir. I'm ready."

"Are you sure? I think there's something you're missing. Another box of nails, perhaps?"

Her lips quirked with humour, but she skilfully managed to stem the urge. Instead, she folded her arms and kicked a leg impatiently.

"No need to look so pouty."

"I'm not pout–" But her words cut off as she, and all her purchases, dropped into darkness.

Before any of the items could pull away from her in the floating nothingness, blobs of Weldir's magic attached themselves to each item. He pushed them all together in preparation for her to take them away again.

She kicked off and shot through the void towards Weldir.

"How are they?" she asked, placing her hand on his shoulder to steady herself from going face-first into the viewing disc.

He rotated them all as if they were on the convex side of a

ball, and Orpheus came into view. Katerina sat between Orpheus' legs and appeared to be huddling in for warmth.

I guess that's a good sign.

Although the Veil was warmer than the surface in the winter, and cooler in the summer, it was still the snowy season.

"Little has changed," Weldir informed her. "And before you ask, our other offspring are much the same. Nathair is also well."

Her cheeks warmed at having the question that lingered in her mind answered before she could speak it. She didn't just care for Orpheus, but for all her children.

"The only one you may be interested in is–"

Before Weldir could finish waving to a different disc, she slapped his shoulder again.

"Is that Merikh?" she asked, before quietly squealing when her legs tried to push her much too close to the viewing disc.

Weldir gently grasped her forearm and pulled her back down so their heads were at an even level.

"Yes," he answered, his tone a little clipped, likely because she'd interrupted him. "He's finally left the ward surrounding the castle. I believe he's heading to the Demon Village."

She pursed her lips at the horned companion next to her son. *Jabez still looks so young.* She figured he was around twenty-five, maybe even twenty-six from his appearance. *He's barely aged since I saw him over fifty years ago.*

It still surprised her how so much could change, and yet so little could in the same vein.

They both wore loose, flowy, low-crotch pants that gathered at the ankle. Jabez's were mauve, whereas Merikh had opted for a deep crimson and had tied them above his echidna spines on his calves. Neither wore shoes, but both had gone for a shirt that appeared more like a short robe.

Look at Merikh, she thought, her eyes crinkling with longing. *He looks so good now.*

Although it was obvious he was copying his counterpart in many ways, even down to the swagger of his walk, nothing could take away his domineering confidence.

Lindiwe found it hard to pull her eyes away from her bear-skulled, bull-horned son. There was so much she wanted to say to him, so much to apologise for, and so much she wanted to learn about him. He was her most intelligent child, and she wondered what knowledge he'd learned, who he'd become, and what his hopes and dreams were.

But he was utterly unapproachable.

He never leaves Jabez's side. And even if she could get a moment alone with him, it was doubtful that it would end in any other way but a fight. One she would not partake in.

He would swing, and she would turn into a Phantom to avoid it. He wouldn't listen, no matter how hard she tried. So she would rather leave him be, knowing he was safe, protected, and sheltered, even if it was at her enemy's side.

"This may be your best opportunity to talk with him again," Weldir suggested.

"No. It's fine. I would rather tend to Orpheus and his needs." She offered Weldir an appreciative smile, grateful that he could see the pain in her gaze and had tried to find a solution. "I should enter that village at some point and see what it's like."

But she wouldn't go around stalking her son while he was there.

"I'd better give Orpheus everything I collected today before it gets too late," she said, leaning back until she was standing upright beside Weldir.

"You could stay and give it to them in the morning."

Lindiwe drew her gaze away from her children to Weldir. At first, his face was barely visible, but she watched as all the chalky streaks of his body coalesced together to reveal his horns and face in full.

She didn't know why her cheeks warmed upon looking at his striking countenance, but her stomach fluttered in reaction as well. There was more of him than usual, perhaps a fifth of him, and she'd never seen this much.

He'd be easier to hold, to touch, and something about that

twisted in her mind in a naughty way.

His face is a sin. She averted her gaze from his pooling black eyes before immediately being drawn straight back to them.

"No. I think it's best if they speak about this tonight, so I can lead him to somewhere deeper in the Veil at first light."

"Do you plan to offer your blood as a sacrifice for the protection dome?"

"Yes. Katerina seems a little... closed-minded. I don't think she'll be amenable to offering her lifeblood, even if it's the cost for her ultimate protection. She'll likely complain about witchcraft and whatever nonsense."

She looked at Orpheus, simply so she could avoid Weldir's intense, unmoving stare. *Sometimes I wish he'd freaking blink.*

"That spell only lasted for a few years, and we don't know if all our offspring have magical capabilities. Only Odie and Merikh have proven so thus far, and it may be because they've eaten Anzúli. We don't know whether this is a natural trait they've inherited or not."

"We have to try." She backed away from him to head towards the journal and the array of tools she'd brought. "If the ward only lasts a few years, then Orpheus can just do it again."

"If you say so," Weldir answered, unfolding his cross-legged position to join her side. "I'll place these within the salt circle so you don't have to carry them."

She nodded and offered a small smile. "I'd appreciate that."

TWELVE

July 17th, 1832

Rustling trees seemed to deepen the foreboding shadows of night, swaying and moving to make it appear as though something might be lurking if one looked too closely. Rocks could easily be mistaken for the warped head of a Demon, or perhaps that was just the Veil allowing paranoia to slip down her spine.

White mist coasted across the ground, cold, wet, and haunted, which made seeing beyond the brush more difficult.

At night, the clacking of branches or the groaning of trees could be mistaken for nightmarish creatures creeping closer. The wind whistled, and sometimes it sounded like whispers or frightfully quiet screams.

The outer ring of the Veil was a terrible place, and as each year passed and more Demons exited the portal from Nyl'theria to Earth, it only grew more dangerous.

Lindiwe had nothing to fear, not when she flew above it in search of the home she sought. It was easy to find from a distance, as the blue glittering dome surrounding it was just bright enough to be seen.

She tipped her wings to bank to the right in that direction and then proceeded to circle it. The gap between the trees was just wide enough to highlight a log cabin home still in its early stages of construction.

Building something of that size would take time and craftsmanship that Orpheus didn't have. He'd restarted multiple times. Mostly because he made mistakes and had to amend them, or his human companion demanded it be expanded multiple times because its initial smaller size was inadequate.

A home was a home.

So long as she ends up being happy with it, that's all that truly matters. Whatever Katerina wanted, both Orpheus and Lindiwe would do their best to give it to her.

Sitting next to a small campfire, a lone pair of eyes lifted up to Lindiwe. Orpheus was nowhere to be seen, to her dismay.

It takes longer for him to hunt now that they're deeper in the Veil. At least he'd mostly learned how to hunt his prey without scaring it off or eating it.

It proved that he was a good boy who just needed time to learn. Time to adjust.

Lindiwe curled her talons tighter, unsure about whether to land or not. Orpheus may be unsettled that she'd been in his territory, and within his protection magic, without him. He may not like her near his precious human.

It's better he's not here. Katerina couldn't use him as a shield, and he'd likely get in the way of them having a cohesive argument.

Deciding this was a blessing, Lindiwe glided within Orpheus' blue protection ward, encasing herself in the dome for safety. She landed a few metres away from Katerina.

She pulled her white-feathered hood back and shook out her curls until they sat comfortably. Then she turned to the woman seated on the ground with a rather nasty scowl upon her remarkably beautiful and pale face. Not even her angered, tight features could steal the attractive shape of her thin nose, plush lips, and angular cheeks.

"*Y-you,*" Katerina sneered with a shivering stammer. She pulled her hands back from where she'd hovered them near the fire for warmth. "W-what do you want?"

Lindiwe's bare toes skimmed the muddy ground, occasionally brushing against a blade of grass that had survived Orpheus' upturning of the soil. He'd removed dozens of trees in just a few short months, including their stumps, and had debarked the trunks to use them for the house. There were still hundreds left, most thick enough in diameter to be used as foundations.

What wasn't suitable would be used as frames for furniture or for her firewood.

"Rain is coming, which is when my magic is best suited for growth," Lindiwe answered, checking behind Katerina at Orpheus' handiwork. "Where is the garden? I want to make sure everything is planted correctly before I grow it."

"What g-garden?" Katerina asked, her pink lips thinning.

Lindiwe's brows drew together. "A fruit and vegetable patch? I gave you both seeds in order to grow some."

"D-do I look like a farmhand to you?" Katerina bit, gesturing to her dirtied dress, cloak, and blanket. "I-I'm not designed for labour. Orpheus hasn't gotten to it yet. I n-need shelter because, as you stated, the rain comes soon and its f-f-f-ucking winter. But he's taking so damn long."

Stemming the urge to cringe in disgust at the woman, Lindiwe shook her head. "Shouldn't food and water be your first priority?"

She shrugged. "He g-gets me food."

"And that's why your home is taking so long," Lindiwe answered curtly. She waved to the barely constructed building. "If you would help him by building your own garden and tending to it, then he wouldn't need to leave every few days to hunt for you."

"I don't know how!" Katerina exclaimed, curling her hands together in search of warmth.

"You know how to read," Lindiwe argued. "You've been reading the journal to help Orpheus build your home, and if you've read it in full, there's an explanation on how to grow your own garden at the back of it. How to turn the earth, plant the seeds, and how much space you need in between."

"I-I've never been good with plants. I k-kill all that I touch."

Lindiwe rolled her eyes, simply because the woman was just being infuriating on purpose. Her incompetence stemmed from a complete lack of trying, which made little sense when she needed food to survive!

It's like Katerina wanted to sit there and be miserable, rather than aid her situation.

And for someone who had grown up using her bare hands to help her father tend to the family farm, Lindiwe just couldn't understand this mindset. When the going got tough, everyone pitched in to help make sure there was food and water on the table, otherwise death would be knocking on their doorstep.

Lindiwe's nostrils flared as she took in a deep, calming breath through her nose, only to release it, and all her annoyance, out of her mouth before she said something callous.

"Use the crates the nails were in to build a fence. It doesn't take much effort to use a hammer and a few nails. If you make the garden and plant everything *properly*, I can keep it healthy when rain falls."

Katerina averted her gaze, with one side of her lip twitching upwards like she wanted to sneer. "T-then you do it."

Something cold and cruel lanced her heart, and Lindiwe rolled her shoulders back defiantly. "I'm not your mother. Do it yourself."

Katerina's bottom lip fell, and her eyes grew wide, like she couldn't believe how Lindiwe had just spoken to her. "How dare you speak to me like that!" Katerina folded her arms across her chest. "Y-you're younger than me. You s-should do as you're told when someone asks for help."

"Younger than you?" Lindiwe laughed. "Katerina, I'm almost two hundred years old."

That made the woman's features pale. "Fucking witch," she muttered, loud enough for Lindiwe to hear it. She hunched her shoulders as she drew her cloak tighter over her body. "M-m-must be nice being young and beautiful forever, e-even at the cost of your soul."

"Oh, how true that is," Lindiwe answered with a dark smirk. "Get off your arse and help. If you sit here much longer, sulking like a bratty child, then you'll be sure to wither away."

Katerina scoffed. "Good."

Unbelievable! Lindiwe palmed her face with one of her hands in frustration. *And I thought speaking with Duskwalkers was hard. At least they* try, *even if they often fail.*

She brought her other hand up and massaged her temples wearily, the conversation sucking all the energy out of her. Finally Lindiwe let out a sigh and then reached underneath her feathered cloak to a pocket sewn inside it. She fished out a stone with an Anzúli symbol etched on it and held it out by its thick red twine.

"Look, we got off on the wrong foot," Lindiwe conceded, reaching out to give the talisman to the woman. "I come with a peace offering."

From the corner of her eye, Katerina assessed it, then backhanded it so hard it flung out of Lindiwe's grasp and landed on the ground. "I don't want anything from you. I don't want your hexes or spells."

Holding back a growl, Lindiwe stomped over to the talisman, picked it up, and held it out to her again. "It will warm you. You'll no longer need to worry about winter, and I have medicinal herbs that will fight back any sickness."

There was even a bathing oil Orpheus would need to apply to her body to hide her human scent. All instructions for everything was noted on a piece of parchment.

"I-I'd rather freeze to death."

"No, you wouldn't," Lindiwe bit out. "Frostbite is a horrible affliction, and the possible death from it is long, painful, and disorientating. How would you like your fingers and toes to rot and fall off while you're still alive?"

Okay, so maybe they wouldn't actually fall off, but they'd definitely rot, and she was hoping that frightening the poor woman would make her see some sense.

It worked.

"F-fine." She snatched it from Lindiwe's open palm and curled her hands around it. "Now wha–"

Katerina's lips promptly shut when the symbol glowed pink, and she proceeded to shudder with a blissful moan. She held it tighter and brought her knees further up, like she wanted to encase her body around it completely.

It wasn't necessary. Just holding it affected the whole body.

"All you need to do is wear it on your person," Lindiwe explained as she pulled a pouch of herbs from her cloak pocket. "The tea is easy to make with a campfire, and it's best if you swallow the ingredients. It should energise you, as much as keep you well, and you only need a pinch, so make it last."

Pouting, Katerina swiped that from her palm as well with her head turned away.

For a few heartbeats, the only sound shared between them was the crackling of the fire. Lindiwe drew her gaze to the tiny, makeshift shelter of logs that was barely enough to keep out the rain. It only looked big enough for Katerina and Orpheus to lie down together, with little space between them.

Space she doubted Orpheus would allow.

It's a shame Weldir can't see through Orpheus' ward clearly. He could only see through the outside of the magical blue dome, like one peeking in through a window but being stuck outside. The canopy of trees often made it impossible to know what was going on. They couldn't check on them properly, and Lindiwe couldn't spend every minute of her days watching them in person from within the forest.

"Well?" Katerina bit out, and she narrowed her stare on Lindiwe. "Is that all?"

"A thank you would be nice."

"Why should I thank you?" Katerina huddled further around the talisman. "You're only keeping me alive to help him. Nothing you're doing is actually for my benefit."

Lindiwe's stomach twisted into a horrible, sickly, nauseating knot because... she was right. The guilt of that was a burning slice against her heart and spirit, and she had to hold back the tears that threatened.

All the anger she'd held onto for the woman due to her less than welcoming behaviour instantly faded. Katerina had every right not to trust her, nor to be amicable about her assistance or presence.

Because all Lindiwe was thinking about was the happiness and wellbeing of her son, at the cost of Katerina's life.

But I really do hope that once she has a warm and safe home, with an abundance of food and water, she'll come to care for Orpheus. It was hard to grow tender feelings for someone when the environment was less than pleasant.

Lindiwe understood that.

If she's happier, maybe she'll trust him. He already seemed to be rather affectionate with her, near purring as he rubbed his skull against her black hair and cheek while holding her.

It was more than Lindiwe had ever gotten.

Although less intelligent than some of his older siblings, Orpheus was sweeter and more malleable. He didn't argue and just agreed to whatever Katerina thought best. He did whatever she demanded, and Lindiwe strove to help him achieve what should have been impossible goals.

Orpheus was trying to appease his companion, whereas Weldir was argumentative and often devoid of emotion and affection.

It was getting better, though. Weldir was turning into someone Lindiwe found her heart flipping for in the oddest of moments, but their beginning... their foundations were rockier than Orpheus and Katerina's. Feelings could develop, so long as their hearts were open to it.

Surely everything he was doing would come to be appreciated. *They just... need time.* Much like how she and Weldir had needed time to get where they were now: they could share in each other's prolonged presence without it feeling stuffy and awkward.

Lindiwe stepped back and bowed her head apologetically at

Katerina. "Build the garden and I will grow it. It will be ready to be harvested straight away, and then you can seed it again."

"I'll think about it," Katerina said, unfurling herself so she wasn't so tightly drawn inwards. She sat more comfortably now that she had a true source of warmth against the bitter cold.

Lindiwe flipped her hood up and willed the shift. She threw back her wings, bent her digitigrade legs, and lifted off.

The last thing she heard was Katerina sneer, "Fucking witch owl."

THIRTEEN

September 24th, 1834

Sneaking into the Demon Village was relatively easy for a being who could fly. All Lindiwe had to do was land on a branch and walk her little owl legs from the outside of a tree to the inside of it, all while ducking around bushels of leaves.

The village was large, and the protective, spiralling walls of gigantic trees weren't to keep out Demons but to block those within from the sunlight, which could destroy them.

When she'd first come here out of curiosity a year ago, it was because she'd finally caved to her yearning to see Merikh in person. Even from a distance, she wanted to see how her oldest living child was doing – if he was well, happy, and cared for.

He was all those things, and more.

He was intelligent enough to hold a conversation with a stranger, albeit reluctantly due to his less than chirpy nature. He'd worn well-tailored clothing, walked with a confident stride, and even bartered for items of his liking with expertise.

And his companion, although someone she disliked greatly, had involved him in everything. Merikh was the half-Demon's bodyguard, a well-known confidant, and... his greatest friend.

It was easy to see their amicable relationship even from afar.

When they'd disappeared together near the centre of the

village by climbing down a set of stone stairs, Lindiwe had wanted to follow, but wisely kept her distance. Within half an hour, more leaves had sprouted across all the trees spiralling around the village, and red flowers, similar to those of a lotus, had suddenly bloomed.

Within minutes, a fragrance she'd never smelt before littered the air.

They'd come to the village for a celebration or festival, which had commenced upon the flowers blooming. Music had played throughout the lively village, with a few dancers, acrobats, and fire spinners offering entertainment.

I'm glad there aren't that many Demons here this time, Lindiwe thought, keeping hidden behind thick clusters of tree leaves.

There was also no festival, and fewer people here. Nor was there music, and the fire-lit lanterns were sparse, offering just enough light for those who did wander through it to see.

She crept across a thick branch, her talons cutting into hard bark, as she kept her owl eyes focused on one individual.

His white skull stuck out like a sore thumb amongst the Demons, who had patches of human skin of varying shades.

It didn't help that Orpheus crept around on his hands and feet to appear less imposing in an anxiety-inducing environment. He was in his humanoid form, something he'd only recently learned he could do, but he'd chosen to be crouched. It made him look more beastly, more frightening, even if his orbs stated otherwise, shifting between a fearful white and curious dark yellow.

No one stopped him from entering, nor did they try to drive him out. They did, however, give him a wide berth when they noticed him, and offered him wary glances.

A small, relieved sigh slipped past her dark beak.

Good. I'm glad he's being received. She lifted a wing to squeeze past a branch as she followed him deeper within the village. *I was hoping that if they've accepted Merikh, they would accept Orpheus.*

No one had told them otherwise. Orpheus would be done here before those who had seen him would finish running to Jabez's castle to inform them about the new 'Mavka' that had entered their village. If all went well, Lindiwe hoped this meant he could keep returning.

Orpheus had already known about this place; he'd just never entered it. Getting him here had been a challenge all on its own.

Lindiwe had spoken to Katerina secretly, and the usually disgruntled and dismissive woman had been weirdly helpful in this regard. Once she'd learned he could obtain various luxuries for her, like a *bathtub*, the woman couldn't seem to push him out of his own ward fast enough.

Being together for a little over two years meant they'd formed some kind of bond, not that Lindiwe really understood to what level from afar. Especially since she couldn't see the intricate, private details of their life within their home.

His communication skills had improved rapidly; his language complexity was deeper, and she seemed to understand Orpheus. Lindiwe didn't know if either of them was happy or not, but they had a form of companionship.

He hadn't wanted to leave her, but Katerina had been very stern and had given him the 'silent treatment.'

Lindiwe didn't appreciate the emotional manipulation, as it obviously distressed him, but he caved to the idea for a reward later. Not that she knew what it was. She overheard Katerina mention the promise of one if he returned with a bath for her, among other things.

They knew Lindiwe would follow to assist him.

As he crept deeper within the village on his hands and feet, he shrank back from those around him each time they neared. It was obvious he found the presence of so many overwhelming, and their stares unnerved him.

They were Demons, and he was used to them being violent towards him.

Even the largest and scariest-looking Demon was nervous about Orpheus when he neared and quickly moved away. They all gave him a wide berth, but some glared at him as he passed. When a couple dared to growl at him, he offered a snarl back in retaliation, with his fur puffing, which instantly quelled their aggression.

Perhaps her most violent child, Merikh, had shown them to back down to his kind. A good outcome, in the grand scheme of things.

Lindiwe winced when a Demon child, probably no older than six years old, saw Orpheus and froze on the spot... then let out a high-pitched cry of terror. Their parent, she couldn't tell what gender, proceeded to wrap their arms around the child's head and bring it to their chest. They gave a protective warning snarl with their fangs bared.

Pushing off, Lindiwe kept her wings close to her body to quicken her dive just as Orpheus' orbs reddened. She grabbed one of his horns with her foot and yanked his head back when it looked as though he was about to roar in confused anger. The sound cut short, and she let go to flap her wings while hovering before him.

Stay calm, Orpheus, she mentally told him, holding his stare. *Remember, no one will hurt you if you don't hurt them.*

She didn't know if that was true, but it was what she hoped.

All of this was a guess.

She waited for his crimson orbs to soften and then turn to his natural blue. He darted his wolf skull towards the child, and who Lindiwe could now see was its father, and snorted out a rough huff through his nose hole. He moved on, showing them, and everyone around them, that he had no intention of harming them.

Seeing as it was safe for now, and that her presence had been given away when she'd been hoping to remain hidden, she flew to the top of a building. When Orpheus went to walk past it, she gave a hoot, and he looked up at her.

She bounced down its slanted roof until she was just above its doorframe, and his skull darted between her and it. The tile roofing clacked underneath her talons when she lightly stamped her foot.

Go inside here.

It took him a few moments, but he lifted his right hand from the ground and held the bag strap situated across his torso a little tighter. When he stepped towards the door frame, he looked up to her for guidance, and she nodded.

He entered.

With too many eyes on her, all curious or unsure of her presence, she was unable to shift into her human form. She didn't know what would happen if they saw her, and she didn't want to draw any more attention to Orpheus than he – or her owl form – was currently doing.

At least she was able to overhear their conversation.

Lindiwe hung onto every word shared between Orpheus and the storekeeper. Snush's voice was mousey, and had a nervous shake to it, but he didn't usher her child from his clothing store. Orpheus must have understood why she wanted him to go inside, because he stated one word, just one, that made the unseen Snush answer with his own.

"Clothing..." Orpheus said hoarsely, his voice grungy but not beastly.

"T-trade?" Snush retorted in a meek and quiet voice.

Whatever Orpheus produced was enough to prove he was serious and had something of value to trade.

She was thankful that she'd discovered many crystal mines within Austrális in her wanderlust, including amethysts, opals, and sapphires. She'd brought Orpheus to the mine closest to his home in preparation for coming here.

By the time Orpheus exited, most of his fur and protruding skeletal bones were hidden away by a pair of black trousers and a button-up shirt. His deer tail was exposed by a slit in the back of his pants, and the front was made with ties that allowed for tightening around his narrow waist. He also had a new bag to go with the first one, and Lindiwe figured Snush had given him multiple pairs of trousers and shirts.

Orpheus scratched at his back and arms as he walked, and

then his backside, unused to the feeling of being clothed.

Yet as uncomfortable as he looked in them, Lindiwe couldn't resist the joyful spring in her steps as she followed him from rooftop to rooftop.

He looks so cute, so handsome! She gave an accidental hoot that would have been a gleeful squeal had she been in her human form. *He looks so dapper in his outfit!*

At the sound she made, he looked towards her with dark-yellow orbs and a head tilt. She held in her excitement and remained still so he wouldn't try to enter the building below her clawed feet. She didn't even know what it was.

Even though he looked more sophisticated, the Demons continued to give him a wide berth. Lindiwe receded back into the twisting, spiralling tree canopy above, remaining hidden as best as she could.

When he approached a cart merchant selling pretty gems and ornament-crafting materials, Lindiwe was surprised by his interest. He sat on his haunches as he inspected it all, as if mesmerised by the pretty shinies.

Before the woman shopkeeper could ask, Orpheus dug into his satchel, which sat above a new one given to him by Snush, and pulled out a handful of broken amethyst crystals.

She shook her head when he shoved his hand at her to trade.

"T-that's too much," she pleaded. "I-I'd only need a few. You don't need to give me that many."

Before she could finish, he pulled his hand back, dumped half of the pieces into his other palm, and held them out to her. Her blonde eyebrows furrowed as she took them with trembling hands and placed them in her wooden trade box next to her. Then she proceeded to place everything he picked up into a large pouch, whether he truly wanted it or not.

When their awkward exchange was complete, the woman picked up an amethyst and gestured to it.

"Thank you, Mavka. I like your trade." She picked up a piece of crude jewellery she'd made, obviously not a well-skilled craftsperson *yet.* "I've never seen pretty stones like these, and I can practise with them. I'm sure others will like them."

He dipped his skull down to her hand and then back to her face. "Orpheus."

Her light complexion paled further as her eyes widened. "Pardon?"

"Name is Orpheus, not Mavka. Orpheus *is* Mavka."

"Oh." She offered a strained smile. "Thank you, *Orpheus.*"

He nodded with a snorting huff and then moved on – a little more confidently than before. He never noticed how the Demon fell back into a chair as if all the energy was sapped out of her, and how the attendant at the cart next to her selling herbs came to her side.

"Are you okay, Coyul?" the man asked.

"By the cursed light, did you see that?" she muttered, fanning herself and attempting calming breaths. "I've only seen Merikh from afar, but I've heard the other Mavka are more violent. I was so worried he'd try to eat me!"

"At least he didn't steal anything," he stated, eyeing Orpheus walking away, only for his eyes to widen when Lindiwe's child grew confident enough to stand on two legs once he left a different cart. "Are they all so big?"

I'm glad the village has a scent-cloaking spell, Lindiwe mused. She turned her attention away from them and brought it back to Orpheus, who garnered more stares now that he was standing at his full height in his humanoid form. *Without it, the smell of their fear might have sent him into bloodlust.*

That, or the aroma of blood from the meat market further in would have.

When he really needed specific guidance, she'd find a place to shift into a human, use black mist to mostly obscure her presence, and leave behind something he would understand.

A single white feather, pulled from her cloak.

FOURTEEN

April 9th, 1835

Seated on a rather comfortable boulder in the middle of a small clearing, Lindiwe moved her writing apparatus with care. It'd been quite some years since she'd used charcoal with her bare fingers, now preferring to utilise a charcoal holder. It was fashioned similarly to a spear, where a polished cylinder of wood was attached to a sharpened piece of charcoal by specialised twine.

Readjusting her journal on her left bent knee, the heel of her right foot had found a place to wedge, so she didn't tip to one side. She noted some of the recent events, as she'd yet to do so.

Dappled sunlight swayed back and forth across her pages, the light wind causing them to flick. The chill in the air was mild enough that it didn't make her talisman radiate with heat, even as autumn deepened. Branches clacked together, leaves rustled, and the subtle squawks of birds could be heard.

Humming a soft tune, she pushed her braided ponytail over her shoulder when it slipped down to her chest.

There was a distinct rustle, like someone dropping from a tree, followed by the quadruple thump of an undoubtedly large four-legged beast landing not too far behind her. After so many years of living on the razor's edge of danger, her human ears had learned to pick up when she was being quietly hunted.

The minute snap of a dry leaf or tiny twig. The clacking of small rocks knocking against each other. The way the area seemed to grow quiet, as if the animals knew of the impending doom long before she did. There was even a sixth sense now where the hairs on her nape would rise under the weight of watchful eyes – a completely different sensation from the gaze of her shadowy partner.

She could almost *feel* the danger, smell it, taste it. It was right there, and with every second that passed, it only grew more barbed – like the universe was cutting its fangs on her demise.

A sharp scratch, like claws digging into hard dirt, and Lindiwe knew she only had a split second to react, or she'd likely be bitten into by deadly fangs or sliced by cruel claws.

And in that split second, she did not move from her spot or stop writing, nor did she cease humming. She turned incorporeal, and a giant monster slipped through her intangible body. The creature struggled to change its position so it could land on all fours, since it had been expecting to tackle her rather than go through her.

Lindiwe didn't lift her head as she turned physical and continued to write.

"You'll need to do better than that if you want to catch me," she informed him quietly.

With a rather beastly growl, her son slammed his big fist against the dirt. The white knuckle bones of his hand glistened in the sun, as did his feline skull, which only seemed to highlight his reddened orbs of rooted annoyance.

"No fair," Leonidas rumbled, punching the ground again before snorting out a huff. He stalked off to the side. *"Never catch."*

The last thing Lindiwe saw in her periphery before he disappeared into the tree line was his short-furred feline tail.

A smile teased her lips as she waited for him to try again.

Leonidas was rather fond of this game. It was a way for her to teach him how to hunt silently, which she'd learned was a valuable tool due to the recent events with Orpheus. She'd done this many times over the last two years and often used it as a way to teach him how to speak.

He was always there, lurking in the shade, watching her, inspecting his prey. He was listening, and she'd pull out various items and show him what they were, explain their names, their origins, where they came from – whether it be a flower, fruit, or an obscure item she had on her person.

If Orpheus was anything to go by, repetition was the key, and she had all the patience to spare. And Nathair had taught her that they could understand language, even if it took a long time.

She thought about all her children a lot, but she couldn't give all her time to just one, even if she wanted to occasionally. Orpheus didn't need her right now, as his relationship with Katerina seemed to be well, although not progressing past platonic friendship. Since she'd taken him to the Demon Village, Lindiwe had travelled across the entire world to greet all her Duskwalker children like she tried to do once a year, if not at least once every two years.

She spent a few weeks with each, taught them what she could, and then moved on in hopes that when she circled back next, they'd retained the information and had increased their humanity enough to understand it.

Then rinse and repeat... forever.

She'd only just returned to Austrális, and considering Merikh was an impossibility, she'd visited Leonidas first before she planned to head to Orpheus.

From her right, quick thumping radiated in her ears.

She turned incorporeal before he could touch her, and he slid against the ground when he landed. He gave her a hiss and paced next to her.

He scratched behind his curling ram horn, as if he was pondering how to win for once.

"What if he actually harms you?" Weldir asked, his voice hinting at mild concern.

Lindiwe shrugged. "Then so be it. It would be my own fault. I can't taunt him and then be mad at him if he strikes true."

"And what of the pain?"

"I've been dealt enough pain in my life that I barely register it anymore," she murmured truthfully.

A purposeful sigh flittered through her mind. *"What if he damages your cloak?"*

"Then you will have to make me a new one, so long as he doesn't swallow the stone." She set down her charcoal holder and watched Leonidas cup his jaw and think *very deeply* while looking off into the forest. "This is the only time he permits my nearness. Even if the game potentially has a cruel ending, it's my way of being able to spend time with him."

Because other than this, Lindiwe couldn't get closer to Leonidas. He sat next to her when *he* wanted to, but if she dared to reach out and touch him, she'd be snapped at by sharp fangs and he'd leave. If she attempted to instigate play, he'd act bored and wander off. And trying to talk to him directly was like talking to a wall, one that had the ability to rudely look at the sky as though it was of more interest.

He's like a feral cat. If she went to pat him or go *pstpstpst*, he'd run off. But if she sat on the ground patiently, he might come and nuzzle his head and body against her. Touch him when or where he didn't like to be touched, and she could be struck or bitten. *At least he doesn't lick himself and doesn't mind water so long as it's not deep.*

All her children had an aversion to deep water, as they couldn't float whatsoever, but she noted that the majority of them liked to be clean and dunked themselves regularly. Especially if they had fur.

"How's Nathair today?" Lindiwe asked, showing that she wasn't being argumentative out of annoyance at his presence.

"He is well. Chasing more conjured fish again." Then she swore she heard the mildest chuckle in his voice as he added, *"I guess we're both playing with our offspring this day."*

"What of Tenebris?"

A small smile curled her lips as she returned to her journal.

"I had to create a new village, as humans from a new town

have been brought to me. I have managed to change the way I consume souls so that this naturally happens now, which has its benefits and drawbacks."

"I'm guessing it drains your magic without your intention."

"Just so. But it also means that this is no longer a task I have to consciously consider. It does make Tenebris ever changing, so I have needed to expand it so these places don't materialise on top of one another."

Lindiwe's smile grew as a sprinkle of sunlight settled on the side of her neck and warmed her. "Have you been looking into the memories of those humans?"

"Hmm, sometimes. More so I can understand what their way of life was like. But sifting through memories isn't something I have been actively doing for quite some time."

He probably thinks he's learned all that he can. Which was pretty evident in the way he treated her these days. He was still quarrelsome when their differing ideologies or morals butted up against each other, but he wasn't as dismissive or emotionally cold as before.

These changes are nice, though, she thought with a smile, opening her mouth to ask him more about his life and Tenebris.

I really like talking to him now.

Funnily enough, a hundred years ago she couldn't have imagined anything worse.

FIFTEEN

April 13th, 1835

Lindiwe pushed her newly braided ponytail inside her cloak so it sat more comfortably, and then she propped up her feathered hood. A light gust pushed past her, making the material flap around her body.

"Are you heading to Orpheus now?" Weldir asked her.

"Yes," she answered, surveying the clouds looming over a forest of the surface world. "You said Orpheus was finally returning home, and I think I've annoyed Leonidas enough."

Orpheus had been hunting for an exceptionally long time – nearly three weeks. To give him his independence, Lindiwe had stayed away and focused on Leonidas, but it had been difficult to do so. Why he was gone from his home and Katerina for so long, neither she nor Weldir knew.

"Are you sure? You didn't even try to teach him his name this time."

She knew he was intentionally teasing her to be *playful*, but it hit wrong, and Lindiwe lowered her gaze to the ground.

I'm... tired of trying. She was tired of them constantly forgetting. And when they finally gained enough humanity to understand that they could have their own identity, she then had to fight tooth and nail to explain that their name wasn't 'Mavka.'

Or someone else gives them a name. Someone they cared

more about, as if Lindiwe's affection was unwanted and bothersome.

Realising she'd grown forlorn, she rolled her shoulders back and plastered a smile on her face. "I don't think he's ready. I'll try again when he has more humanity."

With that, Lindiwe called for the shift, ending the conversation, and morphed into her human-sized owl form.

Flying was tiresome. Although her muscles had changed, she still felt the stretches and aches from using them. She tried to *feel* the air, to see the current, to experience the sky like any normal bird.

She pointed her beak at the greying clouds she headed towards to make sure she wasn't flying into a storm. Although they appeared dark and heavy, there was still an unbroken ceiling, and the rain had yet to begin falling as if the very clouds were crying upon the earth.

She squinted through the gust that cut across her face and feathers from the change in air pressure as she flew beneath the sea of grey. She struggled to orientate herself in the sky, her right wing yanked back as the wind tried to push her to the side. She pulled her wing in, threw it forward, and steadied herself.

Multiple times during her flight, she had to battle the very elements of nature, but nothing was as intense as that first wall of pressure.

She would have preferred to fly above the clouds in bright sunshine, but she wouldn't be able to navigate accurately and refused to risk going in the wrong direction. The first time Lindiwe had dipped above dark clouds to see what was up there... she'd been awestruck. The sun, so vibrant and warm, had been breathtaking, especially with how it had cast varying hues against the *floor* of clouds.

But it was confusing when she couldn't see the ground, so she forced herself to remain below the gloom. If she perceived a static charge against her feathers, she'd immediately dive for the tree line to avoid being struck by lightning.

She hated admitting that had actually happened once. And it

had been embarrassing when she'd died and returned to Weldir's realm for such a strange reason.

Just as the clouds began to disperse, proving her worries had been for naught, the forest fell away, dipping down into a massive canyon.

The Veil looked more oppressive than it used to.

The white mist that lingered all throughout it had thickened by the year, making it appear eerier. The trees were taller, their branches crisscrossing like a network to create a frightful, shadow-casting ceiling. It'd grown quieter, as if the very world wanted to hide from it.

Her eyes homed in on the top of a sparkling blue dome, and she banked a little to the left to head towards it.

I doubt I'll be here long. She just wanted to check in person that all was well, ensure their garden was healthy, and assist them should they need anything.

Orpheus had gone back to the Demon Village on his own twice more since they first went there a little over six months ago and was gaining confidence with each trip. She'd returned temporarily the first time to aid him should he need it, and then the second time she left him to either succeed or make his own mistakes.

What he obtained, she didn't know.

When she neared Orpheus' dome, she found a suitable branch to perch on that allowed her to see within his ward.

Then Lindiwe waited.

He's cleared much of the forest, she thought, spanning her gaze across the log cabin she could almost see perfectly.

Only a few dozen trees still remained within his ward.

The house was well built and looked surprisingly good quality, considering Orpheus' lack of experience. His care and slow, methodical process meant he'd tried to do everything to his idea of perfection. Each timber log appeared to be of similar width, and she remembered watching him compare them to make sure.

The garden fence was a little crude, as Katerina had indeed

eventually made it, but Lindiwe could tell that Orpheus, over the last two years, had somewhat fixed it.

She didn't know what the inside of the cabin looked like. It was his home, and although she was curious, she doubted he'd be okay with her entering it.

She also didn't want to be caught doing so and violating his or Katerina's privacy. *I'd like to be invited in one day.*

As... *silly* as it was, she would have adored being allowed to sit at their table and enjoy a meal or tea with them. A part of her had been hoping that Katerina would eventually warm up to her, so they could spend time with Orpheus together and learn together. Since he had someone he wanted a bond with, Lindiwe might have been able to make a connection with Katerina, who then could have helped Lindiwe and Orpheus get better acquainted.

In reality, she wished Katerina had leaned on her more and seen her as someone safe. Yes, Lindiwe's first priority would always be Orpheus, but she had room in her heart for Katerina.

Kicking her talons against the knob of a branch that was annoying her, she thought, *I would have liked a friend.*

If Katerina became a Phantom, then they could share in that strangeness. She would be someone Lindiwe could help guide with her newfound abilities, and together they'd discuss both the good and bad aspects of their dual lives.

It would mean someone else who was human, but would also live just as long as she did.

To not feel so solitary in this... Lindiwe would have moved the stars and sky for that person.

Lindiwe longed to have an undying friend in this world, especially one who could share in her struggles of being bonded to someone *other*.

But this would never happen.

Although Katerina's behaviour towards Orpheus had become more positive over the years, she still hated Lindiwe.

The woman seemed to hate her more, actually.

She no longer had an issue with taking Lindiwe's help, but

it was always with this awful little sneer of disgust at her magic.

She sighed. *She doesn't have to like me, so long as she likes Orpheus. That's all that matters, really. But it would have been nice...*

If she didn't currently have a hard beak, she might have pouted.

Rustling from a few trees down brought Lindiwe's attention in that direction as Orpheus breached the tree line and entered his ward.

Across his shoulder lay a large deer, with its long legs dangling down the front and back of his torso. In his humanoid form, he approached their home's porch steps, and the carcass thudded against the steps when he placed it down.

"No, no!" Katerina yelled, throwing open the door, and she immediately pointed away from the house. "I don't want you bringing that dead thing in here. Put it away. Out of my sight."

Despite her bossy tone and non-existent greeting, Orpheus' blue orbs shifted to bright yellow, and his deer tail wagged *inside* his trousers.

Lindiwe tipped her head to the side when she noticed the haphazard stitching that kept his tail hidden away, like someone had purposefully sewn the slit shut. *I don't remember Snush's pants being like that.*

"I did as asked," Orpheus explained, dropping low to the ground when Katerina walked down the stairs and placed her hands on her narrow hips. He waved in the direction of the deer. "See?"

Her pink lips pursed tightly as she regarded the creature with disdain. "Yes, I can see that. I'm surprised you were able to find a brown deer with five tines on each of its antlers." Then quietly, and with her face to the side, she muttered, "And in only three weeks."

Lindiwe's gaze drifted over the deer. *Why did she want something so specific?* A brown deer with five tines wouldn't have been easy to find, especially for Orpheus, who would not only have needed to find one, but then not eat it himself.

Readjusting her wings when worrisome dread cascaded across her form, she tried not to let her paranoia get the best of her. *Surely it wasn't to be rid of him for so long.*

Or worse still... to find an excuse to be annoyed with him if he failed or miscounted.

She may want the antlers for decoration. They'd make a nice chandelier for their rustic log cabin. There would be more tines to place candles upon or hang things from.

Orpheus crept closer to Katerina, who didn't shirk his approach, even when he stayed crouched and reached for the backs of her calves. Instead, the woman just raised a dark brow.

"Promise?"

Her lips twitched, and her eyes narrowed in a way that had Lindiwe's feet shifting. Was it a thoughtful expression, a playful one, or anger? It really was hard to tell with her.

Katerina turned her blue eyes to the deer and then lifted her chin. "I guess I did say you could have a reward if you actually managed to bring me one."

She squealed when Orpheus tackled her to the ground, hugging her to protect her from the fall. He began to lick at her neck and jawline.

"I want reward," he demanded, the bulge of his covered tail wagging again.

"Ugh! Don't lick me, Orpheus! I told you how much I don't like that," Katerina complained, pushing at his wolf skull.

He clamped his bony jaw shut and proceeded to nuzzle her instead. "Better?"

A small, albeit silent, laugh escaped Lindiwe as her heart filled with tenderness. *This is nice. She's accepting his affection.*

She wasn't shoving him away, even when her dress was accidentally pushed up her legs, baring them. When he tightened himself around her, partially blocking Lindiwe's view of the centre of their cuddle, there was no complaint or annoyance.

This is what she wanted to see. What she'd been hoping for.

That he'd been accepted, even as he nuzzled her with

woofish huffs and rubbed himself against her entire body like he couldn't wait to embrace all of her. Even when his clothing sank beneath his body and he shifted into his more monstrous form, which Lindiwe figured was for comfort, neither his fur nor protruding bones were rejected.

Why didn't Weldir tell me that things were going this well between them? Lindiwe only visited these two on the odd occasion, mostly to check on the garden and get a peek before moving on, as she wasn't able to interact with them like her other children.

The whole idea of rewarding him for tasks felt like an odd thing, like giving a pet a treat, but if it made them both happy, who was Lindiwe to complain?

"N-not outside, Orpheus," Katerina mumbled against his fur. "And you know I prefer that you don't turn into this form."

Suddenly confused, Lindiwe turned so she could cross to a different branch to see what was actually happening, as she could only really see Orpheus' rump. She peeked at them when a pale leg lifted into the air, but she mostly watched her footing until she found a spot that would offer a better view.

There was a grunt and a snorting huff, but little else was said. His orbs flickered between bright yellow and... *purple?* Lindiwe tilted her head in thought. *I've never seen their orbs turn that colour before.*

Then Lindiwe tried to make sense of what she saw, or where the emotion could have come from. It looked innocent enough – just a hug.

That was until Orpheus backed up enough to make room between them to grab something low, while Katerina's dress was far, *far* too high and settled around her navel.

Something long, hard, thick, and fucking *squirming* caught her eye, and Lindiwe gasped and stepped back... and off the branch she'd been perched on.

She fell out of the tree.

Her back hit the ground with a painful thwack as one of her wings almost made her screech when she landed on the thin bones wrong. Wiggling side to side on her back with her talons in the air, she struggled to get to her feet, finally managing it just as she heard the clash of a groan and a moan.

She lifted her head above the bush she'd fallen behind, but once more regretted looking in their direction and nearly fell back again with a screech.

She hopped away as fast as her bird legs could carry her before she thought better of it and shifted into a human. Lindiwe bolted through the Veil's forest until she could no longer hear anything unseemly.

It was only when her toes caught on an unnoticed arching root and tripped her that she stopped running, her knees scraping against the dirt.

My eyes! her mind screamed as she scratched at her face. *They've been sullied!*

Her following cry was an echo of the horror that twisted her stomach.

"What's wrong?" Weldir asked, as if nothing indecent was happening.

"He has a penis!" she yelled, uncaring for one minute that she was on the Veil's forest floor, about to hyperventilate.

"Well, yes. He is a male, after all."

Her eyes widened, her horrified expression wasted on the empty forest, when really she wanted to cast it upon him. "You *knew*? How?!"

"It's evident in their souls. All our offspring have genitalia that's hidden away. Have you never noticed their slits?"

"Why would I have noticed that?!"

Not once had Lindiwe thought to go *looking* at their privates! Between their thighs was smooth, or so she'd thought... Well, she'd assumed they couldn't reproduce!

"Lindiwe... I don't understand why this would bother you. Humans have penises."

"Yes, but *I* saw *his* penis!" And it had been hard! She'd seen him inserting it!

No mother should see that!

And why... is it... purple? And why did it look like it had tentacles around it?!

Heat bled from her face and her jaw fell. "Did you know they'd been doing that?"

"Sex? No. You know I'm unable to penetrate his ward with my mana. This appears to be a new development regardless," Weldir answered, and relief shot through her that he hadn't withheld that information about their intimacy. Although... the word *penetrate* made her throat swell with repulsion. *"Isn't this what you wanted? For them to have a relationship?"*

Lindiwe's lips pulled back into a cringe, yet she sucked in a calming breath and then heavily released it.

"Sure. I want them to enjoy each other's company, but this wasn't something I was expecting, and I definitely don't want to *see* it, Weldir."

On her knees, she covered her eyes and shook her head, only to start scrubbing her face as if that would help her remove what she saw from her memories.

At least I can be at ease that it's consensual. Because had it not been... well, Lindiwe would have immediately stepped in, packed Katerina's bags for her, and dropped her off at the nearest town. She would have intervened, because no woman should have to suffer that kind of torment.

Oh god, was sex *the fucking reward?!* Lindiwe scrubbed at her face harder, now believing her *ears* were tainted with that knowledge.

Something else crossed her mind. She started to rise to her feet so she could go back there and stop them.

"Oh no. What if she gets pregnant?"

Lindiwe didn't quite see her being the most *loving* mother, especially to a monstrous child. Let alone all the struggles that would come from it, just as she had experienced.

"You needn't worry about that. Katerina is infertile."

Lindiwe mentally threw her hands up because how the *fuck* did he know that? She figured it had something to do with her soul, but Lindiwe didn't care. All she registered was that she didn't need to worry about it, and she fell back to her knees to pray to whatever gods – not Weldir – had the forethought to protect them from that outcome.

I can't come back here. Weldir was going to have to keep an eye on them because she absolutely never wanted to see that again. *I'll make sure the garden is healthy when I can, but Weldir will need to watch over them from now on.* He didn't seem to be bothered at all by *witnessing* that, so he could deal with it!

Then something horrible entered her mind, and this time, bile rose in her throat.

Oh god. My children can have sex.

I have to make them all boys. She peeked at the forest through the gaps of her fingers with stupefied, dazed eyes, as realisation settled over her like a crushing weight. *Their humanity is too low when they're first born. What if they try to have sex with a female of their own kind without understanding they're related?*

Oh my fucking god.

Gross!

SIXTEEN

Soft humming filled Weldir's ears as he watched all his offspring meander through their lives.

The glittering, misty edges of the viewing discs lagged behind ever so slightly when Weldir moved them around, then they reformed once he stopped. The liquid-like, non-reflective pools glowed with differing times of days and seasons. Some were vibrant with colour, like those green and lush in the northern hemisphere, while those in the south were a mix of wilting green, orange, and red – and in Leonidas' case, a sprinkle of snow.

Orpheus he could only see from a slight distance due to his ward, and Merikh... not at all, due to Jabez's ward.

For a long while, Weldir focused on Ari. He was seated in the midday sunlight, while the Demons before him were huddled under the shade of trees to avoid burning. They were deep in conversation, and the Demons didn't seem to mind his disjointed communication abilities.

Ari has made new companions. For how much longer, Weldir was unsure. Most didn't last very long.

Finding their conversation lacklustre and boring, he moved onto a new disc and inspected Ookpik walking across a dewy meadow. Not a single tree was in sight except in the far distance, and streaks of golden dawn hues shimmered across their blue-black feathers and white owl skull.

Weldir moved on, and Orpheus came into view.

He sits alone again, he thought, observing Orpheus sitting in the pouring rain in his monstrous form. Deep into the afternoon, the dark-grey clouds made it appear as though night had long ago fallen.

His orbs were a deep blue, highlighting that he was rather upset about his predicament, when his porch steps weren't very far.

The windows of his home cast a dull glow over him, and at the movement inside, his orbs shifted bright yellow while his deer tail twitched. When Katerina didn't come outside, his orbs receded to a solemn blue, and he looked down with his snout pointed towards the wet dirt.

Hmm. I do not understand why she makes him do this.

This was Weldir's first time witnessing Katerina make Orpheus sit in the rain, but it wasn't the first case of his offspring being banished outside. And if Orpheus moved from his spot at all, it somehow upset her further and prolonged his time alone.

Is this kind of punishment... normal among humans? Should I ask Lindiwe about this? That seemed like the wisest decision, especially with the current dreary nature of the rain.

Weldir leaned back to do a somersault through his realm. Weightlessly floating with utter control, he found the very female he sought before he even finished, and halted with his body upside down so they were at eye level.

She shifted her focus from the journal she'd been reading.

"Yes... Weldir?" By the twitch of her lips, he bet she'd been tempted to call him something else, something *vexing.*

"Would you say it's normal for humans to punish each other by making their companion sit in the rain?"

Her brows drew together into a deep furrow, and her lips tightened. Her gaze grew cold, and she looked off to the side. "No, but it's also doubtful the other person would allow that kind of punishment and actually submit to it. Someone may tell their partner to leave for a few hours so neither loses their head and says or does something they don't mean, though."

But Orpheus cannot conversate well, and he is exceptionally gentle with his female. Unless Katerina was the transgressor in this instance... but then wasn't it best that *she* be the one to sit outside?

He realised it was beyond the depth of his knowledge, and without asking Katerina herself to understand her mindset on the matter, it was a moot point.

When Weldir didn't respond, too busy musing on this, Lindiwe's expression softened.

"How long are you going to stay upside down?" She tilted her head to the side until even her body tipped as well.

"Does it matter?"

She straightened with a laugh. "I guess not." Then she leaned to the right to look around him, and her gaze fell upon his discs. She licked her lips. "I... actually have a question."

"You have many questions. Constantly. What's another hundred?"

She scrunched her nose at him, and with a shake of her head, gave what he *hoped* was a playful sneer. "Is it..." She licked her lips again. "Is it possible for me to see Nathair through your scrying discs?"

"Of course." He waved his hand and a flat disc formed above his clawed fingers. It grew in size, and within seconds, both were able to look upon their serpent offspring with ease.

"Are you telling me that you've been able to do that the entire time and just never have?" Her disgruntled tone informed him he'd probably fucked up.

"You have never asked before," he retorted blandly, as it was obvious.

Nathair was bundled up in his tail, probably napping or whatever it was he did in there. When Weldir looked at Lindiwe once more, her full lips were tight, her arms were folded, and her glare was sharp. Guilt trickled through Weldir's mist.

"You ask about him often. I should have realised you'd want to see him, even if it's from a distance."

A sigh flittered out as she loosened her arms. "I guess that'll do." Then she pushed her journal to the side so she could lean closer to the disc. A small smile curled her lips and crinkled the sides of her eyes. "Look at him. He's gotten so much bigger in Tenebris."

"He consumed a few souls many years ago and it strengthened him." He'd been good, otherwise. He'd adhered to his promise to not eat any more of Weldir's souls.

She reached out and ghosted her fingertips right against where Nathair was, as liquid dotted her long, fanning eyelashes. Her smile only seemed to grow, while the affection in her mesmerising eyes deepened. Weldir was used to seeing that expression.

Never at him, but she'd worn it many times over the years for their offspring.

She looks the loveliest when she wears that expression.

It was utter softness. Contentment radiated from her, as did a tenderness that often sparked Weldir's longing.

He didn't know when he'd begun wanting her to look upon him similarly, only that it sat like a thickness within his mist. He wanted her to not only look at him fondly, but also in a deeper way that he doubted he'd ever understand the full weight of, even once he achieved it. If only those eyes would gaze at him with affection, yearning, and glisten for something more.

I don't understand this need. What they had now should suffice.

Lindiwe no longer regarded him with disdain or disinterest, and she was willing to not only converse with him when he reached out to her through the bond, but she often instigated it. Their relationship was smooth, lacked any tension, and had become... easy.

She'd even begun spending prolonged time within his realm over the last five years since Orpheus and Katerina had met. She read over her journals, fiddled with her other artefacts, and brushed her hair, often styling it. She watched their offspring with him for long periods of time and even slept here on many occasions.

This was all he'd originally wanted. Unity.

Someone to fill his void and let him know he was real beyond his prism. For their voice to fill the silence, and their presence to ease the echoing, solitary loneliness.

He had this.

So why did he wish to feel warmth, even if it was only ever in her gaze? What more could he want?

But there is something else, something I've been seeking, and it has been quite some time since I've had it.

As he looked at his mate, who was glued to the image of Nathair he'd projected, his gaze drifted. It trailed down the bridge of her nose, her full lips, her pointed chin, and then further down to her throbbing jugular. Next it dipped to the neckline of her dress, which framed her soft breasts.

He stared there for much too long.

I tire of waiting.

March 7ᵗʰ, 1837

When Lindiwe touched the flat magical image of Nathair, she hadn't expected it to ripple like water. It distorted him, but it was the closest she'd been to touching him in a hundred years.

Seeing him was bittersweet, as it tore open the scars over her heart at surface level, but it also healed those wounds so much cleaner. She'd always known he was there, alive in his own way, but it was different from seeing it.

Lindiwe waited with a smile, watching the hypnotic rainbows gleaming over his black scales. She wanted to see his skull, hooked ram horns, and orange orbs.

The disc pulled away, yanked by some kind of force, then shrunk before it left behind a fading cloud puff.

She turned to Weldir questioningly.

"Lindiwe..." he started, drifting ever so slightly closer. "It's been a long time."

Oh, Lindiwe knew *exactly* what he was talking about, and it truly had been a very long time. Or rather, it felt like it'd been too long, when in reality, they'd gone longer gaps of time between creating children.

But Lindiwe had felt that gap far more than usual. It'd been harder to ignore the way her breasts would grow heavy, her nipples pinching into aching points, or how her clit would throb while the entrance to her core dampened.

Every minute she spent in his realm, her mind had twisted with the idea that she was utterly encompassed by him. He was everywhere – in her thoughts, against her skin, in her very *breaths* – and it made her all too conscious of his overwhelming, otherworldly presence. Her body tingled more and more until she'd almost caved and reached out.

Had it gone on for much longer, she might have done so.

"I've been waiting for you to ask me," Lindiwe said, rubbing the nape of her neck and laughing with her gaze averted. "I'm surprised it took you so long, if I'm being honest."

"Waiting for me?" His tone was incredulous. "I've been waiting for *you*."

"Me?" Her hand slipped down to her chest as she brought her frowning face back to him. "Why? Orpheus has been fine for years. I haven't needed to return to him and Katerina for months except to check their garden. I could've taken care of a baby during all that."

"You didn't indicate otherwise. How was I supposed to know?" He stilled until even his mist settled its constant hypnotic motion. "Does this mean you *want* to have another offspring?"

The question threw Lindiwe for a loop, simply because she hadn't expected it. He'd never asked her before if *she* wanted another child; he'd only ever sought permission to make one.

Why did him asking her make her heart race and her face flush with heat in embarrassment?

"Well, no," she answered honestly without thinking, more worried about how her hands started trembling when her pussy clenched.

Realising what she'd said, her eyes widened.

"I mean yes!" But she didn't mean that either, because having more children wasn't actually what she wanted! She covered her face when it grew hotter. "I mean, I'm fine with having another, but the act of making another is what I was waiting for you to ask about, and I didn't know you've been waiting for me, otherwise I would have made it clear that..."

She was rambling... and she may have just admitted something she hadn't meant to.

Oh god. I just told him I want to have sex! Shut up!

Not for duty, but simply to be naughty. To have pleasure. To touch and be touched, outside of the promises she'd made all those years ago.

A large hand wrapped around the side of her neck and yanked her closer. Then he rumbled, "You infuriating, vexing, annoying little creature."

His mouth slammed over hers, hard enough to shock her, but gentle enough to incite a muffled moan. Her lips were quick to lock with his, and she slipped her arms around his neck, thankful that he'd moved the solid parts of him to allow it.

A surprised moan mixed with a rasp escaped from her when his hand grasped her breast from *within* her dress. She bowed her chest forward into his hold, uncaring that he'd ghosted through her garment to touch her directly. The tickle of him doing it through her panties had her widening her thighs, wanting him to get to the place that'd been aching for so long.

The ties at her hips keeping her underwear together pulled taut when his hand appeared within them. She didn't mind the slight burn, not when his fingertips expertly found her throbbing clit. Lindiwe instantly bucked to deepen the pressure, and he swallowed her blissful expire.

Even though his hands continued to pet her, one pinching her nipple between his thumb and forefinger, her dress parted down the front. Helping his tendrils to remove it, she let him go long enough to unthread her arms from the sleeves before winding them around his neck even tighter.

She ground against his fingers, just as the ties of her panties were loosened. He could've used his magic to pull the threads apart like her dress and seam them back together as if nothing had happened, but she had a feeling he didn't so she'd shiver when the material traced across her skin as it pulled away.

Weldir broke from the kiss to rub his wetted lips against her throat, and Lindiwe tilted her head back, her own lips parting.

She didn't care that this was happening out of nowhere, that it was happening so fast, or that she was spiralling so quickly it could have been deemed pathetic. Not when he pressed just right against her clit, and she thought she saw stars in his empty, vast realm of endless night.

She'd needed this for so long. The anger she felt at herself for being so silent drove her to claw at him for more.

There's more of him than usual.

She was able to scratch her nails across the top half of his back and not feel a hard barrier. She cupped one side of his neck while her fingers dived into his wispy hair.

She wanted more touch, more pleasure, and his tongue dragging across her skin just didn't feel like enough. Neither did his fingers digging into the heated flesh of her breast, or the drag of his thumb against her nipple. Her arse was feeling unloved, as was the small of her back, and even her sides.

And she swore if he didn't touch her left breast soon, she'd do it herself just to ease the unbalanced ache in it.

"I-if you bring your dick out, I can grind against it," she suggested, beyond caring if that was a lewd thing to say. It would free up his hand so it could caress her in other ways.

Weldir paused, and although he didn't move, she had the oddest inclination that he was looking at her from the corner of his black eyes. Was he surprised that she'd asked, or was it because of her straightforwardness?

Lindiwe was aware her desire was like a candle. All he

needed to do was light her, and she was warm. In the heat of the moment, she was bolder and refused to let her flame blow out until she was completely melted into a gooey puddle.

The hand between her thighs evaporated. She felt the slide of it over her round backside before it shoved her forward... against hard thickness. A barrier finally formed when she went to wrap her legs around his narrow waist, and it gave her an anchor as she worked her hips.

Weldir darted down to take her mouth. With the way his tongue delved, it was only a temporary kiss. Within seconds, he broke away to lower his head, and anticipation thrummed through her. Before he even made it to her breast, she was tipping it up to greet his lips.

A shiver tore down her spine when his lips captured her nipple, and as he used her saliva as lubricant, even more arousal pooled at her core.

Her folds moulded around his cock and spread her wetness over it, making each glide better and hotter until she tingled. Her vision dazed, and she tried to get closer, to make it feel deeper as her pussy clamped around nothing. Each glide over her needy clit and her entrance made her grind harder, faster, until her hips were unceasing and ruthless.

Poor Weldir just accepted it as she gripped what she could of his hair while her nails dug into his back. She let out quiet little cries, trying to push herself towards the smouldering edge of her lust so she could feel its flames scorch her.

"If you're going to ride me," Weldir growled around her nipple, "then ride me properly."

"Wait," she rasped out when he parted their hips. "Why are you–"

A gasp caught in her throat as he slammed her down around his cock, penetrating her deep with one thrust.

Her eyes watered from the bite of pain as her snug pussy clamped down around him in surprise. Yet Lindiwe choked out a sobbing moan and pushed down even deeper to get to the root of him. To feel that stretch until she thought she was splitting in two. Until she felt so full that she couldn't remember what it was like to be empty.

She was so sopping wet that it didn't even matter that she was tight from disuse. Slipping her fingers through his hair, she grabbed his horn to anchor herself as she bounced on his cock.

Had he been human, his nipping teeth around her nipple would have been impossible, but as the middle of his torso was currently missing, he could manoeuvre beyond normality. She didn't care how *weird* that thought was, not when she was so full of his cock that her mind dulled with lust.

She buried her face against the top of his head, wishing he had a scent that she could lose herself in. Or that he'd fucking moan for once so it wasn't just her own pathetic cries echoing around her.

I'm so close. The first time was always the hardest, but once she made it over that hurdle, she'd become a throbbing, climaxing mess.

"Why are you always so quiet?" she whispered around airy pants. "You can moan, you know. I'd kind of like to hear that."

She didn't know why he was hiding them, or if they just weren't natural, but his voice...

That deep, rough, sinful voice... if he gifted her with a broken groan, Lindiwe thought she'd disintegrate and explode in ecstasy. She thought her ears would ring forever, and it would be added to the list of things that sent her on edge with lust when she was alone.

"Moan?" He pulled away from her nipple just enough that if he had any breath, it would've tickled it. "I can pretend to, if you'd prefer."

Lindiwe's movements slowed, then ceased altogether. She pulled back to meet his gaze with a frown. "Pretend?"

Oddly enough, *he* frowned in return, as if what he'd said wasn't absurd. "You know I don't feel anything, so moaning felt disingenuous. I can pretend, though – if you don't enjoy my silence."

With his cock so deep inside her that her lips were flush

against his groin, her heart sped up beyond its normal capacity. It was so fast that she felt it throbbing in her pussy, her wrists, and even in her ears.

Her breaths quickened, and were so short and shallow that they actually *hurt* to produce. Her whisper was so fast that even she barely understood it. "What do you mean, you don't feel anything?"

Weldir brought them face to face as his head tilted ever so slightly. "My physical body is incomplete. I've explained this. I perceive nothing physically. I cannot even smell or taste anything."

Realisation slammed into her like a war hammer. Gasping, Lindiwe shoved his chest so hard that she sent herself flying backwards, her pussy instantly bereft of his girth.

"I thought you meant emotionally! I thought you meant *for me*!" she yelled, covering her breasts with one arm and her pubic mound with the other. "Not physically!"

Tears welled in her eyes as understanding dawned, and she felt far too exposed right then, but she didn't have the will to uncover herself to grab her clothing.

"Lindiwe, I don't understand why you're upset."

At least he was honest these days about his ignorance!

"I thought you were being naïvely callous!" she yelled. "I thought you were saying that it wouldn't feel good because you didn't have an *emotional* attachment to me. I didn't know..."

Her voice broke off when she thought, *Oh god, I sucked his cock when he couldn't even feel it!* Mortification, horror, and embarrassment, all wrapped up into one barbed bundle, had taken root in her chest, and she wanted to crawl into a hole and die.

She brought her knees up so she could cover herself and shuffled her arms in a way that allowed her elbows to hide her breasts. She covered her face with her hands and let out a sob, unable to handle the way her emotions crushed her in that moment.

And despite everything, her stupid body didn't care about how she was feeling. She was still wet, still horny.

"It's not my fault you made that assumption. You should've asked for clarity."

Like she'd been hit with a hateful club, his words knocked her anguish sideways. That barbed ball in her chest grew fangs, as her blood boiled with rage.

"An assumption?!" She lowered her hands just enough to glare at him. "I didn't know I needed clarification! *You* are the abnormality! Everyone feels! *You* are the one who is different. Why would I think I *needed* clarification?! You shouldn't have assumed I knew what you meant by your lacking answer!"

I had no idea he's numb to it all.

To every kiss, to every touch, to the very feel of her skin, her warmth, her breaths. To the way her body moulded around his and the sensation of being inside her.

Lindiwe finally braved unfurling herself to grab her clothing, then squeezed her arms and torso into her dress before yanking it down. She swiped up her underwear, swam over to her cloak – thankful it wasn't too far away – and threw it around her shoulders. Then she tucked her underwear into the pocket for later.

"Lindiwe, I'm sorry if–"

"I don't want to hear your sorry right now!"

She understood this was a massive misunderstanding and that they were both at fault, but it didn't erase the last nearly one hundred years, during which they'd been intimate many times without her knowledge of what he lacked.

It made her feel small and pitiful.

Where all of it, every single bit of it, felt like a horrible lie.

He once said something to the effect of, "So I can see," *and now I understand.* Because he didn't feel anything, he had to see his way around her body. *That's why the first time hurt so much. He couldn't* feel *that he'd made himself too big, couldn't feel he was going too deep.*

She kept coming back to the same thought, and each time

she remembered, her fangs lost their sharpness and left only regret. *I sucked the dick of someone who was entirely numb to it.*

She'd thought she had been... sexy, sultry, naughty.

Absolutely, but all by her-fucking-self.

"I want to leave," she whispered, refusing to look at him.

"I'd rather we talk about this," he stated firmly, in that devoid, emotionless tone he often had. "You were enjoying yourself. I don't understand what the issue is."

"I want to leave!" she screamed, turning physical and out of his reach. "This is why I'm so fucking afraid of coming here and talking to you, because I can't just *walk away* when I want to."

She swiped her tear-stained cheeks before she buried her face once more, this time shaking her head.

"I'm *stuck* here by your whim, your will. And when you feel entitled to it, I know you'll leave me here for not doing what you want." She hugged her midsection as she let out a sob and turned her head away from him as much as possible, only to face the unending darkness *of him.* "So please. Please just let me leave."

If I'd known... I wouldn't have asked for sex. I wouldn't have wanted to do anything with him. I would have just been a good servant and had his babies through his gross wormy tendrils and not given it another thought.

That seemed preferable to the embarrassment that was so white hot it was incinerating her insides into a ghastly, bubbling wound.

"Fine," he bit out.

Lindiwe traded one darkness for another as night danced all around her when she was placed on her knees at the cliff edge of the Veil. She'd landed softly, and she took in the comfort of the real world. How it was cold, and heavy, and so lonely.

"Please don't watch me. Just leave me alone," she pleaded as she keeled forward over her knees, continuing to hold her midsection.

She didn't know if he submitted to her wants, as he never answered, but Lindiwe just cried into the Veil. To the view that was both beautiful and haunted, expansive yet evil.

It all just feels like a cruel joke. He probably thinks he did it for me, but that just makes me feel so pathetic, like I needed it so badly from someone who can only ever 'witness.'

Something rustled in the bushes behind her. She didn't even need to turn around to know that the snarling creature behind her was a Demon that had likely come to investigate her sobbing.

She remembered the last time she was stuck at the edge of this cliff, broken and betrayed, crying as a Demon sniffed at her heels for a meal. It was so vastly different between that day and the way she felt now, but it'd led to her trading her soul for this life.

She'd never regretted it more than she did now.

She stiffened, used her mind like a muscle, and felt out with a tentacle of magic. She grabbed the Demon, uncaring whether it was around its torso or neck, and threw it forward.

Bellowing out a scream, it flailed its arms and legs as it flew through the air and into the forested canyon below.

She felt zero satisfaction.

SEVENTEEN

March 18th, 1837

A small campfire cast its subtle golden aura against the dusty dirt and dry stalks of grass. Above it, a clear sky of stars mingled with galaxy dust.

The dry season brought on cooler nights and drier days, making the air more agreeable. Although a symphony of insects chirped nearby, there were far fewer than normal, and Lindiwe didn't have to fight off mosquitoes.

Tucking her heels up against her backside with her knees to her chest, she stared at the crackling fire. Its glow didn't reach far, leaving the world in darkness. Even though she was out in the open, where there were likely Demons nearby, she wasn't afraid. She didn't even feel the need to change into her incorporeal form to protect herself.

There was truly no need.

Not when a tail with a fluffy tuft tapped across the thick, meaty leg of her companion for the evening. His head was partially hidden by the shadows of night, while his blue-black fur took on orange highlights that revealed the lines of his imposing muscles.

Blood-red orbs peered at her from the darkness, and she kept her gaze averted.

Instead, she looked straight ahead and blinked with tired

eyes. The warm fire tingled against her skin, while a cool breeze fluttered her cloak, causing the feathery hood over her head to tickle against her cheek.

It'd taken Lindiwe nearly two weeks to find one of her children on her own. The idea of flying across the ocean from Austrális had always been daunting, and she hadn't truly understood what kind of exhausting journey it would entail. She'd guessed, but doing it had been hard.

She'd refused to ask Weldir for help.

She didn't want to talk to him at all.

He'd asked her what she was doing when she flew past the shores of Austrális, but Lindiwe remained in her owl form. If she didn't turn human, and was metres above crashing water with nowhere to land, she couldn't answer.

She'd rested on islands when she found them. Some were inhabited by tribal people who had never been touched by Demon claws, and others – those closer to mainlands – had been decimated. Many had been void of life other than flora and a few critters.

It'd taken her a while to realise she'd found the lands of Zafrikaan, but its beautiful landscape was hard to mistake. She'd searched for her children and eventually came across the one before her now.

He lay on his side with his lion skull resting in the palm of his large hand. His tail flicked as he watched her, but otherwise, he remained motionless. The small breeze swayed his thick mane, while his broad chest slowly expanded and collapsed.

From neck to pawed toes, he was thick with muscle. Many of his protruding bones had sunk beneath his flesh, but some remained, like his ribcage, knucklebones, and spine.

She'd once thought his red orbs were an indication of anger or rage as his personality, but she'd been wrong. He was just... hungry. All the time. He hunted non-stop. Even his emotions were greedy and insatiable – like his curiosity.

His main source of prey was Demons. He actively hunted them, whereas he'd often leave animals be – and sometimes humans as well. Although he was an opportunist when the moment struck him.

It was why his mass hadn't changed all that much, considering he feasted regularly. Consuming Demons didn't change her children's forms as much as eating humans or animals – it just made them stronger.

She often wondered if there was a limit.

"You quiet," Ari commented, motionless except for his flicking tail.

A translation talisman radiated warmth next to her left breast. Try as she might, teaching him the native language hadn't gone all too well. Ari had learned... Nyl'kira, the Elven language, from the Demons.

This was an abnormality amongst her children. Many Demons somehow adopted the language of the location they went to, while very few continued to use Nyl'kira. Sometimes it depended on what part of the country they were in, as if language was slowly being taught to each other.

Another point of difference was that although Mavka seemed to be a more universal term, Daesrin was what they called her children here. Whereas Daekura meant dark creature, Daesrin was a nightmarish being.

Besides Zafrikaan, another place with regional differences was Unerica. Then again, both the continents were huge, and human languages could differ as well.

"You not quiet usually," he added.

Lindiwe didn't respond. Instead, she tightened her arms around her legs and propped her chin on her bare knees.

"Is better. Speak too much." He lifted his free hand and opened and closed it like a mouth. "Is rock. Is grass. Is tail. *Annoying.*"

"I can talk, if you prefer, Ari," Lindiwe grumbled spitefully, although her lingering, never-ceasing anger wasn't at him.

"Sayrn. Ari you say, but Daekura call Sayrn."

It was the first time he'd told her his name, and her first time hearing it, so she'd do her best to remember it in future.

Great. Another name has been taken from me. This was the fourth, and she was beginning to lose her enthusiasm for the task.

Then again, I would need to have another child for it to matter. And right now, Lindiwe couldn't think of anything worse. She didn't want to be near Weldir at all, let alone have sex. *I guess it's the wormy tendril for me.*

She'd inform him when she was ready to continue her duty, but there would be no passion in it, no desire. It would be a procedure, and nothing more.

I don't want to have performative sex. She didn't want it to feel like a lie.

She'd been reaching for closeness, for affection. To *share* it and not be alone in her ability to feel pleasure.

She didn't want her sex life to be a fucking joke. She also didn't want to feel like it'd been done out of... out of pity! *I'd just rather not have it at all.*

Part of her was grieving the loss of it, while another was trying everything in her might to escape the constant anxiety. Her pulse had barely settled since, and every memory of touch made the barbed ball of embarrassment needle into her flesh. Her heart ached constantly, the emotion so strong it was like it'd taken root in her chest and grown another organ.

One that constantly flooded her veins with poisonous shame.

Two weeks had passed, and she still wasn't over it.

I know it's my fault for not understanding what he said, but how was I supposed to know? Everyone and everything with a beating heart at least felt things like pain, pleasure, hot, and cold. *He should have better clarified.*

Hell, when she'd offered to give him a blow job, he should've questioned then and there why she'd want to when he couldn't feel it. *That* would've saved them a world of trouble; it was also the act she felt the worst about.

Rather than focusing on it, she was evading the problem entirely.

She'd set out to check in on all her children, without his help.

To find a way to not feel so lonely, even if they often made her feel worse.

She eyed Sayrn's torso and the way he was positioned. She wanted nothing more than to crawl over to him, lie down while she was facing him, and be embraced in a cuddle. Like all Duskwalkers, he was large, likely warm, and she'd bet his fur was exceptionally soft.

That was impossible, and lethal should she try.

And if I die, I'll be sent to Weldir's realm, and I'd rather not.

It was also best that she didn't try to talk to Sayrn, since he was allowing her presence. It was more than she'd been expecting when she saw him from a distance. She thought he'd immediately try to eat her, like he normally did, but he'd spotted her in the sky, regarded her, and then continued his prowl.

When he'd set up this fire, maybe to lure something nearby, she'd appeared through the grass, ready to turn incorporeal. The fact that he'd let her sit down felt like a miracle.

It was better than sitting by herself, miserable.

Watching the flames, she let her mind wander.

He befriends Demons. Many times over the last five years, Lindiwe had witnessed Sayrn conversing with them around a campfire. *He lures them in.* Even though they were fearful or wary of him, they'd eventually sit with him when he allowed it. Sometimes he'd join them in whatever shade they'd found to escape the sun, then gain their trust by not hurting them.

He sought their companionship as if he wanted to ease whatever loneliness he felt.

Then, soon enough, whether it be after a few weeks or months, he'd be metaphorically picking his fangs with their bones. He'd eat his companions when it suited him, as if he was done with them and he let his hunger win.

Then he'd do it again months later.

Maybe he's trying to find someone in particular, and they all end up not being right. It meant Lindiwe was untrusting of his current niceness.

It was a façade.

I shouldn't stay long. Just long enough to immerse herself in his life until he no longer allowed it. *I have two other children on this continent.* One with a hyena skull, and the other with a crocodile one.

The latter was the only aquatic one besides Nathair.

Before long, her eyes drooped as tiredness weighed her down more than usual. Sayrn's orbs seemed to redden further when she copied him by lying on her side, while tucking her hands under her cheek to support her head.

They stared at each other, and his orbs were spooky, masked in shadows when her sight grew murky. Conjuring a protective glittering black dome over her body, she continued to watch him until her eyes shut.

When she woke with bright sunlight showering over her, Sayrn was gone from his spot. The tail brushing over the side of her dome informed her she still wasn't alone.

He was seated on top of it, with one leg bent and the other extended. As soon as she shifted to look up at him, he leaned back on his clawed hands and tilted his skull down to meet her gaze.

He offered her a dark chuckle, at which she crinkled her nose. *He likely thinks he has me trapped.* To prove him wrong, Lindiwe turned incorporeal, and the dome popped.

Sayrn's backside hit the dirt with a thud, and a growl of annoyance rumbled out of him. He was quick to get to his feet as she rose to hers, and he stood over her Phantom form in his humanoid form.

Then he turned away to begin his day, doing whatever he deemed fit, his big feet squashing a shrub of long, grassy stalks.

Unexpectedly he demanded, "Come."

Surprised at the invitation, Lindiwe bounced forward and followed. Hopefully whatever he wanted would be a nice distraction from her solemn thoughts.

It was also the longest she'd ever been allowed in his presence.

EIGHTEEN

April 2nd, 1837

Landing on the ground in her owl form, Lindiwe quickly forced the shift so she could remove her hood. Her movements were unhurried as she walked forward, steady and unwavering in the sunlight. At the same time, she removed a ceramic vial from her satchel and pulled out the cork.

The pop gained the attention of the ghostly woman before her, who lowered her hands from her weeping face. The semi-transparent woman, who was taller than her, shook her head. Her long cornrows and beaded earrings swayed as she backed up from Lindiwe.

She opened her mouth to cry and sob, but Lindiwe pointed the open end of the vial towards the Ghost, and the woman's weeping ceased. Although she'd once sympathised with the deceased and would have attempted to console them in the past, there was utterly no point.

Lindiwe was also desensitised to it all after so many years.

The Ghost's expression went blank before it turned peaceful, as if all her pain, suffering, and worries were sucked into the vial. Her image began to recede, then she turned into a white soul flame.

It was also sucked inside the vial.

Lindiwe popped the cork back in and stowed the vial away

in her satchel. Then she knelt on the ground and picked up a red beaded earring that was half buried in the dirt.

This is quite old, she thought, thumbing its texture. The red was faded where the sun had touched it, and brighter where it had been buried, although caked in dirt.

Next to where it'd been lying was the back of a human skull, which she'd originally mistaken for a rock.

She tsked. *The Demons must have eaten her body, and the scavengers picked over the rest.* She placed the earring in her satchel as a keepsake of the woman she didn't know; it was her way of honouring her. *Either her skull or the earring anchored her here.*

She'd been tethered to this spot, unable to escape or leave it beyond a few metres before being pulled back.

Lindiwe had seen her from a distance. It was how she found all the deceased souls of humans eaten by Demons: by accident.

A cramp twinging across her pelvic floor made her wince and rub her waistline. *Gosh, my period is painful this time.* Most of the time the cramps were easy to bear, but on the odd occasion, they came to sucker punch her in the vagina.

She'd left Sayrn's side when it made her crankier than she already was. She wanted to be alone, but didn't want to be alone, and she was so twisted up inside that she just felt like a hormonal mess.

Since then, she'd been flying over Zafrikaan, looking for Ghosts within the forests or across the grasslands.

I wonder if there's any more here. She scanned the area to see if there were any other items left behind, or the telltale white outline of something *other* being there. *Women don't often travel alone.*

"*Lindiwe.*"

She closed her eyelids and sucked in a long, deep, enraged breath at her name being called.

Just leave me alone, she thought, opening her eyes when she thought she'd quelled the worst of her anger. *How many times are you going to call me before you realise I'm not going to answer?*

She'd speak to him when *she* was ready.

Then she propped her feathered hood over her head to show her disinterest. *I wish he'd just... go to sleep.* Forever. Then they'd never have to have conversations about sex, or children, or anything ever again.

I don't want to hear his stupid, sexy voice, her mind complained as she sulked. *I hate it.*

She didn't, not really, but right now, she was just so full of hurt, betrayal, and spite that she *wanted* to hate it.

"Lindiwe!" Weldir roared when feathers began to form across her nose, and she flinched in surprise because he *never* did that. *"This is not the time for your pesky human silent treatment. Orpheus has abandoned his home to run towards the centre of the Veil, and he is distraught."*

She yanked her hood back, freeing her curls. "What? Why?"

"I'm unsure. I wasn't watching, as I was tending to my souls."

"Where is Katerina?"

"If I was able to see into their ward, I could answer that. Alas, I cannot." Did she hear a snark in his tone?

Lindiwe hesitated. *I said I wouldn't interfere anymore.* Orpheus had to make his own choices and be the leader of his own life. *He could be heading to the centre of the Veil for any reason...* Yet something nagged at the back of her mind. *What if something is truly wrong?*

"Fine. Please take me to his ward."

"I'm surprised you want my aid now, considering you flew across half the world by yourself."

Oh, he was angry with her over that, and likely many other things.

Good!

At least he could *feel* that!

Her lashes partly obscured her vision from her fierce glare. "This is an emergency. I'm not going to waste weeks flying when you can do it in minutes."

"So you'll only deign to acknowledge my presence when it's convenient?"

I'd rather not be in your presence at all! she wanted to scream.

"Why are we having this argument?!" Lindiwe yelled, stamping her right foot and wishing his toes were underneath. "Take me to *our* son's home! Right now!"

The ground came out from under her, and weightless darkness caught her. The moment she saw Weldir out of the corner of her eye, she folded her arms and waited to be transported to the Veil.

When he didn't, and she floated there for too long, she threw her hands out. "Well? Hurry up."

"Infuriating," he growled back.

Dusk greeted her, but the far-reaching shade made everything dark and foreboding, despite the sky being painted in beautiful hues of orange, purple, and pink.

She quickly entered Orpheus' ward and approached the house.

Silence was all that answered back when she called out Katerina's name multiple times. There was no point calling out to Orpheus, since he was making his way to the centre of the Veil.

The lack of any response twisted her gut with worry, and she placed her foot on the bottom step of their porch.

She paused. *I told myself I would never enter his home unless invited.* She steeled herself against breaking that promise and climbed the stairs. As she ascended, a crushing weight settled upon her shoulders and chest.

Lindiwe didn't knock, just opened the creaky door.

Inside was bright with candlelight, and she was taken aback by what she saw.

A large table, gigantic in comparison to a human, sat off to the right. It was bare, with nothing on top of it except discarded gems, twine, and metal, as if someone had been in the middle of creating an ornament. Pushed under it were dining chairs, one designed for a human and one that Orpheus obviously sat upon.

Oh wow. He's done so much more to it than I thought.

Underneath a long windowsill was a metal washbasin with a small wooden bucket inside it. Glass bottles of purple, yellow, and even a pale red filled with unknown liquids, likely some kind of steeping herbs, rested against the wall above the counter.

To the left were two chairs with armrests situated in front of a stone fireplace. The smaller one had an array of animal hides over it to make it soft and comfortable, whereas the larger one was bare wood.

The timber floor was cold against her feet, and she thought it was a shame that it wasn't covered in more animal hides to make it warmer and more inviting.

However, that wasn't what left her in awe.

She'd been right that those five-tined antlers would be used to decorate, and they had been fastened to many others and attached to the ceiling to create a chandelier. Lit candles were fitted to it, which illuminated much of the house.

Attached to it, and the ceiling, were dozens of glittering trinkets. Some dangled lower than others, and they were all so different that some gleamed with pretty crystals, while others had charms made from interesting rocks and bones. More lined the walls, the windowsills, and even the backs of their chairs.

That must be Katerina's handiwork. Lindiwe doubted Orpheus would have picked up this kind of craft. *It looks like she wanted to make their home prettier.*

Which, oddly enough, made it look like a witch's home decorated with amulets, talismans, and spells. If there had been a single plant inside, she would have thought Katerina had changed her mind about witchcraft and embraced it.

Being in this room, with everything designed to allow for Orpheus' height and mass, Lindiwe had never felt smaller.

A hallway to her right snagged her interest.

She opened the first door she found on the right and entered a bedroom. Inside was a massive bed and a box of black clothes.

I'm surprised that's all there is.

She didn't go deep in, as she was encroaching on his space too heavily already. Backing up, she opened the door straight across the hallway.

Inside was a much smaller bed, a cupboard, and a side table. *Do... they sleep in separate rooms? Why?* From what she'd seen over two years ago, sharing intimacy should have allowed them to share a bed. Something caught her eye just as she was about to back out.

The corner of a book poked out from underneath the bed. When Lindiwe knelt and drew up the cover, a pile of journals sat hidden away. She reached out to grab one, but halted right before her fingertips made contact.

She was tempted, bad as it was, to open one and read it.

Lindiwe pulled away.

Although she often detailed parts of her life in her journals, she always knew she'd be leaving them with Weldir, who would read them. Even though she wrote nothing truly private, Katerina likely had. And she wouldn't violate those intimate thoughts by reading them.

She backed out of the room to go to the final door at the end of the hallway. It was lacklustre. It merely held a bathtub and a small bucket to rinse one's body.

Now that she was done with her unguided tour, she left.

Katerina wasn't here, and she didn't know why.

There were no traces of blood or torn clothing, even when she went outside to inspect the state of the garden. There were no claw marks or evidence of carnage anywhere.

"Katerina isn't here," Lindiwe said out loud so Weldir could be informed.

"Then what do you plan to do?"

Flipping the hood of her cloak over her head, she answered, "Well, *obviously* I'm going to go make sure he's okay. That's all I can do."

She'd get her answers regardless.

Not long after Lindiwe began her flight, Weldir informed her of something that had her heart racing and her stomach twisting into horrible knots.

Orpheus had not only approached Jabez's castle, he'd *entered* it.

Why? she asked herself repeatedly.

If he knew about the Demon Village, he obviously knew of Jabez's existence, and what the tall, looming castle in the distance meant. *Does this mean he's met Jabez and Merikh?*

It's unlikely he's in danger. That was the only reason she didn't ask Weldir to take her straight there. *Jabez is friends with Merikh. He doesn't consider Duskwalkers to be enemies.*

Still, another of her children in proximity to him set her anxiety on edge.

Does it have something to do with Merikh?

She couldn't get her wings to fly fast enough, even if she could cover the great distance in an hour.

But would that hour be too late?

No. Neither Merikh nor Jabez knows how to kill a Duskwalker. Even if Orpheus was hurt, somehow or for some reason, things would be fine.

Unless Merikh...

Lindiwe shook her head.

He may not remember it, but Lindiwe knew, deep down inside, that Merikh had retained something about the death of Nathair. Duskwalkers subconsciously learned.

The grey castle finally came into view.

Despite the ache in her wings, and how the muscles along her arm bones strained in protest, she flapped faster.

Right before she could land in the trees to obscure her approach – her white owl form a dead giveaway to her presence – a beastly roar sliced through the air.

Between the castle doors, Orpheus was being shoved out of the entryway by a throng of Demons... with Merikh at the forefront. Merikh used his dangerous echidna spines to drive him back, causing Orpheus to yelp in pain and dart away. Merikh gained a foot of space each time, forcibly shoving him back little by little until he was at the bottom of the castle stoop and in the courtyard.

Orpheus feinted to the left, making Merikh and the Demons lurch that way, before he tried to dart past them on the right. Merikh caught him around the waist and used his shoulder to tackle him to the ground.

Both their orbs were red, but Orpheus' occasionally flickered with white.

Merikh was just too large and strong for Orpheus to fight against; their levels of humanity weren't comparable. Her wolf-skulled child was half the size in muscle mass to his brother and lacked the intelligence to go toe to toe with someone who was skilled in physical altercations.

When they split apart and Orpheus tried to run around him again, with the wounded Demons shuffling inside, Merikh brought his right leg up. With ungodly strength, he kicked Orpheus so hard in the stomach he was sent skidding backwards across the dirt.

"Leave, Mavka," Merikh demanded, backing up towards the castle entryway. "There is nothing left for you here."

Orpheus roared, spun to his hands and back paws in his monstrous form, and lunged. The towering double doors closed before he made contact, and a purple ward shimmered into place. He bashed at the entrance, shouldered it, clawed at it, and bellowed repeatedly, but nothing he did allowed him to get through.

He finally relented, only to pace at the bottom of the stairs with quiet, shuddering whines. Lindiwe landed, and he turned to her with a feral snarl. The bottoms of his deep-blue orbs shattered like glass, and ethereal liquid bubbled away to float around his skull.

Before Lindiwe could turn into a human, she froze, utterly stunned.

Is he... crying? Her mouth gaped as her gaze flicked between each floating drop. *I didn't know they could cry.*

Then her heart broke for him. She was overwhelmed by the discovery that they could feel on such a deeply ingrained level that they could produce tears and weep, just like a human.

She released the magic that maintained her owl form and drew back her feathered hood. "Orpheus, what's happened?"

"They took her." His fish fins flared from the emotional turmoil quaking through his monstrous form.

"What?" Her gaze lifted to the sealed doors behind him. "Why?"

"She said she hated me," he admitted with a whine, and sat down to cover his skull with his arms to hide it. *"I no understand. What did I do bad?"*

Coldness crept beneath her skin and drained the warmth from her entirely. *She said she hated him?* Lindiwe shook her head before frowning to herself. *I don't understand either.*

Katerina and Orpheus had an amicable relationship, from what she and Weldir had watched. They sat in the sunshine when it greeted their garden or tended it together. They snuggled on the grass out the front of their home – or, rather, Orpheus wrapped himself around her while she wrote in one of her journals or napped against him. He helped her with laundry or she sat on the stairs watching as he cut down the forest around their home to her liking.

Lindiwe didn't know what they did inside it, but she'd seen a fraction of it earlier. Katerina had made charms, and Orpheus would have either watched or attempted to help.

Nothing had indicated towards lingering hatred, unless Katerina's strange reward and punishment system was part of it.

But I just thought she was odd. And Orpheus needed someone who was precious and fragile to keep him in line so he didn't hurt them. *She also just came across as kind of bitchy no matter what she was doing.* Lindiwe thought that was part of her personality, and she was a difficult person to like. Which meant Orpheus, who didn't notice these flaws, was perfect for her in that regard.

With a wheezing whimper, Orpheus looked down at his claws. *"Am I a... monster?"* he asked, and his shuddering breath made tears well in her eyes.

"Oh, of course not, Orpheus," Lindiwe said, reaching out to touch him. To pet his beautiful skull and let him know that she accepted him exactly how he was, and to comfort him.

Did she call him a monster? Oh god... Lindiwe could only imagine what else she'd said to him. *He's not a monster.* Maybe a little on the outside, but he was sweet, caring, and always tried so hard. *Humans*, who were truly vile and evil beings that tortured and hurt each other, had more potential to be monsters in their hearts than her children.

Their only crime was eating people, but at least they didn't do horrid things that scarred the mind!

Just as she made contact with the side of his skull, Orpheus struck his right hand forward. *"No touch me!"*

Lindiwe was flung back as a sharp gasp of pain exploded from her lungs. Her backside landed against the ground while she cupped the claw marks cutting across her right biceps and chest.

The cuts were deep, his claws so sharp they rent through the muscle. Thankfully she constantly wore a scent-cloaking spell when she was on her period, otherwise he would have gone into a bloodlust and immediately tried to attack her.

The whine that came from Orpheus was hollowing. He backed up with his orbs a bright orange.

"I am sorry," he whimpered, looking down at his bloodied claws as he shook his head. *"I am sorry. I no mean..."*

"It... it's okay, Orpheus." Lindiwe staggered to her feet with a sympathetic smile.

He continued to shake his head, reaching back to claw at his shoulders before rending his claws down his chest. So utterly confused, so distraught, and in so much agony, he could do little more than attack himself over it.

"Orpheus," Lindiwe called, reaching out once more to show

him that it was truly okay.

"Stay away," he warned quietly, while his trembling form backed up on all fours. *"Bad Orpheus. Evil. Monster."*

Before Lindiwe could say anything more, his teary, orange orbs deepened, and he bolted to the side. Away from her, from the castle, and likely from himself.

She took a step in the direction he went before curling her hands into fists and halting.

Her eyes bowed with anguish. "Oh, Orpheus."

Lindiwe watched him go, knowing that if she were to follow him, she'd only make matters worse. She'd make him run faster, causing him to fret and panic that he was being followed.

Bringing her gaze to the doors of Jabez's castle, a question lingered in her mind. *Why did I not see this coming?*

This had never been on her long list of potential outcomes.

NINETEEN

April 2nd, 1837

Landing within Orpheus' blue protective dome, Lindiwe immediately approached the vacant home.

With hurried movements, she ghosted her way through the front door. Once tangible, she headed down the hallway. Each of her thudding footsteps seemed to make her heart race faster. Anxiety shimmered in her veins, as did anger, confusion, and so many emotions she was struggling to swallow down.

With her throat thick, she entered what must have been Katerina's room... and knelt. Cupping her hand around the bottom of the first stack of journals, she yanked them out from underneath the bed. Then she hoisted them up, placed them on the bed, and grabbed the first leatherbound book.

Lindiwe no longer cared about Katerina's privacy, not with the motherly rage coursing through her. She wanted answers.

The book creaked as she opened the half-filled journal. And with each line she read, her hands shook, her nails dug into the leather, and her eyes scanned each word faster and faster until she was heaving through panted, near-hysterical breaths.

Words jumped from the page, and each one had her stomach tightening with disgust.

Monster. Beast. Ugly. Repulsive. Stupid. It was like Katerina had tried to use every word in the English language to describe her beautiful skull-headed child as repugnant. *Evil. Demonic. Vile.* And if she couldn't find one, she'd use a string of carefully – almost artistically – crafted insults.

An affront to nature. A desecration of the purity of the mortal realm. A grisly eyesore.

The sound of each page turning scraped against her ears, and the feel of them grew coarser as her blood pounded in her fingertips.

She called him a fucking animal and then went on to say that he was as useful as a well-trained mutt.

She never saw him as a person. A being who had thoughts and feelings that were kind. No, she always considered him a deplorable monster, a being of destructive death, even as Lindiwe read through *years* of foul days transcribed.

Her eyes welled with tears at the depth of hate written down.

The journals started not long after he went to the Demon Village for the first time, and they grew more chaotic as time passed.

And it wasn't just hate.

Somehow, Katerina was disgusted by his very presence, the air he breathed out, and even the ground he walked upon. She despised... everything.

She detailed all this fear, all this terror. How she was afraid he'd eat her in the middle of the night or drag her to the pits of damnation.

How her soul, as much as her body, was tainted by just being here.

She lied to him. Manipulated him. The only joyful words were about how she was the master of a Duskwalker that knew how to come, sit, and stay like a rotten pet. Then she detailed how much she despised him for making her do anything positive, as if it was *his* fault that she'd made those decisions.

Every time she patted him? She was disgusted with herself, feeling the need to scrub her hands. Every cuddle she gave him, she did so spitefully. And sex... everything written about it was horribly skewed towards a woman who used it as a form of control and then utterly blamed him for it.

When the weight of the words became too much, her legs grew weak, and Lindiwe ended up seated on the side of the bed. No matter how much she wanted to stop reading, she found herself incapable of doing so. She was so absorbed in learning Katerina's innermost thoughts that page after page turned as if by their own will.

"He never had a chance," Lindiwe whispered as she looked over Katerina's recounts of conversations. "She thought he killed her brother. Someone named Blakely."

"But we know he didn't," Weldir answered.

"I know. And he knew that," Lindiwe said, shaking her head. "He tried to tell her, but he just... he didn't have the capability at the time to properly explain it."

And from what Lindiwe read, it wouldn't have mattered. Katerina refused to believe him, instead calling him a liar. Because why would a vile monster tell her the truth? She remembered what she wanted from their meeting because it aided her hatred and discredited his truth.

When Lindiwe finally couldn't take any more, she threw the journal she'd been reading to the side and drew her legs up, placing the heels of her feet on the edge of the bed. She wrapped her arms around her knees, and a sob broke from her.

"I shouldn't have intervened," Lindiwe said, pressing her face against her bent knees. "I shouldn't have tried to help."

If she'd just stayed out of it and let nature run its course, Katerina wouldn't have survived as long as she had. She would have died either by Orpheus' fangs or a Demon's. Perhaps even sickness would have gotten her.

Katerina wouldn't have 'suffered' for the last five years, and Orpheus wouldn't be running through the Veil with his heart gutted. Lindiwe wouldn't have to bear any of this guilt.

If I'd known that Katerina was so hateful, I would have taken her away long ago. There was never any room for Orpheus in her heart.

Any recounts of Lindiwe in those journals were just as

horrible.

She didn't mind those insults; she could bear them. She may even think she deserved a few, but so much of it was twisted by the perspective of someone who hated her just as much, if not more, than Orpheus.

Because she was human and had done nothing to help. Instead, she'd aided a monster. Katerina called Lindiwe a monster due to her 'witchcraft.' A woman who had sinned and whored her soul to a devil.

Weldir was no devil, and he'd spent much of his time trying to *help* humans. Whether that be by bringing predators and prey to Austrális, or letting her aid humankind, he was... benevolent. He cared for the souls he consumed and wanted to give them a peaceful eden to rest in.

But of course, talking to Katerina had always been an arduous and difficult task.

I thought they were... happy. Well, as happy as the cranky woman could be. *I thought she was beginning to love him.*

He doesn't deserve any of this.

Sure, he was to blame for kidnapping her, as was Lindiwe, but had she just let the hate-filled human be eaten, then all would've been well.

Worse still, Katerina knew that. She'd detailed that she likely would be dead now if not for Lindiwe's aid, and she was *thankful* for it. It meant she could still escape, could still plot to *end* him.

So... why go with Jabez?

Grabbing each journal, she placed them into a pile. She picked them up and held back a squeak when the stack began to topple before she righted it. Then she turned intangible and threw herself through the wall and outside.

Once solid again, she sprinted across his territory and into the forest.

"What are those?" Weldir asked when she stopped to look back at Orpheus' home.

"Journals."

"Why do you have them?"

"Because if he knows how to read, or ever learns, I don't want him to read such filth. Such hatred," she answered, hugging them to her chest tightly. When the top book began to slip, she quickly pushed it back onto the stack with her chin. "I... don't want him to believe the words of a bitch."

"That's quite the insult for you, Lindiwe."

She lowered her gaze. "I know I'm not always the most agreeable person, but I care about everyone. Even if they're different from me, or believe in things I don't, everyone deserves respect. I don't have to agree with them, but that doesn't make them any less of a person. She's a bitch because she hurt my son, thinks of him in a vile way, and wants to kill someone who was trying everything in their power to keep her safe."

Because... although I understand why she was upset about being taken, her actions since then have been less than pure.

One can't fight evil with evil and then call themselves just.

And taking advantage of the ignorant is cruel. Even if that ignorant being had a skull for a face. *Playing games with his emotions, and finding ways to punish just so she* could *punish, was unfair. And then blaming him for her own choices...*

She abused Orpheus any chance she could. Manipulated him. Punished him over the smallest of things just so she had a reason to and then rewarded him simply to keep him compliant. Because a person, no matter who or what they were, could only take so much abuse before snapping, and she knew that. And still, somehow, with all the nasty things she felt guilt over, she blamed Orpheus for making her feel that way.

She blamed him for her *own* actions.

She even noted that had he not been a disgusting monster, she might have been happy. But then those lines were crossed out as if she'd regretted writing that truth.

If only Weldir's magic had been able to go inside their ward so he could see their home properly. Him being trapped to the outside of it and able to look in from the other side had its drawbacks. Even *he*, someone who was inept with human emotions, would have seen how fucking wrong it was. *I would have taken her to the closest village, with coin, and let her find someone else to throw her abuse at.*

Orpheus' only mistake was taking her, but she could have been taken away again just as easily had Lindiwe known the truth.

And that's entirely my fault. I should have done more, should have tried harder to break down Katerina's walls. She shouldn't have trusted what she saw at face value, because it'd all been a lie. All the affection she'd witnessed, the way they'd apparently cared for each other, Lindiwe had never seen the hate in it all.

I shouldn't have trusted Weldir's judgement, nor Orpheus'.

They were both inhuman beings, who wouldn't have understood. *All of Katerina's pain, all her hate... it should have been directed at me. I'm the one to blame, not my son, who just wanted someone to fill the loneliness in his big heart.*

Orpheus was obedient – he'd always been. The fact that he *could* be punished meant he understood commands and consent, and the latter had never been discussed. No, instead Katerina *wanted* that as a way to fuel her hatred.

He stopped licking her when she asked. Sure, he'd made the mistake of doing so, but he'd quickly righted his behaviour. *Because everything was always in her control.*

"Weldir... can you take these and then destroy them?" Lindiwe asked, wanting to unload the weight in her arms.

When she turned incorporeal, one by one, they began to float and then disappear.

Then Lindiwe spun in the direction of the Veil's centre while turning tangible and flipping her hood over her head.

"Where are you going?"

"To Jabez's castle."

"Is that wise?"

"No, but I'm going to do it anyway."

Lindiwe had questions she wanted answers to, and threats she wanted to lay at their feet.

Closing her eyes, Lindiwe pushed her ghostly body through the thick doors of Jabez's castle and his protective ward. Unafraid, she shifted from a Phantom into a human and traversed the grand entryway.

Her bare feet slapped against the cold stone, echoing around her in the dreary and barely decorated interior.

She didn't know where she was going, but she followed muffled voices coming through a set of doors to the right. When she pushed them open, a spacious room lay beyond. There was no throne, as if Jabez didn't feel the need to have one, but there was a lounge at the very back.

Seated upon it was a pale woman with black hair, with a horned, handsome Demon next to her. Lindiwe regarded Jabez's black horns, his surprised red eyes, and his chiselled features with a dull expression.

To his left on a different seat was Merikh, who was draped over it as if with boredom. As if he hadn't just violently shoved his own brother from this castle, from that woman, coldly and cruelly. To their right were a handful of other Demons, but the only notable one was a young woman with patches of void marring her light complexion, bright-red hair, and matching red fox ears and tail.

Jabez had his right arm around Katerina's shoulders as if he was consoling her, but she didn't look too upset to Lindiwe. There was no stain of redness in her cheeks or eyes. Actually, she looked remarkably healthy for someone who had, apparently, just spent horrible, torturous years with a mindless, cruel captor.

Merikh immediately got to his feet with a snarl and bared his fangs at her, the red hue of his orbs deepening.

"You–" Jabez started.

"That's her!" Katerina yelled, pointing at Lindiwe while pulling Jabez in front of her as if he was a living shield. "That's the *witch* who kept me imprisoned."

How many times have I told her I'm not a witch? It's like she doesn't want to listen.

Jabez, the arrogant bastard, leaned back in his chair, squishing Katerina a little before she edged out from behind him. He draped his arms across the backrest of the lounge, placed his left ankle on top of the opposing knee, and cocked a brow.

"You have quite the hide walking into my home," he stated with a disinterested expression.

"You won't let her take me again," she cried, gripping his black baggy pants. "Y-you promised me."

"Katerina, I have absolutely no interest in saving you from the choice you've made," Lindiwe told her as she walked deeper into the room. "You chose to leave, and so be it."

"If you think you can change my mind–"

Lindiwe burst out laughing, and the boisterous sound of it echoed within the room. "Change your mind? I've realised that your mind will never be changed."

Showing no fear, she walked past Merikh, whose bear skull followed her every movement. At the last second, her eyes slipped to the corner to regard him. Only to tsk as she stormed past him.

"I've read your journals," Lindiwe continued. "I know how you feel."

Katerina's blue eyes widened. "Those are private!"

Lindiwe rolled her own eyes. "If you cared for them at all, you wouldn't have abandoned them for anyone to read." Then she stopped when she was in the centre of the room and gave them a mocking smile. "It's like you were hoping they'd be read by Orpheus."

She shrugged a shoulder and folded her arms. "He deserves to know what a disgusting thing he is, and how I was trapped there."

Lindiwe's smile softened. It was false, the face of someone barely biting back rage. "You, Katerina, have always been in control of your own fate. You could have escaped at any time."

"How?!" she screeched, and Jabez cringed at the sound, his pointed ears darting back. "By running through the Veil by myself? I wanted to live! Free! Not get eaten by a Demon."

"Had you been able to open your heart at all to me, had you not scorned my very presence, I would have aided you."

Hell, the diadem Lindiwe had tried to give her may have ensured her freedom, had she not so rudely rejected it.

"You did everything to keep me there! I asked for your help, and you said no."

Lindiwe tipped her head. "In the beginning. I was hoping if you survived that you might come to love Orpheus. I always intended that if it was impossible, I would remove you and take you to a human village."

The woman's lips thinned and her eyes narrowed. "Well how was I supposed to know that? You didn't tell me." Her eyes darted to Jabez at her side before quickly looking elsewhere. Oh, the regret there was unmistakable. "If you told me..."

"Had you not put up a wall against someone over a prejudice that wasn't even true, you would have seen what kind of person I am." Lindiwe waved her hand to the side. "I didn't marry a devil, nor am I a witch. I married an Elven god, one of *his*" – she pointed to Jabez – "and we have been trying everything in our might to protect humankind in any way we can, from *him*, from Demons. The magic you were so disgusted with is Weldir's, and it's not evil, nor is it unholy."

"Are you seriously blaming *me*, the one who was taken from her home? I'm the victim in all this! *You* should have been a decent person and saved me when I asked for it."

"Yes, I can see my faith in you was misplaced," Lindiwe conceded, bowing her head. "I apologise for that, and all the hurt we caused you. Truly. And no, Katerina, I'm not blaming you for all the trouble we put you through. I'm just informing you that had you been less stubbornly closed-minded, you could have saved yourself. A long, long time ago."

Gosh, Lindiwe knew that on an intimate level.

The number of times her own decisions and actions had burned her, with no one else to *truly* blame but herself, was endless. The number of times she could have made a different decision, could have saved herself, and chose *wrong* had burrowed deep in her heart and her psyche.

Lindiwe had made her own hell, and she had to live in that nightmare.

She wouldn't blame Weldir for it. He may have given her the key to the door of *this* life, but she'd willingly opened it.

"That's a horrible thing to say." Katerina lifted her chin. "You are a callous fucking bitch."

"What I read was horrible." Then Lindiwe smiled falsely once more. "And a fucking lie."

Katerina's expression paled before reddening with anger. "How dare you! What I went through–"

"Your faith is entirely vain," Lindiwe said over the top of her. "You disregarded the tenets of your faith when it was convenient for you."

Katerina scoffed. "How would you know anything about my faith?"

"Because before I was forced to make a choice between life and death, I was a follower."

She folded her arms tightly across her chest. "Yes, well, I won't damn my soul like you."

"Katerina, you tainted your own soul long before you met Orpheus. I know that your core beliefs in your heart do not value your god's teachings – the kindness and acceptance he stood for. Instead, you corrupted his love and twisted it to suit *your* desires, your hate, your disregard for the emotions of another *person* by taking what he wrote *out of context* to incite cruelty. Whether it be how you spoke to me or treated that Duskwalker. That is not love. That is not what he taught us. Only *he* can cast judgement, not us."

Instead of refuting the accusations of harm and twisted faith, Katerina screamed, "You can't make me fall in love with someone I don't want to!"

"You're absolutely right, and you shouldn't be forced to. But you saw a monster, and hated him and everything he did because it suited you. You perpetuated lies by calling him a devil brought from hell, and me a devil whore, because it fuelled your anger. You never cared about your survival so much as your undeserving ego."

"Ugh! What would you know?" Katerina turned to Jabez. "Aren't you going to shut her up?"

"Why?" Jabez asked, cocking a brow. "I'm interested in hearing what she has to say." Then he shrugged as he added, "And she'll likely turn into a Phantom and mutter on anyway."

She almost laughed at that, because he was right.

"Orpheus wasn't good enough for you because he wasn't beautiful," Lindiwe continued, before eyeing Jabez. "You being here is proof of that. You chose someone pretty on the outside over someone pretty on the inside. They both eat humans. There's no difference between them in this regard, but one only does so because he thinks humans are beneath him, because they are food for his army, because human life is meaningless to him. And he sees no issue in turning on those around him if it gets him what he wants, or if their usefulness to him has run its course. Orpheus, since meeting you, has tried everything in his power to avoid eating humans. You picked a Demon who feeds on the destruction of humankind and did so knowingly because only an *idiot* would think a Demon to be a saviour. But you did so because that face of his is unfairly handsome."

Jabez chuckled before squaring his shoulders back. "I can't deny any of that. Can I, Merikh?"

A grunt came from behind her. She looked over her shoulder to see he was far, far too close with his arms folded.

Katerina opened her mouth to speak, and Lindiwe closed her eyes while putting her hand up to quieten her. "Whatever else you have to say, I don't care for it. I understand your manipulative, narcissistic mind on an intimate level, and I don't think I want to be subjected to another word of it. I didn't come here to speak with you anyway."

"Then why is it you're here?" Jabez asked, his red eyes drifting down her body before snapping back up. His upper lip pulled into a sneer. "Surely it's not to speak with me."

"Just so. I have a question."

"Hmm. I'm not sure I'm feeling benevolent enough to answer it though."

Lindiwe rolled her eyes so hard it hurt. "Why? Why her? Why a human? Why take her from Orpheus?"

"I believe that was four questions." He leaned to the side to look at Merikh. "That was four, wasn't it?"

"I wasn't listening," Merikh rumbled.

"No. Too busy imagining all the best ways to claw off her head, I see."

His answering grunt was in confirmation.

"Why not her? She's pretty, and I found her quite entertaining as she bossed Orpheus around his home, with him none the wiser to her hateful gaze."

"What makes you think she'll find you any better?" Lindiwe countered. "She hates Duskwalkers, and you didn't consider the impact on your companion?" Then Lindiwe shifted slightly towards Merikh. "She thinks your kind are disgusting creatures that deserve the most painful death. This is what he's brought to you."

Merikh shrugged his meaty shoulders. "Like I give a fuck."

"See?" Jabez said, gesturing towards Merikh. "He doesn't care, and neither do I. As you stated earlier, I have a pretty face. That already makes me better."

He had the callousness to say that right in front of another Duskwalker.

Lindiwe laughed. "You're perfect for each other. Egotistical, arrogant, and self-absorbed." She laughed harder until she had to hug her aching midsection. She may have overdone it just a smidge to be as condescending as possible. "You're going to drive each other up the fucking wall, and I'll be alive to watch it strangle you both because you'll *hate* it."

"You may have Weldir's magic, but you definitely don't

have his foresight."

"Foresight?" Lindiwe stated curtly, because she'd never heard anything more absurd than that power-lacking demi-god having any foresight. "Ahh, Jabez, you have no idea."

"You're beginning to annoy me, Lindiwe."

She wiped away a fake tear. "Fine. I'll say what I really came here for. That woman noted how she wished to kill Orpheus." Lindiwe sobered from her humour and gave them all a malicious grin, even the confused Demons sitting to the right. "If you come near him again, I'll make sure you regret taking her. I'll rip out her spoiled and rotten heart and I'll eat it myself before her dying eyes, then I'll take her soul for Weldir to eat, and she can spend eternity in his realm, and we'll make sure it's worse than the hell she is so afraid of."

Katerina's bottom lip fell in disbelief, and Lindiwe soaked in the utter horror in her expression.

"If you want a real monster, Katerina, I'll give you one."

"That's quite the threat," Jabez said, cupping his jaw. "Kind of makes me want to try."

"I see you were able to regrow your arm," Lindiwe retorted, interlocking her fingers behind her back. "Try regrowing your head."

Then she spun around and headed towards the exit, slowing as she passed Merikh without looking up at him.

"I'm disappointed in you, Merikh," she murmured.

"Me?" Merikh exclaimed while touching his chest with a claw. "What the fuck did I do?"

"You helped."

Then she continued on.

"Is no one going to stop her?!" Katerina yelled.

"There's no point," Jabez responded with a sigh. "She'll just turn intangible and avoid it. She can literally do what she wants."

Exactly.

At least he had some sense.

TWENTY

A time unknown, but one of truth

Sitting on the ledge he'd made for his comfort and convenience, Weldir glared at the viewing disc before him.

The two environments, his and the one in the disc, were remarkably similar. Both were bright with sunshine, both high in the air. Weldir was situated near his special cave – at the top of this mountain. He'd carved this flat area before his cave entrance out of wanting a place to have his thoughts. To sit, like he wasn't just a floating conscience.

Forests, hills, and meadows lay before both of them.

The longer Lindiwe flew, the more Weldir's mood soured – when it was quite disgruntled to begin with.

Rather than having to spend even a moment in my presence, she chooses to fly across the world. Wasting time – she had plenty of it – and wasting energy, although she was a strong female. *This vexes me deeply.*

Orpheus was impossible to be near due to his volatile emotions. If Lindiwe approached him, he'd attack to protect his home from her, while refusing to enter it himself. He was... inconsolable. He didn't know how to be, how to exist, nor did he know how to regulate his emotions, ease his thoughts, and grieve properly.

All of Lindiwe's attempts to help had done more harm than

good.

So she moved on, as she didn't wish to torture him.

And rather than asking for Weldir's aid, she fucking flew across the ocean again! This time, she found herself in Eyropea, and she'd been visiting their offspring on her own.

He hadn't realised how much he valued those fleeting moments with her until she no longer required them. She'd found her own independence, and that annoyed him.

Only because it was done spitefully.

With his legs crossed, he placed his elbow on his knee and rested his jaw on his fist. *Her anger is always stubbornly enduring.* He didn't think he'd done anything particularly wrong.

I told her the truth. It's not my fault she misunderstood.

He was a god. She should have known he was outside the realm of reality.

Now she's stolen my fun from me. Along with her very presence.

Granted, much had happened since then, and it actually hadn't been all that long. What was it? Two months since she'd demanded to leave his realm?

He tried to recount how many sun cycles he'd witnessed, but he'd probably missed a few.

Even after all this time, I don't understand her.

He wanted to. Fuck, he was *trying* to, but she made it needlessly difficult. When she was upset, she wanted to be left alone, and wouldn't speak with him until she was ready.

Is this her way of punishing me? Weldir pondered that thought and then disregarded it. *Lindiwe isn't that kind of person.*

She was a solitary creature, something crafted by their bond. He'd inadvertently made her this way. *No. She is merely upset and is trying to handle it.*

In the same way she moved through grief and loss. She'd leaned on him momentarily in Nathair's death and then had receded into herself. Simply to heal her own heart through time and space, through distractions.

Did any of that matter to how Weldir was feeling? No. He grew more annoyed with each day he *shouldn't* be able to feel the moving stretch of. He should be outside of time, and yet he was dwindling in it.

When she finally landed and turned into a human, Weldir tried, once again, to shorten the mental distance between them.

"Lindiwe, are you ready to discuss what–" Before he could finish, she darted her head to the side dismissively and approached the haunted one she'd seen.

Weldir's mist pulled and pushed away from him in anger, like he'd seen her breaths sawing in and out of her expanding and collapsing chest. His realm rumbled, his emotions so strong they caused an earthquake to tremble through it.

I tire of waiting! His mind roared. *I tire of these human games. Of her ire!* Of her not giving him exactly what he craved: her desire.

He'd already waited for it, and just as he'd gotten it, in the midst of watching her ride him no less, she'd fucking stolen it. The only thing he'd found since the moment he'd been born that *enthralled* him.

Weldir looked down at his arms to see that all the souls he'd collected, and the many she and their offspring had brought him, had increased what was visible. Over a third of him existed, to the point that he was aware his hands to his forearms, his feet to his calves, and his head to the top of his chest, were all visible.

He'd spread his mist far across Earth, and could expand it further should he choose.

Yet he hadn't, simply because it would reduce his physical self. There would be less of it to share... *with her.*

Not that she wanted it.

So what if he couldn't physically feel desire, arousal, pleasure? What difference did it make to her enjoyment of it? Her pleasure? So long as *she* felt it, that was all that mattered, right?

His tolerance regarding her rejection of her own pleasure

was running its course.

He was done with it.

And he was done waiting for this unending ire of hers to fade.

Making a rather devious decision, Weldir transported himself from Tenebris to the void outside of it. Then he waited for his opportune moment.

He watched her turn from an owl into a human and then... a Phantom.

"You will speak to me, Lindiwe," Weldir demanded, wanting to give her the opportunity to heal their wounded bond before he took control of it himself.

She didn't answer him.

So, Weldir yanked her body from Earth and to his realm without her permission. He wrapped a tendril around her ankle, since she was tangible to him, and pulled her closer until their gazes could lock less than a foot apart.

Her glossy curls waved through the floating darkness as she gasped and looked around. She swayed her hand to swim backwards, but his tendril around her leg kept her to him.

"Enough of this," Weldir demanded with a curt growl.

"What do you think you're doing?" Lindiwe asked in a surprised rasp before her face – her pretty, expressive face – shifted. Her lips thinned and she cast him one of her glares. "Send me back. Right now."

Weldir yanked her closer. "No." He darted his gaze down her body with a tsk. "We will resolve this, whether you're ready or not."

"I don't have to." She folded her arms and lifted her chin. "And you can't make–"

Her anger faded, instead replaced by widened eyes as she looked down at her leg. She pulled and yanked, then her heart began to race.

"Why can't I shift?" she whispered.

"I always wondered if I touched you while you were tangible to me, whether I could stop you from changing forms," Weldir stated coldly. "It appears I was right."

"L-let me go, Weldir."

"No." He let the word hang between them, harsh and heavy, and her eyes took on a rather anxious, frightened edge.

At him! Someone who had never gone out of his way to hurt her.

"My patience has run its course, Lindiwe. And I have been a very patient being for a long time."

"Fine!" she yelled. "If you want an offspring, we can make one. But I want you to use your tendril, like before."

"Offspring?" Weldir hummed with dark humour. "I couldn't give a fuck about creating another right now. That isn't the issue."

She drew her brows in tight, obviously not expecting his response.

"What currently vexes me is your silence. You are... pulling away from me."

She curled her hands into tight fists and twisted her head to the side. "I want time to process how I'm feeling."

"You have had *weeks*." His mist tightened against his form. "Surely that is ample time."

For a human, at least.

"I've barely been able to focus with everything that's happened."

It sounded like an excuse to evade the discussion.

A growl rumbled from him. "I don't understand what your problem is. I don't see how my lack of physical perception has upset you. Why does it matter?"

Just his words sent her heart racing, and it throbbed in his mind from all around him. Cupping her hands against her stomach, she drew her shoulders inwards as she kept her gaze averted.

"It just does," she answered in a small voice.

Weldir placed his hand around her knee and drew it upwards, trying to coax her like he usually could; the lithe muscles of her thighs were sensitive and easy to stimulate.

"But you found pleasure in it. You enjoyed it."

She slapped his hand away with both of her own. "Because I am not entertainment!" she yelled, scrunching her face at him in anger. "Because my desire is not for your amusement. I don't want to be leered at, pitied, like my arousal is a fucking joke!"

Weldir snapped his fangs, creating a sharp, clipping noise as he shot forward. "When have I ever led you to believe such a thing?"

"All of it was a lie! A performance that you took part in for *my* sake!"

"I did not lie, female!"

"I thought we were *sharing* something. It doesn't matter that you told me and I misunderstood. It was obvious that I didn't know, and I'm so embarrassed by my own actions, by my behaviour because... because I was trying to..." Her eyelids crinkled as liquid welled along her lash line. She bit her bottom lip, unable to spit it out, then covered her face and shook her head in her palms. "Just... I don't think I can do it with someone who can't even *feel* it. It makes me feel pathetic. Like I'm forcing you to do something you feel nothing for."

A deep, dark chuckle rumbled from him. "That is where you are very wrong."

She lowered her hands to reveal her tear-stained cheeks. "But you said–"

Weldir curled his fingers under her chin and pulled her forward. Her neck stretched as he put them face to face until her nose was close to brushing his own.

"Entertainment? Amusement? My *enjoyment* of it isn't that shallow. And forcing me?" Weldir tsked and dipped his head in a way that made it clear he'd drawn his gaze down her body. "In what way do you have control over anything I do? I do things because *I* want to."

"Then what reason do you have for doing it?" she snapped without pulling away. Instead, her nose scrunched in anger, and he found it cute that she thought she could be scary. "I'm not desperate or pathetic enough to be... to be *pity fucked*!"

The snarl that tore out of him was rather beastly, even for him. He gripped her jaw a little tighter and bared his fangs.

"Because *I* like it!" Weldir roared. "Because the way you tremble when you come stirs me in ways I cannot fathom." He pushed his thumb up to shove her head to the side, exposing her neck to him. "Because when you're close, your heart's rhythm is so erratic that it pulses from you like an erotic drum and fills my realm entirely. And your little pants... your breaths, so shallow and cute, always come out in raspy, long draws when you're about to moan. I know every inch of your body and how it twitches, how it shivers, and how it dips under any caress."

Weldir drew his clawed thumb down her pulsing jugular, hating that it was rapid for the wrong reason. Yet, like her body remembered his touch, the side of her neck prickled with goosebumps.

"Admittedly, I began this simply because it was something you desired, with little care for it, but that changed." When he drew his thumb up, and she gave a shiver at his claw tickling her skin, he perceived pressure across his face – as if he might have grinned at how *honest* her body was. "Your body is such a lusty thing. I may not be able to feel pleasure, but I experience it through you. In the way your eyes grow soft and dazed, or how you stretch into my touch for more without meaning to."

Weldir released her gently, supporting her chin as it lowered to a comfortable position. He pulled back and dipped his head once more to show her he was looking down her body, and his gaze fell on her soft, generous breasts. Her nipples had hardened through her dress, giving away that she was aroused by his words, even if her slack-jawed expression didn't.

"I may not be able to feel desire, or your touch, or the warmth of your body, but I experience it within my mind." He shot his gaze up to greet her puzzled stare. "And my mind is rather perverted, little human." Then he purposefully dabbed his tongue at the seam of his lips seductively, like he'd seen some humans do. "And I very much enjoy watching you."

For once, he liked her silence.

She wasn't arguing with him, wasn't shouting at him. She was stunned speechless.

Had she not desired to leave last time, I would've told her all this. He hadn't wanted her to think she was alone in all this, but she refused to speak with him, and Weldir refused to have this conversation alone in his darkness. *I would have told her because... I tire of hiding it.*

He hadn't wanted to lose those moments of bonding with her. Each time, no matter how small it was, he felt they were breaching the distance between them. He grew more infatuated, and she seemed to soften towards him.

Enough to stay for prolonged periods in his realm.

Enough to remain at his side, rather than scorning him and running away.

So, at the risk of losing it all, Weldir had decided his honesty was the only solution. If he were to be rejected beyond that, if his thoughts and feelings were irrelevant, then at least he would know he tried everything.

Well, almost everything. Weldir would never tell her about his cave of memories, and how many sculptures he had of her. He didn't want his obsession with her to be that intimately understood.

He thought she might run off scared. She'd definitely be mortified, if this situation had taught him anything.

Maybe I could try one last thing?

"But if my unfeeling touch is so abhorrent to you, if it matters that much to you, then you will at least find pleasure by yourself," Weldir stated firmly.

Lindiwe covered her chest with a frown. "What do you mean?"

"Whether it be by my hand or your own, you will satisfy your desire." Humour radiated through his mist when he lowered his voice and said, "I don't think you should deny your hungry little pussy that. It is rather greedy for attention."

Her eyes widened as her lips parted around a wordless protest. Then the brown in her cheeks and chest reddened, and she squirmed bashfully. She'd done a poor job of hiding her breasts, and he witnessed one nipple harden further. Her heart also took on a familiar rhythm, one that was often accompanied by her arousal.

Weldir tilted his head. *Does she like being spoken to like this?* What did the humans call it? Dirty talk?

Lindiwe kicked back to get away from him, uselessly, as his tendril still had a solid grip on her. In retaliation, he extended it so it would tickle the sensitive bundle of nerves beneath her calf muscle.

"What? In front of you?"

"Why not?" he asked. "If you don't want my touch because I cannot feel it physically, then I want to enjoy your pleasure in the way I always have, by watching you." Then he gave a hum as he tried to remember all the human memories he'd delved into. "This isn't an uncommon desire. You humans watch each other masturbate all the time."

"Yes! But I've never..." She trailed off and bit her lip.

"Oh, I know, Lindiwe. I've always wondered why you never sated your desire by yourself."

Her gaze flicked to the side as she gripped the skirt of her dress nervously. Her flush of embarrassment deepened. "It just... we were taught... it feels... and the worry that you might catch me kind of..."

It took Weldir a moment to understand, and he had to sift through many possible reasons as to why she'd be against it.

He sighed. "If you tell me it has to do with that pesky faith of yours..."

Her lips tightened, and she didn't deny it.

All the fun he'd been having in teasing her fucking *died* so quickly he bit out a growl. Instead, he was horribly angered and annoyed, and an emotion he wasn't used to scattered through his mist.

Possessiveness, and perhaps a touch of jealousy.

He yanked her closer by his will until her chest butted up against his, and he looked down at her. "The only god that matters to you now is *me*," he rumbled, holding her doe-eyed stare. "And I am telling you to touch yourself." Then he lowered his head until he was right at her ear and growled, "And I'm not letting you out of my realm until you fucking do."

A strangled, shivering moan escaped her, and she lifted her shoulder like she wanted to escape his voice speaking low in her ear. The temptation to nip her earlobe struck him, but she apparently didn't want his touch, so he didn't.

"It'll be weird if you're doing nothing and just watching me," she whisper-shouted at him.

"I would find it exciting. Rather than my fingers deep inside you, it would be your own, and then you can feel for yourself how wet you get. So much so that you leave droplets of it in my realm."

He pulled away from her and put space between them because if he continued to be within reaching distance of her, he was going to touch her. Lindiwe was lucky he couldn't feel desire. If this was what his mind was like without being physically aroused, he could only imagine what it'd be like if he was.

"Would it make it easier if you couldn't see me?" Weldir asked, casting his body elsewhere while stripping his sight so it remained.

"No!" she yelled, before realising how quickly she'd thrown the word out. "I think I'd feel worse, to be honest. I want to know where you are." He brought his body back, and her shoulders lost some of their tension. "I don't understand where this is all suddenly coming from."

"It's not sudden. You just haven't been privy to my innermost thoughts."

"Then why not tell me sooner?"

"Because I never know with you!" Weldir roared. He threw his hands downwards while gesturing at himself. "I didn't know if learning all this would upset you or not. If you were just trying to make the process of offspring more enjoyable without wanting anything more, and I thought your reluctance to take pleasure by your own hand was simply because you didn't feel the need to, despite how confusing I then found how much you liked it when I touched you. You are my mate, and I don't understand you. You are infuriating, and I have made many mistakes. Fuck, Lindiwe, I have been trying for years to better our matebond. So if I must only be a witness to this part of you, so long as your gaze remains soft towards me, I'm content to have it this way." Then his voice took on a dark edge, as he quietly warned, "But I *will* witness it, or so help me, I will keep you trapped here in my realm and use everything within my power to tease you and break you until you crave my touch once more."

She'd already stated he could use his tendrils on her to create offspring, so he would use *them* to touch her, as they were not technically a part of him. They were just a physical manifestation of his mana.

He winced when he realised he'd threatened her with entrapment, when he'd vowed to himself he never would again. But he was at the absolute end of his fucking patience, and he would make this female *bend* to his will for once. He usually admired how headstrong she could be – it was what made her so resilient and determined, so brave and strong – but it was vexing when it was cast at him.

For once, he wanted this female to cave to him. Be soft, pliable, and give him what he craved. To give him... something.

Regret shimmered through his mist, knowing he likely just did irreparable damage to her trust. *She told me she's worried about being in my realm because I've imprisoned her in it before.* He'd only done so once, and he'd been eating those actions ever since like they were a poison he couldn't escape.

He steeled himself to apologise, to tell her he actually wouldn't do that again, and to try to assuage her fears regarding this. Something he should have done long ago.

Her dress inched up her legs bit by bit as she bundled it in both her fists. His head reared back when he darted his gaze up to her face to find she'd bitten her bottom lip, and her brown eyes had a heated glint to them.

Somehow, the slow glide of the material climbing up her legs made it more sensual than it really should have been.

"You should have just been honest with me," she murmured. "I can't read your mind, Weldir. I thought *you* didn't want anything more beyond what you asked of me in exchange for protecting my soul."

"It's not like you have tried to communicate with me either," Weldir answered with a huff. "You offer silence when you're angered."

Lindiwe's creeping fingers halted, and she cocked a brow at him. "Do you want to argue about my failings, or do you want me to do as you have asked?"

Weldir promptly snapped his fangs shut.

TWENTY-ONE

A time unknown, but one that possessively clings

With each crawl of his mate's white dress inching up her legs, Weldir's mist vibrated a little more. When she flashed the top of her silky thighs and pale-green underwear, he formed a bubble of his mana around one of the ties across her collarbones.

He pulled it and unlaced her cloak.

Her dress glided higher, until she slipped it up and over her head, revealing deep curves and gorgeous breasts tipped with dark-brown nipples. Weldir considered untying her underwear to quicken the pace and save her the trouble – and to sate his greedy yearning.

The flat plane of her stomach dipped once she exposed herself, and she covered her breasts with one arm. His gaze darted up, and he almost produced a growl at her hiding them.

It died when he took in her soft eyes, the brown in them more molten than usual, like glittering bronze. The deep, tawny complexion of her skin allowed just enough nervous red to show through, and it glowed in her cheeks and the tips of her round ears. She nibbled on her fuller bottom lip, making it swell and reveal the pink inner seam.

Her gaze darted over him, her long, pretty lashes fluttering.

This wilful, assertive female had grown all shy. It was so undeniably cute he wanted to reach out and soothe her.

"I'm not really quite sure what to do next," Lindiwe murmured, before thinking better of it while rolling her eyes. "I mean, I know *what* I'm supposed to do, just... I don't know what *you* want to see. If you just want me to get straight to the point."

"I'm in no rush, Lindiwe," Weldir answered softly. "I don't mind what you do."

When her expression grew shyer, even becoming a touch forlorn as her arm tightened across her chest, he realised that wasn't the answer she wanted. *Does she want me to... guide her?* To take some of the control, even from a distance?

Fuck. It would be so much easier to show her.

But fine, Weldir would be honest.

"Show me how you like being touched. Explore your body in the places that make you wetter before dipping into it." With each word, her little heart sprinted faster, and the unease in her eyes evaporated. "I want you to tease yourself until you can no longer take it, and *then* satisfy the ache you give yourself."

He wanted her body to beg for release like it did with him, until it craved, yearned, and hungered for mind-bending bliss. Until she rode her own fingers hard and deep, like she did his, just before she orgasmed.

Lindiwe lowered her arm, revealing her breasts, and brought that hand across the flat area of her chest. "I like it when my skin is touched gently."

Drawing the backs of her long nails down the sides of her teardrop breasts, the sensitive mounds prickled with goosebumps, making her areolas and nipples tighten. She let out a soft, quiet rasp. Drifting them lower, she caressed the outside of her abdomen muscles and then over the dips of her hips until she was trailing the sides of her rear.

"It tickles in a way that isn't uncomfortable." She crossed to just below her navel and then drew her fingertips and nails up the centre of her body. Her stomach muscles danced under her own caress as she met the flesh between her breasts, brushing the insides of those mounds. Then she ghosted above them. "I'm... not used to feeling such softness or being handled with care. Even though I can tell your claws are sharp, you only scratch me in a way that the sensation feels nice, even when you do it harder."

This time when she drew her nails across her body, streaks formed when she pressed them harder. She deliberately scratched up the sides of her neck, then over one shoulder, showing she didn't mind when it was harder, or rougher.

"Sometimes I like how sharp they are, even if it hurts a little."

Her breaths grew shallow when she cupped underneath the perky drops of her breasts until their softness moulded into her palms. She squeezed, her flesh dipping around her fingers, and a muffled, quiet moan hummed from her as she bit her bottom lip.

Then, with her middle fingers barely touching the tips of her nipples, she moved them in featherlight circles. Her breath hitched, and she 'tickled' all her fingers around them, teasing her nipples and areolas, as well as the surrounding skin. More goosebumps prickled along her flesh, starting from where she touched and spreading outwards.

Lindiwe's breath hitched again, her thighs clamping together tightly as her body twitched back and forth while her toes curled. Her brows knitted together, her eyes bowed and crinkled in blissful anguish, as if the sensation was too soft, too light, too much. Yet she didn't stop until her lips parted on a trembling moan.

"Sometimes the caresses are too soft, and it's almost painful," she croaked, cupping her breasts with a hard squeeze.

Her trembling only settled when she clamped her nipples between her thumbs and forefingers. She was soothing the tension she'd given herself, kneading rough and hard – the opposite of how she'd started.

When Weldir's tendril keeping her tangible to him had spiralled further up her leg, he didn't know. It was a manifestation of the excitement that vibrated through his mist at watching her pet herself.

He hadn't expected her performance to be so sensual, or that she'd speak to him during it.

He lengthened his tendril up her leg until it wrapped around her knee. He glided the tip up her inner thigh, and her lower abdomen didn't just dance; it twitched and shuddered as if her pussy quivered in reaction. Her back arched a little as her thighs spread, revealing that her arousal clung to her pale-green underwear in the form of a dark spot.

Her right hand made a path down her body. She pressed on her clit, gave a shuddering moan, and then closed her thighs around her hand as if it was too much.

The growl that vibrated from him was feral, and he used his tendril to pull her leg to the side. "I want to see. Don't close yourself to me." Actually, her annoying fucking underwear was covering where he wanted to see most. "Take your panties off."

Her lips quirked. "What if I'm not ready to?"

Weldir's mist pulsed, and his patient restraint was the only thing holding him back. Patience that was all too close to ending.

"If you don't show me that pretty pussy of yours now, I *will* do it myself."

Her brows darted up her forehead in surprise, yet her fingers pressed harder on her slit as she kneaded her breast. "You promised you would only watch."

A deep chuckle reverberated from him. "When did I say that? I won't utter promises I'd *very* much want to break."

Her lips curled even more, giving her a rather sultry look when she bit her bottom lip as if she *liked* his domineering commands.

"A please would be nice."

"If you wanted a submissive male, then you have bonded yourself to the wrong god."

She giggled, and the rare, mystical sound of it soothed his anger. It caressed his essence, his very spirit, in the oddest way.

She brought her hand to her hip and loosened the tie of her panties. Once the material was loosened on one side, it easily glided down her beautiful long legs and floated away.

She brought her knees up and then hesitated. What had been a naughty, sultry gaze, pinched with unease. Yet, in Lindiwe's often bold and confident fashion, she then spread her thighs and bared herself to him.

Lips parted, the little entrance to her pink cunt was so overflowing with arousal that it'd spread between her folds and glistened on her dark curls.

"You look very wet, Lindiwe," Weldir rumbled.

"I thought it would bother me being watched," she whispered, dipping her fingers down through her slickness. "But I'm actually finding it exciting."

Like a caress to his mind, his mist pulsed with exhilaration. He lurched forward with the desire to take over and show her what was truly exciting, only to pull back. He also withdrew his tendril back down her leg, as he was dangerously close to shoving it into that little spread hole of hers.

I... didn't realise how difficult I'd find it to be a witness to this.

He wanted to aid her, even if it was only a little. Weldir didn't actually want her to reject his touch. He'd been enthralled watching her come apart under his ministrations, *because* of him.

He wanted her to reach out to him, like his touch was superior.

His mind ached to go to her, to envelop her in his mist so it could brush over all of her, but he was unsure if she could feel it.

He'd thought he would be mostly fine with this, so long as she found pleasure and showed it to him, but the slowness was torturous. The lack of control spiked his need to take over. He'd never experienced anticipation this strong, and he found his mind pleading for the next step until she lost herself.

The instant she pressed directly against her clit, her legs spread further and her core visibly clenched. She moaned so sweetly, and her eyelids slid shut. When she moved her fingers side to side in a lazy circle, her head fell back and her silky thighs twitched, spasmed, and trembled.

And this was Weldir's favourite part.

Where he got to witness all the little, intricate details of her body she would be too consumed in her pleasure to notice.

Her heart, so full of need and lust, suddenly quickened, and it thumped around his realm in a chaotic rhythm. Her pulse fluttered fast, and it highlighted the beauty of her slender neck. Any touch to that spot when it was like this could send her over the edge, which was why he often nipped at it, or licked it, or even brushed his horn against it.

Her pupils were blown, eating away at her pretty brown irises, while her third finger on her right hand always trembled when she was this twisted with need. The tiny hairs on her body that would rise in waves were often the precursor to an intense ripple of goosebumps that would cascade down her legs and arms. The corded muscles in her neck would tighten when she sucked in a sharp, near-choking hitch of breath.

Different muscles, slim and taut, would flex. His gaze often bounced between each one, as if following their complex dance, yet he could never guess the next location. They were utterly enticing in their playfulness.

Her bottom lip was now swollen from her constant chewing on it, but usually both were tender from his kisses. The seam of them was drier than normal, but she soothed them with a darting lick he almost missed.

Sure, he should have been preoccupied with her fingers plucking at her body and her melodious, sultry cries as she flicked her clit side to side. Yes, he did find it rather hypnotic, but only because of the resultant symphony. The dance of flesh, muscles, and tendons, the little pants, the shuddering moans.

But it was how her body trembled towards release, how it grew flushed. How he could almost *see* the ache within by the way her hips constantly bucked for more and more, so greedy and ravenous that she stopped caring about anything but achieving her own end. Weldir knew that while she was desperate for it, he could touch in almost any way, explore beyond the boundaries of what he'd tried, and she'd accept it.

Accept him, in the only way she ever truly did.

She dived her fingers lower into the slit of her folds, wetting them to the second knuckle. Then she spread them against her opening as if preparing to enter it, but it gave Weldir quite the naughty peek within her depths. He glimpsed pink flesh that looked plump and tight before she delved her middle finger into the darkness within.

Her lips shut to hum a soft moan, and she tilted her head forward. She opened her eyes, but they were dazed and sightless as she looked at him. He knew there was little she was seeing – perhaps just his darkness, where he hovered. There was recognition there, but her mind was elsewhere.

Lindiwe pumped her finger, and her toes curled momentarily. She angled her hand so the top knuckle of her thumb rubbed against her clit at the same time, desiring more stimulation.

That wasn't something Weldir had ever considered doing.

"Add another," Weldir commanded when she was taking too long. "You like being fuller."

The amber in her molten-brown eyes sparkled with recognition, and she darted her tongue along the seam of her lips. She slipped another finger inside, and its trembling ceased when it was encased in snugness. Her hand thrust faster. Her pussy squelched as she grew noticeably wetter, and the sound was as erotic as it'd always been.

Her eyelids drooped, tipping her dark lashes down.

With each deep thrust, her pants grew shallower and more broken, and her limbs tightened inwards. Then her fingers stayed sheathed, and it was only from her knuckles shifting that he knew she was wiggling them inside her cunt. That she was pressing and teasing the exact spot that had her head tipped back on a loud cry. She moved them together, then individually, only to pump her fingers once more to reveal she'd made herself wetter.

Yet her body didn't relent, and she pulled out to pet her clit so she could catch her breath. Her fingers were drenched in her arousal, a little clear, a little milky, and she used that to caress up and down her slit, keeping her fingers flat. Each time, she made sure to press hard on her clit.

Her melting expression softened, no longer close to the edge but obviously still teetering near it. The first orgasm always seemed to be the trickiest, and then there would be a crescendo of them.

She met his gaze, truly met it, and her petting slowed.

"Why are you stopping?" Weldir had to bite back a growl, although his tone was rough and displeased.

"I don't think I'm going to come like this," she whispered around tiny rasps. "It's like... my body is fighting me."

"Then try harder. I told you, you're not leaving my realm until you have." And he definitely wouldn't let her when she was so close, with her naked legs spread and her pussy wet and waiting.

She hadn't come last time either, and Weldir was still annoyed over it, as she'd ridden him before and *that* had been exciting. Watching her entirely use his body had been so mentally arousing that his mist had started colliding with itself and lumping together in a weird pattern.

So, no, Weldir wouldn't let her rob herself of another orgasm. Not even if she begged to be let go.

His tendril on her leg tightened, making sure she couldn't escape from it.

"It's like it knows it's not... *you*." She whispered the last word, but he heard it, and it shocked him all the same.

Weldir's mist disappeared from around him and instead encased her. The rest of him stayed behind, refusing to further close the short distance between them. His chalky physical self shifted around his limbs and torso erratically, as if the restraint was irritating it.

Lindiwe closed her thighs a little as her shoulders turned inwards and her expression, so full of fire just seconds before, turned shy.

"Can you... help me?"

Weldir was moving in an instant. He didn't need a reason, nor did he particularly care why she'd changed her mind.

He didn't even waste time by floating over. He transported himself straight to her, and she didn't have a chance to register him there before he slammed two fingers, with his claws missing, inside her pussy.

"Oh!" Her back arched and her eyes widened, only for them to grow dazed and then half closed when he quickly began to thrust.

At the same time, he shot his head forward to lick her clit, and although he couldn't feel it, Weldir had used trial and error in the past to determine how hard he needed to apply pressure. He knew how to circle his tongue just right, how to keep his fangs from nicking the sensitive bundle of nerves, and he'd taught himself how to *suck* – although that last one required a touch of his mana for assistance.

One of her hands grabbed his hair, and he made sure it was available for her to do so, while the other grasped a horn.

Except... he wasn't feeling as magnanimous as usual.

He let his frustration and annoyance over how they got here shimmer through, and he grabbed all four of her limbs with tendrils, then yanked them apart. He spread her thighs as far as they could go so she remained open for him to do as he pleased, and he even coiled his tendrils around her legs in a way that trapped her calves against her thighs. Then he brought her arms up above her head and threaded his black tendrils together, so her wrists were bound against each other.

"What are you doing?" she rasped.

"You have done quite enough touching," Weldir said in a low, darkened tone. "Now it's *my* turn."

Weldir upped the ante, and he sucked hard on her sensitive little clit, while thrusting his fingers fast and deep. Lindiwe had done all the hard work for him, and it was barely a few seconds before her entire body went taut.

Her back arched, tipping her breasts upwards, and her limbs trembled all at once. The cry she let out was loud, high-pitched, and satisfyingly close to a *scream*.

He flicked his gaze up her body without removing his mouth from her, then shook his head, knowing it would only deepen her orgasm, and he was quite content with the view. Her breasts, so soft and pretty, jiggled as she shuddered, while her stomach rose and dipped from desperate, erratic breaths. He couldn't see her face, but the dance of her body was enough to quell his annoyance at that.

Then, when her body ceased its quivering, Weldir removed his fingers and mouth from her. He transported himself again, this time to directly behind her.

After he separated his sight from his body, he floated forward, then turned so he could view her, and himself, together fully.

"Would you prefer to know where I am?" Weldir asked as he snaked his arms around her torso. "Like I said, I can only see, not feel, but I do rather like the view of you like this."

Between panted breaths, she said hoarsely, "I'd prefer to know."

Although the way he perceived his surroundings outside of himself was amorphous, he gave it a shape for her human mind to comprehend. Two eyelids, filled with the blackness of his normal eyes, were haloed by a white light. He even added lashes to make them appear less odd, though he always forgot to blink.

Her gaze met his free-floating one, and she looked a little startled at first. Enough so that she gasped in surprise when he cupped one breast, covering it in a dark, chalky hand, while the other dipped low, already wet from her orgasm, and slid along her clit to cradle it between two of his fingers. With her arms still bound above her head, although lacking enough tension that she could bend her elbows, she lurched forward in his arms at his touch.

Her brown curls waved around her face, partially blocking it and his own from being seen, so he used his will to sweep it all to the opposite side. Then he nuzzled his nose against the soft spot behind her ear that always made her breath hitch, especially when he spoke low.

"I like you tied up like this. You look quite defenceless," he muttered, followed by a dark chuckle. "Unable to truly move, unable to get away. Unable to do what you like with that cute little body of yours."

He tightened his tendrils on her limbs just so she could feel the squeeze of them.

When she opened her pesky mouth to say something, Weldir pinched her nipple and clit at the same time, making her words choke in her throat.

"I'd like to try something different." A tendril formed in front of them, then thickened to the size of his thumb – if not a little more. With his fingers, he spread her cunt open for easy access. "You did say you'd prefer a tendril, didn't you?"

"I know that's what I said, but–"

Yes, yes, he was aware that likely wasn't the case anymore. Didn't mean he wasn't still furious over it.

Before she could finish speaking, he shoved it inside her until it bottomed out and the long length of it bent sideways. A strangled moan escaped her, and then more whispered past her lips when he thrust it deep while his fingers teased her clit. He pulled the hood back so he could nestle behind it, then moved his digits side to side. In an instant, her hips tried to buck as her jaw fell, her lips parted, and her eyes clenched shut.

Pleased with himself that he'd been conserving his mana just for this, he made more tendrils form. One wrapped around her waist and hips to stop them from moving, not allowing her even a millimetre, so she could suffer in stillness. He wrapped another around the breast his hand wasn't kneading, spiralling around it until the brown hardened peak was tightly trapped.

"There, is that better, Lindiwe?" Weldir uttered softly as he scraped his fangs against the side of her neck.

"Oh *fuck*," she rasped with a shiver, as she bent her head to the side to escape his voice. Her head lolled against his shoulder, her face pinched, and her moans grew more frantic as his hands and tendrils played with *every* sensitive spot on her body all at once.

It was incredibly satisfying to observe his body around hers from behind, while she was on display, trapped in his chalky black arms or tendrils, all of it shimmering with dark glitter and mist. His onyx eyes were glossy against the matte of his appearance, as were his segmented, tapered horns.

"Oh god. Oh *god*, that feels so good," she rasped out.

Lost to pleasure, she'd never looked as beautiful as she did right then.

The growl that reverberated around his void was deep and beastly. "The only *god* you belong to is me," he rumbled against the side of her throat as he made another thicker tendril form. "And I much prefer it when you moan my name."

He squeezed the new tendril inside her full cunt, and her body put up a brief fight, then relented against his strength, and he gave her no room to reject it. Even if she felt a bite of pain from being overstretched, with both of them attacking, she could do little more than give herself over to pleasure.

He moved them individually, making sure they were hooked forward, so they'd grind against the tender spot inside her.

Now that she'd already climaxed once, the second one came easier. She cried out his name, and Weldir rewarded her with a nip of his fangs, his fingers pressing harder against her clit. Liquid squelched out of her and dripped down his tendrils until drops flicked off from the quick, snaking movements. She fought the others holding her in place, needing to buck, squirm, and grab something, but she could do little more than be trapped as her hands opened and closed.

He watched the intricate details of her body, the ones that only intensified with every passing second. How her heart thumped around him and fluttered underneath her skin so frantically, so erratically, he was surprised it didn't give out and cease its rhythmic drumming. How she grew flushed when her lungs seized, her lips squeaking out a pitiful noise, before her complexion returned to its beautiful, healthy brown when she caught her breath.

How perspiration dotted her forehead and coated her skin in a thin layer that made her glisten.

Every twitch, no matter how tiny, drew his attentive gaze.

That was until her tear-lined eyes, so unique and often sharp, met his, and she stared at him with a semi-lucid hold.

He found it difficult to look away.

I've never had her meet my gaze like this before.

It made it... different. More intimate in a way he'd never thought possible. The corners of her lips even quirked upwards, like she tried to smile but couldn't muster the will beyond her bliss and her next moan. Her third orgasm nearly made her eyes cross.

"Weldir," she cried softly, her features pinching in anguish as she came back down from her climax. "I don't think I can take any more."

But *he* wasn't quite done. She wasn't broken enough, nor had she soothed his anger fully. "Beg," Weldir demanded.

The betrayed look that overtook her face was cute. "What?" she whispered.

"You haven't apologised to me. I was quite wounded, Lindiwe. You stole away my *fun*." He nuzzled his nose and lips against her neck. "Beg me to stop. Plead until I'm satisfied, while I fuck your little cunt with the tendrils you so rudely prefer."

To show her he was serious, his tendrils working her pussy and his fingers petting her clit only went harder. He considered stuffing a third limb of mana inside her but thought she might not be able to handle it. Two already seemed overly girthy for her, since her hole looked stretched around them.

"No," she *tried* to bite out. It came out rather quiet and pitiful.

"Then so be it. I won't stop until you do."

It was all in her control, even if he was dubious about it.

Admittedly, though, she wasn't as wet as before, and wasn't

producing enough slick to make for an easy glide. Yet he knew this female. If she had even a drop to give, she didn't wish to stop, and she knew exactly how to make this all cease if she really wanted it to.

All she had to do was give in.

"I need to use my essence to lubricate you," Weldir told her, figuring the use of two tendrils had aided this dryness quicker than normal. "Is that alright?"

She bit her lip. It took her a moment, but she eventually nodded. He almost wanted to laugh.

Did she want to stop? Didn't she? A vexingly confusing woman as always, but for once, he found it rather fun.

She let out a squeak when he coated her insides with his essence, his seed. Whether this resulted in anything or not, Weldir didn't care. It wasn't the reason he'd done it.

Though he may have given her much more than usual to ensure she remained lubricated, since the pearlescent, whiteish-grey liquid leaked from her and dripped down his tendrils. It coated down to her backside and even seeped up her slit. He dipped his fingertips into it so he could slicken his touch against her clit.

Since Weldir couldn't feel, he didn't slow due to tiredness, nor have his own end to worry about. If she really wanted, he could have suspended this moment for all eternity, never ceasing or requiring a break.

He could be as stubborn as her.

So when her next orgasm took her, something shifted within him. She would give him what he wanted eventually, surely she knew that, but the fact that she wanted to draw this out elicited an unknown emotion in his mind. She was... his, trapped in his hold, his touch, his mind's will, and his realm.

"The next time you want pleasure, Lindiwe, tell me," he muttered against her hair. "If you want this, it doesn't have to result in an offspring. I'm quite content to do this, to touch your body and make it moan, make it orgasm."

He didn't have much to look forward to, much to anticipate.

He didn't feel tenderness or joy in much, but he found it in these embraces. He adored how her gaze went from heated to exceptionally soft afterwards.

When she didn't say anything, and he was unsure if her nod was just the result of her body constantly arching, Weldir released her breast to gently touch her lips. "Speak. Answer me."

"Okay," she whispered against his fingers.

He slipped his hand lower to cup her throat lightly and drew his clawed thumb down her rapidly pulsing jugular, tickling it to make her breath hitch.

The game truly began when their stubbornness met in battle and fought ruthlessly. She wouldn't bend to his will and submit, and Weldir refused to relinquish his prize until she did.

He grazed his fangs across her neck as he made one last tendril form, this one mimicking the spiralling hold the other had on her breast. The soft flesh of her ample mounds moulded around each thin limb, and he pulsated them to make it feel as though he was kneading them, while the ends pinched or swirled around her nipples. He even made their tips meet her peaks to touch them *softly* in little circles, much like she'd done in the beginning. Doing so had her chest arching forward constantly.

He was quite content with his fingers along her slit, and he pushed down so her clit was nestled against the webbing of his index and middle finger. His clawless fingertips wetly slid along the sides of her opening, and occasionally he spread her further for his own view.

Palming his free hand from her throat down her body hard enough that she dipped towards his torso, he placed it low on her pelvis.

"Did you know your body moves here?" He slid his hand to the side to caress where movement shifted forward and back. "A noticeable bulge forms, showing just how full you are of me."

He shoved both his thick tendrils deep, and a small lump

protruded from within. Her back snapped into an arch, and her head tipped to moan into his void. Her shaking only worsened when he pumped them together as one, deep but slow, so she could perceive their every movement.

A whimper escaped her pretty lips. She fought against the limbs holding her in place, her arms constantly pulling and yanking to be freed, as her legs tried to kick.

He gave her hips just a little bit of movement, and she turned into a needy thing. She bucked against his fingers and into the tendrils to quicken their thrusting inside her. The moment he noticed her tells, those intricate details that informed him she was about to come, Weldir quickened the pace of everything to get her there faster.

Cutting his claws across her skin, he left behind lines but didn't slice her delicate flesh as he caressed her pelvis, her hip, then up her spine. The cry that left her was shaky and unbidden.

And as that orgasm ended, Weldir still didn't relent, even when she stayed tense in his hold. Even as every part of her tried to escape, tried to get away rather than squirming for more. She bit her bottom lip so hard he worried she'd draw blood.

"Oh god! Please. I can't take any more."

With a snarl, he grazed his fangs along her flesh. "*That* is not my name, Lindiwe. You are mine, and if I have to keep going until you remember that, I fucking will."

Her eyes crinkled. "I'm sorry."

"That's a good start, owlet."

"Oh fuck. Oh fuck. Please. I'm sorry, Weldir." She sobbed out a whimper. "I'm sorry. Just... *please*. No more."

Within the span of one of her frantic heartbeats, Weldir's tendrils dissipated and dissolved into nothingness. He let her go, and she turned, grasped his shoulders, and melted against him.

He'd expected perhaps a little bit of anger, or for her to shy away from him after he tortured her.

Instead, she curled into him to the point that he needed to cradle her in his arms, and with tear-stained cheeks, wept languidly. Finding it peculiar, but not unwanted, Weldir... held her, and embraced her in the solidness he could still maintain, bringing her that bit closer.

It didn't take long, perhaps a few minutes, but her eyelids eventually slid shut. As she slowly drifted off to sleep, she murmured, "Please don't heal me."

Taken aback by her request and their position, he was unsure what to do with her now.

Do I... keep holding her?

He didn't want to let go.

TWENTY-TWO

April 29th, 1837

Something tickled the edge of Lindiwe's ear. She groaned and twisted her head away to avoid it. Her hands, which were curled up next to her cheek, went to push off the ground... only to be met with nothingness.

Gasping in surprise, she opened her eyes to the weightless void of darkness and lifted her head to see what had been tickling her.

Her cloak of white owl feathers had been carefully placed around her like an unnecessary blanket. She didn't need warmth, as Weldir's realm lacked any temperature, nor did she understand why he'd place it over her.

Her bare shoulder slipped out from underneath it when she twisted to 'sit' in the weightlessness. She curled her fingers around the edge of her cloak to keep it to her naked chest and shield her.

Did he... put this over me because he knew waking up naked would bother me? Lindiwe searched for him and was drawn to the only light.

With his back to her, he was seated cross-legged before fourteen viewing discs teeming with life from Earth. They revealed each of their children, apart from Nathair, who was in Tenebris, and Merikh, whose disc was murky from being under

Jabez's ward.

Lindiwe wrapped the cloak around her more securely. "How are they?" she asked, swimming over to look into the discs as well.

"They are all fine," he answered, his missing head collecting into streaks before fully forming – likely for her benefit so she could see his face. He dipped it to the side at her. "How are you? You slept for quite some time."

Her heart and stomach fluttered in memory of what had transpired right before she'd passed out from exhaustion. Tucking a curl behind her ear, she blushed demurely.

Her racing pulse made all the tender places on her body throb. Her nipples ached from overstimulation, as did her abused clit and pussy. She thought... she could even feel lines of swollen bruises from where his tendrils had bound her, and she peeked down at her wrists. Purple welts matched where he'd held her arms above her head, and she nibbled her bottom lip.

Her thighs were sticky, and there was an uncomfortable, erotic liquid clinging everywhere that made her want to squirm.

She squeezed her thighs together. "I-I'm okay," she said, with a weak smile.

She was more than fine, while also simultaneously freaking out. She felt... satisfied, content, and not just physically, but... emotionally? He'd been so honest, and over something she'd never in a million years expected from him.

He wanted sex? Even though he couldn't feel it? He wanted to watch and be a part of it, be naughty because it somehow made him feel good *mentally*?

He's more of a pervert than I thought. The emotionally void demi-god wasn't as unfeeling as she'd assumed.

No. That's not true. He'd... become this.

His rejection from when she'd first offered sex still rang in her mind. He hadn't cared for any intimacy back then. Pointless, he'd said.

Something had changed.

And Lindiwe worried about what that meant.

Could he feel something more for her, or was it limited to sex and intimacy? She knew he wanted to deepen their bond, but was that through logic for the cohesive unity of their marriage or... because he actually had a heart he could give?

He doesn't have a real heart. Her own panged at the realisation that it was very unlikely Weldir could... love. There was a physical reaction that came from such an emotion.

He probably could feel tenderness for her, contentment in their relationship, but the mind-altering, life-changing adoration she'd longed for as a young girl... that came with aches and pains that were special. Like the emotion was so strong it clawed into one's spirit until it tore it in two and let someone else inside.

If sex like *that* was going to be in their future, and she could have it freely outside of duty, she worried her own feelings could become tangled, twisted, and confused in ways she may not be able to handle.

I don't want to fall in love with someone who can't return it. It'd be too painful otherwise. *And we can never really be together.*

Strengthening her resolve on the matter, Lindiwe decided she could be content with affection through the most basic carnal need.

A giddiness struck her. *I guess this means I can be honest and naughty about it!*

Satisfaction thrummed, and she offered a real smile. "I think I had the best sleep I've had in a long while," she admitted.

"Yes. You snored quite loudly."

Lindiwe laughed. "I bet I did." Then she showed him her wrists. "I'm surprised all these didn't wake me."

He gently cupped one of her hands and brushed his clawed thumb over her bruises. "Do you want me to heal you now?"

Lindiwe pulled her arm from him before he could even try. "No. I'd rather you didn't."

His head cocked, making pieces of his face break off and collect in his wisping hair. "I... don't understand, but as you wish."

Peeking at each of the viewing discs, she pulled up the falling cloak and then looked around. "Where are my underwear? I'd like to put them on."

"Your panties?" He looked forward into the disc before him. "I've lost them."

Her curling lips flattened with humour. "That's entirely impossible, Weldir."

His lips parted, revealing straight teeth and canine fangs, as he let out a sinfully deep chuckle. "Very true." A tendril pulled from below them, and on the very tip floated her pale-green underwear, half untied. "I considered keeping them."

Lindiwe reached out, slipped them up one leg, and then tied the loosened side at her left hip. "Alright, and now my dress?"

"I lost that too." He dipped his head to the side at her pretend pout, and he chuckled once more. Another tendril formed, this time with her altered Anzúli dress bundled in it. "You know, I think I should implement a new rule within my realm."

She reached out for it. "Oh? And what's that?"

He ducked it out of her reach. "Along with remaining as a Phantom in my realm, you should also be naked in it." He waved the garment side to side. "It would make things easier, as I'm hoping you'll be here for more erotic reasons in the future. You did promise me."

"I don't remember promising anything," she answered with a grin.

He yanked her dress further from her. "Little female, you know I can keep you naked here until you agree, and can strip you of your clothing with nothing but a thought in the future."

"I'll think about it," she lied.

Weldir tsked, just as the bridge of his nose wrinkled lightly. He handed her dress to her. "That's your way of saying no."

She raised it above her head so she could slip her arms through the sleeves and shimmy it down her body. "You can't just make up rules and expect me to adhere to all of them."

"Not to boast," he hummed with mirth, "but I am a god, and

this is my realm. I may do as I like."

Lindiwe rolled her eyes at his harmless arrogance before shifting her cloak over her shoulders and doing up the ties. "I think I'd like to return to Siran. I haven't seen Anubis since before I went to Unerica."

Anubis had tightly spiralling markhor horns. She'd given them that name since they bore a jackal skull, and it had reminded her of one of the Hygyptian gods.

Admittedly, with everything that had happened with Orpheus, she'd struggled to stray from Austrális for too long. Many of their newer children, like the two in the Sing Empire and the one in Pyrssia, she hadn't visited since. She tended to give them space in their adulthood – after spending an initial year with them to help them through the beginning trials of their lives.

It was time to return now.

She cupped low on her pelvis. *Especially if I end up becoming pregnant again.*

Considering the amount of seed he'd used to 'lubricate' her, enough to leave its evidence all over her thighs, it was doubtful it wouldn't take.

"You could stay here for a little while longer," he said softly.

Warmth flared in her cheeks again, and she averted her gaze when her stomach fluttered with a strange tenderness. As tempted as she was, as much as she'd like to... *I don't belong here.* Her presence could only be fleeting, as it'd always been. *I can't live in this realm with him.*

When she brought her gaze back to his carefully blank expression, the giveaway was his eyes, which were so focused on her that her chest squeezed.

"Maybe I can stay for a little while," she conceded. A few hours wouldn't hurt, surely. "I want to check up on those I haven't seen in person since giving them their skulls and horns before I stay in Austrális again."

"You plan to go there again? Why?"

"Because if we have another child, I don't want to be too far from Orpheus... who may need me."

Because things revolving around him still concerned Lindiwe, and she was hoping that she could do more to ease his distress and loss. There had to be some way she could help, maybe by giving him a new companion who may, one day, love him for all the goodness inside his heart.

The more children we have in Austrális, who may end up protecting each other against Jabez, or maybe even Katerina, the better.

Jabez wanted an army?

Then Lindiwe would make her own.

TWENTY-THREE

A time unknown, but another life begins

Weldir could perceive his strength waning rapidly. His mana was being eaten by the very soul he'd sworn to protect, as penance for consuming it beyond his normal duty.

Its white flames flickered and flashed within the rapidly moving, agitated layers of his physical self, and reflected off the sweat coating Lindiwe's ashen skin. The luminous soul brightened the dimly lit hotel room she'd hired for the evening, a place that was warmed by the fire that pushed back the early winter chill and was safe from Demons.

Perspiration dotted her face and soaked through the tunic she was using to cover herself while keeping her legs free. Everything was quiet after hours of screaming and grunting, except for how she let out pants of relief through chapped lips. She was exhausted, and by the trembling of her legs and arms, Weldir knew she was weak.

But the worst part was over.

She sat on her knees upon the wooden floor with her cheek resting on the grey sheets of a lumpy bed.

She'd chosen the human establishment, as she trusted in the strength of Weldir's magic to keep them safe. He could sense the mana of a scent-cloaking spell she'd activated, which ensured their offspring wouldn't attack her immediately upon being brought into her world. She'd also learned from the Anzúli how to create a sound dampener within a hollow space, and the symbol scribbled with coal upon the ground still glowed a faint yellow.

He'd long ago hovered in a kneeling position next to her, as standing over her often distressed her when she gave birth. He couldn't touch her – his hand would merely go through her body – but he hovered his arm over the bed as a reminder that he was there.

She'd reached for his dark clawed hand many times, only to grip the sheets.

He tried to do this often, to be by her side when she felt the most vulnerable. If they were out in the forest, he'd kneel in front of her so she had something to focus on. He knew his ability to praise wasn't great, but he'd practised over the many years to soothe her with his voice.

At first, she'd seemed nervous about doing this in front of him, but even from the beginning, he'd seen that she preferred it. She hadn't wanted to be alone, and needed someone to fill the space to distract her from the pain and fear.

After so many times – sixteen from his count of offspring, although two had come at the same time – she was at ease with his presence.

She knew his time here could only be limited, as the soul he'd consumed, which consumed him in return, would fester and weaken him the longer he held onto it.

"You have done well, as always, owlet," Weldir offered.

She brought her weary eyes to him and offered him a tired half smile. When movement made her flinch, she pulled back from resting against the side of the bed and lifted her hands.

A Mavka no bigger than her cupped palms stirred.

Their featureless oval face pried apart, revealing their jagged mouth, and they hacked a mixture of blood and darkness. Their slitted nose holes flared, but with all blood scents muted, and Lindiwe unafraid, they merely relaxed into her palms.

"Are you ready to depart?" he asked, pushing out a puff of

mist to leave behind so he could return her to this location.

She winced as if a contraction cramped her stomach and nodded. "Yes."

Weldir's form retreated as he released the hold on the chaotic dead soul currently feasting on his mana, and he was pulled back to his realm. He brought Lindiwe with him.

Before she could turn incorporeal, and therefore tangible to him, he already shoved a tendril into the Mavka within her hands. He couldn't touch their physical body, but he was able to caress their soul and force the shift so they, too, would turn ghostly and within his reach.

He couldn't do this with Lindiwe, and he often wondered if this was due to her soul being outside of her body.

As Lindiwe shifted, he cleansed her of the afterbirth she had yet to expel and then healed her wounds. He also cleaned her and their offspring, and she sighed with relief.

Weldir petted their newborn offspring. They were tiny in his large hand, able to fit entirely in the palm of it, and looked fragile. He hated the limpness, and that he could only greet their offspring while they slept, but being on *this* side of life and death forced them into a slumber.

It was useful for her, but an annoyance for him.

Just once, I'd like to have one of our young offspring teeming with energy and life as they crawl over me, like they do with her. He'd like them to pester him as they swam through his realm, forcing him to chase them.

He'd once made the mistake of letting them go, and they turned physical. Their shrieks as they frantically searched for her, alone in the scentless, floating darkness, ensured he never released them again.

Instead, he just focused on their light breathing, and how he could hear their heart beating within his realm, filling it alongside hers. He pressed his foreknuckle under their rounded jaw to caress them, which accidentally rolled their head into an unnatural position while they lay limply on their side.

"I have them for now," he told her. "I can send you back to

rest comfortably."

"Actually, could I stay here?" Lindiwe asked, and he caught her pushing a curl behind her ear.

It was only then that he noticed her satchel in her hand, and he must have missed her seizing it between the seconds he left her side and then brought her here. He'd noticed it on the ground next to her earlier and hadn't thought this was why.

"Of course. Do you plan to return to that establishment at all?"

She shook her head as her eyelids drooped. "No. I have everything. I only paid for the night to give birth. I'm happy to return to the forest where they belong when I leave."

A sense of tranquillity shimmered through his mist that she was choosing to remain, and found his realm a safe and comforting place to sleep. Especially after all these years where she'd rejected his offer.

"I will hold on to them so you may rest."

She perked up with a smile and dug into her satchel to retrieve her dress. "That's okay, I'm not feeling all that tired since you healed me. They also didn't take as long to come as usual."

"I see." He tried not to make it obvious that he wanted time alone with them before she would forever have them in her world. "In that case, I'd like to speak with you regarding something."

In the middle of getting changed, uncaring that she was naked momentarily before him, she cocked a single brow at him.

"Should I be worried?"

"Depends. I'm always unsure with you." Humour vibrated through him at the unamused look she gave him, then he glanced down at their offspring and patted their back. "Will you be alright on your own for a short time?"

"Sure, but why? There's more of you than usual. Your power has grown." Her lips pouted, as if she was a little disappointed by the potential solitude she had once so fervently wanted.

"That is because I haven't been completing my duties."

He'd been putting off consuming a large portion of souls and placing them in Tenebris. It was for her, even if he'd never tell her that. He'd justified the wait because a few months was a blip in time comparatively, but the souls were beginning to pile up, and he needed to tend to them.

He was finding everything... tiresome. Tedious, even.

Between consuming souls and giving them a home, keeping Tenebris bright and playful, spreading his mist, and barricading Demons from returning through the portals to Nyl'theria, his power and mana were constantly being drained. And there was also the mana she used, as well as Weldir frequently having many viewing discs summoned.

He was strong now, but it was only because he hadn't been doing half his duties. Now that they'd resolved the foundation-breaking issue, it was time he returned to them.

And it came with sacrifices.

"I have perfected how to consume a large number of souls while their fate tethers give them their homes and places within Tenebris with little effort and thought."

He'd made it automatic, a spell that had taken him since meeting her to perfect. That, too, cost him mana.

Lindiwe came closer to pet their offspring, and he was very tempted to run away with them so she couldn't take them before he was ready to relinquish them.

She used the pad of her index finger to pat between where the baby Mavka's eye holes *should* have been. "How long?"

"A few months."

Her eyes drifted up, and he made his face form so their gazes could meet confidently. It was... odd, having her this close of her own volition if it wasn't sexual. They were almost face to face, and he rather liked this innocent nearness.

Her eyes flicked back and forth over his horned features. "Do you want me to wait to give them their skull and horns so you can witness it?"

His mist tightened against him, and Weldir was surprised by

the offer, and... appreciative of it. "Yes. I would like that."

She gifted him a rather large smile, and if he wasn't mistaken, it was soft and tender in a humoured way.

"As you wish," she said, repeating the words he so often said to her.

TWENTY-FOUR

July 11th, 1838

A thin layer of snow blanketed every surface it could collect upon, like the bare branches, the hard ground, and the rocks. The forest looked barren, grisly even, especially as the flora wasn't used to such low temperatures.

Many spindly trees native to Austrális had wilted and didn't look as grand or strong as they once did. They were acclimatised to harsh and hot summers, and barely cool winters. In their place, trees similar to evergreens, fir, and pine had grown, spread outwards from the Veil by creatures that unknowingly carried their seeds.

The Veil had a massive impact on Austrális, messing with its climate and the very way the landscape functioned. With no barren desert, it was unmistakably different.

Then again, Lindiwe was the only human who had visibly witnessed its slow change, and was the only one who complained.

"I only hate the snow because it's not meant to be here," she said, with her back resting against a boulder. "I hate what it means, how it came to be."

Her child, barely bigger than a newborn, gave a quiet trill in answer. Her lips quirked as she grabbed their soft, malleable hands, so they could curl their little fingers around her thumbs.

They were supported on her lap with her knees bent to give them something to rest their back on – and stop them from rolling off.

Her smile instantly died.

They were cute, as were all her children when they were babies. They bore no skull, no horns, and were still tiny and clinging – although this one was clingier than most.

They also had a nasty habit of getting upset if any living thing came near her. It didn't matter if it was their brothers, Orpheus and Leonidas, another human, or even a meek little bunny. This child, compared to her many others, was possessive of her, her scent, her presence.

It made doing anything but spending time with them difficult, and she often had to shove them inside her clothing to block out any foreign scents by encasing them entirely in her own.

Then again, Leonidas was being Leonidas, still trying to play catch and kill, and barely listening to her. Orpheus, on the other hand... he was still impossible to approach.

He hadn't been humanoid for quite some time, and the scars on his heart were lasting. He was easier to agitate, more possessive of his territory, and violent.

But she knew he was getting used to her presence again, getting used to the hurt he constantly carried in his much-too-deep-blue orbs. He prowled his territory, and he'd *finally* re-entered his house after months of refusing to do so. Mainly to sit in the quiet dark, and whatever else he did in there, but she could hear him whimpering in the loneliness of those walls he built for someone else.

At least he'd gone inside. That was a start.

Lindiwe also had more pressing issues. One in particular constantly nagged her almost every single minute of every day. It had her mind tingling with anticipation, unsatisfied, and also had worry eating at her.

"He told me he'd only be gone a few months," Lindiwe muttered, as she played with her baby's bendable fingers. "It's been over a year."

She'd given birth in June of last year, and it was now the middle of July in the year eighteen hundred and thirty-eight.

All that time, Lindiwe had waited for Weldir's voice to fill her mind. To wake up and resume being a distant presence in her life that she didn't want to be so distant anymore.

"I... can't wait much longer."

As much as she wanted to adhere to her unspoken promise, Lindiwe had to move on. She had to continue her life, checking on their children and progressing in some form.

She let go of their hand to place her palm on the fleshless, cleaned fox skull strapped to her waist. After eight months of waiting, Lindiwe had stumbled upon Demons chasing a fox in the dead of night and intervened to take their kill. She'd given what remained to this child, which offered them their skeletal bones and fluffy fox tail, but she'd kept the head.

She'd been saving it for Weldir's return, knowing the creature didn't have to be recently deceased to give them their skull.

I even know what animal I'll use to complete them.

They'd managed to get to a bird before she took it from them, so they had a cute patch of feathers around their neck. But she intended to give them deer antlers when she decided they were ready to reach mindless adulthood.

I've... already picked their name too.

Lindiwe had seen many foxes during her travels. One of her children from Unerica bore such a skull with pronghorn antlers. Like many native cultures around the world, she'd fallen in love with the people there, their way of life, and even their language – and they'd been kind enough to share it with her.

It was why she'd named that child Inali, meaning *black fox* in their language – a name often associated with strength, bravery, and cunning. And her child needed all of those to battle against the Demons.

But I plan to call you Fennec, like the big-eared foxes I've seen in Zafrikaan. She moved their arms up and down for them, making them celebrate their name they'd forget, and may never know. *They are so cute and fluffy, just like you'll probably be.*

She'd had so much time, all of it alone, that she'd been able to plan all this.

Lindiwe was ready to let go. She was ready for them to go off into the big world by themselves and be the monstrous servant Weldir wanted. To become their own person, and make their own choices and mistakes.

To live beyond her and move past infancy.

"All he has to do is hurry up and come back."

The constant silence worried her. Weldir hadn't slept for this long in over a century. A few weeks to a handful of months – that's all she usually had to wait. In the past, she'd done it joyfully. Now, though?

One thought kept coming to mind.

I'm... horny. She didn't even have the will to blush right then. It was true, and he'd told her she could have it whenever she wanted.

So where the fuck was he to give her that? Hmm? Why, right when she was prepared to reach out to him for it, for mind-bending, spirit-altering bliss, was he *missing*?

She didn't think she'd even be mad at him if his voice just suddenly popped into her mind right then. She'd gift this child their fox skull and antlers, and then jump Weldir's shadowy, non-existent bones so quickly he'd no doubt be unprepared for a clawing Lindiwe.

This long wait was gruelling. No... it was rude, and torturous!

I also don't like how much I... miss him.

His presence in her mind, the sound of his husky voice. The way that if she really needed to, she could turn to him for comfort or strange advice.

How she missed the weightlessness and emptiness of his realm.

Because it was safe.

Because... *he* was there.

October 3rd, 1839

The silence continued.

September 27th, 1840

And continued.

April 7th, 1841

Until Lindiwe stopped calling out, expecting a response.

TWENTY-FIVE

February 3rd, 1842

The mist keeps receding, Lindiwe thought, worrying her lips as she walked through the forest of the Veil.

It wasn't until it was gone that she'd understood that Weldir's magic had made the shadows of the Veil seem... deeper. Darker. More foreboding, and less haunted in a nightmarish way.

It's like this everywhere.

No matter where Lindiwe went, no matter what continent or country she flew to, Weldir's black mist had shrunk. It was thinning, its reach pulling back and fleeing from the hundreds of forests and meadows it'd lightly swept between.

It was slow. Perhaps a centimetre or so a day, but after five years, Lindiwe had noticed its decline. She'd trained herself, after all, to know how far his reach had gone. To know when she'd entered it, when she could greet it.

The souls she carried on her person took longer to ferry to him.

Before long, it would only surround the shimmering portals the Elven god, Rökul, had left behind. That was likely a problem to face in many decades, but this constant withdrawal had her on edge non-stop.

Why was it fading? Why had Weldir disappeared for so long

when he'd told her it would be temporarily short?

Something was wrong. This stretch of time wasn't simply Weldir being a demi-god who had let the hours – years – slip by. He wasn't merely distracted and had forgotten to respond; this was different.

He was asleep, and instead of his mist thickening and spreading, it was... disintegrating. He was permanently *losing* power.

And that was the one thing he wouldn't stand for.

"I can't keep thinking about this," Lindiwe muttered firmly while clenching her hands into tight fists. She softened her grip as she raised her right palm and made black mist puff above it. "He has enough that my abilities haven't faded."

She just... used them sparingly.

Lindiwe didn't want to harm him, but she also needed it to survive. To check on their children from afar.

Bringing both hands together with a slap, she then pulled them apart, and glittering black formed between them. A ball of shadows rotated to life before it flattened when she spread her hands further apart.

A disc formed, and all Lindiwe needed to do was think of the face she wanted to see, hold their name in her mind, and they'd come into view. An image of Dymphna brightened the viewing disc, and he was as she'd last checked on him in person – perfectly fine.

He'd been given the name Lurion years ago.

She had no idea of its meaning, only that it was Nyl'kira and given to him by Demons he'd once befriended. Those Demons had died long ago. An accident and hazard of being near Lindiwe's children, who easily fell into a rage and were unable to distinguish between friend or foe.

He'd not befriended any others since then, afraid of his own strength and bloodlust.

Lindiwe closed her hands, and the viewing disc faded entirely. She'd already checked on her children before coming here, and she wouldn't waste Weldir's magic when he may need it most.

There were also more important matters to attend to.

Lindiwe stepped across a groove that had been carved in the ground by a metal spike, and she was careful that her bare feet didn't kick any dirt into it. She inspected the line of salt within it, finding it adequate.

Then, lifting her gaze to the log cabin home at the very centre of a clearing, she noticed Orpheus waiting for her at the top of his porch stairs.

I hate the colour of blue in his orbs, she thought, approaching him as he sat on his backside with his hands at his sides against the ground to support his position. *It's so much deeper than it's supposed to be.*

What should have been an ethereal sky blue, was now dark like the frightful depths of the oceans she often flew across.

Keeping her distance due to his preference, Lindiwe halted a few metres away from the house. Any closer and she'd be snarled at, even if her presence in his territory was welcomed this day.

"Are you ready?" she asked, cupping her hands near her stomach as uncertainty pulled taut.

"You no know if this will work," Orpheus answered, his voice deeply distorted due to being in his monstrous form. *"What if only hated?"*

Despite his longing to remain near his home, Orpheus had left it on the odd occasion. Lindiwe had watched solemnly as he'd tried to befriend other humans wandering the surface recently, only to be spotted. Only to be screamed at and run away from, driving his bloodthirsty instincts to the surface until he rent them to pieces with his claws and fangs.

His humanity had grown, but it'd come at a cost.

His understanding of language had deepened, and he could articulate his thoughts better, but... it meant he puzzled over the final words Katerina had said to him. He felt them more, believed them, deciphered their true meaning, and he'd been able to look back on their time together with an understanding that he didn't have before.

"I have already spoken to the village, and they are aware of what will happen. I already have their approval."

"What if I destroy human?" His wolf skull drifted to the side as he looked around his territory. *"Protection stay long time."*

"Then you will wait for it to fade and try again."

Lindiwe hid her reservations, her uncertainty, and how much she thought this would... fail.

That Orpheus, like all her children, would remain alone forever.

I just need one human... If one could see past what he was and love him for the good he had inside, then wasn't the possibility worth it? Even if it took a hundred years or half a millennium, if there was just the tiniest thread of hope, wasn't that worth following?

It would be better than sitting here alone in the dark for the rest of his life. He needed to somehow look to the future, rather than dwell in the past.

Even if he killed and ate each one, they would gift him intelligence he could use to charm the next person.

Her right hand curled into a fist once more. *There has to be one person in this forsaken world...*

"Follow," Lindiwe demanded. "That's all you need to do for now."

With a snorted huff, Orpheus climbed down the stairs on all fours as she pulled her feathered hood over her head.

When she was in her owl form, she took off west, and he sprinted after her.

Not in rage, but in faith.

She hoped to the spirit of the void that it wasn't sorely misplaced.

Landing at the forest's edge near a walled village, Lindiwe allowed her human form to come to the surface. Her curls bounced around her cheeks and shoulders when she pulled her hood back, and they were swept to the side by a light, warm gust.

She waited for Orpheus to catch up, and he followed her scent to greet her. She kept herself still, letting him come as close as he chose, and then reached into her satchel.

"I think it's best if you use this to block out any potential fear or blood scents," she told him, holding out her hand.

A cloth saturated in a heavy, clogging perfume tingled her nose. He gingerly pinched it from her palm, held it to his bony nose hole, and sniffed it. Orpheus immediately choked and gave two wheezing sneezes while pulling it away.

"Awful. Bad smell."

"I know it's not the most pleasant, but your sense of smell is keener than a human's. You need to tie it around your nose, and likely inside your mouth to hold it in place."

Orpheus' tongue poked forward with a blergh, but he obediently did as he was told. He sneezed a few times, and his blue orbs turned white and started to waver as if they were about to shatter and produce tears. He adjusted to it and began to breathe through his mouth with shuddering pants instead.

"I also have... this for you." She pulled out neatly folded black material and unravelled it to reveal a cloak. "It might work in your favour to make your appearance initially easier for humans to look upon."

Orpheus took it and inspected it thoroughly. *"Hide?"*

Lindiwe hid the worst of her wince, so that it only twitched one cheek. She felt awful that she was having to do this, explain this to him, but it was the truth – and it was best he knew beforehand.

"Your... appearance might be a little frightening. A living being walking around with a skull and horns is abnormal, as is your body. It would be best to shield it, even a little, until you gain the trust of your new human."

"Yes. Ugly."

"Not ugly," Lindiwe rejected darkly, her jaw clenching at the fact that he even knew what that word *meant*. "Just different."

Orpheus fumbled with how to put it on, throwing it over his head like a sheet. She couldn't help her quiet, hidden laugh as she stepped forward to help. Taking it from him, she waved for him to lower his head.

"There's two holes for your horns. You have to poke them through first." She slipped them over his impala horns at the same time to show him, and her fingertips tingled at touching the hardness of those bumpy spirals.

I've never been able to touch him before. She even sneaked a caress over his cloth-covered wolf skull when she adjusted the fabric. Then she secured the ties around his neck.

Shoving his arms to the side, he pushed the cloak open and brushed his claws over the dark material. Then, before she could direct him to, his form shifted, and black clothing rose to the surface when he became more humanoid.

He knows this is a better look for humans.

Which was a saddening thought to Lindiwe.

He still looked dapper and gentlemanly, albeit a little spooky, like a grim reaper with his cloak. But it did help to hide the more animalistic parts of him. If it wasn't for his skull, horns, claws, and pawed feet, he could have passed for a very tall human.

"Maybe you should sheath your claws," Lindiwe suggested, and he promptly complied.

She pulled the cloak in tight over his chest, surprised he was letting her be this close to him, while remaining wary of a lethal strike. Perhaps her actions were foolish, but Lindiwe trusted him.

She trusted Orpheus. He knew his own strength – knew he could harm easily. Everything he did on purpose was gentle. It was careful, hesitant.

"There." She let him go and stepped back, then turned to the side to look upon the village gates. "All you need to do is follow me inside and heed my directions."

"What if I hurt?" Orpheus asked, and brought both hands to his abdomen nervously. His orbs morphed to white when his bony snout lifted towards the village.

"Orpheus." She let out an exasperated huff. "You're forgetting who and what I am."

He pointed a grey finger at her. "Witch Owl."

Her annoyance deepened, enough to make one eye twitch, but she didn't correct him. He knew her name, but apparently this title was what he, and fucking Katerina, had decided she would be called.

"If you go into a rage, I'll be here to stop you." Pushing her bangs back, Lindiwe sighed. "Just... let's go."

The hard dirt of the forest changed to soft grass of a cut meadow – leaving no shade for the Demons to hide in – as they headed towards the village. Spear-wielding soldiers at their posts on either side of the gates lurched forward upon seeing them and immediately ran inside to inform everyone of their approach.

And yet the gates remained open.

Lindiwe peeked over her shoulder at Orpheus. His hands were up near his chest in such a sweet, yet unconfident way. Her child, as monstrous and scary as he was, felt fear.

Of himself. Of failing. Of hurting those they were about to meet.

How anyone could see him as evil when he could behave this way was beyond her.

The entrance to the village was remarkably vacant. She'd expected to be greeted by a throng of gawking stares. *It appears they've told everyone to remain inside their homes.*

In the middle of the town's entrance were eight humans. Six soldiers clad in iron armour, the mayor in a well-tailored navy suit, and a woman whose skirts were white with a brown overdress. The ninth person bore a white mask with one side painted lime green, and their white Anzúli robes, etched with purple symbols around the seams, fluttered in the wind.

The masked Anzúli, who the humans called either a Priest or Priestess, bowed their head to Lindiwe with respect. *They* were the only reason this was happening at all. Her friendship with the Anzúli people had garnered so much trust that mattered in this very moment.

She could never have guessed this was where it'd all been leading towards.

Where her request, her favour for all the good she'd done for them, would be at the cost of a sacrifice.

Despite the pang of guilt, she kept her features cool and indifferent as she tipped her head in return.

Harry, the mayor, fiddled with the bottom button of his vest as he looked over her shoulder with wide eyes. Perspiration dotted his tan forehead, and the sickly pallor of his face informed her that he was terrified of the tall creature casting a shadow over her.

The woman at his side – middle-aged, perhaps in her late forties or early fifties – hadn't shifted or flinched at all. Her lightly tanned face sported an array of sparse wrinkles, and her short, straight blonde hair had a sprinkling of grey throughout. Her brown eyes held nothing, remaining emotionless.

She'd found purpose in the role she was about to take on. At least, Lindiwe assumed this woman was the offering, considering there was no one else here.

"So it's true," the Anzúli said, tightening his arms behind his back. "You truly befriend the Duskwalkers."

"Yes," she confirmed without hesitation, before waving to her side. "This is Orpheus."

He grunted at the attention upon him, and his right hand came forward a little to... twitch his fingers at them? *Is he attempting to wave?* If so, she found that rather cute.

"This is Lydia," the Anzúli said, waving towards the woman.

She pinched the sides of her skirts and curtsied. "Hello."

"Are you willing?" Lindiwe asked, meeting her gaze directly when she lifted her head.

Taken aback, her eyes fluttered, and she halted. "Y-yes. I know of everything and agreed to it."

Lindiwe's tone darkened and became firmer. "But were you coerced?"

"No." Harry stepped forward with his hand placed upon his chest. "We spoke about this in the village hall, and Lydia offered herself."

"I didn't ask you," Lindiwe snapped, and he started in response and stepped back. "I want to make sure she understands what this entails. That she won't be returning here and will go to the Veil with Orpheus, and there is a chance she may die."

Lydia's lips thinned, and her eyes narrowed. "Yes, I understand all of that."

"Are you sick?"

She shook her head. "No. I'm a very healthy forty-eight. I chose to do this because I have no family. No children, no husband, no one but friends who will miss me. It is for *their* children that I do this."

"So you are willing, you are informed, and you are pure of disease."

The tension in Lindiwe's shoulders eased. The last thing she'd wanted was for someone to be forced into this role or be ill-informed of the potential terrors they may face. She also didn't want the humans to pass off the sick, and for them to die before Orpheus could gain their trust.

They may not even survive the journey.

"Then alright." She gestured for Orpheus to come forward, and he tilted his head at her waving hand before doing as instructed. Lydia came forward upon request, and they came face to face with each other. "Hold each other's hands."

Lydia's hands shot to her chest when Orpheus' came forward, and she hesitated. For the first time, she looked unsure, but then gingerly placed her own in his. His touch was gentle as he wrapped her hands in his much bigger ones, and Lydia's posture unstiffened.

Lydia laughed dryly. "It feels like I'm getting married to a Duskwalker."

Lindiwe appreciated her attempt to unravel the awkwardness they obviously both felt. It also made her heart twist. *I like her a lot.* She could only offer the woman a sad smile. *It's unfortunate that she'll likely die.*

She may have been perfect otherwise.

The Veil was far, and Demons loitered above the surface and in it. How Katerina had made it alive to the house Orpheus had built was purely luck, *bad* luck, and Lindiwe was sure fate would rear its ugly head once more.

"You'd be a very pretty bride," Lindiwe said to play along.

"Bride?" Orpheus asked, tilting his head as his orbs shifted to dark yellow in curiosity.

"It's what we call a woman when she's about to bond with her future husband. They're always beautiful, and often in a lovely dress."

"I... see." His tone came across pensive.

"Do you remember how to do this?" Lindiwe asked, and he nodded in answer. "I think it's best if you breathe through your mouth." Then she met Lydia's gaze. "This may hurt a pinch."

The woman's eyes widened right as Orpheus' claws shot forward. Two slipped beneath the thin skin of her wrist, and she gasped in shock and yanked her hands from his. But it was enough.

A few drops of blood touched the dirt, the bargain for the spell was given, and blue light shone from it. Within seconds, his magic spread across the ground as shimmering, sparkling blue made the air swirl around them. A protective dome began to form over the village.

Lydia, holding her nicked wrist, gasped softly as her eyes lifted to follow the magic's path. The soldiers, Harry, and the Anzúli also looked up, the azure light highlighted upon their faces. The initial brightness dulled when it was complete, enough to show it was there, but it wouldn't be overly distracting.

"The bargain is complete. In exchange for this offering–"

"Bride," Orpheus cut in. "She is my bride, yes?"

Lindiwe paused and gave him a perplexed frown before continuing. She hadn't expected him to say that, nor to speak over her.

"–your village now has a protection ward that will last ten years. He may, or may not, return to place a new one here, or upon the other village and town nearby." Lindiwe brought her gaze to the black mesh eyeholes of the Anzúli's mask. "Now that you've seen the truth, and what his power can do, I expect you'll share this information with the other mayors?"

"Why will he not return here?" Harry asked, his light-brown eyebrows furrowing. "We are happy to continue this arrangement if it keeps the Demons from attacking us."

Because expecting Orpheus to remember which village, when they're so close together, is asking too much. If he forgot, or mistook which one he was supposed to approach, Lindiwe had prepared all three.

"This is what has been agreed upon," Lindiwe stated. "It's also not up for discussion."

He grumbled and folded his arms, but remained quiet, and that's all she cared about.

It was unwise to remain for too long, especially as she could see a few heads beginning to poke from windows and doors, all curious about the new protection ward. She ushered Orpheus and Lydia from Staton Village as quickly as she could.

The gates closed behind them with a boom when they'd traversed halfway across the meadow. When they made it into the tree line, Lindiwe stopped them.

"This is where I leave," she announced.

"Y-you're leaving?" Lydia darted her gaze to Orpheus before stepping to the side. "I thought you'd be remaining with us."

"Orpheus will take you there by himself. I can't join you on this journey." Then she turned to Orpheus, who dipped his skull to greet her gaze. "This is also where my help ends. This is the last time I will intervene. From now on, you will do this on your own."

Lindiwe wouldn't be here to watch human after human die, and for her son to be hurt over it time and time again. He wanted a companion, and hopefully she'd done her best to facilitate that for him one day, but this was where she had to stop. Where she had to protect her own heart, shield herself from guilt, and step back.

Orpheus had to make his own choices, his own mistakes, and learn on his own.

The most she would do was grow the garden.

TWENTY-SIX

November 5th, 1848

Lindiwe hesitated at the boundary of a protection ward. She desperately wanted to go inside it, yet was utterly resolute about not doing so. The person inside didn't want to see her, speak with her, or be anywhere near her.

With the side of her right hand placed between her breasts, as if she could still her heart, she considered... leaving. Why force this bond when it was obvious he didn't want it? Why try, when it always seemed to do more harm than good?

But this is the first time he's been alone in almost ninety years. It was the first time she could truly speak with him privately, without the influence of another, without having someone cruel to feed off. *I may never get another opportunity like this again.*

His solitude might be fleeting.

This could be her only chance.

She'd flown straight here from across the oceans, from the other side of the world, all by herself, just for him.

To stand here and then turn back would make all that effort pointless. The week she'd taken to get here, resting for fleeting hours before taking off again, would have all been for naught. She'd even flown through a storm and injured her left arm, but prevailed through strength and will.

The entire time, she'd prayed Weldir would awaken and save her the strain. Would aid her and bring her here within the blink of an eye.

His prolonged silence continued, even eleven years later.

Thankfully little had happened in that time.

Her children had grown and evolved. Their humanity and intelligence had deepened, and their battles with Demons remained unending against the horde. Lydia had died before she and Orpheus could even make it to the Veil. Demons had come, attracted by her human scent, and his enraged mind eventually turned on her as she'd fled the carnage.

Lindiwe really wished she hadn't watched from afar.

She'd already protected one of his companions from death, and that hadn't gone very well. The human that forever stayed by his side needed to survive on their own terms, and Orpheus needed to learn how to control this side of himself. How to push back the bloodlust, keep it in check, if he wanted one to survive in his world.

Not all would be as heartless and fearless as Katerina.

Leonidas was doing well, but wandered often. It was hard to follow someone who constantly journeyed and didn't particularly listen.

Fennec... well, *he* was still just starting out. Lindiwe had gifted him his skull and horns years ago, and had also made sure to do so near a group of travelling humans. He gained his gender quickly in comparison to her other children.

I haven't been back to Austrális since I helped Orpheus.

For the better part of five years, she'd watched her children in Austrális through a viewing disc. She could only conjure one at a time, as she just hadn't mastered the ability like Weldir, but at least she could see them whenever she wanted.

She hadn't expected that when she'd finally given in to the pointlessness of trying to check on Merikh by scrying for him, she'd... see him. She had thought it would just be indistinguishable murkiness.

When his bear skull and bull horns came into view, she'd

stared at him with shaking hands. It'd taken her less than five minutes to make her decision to cross the harsh oceans to come here, when she'd realised he was alone.

In his old home.

Her gaze flicked up to the red dome he'd placed over what used to be Nathair's waterfall and lake, and the entrance to Merikh's cave. Dawn brightened the world in a golden glow, allowing her to notice the dark silhouette of a large person moving within the shadows of his cave.

He was right there, and a lead ball of worry had rolled around in her stomach for the past half an hour until nausea twisted it.

But that wasn't enough to keep her at bay indefinitely, and she eventually shoved her way through the red dome and entered his territory. Grass crunched under her feet as she approached the entrance to his cave, where the thud of heavy pawsteps echoed.

All sounds ceased before a short growl was followed by a deep huff. Then he resumed whatever he was doing inside, and rock against heavy rock scraped together.

She placed her hand on the Veil's cliff wall and intended to slowly, and coyly, poke her head inside.

"You have some hide coming here," Merikh said in an unnervingly quiet tone. "Then again, I should have expected it."

Lindiwe peeked inside, and his back was to her. He looked over his meaty shoulder to regard her with one red orb, and it flared bright in anger when their gazes met. His back, forearm, and calf spines flared, a warning of lethal danger should she approach any further.

He snorted out a puff again and then finished placing a slab of cut stone atop a rectangular base of rock. He readjusted it until it was centre, then seemed to stare down at it.

Without drawing his sight from the bench he'd made, he snapped out, "What do you want?"

"To see how you are."

"To find out why I am alone, no doubt."

Her shoulders rotated inwards at the truth of his assumption.

She brought her hands together to pick at the ridges of skin around her nails, unsure of what to say now that she was here and he hadn't immediately forced her away. She fidgeted, shifting her weight from one foot to the other.

Merikh placed a meaty hand upon the bench, and his sharp claws clicked against the stone. "How right you were." He tapped his middle claw repeatedly. "But you were wrong about one thing. It's *me* she drives up the fucking wall."

"Katerina?" Lindiwe asked, perhaps a little too hopefully.

"We thought her hatred of Mavka would be limited to Orpheus, but no. She hates us all, hates the Demons too. She only seems to tolerate Jabez, but even then..." His bear skull shifted to the side a little and faced her just that tiny bit. "She's... frustrating. How Orpheus did not kill her is a miracle. I would have torn her head from her body the moment she tried to speak to me the way she does."

"She was good at hiding it, I think."

He let out a soft growl and shoved away from the bench with a swipe of his claws. Then he crouched next to one of the many bags lying around, and his bull tail tapped the ground silently, the furry tuft on the end making little stones roll away.

"We see it." He stood with two items in his hands. "He sees it. He just does not care. Finds it funny – only because she is smart enough not to do it to him."

Her lids lowered into a glare. "He doesn't care how she treats you?"

The snarl that burst from him shook her bones, and the chomp of his fangs that followed it had her gulping.

"Of course he does! There is just no way to appease her, and I have tired of it. She lies, and then cries when no one believes her, especially when her accusations about me are ridiculous." Then, as he placed a board and a handful of fleshing and skinning knives upon the bench, he grumbled, "She's more at risk of me clawing her than anything. *Those* threats are true. He knows it. He does not care about that either. Finds that funny too."

It sounded like Jabez was staying out of the middle of it, probably hoping they'd resolve it themselves.

But if our relationship is anything to go by, when Merikh hates, he hates forever. He held onto his grudges just as passionately as his mother.

He turned from the bench. "Have you come to gloat? That will piss me off."

You're already pissed off. His movements were jerky and strained, proving he was a dangerous spark just waiting to ignite.

"No. I only came to talk to you, since I've never been able to before."

When he dropped to crouch again, this time he hung his arms over his knees, and stayed there. "I do not want to talk to you."

"Merikh, what happened back then–" Lindiwe bit her lips shut when he let out a snarl so foul, it thickened the air. The tiny hairs on her arms lifted, warning her of the imminent danger.

He swiped the half-emptied bag up, stood, and spun to the bench. He carelessly tossed it onto the hard surface, followed by the *crack* of something ceramic breaking inside. A sweet-smelling liquid perfumed the air as it saturated the bag.

His echidna spines raised, and even seemed to tremble, as a continuous growl reverberated within his cave. His orbs darkened to crimson, and he placed his big hands upon the bench as his bull tail flicked to the side.

Once more, he tapped his right middle claw against the stone.

"How... did I do it?" Merikh asked in a low voice. "You said it was not you, but me who killed the serpent one. How? We played many times, both dying and returning."

"I... can't tell you that," Lindiwe answered.

"Why the fuck not?!" he roared, turning to her. "You must know! All I remember is you collecting his skull. Everything else is... murky."

She took in a steeling breath. "Because if you share that information with Jabez, he could use it for the wrong reasons."

"He would never hurt me."

"It's not you I'm worried about."

His orbs shifted to orange as realisation dawned. "Orpheus."

"And the others." She braved taking a step forward. "Can you, with absolute certainty, tell me Jabez wouldn't then use that information to potentially give Katerina what she wants? It goes beyond your friendship and could have a disastrous impact. Do you really want to be responsible for the deaths of *more* of your siblings?"

"Siblings?" Merikh reared his head back. "Do not tell me that Orpheus is..."

"Yes, he's your brother."

He tilted his head at her, and his orbs flickered with dark yellow. "How do you know that? How do you know... anything? I doubt even Jabez knows this, and he knows all that happens within the Veil."

That was doubtful, but Lindiwe wouldn't correct him.

"I just do."

"How?! No more of your secrets!"

She winced and stepped back. "I can't tell you."

"Tell me or leave!" he yelled, pointing towards his exit. "You infuriate me. You will not tell me what I desire, and only share things I do not understand. I hate this about you."

"You don't know me to hate me!" Lindiwe shouted. "From the moment you were born, you have been this spiteful little thing, always biting me or those around you. You snapped and snarled, even when you didn't have a skull to be frightening."

"Born?" His head reared back once more. "You've known me from the beginning, from when I do not remember. You know where I come from?"

"Yes."

"Tell me."

"I can't."

Merikh roared and then lunged forward. Lindiwe gasped and turned incorporeal, and he chased her around the outside of his cave with swiping claws. "Tell me!"

He wouldn't stop, even when Lindiwe stopped moving and just stared up at him.

More than ever, she needed Weldir's voice. She wanted his advice, his ideas. *Should I tell Merikh or not? He may leave Jabez's side, but it could have consequences.*

Could those consequences work in her favour? Would Merikh round up the other Duskwalkers and unite them, or would he doom them? Would he... care?

Lindiwe wanted to tell him. He deserved to know everything.

What could Lindiwe achieve if she brought him to her side? *Could it repair our relationship?* She wanted that more than anything.

"Fine," Lindiwe conceded with a sigh. "I'll explain everything, and what you do with that information is your own choice."

With frantic, rabid huffs, he backed up enough that she could view him properly. His muscular body wasn't as lean as it'd been five years ago, but he still had a few protruding bones, mainly some ribs and his hand knuckle bones.

"I am your... mother," Lindiwe admitted, giving him the least amount of information to start with to gauge his reaction.

His bear skull tilted. "Like a female creator?" He patted his thin stomach. "The one that grows life? How can a human make Mavka?" He pointed at her belly. "Too small."

Wow. That was remarkably easy. For once, she had a reason to thank Jabez, as he'd given Merikh knowledge about such things.

"Weldir is your father."

"Who is this? This Weldir?"

A frown pulled her face tight. "Weldir. Did Jabez not give you his name? You know, the spirit of the void?"

"What?!" he snapped out, backing up a step. Then Merikh cupped the end of his blunt snout and tapped a foreclaw against the side of it. "I see. He would be interested to learn this."

Her brows furrowed deeper. "You aren't upset by this?"

"Yes, but if you are telling the truth, then it makes sense as to why *he* does not know where I come from, why I cannot die, why I am the way I am." His bull tail swished side to side. "I thought you did not like the spirit of the void? Sexless, Jabez said."

Lindiwe's cheeks flared with so much heat she was surprised the ends of her hair didn't catch fire. She couldn't believe her own *child* had said that to her or knew such a thing!

"I don't." Then Lindiwe quickly corrected herself. "I mean, I didn't. It's... complicated."

"Younglings are usually made from affection, yes?" Then he scratched the side of his snout, with his orbs darkening in their yellow hue. "But not for Jabez. No, he only knows pain."

A weak and panicked smile rose. "N-not always from affection."

"I was not created that way? No love? Then how is it I am here?"

I can't believe I'm having this conversation with him. This wasn't how she'd expected it would go. She thought there would be stomping, huffing, and growling. That he would be angered to learn all this.

He just seemed... curious.

Should she be giddy about that? Honestly, she was just happy they were talking without it being an argument.

"Part of the reason I bonded with Weldir – uh, the spirit of the void – was due to a transaction. My soul and my presence and usefulness on Earth in exchange for servitude. One of the requirements was that I make children for him. Y-younglings, I mean."

His orbs flickered with blue, and her heart squeezed in sympathy for him. She didn't think he would have cared that he wasn't born from love. *I'm surprised he would even know that or want it.*

His shoulders lost their tension and fell as the solemn hue remained in his orbs. "Then why is it I am here?"

How do I explain this to him? He wanted to know, but he

might not find the answer... pleasant. *But he has a right to know.*

She gripped her left forearm to distract herself and averted her gaze to the side. "He wanted servants. Younglings who would collect souls to help empower him. None of you know it, but each time you eat a Demon, you take the souls they're unwittingly carrying on their person and cleanse them. When you return to the Veil, to his mist, he takes them from you, and it strengthens him."

Nothing else was said, and the silence between them weighed heavily on her. His breaths drew in and out, deeper with each one, and she found her own mimicking them by accident.

Their increasing rate made her heart flutter nervously.

"*That* is why I exist?" he asked with a dark, foreboding tone. He pointed a claw at his chest, and when she brought her gaze back to him, his orbs had returned to their normal scarlet hue. Then they shifted to crimson. "*That* is why I am here? To be a fucking servant for a being of the void?! I fucking *aid* him?!"

"He's very thankful for it," Lindiwe said as she lifted her hands placatingly. "He also cares about you all very deeply. He watches over you."

"Thankful? I don't care if he is thankful!" Merikh roared. "He is our enemy! *You* are our enemy. Being created by you is one thing, but *this*?! This goes against everything." Then he placed his hands over the top of his skull and gripped his bull horns. He turned to the side with white flashing in his orbs. "Jabez will be enraged when he learns of this. I *empower* the very being in his way!"

Lindiwe was thankful she was still incorporeal because when she reached out in hopes of placing a soothing hand on his biceps, he slashed his hand out and his claws went right through her head. She retreated, putting much-needed space between them.

"You don't have to tell him," Lindiwe suggested.

"Of course I do! He is my *friend*, and he will want to know. He will hate me if I withhold this from him and he learns of it."

"Merikh..." Lindiwe didn't know what to say or do to calm him.

"Leave!" he bellowed.

Lindiwe cupped her hands to her chest. "Merikh, please."

"Is that all I am? A fucking *tool* to be used by you? By him?! I have seen what servants are, how their wants matter little to those above them. If that is all I am – not created from affection but to be used – then I have nothing else to say to you."

"I care about you!" she shouted, thankful she couldn't cry in her Phantom form, as tears would've spilled by now. "From the moment you were born, I loved you."

"I don't care! You brought us into this world and then abandoned us in it. To ferry *souls*."

"That's not true. I've always tried to be there."

"And yet you weren't!"

Before Lindiwe could utter another word, Merikh roared, his orbs darkened into a nightmarish red, and he shifted into his more monstrous form. He attacked her ghostly body, and nothing she said to try to console him worked.

Whether it be anger, confusion, or loss, it was just too heavy for him to carry. He couldn't regulate his emotions; all he knew how to do was maim when he couldn't escape pain.

Lindiwe retreated, and he chased her intangible form. Enraged, inconsolable, he fought air.

She slipped inside a tree and waited while he slashed at it with deadly claws. When he wasn't looking, distracted by the trunk as if his bloodlust saw it as a living, breathing Lindiwe, she fled.

The cracks and groans of it being destroyed until it eventually fell reached her ears even when she was deep inside the Veil's forest.

Only when she was so far from him and his massacre that she was no longer in earshot, and her scent would be difficult to chase, did she turn into a human. Pressing her hand against a thick tree trunk for support, Lindiwe breathed through her anxiety, her regret, and the guilt that festered within.

I shouldn't have told him. I shouldn't have said anything.

It didn't matter that he wanted to know, deserved to know; apparently this knowledge was just too much of a burden for her children to bear. They weren't human, and they didn't understand the weight she, or they, carried – not like her.

I really, really fucked up this time.

He will tell Jabez. She didn't think it would matter, but she'd just pushed Merikh further away from her. *Does this mean I shouldn't tell... any of them?*

"Curses, Weldir! Where are you when I need you most?!" she screamed out, before gasping at a roar in the distance and the loud thumping of a four-legged nightmare heading her way.

Merikh had caught the thread of her scent and was hunting it.

Lindiwe flipped her feathered hood over her head and transformed long before he could find her.

I'm so tired of learning as I go and failing constantly.

Why could nothing go right?

TWENTY-SEVEN

February 23rd, 1872

The unbridled, unyielding rage that seethed beneath the surface of Lindiwe's very flesh was scorching. It boiled in her veins, in her muscles, until it clutched her bones. It was so lethal it was like a living, breathing, dangerous aura that pulsated around her.

And as Lindiwe stormed between the beautiful, tall flowery hedges that acted as thorny fences for a pathway, her heart swelled with the way the world reflected her unrest.

Behind the small castle she kept her hateful stare on, lightning cut across the sky in blinding flashes. It crackled and boomed, and the thunder seemed to rumble the very ground, so loud, so deafening, it rang in her ears.

The grey clouds, heavy and angry, kept out the midday sun, making everything bleak. The rain had yet to pour, but she could see the wall of it heading towards her in the distance, sped along by violent winds. It was powerful, and the rush of it exhilarated her down to her very spirit.

Her worn and torn feathered cloak fluttered across her body, pulled tightly around her. A downy plume tickling her cheek slipped loose and flew away, as had many others in the decades it'd been since Lindiwe last heard from Weldir.

Soon... she doubted she'd be able to fly.

Her dirty white dress clung to her torso and limbs, while her bun kept her curls out of her eyes.

Demons intercepted her, trying to bar her entrance to witness this sad and pathetic attempt at being kingly. Jabez didn't need a castle or a throne; he needed a fucking grave.

She'd help give him one.

Despite how much this would likely impact Weldir's dwindling magic and fading mist, she made shadowy tentacles form.

Most of her opponents were medium-sized Demons on their way to completion. Half humanoid, half disgusting vermin, they either walked on all fours, slithered on their serpent tails, or squawked on bird legs.

With little thought, she shoved more magic into the tendrils to give them a burst of power. She lifted the Demons and *tossed* them to the side to clear a path.

The castle doors were closed, the purple shimmering ward in place. Lindiwe scrunched her nose at it and phased through it by turning into a Phantom momentarily.

Jabez greeted her in the foyer with more Demons – those who were more humanoid – surrounding him.

His red eyes were cold as he met her gaze. His long white hair was tied back in a neat ponytail, and it fluttered to the side by some unknown draft. His white tunic was tucked into loose, flowy, low-crotch burgundy pants, and she noticed a handful of strange black markings that hadn't been present on his skin the last time she'd seen him.

Or maybe she hadn't noticed them.

A few of his fingers had black rings, which appeared like tattoos, while one of his forefingers had little arrow markings. There was a pattern peeking through the vee in his tunic – a spiral of runic symbols of Nyl'kira – but she was unable to see what it said.

"Where is she?" Lindiwe demanded, making her stance wide when she stopped. "I believe I have a promise to deliver."

Her eyes scanned for the infuriating woman, who she'd promised she'd eat the heart of if she interfered in Orpheus' life.

She was missing, as was Merikh.

Then again, Lindiwe hadn't expected Merikh to be there, not after what had transpired between him and Jabez. Their 'friendship' wasn't as strong as either of them thought. This silly half-Demon had turned on the bear-skulled Duskwalker not even *days* after she'd told him the truth of his origins.

And Jabez had to know he was an idiot for doing so.

He'd lost his strongest and deadliest companion, one who had been utterly loyal to him, over something that changed *nothing.* Her son still hated her – probably Weldir, too – and now roamed Austrális alone to cause havoc.

Merikh wasn't their ally.

At least he'd no longer be an obstacle.

Jabez folded his arms and rolled his shoulders back in a show of superiority. His sharp fangs, like the outside row of a shark's mouth, peeked past his full lips when he said, "As if I would let you near her. She's hidden away."

Lindiwe lifted her gaze to the tall ceiling before letting it fall to the second level's railing. She shifted her focus to the right, where there was a hallway beyond a grand staircase.

"That means I will just have to look for her."

Turning incorporeal, she lunged forward, and the Demons surrounding Jabez snarled and roared as they leapt for her – only to pass through her intangible body.

Lindiwe floated towards the second level. To her right, Jabez jumped over the railing of the staircase and landed halfway up it. By the time she got there, Jabez was already at the top of the stairs and attempting to block her path to the hallway.

She floated through him and headed straight down it, then shoved herself through a wall and landed inside a decently furnished room. By the strange nesting that was happening on top of a single bed, it likely belonged to a Demon who lived with them.

Rather than go back into the hallway, Lindiwe flew herself forward, passing wall after wall as her head turned one way and the other in search of the pretty, black-haired woman. She stopped when she accidentally floated through the castle's stone wall and outside, then quickly shunted back so she didn't start falling.

She went to the other side of the building, past the window at the end of the hallway, its yellow-and-red curtains closed. Then she headed in the other direction, passing rooms in her search.

A door slammed before she could get to the end, and she threw her body to the left through a wall. All she saw was the side of Jabez, who had leapt onto the landing's railing, and a pair of pale legs. He jumped to the ground level, and Lindiwe went after them.

By the time she reached them, Jabez had fled to the left of the castle's entrance into some kind of ballroom. A throne, which was hardly more than a sad wooden chair, sat behind them.

The room had decorations, but they all clashed. Stone sculptures that weren't well-crafted appeared to have been made by a Demon artisan, considering the demonic depictions in them. The bust of a sculpture of a horned creature she'd never seen on Earth – likely one from Nyl'theria – sat on top of a stone pillar.

The floor was layered with mismatched red rugs, enough to soften the surface and ease the chill that surely came up through the stone. Wrought-iron chandeliers hung in single file from one end to the other, with eight candles in each, all of which were lit and gave the room decent visibility.

With their curtains pushed open, large windows on one side allowed the lightning to flash intermittently, and it cast its hot light over Jabez and Katerina, who were under a pink, semi-translucent dome. She hid behind his towering form, the woman only coming to his ribs.

A small army of Demon soldiers stood between her and them.

"You think any of this will stop me?" Lindiwe gestured to the ridiculousness of it all. "You are only delaying the inevitable. I will kill that woman."

"Considering I'm the one who killed Orpheus' little male companion, shouldn't I be the one your anger is directed at?" Jabez asked, cocking a white brow.

"Would you have intervened had she not requested it?" Lindiwe eyed the dozen or so red-hued gazes upon her and lifted her upper lip in a sneer.

Jabez didn't answer, and that was truth enough.

No, he wouldn't have, and he didn't even deny it. There was no point in lying. He wouldn't have fucking cared if not for *her*.

And why? Why take away the very first companion after over thirty years who had *survived* the journey to the Veil? Orpheus rarely had constant crimson orbs, but they had lasted long enough to bring her to his side and ask what had happened to make him so annoyed.

Because he'd watched it happen.

Because Jabez had killed that human in front of Orpheus and then left his bleeding corpse for him to eat while he fled!

And what for?! So that Orpheus failed? Was alone? Suffered? Why go to such lengths just to hurt him, when they were an entire forest apart? He was trying his hardest to move past his own hurt after thirty-six years, and Katerina had a new life here.

One where, apparently, she was undying.

The vile woman peeked around Jabez, barely looking a day over thirty, and she'd been around twenty-two, maybe twenty-three, when they'd met. At some point since Lindiwe had last seen her, Jabez had figured out a way to stop her from ageing.

That worried Lindiwe... what else had he learned or discovered? How much of a dangerous threat had he become?

"You know I can move through your wards," Lindiwe said, eyeing the useless pink barrier separating them.

"But you must turn *physical* to harm her." The smirk that grew on his smug face was malicious. "And we both know I'm faster than you. I'll end you before you touch either of us."

"I would just come back to life through Weldir and return

here."

Maybe...

She could also end up staying dead, or worse, be stuck in his void while he endlessly slept.

Jabez was right about one thing, and it was unlikely she'd be able to make a killing strike in such a small space. Not without some distraction.

Let's see how strong his magic is... when it has an entire castle collapsed on top of it!

She turned tangible, and the Demons, most in clothing, lunged. Their strength and speed meant those at the front were at her within a second.

But she only needed the span of a single breath.

Pulling in a vast amount of power from Weldir, a dark ball of hard magic formed between her hands. She yanked her arms apart, and the ball expanded, pushing back the Demons in all directions.

It moulded around Jabez's ward, his power stronger than hers, and they, under the ward, remained in the centre of the room. The others were flung against the walls or shattered the windows when they were thrown outwards.

The walls creaked and groaned while the building rumbled and shook. Stones dislodged, and when they gave way, they flung outwards as rotating boulders that crashed outside. Once the supporting walls were broken, cracked, and crumbling under the strain of her magic, the ceiling instantly toppled inwards.

Before a ledge of ceiling could land on her, Lindiwe turned incorporeal, rendering her magic inert. But the damage was done.

And as the castle tilted to one side and collapsed inwards, she shot forward through the falling rubble. The flurry of dust and carnage was difficult to see through, especially when it obscured her line of sight. In the encroaching darkness, she followed the only light she could see – a pink shimmering dome.

The moment she was inside it, Lindiwe turned physical and

conjured a shadowy blade. She had to orientate herself to strike Katerina in the heart, and the woman's blue eyes widened. Just as she sucked in a breath to scream, Lindiwe lunged to stab her chest.

Claws gouged into her right biceps.

With one of his hands high on her biceps and the other around her elbow, the instant he grabbed her, he used the momentum to shove her arm downwards quicker than she could figure out what was happening.

He shoved his knee up at the same time her arm came down, and her humerus bone snapped.

A bloodcurdling scream burst from her. Turning into a Phantom proved futile when she flickered in place against the white-hot pain. The shock of it halted her as tears welled in her eyes and bile rose in her throat, her body rejecting the agony.

She made another dagger form and slashed it at him. She cut a deep gash down his face before it stabbed into his arm, but he only glared. When she pulled it out to attack again, trying to get him to let go, Katerina bounced forward with a grunt. The woman wrapped her slim arms around Lindiwe's left arm and held it in place so she couldn't defend herself.

Jabez then twisted, and Lindiwe tried everything in her might to get away. Her skin tore, and the already broken bone crunched and further separated as he stretched and mangled her arm before he yanked it off.

"An arm for an arm," Jabez sneered, tossing it to the side.

Her dismembered arm slapped against the inside of the pink dome, splattering blood across the surface before it hit the ground with a thud.

Freed from Jabez, Lindiwe dropped to the ground to kick Katerina's ankles and make her release her arm. Her heart was racing, adrenaline and fear of more pain rushing strength into her bloodstream – which only made her pulse dangerously faster.

Lindiwe's sight warped in and out while she tried to get her bearings. The inside of her mouth was flooded with drool, and she swallowed it to push down the nausea that cramped high in her gut.

Tears of agony had long filled her eyes, but she couldn't stop to register anything other than the need to escape.

Phantom. I need to shift.

Covering the bloodied stump of her right arm, she fled while attempting to morph forms, and flickered between the two. Jabez chased her around his dome as Katerina screamed and tried her hardest to avoid getting in the middle of them.

Darkness surrounded them completely, the layers of Jabez's castle still on top of them.

Ducking underneath Jabez's arms, using his Elven height against him, she managed to suck in a breath that pushed clarity to the surface. She let go of her injury and made a thin blade form in her hand. When her back shunted against a shimmering magical wall, she stabbed it backwards as hard as she could muster.

The thinness of the blade ensured she was able to stab through his ward. She hadn't known it would work, as it depended on whether the ward was made to protect against slashing, impact, or penetrative damage.

It was enough that she was able to slice sideways.

And with her momentary clarity, she was able to turn intangible... just as his castle came down on top of them. He roared when they were buried alive under what should have been an unbearable weight.

But Lindiwe knew they weren't crushed, based on the constant sounds coming from within, even when she floated upwards through the rubble.

"Stop fucking screaming!" Jabez bellowed. "Or I'll end you myself!"

Katerina instantly went quiet.

When Lindiwe exited through the top of the ruins, half of the building had collapsed, while the other side creaked and groaned as chunks fell. The Demons she'd thrown against the walls were already climbing through the outer parts of the debris. They shook their bodies and hair of dust and rocks before dragging their sorry arses away to the surrounding areas.

I have to get somewhere safe. The fact that she could stay a Phantom was a miracle, but her strength was waning.

She doubted she'd get far in the middle of the Veil, but it was less inhabited compared to the outer rings. If she could find somewhere to stem the bleeding, she had medicinal herbs she could use to aid with the pain and potential infection.

Lindiwe didn't consider this a failure.

She may not have killed Katerina or Jabez, but she was sure she'd frightened the shit out of them. She'd proved she was someone to be wary of, and that her threats were anything but empty.

She was deadly, and would only be more prepared and cunning next time. She had all the anger, determination, and will, and all the time in the world to be locked in battle.

The winds picked up speed, and the first pattering droplets of rain fell through her transparent body. Thunder rumbled before a flash of light forked across the dark sky, and it mimicked the aura of her rage.

Fuck you, Jabez.

TWENTY-EIGHT

A time unknown, but of memory fragments

Weldir's subconscious twitched.

It shifted, spiralling further and further apart, until his hold on the tethers unravelled into invisible fraying strings. He felt no desire to pull the pieces taut. He lacked the strength, will, or even the thought to do so.

Instead, the weightlessness crushed into him and pushed him deeper into the waves of his memories.

Of darkness, of nothing but his own echoing roars. Of heavy loneliness and abandonment that never ceased its yawning gulps.

His subconscious twitched again, and it twisted in reaction, pulling in on itself, only to scatter like dust.

His own voice muttered to him incoherently as moments of madness festered within the ache of his mind. The dullness of living for eternity, in his own self-made suffering, was his imprisonment.

Memories flickered, all the same. Just a string of indecipherable thoughts. Then a face, beautiful with a mix of brown and gold, appeared for a millisecond. It was gone before he could truly discern who it was. Their face returned multiple times, each time growing more withered and drained, and the golden glow radiating from their very being became lacklustre.

The darkness *always* returned. His darkness.

Another twitch, and this time his subconscious stretched in two different, twisting directions.

Then he managed to grab ahold of a memory when it blessed his everlasting void, and it played out in his mind.

A set of green hands, the soft flesh of their palms paler and near cream, picked up his prism. He felt nothing, despite knowing he was no longer lying upon the bed his mother, the Gilded Maiden, rested on.

Bright-green scales covered the hands as the sides and backs of them came into view. Cream-coloured claws chinked against whatever was keeping Weldir contained. Then the darkness parted like a curtain, and a strange, humanoid face with short dark-green hair was revealed.

The facial scales appeared soft and malleable, allowing the reptilian flesh around his yellow eyes to crinkle. The spikes framing his eyes and brows moved with his frown, and a forked red tongue licked at his dark-green lips, which incidentally revealed his sharp, thin fangs.

He looked Elven formed: a broad jaw, high cheekbones, and arching brows. His long, pointed ears twitched, tipped with little spikes upon them. Yet his face lacked a proper nose; it was only two little slits with a slightly convex bulge where there should be one.

He'd never seen this male before. As he eyed the spikes jutting out from the corners of his jaw, and the scales lining his neck, the rest of him faded from view.

"I know you are in there, dark one," the being, likely an Elven deity, stated. His voice was soft, rich, and smooth, and oddly had a calming influence upon Weldir's subconscious. "I have felt your power shifting and changing as your prism lies in my mending vines."

He remained silent; no one could hear him beyond his prison.

The bright, indistinguishable background sped past in a downward fashion, as if the male lowered to sit upon the ground with the crystal prism in his hands.

"I hope you don't mind, but it's time I introduced myself."

Yellow mana rippled from the male's fingertips like water.

Weldir's mist perceived an intrusion, and he spun in a circle to find the male behind him. He was in the far distance, searching the endless darkness, so Weldir transported directly in front of him.

He wore a pair of loose white pants, and a sleeveless shirt made from vines and pink flowers. His clawed bare feet were also adorned with green leafy-patterned arching shoes that lacked soles, with little pink flowers. Over his shoulders he wore a half vest made of thick, scaly brown material.

The male spun, his head moving one way and then the other, and almost passed over Weldir. Yet he stopped, and his yellow eyes slipped back, then widened when they fell upon him.

"So, you have truly gained some kind of form." He pushed forward in a way that was unnatural, as if the makeup of the prism didn't affect him. "But it's still not whole."

"It's a manifestation," Weldir answered, unsure if he'd be heard or even understood.

The male whisked his hand through his mist. "Of mana?"

Weldir's entire being pulsed without his control.

"It is real. I can feel this is a part of you, a solidness that isn't complete or truly tangible." The male then lifted his yellow eyes with slitted pupils to meet his gaze. "It's more than we hoped. It means you have a semblance of... control."

Weldir lifted his arms to look down at his body, seeing it in its entirety. He also saw the constant mist that shrouded him wherever he went.

"Who are you?" Weldir shifted to look behind him, to where the image of this male still existed beyond his prism. "And how are you here? How have I not eaten you?"

"It's a projection." He waved down at himself. "I'm not truly here – merely an illusion – and you cannot destroy what isn't real." Then his thin lips pursed. "Although I can feel you eating away at the mana the longer I do it."

Weldir waited patiently for him to answer all his questions.

"I am Leyfr, the god of forestry and flora. One of your potential sires, and one of the last three deities remaining on this plane." He gestured towards his own face beyond the prism wall. "I'm the one who has been keeping Almethrandra alive within my mending vines and monitoring your progress in her stead."

His gaze slid down Leyfr completely, and he expected that by the time he looked back into his eyes, he would regard him differently.

He didn't.

He felt nothing for his potential sire. Just emptiness.

Not due to hate, indifference, or abandonment, but simply because... why should he care? Weldir was an adult and lacked any connections. He wouldn't turn away from this bond, but it mattered little to a being who was imprisoned without an end.

"You seek something from me."

Leyfr's spiked brow cocked. "I was hoping to see how far you'd come in controlling your power."

"Do you need it?" He regarded the reptilian Elven god once more. "Forestry and flora? Whatever it is you seek, it is out of the realm of your capabilities. It's not life you wish to grow in the dirt, but something else entirely, and my mother is still incapacitated and of no use."

"I see," Leyfr said with a hum. "It appears I was right. You may be ill-formed, but your mind is stable. The foundations of you aren't inherently evil."

"I'm not evil at all."

His lips pulled into a grin. "Yes, I can see that. You must understand, our first meeting of you was during the destruction and carnage you wrought. Almethrandra had hoped you were benevolent, as you saved her by healing her of the Daekura venom she absorbed. But... we didn't know if you desired such things or if it was accidental."

"I have little recollection of my birth."

"You are a facet of death, which shouldn't be possible when

we already have a being of death. Every living thing your shadows touched was eradicated from the inside. You consumed their spirit and destroyed the vessel that housed it. But there is more to you; I have been able to sense it from my vines. You can manifest your mana, touch what no one else but Yanyas, the god of the afterlife, can. Souls." Then Leyfr lifted his arms and spun in a circle. *"You are the Warden of Darkness, and your shadows can manifest and reach out in a swarm. They have completely blocked you inside this prism so that not even we can see you."*

"I am broken, and my power is insignificant," Weldir admitted freely. He lifted his arms to show the tiny dots of solidness. *"You can see me, but I can sense there is little of me."*

"Care to expand it?" Leyfr asked, making Weldir lift his gaze to his once more. *"A strange child, part Demon and part Elysian, was born some years ago. He, too, was imprisoned for things he couldn't control, and led a massacre upon gaining his freedom. During that freedom, he took a portal stone and has opened up another avenue."*

"A portal to another realm?" Weldir's mist shifted in thought. *"Do you wish for me to aid him? How will this benefit me?"*

"Aid him? No. We are hoping more will follow behind him. We want you to stop Demons from returning through his portal, then consume the souls of the humans they've eaten."

"How? I'm trapped here."

"I can take a piece of your mist with me, a flicker of your mana. A link between you and that world." Leyfr hummed as his eyes slipped to the side pensively. *"Well, I wouldn't be able to do such a thing, but Rökul sure can."* The male tsked and scratched his pale claws through his dark-green hair. *"It really is a shame that the first one you consumed was Taoveen. She was a creator and could have given you a body in which to house your scattered spirit."*

I know these names from Mother, *Weldir thought.*

She'd shared with him many of her own memories, which helped to puzzle out all the pieces of what Leyfr spoke of. He'd seen all of Nyl'theria through her perspective when she let her consciousness wander aimlessly.

Leyfr offered him a smile. "If you consume enough souls and grow your power, you may be able to stabilise your form and become complete."

"No. I don't have the capability to give myself a physical body. This manifestation is at the edge of my limitations."

Leyfr's hopeful expression fell. "You do not know that."

But he did.

Weldir's brokenness, his incompleteness, could never be fixed on his own terms. It would require assistance that he was unsure if even his mother could offer.

"I don't need false hope. It is an emotion for those who can feel it," Weldir answered coldly. "I'm willing to agree, simply because it will give me the freedom I lack now, although cruel. Thank you for not wrapping this request in a façade of liberation that is untrue to hide that cruelty."

Leyfr's head reared back, and his spiky, pointed ears shot back. "Cruel?" He waved his clawed hand to the side. "I earnestly think this would be beneficial for you. A way to grow your power, and one day give you true freedom."

"Freedom you cannot guarantee," Weldir rebutted. "A way to leave my prism through projection, as I have just learned the ability from you being here, but to a world I cannot touch, scent, or taste. To show me what I cannot have, and likely never will."

His eyes crinkled when they bowed with sadness. "Weldir... Almethrandra might have such capabilities."

"Once more, there is no guarantee that she does, or that she will upon her waking, if she ever awakens. I have agreed to your request. Is there anything else I should know, any rules I must abide by?"

"So long as you abide by our morals, and don't feed upon living beings with an evilness, Almethrandra will always welcome you. You may not see it, but she cries for you in her sleep."

"I know."

The memory was so real that when Weldir's hold on it slipped, it shocked him into alertness. His subconscious twisted and tore apart.

Weakness tried to pull him under, like a human breathing in water and drowning underneath a wave right as their fingers were skimming the surface they'd been reaching for. He perceived the hold on his thoughts, his alertness popping like bubbles.

Until a new face, a much more recent one in the longevity of his life, reflected in a bubble.

Someone beautiful, whose brown eyes had flecks of golden amber, and long, dark, curling lashes. It was just a flicker, but her neck arched back, revealing the long column of brown skin. A breast tipped with a dark nipple arched into view.

Weldir's mind exploded.

His vision spun one way and then the other.

The pieces of him that usually made up his solid, physical self were spread throughout his consciousness. His mist had expanded, thinning as it drifted and spread out from him. With a clench against his mana, he sucked it all inwards until he righted himself.

When he looked down at his hand, its silhouette warbled and jiggled, then eventually settled.

Before he could register anything else, Weldir knew, with absolute certainty, he was weak. His power had been stolen and siphoned.

Something is wrong.

He immaterialised and transported himself to Tenebris.

Shock struck him as he looked up, down, and then all around at his crumbling realm.

Tenebris was like the inside of a ball, with a sphere of permanent bright-blue sky in the very middle. Meadows, forests, and human cities rolled along the outside, and looped in on themselves.

Fragments had fallen. They hovered inwards towards the sky from every direction, as holes filled with glossy shadows littered everywhere. The mountains in the distance, the trees, and even the blades of grass beneath him had a transparency to them. Everything was dulled and see-through, letting darkness shift their colours.

Weldir quickly shot himself backwards to find the humans. They were asleep, but none of them were in motion. They weren't alive, playing out their fondest memories with those connected to their fate threads. They were lifeless, their eyes hollow and cloudy.

Pressure pulled across his face and the tops of his ears, like their points had tipped back, as he scanned the slanted, breaking horizon. A hollowness filled his mind.

How did this happen? How long have I been asleep?

He waved his hand to reveal his own fate strings, all the different colours threaded with black, representing his own soul. Each colour reflected the base orb hue of each of his offspring, and one multicoloured string represented his mate.

He pulled on the only one that didn't lead out of Tenebris and yanked himself forward.

All his questions were answered when he reached the other end.

Nathair lay on his back with his tail looped in multiple figure eights. With his fingers rigid, his hands unnaturally locked, his jaw open and pressing against his left shoulder, and his humanoid torso pulled so taut that it arched, he quaked upon the fading ground.

He seized quietly, almost lifelessly. His twitches were so minute that, maybe to a human's eye, he may have been motionless. But Weldir could see them rippling beneath his black-and-rainbow glistening scales.

He has grown exponentially. Nathair had doubled in length, if not more, in his absence. Although very few of his skeletal bones had sunk beneath his flesh, more had protruded along his longer and girthier tail. His waist no longer narrowed in a starving, sickly way, but had thickened with meaty muscle, as had his bulging chest.

His fins had lengthened and currently twitched all down his sides to nearly the tip of his tail.

His usually orange orbs rotated with a kaleidoscope of colours, constantly shifting and never holding one for any length of time.

Lowering to one knee, Weldir waved his hand over his eldest son's chest to look at his orange soul. Shards of white flaming glass had embedded themselves within his spirit.

They've burrowed deep, Weldir thought, turning his palm up and trying to call them out from within him. They weren't new and shallow, like the last time Weldir had removed the remnants of the deceased souls Nathair had eaten.

While I was asleep, he must have gone into a rage and then rampaged through the nearby village. And the memories from the humans had incapacitated him until he was stuck in an ongoing seizure. *No wonder my mana is so low.*

He barely had enough to stay conscious.

A deity's mana was created by the aura that surrounded their soul. The larger their aura, the thicker it was, the more they had to expend. If they ran out of it, they had the potential to go *beyond* their capabilities and begin using their essence, their very self, for power.

That is also how a god permanently lost an arm, an eye, or worse, extinguished themselves forever.

For Weldir, the second consumption of a soul feasted on his aura like a plague until he ceased using it. He considered it a penance, a punishment for violating another's soul in immoral and unimaginable ways.

When Nathair consumed souls, the initial shatter of it left behind the human's memory fragments – little shards of glass that refracted pieces of their life.

Once a soul shattered, it didn't feast upon his offspring, but the power surrounding it: Weldir. Nathair had no mana here in Tenebris to offer the souls. They festered and fizzled with gigantic, yawning mouths, like a whale eating krill. And a shattered soul gulped and gulped as it tried to put itself back together before slowly evaporating when it couldn't stabilise itself.

Considering how deep these are, it's evident it's been an exceptionally long time... Nathair roared and twisted as the shards began to dislodge. *He almost destroyed me.*

My mist has receded. I can feel my reach on Earth is minimal. He looked up at his poor realm. *Tenebris was close to dissolving.* He was surprised he hadn't woken to screaming.

Some of Rökul's portals... don't have my barriers on them. He checked to make sure Jabez's did, and it was thankfully still in place, but half of the others had disappeared.

His power just hadn't been able to maintain them.

Lindiwe will have to help me. She would need to fly to all those that were preventing Demons from returning to Nyl'theria, so he could lay down new mist. Once she showed him those locations and he could transport to his mana there, he could conjure new barriers. *I must do so in person.*

When Nathair gouged into his own neck, shredding his flesh and gills – and coincidentally his soul – apart, Weldir made tendrils form across his huge body. Nathair's orbs, still shifting between colours, shattered as ethereal tears began to float around his serpent skull.

Weldir placed a hand over the side of Nathair's brow bone and stroked it comfortingly. "I know it hurts, but I must get them out."

The more the shards ripped through his soul on their exit, the more Nathair squirmed and fought. He wriggled on the ground, trying everything in his might to escape. He let out a scream that made Weldir pity him, but he couldn't stop.

At the same time, he tried to heal Nathair's soul of the damage he'd done to it. His wounds were deep, like skin had grown over splinters of glass that'd burrowed into muscle.

When the largest shards were gone, the flickering rainbow in his orbs slowed, but did not cease.

There must be more. Weldir started over, pulling out smaller shards; those were difficult even for him to see. He repeated the process, removing fragments while healing him at the same time – even at the cost of his low, dwindling mana.

When Nathair stopped quaking, but didn't wake up, Weldir stopped and pulled his serpent skull to the side by one of his dark, hooked ram horns. He peered into white orbs.

I cannot see them, he thought hopelessly, as he waved his hands over his offspring's unconscious form.

Deep within Nathair's body, shards glittered in answer, but they were so tiny that Weldir couldn't see them properly. He couldn't even perceive them with his mana. It was like looking for a crystal of sugar in a sea of salt, no matter how much he tried to call them out of Nathair's body.

"I'm sorry, but this is all I can do," Weldir told him, placing his fingertips gently on the centre of his bony forehead. "Sleep. You have been awake for long enough."

Nathair's orbs blackened, and he went limp.

"I have failed you." He'd let his offspring be harmed under his care.

Had he not already been deep in slumber when Nathair did this, Weldir may have been able to stop him. Regardless, he wore the blame.

He tipped his head back to look at the fracturing sky. *Will Lindiwe be angry?*

How many of her years had he missed? How many of their offspring had evolved?

I didn't see what skull and horns she gave our last offspring.

And he didn't have enough power – between keeping Tenebris in its current state, but stable, and saving Nathair – to remain awake any longer.

She will have to wait a little longer.

TWENTY-NINE

A time unknown, but of strange fondness

Weldir's mind twitched as he gradually returned to consciousness. In the weightless nothing, he spanned his sight over his body.

The inky spots that usually made up his physical form were minuscule. He'd barely gained a fraction of what he'd lost. At most, his fingertips would be visible, which was nothing in comparison to the third of him that had been available before Nathair's carnage.

Weldir tipped back to float to a different part of his outer realm, and Lindiwe's citrine flaming soul brightened his sight. He enlarged it so it would better fit in both his palms. One hand cupped the bottom of it to support it from underneath, while his other wrapped around its back. Although it was vertical, it appeared to be lying on its side.

Her soul was brighter before.

Before he'd been absent, the coal markings on it, highlighting her emotional and mental pains, had been minimal. They'd returned with a vengeance in his absence.

He stroked his mate's tiny flaming likeness, more to soothe himself than her.

Floating close by were the broken pieces of Nathair's physical skull, with tiny bubbles of his mana keeping them tangible to him. Seeing it prompted him to immaterialise and check on his serpent offspring.

Tenebris remained the same without his intervention: slanted, fragmented, and suspended in time while in the middle of collapsing inwards. Crouching onto one knee, he brushed his palm over one of Nathair's hooked ram horns to check that his orbs were still black, signalling they were closed.

He hadn't moved an inch under Weldir's sleeping spell.

I cannot wake him, not yet, he decided, lifting his gaze to his broken realm. *I cannot fix this yet, either.* He'd only recuperated enough mana to stay awake. Wasting it on a selfish need to see Tenebris flourish didn't negate the fact that he had responsibilities that went beyond it. *I have to place new barriers and lay new mists.*

He didn't have the power for that either.

I also wish to see Lindiwe. There was this mist-vibrating need to make sure she was well. To see how she'd fared. If... she was angry with him.

The last one might have also been the reason he hadn't immediately reached out to her. He didn't wish to face her ire when he was already dismayed and dispirited over his current state. *At least I cannot feel her in my realm.*

She'd somehow managed to stay alive on her own on Earth.

Her use of my power likely consumed the little I replenished during my slumber all these years. He wasn't upset by this, but thankful for it. *If she'd been trapped here for however long I've been asleep...*

That would have been horrifying for her.

No. I cannot wake Nathair until I have fixed everything and made sure he won't do this again. He wouldn't survive it, and Nathair, along with all the souls in his realm, would cease to exist entirely. His essence was volatile, and it would consume everything in its path to survive, including feeding upon his deceased offspring.

He wouldn't even know he was doing it.

Weldir sighed. *If only I could eat living souls.* He could, but he just shouldn't. *That is unlimited power that doesn't harm me.*

He could consume them in the way he did with Lindiwe's soul, where they were bonded to him. Just pure, unadulterated power. But she wanted this to be a closed bond, and he'd adhere to that wish.

He did have another realistic option, and now that he'd checked on his offspring and the state of Tenebris, he left to go there.

The overwhelming number of souls waiting for him was daunting. Hundreds of thousands of tainted souls, all broken and sickly, floated in hordes of white flaming light.

With a flick of his mental will, he lifted all those that were untainted upwards, and he snapped his right hand to the side to dismiss the diseased ones out of his view. With a tug of his mind, he pulled all the clean and unharmed souls closer.

He halted in surprise.

There are hundreds of them. Lindiwe and his offspring had collected far more than he ever expected. Or was this just the evidence that an exceptionally long time had passed?

He shrunk them until they all fit onto one hand, lifted them, and then let them float within the cavern of his mouth. He swallowed, and a burst of energy pulsed through his mist — enough to give him the majority of his hands.

It wasn't a lot, but since he'd rested more, it brought him to proper alertness. *I imagine this is what it's like for humans when they consume caffeine, like coffee or certain teas.*

He instantly wasted some of the mana he'd gained by putting all the new souls within Tenebris to sleep, since it wasn't stable enough to let them drift in their fondest memories.

Now I can cast the spell I want. A single viewing disc, smaller than usual to preserve his energy, rippled into existence.

The sight of Lindiwe instantly made his mist collide with guilt. *Her cloak is in tatters.* Barely any feathers clung to the white material thrown over her shoulders.

The dress she wore was a plain pale green with short sleeves. The bust was high, hiding her ample cleavage, and a leather belt cinched the waist in to give it more shape. Her cloak hood was back, showing her hair was loose and a little tangled as she knelt within a garden.

With her right hand, she plucked herbs from their stems and yanked cruciferous vegetables from the earth or their roots. After carefully placing them in a basket, she stood, grabbed the handle to lift it from the ground, and strode to a little cottage.

It was obvious that she inhabited it.

A journal sat on a table that had two chairs tucked underneath it. A fireplace brightened the inside along with the open wooden blinds that allowed the sunshine in. A wooden bench, which he figured was some kind of lounge without padding, had been pushed against the wall next to the biggest window.

A pair of barely used flats were next to a doormat, on which she wiped her feet before heading towards the kitchen area. One-handed, she carefully placed each item she'd collected onto a thin tray. Then she opened a low-burning hearth, placed the tray inside, and moved to stir a bubbling pot.

She isn't cooking food. Medicine or some kind of Anzúli alchemy, perhaps?

Her face, although clean and healthy, was entirely devoid of emotion. There were no dark smudges of tiredness at the inner corners of her eyes, but her gaze lacked the usual life he expected to see in it.

The fire of his mate, who looked at the world with unbending determination and will. Who had always appeared ready for battle, whether it be against nightmarish creatures or the curse of intelligent, sentient existence.

It was all missing.

Despite this, a sense of... calm pushed through him. He hadn't realised his mist had been buzzing with worried tension until he saw his mate was well. No doubt she was unhappy, but she had found a place to reside that was safe and comfortable.

"Lindiwe," Weldir called.

A gasp parted her lips, and she lifted her face from the

simmering pot to the sunny window in front of her. She dropped the wooden spoon inside the pot, and it clunked against the edge, slowly slipped to the side, and sank within the thick, bubbling broth.

"Weldir?" she whispered.

"Yes, owlet."

Tears welled in her sparkling eyes and instantly spilled over. He hadn't expected tears; he thought she'd go into a tirade about his disappearance. She covered her face with her right hand, and her shoulders trembled inwards as she heaved out a quiet sob.

"I've been so worried about you," Lindiwe cried, wiping her cheeks with the back of her hand. "I didn't know when or if you were ever going to wake up. I knew something was wrong when I saw your mist fading, and I knew using your magic would only further harm you."

A shaken, shuddering breath, like it didn't know if it wanted to exhale or be sucked in, broke from her. As if she needed to steady her legs, she placed her hand upon the oak bench and just let her tears fall freely. Each one that landed on the wooden surface darkened it with a wet splotch.

"It's been *years*. What happened?"

"Nathair consumed a few dozen souls while I was recuperating my mana," Weldir informed her. "Our offspring is not well, and has not only damaged himself, but me as well. Everything we have done, all the souls we have collected together... all the power from them is gone."

Lindiwe slapped the table with her hand. "I don't care about your power right now!" she yelled through a sob. "It's been sixty-two years, Weldir!"

He was stunned into silence. *It's been that long?*

"What I've gone through..." Lindiwe said through shaking lips, cupping her side. "I've been stuck in Austrális for twenty-five years. When our children needed me, I could not be there. When I needed you... you weren't there."

"I am... sorry, Lindiwe." His mist pulsed in and out due to the collision of mingling emotions. Guilt, despondency, sympathy. "You wished to know what has happened, and my fading mist is the reflection of my mana depletion. I've been slumbering and drawing back subconsciously to *survive*."

Anger flashed across her face at his mentioning once more of his power, only for it to fade.

Her eyes softened with uncertainty. "Survive?"

"Had Nathair consumed any more before succumbing to the fragments, I would have ceased to exist."

"How is that possible?" she cried, shaking her head. "You are a *god*! You aren't allowed to die on me."

"Demi-god," Weldir corrected, like she usually did. "I don't have the same benefits as a fully formed deity. Useless and not all-knowing, as you once said."

Her lips shook as she weakly admonished, "Don't say that." She licked them to soothe their trembling. "Can you just hurry up and bring me to your realm?"

Taken aback by her request, he regarded his mate differently. He didn't know why. Perhaps it was because he never thought she'd cry for him, over him, or make it sound as though she... *missed* him.

"There is little of me to see," he admitted.

"I don't care." She grabbed the long handle of the simmering pot and pulled it away from the heat. She waved at the internal stove. "The coals in there are so low for drying those herbs that it'll safely go out. It's just medicine and scent-cloaking ingredients for the nearby town. Everything else I want from here... I can come back for later."

Seeing as she was set on this, and arguing with Lindiwe could often prove futile when she had her heart set on something, Weldir submitted. He pulled her from her world and into his.

The first thing she did when she came into view was search for him... even when he was right in front of her. She squinted in the darkness, only for her eyes to widen when she caught his light mist in her periphery.

Her cloak swayed around her, slowly continuing to move in

the direction she'd been turning before halting. "Oh, Weldir. Look at you."

He tipped his gaze down, knowing what she saw was nothing but a handful of small streaks and the cloud of his mist. Not like before, where a good portion of him had become visible, tangible, *touchable.*

"As I mentioned, there is little–" He lifted his gaze just as her cloak finished opening on her left side, and his words cut off. "Lindiwe... your *arm.*"

He transported to her side and brought what little he had to his fingertips to reach out to her. She had yet to turn into a Phantom, so there was no point in him trying to touch her, but it wouldn't have mattered. At some point since his disappearance, Lindiwe had lost the limb.

Halfway down her biceps was a stump, the keloid scarring taut.

Guilt trembled through his mist again, but it was utterly overshadowed by the intense rage that vibrated all through his realm. The growl he produced rippled his darkness, his void, and he perceived it all the way to his gut – in Tenebris.

"Turn Phantom *now,*" he demanded.

She immediately did, and he used his fingertips to touch her and lift her arm. Then he linked her soul to her body and pushed mana into it to regrow the limb for her.

Without his intervention, Lindiwe did not heal. She did not change either. Unless she was within his realm, their bond kept her the same; she didn't age, and her hair didn't lengthen if she cut it. His nearness, while she was a Phantom, helped to reset her physically.

"How did this happen?" He lifted his gaze to glare directly into hers, his ire not *at* her, but *for* her. "You are usually so careful."

The fact that he'd been gone so long and she'd survived every one of those years was testament to that.

She grabbed her newly healed arm and pulled it away from him. "I had an altercation with Jabez."

Weldir snapped out a snarl through chomping fangs, and his mist visibly pulsated, to the point that her eyes widened in surprise.

If I could, I'd take that male's life force and snuff it out. Frustratingly, he couldn't do that! Leyfr had made him promise many things, and one of them was to not destroy the life of a living soul by his own mana.

Technically what he'd done with Lindiwe was a *bend* of that rule. He hadn't killed her, not fully, as she was still alive – despite her technically being dead.

And no one had told him he couldn't claim a mate or have offspring who could *potentially* do what he'd sworn not to.

Many times over, he wished to disregard all those things and do what he wanted. Eradicate the Demons from within, destroy anything and everything that annoyed him.

But he didn't want to be the evil creature they feared him to be. Even just one soul would be a violation, and as if Leyfr knew Jabez in particular would instigate his ire, he'd made sure Weldir swore not to interfere with that male.

The forest god's morality was entirely detrimental to Weldir's more destructive desires. Sometimes adhering to his rules was dispiriting.

"No one is angrier than me," Lindiwe pointed out, her lips pursing as if she could sense the maelstrom of fury within him. "If it makes you feel any better, I cornered him when he was above the surface and placed a ward over him."

That piqued his interest, knowing his grudge-holding, strong female could be ruthless when given the chance. "Does that mean he's gone?"

That'd make him rather ecstatic.

She rolled her pretty eyes with a pout. "I wish. I waited until the sun rose and then released it. I thought the sun would instantly burn him like other Demons, but it only wounded him while he escaped into the shade."

Her eyes flicked all around without his face being visible. She didn't know where to look, how to find him, and there was too little of him to help in that regard.

"So much has happened since you've been gone." Then her eyes grew incredibly soft, their whites pinkened, and new tears formed. "I really want to hug you right now."

Once more, Weldir was stunned by her crying. He also wasn't quite sure how to respond to it, as this was new territory for him regarding her. His mate wanting to hug him, cry for him, be all soft and *cute?*

"I... thought you would be angry with me," he admitted, hoping she'd help him understand.

She gave a tearful laugh. "Oh I am. But I'm just so thankful you're okay, and that you're back. When you didn't come back to witness Fennec gaining their horns and skull like you promised, I knew it wasn't your fault."

When she cupped both her hands to her chest, he braved reaching out. "I cannot give you what you seek right now, but I can do this."

Collecting every piece of his self into his right hand, all his fingers solidified to their base knuckles. He cupped the side of her tear-stained cheek and brushed it with his thumb to wipe some of the moisture away. His mist pulled in tight when she... *leaned* into his meagre touch trustingly, affectionately, and something about it changed something within Weldir.

I like this side of her. He came a little closer, wishing there was more of him to share with her, and that he could bring her into an embrace he couldn't feel but longed for all the same. *I like this... tenderness.*

"Would you care to stay awhile and tell me all that I've missed?" he asked, refusing to pull his hand away from her cheek. He drifted it down the crease of her nose and even rubbed over her full lips.

"Yes. Please, yes. I want to stay here."

His mist swirled around him in mini whirlpools, and that had never happened before.

We can lay my mist upon Earth later. He would tell her how he needed her help *after* he spent time with his female. His mate, who was being exceptionally soft with him, had no idea how captivating he found it.

For once, he didn't care about strengthening his power, his reach, or even his duty. He didn't want to shadow this with impatience or expectations.

He just wanted to spend time with her in his realm, surrounded by his darkness, her voice and presence filling every inch of it the way he'd long ago begun to want it to.

It was also the first time he'd wished there was more of him, simply so he could seat her in his lap while they spoke.

She had years to share with him, and he would be a grateful listener.

She also likes watching me fix her cloak.

And considering its poor and sorry state, and his low mana, it should take him some time. More for him to spend with her. For once, he didn't think he needed to use that as an excuse.

She wanted to be here as much as he wanted her to stay.

THIRTY

August 17th, 1900

Approaching a swirling yellow portal in her snowy owl form, Lindiwe landed before it, shifted, and removed her feathery hood.

Nearly a year had passed since Weldir's return, and she was thankful they'd had many spare owl feathers for him to fix her cloak with. She'd been without the ability to fly for nearly twenty-five years, as it was impossible to fly with a missing arm, and therefore, wing.

She probably should have taken better care of the garment by folding it away neatly and storing it safely, but her cloak was a part of her now. It was an extension of herself, and not wearing it was like being naked and exposed. She also hadn't wanted to die, be trapped in Weldir's realm, and have it go missing. A human may have picked it up or stolen the mana stone – not knowing its owner would one day come back to retrieve it.

Although she still had a lot of pain and trauma to mentally deal with from his disappearance, she was... happy.

He was back; that's all she needed to remember. And things between them had noticeably shifted.

For once, the time apart had allowed her heart to grow fonder. She believed it had to do with their intimacy right before he was shoved into a near-death slumber.

But it wasn't the sex, despite that being an exceptional bonus. No, it was his openness, his honesty, and his truth that had built the foundations of trust *beyond* their bargain. For every single one of those years alone, she remembered the words he'd said to her, the way he'd touched her with care, and the possessiveness he'd displayed.

Their impact was enough that if she remembered them late at night and under the covers of a soft bed, she'd find her fingers gliding into her underwear so she could give herself relief. Orgasming like that had felt hollow when it wasn't her hand she wanted, but his. Or his mouth, cock, or tendrils.

Funny how her opinion and mindset had shifted from just one very naughty conversation.

None of that removed the ache in her heart, and the new fear that he'd disappear again. Possibly forever. Anxiety ate at her constantly, nibbling away until it'd burrowed deep, and tightness clutched her chest.

Almost once a day, Lindiwe called out to him to make sure he was still there, still awake, still... alive.

But there was something else behind the anxiety, a tenderness and yearning that hadn't been present before. The need to hear him constantly, see him more, and be by his side.

If it wasn't for the fact that Lindiwe was charting across the globe to aid Weldir as his hands and feet in a world he couldn't touch, she would have asked him to transport her here so she could have an excuse to be in his realm. Be near him.

It's taken me nearly a month to find this portal, she mused, stepping closer to it confidently. *I've never been to this part of the world.*

Which was surprising, considering how far she'd travelled over her two hundred and thirty-nine years of life. She'd also been in North Unerica for many years and had never travelled to South Unerica.

Releasing the clasp of a special vial, similar to the one she used to collect souls, a tiny, cute puff of shadowy cloud hissed out.

"Thank you," Weldir said as black glittering sand, so small it was almost invisible to the naked eye, surrounded the portal's yellow swirl. *"This is the last one on this continent. You only have one more to travel to."*

Weariness made her eyes heavy, and she wanted to groan, complain, and stamp her feet. She deserved a break. Lindiwe had been travelling the world, helping him lay down his mist, for nearly a whole year.

To say she was tired was an understatement, and there were things she wanted to do.

I haven't seen some of our children in over twenty-five years. Weldir had missed out on so much, but so had she.

"I dislike that you cannot see me," Weldir said, making it known he was right there, but completely invisible.

She offered his cloud a smile with false recognition in her eyes, hoping she was looking in his general direction. "You could take me to your realm for a little while, then I could see you." She turned slightly, so she was facing the portal more. "I know doing this drains what little magic you have, so maybe we could rest for a short while together? You can place me somewhere closer to the next location so I don't have to fly such a distance. You did say it was quite far north."

Greenisland, he'd said it was called.

A decadent chuckle flittered through her mind. *"You're starting to make me think you like being in my realm."*

Her cheeks warmed, and she lifted her gaze to the side. "Maybe a little," she admitted, placing her hands behind her back and interlacing her fingers coyly. "It's my... safe place."

"Safe? You once said you hated being there because you were afraid of being trapped in it."

A sigh slipped past her lips, and she closed her eyes while dipping her head to the right. "Well yeah, I don't really want to be stuck there with nothing to do if you aren't there. I would've gone insane had I died and returned to your realm while you were sleeping." She opened her eyes and shifted them to the general location she believed he was. "But if you're awake, I find it safe. Nothing can hurt me, and you've proven you won't do that to me again."

Hearts could change, they could be healed, and trust could be earned – even when it had been severely damaged.

She felt comfortable enough to sleep there peacefully, while knowing he would be awake the entire time. She was content to read her dozens of journals and spellbooks, or re-familiarise herself with all her personal items.

Heart-stuttering and body-quivering naughty things happened in that darkness. Her thighs clenched when her clit and pussy throbbed in longing.

But intimacy is entirely impossible right now. Because she didn't want his tendrils – she wanted him. His hands, his mouth, his cock, even if he couldn't feel it. She yearned for him to whisper sinful threats, promises, and compliments in her ears while he watched, which made it all the more perverse and erotic.

Her fingertips itched to claw at his back or barriers for more, or to grab his horn or hair and tug hard as she came. And to be kissed... Lindiwe sometimes had to stifle a moan because she missed his lips more than she cared to admit, and the way they made her own swell.

But his physical body hadn't grown in the past year.

He was using every drop of power he gained to spread his mist and barricade these portals. He hadn't even tended to Tenebris or woken Nathair, and only healed and consumed a few dozen souls a day to slowly whittle down the vast number waiting for him.

Lindiwe sighed. *I miss sex.* She'd missed it for the past sixty-three years, and knowing she'd be going without for even longer was making her have perverse thoughts. Especially now that he was back within reach – but bodiless.

At some point, I'm going to give in and masturbate.

When he'd been slumbering, she'd clenched her eyes and moaned his name, as if the way she called to him with desperate, aching need might wake him.

It never did.

"I'm... glad you finally feel that way about being in my presence," Weldir eventually said, his words slow and careful. *"You have always been welcome in my void."*

The heat in Lindiwe's cheeks deepened at her less than pure thoughts.

"I don't think we've placed any children in this part of the world," she said, trying to distract her mind and evade the vulnerability in admitting how she now felt about his realm. "Nor are there any in the next place I'm going. Is that something you are going to want to change soon?"

That had likely been the plan after Fennec was born.

"Is that something you want?" Weldir surprised her by asking.

"I'm more trying to strum up a conversation about your plans for the future."

"We can now, but I would have to use my tendril to do so."

Her smile twitched with strain. "I'd rather not do it that way."

"I'm sorry, owlet, but I cannot–"

Lindiwe threw her hand up with a strained laugh. "It's okay, Weldir. I understand, and I'm happy to wait however long it takes." Then she looked up at the bright sky and let the sun warm her face with a small but genuine smile. "Just know I'm ready whenever you are."

She gasped when she fell backwards as she was sucked into weightless darkness before she was caught in the comforting ether.

Parts of Weldir's face formed, enough to dot an eye, cheek, and the opposing side of his nose and jaw. He shoved his face less than an inch from her own to glare at her.

"This kind of teasing is unfair," he growled, yet it had no edge to it, just a yearning desperation.

Teasing? She was only being honest for once!

Yet knowing his growl was due to the frustration of needing to hold back had her nipples instantly hardening against the material of her dress. She almost wanted to arch into the sound of it, like it was a tangible thing that could erotically caress her all over.

Watching a patch of solidness move across his mouth, she waited for the perfect moment and then lunged forward. She pressed her lips to his when they were fully formed.

"Then hurry up and grow your magic so you can do something about it," she teased.

When she pulled back, her hair waving over the sides of her face, his lips parted, and he appeared dumbfounded by her kiss and playfulness.

"Vexing little female." He drifted away with a tsk, his mist visibly warping in and out. "You taunt me at your own peril."

I'll wait with anticipation for whatever that means, she thought with a mischievous smile.

A time unknown, but of peaceful contentment

With the tip of a blunted claw, Weldir stroked across her cheek and pushed a stray curl behind her little human ear.

Lindiwe's face pinched, her mouth tightening as her closed eyes clenched further, then she burrowed her cheek against her hands. Her soft, barely noticeable snores of sleep quietened and then ceased when his claw tip followed the line of her round ear and down the arch of her neck.

She stretched into it and softly rasped, *"Weldir."*

The satisfaction in that singular word, coming out on a sweet expire, was strong enough to make his mist swirl like a tornado.

He brought his knees up so he could sit cross-legged next to her sleeping form and watch her twitch and her closed lids flicker back and forth from her human dreams. Her cloak completely shielded her while she was curled up in a ball, resting so similarly to how her soul did.

Unashamedly, his gaze perused the becoming features that made up his mate.

The line of her nose, her plump lips parted ever so slightly, her pointed chin, and her sharp jaw. When another curl drifted across her arching brow, he pushed it back as well, and the end cut across her high cheekbone. Her hair was currently being a nuisance as it fluttered all around her in his weightlessness, tickling her and disturbing her rest, but it was as glossy as ever.

She took great pride in maintaining it while within his realm.

He didn't know if she was aware that he watched with rapt interest as she combed silkening oil through her curls to reduce any frizz. The loose, coiling patterns never seemed to be the same, each one unique and charming, and highlighting that her hair wasn't just brunette, but had these varying tones that only enriched her.

Weldir was unsure when he stopped seeing her as just a blob of base features, such as a human face, a woman's body, brown skin, brunette hair, arms and legs. When had each one of those facets deepened in his mind to where he saw the depths of them? At what point did he notice that her hair wasn't just a dark brown? It was also chestnut, cinnamon, and dark copper, among an array of other colours he didn't know how to define.

He did know it had started with her expressive eyes.

The pooling, rich depths of mahogany had begun to feel like they could consume his shadows if he looked long enough. It was only when he'd noticed the flecks of golden amber that more about her slowly came into focus.

Now he couldn't imagine *not* noticing all the unique beauty that made up his mate. But he still didn't know how he'd gotten to where he'd rather stare at her while she slept than do anything else.

She's changed, he thought, taking in the calming, rhythmic pattern of her heartbeat and quiet breaths. *I'm unsure as to why.*

Somewhere in the last sixty-seven years, Lindiwe's demeanour had shifted, and it had been noticeable from the very moment he'd woken up five years ago. She was still his passionate female, all fire and vengeance, all cutting glares and lethal venom. But... the smouldering flames quickly sputtered out with him.

She no longer held onto any anger towards him, and any annoyance was often overshadowed by an odd playfulness and a wry smirk. There were teasing words and jabs that often left him a little puzzled and unsure how to proceed.

When he first woke up and had been able to sense that a very long time had passed, he thought any tentative bond between them would be shattered. He'd broken promises, had essentially abandoned her when she could have needed him, and provided unanswered solitude and isolation.

Somewhere during their separation, things had not worsened, but bettered. How that was possible, he didn't know.

Especially when there was unshed pain that lingered in her gaze, and internal wounds that she'd shared but not unburdened herself with. How an echo of loneliness came from her and often mimicked his in a spiralling parallel.

I like it. These changes, this softness and constant reach for him, left behind a tender sentiment to shiver through the cloud of his shadows. *I'm growing fond of this side of her.*

Their bond was strengthening alongside Weldir's affection for her. And his deep, darkening obsession with her had begun.

If he wasn't with her in this part of his realm, speaking with her through a viewing disc, fixing Tenebris, or consuming souls in a safe way that didn't drag him under, Weldir was in his cave of memories.

Being there annoyed him as much as it transfixed him, living in the moments of her pleasure nostalgically, while furious that he was unable to add to them. Not in the way he – and apparently *she* – desired.

I'm growing stronger. Lifting his right arm, he collected all his solidness to gauge his power levels, and it encompassed his entire right hand to his right elbow. *But this is not enough.*

Not to resume their intimacy – especially as he constantly put off growing his mist now that she'd helped him lay it all across the world again. Fixing Tenebris was taking time, effort, and mana he didn't have to spare, and Nathair still lay asleep within it. All the souls within slumbered, and it made his afterworld dreary and depressing – he now hated being there, when he once enjoyed watching it teeming with life.

Five years wasn't enough to regain what he had built over the course of nearly two human centuries.

The only silver lining was that his well of mana stores, although empty, was deeper. He had more souls within Tenebris, and each one offered him just a speck of power every day to feed him. Those tiny fragments of power, as a collective, as a whole, were likely the only reason he'd survived Nathair's carnage, and why he'd woken up when he had.

Lindiwe has been helping as well.

In between searching for souls for him, she'd come to rest here – freely and comfortably – before spending time with him. They sat together and watched their offspring through viewing discs, as if she hadn't spoken to him the *entire* time she'd wandered the world, noting anything and everything that could be of interest to him, just to share her voice as he offered his own.

Humoured when a curl caught on her long, dark lashes, he brushed that one back as well. Contentment from doing even this simple act vibrated through him.

Especially when she arched like a naughty little female who wanted to be petted, even in sleep.

If only I didn't need to right everything once more first.

He would've given her exactly what she sought.

THIRTY-ONE

November 21st, 1908

I can't take it anymore. Lindiwe mentally groaned, ghosting her hand down her abdomen.

Lying on her side, she peeked open her eyes to check on the smouldering coals of her dying campfire, its light low and its heat faded. Nearby, the lake she'd washed in earlier trickled in the distance, a gentle cascade of nature's music.

The waxing crescent moon offered muted light, but it barely reached her under the shadowy protection ward she'd placed around herself. She was safe, her scent masked under a magical cloak, and she was hidden from unwitting interlopers under the dome and her blanket.

She burrowed further under the thin material until just the top of her head was exposed, then dipped her fingertips into the waistband of her underwear. Doing this out in the open was nerve-wracking, but a woman had to take her opportunities when she could. Especially when she was tired of the ache that constantly pestered her.

This wasn't the first time Lindiwe had sated her lust since Weldir's return, but the longer it went on, the harder it was to resist the temptation.

Especially when she had his deep, body-tingling baritone in her ear constantly, including right before she'd drifted off earlier this night. She always found it harder when she was falling asleep, as twisted, heated images flickered behind her closed eyelids. They bled into her dreams until the hot pulsing thrummed in her nipples, her clit, her very blood.

Times like now, when she woke to find herself panting and needy, she desperately wanted to call out to the one being she desired to take care of it.

But she couldn't yet. *There's still barely anything of him.* What Weldir recuperated, he used almost instantly. That was okay, kind of. She'd done this dozens of times now, both during and after his disappearance.

Lindiwe lifted her leg so she could wedge her hand further within the tight material. When her fingertips touched soaking flesh and her sensitive clit, she shut her thighs and rocked the throbbing bud against them. She let out a soft expire as she moved her fingers side to side in a hard and lazy motion, then bit down on her lips to muffle her noises.

She reached into the low neckline of her dress, accidentally exposing her breast, and kneaded it. She pinched her nipple between two fingers, sending a jolt down her body that coiled in her belly and made her core clench.

I'm so horny. All the fucking time. Her touch-starved body hungered like nothing else. She'd rather have the need to eat than the aching, pestering need to be stretched open by his shadowy girth and pounded into until she lost consciousness.

I want to be bitten, she thought with a whine, remembering the feel of inhuman canine fangs nipping hard and mean. *I want to feel his claws against my skin.* Like little threats that could do so, *so* much damage, and did nothing but send her skin tingling until she was frantic for them to cut deeper.

I want his hands on me, his lips. Gosh, his fucking *lips.* That semi-emotionless man would never know just how much power he had over her when he peppered kisses over her skin. The way they brushed down her neck until she arched it, or made a path that had her thrumming with anticipation when he went lower. And if he went past her breasts, and his tongue, usually coated in her saliva, joined the foray down her stomach, the temptation to shove his head between her thighs was nigh overwhelming.

It's been so long since I've had his cock inside me. His shadowy, hard-to-define, hard-to-see cock. *It fits me perfectly.* It stretched her to the brim, stuffing her until she wanted to go cross-eyed.

Her fingers worked faster, and she shivered when her clit twinged in a way that made her insides quiver and clamp every single time. Her movements became unsettled, the blanket slipping down her heated ear as she tried to press harder so she could repeat the jolt. The second time, so much more powerful, had a stifled moan falling from her.

Rolling her nipple between her fingers, she tried not to arch into it when it felt just right.

Nothing came to disturb her in the middle of the night. Not even a stick cracked in the distance. Just her, her hand, and the sound of trickling water, her pants, and the moans she tried desperately to hold in.

She bit her lips shut when a louder one tried to make its way past them. *Mmm. I'm getting close.* It was slow, lazy, but she didn't mind so long as her toes curled and she broke apart under the covers.

The ground came out from under her.

Without warning, the minuscule light of night was snuffed out by utter darkness. A gasp exploded from Lindiwe as she ripped her hands from her body to right herself from the inertia of falling.

"Hello, little female," Weldir greeted, far too close. His face, which had pulled together almost in its entirety, was only a few inches from hers. "What were you doing?"

"Nothing!" she exclaimed, surprised at being interrupted in the middle of pleasuring herself, rather than wanting to lie about it.

Seeing him did nothing to quell the way her heart had already been racing with need. Instead, it quickened in her veins. The very being she'd been thinking about was right there, and she didn't know if she wanted to jump his weird shadows or expire from embarrassment.

A thin tendril wrapped around her wrist and lifted her hand between them. Her very wet fingers glistened, and the warmth that swelled into her cheeks made her squirm. She had always thought she'd want to be caught, but now that she had been... she couldn't stop the mortification hammering through her.

"This doesn't quite look like nothing."

Lindiwe yanked her hand to hide it, but his tendril stayed firm. Actually, it twisted up her palm and around her fingers to stop her from curling them downwards. When he didn't let go, Lindiwe narrowed her gaze and tried to distract him.

"I don't have my bag, Weldir," she complained.

"I'm... disappointed, Lindiwe," he said, despite his tone not really sounding so. It came across as pouty, more than anything. "If you're going to play with yourself, the least you can do is let me watch. Although I did find your attempts at hiding those little moans of yours rather cute."

Lindiwe wanted to disappear as her ears heated further. Yet his stupid grin, when his expression was usually deadened and unmoving, had her stomach clenching.

"I thought we had established that if you wanted pleasure, you'd tell me," he said, as she felt the slip of material over her left breast.

She looked down to find a second tendril had pulled the neckline of her dress to the side. Now both her tits were out, and she hadn't realised the right one had been free to begin with!

But she didn't feel the frantic desire to cover herself. Knowing they were free, and that Weldir had been the one to expose her further, only made her more aware of them. And of his gaze on her hardened nipples – which had them begging for attention.

"I didn't think it was fair," she whispered, only for her breath to catch when part of his face melted away and his newly formed fingers glided up the inside of her thigh. "I know there isn't much of you right now, and I didn't think watching would be... enough."

Not for her, at least. And if last time was any indication, she didn't think it would be for him, either. It'd be like torturing them both, and he wouldn't even be able to truly feel that suffering like her.

"But there is enough," he rebutted, tracing a claw along the sensitive line that made the muscles in her leg tremble wildly until she parted it more. "And I really have tired of waiting." Something foreign pressed on her clit through her underwear, hard enough to make her thrust into it, as he said, "You can repay me for not letting me watch by letting me take over."

Before Lindiwe could agree – because now that he'd suggested it, she couldn't think of anything better – he slammed his mouth over hers. She instantly melted into the kiss, and her whole body lunged forward to wrap around his. Every limb passed through air, and she cringed in shock before his tongue slipping between her lips distracted her.

Whatever he'd collected of his hand, as it wasn't fully formed, ghosted through her underwear and touched her pussy directly. She shuddered at the contact, messy and uncontrolled as if he couldn't see, yet she didn't care. It was him, it was perfect, and she wanted more.

One of her arms pushed up as a barrier formed, giving her something to claw and anchor herself with, while something strange happened to her other hand. A tendril poked her palm, thickened at the end, and then split into five. It interlocked between her fingers like a hand, and she squeezed it in welcome.

Moaning into the kiss, she hastened her lips, eating at his mouth with quick pecks that deepened each time. His tongue moved in practised movements, soft and pliable but never giving way as it dominated hers. She was glad he couldn't feel, since she pressed so hard in hungry desperation that her lips swelled.

"This needs to go," he whispered against her mouth as her blue underwear was untied and removed.

Despite not being ready to relinquish the kiss, she arched her neck to the side and let out a soft cry when he brushed his lips over her pulse. She spread her thighs, wishing her heels had something to pull on so she could deepen the way he petted her clit.

"Please, Weldir," she pleaded around quick, shallow pants, looking for his face, his horns, and finding nothing – as if only his nose and lips were present. She didn't care about that right now. "I need your fingers inside me."

She was tired of feeling empty. She wanted to be pumped into, to feel whole from within. To be sent into mind-bending bliss so she could forget the long, frustrating wait. She was so damn pent up.

His mouth, wetted by hers, clamped around her nipple. He licked it in a wide and long stroke, while whispering huskily, "I think you want something much bigger."

Her head snapped back, her body arched tightly, and her lips parted on a raspy cry when a thick tendril – girthy, hard, and long – penetrated her deep. The stretch was harsh and sudden, but its evidence, that light pain, was rapture as her soaking pussy clamped and clenched around it in utter delight. Stars dotted her vision in the usually empty ether. They glittered and pulsed when the tendril started pumping right where she needed it to, while his fingers pinched behind her clit and moved in circles.

And with his tongue swirling around her nipple, all three had tears of need welling.

"This is all I can give you right now." His sinful voice layered with arousal was like a naughty stroke along her senses.

"I don't care," she rasped, squeezing the digits of his hand-like tendril while her nails dug into his barrier. "It just feels good to have you inside me again. I don't care what it is."

A quiet growl rumbled all around her, an echo of his satisfaction at her honesty, and the tendril inside her thrust faster. Her eyelids flickered and her jaw fell. He licked over her nipple, and it was a little drier now, a little coarser against the peak.

She arched when his tendril hooked forward right against her G-spot, and she cried out. "Oh fuck. Right there!"

Pushing her hips forward, she wasn't able to make it go harder as it wiggled and pumped, and she became frantic in her attempts. One of her hands remained interlocked with his strange tendril and the other gripped his barrier as she kicked, her hips bucking back and forth. But when she gained no momentum, it made her more desperate.

"I need you to come for me, Lindiwe. I don't think I can maintain this much longer."

He didn't need to tell her that. She was right there, her pussy quivering and spasming, so close to coming. She arched one way, and then back, while her legs closed – unimpeded by an actual physical person.

"Oh god," she moaned, only for Weldir to snap out a snarl at her for doing so. "I'm sorry! I'm *sorry*. Oh g–, oh fuck." Her eyes clenched and her body locked up. "Don't stop. Please don't stop. I'm com–"

For a split second, her heart was going to burst as her next breath caught in her lungs and halted them. Liquid heat flooded her insides as she came around his thick, shadowy tendril. The scream that eventually exploded from her as she shook and trembled was from *years* of pent-up need finally getting an outlet.

She came so unbearably hard, the dam of it so intense, it almost bordered on pain, and she revelled in every second, every twitch, every clench. She undulated, she cried loudly, and she clawed at him any way she could.

When she relaxed, he stopped, and she almost wept.

It wasn't enough. She wanted more; she needed it. She was so twisted up with longing that she wanted to become a satisfied, lewd, twitching mess within his floating realm. "Please don't stop."

"My control on my form is weak. I'm likely to evaporate if we continue."

She wiggled her hips side to side, trying to stir his tendril into moving again as aftershocks continued to pulsate from within. She opened her eyes to look forward, knowing he was watching from somewhere in front of her, and her face pinched with anguish.

She wanted to plead and beg, but knew it was unfair. He was trying, and he'd already made her come despite his limitations, but she'd been waiting for over seventy years for this.

Sometimes living forever had the most frustrating drawbacks.

"That is quite the adorable face, owlet," he said, with the hint of a dark undertone. "If you reward me, then I'll continue. If I evaporate, I'll try to maintain my tendrils for you."

Lindiwe gave him a lopsided smile, her mind a little dazed. "Okay."

The oddest sound came from him. She was unsure if it was a rumble, a growl, or... a groan. "Now *that* face..." he trailed off, leaving his sentence unfinished. He lifted his wet, cum-coated fingers away from her pussy to show her. "I've always been curious about what you taste like. I'd like for you to tell me."

"What?" she whispered softly.

"Open those pretty lips of yours."

Oh god, no. She stared at the evidence of her orgasm coating his fingers, and the urge to open her mouth absolutely did *not* come to her. She only complied because it was a small sacrifice if it meant more pleasure.

Weldir slowly slipped his fingers between her parted lips. She winced but willingly sucked on them, and the points of his claws dragging across her tongue was the strangest, yet most erotic experience. He pulled them away so she could speak.

"Kind of... tangy?" Despite her aversion to the taste, she found herself licking her lips. Not for more, but because it felt... naughty to have her own cum on her tongue.

A deep chuckle filled her ears, and her shoulders turned inwards self-consciously.

"I'm now realising that was a rather foolish request. I have no idea what tangy – or even sweet and spicy – tastes like."

Her shoulders eased, and she laughed in return.

"But you have done as I asked." His fingers disappeared, and his head came forward so she could see that over two-thirds of his face was visible. "It will be easier if I just use a tendril. I should be able to maintain that."

To demonstrate, he pumped it just once, and she spread her thighs for it. His face disappeared, and she tried to see where it went.

Her whole body cascaded with prickling goosebumps when it made its location known, behind her ear.

"But I won't be giving you my essence this time, owlet. The only result from this will be pleasure." His tendril started to move, slower but harder, deeper, and she perceived every undulating inch within her. "And if I catch you again fucking this cute hole of yours, know that you risk coming to my realm. No matter where you are, or what you have planned, I will bring you here, and I will do as I please with you."

Lindiwe's heart fluttered as the weight of his threat hung over her. It'd be like the most perverse game of hide-and-seek, except she'd be hiding that she was touching her pussy without him, and he'd be waiting to catch her at it.

That only taunted her.

She'd probably end up doing it more.

Lindiwe would also be a poor player, no doubt wanting to be caught, but still competitive enough to try and evade him. But no matter whether she won or lost, both would result in an orgasm.

Which was a wonderful conundrum.

THIRTY-TWO

Staring out over the horizon of Tenebris, Weldir was satisfied with the state of his realm.

It had taken numerous years with his low, easily diminished mana stores, but it was finally as glorious as it had once been. *This took too long. What year did Lindiwe say it is? Nineteen-seventeen?* That meant it'd been eighteen years since he'd woken.

The process had taken longer due to the number of newly consumed souls without homes, all of whom had just been floating around in an unconscious state. New towns, new structures, and new terrain had been formed, which delayed this tranquil view.

His mist's reach on Earth was nowhere near what it had once been. He'd barely made a dent in it, in that regard.

Sitting on the flat area right outside his cave of memories, he could just see the edge of a small lake. *Nathair is doing well, despite his changes.* Weldir had released the spell on him a few years ago, uncomfortable with the idea of having his offspring in a prolonged sleep state.

He'd also missed the serpent Mavka's antics, his humour, and good-natured fun. But it hadn't been a pleasant greeting.

I originally put him to sleep so he couldn't consume more

souls and weaken me when I was already feeble, but... Weldir sighed as he pulled his gaze away from the sobering direction to look at the curved horizon. *I didn't know his mind had been corrupted.*

Human memories plagued and tortured him. *It was too long.* Nathair had been living with those human soul fragments for too many years, and they'd shattered bit by bit, leaving behind pieces he just could not remove, no matter how he tried.

Had I stopped him... had I healed him before they burrowed so deeply, I could have extracted them all. Weldir's absence had done far more damage than he'd realised, and both his mate and offspring had borne the burden of that.

There was little he could do to change the past. He just tried to help his offspring adjust and deal with the intense slips of lucidity. Currently, Weldir knew he lay awake but dazed, his body contorted, as his orbs shifted colour depending on the context of the fragment that had yanked him under.

I'd hoped to converse with him now, since his humanity has increased exponentially. But Nathair had lost his voice, and when Weldir looked at the shards of glitter, they were the worst around his skull, throat, and chest. All locations that were close to that big maw of his.

Hopefully this is only temporary. If not, they'd have to figure out a new way to communicate. *Humans have sign languages that vary from culture and country.*

Just as he mused on how and where to start, a voice called out to him. One that was familiar but had never uttered his name.

A flick of his mind brought up a scrying disc, although limited in its view from outside a ward of magic, and a bear-skulled Mavka stood within it. His strong, meaty arms were folded across his muscular chest, and he tapped a semi-humanoid, pawed foot on the ground. His red orbs were crimson, and a little darker than their normal hue.

Merikh had the hide to look disgruntled when *he* called out to Weldir.

He stood inside his red protection ward, wearing a set of black knee-high breeches. A simple, sleeveless brown garment covered his chest and was tied in a way to avoid his back quills.

With another flick of his mind, another disc formed of his mate. Crouched within a river, she was searching for nuggets of gold again, so he could reshape them into the coins she wanted for use as money. It was a rather ingenious idea of hers, and one she'd discovered over a century ago.

She had a funny aversion to stealing from humans.

"Lindiwe," Weldir called.

"Yes, Weldir?" she answered without missing a beat, pulling a small pebble from the water. She cleaned it of sediment, found a white stone, and then tossed it behind her.

"Merikh has called out to me."

Her head perked up at that, making one of her double braids slip over her shoulder. "What? Why?"

"I have yet to find out." He looked between the two discs, then let his eyes linger on Merikh. "Do you wish to be there when I speak with him?"

Her head lifted to the opposite riverbank, and her lips pursed in thought. Her gaze fell, and there was deep, unshakable, and dispirited pain in her eyes.

"No," she answered in a small voice. "I think it's best if I don't." She shoved both her hands into the water and began turning over the riverbed's sediment. "I'll only make matters worse. It's obvious he hates me, so if there's a potential for you to form a relationship with him, I don't want to be a hindrance by being there."

She has stepped away from all our offspring. Lindiwe wasn't as involved as she once had been.

None of them liked her presence, and she'd worked out that it had something to do with her magic. Her scent-cloaking spell, the one that protected her from being hunted, was the one they disliked the most.

But he thought it was deeper than that.

She'd been with them through every beginning stage of their

lives and pestered them when they wanted to be left alone. She had good intentions. Without her teaching them, they wouldn't be as knowledgeable about the world or able to have coherent conversations.

But it'd annoyed them.

Lindiwe had also learned that in the twenty-five years she couldn't travel due to missing her arm, they didn't actually need her. He'd seen the deflated way her shoulders had fallen, the dejected anguish in her gaze, how she'd looked off into his void as she'd spoken about it.

It'd been a while since she'd visited any of them, and she focused all her time on wandering the world in search of untainted souls for him.

That, and playing their fun little game where her hand went diving into naughty places and he tried catching her doing so.

"Weldir!" Merikh *growled* it this time, his arms tightening across his broad chest. "Fucking Jabez. He told me saying your name would fucking bring you here. Now I just feel like a dickhead shouting into the Veil."

"As you wish," he said to her, before pulling himself from his realm and into his mist within the Veil. "You called?" Weldir greeted, causing his offspring to halt his retreat.

Merikh drifted his bear skull to the side to look over his shoulder. "So it does work?"

"Indeed. A deity's true name is a link to their conscience. It's why we don't often share it with mortals." It's why his mother was known as the Gilded Maiden, otherwise she'd be pestered by thousands of Elysian Elves.

Merikh turned around and drifted his scarred snout one way and then the other. The claw marks across his snout were likely due to the altercation he'd had with Jabez years ago when their friendship had ended abruptly, and probably violently.

"Where are you?" Merikh asked, once more folding his arms in a way that could only be described as defensive. "I refuse to talk to the air."

"I'm on the other side of your ward. I'm incapable of being

seen or interacting with this world. This is all you will get."

That wasn't true, but complicating it by consuming a soul to the point of destruction was unwarranted.

"I wanted to speak with you, learn who my father creator is. See what you look like, sound like, what your realm looks like and why you hide in it constantly."

"Hiding is a strong word, and wildly inaccurate. There is little reason for me to be present on Earth when there is nothing I can do on it. I cannot even shake the tree behind me or enter your territory through your ward. I am limited to my mist and where it can reach. What point is there in attempting to interact with a world that can do little more than hear me?"

"Fair enough. I was told your power was limited. Does this mean it's impossible for me to go to your realm?"

"No," Weldir stated honestly, but...

In order for me to do that, I will have to create a portal. Weldir already knew he couldn't pull his offspring to him like he could Lindiwe. He looked down at his hands and collected the physical parts of him to them until both formed – and nothing more. *Can I handle such a thing right now?*

He closed them and brought his attention back to Merikh. *This may be my only opportunity to heal some of the broken bond between him and Lindiwe.* By giving him what he sought, would that soften Merikh's ire towards them?

"Then take me there. I want to know what is within your so-called void."

"It's not that simple. I can take you to the outer edge of my realm, but if it's Tenebris itself you seek, I will have to consume you, and it could kill you. You may become stuck there."

"So you have no idea? What if you don't kill me?"

"That is a possibility, but are you sure you would want to risk that?"

Merikh tilted his head and grunted, cupping the end of his snout as his chest expanded and decompressed on measured breaths. "Would you be able to remove me if it appears you are about to consume me?"

"I can try, that is all." *Perhaps I can pull him from me if he's at risk of completely transcending to the afterworld.*

Merikh shrugged, then loosened his folded arms and rested his hands on his narrow hips. "I have very little fear of dying, and I want to see where my creator comes from. Where I am from, in the most abstract sense."

"You've surprised me, Merikh," Weldir freely admitted.

"One thing I've learned at Jabez's side is that knowledge is power, as much as is fear." His tail swished, and the tuft of black fur at the end fluttered through a sunbeam. "I want answers, and those answers may help my endeavours."

"And what endeavours are those?"

Merikh's orbs reddened at Weldir's prying, and his silence told him he'd learn nothing of his offspring's goal.

"If this is really what you request, then I'll have to confer with Lindiwe before agreeing."

Merikh parted his fangs and snapped at the air irritably. "What does she have to do with this?"

"I will return shortly." Weldir retreated to his realm so he could speak privately with his mate. "Merikh has requested that he be brought to my realm."

He conjured up her viewing disc as he spoke and found her kneeling next to the riverbed with small chunks of mud-covered gold. While she cleaned them in the water, her lips pulled tight. "If that's what he wants. But can you do it?"

"Yes, however..." Weldir paused, hesitant about his next words. "It would require the use of a portal, or two."

She stopped and lifted her head. "But that would mean..."

"Yes. It is likely I will have to sleep in order to regain what I have lost. I know I don't have much power to spare, but this has the potential to open an avenue for you."

She brought her hands together to fiddle with the nugget she'd been cleaning and looked down at it. With her hair tied back, it allowed him to watch anxiety cut across her features.

"What if you don't come back for a long time again... or at all?" she murmured quietly.

"I can block Nathair from going beyond a border I set, and this would only be temporary. I'll attempt to lessen the damage so as to not be absent for too long. Possibly a few months."

"You said that last time."

"I don't have to do this," he offered.

Her thumbnail picked at a particularly sharp ridge. "No. Do it. Thank you for asking me, but you're right."

He returned to Merikh and then tried something new. *I know my mana and mist cannot pass through their wards...* But could *he*? To test this, he floated forward and unexpectedly passed through Merikh's dome. *So it's only my mana?* What he was now was a fragment and a projection of his soul.

"Lindiwe is now aware."

Merikh grunted at his voice and how it had gone from in front of him to his side. He leaned forward, as if the proximity might help him see Weldir, which it wouldn't.

Weldir opened his mouth and shoved his hand and then arm into it until he knew his fist was within Tenebris. He called a soul at random to his fingers and pulled until it passed through his fangs.

Merikh's orbs morphed from red to dark yellow, and he tilted his head at it floating above Weldir's hand.

Surprised, he asked, "You can see it?"

"Yes," Merikh responded gruffly. "Why is it white?"

"All souls that are deceased are white. They lack their normal, healthy colouring, completely sapped of life."

Using his thumb claws, Weldir tore it in two and called a portal to form out of the chaotic energy that burst to life. He then quickly ushered Merikh through.

The moment he joined the bear-skulled Mavka in his darkness, he decided to close it. Keeping a portal open drained his mana fast, and he'd prefer to safely calculate the loss of two souls, rather than the potential unknown of Merikh's time here with just one.

"This is your realm?" he asked, waving his arms and kicking his legs in the unfamiliar weightlessness. "It's empty."

"It is."

Merikh stopped moving and looked directly at him now that he could be seen. The dark yellow in his orbs deepened, and he drifted his snout down and then back up.

"You really are a being of shadows."

Weldir opened his arms and shrugged.

"I am what I am." He shrank Merikh, whose head reared back at Weldir growing. "I cannot touch your physical body, but I can touch your soul. Like I said, I will have to swallow you."

Merikh belted out a yell when Weldir picked his soul up by the nape of his neck and lifted him.

"Wait, fuck." He pushed at the air in panic. "Won't that hurt? I'm covered in fucking quills!"

"I don't feel pain."

Opening his maw, although doubtful that Merikh could tell with how little there was to truly see of him, he placed his most aggravating and arrogant offspring upon his tongue. He swallowed him whole, and the Mavka roared the whole way down.

Once Merikh was past the point of no return and had fallen into the vast space of his stomach, Weldir yanked on their soul tethers. He came to Merikh's side as he fell, legs kicking as the ground rushed closer. Weldir observed his body to make sure his life force wasn't being eaten at the same time.

He'd made sure he had a good hold of Merikh's soul tether in preparation, but there was no need.

"Shit!" Merikh shouted, before he stopped mid-fall barely a few centimetres from the ground. Weldir softly let him down, and Merikh bounced to his feet and spun around until he found him. With claws at the ready, he swiped to grab Weldir's throat while shouting, "You gave me no warning!"

He grabbed air, then looked down at his palm. Then he swiped the claws of both hands through Weldir and his mist, and his growls grew infuriated.

Weldir watched with abject boredom, waiting for him to get whatever fury out of his system.

Something became apparent when Merikh tried to strike at his face. Weldir threw up his arm so Merikh would stop. He shifted closer to his hand and noticed tiny pinpricks of red had formed at the ends of his claws.

"You're dying," he stated. "It's slow, but I'm consuming your soul. You're transcending over to my afterworld."

Merikh looked at his claw tips. "It's red?"

"Yes. Your orb colour reflects your soul, and it encompasses your entire body."

This brought on a list of questions. *Is it him or the size of his soul that is slowing the process? Does that mean I can bring Lindiwe here?* He'd like her to see Tenebris.

No. I don't want to risk completely killing her, as she's human.

"How long will it take?" Merikh huffed out.

"I'm unsure."

"This is your realm?" Merikh lowered his hands to look around. "It still looks so dark and haunted."

"Haunted?" Weldir surveyed their surroundings, and the bright sunshine that cascaded over everything. "What is it you see?"

"White mist and low light, like we're in a spooky, cold forest."

"Hmm. Interesting. It appears you can't see Tenebris at its full capability, as you aren't dead. It's actually a world that would reflect Earth, if it were perpetually day all the time and remained untouched by Demons."

Merikh grunted. "You tried to create a haven? Of *death*?" He dropped his head to the side with a sigh. "That is all I wanted to know, and I'd rather leave before I'm permanently stuck here."

Weldir considered telling him that his sibling was here, but he knew the answer almost immediately. *Nathair cannot respond right now, and I don't think it will do Merikh any favours to learn that he's technically alive here, and suffering.*

That could deepen his guilt and loathing.

One day he will learn of it, but not now.

"This time, should I give you warning?" Weldir stated with the mildest hint of humour.

Merikh refused to pull his sight from the world. "Actually, before I go, I have one final question." His fingers twitched, and then he rubbed the pad of his thumb against his claw tips. "How does a Mavka die? What is our weakness?"

"Depends on what you wish to do with that information," Weldir answered plainly.

Merikh tilted his head to the side, but didn't stop pointing his snout towards the horizon.

"I understand now why she didn't tell me. I likely would have told Jabez, and he would've used that information against Orpheus, or even myself." His orbs flickered with blue, and he grunted before they flared with red in a rather unnatural way, as if he focused on the stabilisation of his emotions. "I deserve to know. The feline-skulled Mavka has grown interested in my presence, and it annoys me. He's so fucking curious, and he will not let me be, and I am..." Merikh regarded his deadly claws again, his fingers shaking, before curling them into fists. "I'm angry. All the time. I don't want to be the reason another of our kind dies."

His orbs morphed to orange, and they held that colour. Actually, they deepened the longer they were here.

"Your skulls aren't as indestructible as you believe," Weldir eventually answered. "It may take overwhelming strength, perhaps only that of another Mavka, but if broken... that is the end."

His voice was small, low, and it didn't match his usually boisterous and confident personality when he asked, "He's here, isn't he?"

"Yes."

Merikh grunted and turned to him. "I'm done. Take me back to Earth."

"You don't wish to see him?" Weldir asked, truly curious.

His orbs flickered between blue and orange, highlighting the way guilt and sadness warred inside him. "No."

Weldir didn't try to convince him otherwise, nor press him further as to why. He took his offspring from Tenebris as he'd asked.

I was right not to tell him of Nathair's condition. If this was how Merikh felt — that he *could* have empathy for his own siblings — then knowing that Nathair was suffering would only deepen his hurt.

It's not his fault. They didn't know.

THIRTY-THREE

A time unknown, but of adapting

Heavy, laboured breathing filled Weldir's ears as he coalesced his physical self into his hands so he could present them.

He positioned his left palm flat but facing up and then placed his index, middle, and fourth fingers of his right hand in the middle of the left to sign 'M' at Nathair. His offspring mimicked it, and Weldir removed his fourth finger to create the letter 'N.' Then they continued onto 'O,' Weldir dipping into the memory of a soul that knew sign language to relay the next letter of the alphabet.

Austrális sign language was what Weldir had decided to base his teachings on, and then they had both agreed to create their own language that could incorporate Nathair's orb colours. He didn't have flesh upon his bony face to make expressions, so most signs weren't possible to their full extent.

He wanted Nathair to decide what each gesture signified, and to structure his own sentences. He believed this would give him a sense of control over his communication abilities.

But if we create a structured base from one culture's alphabet, it'll make the process easier. They could begin communicating by finger spelling, and Nathair could see how to formulate gestures from an example.

Once they were done, Weldir showed him how to finger spell

his own name.

He took two fingers from his right hand and pressed them against his left palm for 'N'. Then his right index finger touched the tip of his left thumb: 'A'. His right index poking the side of his palm right below his left pinkie signified 'T'. All four fingers of his right hand brushed from the centre of his left palm up to his fingertips to sign 'H'. His right index finger touched the tip of his left thumb again: 'A'. Then his right index touched the tip of his left middle finger for 'I'. Hooking his right index finger until it almost made a semi-circle, he pressed it against his left palm to indicate 'R'.

"N-A-T-H-A-I-R," the serpent Mavka copied, before pointing to his chest to signal himself with bright-yellow orbs of joy.

"Yes. That's your name."

Then Weldir started a different word.

With his hands steepled, he interlocked all his straightened fingers together except his thumbs: 'W'. Then his right index finger touched the tip of his left middle finger for 'E'. His right index finger pressed against the centre of his left palm to sign 'L'. He made a backwards 'c' shape with his right thumb and index finger and pressed the tips against the length of his left index finger, indicating 'D'. His right index touched the tip of his left middle finger for 'I'. Finally he hooked his right index finger until it almost made a 'u' shape and pressed it against his left palm to spell 'R'.

"W-E-L-D-I-R," Nathair mimicked, his orbs brightening.

His offspring moved his right fist in a knocking motion to signal 'yes' that he was happy. 'Yes' and 'no' were the first things Weldir had taught him. It gave them the most basic way to communicate, and not utilising a nod or a shake of his head meant Weldir couldn't accidentally misunderstand him.

Pride radiated through his mist as he watched Nathair repeat the alphabet seamlessly, as if he hadn't just been taught for the first time. It revealed the depth of his intelligence, his memory, and that Weldir had been right; all the souls he'd consumed had increased his humanity tenfold.

"H-E-L-L-O," Nathair finger spelled.

Weldir waved at him in return, as that was a common way to greet a person in any language and culture – and even how the Elvish did it. Nathair grumbled and waved back, and likely committed it to memory.

Mischievous humour made Weldir's mist shimmer with vibrations. "I can teach you how to say 'fuck you' as well if you like."

Nathair knocked his right fist in the air.

Weldir lifted his middle finger while keeping the rest of his fingers down. A chuckle left him when Nathair not only mimicked him, but shoved his big hand through his misty head. Nathair answered with his own throaty, chesty chuckle – which sounded different to the laughter that used to radiate from his mind.

Then Nathair groaned as his orbs flickered white, and he shuddered deeply. He lifted both hands around the sides of his serpent skull but didn't grab it, as there was a chance he'd try to crush it by accident.

Which would kill him – forever. Had Nathair's body not locked up into a seizure while Weldir was forced into a catatonic state, his offspring could have torn at his own soul and destroyed himself entirely. A slip of luck, all things considered.

Weldir watched his offspring struggle to keep a human memory at bay and listened to how his heavy breathing grew more laboured. He said nothing, made no note of it, nor did he bring attention to it when Nathair managed to pull it back with his shoulders drooping.

Weldir didn't even ask if he was okay, as that annoyed him.

Nathair's orbs flashed an embarrassed reddish pink, and he tipped his face away slightly to hide it.

He didn't need a voice to tell Weldir how much he hated this, and hated how he'd done this to himself. It was obvious in his body language, and he had *a lot* of body.

"Weldir," Lindiwe's voice practically growled.

I find it rather cute when she does that. She tried to show she was mean and scary, and it merely tickled his humour.

"Yes, Lindiwe?"

Nathair was used to him answering her in his presence.

"I just watched Jabez take Orpheus' offering and fucking run off with her into the Veil," Lindiwe said, and when he brought up a viewing disc of her, the image of her looking at her own much smaller version became apparent.

A small offspring with a maned-wolf skull rested in her lap and used her dress as a hammock while they napped. They'd been with her for quite some time, and it was the first they were intending to place in South Unerica. Weldir had finally expressed his desire to begin this venture once more, and Lindiwe had accepted immediately.

It gave him the impression that she'd missed it.

"I believe you said you wouldn't interfere."

"I know what I said." She stuck out her bottom lip. "But I *warned* them years ago, and you'd think after I destroyed his last castle, they'd take the hint and stop. I don't know how he's getting through the salt circle. He can't when Orpheus is there."

"Didn't you say that the offending person has to have hostile intentions? If Jabez has figured that out, and he means no harm to the human directly when passing through, then..."

"Conniving bastard."

Weldir made sure she couldn't hear his chuckle. *I like it when she's all twisted up like this.* Of course, only when it wasn't directed at him.

"You're in another part of the world, and I've told you that I don't wish for you to engage him again."

He was still furious she'd lost an *arm* – no matter that it was temporary in the end. No amount of harm to her was worth Jabez's demise, no matter how she, or he, wished it for the safety and security of their offspring.

"I'm sure I can think of something where I don't actually need to fight him."

"So long as he doesn't harm you, you may do as you wish."

Her beautiful face pulled into a tight expression, and her eyes narrowed at the small disc, no larger than a handheld mirror that floated between both her hands. She lifted her gaze away from it to watch the frothing waves crash upon the sandy shore before her. The horizon was nothing but ocean.

A serpent skull slid in beside him to watch Lindiwe silently. He pointed to the water.

"S-P-E-L-L?"

"You want me to spell the word ocean?"

Nathair gestured yes, and Weldir complied. Then his offspring made a wave motion with his left hand in a backwards direction. *I see. I'll have to teach him how to spell a word, and then he will have to come up with the corresponding word sign.* That complicated things, and would make this journey longer, but so be it. They had ample time, and Weldir was willing to be dedicated to this task; he would spend every moment he could with Nathair until they completed it.

He spelled Lindiwe's name, so Nathair could do so with his fingers. Once more, his orbs brightened to yellow.

"Weldir..." she started, her glare strengthening at the waves. "How... strong are you right now?"

"Decently so. I haven't spread my mist for quite some time to recuperate my mana store, just in case."

He wanted to keep their options open should he or she need his strength *without* him being forced to slumber.

He'd kept his promise last time and had only been missing for three months. It'd been seven years since then – at least, from what Lindiwe had told him. It was now nineteen twenty-four, she'd said.

Then again, it could've been a week to a year ago since she'd told him, as his concept of time was skewed. It didn't help that if she moved around the world too quickly, he'd lose track of the seasons, as Earth's hemispheres had opposite rotations. If it was winter in the north, it was summer in the south, and she could often experience the same season twice in a year.

Her shoulders lifted sheepishly while she brought her chin

in, and a rather malicious grin curled her lips. It was an unusually evil expression on her sweet face.

"Would you be willing to use a soul for me?"

Taken aback by her request, he was unsure if he had enough power to maintain such a debilitating usage of it. "Why?"

"What if I enter his castle, place a ward around the room they're in, and you open a portal from within the ocean into it? I wouldn't have to fight if we did that, and then I can just drown them both. Two birds, one big gulp of water."

Weldir offered silence. What could he say?

That does sound like a suitable and rather ingenious plan, despite how that will impact me.

A question arose, though.

"Wouldn't you be trapped in the room with them? You cannot turn into a Phantom and wield my mana at the same time. You must be physical for it to remain."

She fiddled with her fingers. "I'm not afraid of drowning, when it'll just bring me to you."

Weldir allowed a curt growl to push through their bond.

"Oh, come on! Technically I'd be doing it to myself, and it's not like I would be *dead* dead."

"And what if Jabez survives beyond you? He is an *Elf*, Lindiwe. His lungs are bigger and stronger than yours."

"His doors open inwards, so the water would lock them in, and if I did it in the middle of the day, his only escape would be out the window and into the sun."

"What about Valko?" he asked, reminding her of their current maned-wolf offspring's infant state.

"I can just leave them with you."

That perked Weldir's interest, as it was rare he was able to interact with his own offspring after the night of their birthing. Still...

"I don't like this."

"Please?" She fluttered her long, pretty eyelashes and pushed her bottom lip forward a little.

Something became startlingly apparent to Weldir in that

moment. He was undeniably weak to this human female, and unfathomably smitten with her at the same time.

Two very tender things that could spell disaster for him.

Weldir sighed. "Fine."

It's not like she'll die permanently.

And he was excited to see her, as it'd been quite some time.

Or had it only been a few days? The time apart from each other was beginning to become intolerable, especially when they'd begun to spend much of it together.

I think... something is wrong with me. Was it normal to be this obsessed with his own mate, constantly captivated by her, and longing to be near her? *Our intimacy is ruining my mind.* He'd been spending too much time in his cave of memories. He also hadn't added enough to it.

He looked down at the fifth of him he'd managed to gain, knowing he was about to lose it once more.

I've been hoping to fuck her properly at some point. Not just with his hands and tendrils, but with his cock. Like before, where she'd cling, moan, and scratch at him while he pounded into her. It was much easier to break his mate until she was a malleable puddle for him. *I very much miss doing that.*

So be it. A little longer I will have to wait, then.

Which was a fucking shame.

THIRTY-FOUR

August 24ᵗʰ, 1933

Wiggling her fingers while crouched on a tree branch, Lindiwe leaned to the right and then left, following the progress of an anaconda on the forest floor as it prepared to strike an unsuspecting critter. The prey it was after was partially hidden behind the leaves of a tall shrub.

Just as the anaconda parted its segmented jaw slightly, Lindiwe lunged from above. Its big head thunked against the dirt and squirmed below her. Its long, lengthy body looped one way and then the other, while its tail flicked fallen leaves around with a loud rustle as it tried to get away.

Once she straddled it safely, a shadowy dagger formed in her right hand, and she lanced it vertically behind its skull. It squirmed for a little longer before contorting tightly, and then... went languid.

The instant she evaporated the blade, blood welled around the wound. She released her scent-masking spell, and the child clinging to her chest lunged.

Their jaguar fangs were sharp and strong as they bit into the back of the anaconda's neck. Their white feline skull caught a small patch of sunlight peeking through the maze of twisting canopy above. It glistened across smooth bones before scarlet covered the young Duskwalker's snout as they feasted.

Their newest child wasn't even halfway done before their cute little legs began to fuse together. The further they ate down its tail, the more their legs became one until they grew their own.

Ha! I knew that would work.

Despite this child having a jaguar skull, she'd purposefully not fed them any more of the large forest cat native to Zazil, a country within South Unerica. She'd wanted to see if she could make them semi-serpent if she fed them a snake, and she was pleased she was correct.

That just leaves your horns, she thought, dusting her hands, then became incorporeal to ensure they didn't turn on her. *I feel a little bad that I'll have to take the nearest city's cattle.*

Other than the rare wild deer that had survived the Demons, Zebu cows were easier to find, and the city had quite a few of them to help feed their people. Another breed of cattle was what she'd given to Valko, the maned-wolf-skulled Duskwalker.

Lindiwe winced at her mistake. *Maybe I should have found Balam a smaller snake?* They were quite large, and she was sure that'd mean they were heavy.

Balam pushed up with their little humanoid arms and sniffed at the air. Their head dipped a little, their neck unable to support it fully.

When they slowly wandered off with a sooky little hissing wail, Lindiwe turned corporeal for them. They immediately slithered over and climbed her legs with malleable claws, grabbing onto the bottom of her skirt.

She picked them up and then helped them curl their tail around her torso to teach them they could do it. When it registered, they held on tight and buried their snout into her bosom. They rubbed against her to cover themselves in her scent, like usual.

"Ugh. I was right. You're heavy now," she said with a groan.

It was unusual for her to have to cock her hip to hold them, but they had to be the size of a human one-year-old, despite only being about three months old. And that was only counting to halfway down their tapering tail.

"I wonder if I'll still be able to fly with you."

"Walking through that forest will be dangerous," Weldir said, his rich voice distant as always when he spoke to her through their bond.

"Eh." Lindiwe shrugged and then headed in the direction of the city – she hoped. "It may be teeming with Demons, but they hunt me at their own peril."

Still, Weldir had a good point.

Deciding it was safer, Lindiwe switched back to her Phantom form. Not because of the Demons, but due to the number of poisonous frogs, and venomous spiders and snakes. She was more afraid of *them* than any nightmarish void-fleshed monsters lurking.

And I thought Austrális was bad.

"It's been a while since I went to my homeland," Lindiwe murmured, looking around at the shaded forest.

"Do you want to return there for a little while?"

"No. I was just comparing the deadliness of the fauna between the two. I'm going to collect more souls for you in North Unerica, and then you mentioned you wanted one more child here, and one around Pyrssia, the Sing Empire, and near Siran. We only have one in each of those locations, and the Demons' numbers have been growing there."

"As well as Greenisland, as we have none there thus far."

"There too. A-and Austrális? I'd like one more there, just in case."

A sort of giddiness ran through her, revealing that Lindiwe's mind had grown... perverted. More children meant more intimacy between all the touching that was already happening.

She was learning that when she was comfortable and her desire welcomed, she could be quite the tease. It seemed to be having a weird impact on the shadowy demi-god.

Gosh, I miss actual sex, though. Weldir was still expanding his mist's reach, and although he'd covered many great distances, it wasn't the same as it once was.

She hated this slow progression. She wanted it, and she wanted it fucking *now.*

Well, at least I'm getting plenty of orgasms, she thought. *But I don't like how weird my mind and body are getting about having babies now.*

The thought of having one, knowing that something of Weldir's was growing inside her, was making her have heart-panicking lewd thoughts. She didn't like that it was beginning to turn her on, and she often felt the need to scrub her mind of unclean, impure, depraved thoughts.

It also brought on a deep sense of fear.

One that sat in the forefront of her mind constantly and was one of the reasons that she was trying to avoid being in his realm and presence as much as possible. Which was difficult, considering she was horny a lot – probably a healthy amount – and he kept catching her masturbating when she was trying really, *really* fucking hard not to be caught anymore.

Weldir had, unwittingly, offered her a freedom she hadn't had before: sexual control over her own heart, mind, and body. She'd never realised how much she needed that, or how it would also end up leading to all this.

My heart keeps hurting whenever I look at him. Or talk to him. Or think about him. Or anything involving Weldir, really.

And it wasn't a cute little tender pang, either.

It was a horrible, heart-wrenching clutch that was so strong, it was tearing the tendons holding it in place. It caused a nauseous pit in her stomach that made it hard to swallow or breathe. The more they touched, the agony of it worsened.

I think... I'm– She shook her head. *No. Don't even think it.*

She doubted he'd be capable of truly returning that affection, and... even if Weldir *could* experience love in the same way he could perceive desire, there was a glaring issue. One that would always be present. One that would not change. One that made her heart hurt so bad she wanted to cut it out of her chest cavity with the very shadows she wielded.

They couldn't be together.

He's stuck in that world. Yes, she could visit him, but it wasn't *real.*

He couldn't be in the mortal, living world with her. He couldn't breathe air with her, couldn't touch the wilting petals of autumn, feel the sun, or... the warmth of her skin. Their relationship would be a falsity that continued on, and on, and would for as long as her soul belonged to him.

And that was so saddening that on the odd occasion, she found tears forming over it. Too many times she had to swallow the lump in her throat, push down all this tender affection, and smile.

Lindiwe no longer believed he was just 'pretending' in order to make her content. That he was, unmaliciously, playing the part of a supportive husband. She could no longer deny his care, consideration, and... kindness. It was always there. *He* made himself available in any and every way possible – sexually, emotionally, and even mentally.

He may have disappeared for many years, but he had tried to support her through many of her personal trials. Sure, in the beginning he'd failed often, and had been accidentally callous, but now? Now Weldir could almost be sweet, on top of the fact that he'd always been patient, and he tried his hardest to compromise.

He showed interest in everything she did, as well as in their children and their progress.

He wanted her near, always. She'd denied that for a long while, but it was apparent that he preferred her in close proximity.

I wish this wasn't happening. She had been growing fonder of Weldir to this point. Of a literal entity of mist, shadows, and a dark void. One who could not truly leave his realm. She couldn't even *see* him when he did, even if he was standing right before her.

I don't want to stop being intimate. A woman had needs, and she deserved to have them met. *But I can't fall in love with Weldir.*

Love had to be an impossibility, when their realities would never meet and become one. It would be utterly pointless otherwise, and only ever painful.

So when did her lust get away from her to allow this foolishness? She'd known from the very start that she couldn't allow it, so why did she? Or was it Weldir who reached his ghostly hands into her chest to pull on her heartstrings, just like her soul?

I need to figure out a way to stop it.

Lindiwe didn't want to go back to hating him, but she couldn't swing entirely in the opposite direction either. She needed to barricade her heart from him. Lock it so tightly behind a protective, impenetrable cage that he couldn't pry the door open.

Lindiwe worried what would happen to her otherwise.

THIRTY-FIVE

May 15th, 1972

Lindiwe had tried; she really did.

She'd tried not to let the festering, growing infatuation turn into full-blown yearning. With human nails and teeth, she'd fought like a rabid, injured creature desperate for self-preservation, striking at the adoration in fear of more harm. She'd hidden it behind false laughs, weak smiles, and light conversation, pretending the pit in her chest wasn't yawning wider with each passing year.

It'd been a losing battle.

So much had happened in the thirty-nine years since Balam was born. Three more children had been born, as promised, within Greenisland, Peryu, and in Turkcul. She'd collected too many souls, each one proving that humankind was slowly dying as towns and cities were decimated to leave behind ruins.

She'd even witnessed the downfall of her own home; the place a little piece of her heart had always remained. It'd stood proud and strong for nearly three centuries, but Rivenspire had met its end. And Leonidas, who had been called by the warning bell, had arrived at the end of the Demons' carnage just as daylight was greeting the horizon.

She'd collected knowledge where she could, filled in her journals until she had a nearly complete encyclopedia of the world, its flora, and its fauna – many of which were now extinct.

The years had passed by in a rush, and she'd flown over much of it in her owl form. When the trickle of time had sped up for her, she didn't know. When had she started feeling outside of it? Somewhere along the way, she'd lost much of her humanity and had done things she never thought she was capable of. The way she'd grown desensitised to the destruction caused by her very creations, and how her altruism was extended only to them, proved she was far removed from who she once was.

They were also the very reason she was no longer welcomed within Anzúli temples. To them, she was a corrupt being who tainted the very stones she walked upon.

She never thought that helping Orpheus would lead to her being cast out by them.

She didn't care. She'd learned all she needed to from them, and this all just meant their usefulness to her had run its course. They'd also begun having twisted ideologies that were different from those who had first stepped foot on Earth centuries ago.

Talk of harbingers of bad omens and cursed towns became rumoured whispers as the teachings of the Anzúli grew more frightening. Their people were dying and being eaten. They'd been here too long, their bloodlines mixing with humans just to preserve their numbers, and now primary skills were withering away to basic alchemy and chemistry.

None of this instilled a sense of hopelessness like her thoughts on Weldir.

Nothing about them had changed. It was the same.

Nearly forty years had passed, and the only difference between them was how many children they had, and how much power he'd achieved through them, and her. The only thing that had grown between them... was the way Lindiwe cherished every moment with him in a way that was wrong and heartbreaking.

The heart flutters, the stomach butterflies, the shy push of a curl behind her warmed ear. The hidden glances at his side or back as he watched his viewing discs while she went through her belongings in his realm... all of it was killing her slowly.

Her heart was bleeding through her chest, and she didn't know how to stem it. Yet she kept returning, unable to stay away, as if she needed his nearness to save her. Like she had poison coursing through her veins and the antidote was his shadowy void.

Her desire was selfishly hedonistic, often taking the forefront when her heart *screamed* for her to stop and save herself.

Only for guilt and fear to rear their ugly heads when she came down from the high of her orgasm, or the light of Earth woke her from her hazy, erotic dreams, and all the anxiety she'd forgotten about for a little while came crushing down on her tenfold.

Which was why, when Weldir's clawed hand began to tickle up the inside of her thigh, Lindiwe flinched away. His fingers twitched when he paused, and she greeted his onyx eyes shyly. Her pulse had long ago started to race, and she was unsure if it was excitement or terror as it drummed in her ears.

The weightless shadows held her firm, even when her heart sank.

"Are you okay?" Weldir asked, his head tipping downwards to look at her body. "You don't usually shy away from my touch."

Cupping her hands to her chest, she offered a weak smile. "I'm just a little nervous."

His quiet chuckle made her insides quiver, untwisting her stress and worry with its handsome baritone. His very voice did even more as he said, "We have done this plenty of times."

"I-I know, but it's been a while since we did... *this*," she murmured quietly, eyeing the fullness of his perceivable form.

At least a third of him existed.

He'd already admitted to holding onto his power rather than spending it, so they could finally have sex. Proper sex, and not Lindiwe half holding barriers because he wasn't really there.

He was able to cover his entire head all the way to the middle of his chest, as well as his arms to his fingertips. She didn't truly need his middle, his legs, or all of his biceps. Just the places her arms would rest, her legs would cling, and her nails would scratch, while still offering a face to look upon.

"You truly can be a contradiction, Lindiwe," Weldir said, drifting a little closer. "How can one female be both shy and bold at the same time? This part of you melts away entirely when you're receiving pleasure."

Heat swelled in her cheeks, and she pouted a little. "I don't know."

Before she could say anything more, Weldir pressed his shadowy lips against hers, and her mind sputtered. All it took was one peck of their mouths for Lindiwe to moan softly and wrap her arms around his neck. Her nails dug into the back of his chalky shoulders when they deepened the kiss at the same time, and Lindiwe licked across his weirdly smooth tongue.

I wish I could taste him. He tasted like absolutely nothing. He had no saliva to mingle with hers, no warmth in his flesh. *He doesn't even have a smell.*

When a set of narrow hips slipped between her thighs, She wound her legs around them. The surrounding space suddenly felt less empty, like she'd been waiting forever to cling to another being with her entire body.

Weldir pulled his mouth away from hers, and his nose trailed a path down her jaw, and then her neck. "Do you want me to use my mana to remove your clothing, or do it like normal?" he asked, his voice low and soft at her throat.

"Like normal," she whispered back.

The back of her dress was lifted up her body, and the drag of it slowly creeping over her skin formed prickles in its wake. It felt especially nice brushing over her hardening nipples, and she lifted her arms to help remove it.

When she brought her arms back around his neck, she loosely gripped the end of a tapered horn while he set back in. Kissing and nipping, he moved one hand to cup her breast and gave it a light squeeze.

I wish he had breath, she thought, when his lips trailed lower. She wanted to know if something so light and invisible could have an effect on her – like an unseen caress that was present wherever that playful mouth of his went.

All her thoughts disappeared when something long, hard, and thick slipped over the crook of her thigh. *Oh god. It's his cock.* Her hips surged forward to get it nestled between her underwear-clad folds and nuzzled against her clit. *Okay. It's happening. This is actually happening.*

They were going to have proper sex. Well, as proper as it was between a human woman and a shadowy entity that couldn't feel anything.

All the small, sensitive veins in delicate places pulsed – her wrists, her breasts, and between her thighs – and the pool of arousal at the entrance to her core dampened.

Needing to quicken the pace, she flattened her hands and dragged them over his shoulders to touch him. They palmed down his chest, and one brushed over a tiny nipple before resistance faded and she touched air. She quickly brought them down to tug on the ribbons at her hips and remove her panties.

Then she slipped her arms around his shoulders again and pulled him in for another kiss. One breast squished against him, while the other floated in the weightlessness and ached for the same pressure.

"Are you going to grind on me again?" Weldir asked with a low chuckle. "I did find that fun to watch."

Fun to watch. She closed her eyes tightly to disregard how weird that was.

He pushed up, and his shadowy cock ground against her clit. Her body instantly melted at the sensation, and she pushed her hips down to grind deeper. A raspy moan whispered from her between kisses, and another broke free when his hand kneaded her backside while working her along his length.

Desire coiled low in her belly, her skin itched to be touched all over, and lustful heat swelled in her skin. The long girth of his cock massaging all along her pussy lips made her insides ache.

What she wanted was *right there*. So close. It even slipped right over her entrance, and she wanted nothing more than to have her body swallow it. Swallow it so whole it went missing, so she could cuddle it in heat and wetness.

"Inside me," she begged hoarsely, grinding harder.

"You don't want me to prepare you first?"

Lindiwe shook her head in answer.

The question was sweet, caring even, but seriously... screw that right now. She didn't want gentle or kind; she wanted to be fucked into oblivion so she could just forget *everything* except existing within bliss.

For a moment, she didn't want her heart to feel heavy. It never hurt when they were being intimate, and that's what drove her forward faster into this. Pleasure mixed with escapism. A distraction from the painful tenderness, so she could experience newer, better, different sensations across her skin.

His left hand continued to squeeze her breast, his thumb intermittently flicking her nipple. The other stayed with her arse, the grip firm and controlled as it helped to move her. Just as she slid upwards, he lowered his hips and created space between them.

Lindiwe knew he'd used some of his magic to position himself, like it was that easy for him, but she still gasped when the tip nestled against her opening. When she started stretching around the head, any pain was drowned out by the sense of delicious fullness that overcame her.

Her lips parted as it sank deeper in, and she tipped her head back. She was so wet that the only resistance was how narrow she was compared to the girth, and she clenched around it before relaxing around each inch. She was thankful it was slow, her body adjusting to it in a way that didn't hurt but was welcomed.

His lips and tongue, covered in her saliva, clasped around her other nipple and her hips bucked. Her pussy slipped down his cock a little faster in a sudden jolt, but it was forgotten against the prick of his canine fangs and sharp teeth cutting across the hard bud.

Had he been human, or properly formed, this would have been entirely impossible, but Weldir had demonstrated many times he could detach parts of his body. His middle section? Likely non-existent right now, and it meant when he bottomed out within her, his mouth could firmly – perfectly – stay where it was.

After only a second of adjusting, the nagging need to move hammered her. She gripped the end of one horn, kept her arm firmly across his shoulders, and shunted her hips forward. He slipped out, and then in when she went backwards.

Her eyelids flickered when he hit the perfect spot, and she quickly chased it. As she moved back and forth, she also lifted slightly, trying to get his big cock to keep rubbing just right. A shiver ran rampant down her body, making her squeeze him just as a soft cry left her.

Weldir didn't move his hips. He didn't need to, as if he knew she'd find her end on her own and didn't wish to impede it. But as Lindiwe moved with hastening hip thrusts, her mind spiralling, all she heard was the echo of her own voice. In the utter quiet, her moans and pants rang louder and louder in her own ears.

There were no groans or growls mixing in to make a harmony of low notes with her high ones. No symphony of pleasure, no song shared between two people. She sang alone, and it had never bothered her in the more recent past because the touching had been entirely about her.

She never touched him unless it was a minor brush of her palm down his chest, as she sometimes forgot he couldn't feel it. There was no need to lick, kiss, or nip his neck unless it was to tingle her own lips. There was no need to stroke his cock, or play with it, and she'd refused to when she knew the enjoyment of it was purely mental – she just couldn't play pretend in that moment without feeling foolishly embarrassed.

As she moved on his cock, for a moment, just a single

second, her hips stuttered at the same time as her heart. *I wish he could feel it.*

She wanted to know how Weldir would react if he could feel the way she snuggled his cock tightly, or share in her heat and heartbeat, and had his own to offer. Would he be sweet or feral? What would he be like if he was actually aroused? Would his mouth be naughtier, his word dirtier?

I want to know what his moan sounds like. Her hips moved a little faster at the thought, and she angled them just right so she could feel him constantly petting her tender spot. *I bet it's so deep. It'd sound so nice, so hot.*

Hurtling herself to bliss with horny longing, she produced a shaken moan. *Oh god. I'm so close.* She was getting there faster than usual. Eyes crinkling, she looked up at the empty ether, and thought, *I want it. I want him to groan, moan, or growl right in my ear. I want to feel his breaths.*

The need was pure agony, and her imagination of it so wild, so erotic, that her eyes rolled back when she started to come. She lost her controlled momentum and bounced frantically, each spasm spreading out across her groin until her very pelvis ached. She squeezed him so tightly that he just kept pressing against her G-spot and her mind numbed out while she released a high-pitched, bliss-filled scream.

"That's quite the lewd face, Lindiwe," Weldir rumbled against her breast.

He shouldn't be able to see it from where his head was. She was grinding against an absent body, while his sight was watching from elsewhere.

Yet his deep, sinful, near-criminal voice, having that little inhuman bass to it, had her shivering and her skin tingling.

"I've always wanted to see you ride me," he said, licking across her nipple in a long stroke. "I think this might become one of my favourite memories of you. Riding me, using my body for your pleasure."

"Weldir," she groaned in answer, as her body continued to uselessly milk his cock.

When she softened, his palm on her arse began to move her. Leaning forward, she rested her brow against the top of his currently solid head to balance her dizzy, swirling mind. She tried to get back her momentum, to just live in the moment, and the twitches that assaulted her whenever he hit just right helped.

Her first orgasm had come on faster than usual. The intensity of their bodies meeting was more profound this time because he used his cock, and she could cling to him like they were having proper sex. And the echoing loneliness in her chest wasn't as prevalent when she was being filled to the brim like this.

"I can feel you so deep inside me," she whispered airily, closing her eyes against his wispy hair. "It feels so good."

"I know it does. I can tell by your face that you're enjoying my cock."

I want him to say it feels good too. All these impossible wants, and no solutions to achieve them.

"Faster." She needed him to take some of the control, so her mind would just shut up. "Please, Weldir."

He pulled his head away. "As you wish, little female."

Lindiwe's back snapped into an arch and her head tossed back when his hips started to pump into her from below. She didn't need to do anything more, didn't need to buck her hips, or meet his thrusts. His speed was impossible to match.

All she could do was bounce and jiggle in his partially existent arms. Both his hands grabbed her arse to hold her as still as possible while he pumped. Her knees spread further apart, and she held on for dear life when it felt like he was trying to fuck the very breath out of her.

"Oh fuck!" she rasped, barely able to get words out past her ragged pants. "Oh Weldir. Oh f– I'm going to–"

The inhuman god went faster, and Lindiwe's mind blanked out as she let out a scream so powerful it was *silent*. She clawed, she kicked, and her pussy quivered and spasmed.

He didn't stop, didn't slow, and her climax continued on, and on, until she was a near-sobbing mess. He didn't even soften his movements when she came down from rapture, and all she could do was blissfully experience the torture. It was too much; it was perfect. She wanted more; she was getting too sensitive. Her hands and hips pushed at him to get away, yet her legs and pussy clung so tightly.

She never asked him to stop, never pleaded for it to end.

And one thing was certain: the moment he took over, she stopped thinking about anything other than the all-consuming bliss.

THIRTY-SIX

May 16th, 1972

When did the weightless shadows become comforting? When did Lindiwe begin seeing this place as her home? When did it start to feel safe and welcoming? When did she begin to feel those things, and more, about its owner? When... when... when?

These weren't questions she could answer.

His onyx eyes, so inhuman and strange, once filled her with fear and dread. Like the piercing, unfeeling gaze of a god looking down on a mere mortal being. It felt like his pitch-black orbs would change her, corrupt her, *break* her.

She never expected that she'd one day find them... beautiful. They peered with such interest and curiosity, with such intensity and care, even if they lacked any perceptible emotion. They were keen and watchful, and Lindiwe had been sucked into those glossy pools of darkness many times over.

So when had she begun to look at him the same way, with curiosity, and see not his lacking exterior, but into his very cloud and find it ethereal?

Why was she here, now, half-awake in his realm, but unable to tear herself away from sleep because it meant facing reality? Why was she sore in the most wonderful way, tender in all the right places – as if her whole body had been worshipped – but it couldn't overshadow how she was bleeding out?

Why does it have to hurt so much?

More than ever, her chest ached beyond recognition. There were wounds in places the eye couldn't see, and no medicine or spell could heal. Her heart felt battered and bruised, like it'd been punched and jabbed at repeatedly.

And she had no one else to blame but herself.

Something brushed her cheek, perhaps the back of a knuckle or a claw. "Why are you crying, Lindiwe?"

Her eyes snapped open and she sat up. *I'm... crying?*

She didn't even look at Weldir as she touched her cheek and peered down at her wet, tear-stained fingertips. Seeing them made her chest tighten, and more spilled over.

Lindiwe bit her lips shut, her vision blurred, and droplets began to drip off her nose and jaw. *I can cry like my children.* Here, in this place, when they departed from her skin, they lifted off and floated around her face. They didn't glow, they didn't look as pretty, but they hovered around so she could see the evidence of them so cruelly.

Lindiwe didn't sob. There weren't any whimpers. Her pain was so profound that her body didn't know how to expel it other than to cry silently and listlessly.

"I... can't do this anymore," she whispered.

She thought sex would make her feel better, but the momentary numbness only made her feel worse. It made her reality sink deeper in and inform her that it was all... hopeless.

All the longing and yearning in the world wouldn't change a thing. She was wishing for things she could never have, and the crater of yawning loneliness was only growing wider.

"Do what?" Weldir asked, his voice lovely, yet his tone so dull. "Sleep here?"

Holding her cloak to her chest to shield her nudity, thankful he'd covered her in it, she searched for her dress.

"I can't be here anymore," she told him, quietly and calmly to hide the fear and panic settling in. "I don't want to be intimate anymore."

"What?" Weldir asked as he followed her. "Why?"

Lindiwe threw her dress over her body, then threw her cloak around her shoulders. She swam for her underwear, tied one side, and then slipped it on to tie the other at her hip.

"I just don't want to."

"But you enjoyed yourself. A lot, if your moaning and pleading for more were any indication." When she refused to look at him, her expression pinching in sadness, he came to her and placed a bent forefinger under her chin to make her meet his gaze. "Did I do something wrong?"

Before she could greet those captivating, glossy midnight eyes, she snapped her head away.

It was wonderful. He was being wonderful, and that was the problem. *It was so good that I thought I was going to melt.* Even now her body thrummed with satisfaction, singing from all the perfect touches, caresses, and thorough pounding.

Her lips trembled and her voice cracked when she said, "I don't want to pretend anymore."

Her pulse raced at that realisation, and it bled poison into her veins. Her skin was cold, but she was burning up, and she wanted nothing more than to go back to sleep so she didn't have to deal with how she was feeling.

"Pretend? Lindiwe... I do not understand."

Clenching her eyes shut and curling her hands into tight fists, she shouted. "Of course you don't! What could an emotionless, heartless *demi-god* know about how a *human* would feel?!"

"I have done all I can to meet your expectations," he answered, his tone finally holding some substance. Cold annoyance. "It's unfair of you to state otherwise. I'm not devoid of emotions, as you so callously throw at me, and you know that."

"But it's not enough!" she yelled, finally tossing her head to the side to look at him. She hated the way tears continued to fall, but her rage, the vengeance she felt for *herself,* for her bruised and battered heart, fuelled her forward. "You react with *anger* because you think you have been wronged or disrespected. You experience *desire* because it is entertaining, because it gives you something to look forward to. You know sadness and sympathy because it is *logical.* Your loneliness comes from wanting to fill the utter emptiness around you."

His expression didn't flinch, but his mist did pull in tighter. "That is very true. I *feel* through my mind."

"That is not true feeling! That's a façade of the consciousness." She darted forward, incidentally making him pull back in surprise, until she placed her palm over the left side of his chest. Her fucking hand ghosted through him. "You don't have a beating heart. You don't know what it feels like to have it bleeding out in your chest as you yearn for impossible things from an impossible being."

"I have tried for you. Is that not enough?" He created space between them and waved his clawed right hand through the air, as if to gesture to some unknown thing. "I have attempted to be a fitting mate."

"Because logic tells you to! Because, as you once said, affection allows for a cohesive bond."

Weldir growled as *he* shunted forward, his nose crinkling and *finally* showing an emotion. "I do care for you, Lindiwe. I have grown very fond of you over these years, and I have attempted to make that known."

"I know that! I'm not a fucking idiot. But you experience it all the same way. Your anger, lust, affection, dedication, and care all come from the same place. It doesn't exist within the real, living world."

"It exists to me!" he roared.

"Because you are not real!" she screamed and pointed to the ether. "I don't belong in your lifeless, lightless void! I can't *live* here, and you can't exist in my world, the *living* world."

His tone became deflated and almost sounded... hurt. "That's not fair, Lindiwe."

It wasn't fair. She also knew it wasn't his fault.

I love you. I love you so much, and it pains me every single day because you can't be with me.

Weldir couldn't change. He couldn't suddenly grow a body

and join her, and that was heartbreaking. She wanted it more than anything. She wanted to share her world with him, walk in it with him, holding his hand and feeling warmth in his touch as he felt the sun, air, and grass. Smelt the trees, the dirt, and the flowers. To experience what cold rain felt like on a hot summer's day, or the sun warming him from the outside in on a winter's morning.

Pretending that it was one day possible was slowly killing her. She yearned for it with every passing day of the *thousands* that they had distantly spent together.

And I can't tell you that. There was utterly no *point* in telling Weldir that she somehow, foolishly, had fallen in love with him. That she wanted a proper life with him where he wasn't in some faraway, unknown realm made up of shadowy, dark ether.

A cruel, lonely, and sad space just for him.

Lindiwe didn't know if he loved her, if he could even experience the true, wonderful depth of it. If he did feel it in some semblance, then she didn't want to know.

She didn't want this to be even more painful than it already was. For her, and for him too.

Because she knew one thing for certain: love wasn't supposed to *hurt*.

It could be saddening and frustrating. It could have moments of jealousy and possessiveness. It should always be filled with comfort, affection, and soft caresses. There would be fights, and there would be times of weakness and selfishness. There could be aches and pangs.

But it shouldn't feel like this.

It shouldn't feel like her heart was on fire and sending flames into her bloodstream. Her chest shouldn't feel so tight she thought she was strangling on every breath.

It shouldn't be this absent and lonely.

It shouldn't feel this distant, where he could feel nothing and she had to feel for both of them for... forever. Alone, and never truly sharing that sensual bond, something that Lindiwe craved every day with him, with no solution in sight. Especially when he spent so much of their time slumbering and leaving her to experience every aching second of life.

I feel like I'm breaking into a million little pieces. And she kept leaving them behind for Weldir to hold onto, to cherish in his inhuman way. *I can't keep feeling this way.*

It'd taken her nearly three hundred years to fall in love with this person, and she feared it would take twice as long to fall out of love with him.

They'd been intimate properly for only a hundred years of that time, and it had been sporadic but intense. Yet, he slept through seventy percent of their relationship, leaving her on her own, and she sat here... waiting for him. Always loyally waiting.

And she experienced every. Single. Second of those long years. Sad, lonely, and filled with longing for him.

For once, she'd like to wake up in his arms and feel *all* of him, feel warmth, love, affection, like she was the most exquisite woman in existence.

Not nothingness, not cold shadows.

"I want to leave," Lindiwe eventually stated, uncurling her fists as regretful determination sunk in. "I don't want to stay here in your realm anymore. I don't want to be intimate or have sex again."

"I truly don't understand what has brought this on. And you're always so secretive when it comes to your thoughts."

It was true, and she couldn't deny that. *But I don't want to tell you I love you, then hear you say it back and not believe it. Or for you not to say it at all. Or try to convince me that this isn't the best option because, no matter how much I wish it, you will never truly be with me.*

Lindiwe cupped her hands together and placed them on her stomach when it rolled with sickly waves.

"I will do as we contractually agreed in the very beginning. I will be your servant, as you asked. If you want more servants, I will grow more Duskwalkers as I promised, but if I'm pregnant from this, I would like to wait a while before having another. We will use tendrils like in the beginning, in a non-invasive, nonsexual way."

She wanted it to feel like a procedure, and not something that had her clawing for more with mind-numbing rapture.

"You're the one who asked for this in the first place," Weldir snapped back with a growl.

Her shoulders lifted self-consciously, and she looked down at her knees. "That's the thing about consent. I can give it, and I can take it away." Then she fiddled with the seam of her cloak. "And we both know you won't keep me here to coerce me otherwise."

He may have done that in the past when she'd refused to climb down from her cliff of anger and hatred towards him and her situation. But it'd only ever been once.

She'd thought it meant he was selfish and manipulative, but one fault over hundreds of years of the opposite exposed the truth. Weldir was kind and patient, but could react in thoughtless anger, just like anyone.

In a mere few hours, he'd attempted to communicate through it even when she refused.

That was one of Lindiwe's faults: her anger drove her to hold grudges in silence. Something he'd... accepted and often allowed despite how it annoyed him.

Lindiwe peeked at him, and his lack of response and his stillness informed her he had no idea how to change her mind.

I promised myself I wouldn't feel this way about him, so where did I go wrong? Why did she mix affection with pleasure? Why did he have to disappear and make her realise how much she needed his presence? And not because he aided her, but because he was a comfort in her life, a safe place to be.

She'd gone through so many metamorphoses over the years. From Lindi to Lindiwe. A raven to an owl. From a human to a Phantom to the Witch Owl. From hating Weldir to loving him.

How much could one person change before they lost themselves entirely? *But I don't want to die inside.* She didn't want this pain to become her new form and change her in the worst way possible.

"Does this mean you will ignore me like before?" Weldir asked darkly.

Her drying tears renewed as she offered him a weak and broken smile. "No. I'll always answer when you call for me. I may ask you to help me move across the world quicker occasionally, or for one of my belongings I keep here, but my stay will be limited to those things." Her smile grew more tenuous when it wanted to fall. "Now you can focus entirely on expanding your mist and reach, without worrying about me or my needs."

His chalky, flaky brows drew together. "Doing so will mean I will likely sleep more to recover what I temporarily lost."

"I know." She hated the way the salt in her tears seemed to abrade her swelling cheeks and sting her eyes. "I'd like to leave now. Please."

A tendril coiled around her ankle. She wanted to tug away from it when it broke her heart a little more, especially as it was likely a sign of his anxiety or sadness.

"At least tell me why, Lindiwe. You were... changing. I've known for a while you were growing fond of me, of being here with me."

"I'm really sorry." Sincerely, she was sorry, but she also had to protect herself from the one being who could destroy a part of her even he could not heal.

"Why are you telling me all this while crying as if it upsets you?!" he roared, just as his tendril coiled further up her leg. "You are being needlessly confusing, little human!"

Because the answers he sought would only do more damage to both of them. Why deepen his potential mental fondness of her and make him yearn for something that was impossible?

If I'd known I would end up falling in love with you, I never would have given you my soul.

There were many regrets she had in her life, but nothing this horrible, or painful, or made her truly wish she could turn back time and change it.

I wish it wasn't me you found at the edge of the Veil. It would have been better, and easier, had she just bled out or been eaten.

His tendril squeezed her lightly. There was no malice in it, no cruelty. He was holding on, and she wanted to believe it was because he didn't want to let her go, fervently, *desperately*.

And that made her want to change her mind.

Her stomach twisted, but she wanted him to know at least one very important thing. So that he wouldn't blame himself.

"You did nothing wrong, Weldir," Lindiwe finally answered, quietly, softly, and with utter sincerity. "You're right. I do care about you, and you've done everything you can to be patient with me – often when I don't always deserve it. But I don't want to pretend anymore. I also don't want to pretend that I'm okay anymore. There are issues that can't be resolved."

"Well, yes, but I am content with how things are."

"I'm not. There are things I want that I can't have, and wishing on impossibilities will only break me." She lifted her gaze to greet his, and she crinkled her eyes with swallowing sadness. "I've spent three hundred years making sure that doesn't happen."

Lindiwe was on the brink of totally losing her humanity.

What would happen if she did?

THIRTY-SEVEN

December 18th, 1972

Lindiwe wiped her brow with her forearm before shielding her eyes from the intense summer sunlight. *Ugh. Summers in Austrális are always so humid.* She was baking in the heat.

A disgusted cringe marred her face as she beheaded the fruit bat she'd caught. Her scent-cloaking spell worked perfectly to prevent the two little Duskwalkers wandering around her from attacking it.

One of her babies, as she'd had a set of twins, came to investigate the noise she'd made. Little black-feathered wings twitched as they sniffed around, unaware they'd just placed their tiny paw in a growing puddle of scarlet.

"You get the head this time," Lindiwe told them, since she'd given them the body of a raven last time. "And you can have the body this time," she continued, as she searched for the second baby Duskwalker.

Her eyes widened, and she made her shadowy dagger disappear as she rushed to her feet. "Oh, for fuck's sake! Where did you get a lizard from?!"

She couldn't even tell what kind was dangling from their raven beak, only that they were trying to rip it in half with the tail already missing. She dived for it and grabbed the lizard around the head to yank it away.

A shrill cry came from her right, and Lindiwe snapped her head in the direction of the sound.

"No! You've already got wings! You're supposed to share that with your sibling," Lindiwe yelled, as her winged child began eating the body of the bat she'd intended to give to the one she was currently tug-of-warring with.

The lizard tore in two, and her arms cartwheeled when she fell to her back. The top half of the carcass spun as it flew through the air... and landed on top of the baby that was in the middle of growing a bat skull while they ate. They immediately turned to the offending assailant and attacked... half a dead lizard.

From her prone spot on the ground, she peered past her feet to where her raven-skulled child grew a lizard tail and feet. Scales reflected purple, blue, and black as they appeared across their flesh.

Her head fell back with a thud, and she shook it. Then she threw her arms into the air and kicked her legs immaturely with a frustrated yell.

"I wanted you *both* to have wings! One with a bat skull and raven wings, the other with a raven skull and bat wings."

She wanted the world to know they'd shared everything they'd eaten in their evolution and had been created at the same time.

Throwing her arm across her face, she sighed and just lay there defeated. It was too late. Now one was part lizard, tail, paws, and all, and the other wasn't – although she was sure they'd sport some scales here and there.

You know what? This is probably a good thing. Flying Duskwalkers were terrifying things, but she just hadn't been able to resist the temptation. *Even if it means I can't fly with them both in the future.*

She tsked. Just as she went to sit up, two little creatures climbed on top of her – one up her right arm, and the other up her left leg. When they both made it to the middle of her torso, their skulls clunked together and they snarled at each other.

One tackled the other, and they both fell off her. Trills, growls, and squeaking roars became her background noise as they rolled around in a fighting heap. Neither was about to hurt the other, no matter how they struck with bendy claws and bit into each other's indestructible bodies.

She relaxed on the ground with her arms and legs out wide. *They'll tire themselves out.* They always did.

Their fighting ball came back to smack her in the side of the head. One backed up and landed on her forehead, incidentally poking her in the eye, before the other tackled their twin off her face and to the ground on the opposite side. Once more, they locked limbs and rolled around.

She watched them for a moment before she looked up at the blue sky and white clouds softly floating overhead. Other than their noisy sounds, the only other things she could hear were the trees rustling and a wind chime.

With her lips pulling downwards, she peered at the wooden tubes fluttering in the easterly wind. *I'm glad I bought that. It sounds nice.* Her eyes then drifted over the small hut that Lindiwe had built... in the centre of the Veil.

A black protective dome surrounded it always. She'd asked Weldir if she could have one permanently, and he'd agreed to it without hesitation.

Her home was modest. Kind of.

It was situated near the centre of the Veil where it was safest, and was only spacious enough for a bed, a small stove, and some room to move around. The roof was slats of timber, and the outside – the only walls of the structure – was constructed from clay bricks. She'd thought about painting it, but she didn't care all that much about it, only that it had a safe place for her to return to and sleep.

There was no garden, as the trees surrounding it let no sunlight pour down except for where she lay.

But it was hidden, and small enough to likely go unnoticed.

I still can't believe I managed to build it while pregnant. Then again, having the ability to use tendrils and tentacles of magic to do all the heavy lifting was an invaluable asset.

It was her way of finally having a home outside of Weldir's realm. A place just for her, and her sad thoughts. A way for her to move on mentally, even if she was struggling to begin that journey emotionally.

As promised, Lindiwe responded to Weldir when he reached out, but she left out all the playfulness. She put up a mental barrier between them, hoping one day... it would exist between him and her heart.

She let her head fall back and looked up at the bright sky once more.

I miss him already.

Only a few months had passed, and she missed the amicable way they spoke almost every day. Where she would share what she was doing, and he'd talk to her as he completed his duties. Where she considered being naughty by teasing him until he snatched her from Earth, or she just downright asked him if he wanted to be intimate.

They'd begun sharing their innermost thoughts, and she missed knowing they could rely on each other as a sounding board. She mourned the loss of being able to sleep in his realm safely, blanketed in utter protection, while he watched over her. Where she'd feel him tucking her cloak around her in sleep or brushing her hair from her face, so it didn't disturb her.

She missed his care, and the gentleness he'd begun showing her quite some decades ago. The sweet, oddly tender moments that had begun to steal her affection bit by bit.

This sucks. I hate feeling this way.

She wanted to go back on her decision and crawl back to him, but she... couldn't. Even if it made them both unhappy, Lindiwe didn't want to live in her suffering and make it worse with every moment they spent together.

But I really, really miss him. Enough so that the ache in her chest just burned constantly with no end in sight.

She lifted her right hand so she could look at the blazing sun between her fingers. *I feel so awful for everything I said.* But all of it was true, and he couldn't deny any of it. *He's made it known that this separation upsets him.*

Guilt constantly nipped at her, and that, too, was a difficult thing to swallow. *I don't want to hurt him,* she thought, as she swayed her hand through the streaks of sun so it would glitter between the gaps of her fingers. *I wish it didn't have to be like this. I wish we could be together.*

But this wasn't a fairytale where love could triumph over all. He wasn't some prince who could sweep her off her feet, and she wasn't some pure-of-heart maiden who only needed a kiss to have everything she wanted. No, she'd long ago become a villain, a creator of destroyers, and this was merely her penance.

This was reality, and reality came with limitations – ones that not even a half-formed demi-god could change.

I'm really sorry, Weldir. She could no longer recount how many times she'd apologised to him now, without offering the answer as to why it was all happening. *And thank you for still being kind to me, despite your annoyance.*

After a few minutes, two sets of tiny hands climbed up her right leg. She grabbed a baby with each hand and placed them on her chest. She made sure their skulls didn't bash together when they nuzzled just below her breasts. Then, like they always did, they curled into each other to cuddle while letting her slow breaths lift them up and down on her belly.

They fell asleep as she scratched the backs of their necks, and they both stretched into her petting at the same time. *I think I'll keep you two young for a little longer than the others.*

They were a wonderful distraction, and very adorable together. They liked to snuggle, they were often affectionate with their little head rubs and licks, and they'd never bitten her – just each other.

I wonder what horns I'll give them.

Lindiwe thought long and hard about this, as it was better than the alternative: thinking about Weldir or her myriad of adult children who wanted nothing to do with her.

A goat's perhaps? She didn't know, and she would figure

that out later.

I wonder what orb colours you two will have?

Lindiwe was always a little excited and nervous to find out.

I know he'll watch when it happens, she thought with a sad smile. *He's probably watching right now.*

THIRTY-EIGHT

A time unknown, but one of disgruntlement

Keeping his eyes on a viewing disc of his mate, Weldir sat cross-legged, one hand gripping his knee while he rested his chin on top of the enclosed fist of the other hand.

Nathair, lounging back upon his tail like it was some kind of chair, lifted his hands in Weldir's periphery. His signs were deliberate and often held pointed intent.

"Why haven't you greeted her?" Nathair tilted his head with his orbs morphing to dark yellow.

"I will when I'm done," Weldir stated dully.

Although he was in the middle of extending his mist, he could do both at the same time. He just didn't want to. *I doubt she cares.* Or maybe she did, who fucking knew?

He disliked this change, and no poking or prodding on his part had aided the situation; she was steadfast about maintaining their distance.

Her soul has changed again. What had been glowing brightly with pure citrine flames now bore charcoal. The left breast, up the side of its throat, and half its face were blackened like coal. He'd long ago learned they were depression markings, and it... upset him that his female wore them – again. After years of not having them, as if she'd grown happy with her life and their bond.

The darkness had only developed after that day.

She said I have done nothing wrong, yet she punishes me regardless. Therefore, Weldir had surmised that she had lied, and he was at fault somehow. *I don't know how to help her heal these markings if she will not share with me her pain.*

He was waiting her out, seeing if whatever thing he'd done to offend her would eventually fade and they could resume as they once had.

It hasn't been long. Perhaps a year and a half? It was difficult to tell when he'd been asleep and hadn't long woken.

He'd consumed all the souls waiting for him after finally perfecting the process to occur automatically. He'd checked on all of their offspring, and they were all well. He'd checked on her to find she was still at her little hut that was barely big enough to be classified as a home. Or maybe he was just annoyed and jealous of the inanimate object because he'd thought she'd begun to see his realm as her home.

Then Weldir had come to Nathair and found him to be lucid. Since that lucidity could be temporary and fleeting, he'd put all his energy into Nathair so they could continue to build his vocabulary.

He learns fast, he thought, letting his gaze slip to Nathair when he shrugged and lounged back once more. *Then again, a number of human years have passed since we started.*

Seeing as his offspring no longer felt chatty, and Weldir was often subjugated to his whims regarding that, he brought his focus back to his female who didn't want to be his mate right now.

Why should I care if this is what she seeks? There was still an amicable friendship there. She may not have returned to his void except for the night of the twins' birthing to be healed, but she wasn't avoiding him entirely. She didn't seem angry at him, nor was she acting like his voice was an irritant.

She spoke kindly when he reached out to her, and her responses weren't curt or designed to end the conversation. She always left them open, but he didn't know how to continue them without her assistance. He didn't have enough excuses.

If this is what makes her content in our bond, then fine.

This was what he'd once wanted. He'd never imagined more until she decided it. He'd been quite content with friendship and unity within their joint duties, as that was all he'd originally sought.

But it wasn't fucking fine.

He was greatly vexed by it, and going to his cave of memories only made him angrier. The last time he'd been inside it, his fury and rejection had caused him to crack his newest creation of her diagonally in half. He was annoyed by the obsession to make it, and that she wouldn't give him more to add to his cave.

He'd fixed the statue and then quickly left, and hadn't returned since, when he was usually quite infatuated with his memories of her.

"Weldir," a voice echoed from within his mist.

He knew that familiar voice, and like the last time it called out to him, he was surprised to hear it growl his name.

His gaze shifted to Nathair beside him, whose orbs were white. *He's slipped into a daze.* It could be hours, days, or weeks before his mind returned to consciousness.

He collected his mist tightly against his form, hating that this was happening to his offspring and he could do nothing to assist. Especially when he was partly to blame.

At least this means I can leave without informing him as to why. Nathair was nosy and curious all the time with nothing but Weldir to entertain him.

He dematerialised and transported himself to the outskirts of the Veil, between the forest and canyon walls. Waiting for him at the border of his red protection ward was Merikh. Arms folded and shoulders stiff, the sun on his back caused his bear skull and horns to create a shadow through Weldir's invisible form.

"You called?"

"Bring me Lindiwe," Merikh stated instantly.

"Why?" he asked, a touch more defensively than he intended.

Their interactions had always gone unpleasantly, and Lindiwe... was always distraught afterwards. He also had this remarkable sense of protectiveness towards his mate, and he didn't wish to add to her sadness if there was a way to prevent it.

Although he wanted them to have a bond, Weldir would rather they didn't meet if Merikh only intended to be unwelcoming.

"I have absolutely no desire to speak with you," Merikh stated in an odd tone. Like he was trying to hold in a growl to sound cold and indifferent, but failed.

"Why not? From my memory, we parted ways last time amicably. I see no reason why you would be disgruntled by my presence."

"I'd rather not speak to my *master* if given the choice, especially as I have no interest in being your servant."

"Master? That's a rather profound statement. You're my servant, whether you wish to be or not. You cannot undo the souls you have brought me, nor can you prevent yourself from bringing more in the wake of your constant destruction."

A rolling, huffing growl came from his maw. "I will never have need of you. If I wish to speak with her, I will call you, as I cannot call out to her." His arms tightened, and he rolled his shoulders back more defensively. "I met you, saw your realm. My curiosity was sated regarding you. Other than that, you are nothing but a reminder of what I am and why I was born."

"If that is how you feel, I see no reason to discuss this further."

Dark yellow flickered in his orbs. "That's it? You don't care?"

"Why should I?" Weldir asked, genuinely confused. "If this is what you want, then there's no reason to convince you otherwise. It changes nothing."

The only offspring he'd ever spoken to was Nathair. He was

the only one who could ruffle his mist if he became absent.

Merikh grunted. "I thought you'd at least give some sort of a shit."

Weldir chuckled lightly. "I don't have a physical body, so I cannot do that for you. Quite an odd request."

Merikh choked on his own spit and staggered forward. "That's not what I meant! I did not mean *literally*!"

His laughter deepened. "I know. This will be the last time I come to you when you beckon. You will now be at the whims of your mother, and it will be up to her if she wishes to grace you with her presence."

Weldir left and transported himself to within his own magical dome – one he didn't cast but freely allowed in his mist. His body, invisible as it was, created no shadow over Lindiwe.

Despite it being winter, she lay upon the ground in the sun, and was apparently trapped there by their twin offspring snuggling on her belly again. He had an inkling she did this on purpose. Her eyelids were low and drowsy as she looked up at the sky. Swaying shade cast diamond patterns across her legs and dress.

Once more, he was hesitant to greet her.

But he easily gave in. He wanted to hear her voice anyway, as it was no longer a frequent gift.

"Lindiwe," he called.

Her eyes snapped open fully, and she sat up with a gasp. She threw her arm around the twins just in time to stop them from rolling off her lap as they squealed from suddenly being hurled forward.

"You're awake," she rasped.

He didn't know why she smiled, as if she was pleased about this. More and more, she puzzled him, and he was finding he understood less as the months passed by. She was happy he was back, despite apparently wanting little to do with him?

She never saw him beside her, but that didn't stop Weldir from wanting to reach out to her, knowing they were intangible to each other.

"Yes." He was unsure if it was cowardice in the face of all this or just anger that had prevented him from telling her.

Curls fell around her cheeks, haloing her beautiful face while simultaneously hiding it when she looked down. "I've been waiting for you to come back."

Weldir's mist pushed out from him in surprise. "Why?"

Had she changed her mind? *Should I have reached out sooner?* Did his absence again upset her and wake her up to this foolish, infuriating distance between them?

"I know you like to watch them grow into adulthood," she murmured, before petting a tiny raven skull and a fruit-bat skull.

So nothing had changed, and he'd gotten excited for no reason.

"You waited for my return to grow them?"

Her smile became saddened. "Yes. I've already picked what kind of horns I want to give them and know where to find them."

As much as he was annoyed, his mist shimmered with mild joy. She thought about him, what he desired, and even waited for his return for such a reason. He appreciated that.

"Thank you. Unfortunately, we have other matters to speak about. Merikh has requested your presence."

Her brows drew together until her frown crinkled her forehead. "What? Why?"

"I don't know why."

July 2nd, 1973

Standing in front of Merikh, whose arms were folded defensively, Lindiwe regarded him as he towered over her. His orbs were more crimson than normal, and as usual, he had a menacing aura about him despite the bright, wintry day.

Considering he'd asked her to be here, she found that rude.

"You asked to see me?" Lindiwe greeted.

"Yes. Hold out your–"

Before he could finish, a tiny bat skull poked up through the base of her feathered hood and squawked at him. It was then yanked down as her raven-skulled baby fought to poke their head out of the loose gap as well.

"Sorry, pardon me for a moment." She reached within her cloak, sightlessly grabbed one baby, and moved it to the other side. Both their heads then stuck out at the base of her hood, and they sniffed in Merikh's direction. "I've never met another being while holding them, so they're probably interested in your voice and scent."

"You have more," Merikh said all surly and snappy. "Isn't there fucking enough of us?"

"You have no idea," she answered with an eye roll.

And Lindiwe didn't plan to inform him just how many. It'd just piss him off.

"Whatever. Hold your hand out," he snapped.

When he raised his big fist, she hesitated before lifting her palm through his ward. He lowered his fist, then partially opened it, and something tickled her skin. His foreclaw grazed across her flesh when hc dropped whatever he was holding and pulled away.

She brought it close so she could inspect it. A bundle of dill was tied tightly with a white ribbon, and it had two bells and a tiny bone dangling from it.

"What is it?"

"A protection charm. If tied at each corner of a house, it stops anyone from entering unless they've been invited."

"Okaaay." Lindiwe curled her fingers around it and brought her gaze up to meet his orbs. "But why are you giving it to me?"

"There was a city that was destroyed, and it had a temple connected to it. A Demon brought much of its written knowledge back to her den, and she read a few texts to me while teaching me how to read. This was a spell we discovered in one of them."

A city with a temple? Her fists tightened around the charm. *He probably means Rivenspire.* It was only a little northwest from here.

Her brows furrowed as she looked up at him in puzzlement. "You befriended a Demon?"

"It was short-lived. She was murdered for befriending me."

Lindiwe's eyes widened. *"She?"*

He produced a rather curt growl, informing her that this wasn't up for discussion.

He made a friend, not only with a Demon, but a woman? Lindiwe didn't want to know what that meant. *And she was killed because of it?*

How... sad.

I didn't know he sought companionship after what happened with Jabez.

Merikh's claw pointed at her fist. "Give this to Orpheus. It should stop his offerings from being taken, or his home from being invaded by Demons."

As nice as this was... "Why do you care?" She couldn't help the way her eyes narrowed in untrusting spite at him. "You were the one who helped start all his suffering."

"This is my way of making up for that. I know they are trying to figure out a way to kill Mavka, and although I don't want to be within sniffing distance of any of my siblings, I won't allow myself to be the reason another of us perishes."

Is it guilt? This added a layer of complexity Lindiwe didn't foresee in Merikh.

"And yet, *you* are adding two more to be targeted. How stupid and selfish," he bit out.

Lindiwe scoffed at that. "I'm hoping Ingram and Aleron will protect each other."

Like you and Nathair once did before you killed him. Her cheeks pinched in resentment, but she quickly smoothed her features.

"What kind of names are those? Just as useless as the name *Orson* for a Mavka."

"Your name was special to me," she grumbled defensively. "Their names mean 'raven of peace' and 'the winged one.' Just because you don't like your name, doesn't mean theirs are bad."

"Everyone and everything will hate them regardless. You're birthing more creatures that don't belong anywhere in this world."

Is that really how he feels? Like he doesn't belong anywhere? Lindiwe averted her gaze because she didn't want to invalidate his pain, but she also disagreed. Or maybe she wanted to believe he was wrong, and they'd all find their place eventually. *If he would stop being so aggressive and short-tempered, he's intelligent enough to gain companions...*

"That is all I wanted." He waved his hand in a shooing manner. "Now go give that to Orpheus. Hopefully it helps him."

"Wait," Lindiwe yelled while reaching out, before quickly drawing her hand back when his quills flared dangerously. "What if we find a way for you to fit in?"

"Fit in?" he stated darkly, then let out a cruel laugh. "That's impossible. Mavka don't fit in anywhere."

Her eyelids lowered into an irritated glare. "You offer a magical charm and then disregard the potential for magical aid."

"Alright, fine." He folded his arms. "I'll bite. What do you have in mind?"

"Weldir?" she called, causing him to tilt his head questioningly.

"Yes?" he answered through the bond.

"Do you think it's possible to make a glamour with one of the remaining mana stones we have left?"

"I don't see why not. It's not a particularly difficult spell. You would have to sacrifice one of your items, though – like with the diadem."

Oh, right. The diadem. Lindiwe looked up at the sky. *I'm glad Orpheus still has that.* She'd left it on his dining table quite a few decades ago. Considering she'd seen that offering wearing it before she died, Lindiwe knew she'd read the inscription for Orpheus, and he continued to give it to all those who survived the journey afterwards.

She lowered her gaze to Merikh.

"I have a necklace he can wear around his neck." She eyed

his quills, and her lips pursed. "Maybe not around his neck. Around his horns?"

"I will make it now."

Lindiwe nodded. "You want to fit in? Then we'll give you a glamour that lets you walk among humans."

Merikh tilted his head with dark-yellow orbs. "Aren't they going to be concerned about my height?"

"You'll be surprised by how tall humans can get."

And you're still my shortest child, whether you know it or not.

He pointed a claw at her hand again. "That charm is in exchange for it. I don't want to be indebted to you."

I don't know why I expected a thank you. But one would have been nice.

"This also changes nothing between us," he added.

He would never know how much that wounded her. "I know."

For a very long time, she knew building a connection with him was doubtful. *But I can always hope... and keep trying.*

"I'm sorry for what happened–"

Before Lindiwe could finish, Merikh turned away.

"Leave it within my ward when you're done. I'll find it when I'm ready." With that, he walked away to enter his cave.

She knew there was no point in following. He'd emotionally shut her out, and she knew all too well from her own actions that nothing would let her in.

Sometimes... he's too much like me.

Yet he lacked all the other good parts of her, the ones that could be kind and forgiving. Loving and accepting.

Why does he hate me so much? As she looked down at the swaying grass, tears welled in her eyes. *He's the one who ruined everything!*

Pulling her hood over her head, Lindiwe transformed into an owl before a single tear could form. She tucked the pain away, just like she did everything else, and lifted off to head towards Orpheus' home.

I'm... tired of being blamed for things that can't be changed.
She was also tired of wishing they would.
But once more, reality was cold, cruel, and hopeless.

THIRTY-NINE

April 17th, 1979

A welcoming glow allowed the village before her to glitter with warm light. Tall buildings, many two or three stories high, all had different styles of roofing: straw, tiled, or wooden. Pathways had been properly paved with cobblestone or grey brick, and all led to the village's circular centre – where a tall statue of a man stood. Crowds of beings weaved through each other, like colourful bodies of water constantly colliding, their clothing ranging from simple cloth to high quality.

Their hair and skin were all different shades, but most had patches of human skin tone. And there was always one consistency: red eyes.

The Demons below, most of them fully formed in some way, all bore different horns, antlers, or animalistic ears. Many still had inky, void-like patches on their flesh.

The giant spiralling trees completely keeping out the sunlight swayed, and leaves constantly fluttered down like pretty green confetti. Material draped above, extending from the centre of the spiral and attached to the many base branches of the surrounding tree trunks, adding cheerful colour. Thankfully the aroma of meat didn't clog the air – as much of it was human meat – but the smell of herbs and spices wafted all throughout. Music rang out, tasteful and charming, and occasionally had

Lindiwe's shoulders bouncing side to side in a little dance when the rhythm was just right.

Spiral Haven had come a long way over the last two centuries.

There was no dreariness, no hostility. It looked like any other town, minus the Demons and the strange walls surrounding it.

Couples walked hand in hand while children played, and a smile often crept onto her face. It also made mild jealousy form, as she'd never experienced what being a parent in a happy family was like.

"This place really is beautiful, Weldir," Lindiwe said, as she lifted her fingertips out to a glow bug when it came near her. She didn't disturb it, just followed underneath it in case it wanted somewhere to land. "It's unfortunate you're unable to see it."

He could hear her, but his magic couldn't penetrate the area due to the barrier. Somewhere far beneath the ground, a mana stone made the bottom of a deep pond grow bright green. It ensured the trees remained lush and healthy, but it also prevented Weldir from entering. She was unsure if that was intentional or not.

"Perhaps one day."

Lindiwe didn't need to pretend smile, as he was unable to see her through a scrying disc. She was away from his gaze here.

It might be why she often lingered a little longer than she should.

She was situated on top of a roof's ridge, at the crest of the establishment. Verlem's Hats, it was called, where head adornments were crafted and sold to fit all the varying horns, antlers, and ears.

It was the perfect perch for Lindiwe, as she sat with one foot up and on the edge, and the other dangling down. Her feathered hood was up, ensuring a quick transformation, and the trees surrounding the village allowed for minimal wind to billow her clothing around.

With a stern, watchful stare, she waited for the inevitable.

In the crowd, a Demon picked up a piece of jewellery from a cart merchant, and their touch disturbed the anchor. A Ghost appeared next to them, covered the sides of their head, and wailed. Everyone cringed or flinched, pulling away as the customer tossed the item back down in disgust.

Just as the attendant and customer began to argue, Lindiwe forced the shift. She dropped off the edge of the roof in her owl form, glided through the air, and landed in a nearby alleyway.

In her Phantom form, she was mostly ignored. She was just another Ghost among many that popped up here.

It was only when she turned physical and reached out to the discarded ring that she was looked upon warily. She stared at both the merchant and customer with a piercing, silent statement: don't interfere.

"A human?" the customer snarled, raising his claws to grab her.

The attendant grabbed his arm to stop him. "Don't," she bit out. "That's the Witch Owl."

Lindiwe grabbed the ring, and the deceased human's spirit came to life. The haunted one, a man, looked around and then screamed at his surroundings. Whether he knew he was dead or not, she didn't know.

Already in her hand was a glass vial. She flicked her thumb over the cork to remove it, pointed it in the spirit's direction, and he went quiet. He sighed, as if sensing she was there to aid him, and he was sucked inside without a fight.

"There. The ring is no longer an anchor," she stated, respectfully placing it back down upon the leather table covering.

Pushing the cork back into the top of the vial, she turned incorporeal. They stared at her, their red eyes wide, until she faded into the crowd. Down an alleyway, she transformed into an owl and obtained herself a new perch.

A few Demons turned their heads up at her. Many shied away when she greeted their gazes, daring them to do something about her presence, while others glared back in distaste.

A charge crackled the air.

It was quick, like lightning flashing behind her, and it set her teeth on edge. The hairs on her arms and nape lifted at the disturbance, as if the air snapped with cold.

She'd never experienced anything like it.

Pushing off, she shifted into her Phantom form, turned in the air, and floated – whereas most would have fallen.

Who she saw made dread sink into her gut.

Jabez crouched with his hand swiping the air right where she'd been half a second ago.

Realising he'd missed her, he rested his forearms on his bent knees and balanced himself on his toes. He looked rather menacing as he stayed low. His long white hair was messy and haphazardly rested around his dark horns and ears. A few strands fell to obscure his left eye.

He was silent as he glared at her, his expression holding nothing but cold malice. He looked... deranged, in comparison to when she'd last seen him.

The dark circles under his eyes hadn't existed before, and his hair was usually neat – sometimes even tied back. It was also odd to see him without a shirt on, as he just wore dark-crimson loose pants.

His markings have changed as well.

What used to be strange, runic symbols had changed into black streaks that went up his arms, sides, neck, and even into his hairline. It made his features appear sharper, demonic, and ruthless.

They didn't hide that the young man she'd met centuries ago, who couldn't have been older than nineteen, had to be at least in his mid-thirties now. He looked tired and indifferent to chaos.

That was the weight of his silent stare.

His nose wrinkled, and he bared his sharp, shark-like fangs. "I told you to stop coming here," he stated with a quiet growl.

She tilted her chin up. "It's not like you can stop me."

"We'll see about that."

Then, within the blink of an eye, he was... gone. He hadn't

twitched to move, hadn't leapt to the side. Just vanished.

Floating in the air, Lindiwe searched her surroundings. She couldn't see or hear him. *He couldn't have just disappeared.* She drifted closer to the building. *Where did he go?*

Lindiwe searched in every direction and even hovered to a new location. *Maybe I should stick to the shadows again.* She hadn't been in the village long, maybe an hour, so she hadn't expected him to suddenly turn up. *It usually takes him a few hours to get here once he's been alerted.*

It took him a while to run here on foot.

Wanting to make sure she couldn't be followed, as she still had a few more Ghosts she knew she could collect here, she sunk within the random building below her. Then she passed through the walls, surprising Demons as she moved to the next building over and shrouded herself in shadows.

I should be able to collect a Ghost before he reaches me. So long as she stayed hidden until that very moment, she wouldn't be caught.

It was difficult to do on the ground and in the shadows, so she found a secluded spot within the human items market. She'd already cleared out most of the meat market, but it also depended on whether the butcher touched the human's corpse while she was near.

A scream caught her attention, and Lindiwe observed what had been touched and noted it. She waited until another spirit made itself known, then Lindiwe hovered out of the shadows with haste towards the first, using the second as a diversion.

Just as she went to touch a slipper on a table, a large hand wrapped around her forearm. It tugged her forward towards the assailant, with a semi-clawed hand coming down to strike her throat. She gasped, turned incorporeal, and gave her back to the crowd to face Jabez.

He didn't sneer, didn't grin, but his eyes were sharp and fierce.

And he hadn't been there a second ago.

"Next time, I won't miss," he said, before instantly

vanishing.

He actually disappeared! Her eyes widened as she floated back. *What the fuck?! Since when can he do that?!*

"Uh, Weldir. Something strange is happening." She backed into the crowd to hide. "Jabez just disappeared into thin air."

"Disappeared, how?"

"It's called teleporting," Jabez muttered low in her ghostly ear from behind.

She gasped and slapped her hand over her ear as she turned around. He was gone.

"It's a new ability," he said in her other ear. When she turned that way, he was no longer there. "It means wherever you go, I can follow, even if it's to the ends of the Earth."

Lindiwe spun, and he stared coldly down at her.

"Teleporting?" she asked... both of them.

"That is a very dangerous ability for its user, as it's possible to migrate into a wall or another person. Only certain individuals can avoid that, and it requires practised skill."

Jabez's height had always been daunting for her as a human, but with his face shrouded in shadows, his red eyes seemed to gleam more than usual. "You won't notice me, won't see me, won't hear me, until it's too late."

But I did sense it. Maybe she was just used to detecting magic so she could feel for Weldir's mist when it was invisible, and in the process had trained herself to perceive magic. To sense when it was around her. *When he first teleported behind me, my skin crawled like when the clouds charge right before lightning.*

She backed up and then floated to the top of a roof. He teleported in behind her, likely wanting to flaunt this new ability to incite fear or wariness.

She hadn't felt the charge, as she couldn't perceive anything when incorporeal.

To test her theory, she became tangible, turned, and ran down the slope of the roof. She sensed a charge from her left and ducked to the right to avoid his fist. He frowned before chasing after her when she sprinted away.

He appeared before her, but she ghosted straight through his body and then shifted to human once more. She dodged every strike, evaded him every time he teleported around her, until... a punch landed.

Jabez was just too swift, his Elven side making him fast, and she fell sideways. Her body skated across a rooftop, dislodging tiles, and she turned intangible to narrowly miss his foot coming down on top of her head.

"Do you know how long it took me to perfect this?" he bit out, darting after her when she sprinted away in her Phantom form. "How many injuries I had to sustain? How many times I almost died, just to make sure you can't fucking drop me from the air again, or try to drown me, or burn me fucking alive?"

Lindiwe could admit to doing all those things.

She'd grabbed him by the shoulders in her owl form and dropped him from unimaginable heights, breaking his legs when he hit the ground. It was just unfortunate that before she could get to him on the ground, he'd already learned how to make portals and had crawled through one. This had been *after* she'd drowned him and Katerina with the sea, thanks to Weldir's assistance.

He'd narrowly escaped all of those attempts on his life. She'd snuck into his castle while he slept and tried to stab him in the heart, but he was always alert and managed to catch her before she could strike. She'd tried to do the same to Katerina, but her scream had alerted the castle, and Jabez had created a portal to save her.

Jabez had managed to land a few strikes, sometimes forcing her to retreat before she could shift into her incorporeal form.

If he saw her in the wilds, he'd chase her until they battled, and she'd do the same thing. They were like two magnetic elements; whenever they neared each other, they had this overwhelming need to kill – without ever being successful.

Many of their battles had happened within this village.

It was his. He hated her in his lands, and he had made that

known many times.

She eventually stopped running and turned physical when he teleported a few metres in front of her – she'd been intending to float to a new rooftop and then out of the village, admitting defeat.

But there was an avenue here, one she didn't particularly want to give up just because of his new ability. *I won't be able to come back here and collect souls properly.* He had some kind of scrying ability, and he checked on the village often. It was how he was being alerted.

"So, you've figured out a way to evade me completely," Lindiwe grumbled.

"Just as you have always evaded me," he said, his cold, crimson eyes glancing over her with disdain. "I realised that I'd been pouring all my efforts into offensive abilities rather than defensive. I started rectifying that mistake decades ago."

I can either give up on collecting souls here, or... Before she could finish that thought, he disappeared from his location and reappeared directly in front of her within an instant.

She shot to the left while turning incorporeal and floated to a different rooftop. He followed her, teleporting in front of her, not allowing her space no matter where she went. If she fled now, would he follow her through the Veil to make his point?

"Aren't you... *tired* of this?" she asked, gesturing at their surroundings and herself at the same time. "If neither one can reach the other, why bother?"

"Because luck can only get us so far, and I'm faster and stronger than you. I will eventually grab you."

She threw her hands up. "To what end? I'll just come back."

"Until you stop interfering," he said quietly, unnervingly.

"Then stop trying to hurt my children and I will!"

"Then tell Weldir to drop his ward on my portal. As I once told you, all your suffering starts with him, and that includes your offspring."

The malice in his eyes was darker than it used to be.

It was the gaze of someone who had completely cut out

anything good within them. He was no longer the light-hearted boy she'd once known, someone who once said he didn't want to be a ruler. There was no light in his eyes like she'd experienced by the waterfall as they laughed together.

He was corrupted by his goal, and the chaotic, bloodthirsty journey of it. His heart was likely filled with poison, and his words were meant to be nothing but venom.

He was arrogant, rightly so, and his new power would only make him more dangerous.

"You know what he wants is absolute," she argued. "I can't convince him to do anything he doesn't agree with."

"Then this will continue."

He tensed, as if to dart forward or teleport, and she held up her hands. "Wait!" she yelled. "Just wait."

His pointed ears pulled back as he let out a small snarl. Yet he quickly soothed it and straightened his shoulders, adopting an icy gaze.

Lindiwe waved her hand back towards the village behind her. "I know you care about Spiral Haven. Let me do this. Let me rid it of the spirits of dead humans. The haunted ones."

"Why? So you can empower Weldir? I won't aid him by allowing it."

"Because it disrupts the peace here," she explained calmly. "You and I both know their screams upset the people. Sure, it may empower Weldir, but I will keep coming back here to do it, no matter how you try to stop me. You will just make that process slower and will incidentally be the reason visitors stop returning when it's entirely riddled with Ghosts."

Jabez lowered his eyelids in annoyance and placed his arms behind his back superiorly. "They will adjust. They're easy enough to ignore once you're used to them."

"What about those who can't? Or the children who are easily frightened by them?"

Surprisingly, his right ear twitched when she mentioned the young, and his red eyes narrowed. They quickly dulled.

"Haven't we destroyed enough buildings that need

repairing? Or almost harmed the innocent in our fighting?"

"It's barely considered fighting when all you do is run like a coward."

"I'm the only one who can rid you of this problem, as no living thing can remove or touch them. The cost of that is I take them and give them to Weldir, but what's a few extra souls when he already collects thousands?"

He regarded her suspiciously, and he brought his arms forward so he could cup his jaw.

"You're speaking of creating a balance. Payment, essentially." His gaze softened as he looked over the village, and he tapped his lips as he thought. "You want this place to be a location of truce. Where we don't fight, even if we are in proximity of each other."

That wasn't what she intended, but... "Yes, that would be beneficial. I have no ill-will towards Spiral Haven, as you have seen. Why not let this be neutral ground?"

"Because I hate seeing your fucking face?"

Lindiwe couldn't help rolling her eyes. "The feeling is mutual, Jabez. You're literally so self-involved that it's utterly sickening."

"You'd be surprised by just how wrong you are about that," he murmured, still tapping his face. His red eyes darted to the side at her, and his lips thinned. "What else do I get out of it? I already let your abominations meander through it safely."

Seeing as they were having a relatively safe conversation, she needed to show she was trustworthy by being vulnerable.

"What do you want?" she offered, turning tangible.

His brow cocked in surprise, but he stayed right where he was. "What you're asking for goes against the very thing I'm trying to do. It has to be something good."

He continued to think, but the exaggerated manner in which he looked up at the spiralling, branched ceiling informed her he already knew what he wanted. He just made her stand there in anticipation.

Lindiwe was officially bored with his antics.

Finally he placed his hands behind his back, leaned forward a little, and had the audacity to demand, "Kneel."

Tipping her head forward to look up at him through her eyelashes in irritation, she sneered. "You're joking, right?"

"I think I would find it quite entertaining. I am a king and therefore should be knelt before.

"I kneel for no one," she retorted. "Least of all you."

"Not even Weldir? Considering all your offspring, I'd think you'd be used to kneeling for a male."

She shuddered. "You're still disgusting."

Jabez threw his head back and gave a deep, boisterous laugh. He brought his right hand forward and waved it dismissively.

"I'm fucking joking, you uptight prude. You're just as easy to make squirm as you were all those years ago."

Gosh! I want to kick him in the shin!

He gestured with his clawed fingers towards the village. "Bring a trade, something that is difficult to get but would be invaluable to the merchants, even if it's low in value for a human. Iron, dyes, silk cloth, even books. Benefit Spiral Haven. The payment of souls is nothing but to your benefit. Do more beyond self-gain to aid the people here who want to improve the lives of others. That will be your price of entry."

Taken aback by his request, it rendered her silent. She never expected him to ask for something so simple or selfless.

It didn't erase the fact that he was a violent psychopath who targeted her and her children when it suited him. It didn't even make her see him in a new light. It just revealed he could be cunningly benevolent, and often just chose *not* to be.

"How should I give it?" she asked.

"I will have a box made. You will leave an item in it for each time you enter, and I'll share your contributions with those who would enjoy them the most."

"And you'll inform the occupants to leave me be when I work? Some do try to catch or attack me."

"That sounds like a you problem." When she gave him a glare, he rolled his eyes and let out a big sigh, like she'd asked him for the moon or something. "Fine."

Then, Jabez teleported right in front of her. Lindiwe looked up at him, meeting his glare head on, but was ready to change forms if needed.

"But outside of this place, only hostility exists between us – unless Weldir drops his ward. I can be forgiving, Lindiwe."

"I have no interest in being your friend, even if given the opportunity."

She finally gave in and kicked him in the shin and then turned incorporeal before he could do anything about it. As he growled and held his shin while hopping on one leg, she poked her tongue out at him and let her intangible form sink to the ground.

We should have had this discussion years ago.

FORTY

June 8th, 2014

"Weldir!" Lindiwe shouted, her hands shaking while maintaining a viewing disc. "Oh god. *Please* be awake! Weldir!"

"I'm here, Lindiwe," he answered calmly. *"I've been awake for quite some time."*

He didn't tell me? A cold sadness dripped against her chest, even if... that was what she'd wanted – distance between them. *Wait.* She clenched her eyes shut and shook her head. *That's not important right now.*

"I can't see Leonidas." She *refused* to call him Kitty. When she'd learned of this name, she'd tried to explain to him what his actual name was.

He didn't want it. Apparently Kitty was more suitable to him.

She'd been considering teaching him his name nearly two decades ago, as he'd become rather intelligent, but Lindiwe had grown... *tired* of trying. Her children didn't want her, and she was always failing with them, so... she stepped back.

She needed to shield her heart from them as much as Weldir, and she'd completely stopped trying to connect with them. She was the Witch Owl, a strange being that created unease in them, and she'd long ago learned that's all she'd be.

In doing so, she became colder, more resilient to their dislike, and... deadened inside. She'd shifted beyond what her humanity could handle, and fully accepted that she was different, a Phantom, not only in species but to the world.

She didn't need a place to exist, except within herself.

She gave them names, but they only existed to her and Weldir, as they'd inevitably gain their own. It had become a recurring thing.

Sometimes they found each other, and the older ones helped the younger ones, like Fennec and Orpheus. Or Merikh with the twins, who had discovered him and didn't seem to understand he wanted to be left alone. Or Ari with Fisi, the hyena-skulled Duskwalker, and Kambarah, the crocodile-skulled Duskwalker.

"I cannot see Leonidas either," Weldir eventually answered. *"The image is murky and indecipherable."*

She hated how calm he sounded when she was so panicked.

"Then where is he? Why can't we see him?" And how long had it been since he'd gone missing?

I've been so busy with Auberon for the past week that I only checked on everyone today, she lamented. None of them usually needed her.

She surveyed the cave she was resting in somewhere high in the mountains of Pyrssia where Auberon, a second bear-skulled Duskwalker, lived.

"We both know the answer to that question, even if you don't want to admit it."

Lindiwe said she wouldn't interfere, except if their lives were in danger. It didn't matter that she was halfway across the world.

"Please take me there," she demanded, tucking her journal away and stashing it into her satchel. She threw it over her shoulder.

She was brought into a darkness she hadn't visited for quite some time, as she hadn't left that continent in years.

She glanced at Weldir, noticing his form was barely one-eighth, and a cruel loneliness crept inside her. *I hate coming here. I hate seeing him.* It reminded her of what she couldn't have, and all her painful wishes that'd never be granted.

Her unrequited love that was often too much to bear.

The awkward uncomfortableness between them was so thick she doubted she could bite through it and swallow without choking. She shifted her gaze away.

Thankfully, it only lasted a few minutes.

Transported right to the fringes of Jabez's lands, Lindiwe took in his newer castle that had stood for many decades. It was larger, more imposing, and utterly dreadful compared to the last. What had once appeared like a humble estate, modest in size for a 'king,' now stood as a daunting pillar of chaos amidst a haunted forest.

The structure was grey, and the bottom level was tall enough to fit a giant depicted in tales. The firepits illuminating the front entrance gave the impression that it was the doorway to the palace of damnation. The dark clouds on a moonless night gave it a foreboding aura, and the Demons patrolling made its warning clear: approach at your own peril.

Lindiwe stuck to the shadows so her colourless Phantom form was harder to see. She had no need to enter through the front doors and chose to go around the side to float through a wall, ending up in a dark room.

Staying intangible, which made her unable to be scented or heard unless she spoke, Lindiwe began to investigate the castle. She poked her head out of every door or wall first to check if it was clear before exiting into a new room or hallway.

Red carpet lined the hallway floors, while dimly lit candelabras created flickering shadows. She hid in many of those dark spots to avoid patrolling Demons in her search, most of whom were midway or fully developed.

Jabez sat in his throne room, lounging on his chair irreverently and looking bored, while Demons spoke to each other in the hall.

Katerina read quietly off to the side in an adjoining area with two guards, one protecting her back and the other in front of her.

There was no opening, not one where Lindiwe would be able to strike before Jabez teleported to her side – or created a portal to her.

For once, I'm not here for them.

She lingered within a wall so she could listen to their conversations and see if she could get a hint of what he'd done with Leonidas. Or if Jabez had him at all.

What if he's decided to become Jabez's new guard? She could see Jabez replacing Merikh easily.

A muffled roar, buried deep, bellowed from below her feet.

"Can someone shut that Mavka up?" Jabez commanded, palming his face in annoyance. "If it's not going to give us the pleasure of dying, the least it could do is be quiet."

"Y-you want one of us to go down there?" a Demon nervously asked, his hand gripping the front of his shirt.

"Did I stutter?" Jabez asked, lifting his hand off his face slightly to glare at the offending Demon from the corner of his eye. "I'm tired and annoyed from dealing with it already. Are you insinuating that only *I* should do it? What point is there in having servants then?"

"No, Your Majesty," a woman cut in. Dressed in tight leather, she threw her hand out to the fearful one. "But none of us will survive if we tend to it. Should I call for Woik to place a sound-dampening spell?"

"That will take time," Jabez retorted. "You will have to travel to him and return with him."

"Not if you retrieve him, Your Majesty."

Jabez's nose crinkled tightly as he bared his fangs. He was gone in an instant. He returned a few minutes later holding the arm of a large, burly, horned man.

"Deal with it. I'm leaving." He exited the throne hall into the adjoining room, and his voice echoed from within. "I'd like to go for a walk."

"I want to stay here," Katerina sneered in answer. "It's winter. Go freeze by yourself."

"Your impertinence is beginning to annoy me, Katerina. I

give you everything you want, and you can't even go for a stroll with me to help me clear my thoughts. It's not difficult to wear a warm cloak."

"Except you can't give me the one thing I desire because you keep fucking failing."

His voice grew quieter, but the menace in his tone was apparent even if Lindiwe couldn't discern what he said. It was a warning, one that would have set even her on edge had it been muttered with such unnerving calm at her.

There was no crash as if something was thrown in anger, no shattering of glass. His temper wasn't childishly explosive. Yet when she poked her head inside just enough to see, he was gone, and Katerina's expression was pale and spooked. She muttered profanities while snapping her book shut.

Lindiwe didn't care about whatever messed-up dynamic their relationship had. Or that it was obvious Katerina was impatient for the demise of Lindiwe's children and was punishing Jabez for it.

She quickly followed after Woik and the woman who'd suggested his presence. Woik was a tall Demon, perhaps close to encroaching on Jabez's height, with muscles nearly twice as big. Yet he walked with a dignified grace and silence unexpected for his size.

He was taken through a doorway that opened to a spiralling stone staircase. A guard behind them grabbed a torch from the wall just outside to brighten the dark descending tunnel.

Growls, snarls, and pitiful whines echoed from the belly of the castle, and each step down brought them closer to it. It frayed Lindiwe's nerves, and she desperately wanted to pass them and go to her precious son.

But she needed to remain undiscovered, especially as she had no idea where she was going.

The moment their approach was scented, Leonidas bashed against the wall.

"My barrier is still doing well to keep it contained," Woik stated, baritone voice soft and gentle.

He knelt in front of the wooden door that didn't shudder, even with Leonidas trying, with all his might, to hit it. The barrier protecting it trembled instead. Woik drew a symbol on the ground, a mix of triangles she couldn't decipher, and placed his hand over it.

He grunted as orange wafted from between his fingers like smoke. Sounds of the distressed Duskwalker dampened before fading completely.

He then stood and rubbed his wrist.

"I understand his majesty doesn't wish to maintain this kind of magic, but I'm unsure how long I'll be able to keep both present at the same time. I'll remain in the castle so I can warn him if it fails, and he can apply them himself."

"Do you know why he won't?" the woman asked. "It doesn't seem that hard, and his abilities are much stronger than yours."

He turned to the woman and narrowed his white brows at her. Pointed Elvish ears flicked. "Do you really have that little understanding of the significance of what he does? The deepest well has an end if you drink from it constantly."

The woman averted her gaze. "This just seems so minor."

Woik reached up to scratch at his short white hair. His skin was a light tan, likely from eating many humans, but he'd retained many Elvish features.

"Think about all he does. The sun barrier on the castle throughout the day, the scent cloak in the village at all times, the constant need to teleport, the wards he requires to sleep safely, and he must battle constantly to maintain his position on the throne. He must save his reserves, or he will have nothing to expend when he needs it most." Woik then waved towards the silent door. "Demanding minor assistance is not a sign of weakness, but of someone who understands that not doing so and failing means death. It's not laziness; it's intelligence. He's tired, he's spending too much, and it's *irritating* him. Only a fool would fail to see that all this expenditure is taking its toll on a mortal being."

He then turned to leave up the staircase. At the bottom of the dark, winding, ascending corridor, he gave her an unfeeling stare from the corner of his eye.

"I suggest you relay that to the other guards within this castle before your insolent words cause him to think your loyalty is shallow, and he removes you... *violently.*"

After he left, the woman shuddered as she peeked at the other guard. "Scary."

Their footsteps padded after him quickly.

Now that she was alone, Lindiwe turned to Leonidas' dungeon cell. She cupped her hands nervously, unsure if she wanted to see the horrible state of her child. She quickly squashed that down and passed through the door, and magical barrier, freely.

Now that the smells of people were gone, he no longer attacked the door, but he bashed against every surface for freedom. He looked fine. There wasn't a single wound on him, but Lindiwe knew better.

The overheard conversation from earlier was enough proof that they had tried all manner of things to kill him. His trembling limbs and white orbs, constantly spiralling with red before being engulfed in fear, proved he wasn't okay.

On all fours in his monstrous form, he paced as he whimpered, only to snarl and run headfirst into a wall, bashing it with his curling ram horns for freedom.

"Leonidas," Lindiwe whispered, turning physical so he could smell her familiarity even if it often unnerved her children.

Leonidas backed up into a corner, the vortex fire of his orbs rotating into crimson, but he didn't attack. He defended himself like a skittish creature that had been tortured, swiping his claws whenever she neared. When she came too close, he slammed his hand down, parted his feline fangs, and hissed.

"Please calm down," she cooed, lifting her hands up so he could see they were empty. "I'm not going to hurt you, little one."

Darting forward in a blur of chomping fangs, he locked his

jaw around her arm faster than she could turn incorporeal. Lindiwe screamed as she turned Phantom and floated away from him while holding her elbow to support her injured forearm.

That's not like him. He wasn't enraged; she wouldn't have approached otherwise. He'd chosen to bite her consciously, and Leonidas wasn't inherently violent like many of her other children.

The taste of her blood sent him over the edge, and he sprinted from one side of the cell to the other in search of more. He attacked her ghostly body, not understanding it wasn't touchable in that moment.

I won't be able to help him while he's like this.

"W-Weldir?" Her form wavered. She didn't need to be human right then to sense her own panic, fear, and worry. "Are you able to make a portal here if I bring some of your mist?"

"No. I don't have enough mana to sustain it right now."

Her eyes bowed in distress. "Please?"

"If I do, I have no idea how much damage it will do, and how long I'll slumber as a result."

"Please?" she begged. "There's a barrier, and I doubt I'll be able to get him out of the castle before he's recaptured."

Jabez would just teleport him back here if he got his hands on him. And in a tight environment that he knew better than a crazed Duskwalker desperately searching for an out, even if it was right before him, every minute they took to flee would only ensure his recapture.

"You know there is another option."

"I can't!" she yelled. "Please. *Please* don't make me do it."

"You're sacrificing my ability to help in the future over your emotions. If another of our offspring requires immediate help, you may be too far to give it. Is your guilt worth that?"

He was right. She knew he was right.

That didn't stop the tears that instantly welled when she turned physical. It didn't assuage her anguish and disgust, nor soothe the frantic pace of her heart. It didn't make her feel any better as she clamped her injured arm to her abdomen for support and threw her left hand forward.

Thick shadowy tentacles snapped around Leonidas' body. He fought them, and his distressed snarls only gouged into her chest further. He was so strong that his arms constantly pushed his chest up as he writhed to be freed.

His right arm came out from under him and his chest slammed against the ground.

"I'm sorry," Lindiwe cried, summoning a blade into her trembling, uninjured hand. "I'm so sorry."

Leonidas' beastly roar shook the very foundations of who she was. His feline tail curled, and his fur lifted in aversion when she stepped closer while crying.

"I'm so sorry!" She screamed it this time as she brought the blade down just behind the base of his skull.

Leonidas let out a heart-rending squeal, and she answered it with a shuddering cry. She wasn't strong enough to do this in one swing, and she had to bring her blade up again and steady her hand so she could hit the same spot. She hated that he kept moving until she cut through his spine. His orbs bled to white. What should have been a fatal wound meant nothing to a Duskwalker.

"Why?" he whispered, the betrayal in it evident.

She shook her head, unable to answer while biting her lips hard enough to draw blood as she brought her blade down one last time. In an explosion of glittering sand, his body turned into a giant cloud and disappeared.

All that remained was his head. His beautiful feline skull and sandy ram horns.

Her blade disappeared as she grabbed his horn with one hand and lifted his weighty skull. When she turned incorporeal, it came with her – it wasn't something she could do when their bodies still existed.

They had to be temporarily dead for her to bring them to *this* side of life and death.

She carried it tightly and narrowly evaded being discovered

as she fled the castle. Each second weighed on her conscience painfully, and she struggled to maintain her form under the heaviness of her emotional anguish.

She made it outside into the dark of night and sprinted with the remains of her stolen prisoner. She went as far as she could; the castle was far away and hidden behind the canopy of leaves before she finally gave in. Thrown from her Phantom form, Lindiwe collapsed to her knees and held Leonidas' skull tightly, hugging it to her chest with all her might.

"Why?!" she yelled, as hot tears dripped from her jaw and splattered against the dirt. "I never wanted to do that!"

She never wanted to harm her own son – only to save him. No mother should have to do such a thing, have their child's blood splatter against her hands and feet, staining her dress, her very mind, as she hacked their fucking head off.

The unfairness of it was unbearably cruel.

On her knees, she cried against his big head. Her shoulders heaved, and she hiccupped, struggling to catch her breath through her sobs.

Why him? Why was Leonidas taken? Why did any of her children have to suffer at the hands of that evil vixen and her brutal guard dog?

Because none of the others would have let any Demon near them, and Merikh was too smart to get caught.

Orpheus hated them more than anything. Fennec was wary and territorial, but he never wandered far into the Veil. And the twins, Aleron and Ingram, were more dangerous as a synchronous unit than any living thing in the world. Because Leonidas made himself vulnerable – he was curious, befriended Demons, and wanted to learn.

Weightlessness suddenly took her.

Lifting her head with a sob, she peered into the dark void. Weldir looked so distant that she could barely make out the imprint of his minimal solidness.

"Change forms, Lindiwe."

Adhering to his command, Lindiwe shifted, and her tears

renewed. Then he shot forward, and her swollen face was tucked against strange firmness. A limb held the back of her head, while the other rested low and held her hip. The body she was pressed against felt wrong, as there was no defined muscle or malleable softness. It barely made a discernible shape.

"I know you said you don't wish to pretend, but this is all I can do for you."

The limbs around her were tendrils, with their ends split into false hands. His body was nothing but a barrier, smooth enough to be hugged, but not real. The only part of him that seemed to exist was the crook of his neck her face was pressed up against, up to the edge of his jaw and pointed ear.

Lindiwe let go of Leonidas' skull, knowing Weldir would keep it utterly safe, so she could wrap her arms around his barrier as if it was his midsection. The anguish in her next cry was pronounced enough to ring in her own ears.

She embraced him like her life depended on it as she sought the comfort he was generously offering. Lindiwe clung to him desperately. She clung with every inch of her body, every ounce of strength, as she scratched with the need to crawl deeper inside of him until he swallowed her whole and numbed away the anguish, the loneliness, the regret.

"I know this was hard," Weldir stated softly. "I know this was something you never wanted to face, but your strength and bravery in that moment is a reflection of your selfless devotion to him. To all of them. You should be proud of your savage mercy, as I am proud of you for doing it."

His tendril hand patted the back of her curls, being so gentle with her as she trembled in the wake of this kindness. His words somehow deepened her wounds and healed them at the same time.

Right then, she didn't care if this was real. She didn't care that she wasn't really hugging him, when she knew he was at least *there* for her in the only way he could be. That his consciousness was welcoming her and trying to help her through one of her most painful moments.

She wasn't alone.

"I am sorry that you must always face hardships in my stead."

FORTY-ONE

September 28th, 2022

"This human has lasted much longer than the others," Lindiwe muttered to herself, as there was no one listening.

No one watching.

Weldir had been asleep for quite a few months, after exerting all his energy into growing his mist.

"It's already been two weeks since Orpheus brought her to the Veil. The most someone has lasted was eight days, and he eventually ran off into the Veil to be eaten."

Lindiwe's faith in Orpheus' newest offering was justifiably... non-existent.

She'd likely die like all the others. Lindiwe was aware this made her callous, but her heart couldn't take hoping, only for it to be squashed. For Orpheus' attempts to be squandered and unappreciated.

Sitting on her bed in her little hut in the middle of the Veil, she hugged her upright knees with her back against the wall. With her cheek upon her knees, she kept her other hand out below the scrying spell so she could watch the pale woman run at Orpheus with a short sword.

She swung so confidently, yet her stance was pathetically unskilled. With his arms crossed, the wolf-skulled, impala-horned Duskwalker easily evaded the human's swings as she grunted and screamed through clenched teeth.

Is she learning so she can try to kill him? Did that make Orpheus a fool for trying to teach her something he didn't know how to do himself? *She'll probably try to escape again, just like before.*

How she didn't die after being taken by the arachnid of sorrows, a rather nasty Demon with much Elven magic, was beyond her. *She did protect his unconscious body and drag him inside the protection charms for his safety afterwards, though.*

Reia was a mystery to Lindiwe.

Then again, she'd seen what people would do in the name of survival and self-preservation. This woman had survived two weeks, but someone else had survived five years.

The sun was dim behind collecting grey clouds, and the muted light reflected off the woman's sword. They stopped and discussed teaching her how to wield it.

Then Orpheus made a sound, and her chest felt a little lighter.

I don't think I've ever heard him laugh before. A small smile curled her lips as she looked at him with motherly affection.

"You won't be able to hurt me, my little human. You will not be quick enough, nor strong enough." With his arms folded, he stepped in front of her so they were facing each other. "I will carve you a wooden sword if it looks as though you might, but until I do, you will train with this. I will make sure we are careful."

It's been so long since I saw his orbs be anything other than blue or red. It's nice to see them joyful for once.

The woman, short and of average physique, blew a few strands of her long, straight blonde hair from her eyes.

"You're awfully arrogant for someone who has never seen me fight." She stepped back and pointed her sword up at his bony snout brazenly. "I was pretty effective at killing those Demons to protect your sorry butt while you were unconscious."

His chuckle deepened, and Lindiwe found herself laughing along with him. "I'm sure you were, but let's make you better."

Okay. So maybe she isn't too bad.

Orpheus seemed genuinely content with her, and she didn't appear to harbour any ill-will or resentment.

Reia swung carelessly as she chased Orpheus in a circle.

She tried with all her might to cut downwards, and the point hit the dirt and became lodged. Her green eyes widened, and she failed to remove it no matter how much she wiggled it up and down.

Orpheus wrapped one of his palms around the hilt of the sword, which so happened to encompass her small, nimble hands, and helped her to dislodge it. She didn't gasp and shy away from his touch, nor did she swat it away with disgust.

They resumed the poor lesson.

She said something that did make Lindiwe feel a little better. "Wouldn't it be better if you had your own sword so that I could attack it? It might help me learn."

She doesn't want to go out of her way to harm him, even if it's an accident. That was a welcome change. Although her movements seemed careless, it looked like she was holding back from hurting him.

Orpheus turned his skull upwards, and Reia followed his gaze.

"That is a good idea, but something we will have to try tomorrow." Grey clouds, which had already started thundering above Lindiwe, finally shaded the clearing out the front of his home. "It is going to rain."

That's true. She listened to the rumble of thunder. Her wooden shutters were closed and rattling against the wind, but her talisman kept her warm even without a fire. *She's been there a long while. Her food resources will be low.*

It was lucky that Lindiwe was nearby. She always had this anxiety whenever she knew ten years had passed and it was time for Orpheus to find a new offering.

After a hundred and eighty years, Lindiwe tired of this. She tired of his sadness that would inevitably come once Reia was gone. She worried that this momentary contentment would only bring on a deeper sorrow than usual.

Lindiwe often regretted having put Orpheus on this path, but she also knew this hope was what kept him going. Like a puppy chasing his tail, he didn't care if he got hurt, so long as he eventually obtained his prize.

Crawling off her bed, she mentally prepared herself for the journey, feeling remarkably empty inside. She threw her cloak around her shoulders, tossed her hood over her head, and stepped into the encroaching storm. She shifted into an owl before lifting off to battle the winds.

It didn't take her long to arrive at Orpheus' home situated in the middle of a large clearing. The rain had already come, wetting her feathers, but she was warmed by her talisman radiating a mild heat throughout her body.

She landed on the outskirts of his salt circle.

Demons loitered around Orpheus' home whenever he had a human there, lured by the promise of meat from his past failures. When one rushed for Lindiwe in her owl form, she curled a tentacle around its neck, snapped it, and tossed it into the forest.

She waited for her opportune moment: when Orpheus was at the back of the house.

Then she started the annoying dance required to summon her growth magic. She bounced side to side, hopping from one taloned foot to the other, while lifting her wings up and down slightly. Reia was seated in a chair on the porch, showered in a glowing light that came from within as she ate from a bowl.

Lindiwe had no qualms about making her presence known.

It wasn't the first time she'd shown herself to an offering, and she doubted it would be the last. She just hadn't spoken to any of them since Lydia, the first.

She also hadn't spoken to Orpheus since then, either.

What's the point of getting to know them? She refused to intervene anymore, unless it was to be a silent waking hell when *others* touched things that didn't belong to them. *So long as I've done my part, helped in this small way, that's all that matters.*

Just before she was almost past the side of the house and near the garden, feeling the call of magic that tingled in each raindrop, she turned her head to Reia. Their gazes met momentarily.

"Orpheus!" Reia screamed, backing away towards the safety of the doorway.

It only took a moment for him to rush to her, and his gaze followed the direction she was pointing.

"It's the Witch Owl," he explained, as Lindiwe hopped away and continued her dance.

The Witch Owl. That was all she was to him. All she was to any of them. Even those far away in distant lands called her something similar, although never those exact words. Just *owl*, in some form.

It was like they saw her as some strange entity. Not their mother. Not their friend. Not someone they could trust.

Orpheus went on to explain what she was, much of it incorrect. She only ever approached him in her owl form, and he was quick to vent what had triggered his temper or agony at a silent bird.

Once she was in the middle of the garden, she threw her wings up and bounced in a circle. The turned soil began to glow around stalks and hidden seeds, and little sprouts flourished in the embrace of her and the rain.

"I believe she is the one who gave me the amulet circlet, but I am not sure. She has only spoken to me once when human."

Lindiwe faltered a step. *Once? I have spoken to you hundreds of times, Orpheus.* Realising she'd stopped dancing, she picked up her pace to make up for the lag. Maybe he saw all those moments as a collection of one time, or his memory was partially broken from the years of mental and emotional pain.

Perhaps he'd tried to forget all those moments with Katerina that involved Lindiwe to escape the hurt. He didn't understand how the passage of time worked, and perhaps his suffering made him feel that forever had passed, as if it had all dragged out slowly.

His humanity was low back then. His obsession with a cruel woman could easily dismiss Lindiwe's presence while under the thumb of emotional manipulation and torture. *He remembers his name because it was called out to him a hundred times. Remembers her face, as it was there for thousands of days.*

She finally stopped dancing when the earth glowed bright green on its own. Orpheus came past the fence of the garden and paused mid-stride to stare at her. He was quick to snort out a huff and continue patrolling.

There was no greeting. Just nothing.

This hurts. Doing this hurt. Being forgotten hurt. Being considered untrustworthy, when she'd poured all of herself into her children, hurt. *Why does everything have to hurt?*

All her love was ignored. Her love was never returned.

She found herself growing emptier, especially in the wake of her choice to put space between her and Weldir.

I tire of always hurting. It was slowly breaking her beyond repair. It was eating her from the inside out. It was ruining her, desensitising her, twisting her.

Lindiwe pulled back her hood, then transformed into a human and lifted her face to the cool rain. It'd been a long time since she'd cried; after beheading Leonidas eight and a half years ago, in fact.

I feel like I'm all out of tears. How many had she shed? Enough to fill an ocean and drown in it?

Despite it all, Lindiwe reached into her cloak as if nothing was the matter and began planting seeds. *I wonder if this human would like a lemon tree.* Something sweet and bitter.

She picked an empty spot in the garden while it was still infused with magic and used her bare hands to make a hole. Then she planted the seed and waited for a lemon tree to grow. Lindiwe stayed there for a little while, watching it grow, while raindrops splattered against her head, her nose, her shoulders, and her sorrow-filled chest.

I miss you like an ache, Weldir.

And she wished that didn't hurt either.

FORTY-TWO

October 13th, 2022

Sharp talons dug into the bark of a massive tree branch as Lindiwe stared at Spiral Haven from above in her owl form. She'd removed most of the spirits of humans from it when she first got here, ensuring that the likelihood of one popping up was low.

It was all in preparation for the people who had just entered the village. All three were shrouded in black cloaks, and it did much to hide their wolf, fox, and deer skulls from being noticed. Although two beings were over seven-foot-tall Duskwalkers, the little one, who barely came to their chests, was a brave human in disguise.

Reia constantly adjusted her deer skull so she could see through its eyeholes and stuck to the shield of Orpheus' cloak. A scent-masking spell stopped her human smell from being detected. If she strayed too far from him and got lost on her own, she'd likely be discovered.

Lindiwe intended to intervene if that happened, but she also had other motives for being here.

It's nearly been a month since she was brought to the Veil. Reia had somehow managed to survive longer than any other offering.

She cares for Orpheus. It was apparent that she felt

something tender for her son, and that was bringing on foolish hope. *Could she be the one?* Was Reia finally the human who would, of her own choice, stay with Orpheus? *We've waited so long for this.*

It was a shame that Weldir wasn't here to witness this. If he had a real ass, he might kick himself in disappointment for still sleeping.

Unfortunately, Lindiwe had an irritant as a companion this eve.

"Heeeeere, pretty birdie," Jabez cooed at her side, his hand out as he clicked his fingers like she was a cat.

Piss off, she wished she could say, flapping a wing dismissively as she side-stepped further down the branch and away from him.

"Awww, don't be like that. What happened to our truce?" When he went *psst psst psst* at her again, following her while crouched, she gave him an angry hoot. "Are you still fucking mad about the feline-skulled Mavka? That was almost a decade ago."

I hope you fall off this tree and snap your stupid neck. Of course she still hadn't forgiven him for what he did to Leonidas! He could rot and burn for all she cared.

When he wouldn't stop pestering her, Lindiwe glided to a lower branch. The bastard fucking followed her by teleporting!

She yanked her hood back and scrunched her face at him angrily. "What do you want?"

"I'm bored. Entertain me."

She wrapped a tentacle around his neck and yanked it. He teleported on the spot to be free before he could go flying.

"That's not nice. You know how boring it is to live this long – take pity on me." He probably thought he was being humorous and light-hearted.

"The only reason I'm not trying to stab you right now is because this is neutral ground."

Jabez sighed and sat down with one leg dangling over the side of the branch. "This human has lasted quite a while. If this wasn't neutral ground, I might've snatched her by now." He leaned back on straightened arms until all his long hair dangled like a white curtain. "Then again, we never agreed Mavka would be included in that truce. If you won't entertain me, I'll find other means."

The threat was there. It hung over her head silently. Unspoken but utterly terrifying because he was talking about stealing away their hope.

Bastard. Fine.

Lindiwe sat down as well, ensuring there was a gap between them. Jabez shifted over until their shoulders almost brushed.

"Come now. I don't bite."

Lindiwe placed her hand on the coarse bark and pushed away. "That's a lie, and we both know it."

He'd almost bitten her multiple times.

"It's interesting watching them, none of them the wiser that two people on opposing sides are observing their every move." Jabez disappeared, only to reappear moments later with two apples. He dumped one in her lap before taking a bite out of his own. "Have you come to make sure he doesn't fuck it up?"

Cupping her hands around the apple, knowing Jabez wouldn't stoop to poisoning her, she brushed her thumb over its smooth surface. "Yes. I also plan to help them obtain some useful things. Items that they wouldn't think to get."

"Want some help?"

"You know anything I tell them to get wouldn't benefit you."

He took another bite of his apple and then pushed the chunk into his cheek to talk. "Eh. Sometimes it's fun to give the opposing side a hand, just to see them flounder regardless."

"Do you intend to intervene?" Lindiwe asked darkly.

"Hmm. Haven't decided yet."

Lindiwe could feel the foreshadowing, the lie that must be present. *It's why I plan to help today.* Reia was a strange, although strong, person. She was getting better with her sword, but she needed help. *And Fennec could use a book on how to build a house, like how I gave one to Orpheus.*

"Although I didn't know it at the time, I have my answer," Jabez stated, and the tiny hairs on Lindiwe's arms lifted.

She looked at him, and his cold red eyes were intense as he peered at her from the corner of his eyelids.

"Answer to what?"

His lips quirked. "Wouldn't you like to know. How's the feline Mavka?"

"You have some gall asking me about him after what you did."

"I did to him what was done unto me. Then again, that's not entirely true, as I did do a little more than that."

Her stomach knotted with understanding and dread. *He's better, since it's been a few years.* Leonidas was resilient, probably more so than his siblings, but there were scars in places where the eye could not see.

Cutting off his head to save him had been hard, but she'd also been there when he came back to life. He'd been thankful after she explained why she did it. A small amount of trust had grown, but he was skittish around most beings now – understandably so.

She wanted to ask Jabez how he could do that to another living creature, but she was also acutely aware of how hypocritical that would be. Like he said, he did what was done to him... by her. She would probably do more if she had the opportunity, like cut out his beating heart and show him how sickly and broken it was.

When did Lindiwe's spirit grow so corrupt that she would even consider doing such a horrible thing? *I'm a monster, as much as he is.* She'd known that for a long time too.

She was more of a monster than her children, even if she didn't look like one. *Everything I do, everything I touch, rots.* Perhaps she was unlucky or cursed.

"How'd you save him anyway?" Jabez asked, extending his hand and dropping his apple core. He looked down, watching it fall, and then tsked when it hit the ground, like he'd been hoping it'd land on someone's head. "I've always wanted to ask how he got out with the barrier still in place."

"I... cut off his head."

He didn't laugh, didn't make a joke. The silence was surprising, and when she lifted her gaze to him, he cocked a white brow.

"I never thought you'd do such a thing." He looked down at the apple in her lap, rolled his eyes, and then snatched it so he could eat it when it was obvious she wasn't going to. "But that's the price of war. You find yourself doing unimaginably horrible things, even when you don't want to."

Lindiwe was unsure if he was talking about his own actions or hers, even when his ears were pulled back in a way Lindiwe knew meant he was being coy or hiding the truth of his emotions.

"I can't do this anymore," she said, getting to her feet. "I can't sit here and pretend we're on amicable terms when I want nothing more than to scratch your eyes out. You are the one at war, all by yourself."

"Fair enough. I did just come here to annoy you, after all. However, Lindiwe..." he trailed off.

She considered ignoring him and not giving in to the weight of her name and how he said it. To not give him the satisfaction of turning and meeting his malice-filled gaze.

She failed... and greeted him.

"We have been patiently waiting nine years. It's not my revenge to take, but hers, but my war has always been more important to me than her wishes. I suggest Weldir lowers his ward now, or prepare yourselves to suffer the consequences of inaction."

"I told you, we have no–"

"You are almost out of time. Heed that warning now, as this is my way of offering kindness."

Then he was gone, and Lindiwe's blood pumped with alarm.

Reia was in danger. Then again, she had been this entire time. It'd never been a case of *if*, but *when*.

I need to prepare them for any outcome. Orpheus likely told her of Jabez and the danger he presented, but that didn't stop her from being snatched. *If she can just give me time to get to her side and help, if she can wield her sword and protect herself, then...*

Maybe Reia could survive long enough that it no longer mattered. *If she would just give him her soul...*

She hastily shifted into an owl, all so that she could lure Reia to a bookshop where she'd leave behind tokens for her to obtain. Feathers that stuck out from the spines of books.

Weldir, I really need your help right now.

Please wake up.

FORTY-THREE

October 23rd, 2022

I want to keep watching them. Lindiwe had never been this interested in any of Orpheus' offerings, but things had also never gone this well before. *But I can't stare at their house all day.*

After safely returning from Spiral Haven, Orpheus and Reia had spent much of their time inside for nearly two days straight. She would have thought they'd died if it wasn't for the fireplace and candles illuminating it at night. The salt barrier kept her from seeing with her scrying spell due to magic keeping her out. She wasn't privy to anything personal that happened between them – she just kept her fingers and toes crossed that all was going well.

Most days, Reia went outside to train with her sword. Orpheus was often by her side, helping in his own way.

All Lindiwe could think was: *He's matured so much.*

Seeing him interact with another being who not only accepted his presence but welcomed it was new. She hadn't realised that Orpheus had grown so much, despite his humans often perishing – many by his own fangs.

Reia was cute, in her own way. She was a stern person, who obviously didn't let anyone push her around, yet her cheeks were quick to stain with a blush. She often made herself flustered, especially in Orpheus' presence.

Was it enough? It felt like they were racing against time.

Her anxiety was growing by the day with Jabez's threat lingering over her head, and she hated this wait. This feeling of uselessness. As much as she wanted to, she couldn't linger in the trees day in and day out like a creep.

Lindiwe was aware of the... *intimate*... nature of their relationship now, and she just couldn't bear to snoop in person and witness it. It felt sickeningly wrong. She'd caught a glance in her viewing disc of an outside dalliance, and she'd waved away her scrying spell so quickly she'd bashed her hand against the wall.

It was making it difficult to monitor them.

One thing I know for sure: Jabez won't attack while Orpheus is there. He wouldn't win, even with his teleporting ability. He'd never been able to do so in the past, and he couldn't enter the salt circle while Orpheus was there.

Unable to subdue her unease without checking on them, she brought up her viewing disc to see they were outside together.

Reia was on her hands and knees, tending the garden happily. He held a basket for her as she placed vegetables in it. Orpheus' tail, no longer hidden away due to someone else's disgust, shifted slightly in joy whenever Reia smiled at him – like he was just waiting for it patiently and sweetly.

This is what I always wanted for him. Someone to see who her children really were, and that they were beautiful, kind, protective, and deserving of love. Orpheus doted on her every way he possibly could, and it was nice to see someone not abuse that.

And this particular someone had opened her arms to Orpheus first, rather than it seeming like he was clinging to her skirt for scraps of affection.

They went back inside, then not long after, stepped onto the porch together.

Lindiwe's heart nearly exploded with joy when Reia stepped closer of her own volition and slipped her arms around his midsection for a cuddle. Obviously surprised by it, it took him a moment to wrap his arms around her shoulders and draw her in tighter.

His orbs morphed to a bright pink.

Lindiwe sat up straighter and leaned forward to see better. *I know because of Aleron that their orbs can turn that colour, but I've never seen it happen before.* Her pulse raced in excitement. *What does pink mean?!* She'd been waiting since Aleron's birth to know!

Whatever it signified, it was obviously a pleasant emotion.

Is it... love? Her lips pursed in thought. *Then why did they never turn that colour for Katerina? Unless... did Orpheus never love her?* Then again, how could love form when all Katerina did was throw salt into his garden of affection, rather than tend to it with nourishment? Obsession, fascination, curiosity – these things had been apparent, but perhaps never anything as deep or as tender as love.

Orpheus' orbs shifted to bright yellow during their conversation. "You are funny, my little doe. If they do not fear Mavka, then they will not fear you and your little sword."

Reia lowered her sword with a pout. "That's not nice, Orpheus."

He answered her with a light chuckle.

They're going to practise. They did this almost every day, then they would go inside so Reia could cook, bathe, and whatever else it is they did. *I'm glad she's finding the book I told her to get useful.*

Seeing that they were fine, together, safe, and most of all, happy, Lindiwe changed the image to a different child. Although she had the ability to bring up multiples at the same time, she refused to weaken Weldir when she didn't have to.

You worry me, Leonidas. After so many years, he'd found the courage to return to the centre of the Veil. He didn't linger, often wandering the surface where it was safer, but he currently approached the village.

He eventually headed inside it, and the spell around it

stopped her from scrying on him.

She moved onto Merikh, who had immersed himself within a new human city. His glamour allowed him to weave through the crowd of people without issue, and Lindiwe had no idea what the citizens saw. The blue mana stone hanging from a silver chain, tapping against his bony forehead, only glowed when he was in the presence of humans.

Oddly enough, he said he wanted to fit in, yet he was surly with everyone he spoke to.

She couldn't help smiling when she summoned Ingram and Aleron to the forefront. They mirrored each other's movements in reflected parallel as they wandered through the Veil. A poor, unsuspecting Demon caught their attention.

Perhaps due to their special bond, it was rare that they attacked each other when they were enraged and mindless. They argued with growls and snarls, fought a little over their prey, but never truly turned on each other with hostility.

The Demon was ended quickly, and they played tug-of-war with its corpse.

Now that she'd started, she couldn't help checking on them all.

It was easy to lose herself in their moments as she watched them. She lingered each time, feeling the waves of loneliness slowly creeping up the sands of her psyche like an incoming tide. She was used to it, and that was why she found it easier to become a spectator.

Her home had become a prison of solitude.

The afternoon crept in, and Lindiwe lay on her hard bed on her side. She got lost staring at Odie. *It's been a while since I saw him.*

"Weldir?" Lindiwe called, just to know if he was there or not.

Silence greeted her.

I'm tired, she thought, as her eyes grew heavier.

She summoned a different child, and a jackal skull came into view.

I really wish he would wake up. He's able to watch over them all at the same time. Maybe then Lindiwe could close her eyes and properly rest, as she hadn't been able to since Reia had successfully travelled to the Veil.

It comforts me to know he's there. Even if she had to keep her heart closed off to the best of her abilities.

Her eyes drooped under the weight of her constant restlessness and unease, the nights of difficult sleep catching up to her. She finally drifted off while watching Balam, her jaguar-skulled son, hunting through the jungle.

When Lindiwe's eyes peeked open, day was about to break. She stretched, her back arching off the bed, until she felt a twinge just above her hip.

She began her mornings like most.

Deciding on whether or not she actually wanted to eat, since it was no longer a requirement but more for enjoyment. Then she pulled her journal out and detailed everything noteworthy from the day before, leaving out her thoughts and feelings. She'd never been interested in going back to read over her journeys to experience her mental decline.

Most of the Duskwalkers in the southern hemisphere will either be asleep or just going to sleep. Reia is also human, so she and Orpheus should be asleep at this hour.

She scried for those in the northern hemisphere, the many that there were. Once done making sure none of them needed her – they never did – she tended to her herb garden. Having medicine was useful, and she often made her own soaps, shampoos, oils, and other care products. She liked to be *clean*, even if all she had to bathe in was river water.

Midmorning came, a time when most of her children in Austrális or South Unerica would begin moving. The rotation of her duties continued, and she brought up her first viewing disc as she packed her basket to go bathe.

Expecting to see Orpheus' home when she scried for him, she halted midway through collecting a final toiletry item. He was in the forest, chasing after some unseen thing, with orbs stark white.

Her basket and everything in it clattered to the ground when she knocked it to the side as she scrambled to the hook where her cloak was. She almost tripped face-first into the wall, and the hook ripped through the hood when she grabbed it to stop herself from falling.

It was fine – it was still intact.

"Fuck," Lindiwe snapped out as she threw it around her shoulders. "Fuck. Fuck. Fuck!" She grabbed the handle for her door and yanked it back, shoving herself over the threshold. "Reia!"

Because Lindiwe knew one thing for certain: Orpheus wouldn't be heading towards the centre of the Veil, in the direction of Jabez's castle, if she wasn't there. She'd seen it in the distance, watched as his snout lifted in that direction with a whine.

"She was taken." Lindiwe threw her ripped hood over her head, and a loose feather fell down her face. "Curses. I thought they were fine!"

She transformed and lifted off in her owl form. She couldn't see Jabez's castle from where she was. She'd made her home on the complete opposite side of the inner ring of the Veil.

How?! Orpheus hasn't left his home in days! Why did he leave her by herself?! To fetch water? To hunt? To chase after a Demon? The reasons could be endless. Lindiwe felt it in the pit of her soul that it wasn't Reia's fault. That she didn't run away or willingly go with Jabez.

It's different this time. They may have only been together for a month and a half, but Reia was gentle with Orpheus. She didn't disdain his presence; she inserted herself into it with a big smile that even warmed Lindiwe with tenderness.

Shit. Shit. I'm so sorry, Orpheus. Lindiwe flew hard, using all her might and the calm winds to get there faster.

But he's so close to it. He must have been running since yesterday. Perhaps it'd happened only a little after she'd stopped watching them. Damnit. Was that why they'd been talking on the porch?

Orpheus has never gone after a taken offering before. If they were taken, he knew they were lost. *For him to go after her...*

It meant she was special to him, and he trusted that she'd want to be returned to him. History wasn't repeating itself.

Would they be too late? Was Reia already dead? *For once, can luck just be on my side?* But what use would Katerina and Jabez have... for keeping her alive?

Hope was slipping through her fingers.

Trying her best not to be seen, Lindiwe landed on the pathway between two tall, thorny hedges and turned into a human. She didn't remove her feathered hood as she brought her hand up to create a murky viewing disc, everything grey and indistinguishable.

He's already here, Lindiwe thought, lifting her gaze to the ominous castle.

Closing her hand to undo the scrying spell, she then shifted into her Phantom form. Darting forward through the neatly trimmed hedges, she shoved her intangible, ghostly body through the outer wall.

Landing in a random hallway, she then headed straight for the throne room. *If he went anywhere, it would be there.* A place where all his sadness and grief started. *It worries me that he's here after what happened with Leonidas.* Orpheus had already suffered so much emotional turmoil, he didn't need to be physically tortured as well.

And she imagined if Katerina got her hands on him, she'd make it far crueller. There would be no end; she'd probably get off on it too. No doubt teasing him, brutalising him, and digging into his mind just as sharply as any blade she'd wield at the same time.

Passing through the wall, Lindiwe poked her head inside and only saw two of them. The fact that Katerina was facing Orpheus alone wasn't a good sign.

Where's Reia? And more importantly, *Where's Jabez?* Orpheus didn't even seem to understand the significance of that.

In his monstrous form, he stepped to the side to go around Katerina, who was standing at the top of a set of podium stairs.

"I'm telling you that I want to go with you," Katerina said, her brows creasing. "I told you where she is. She is with the Demon King. Why do you keep asking about her when you have me?"

Confusion laced Lindiwe's mind. *Why would she say that? She hates him.*

Lindiwe knew Katerina and Jabez's relationship was a mixture of like and hate, and stemmed from transactions rather than true affection. A way to appease his loneliness while providing her protection, his desire for companionship in exchange for indulging her need for revenge. Broken trust meeting broken trust.

Neither cared about the toxicity, so long as they obtained what they sought. Filling the void of desolation was hard, so finding someone to rely on, even if it was barren of emotion, was better than being utterly alone.

It was why she doubted Katerina would've had a change of heart. *She's up to something.* The question was: what?

Lindiwe could only imagine how confused Orpheus must be to be presented with someone he once thought of fondly. She was offering herself up, but Lindiwe knew... it wouldn't matter.

The pain in Orpheus no doubt stopped him from wanting this woman back, but she represented the very first ease of companionship. He likely didn't miss her, but the space she'd filled, and had never truly understood why it was taken from him. He didn't know what he'd done wrong, when his actions had never contained malicious intent. He wanted to fall in love and didn't know how, and no one cared to show him.

He'd acted on instinct. Because instinct didn't need a reason; all it said was to protect, provide, and nurture in every form it took.

And he wanted someone to reciprocate that base instinct.

Lindiwe didn't need to hear his next words; she knew what his decision would be.

It would be the woman who reached out to him first, with a smile and adoration in her green eyes. Someone who invited him in rather than pushed him out. Who, even if she seemed surly at times, often thought of his best interests and knew the hidden kindness in his heart existed.

Enough to teach him how to be compassionate, even to a strange Duskwalker with a fox skull and antlers.

"Because I don't want you. I want to find Reia."

He's... facing his past and choosing his future. Not just because it filled the lonely void, but because it filled it with utter warmth. If he wanted to appease it, he would take just anyone offering themselves.

He would've taken this callous woman.

"You will regret that, Orpheus," Katerina sneered, and her hands tightened behind her... around a dagger.

Has she truly gone fucking mad? Stabbing him would do nothing but enrage him. *She wouldn't do that. She wouldn't be so stupid.* Katerina was a fool in many senses, but she cared about her life above the cost of anything else. *So what kind of trap has been laid?*

Where was Jabez hiding, and when would he reveal himself?

She said Reia is with Jabez. Does that mean she's actually alive, or is it just a ploy to keep him here until he returns? I need to search the castle. Maybe the dungeons?

Relief violently hurtled through her like the heavy wet winds of a cyclone when the blonde-haired woman appeared out of nowhere. Jabez materialised behind her, clutching his groin with a hiss through clenched fangs.

Reia tackled Katerina to the ground and punched the black-haired woman in the face so hard even Lindiwe winced when her head smacked against the ground. A skirmish immediately broke out, and Orpheus dived for Jabez.

Lindiwe didn't know how to intervene, or if she should. *I could just end up being a distraction. I could confuse the situation.* Orpheus might turn on her, or the two humans fighting.

Although Orpheus and Jabez weren't on even footing – one smarter than the other, one faster and stronger than the other, who could now teleport away – Reia had the upper hand.

They don't know how to kill Orpheus, and so long as Reia survives... Lindiwe would jump out if it seemed like she was truly in danger. *Jabez won't be able to get near her before Orpheus comes to her side, and he wouldn't do something that could put Katerina in danger.*

Screeching, Katerina managed to kick Reia off her. Reia slid across the ground and stopped near her discarded sword. She rolled to it, albeit not gracefully, and picked it up with a determined, narrow glare.

Yes! Atta girl, Lindiwe exclaimed in her head.

Then the most frightening thing she'd ever heard echoed within the throne room.

With a low chuckle, Jabez said, "That skull of yours will be nice when it's broken into pieces."

Lindiwe shunted back in shock, and into the empty room behind her.

What? How did he learn... Merikh? With her eyes wide, she looked down at the rough carpet. *No. He wouldn't have. He gave me those charms for Orpheus, and he knows the dangers that knowledge presents to himself and the other Duskwalkers.*

The answer was obvious.

Jabez said he's been waiting nine years. That's when Leonidas was taken. Although she couldn't feel it, she curled her hands into tight fists at her sides. *Were they waiting for Orpheus to get a new offering, hoping she'd stay alive long enough to become bait? Why else wouldn't they have taken Reia sooner?*

'It's not my revenge but hers.' That's what Jabez had said. *Because Katerina would be angry if she wasn't the one to kill him?* Had all the pieces aligned for them perfectly? Leonidas, Orpheus, Reia. Did they think that fate was in their favour to make the perfect lure, right after discovering the truth?

They held onto this secret until the opportune moment. He spoke to her and threw it in her face, knowing the whole time, while she thought they were still safe. *He had such a horrible plan, and sat down next to me, watching his lure solidify herself as bait, and even offered to aid her.*

Cold, ruthless cunning. Heartless evil in the form of a man.

Lindiwe shot forward to save them. *Orpheus shouldn't have come here!*

She immediately paused as she registered the two women in front of her.

Scarlet splattered to the ground in a growing puddle, as Katerina coughed up blood from between her lips. A sword had been shoved through her midsection, with Reia low on the ground keeping it in place.

Jabez called out to Katerina, alerting Orpheus, who charged and brought Reia into a protective embrace.

Lindiwe was too shocked to move or truly hear what they said. *She killed her.* Reia had done the one thing Lindiwe hadn't managed to do, no matter how she'd tried. *Does this mean this is... over?*

No. They would keep being hunted, but now their weakness was known. There was no reason to hold back anymore.

Orpheus held Reia tightly as he stepped back towards the exit, where guards were likely outside waiting to be let in. He didn't need to fight so long as he could run with her.

Yes. Leave. Get out of here.

If only Lindiwe could turn them incorporeal with her.

What followed happened so fast. Something glinted through the air and made contact with Reia. She arched into Orpheus and gripped his fur tightly in pain. *A dagger?* It was the one Katerina had dropped.

Lindiwe didn't know what to do when the scene played out before her. She couldn't be overjoyed that Orpheus finally learned how to make a small protection dome – the bargain for the magic was the blood of the one they wanted to protect. Not when Reia was lying in his arms utterly protected, but dying anyway.

I can't watch this. It was too much, too painful. *Come on, Reia. Just do it!* They still had time.

It was why she hadn't interfered. Because when she did, everything always went terribly wrong. *Please...*

"How do I give you my soul?" Reia rasped.

Yes! The words Lindiwe and Orpheus had been holding their breath for had finally been uttered. *Is it too late?* She looked over Reia and her wounds. *I was this close to dying when I gave Weldir my soul.* Maybe she just wanted to have faith that it would work out.

When Reia's flaming soul emerged from her chest, bright orange and full of life, she knew everything would work out.

Eat it, Orpheus. All you have to do is eat it before it turns white. Before it, and she, died.

And he did.

Lindiwe grinned so damn wide.

Not even when Reia crumbled in his arms like ash, did her grin fall. His whines and ethereal tears were heartbreaking, but they would be short-lived. The fight that broke out afterwards was frightening and the most ruthless battle she'd ever seen, but her euphoria didn't wane.

Her son, in that moment, was wilder and fiercer than ever, putting Jabez on the back foot. Evading and defending, his teleportation was slower than Orpheus' rage. Jabez's arm was severed, the same one Lindiwe had dismembered years ago. Injured and angry, and seeing this was now a losing battle, Jabez created a portal and kicked Orpheus out of his home.

The moment it shut, he placed his hand over the stump of his biceps and cauterised the wound. Heading towards Katerina, he made a circle with his thumb and middle finger and put it to his mouth to whistle.

Lindiwe chose then to emerge.

He halted and then lowered his head to sneer. "What kind of coward watches from the shadows?"

"Hmm. Wasn't quite a shadow, more like a wall," she answered nonchalantly with a shrug. "And sometimes it's better for others to battle it out. I knew he would win."

A lie, of course. Lindiwe had been terrified the entire time.

"I wouldn't call it a win. I killed his fucking human, or did you miss that?" His red eyes flicked to Katerina when Lindiwe neared her corpse. "Get the fuck away from her."

"Did she die, or did she *fade*?" she remarked, before kneeling next to the foul woman's body. "Stop me if you think you can. But I'll be taking her soul, just as I promised. Too bad she can't watch me eat her heart out first."

Jabez snarled and disappeared, but before he could get to her, Lindiwe turned incorporeal once more.

"Here's the thing, Jabez. I've known for a long time that a soul can be given, and a soul can be taken." While she was intangible, and with his sorry self standing over her, she punched her ghostly arm through Katerina's still chest. She felt resistance, but that's all she perceived as she yanked out the bitch's soul.

She looked up at Jabez's enraged expression, his long hair curtaining around the sides of his face, and gave him a bright smile.

"You both brought this on yourselves. Have fun with her corpse."

Then she leapt back and through the wall, and continued to bounce from room to room, until she made it outside. He didn't follow – what would be the point?

Once in the sunlight, she looked down at Katerina's soul, free of any scarring, spots, or anything that pertained to an injured person – whether that be physically or mentally. A pure soul that reflected nothing of the rottenness within.

I considered giving you to Weldir to take you to the

afterworld and empower him. Not to torture her, as that had always been a lie, and something she doubted either of them could stomach. *But I've changed my mind.*

She wanted this woman's existence to cease entirely. Never to be returned, even by accident.

It was asleep now, limp and at peace.

She held onto it with both hands, dug her thumbnails into its centre, and yanked in two different directions. Katerina's soul tore apart, and nothing special happened.

Lindiwe didn't suddenly gain newfound power. There was no gust of energy, no pulsing of magic. All that followed was the sense of triumph as it withered away into nothingness, gone forever.

She looked up at the sky. Things were going to get harder from now on, but she appreciated this moment of joy. *You're probably running after her memory right now, so let me help you go home.*

You finally have your bride, my sweet Fenrir.

FORTY-FOUR

October 25ᵗʰ, 2022

After placing a white feather on the windowsill of Orpheus *and* Reia's bedroom, Lindiwe peeked inside. Both were naked and partially covered by their blanket, his arms around her with his hands squeezing her in sleep like he feared she'd disappear. Reia's head and delicate fingers were buried in the fur of his chest.

Hopefully Reia sees my feather when she wakes up, she thought with a warm smile at their snuggling.

If not, Lindiwe would have to find the opportune moment to speak with her privately. After what had happened, and how he'd almost lost Reia, she doubted Orpheus would be feeling inclined to allow anyone – let alone someone he barely trusted – near his precious *bride*.

It will also be easier to speak to her alone.

As she perched in a tree to rest during the long wait, dusk blanketed the Veil with oncoming darkness. Every time the feather fluttered away, she used a tentacle to put it back.

Eventually, blonde hair rose above the sill as Reia sat up. Her eyes blinked lazily when she peered outside, likely gauging the time of day, then her gaze narrowed. *Good. She's seen it.*

Before long, she exited the quaint log cabin home with a white gown on – a wedding dress of another offering that had yet to be dyed a colour.

"Hello. It's a pleasure to finally meet you," Reia said, lifting the feather Lindiwe left behind. "You keep leaving me these."

"And you keep following them. You've been a very good human in letting me guide you," she answered with mirth, happy that everything had worked out, despite the fact that it all could've easily ended in tragedy.

"You're lucky I have. It's only because you made the garden grow, and that Orpheus trusts in you, that I was able to follow your clues to the bookshop."

"Perhaps it is instinctual that he trusts me." Lindiwe said this but knew it wasn't true. Their instincts told them *not* to trust her, but with Orpheus in particular... perhaps it was the past he couldn't remember well that allowed Lindiwe a presence in his heart – despite how much someone else had tried, fervently, to make him turn against her. "Are you not going to step out of the salt circle?"

Reia stepped forward bravely, and it was in that moment Lindiwe truly became smitten with her. *Orpheus needs someone like this. Someone courageous in the face of everything that could be dangerous to help him out of the broken shell he's been forced to hide in.* Stern, yet kind.

"Did you know I was going to be taken by the Demon King? Is that why you gave me all the books?"

Yes... But also no. It had never been certain that Jabez would, although it'd always been likely. Being prepared for the future, whatever it may have been – either Jabez or a stray Demon that tried to rip its claws into her – had always been Lindiwe's goal.

She also didn't want to give the impression she was omniscient, when she absolutely wasn't.

"Not at all, but it wasn't hard to guess what would happen. You wanted to learn how to wield a sword, and I provided a way for you to be taught. History wanted to repeat itself, but it did not expect a girl to be her own knight in shining armour."

A snort of laughter burst from Reia. "I got stabbed in the back by a dagger and died. Some hero I was."

Lindiwe lifted her gaze towards the house and the direction of Orpheus.

"But you were his. You killed his past and gave him a future he has always sought." Pride swelled in her chest, as well as gratitude, even if she tried to hide it in her expression. She kicked her legs to give the impression that this was all meaningless to her, despite how she'd been worried every minute of every day. "How does it feel to be a Phantom?"

"Like I can escape the world." Reia folded her arms and lifted a brow. "You knew I would become one if I gave him my soul, so why didn't you tell him?"

"Sometimes mystery leaves us wanting more."

Because they didn't actually know what would happen, only that their child could have a bride. Their abilities beyond that were unknown, as was this bond.

"Then what of the children's book? It was very funny where you left your feather. *Beauty and the Beast*, really?"

"Didn't you enjoy reading it to him? Your story is not the same, but you still fell in love with someone most find hideous."

Someone no one else wanted to love. Which made her a pillar of hope for dozens of her children across the world. Lindiwe planned to share this possibility with all of them.

"But the beast was a dick in the beginning, and Orpheus was kind to me the entire time."

"He was also worse. You were almost eaten many times," she reminded her. "I didn't think you would survive, and yet here you are, speaking with me as though I have done something wrong."

She sighed. *Why does everyone treat me like I'm the bad guy?* She was trying her hardest to help, but she also had to protect herself and her bruised heart. She had to distance herself, otherwise she worried she'd grow... *tired* of wanting to be here.

Living forever was hard. It was harder when she felt alone and had been made an outcast by the very creatures she sought to love and be loved by in return.

If she let them hurt her too much, and with her future with

Weldir despondent, Lindiwe wondered if there was a point where she just wouldn't be able to take it anymore. She may be a Phantom, and to everyone some strange, otherworldly spirit, but in actuality, she was human.

She had limits.

She might want to stop existing if she didn't barricade her own emotions and protect her heart, and then they would no longer have her when they truly needed her the most. She knew that was why she kept living on – for them – even when sometimes she didn't want to.

Weldir doesn't really need me anymore.

She'd given him enough servants to obtain and cleanse souls for him. The few that Lindiwe retrieved during her travels were meagre in comparison. Her role was almost complete in this regard.

I promised him that once he woke up again, we'd finish what we started. The Sing Empire and Pyrssia still only had one each, and it was the last major landmass that didn't have many Duskwalkers. *After we place a few there... what need will he truly have of me?*

So, she had to emotionally distance herself from her children enough to stay present in this world, just so she could take care of them. Not that she was *unwilling* to try and form a bond.

Lindiwe manoeuvred herself so she could swing upside down from the tree branch while still facing Reia. *Maybe I should one day try being a bat?* She could take on any form she liked.

She was also childish when she wanted to be, and she knew trying too hard to become a mother figure to this woman, or someone she could befriend, would only scare her off. *I'd rather she think me odd than an enemy.* Someone to keep at arm's length, so she could do the same.

Then again, Lindiwe *was* odd, considering the life she'd lived and the beautiful beings she'd given birth to.

"Can a mother not care for her child?" Lindiwe asked when Reia questioned her motives.

She wanted to laugh at the young woman's shock, but kept it in. Hopefully Reia would explain what it meant to Orpheus, only so they would rely on her a little more in the future. They didn't have to like her, just trust her enough to know that she always had their best interests in mind when giving advice.

"So, you're just here to help your children? What about the others, then?"

She went to explain the depth of her situation, and about the other Duskwalkers – all of them. To explain that everything was more complicated than they could ever imagine.

Something stopped her.

Sometimes it's best to let them believe their world is small.

What use was there in telling them about Duskwalkers they'd likely never meet in person? Why complicate it for creatures who already struggled to understand life and the world?

One thing Merikh has taught me... the less they know, the better.

She'd never tell another why they were truly born, after learning how much damage it could do. She'd rather they question their existence than know it was due to a selfish and yet selfless reason – to aid Weldir but also help humans.

She told Reia about the other Duskwalkers only pertaining to Austrális – those she may meet in the future. She also left it open-ended just in case Weldir wanted more here, or across the world. The many tomorrows to come were uncertain.

Regardless, she'd come here for many reasons: to reveal part of the truth, plus her and Weldir's presence, but also to share information. She didn't want to leave Reia unprepared for the possibility of pregnancy. *Weldir said it's likely they'll become compatible if the human shares their soul.* It'd changed Lindiwe, after all.

If they can heal, create protection domes, and, uh, other sexual things, then surely there is a way to prevent pregnancy. All they needed was a reason to learn.

Orpheus had even learned how to make wolf illusions, just

like the spell she'd discovered in the Anzúli temple so many years ago. How? She didn't know. Perhaps he thought if it appeared he had companions, the Demons and Demonslayers would leave him be when he travelled the same path he took every ten years.

For once, I'm going to be like Weldir and... guess.

Hopefully it was true they could prevent pregnancy.

If not... oops?

FORTY-FIVE

March 13th, 2023

Humming, Lindiwe watched her newest baby scamper around a small meadow in the bright morning sunlight. Snow covered every inch of the ground; it was too soon to begin melting with the early spring chill.

They were young, barely a few weeks old, and had no distinguishable features yet. Their blobby, baby-like form was the same as all her children when they were first greeting the world. A tiny oval snout with two slits made up their nose, and they had no eyes or even impressions where they should be. Two little holes marked where their ears were.

A small smile crept onto her face as they explored, sniffing anything and everything of interest. They didn't seem to mind that their claws and fingertips bent backwards as they dug, or the iciness when they bit around snow, chewed it, and then spat it out with their purple tongue curling at the taste.

Her smile cracked when her stomach twisted with nausea. Seated upon a stout boulder, she covered her gut and tried to swallow down the saliva flooding her mouth, which informed her she was moments from puking if she didn't soothe the urge.

Her stomach gurgled, bubbled, and heat travelled up behind her sternum.

Losing the fight, she bent forward with a hand on one knee

and expelled the empty contents of her stomach. It was so warm that the blackness staining the snow began to melt it. Tears welled in her eyes as she heaved multiple times, trying her hardest to see so she didn't vomit on herself or her curious baby.

At the noise she was making, or perhaps the smell, they came running over with a trill. Lindiwe scooped them up before they could step in the black puddle she'd made, as her body continued to heave even when nothing came up. Screeching with hands reaching out and making grabbing motions, they fought to get to it, and she utterly refused to let them play in it.

Once she was done, and managed not to get any on herself, she leaned back to breathe.

"You should eat. It makes you feel better," Weldir said through their bond.

"I know it will make me feel better, but it sometimes makes it worse," she answered, as she looked up at the colourful sky slowly shifting to blue.

Lindiwe wiped her mouth with the back of her hand and then reached down to grab a fistful of snow. She wiped her face, then put some in her mouth, let it melt, and swirled it around before spitting it back out.

"It seems particularly bad this time."

Lindiwe gave a mild snort of laughter. "Maybe having two children back to back wasn't wise."

"It was your idea."

She rolled her eyes, got up, and walked away from her mess with her baby curled up under her arm like a ball. "I know having a second baby only a few weeks after the first was my idea, but I'm hoping if I grow them closely like Ingram and Aleron, they'll form a bond like them. I wish I had realised sooner, as I may have paired up all the Duskwalkers."

"You cannot change what has happened."

Snow crunched under her footsteps as she walked into one of the forests of Mongulien. The people here were good, kind, and hardy, which meant many of them had survived in the destruction of history.

The Demons kept coming, but they were wary of the humans here, just as they were wary of the countries surrounding it. This was the perfect location to raise these two, as the country sat between the Sing Empire and Pyrssia. She planned to leave them a little east, where the two countries bordered, and let them roam freely.

"How is Nathair today?" Lindiwe asked, changing the direction of the conversation.

She kept an eye out for any noise or movement, knowing the hibernating animals would emerge soon in search of food now that winter was over.

"He's still lucid, but he isn't interested in speaking with me much."

Pausing to sigh, she pushed her fidgeting child to her chest so they could cling to her properly, then scratched behind her ear. Her loose hair tickled the back of her hand, and she patted it down to neaten it.

"He's doing better regarding the fragments, but I think he's truly begun to realise that there is no life here. He cannot move forward when there is nothing to move towards."

As much as learning this upset her, they'd known about Nathair's mental decline for quite some time. His sudden increase in humanity meant he understood the hopelessness of his new life.

The fragments had been a distraction, but he was better at controlling them. Learning how to speak through sign language had also been a welcome challenge because it gave him something to focus on, rather than dwell. But he and Weldir had, apparently, been able to speak for decades, so all that remained was a hole in Nathair's life.

One in which he dwelled in impossibilities, just like her.

Lindiwe raised her face to the sun when it peeked through the trees. *I bet he's questioning why he's there, and how unfair it is.* She continued walking on her aimless path. *He used to watch us with Weldir, but he's stopped doing that too.*

He was mentally shutting down, right after snatching his

mind back from the human fragments that pestered him. They were still present, and sometimes he lost the battle, but he was better at dealing with them.

She was thankful to remain updated, but it was... hard not being able to do anything to help. He was there, even further from her reach than Weldir, and there was nothing she could do about it.

Weldir worried he'd consume her entirely if she went to Tenebris. She was human. She may not survive the 'great swallowing' she'd once called it with a disgusted shudder.

Placing a hand on her stomach when it grew queasy, she then rested it lower. She rubbed the outside of her growing womb, her belly still flat, as it was too soon for her to start showing.

They'd both been conceived by a tendril, Weldir begrudgingly agreeing despite never trying to convince her otherwise. He'd given up on trying to change her mind about intimacy, as five decades had passed and she'd not once wavered in her decision.

She'd hated the entire process, but it did make her heart feel lighter. It also made guilt deepen to the point she wanted out of his realm so fast, she would have ripped apart the fabric of space and time just to flee.

"Thank you for letting me know about Nathair."

Silence fell between them, which was perfect. It allowed her to begin her hunt for food.

When she first spotted a marmot, she considered killing it but didn't want to risk the sickness they sometimes gave to humans, despite being a delicacy in this part of the world. She'd tried it before but didn't wish to risk it while pregnant. Instead, she captured a hare.

Then she made herself a fire on top of a flat piece of rock, skinned it, and cooked it. The process took some time, pushing her into the midmorning when she started eating. She was midway through when a Demon came to inspect her smoke and the smell of meat in the air.

She covered herself in a protective dome, and it proceeded

to snarl and bash at it. She didn't give it another thought, even when her baby growled back while scratching at the inside of the dome to fight it.

Cutie. It's in their instincts to fight Demons.

"Lindiwe," Weldir called, when she was taking her last few mouthfuls of meat. *"A group of humans has stepped into my mist bordering the Veil."*

"So?" she asked around a warm bite. "If they want to die, then that's their choice."

"There's a bound woman with them."

That made her pause, and she pulled her meat away from her mouth to frown. "But the occultists are mostly gone. None have sacrificed women in over a century."

"These people don't look like occultists. Most of them are armoured."

"Like from a town?"

"I believe so. They have crests on their armour. I think the woman is a criminal of some kind. They've mentioned a murder."

She lowered her food entirely. "Throwing someone into the Veil for a crime is barbaric. She must have killed someone of importance if they marched all the way there just for her."

She probably pissed off the wrong person, and they wanted to make an example out of her. I don't see why it matters to us. Humans were cruel. Enough to stab Lindiwe and leave her to die and be eaten. Enough to do other vile things to each other.

"I thought you'd be interested to know. And that they're very close to Fennec's cave."

"Then he'll gain some humanity – unless the Demons get to her first," she murmured, taking another bite.

"I'm... surprised by your response."

Her gaze lowered to her fire in shame. *I can't save everyone.* She'd turned her back on humankind a long, long time ago. *I can only care about my children. They're my priority.*

Yet, her next bite was harder to swallow, and she gave up on her meal entirely when she just felt sick for all the worst reasons.

I guess I could save her. But to what end? To leave her in the forest on the surface just to be eaten? *I would have to walk with her to a nearby town and hope she isn't arrested again.* Not saving her life could save her from living in a prison cell for the rest of her days – which was more merciful, in Lindiwe's opinion.

Then a thought crossed her mind, and her shoulders lifted self-consciously.

"*How* close to Fennec's cave?"

"Enough that he would find her with ease from where she falls."

Her mind rotated with an idea. *I told myself I wouldn't interfere anymore.* She rubbed the side of her neck. *But... I know he seeks a companion like Orpheus.* She pulled her hand away to look down at her palm. *What do I do? Let her die, or give her a chance at a new kind of life?* Her hand held no answers, and her next question sent dread through her chest. *What if she's like Katerina?*

She curled her fingers until she made a fist. *What if she's not?*

A resigned groan came from her, and she threw her mostly eaten meat into the fire. She stood, kicked snow onto the flames, and picked up her featureless, unnamed baby.

"Okay. Take me to their location."

"If you intend to save her, you don't have much time left."

"Then let's be quick."

As soon as Lindiwe was thrown into midafternoon sunshine, she immediately leapt into motion. Just as she arrived, the tanned woman, who had shoulder-length dark hair, was shoved off the canyon's cliff.

She pulled her hood over her head, ran in the woman's direction while holding her taut belly, and jumped off the cliff.

Her heart was already racing when she leapt, and it only grew more rapid when she transformed into an owl.

The woman's scream ended about halfway down as she passed out from the inertia of falling, and Lindiwe kept her wings close to her body as she dived.

Curses. I'm not going to make it, she thought, when the ground came hurtling towards her. *No. I can do it.*

She flapped her wings to go faster, and faster, trying to beat her falling speed.

"Lindiwe. You mustn't hit the ground. You may injure—"

She gave a bird shriek to shut him up. *I know I can't risk my own death!* She would never do anything to harm her unborn child just for the sake of this woman's life, or Fennec's potential happiness.

Lindiwe rotated her own body and managed to lock her talons around the woman's side and a leg. She spread her wings right before they could hit the ground, caught the wind, and shot into the air. She flapped her wings when she began to lose height, and the unconscious body swaying made her veer to the right.

Fuck! She threw herself to the side before the woman could smash into the rock wall, and they were shunted to the left. *She's too heavy.* Lindiwe could only fly with the equivalent of what she could carry, and *any* size of person was a struggle.

She'd seen from a distance that the woman was a little plumper than most, but that hadn't deterred her. *We don't have to go far.* She could see the entrance to Fennec's cave and the salt circle he had carved around it.

I just need to place her gently down in front of it.

Her talon slipped from where it gripped a soft torso. Lindiwe released her hold to avoid clawing into the poor woman's skin, and she screeched when all she held onto was a leg.

Oh shit! The momentum of her body swaying was too difficult for Lindiwe to counteract with her tenuous hold on one foot, and they swung sideways. The woman's body dropped hard, and her wings couldn't battle the fall. She tried with all her might to flap and regain control, but she just couldn't do it while carrying another person.

She was only so strong, especially in the air.

Damnit!

She let go to save herself, hoping the woman could survive the small fall without bleeding out. It was too late. Lindiwe shrieked when she crashed into the wall of the Veil's cliff headfirst.

She instantly blacked out when she made contact.

A time unknown, but of worried disgruntlement

Watching the situation unfold, Weldir called Lindiwe to his realm when she hit the rock wall, passed out, and began to fall. He caught her owl form in his weightlessness.

Blood coated her feathers around the crown of her head, and it leaked from her nose holes and beak.

And Weldir could do nothing.

She was physical and out of his touch. He couldn't heal her and merely had to wait and hope she'd wake up on her own. Unbridled fury gave his growl a dark edge, and he called her soul to his side so he could inspect it.

The wound doesn't appear to be too bad. It hadn't left a permanent mark on her soul, so she should hopefully wake on her own. He noted that their unborn offspring was fine and hadn't suffered any damage – that's *if* they could be harmed at all while in gestation. They were indestructible until they gained their skulls and horns.

That wasn't enough to soothe his anger.

He drifted his gaze to his mate and the way her snowy owl form appeared brighter in his shadows. The smear of blood was stark against her white feathers.

He hated that she was hurt and there was nothing he could do about it. Like always, he was stuck on *this* side of life and death.

His mist shimmered and vibrated around him as his growl deepened. *We will have words about this, Lindiwe.*

Had he known this would happen, he wouldn't have told her about the human female. He wouldn't have helped, even if it appeared they seemed to have had the same idea.

Orpheus had a bride; hopefully Fennec could have one as well.

His viewing disc showed that the little female Lindiwe had tried to save had surprisingly survived the small fall – and had landed right on top of an unsuspecting Fennec. Weldir believed this had actually saved her from death, or any major bleeding wounds that would have made her a meal for his offspring.

There was hope for her yet.

Closing his clawed fist and sending his mate's soul away, he thought angrily, *This better not be for naught.*

FORTY-SIX

April 11ᵗʰ, 2023

After landing in front of her cottage, Lindiwe turned from an owl to a human, proceeded to drop to her knees, then grabbed her hair and had to swallow down the urge to scream.

"She's pregnant!" she exclaimed, so utterly stressed out about this news that her breaths were frantic, shallow, and her heart raced. "She hasn't even known him for a month! Oh god, this is so bad."

Ready to start ripping her hair out, she untangled her fingers so she wouldn't. She covered her face and shook her head.

"How could this happen?!"

"Well, she did give him her soul readily, and they must have had intercourse since then," said Weldir, being utterly unhelpful and obtuse about it. *"What is that human saying? 'When a mummy and a daddy–'"*

She couldn't believe the trickle of humour in his alluring baritone voice!

"I know *how* it happened, just not how they got to the sex part!" She leaned back and crinkled her eyes at the sky dramatically. "I didn't even have time to prepare them! He shouldn't have known what sex is, or that he has a penis. Things like this should have come much, much later. I was hoping to give them some advice once their relationship progressed, but they went from barely knowing each other to being intimate."

"Isn't this a good thing? It means they like each other."

She shuddered, simply because it had been so awkward having to tell her own son he'd gotten his bride pregnant. Then she'd explained what babies were and how they were formed.

I had to have the birds and the bees conversation after *the bee already fucked the bird.* She wanted to wail because this was all so backwards.

Once she finished getting her anxiety out of her system, she sighed and let her arms fall. The backs of her hands rested against the grass, and she was so tired from being on edge for hours that she just wanted to close her eyes forever.

"Don't get me wrong, I'm happy for them," she said, staring up at the cloudy sky. The rain had come and gone, but the dreary weather continued to linger and threaten them with another downpour. "She seems nice, and she cares for him. She's a little shy and reserved, and it's obvious she's pretty depressed, but I can imagine how confusing this all is for her. She was thrown into the Veil, barely saved by me, became the bride to a Duskwalker, and is now going to have his baby all in less than a month. It's... a lot. For anyone. I had time to adjust to all these strange changes. Even Reia is still adjusting. Delora has been thrown into the deep end of the lake headfirst."

It's a lot for me to take in.

She'd had no intention of staying in Austrális once she'd given birth. She'd actually been in the mountains of Mongulien with both her babies when Weldir informed her that Orpheus had called out for *Magnar,* as that was Fennec's new name apparently.

She'd been over the moon when she'd learned that Magnar had discovered how to heal, had protected his new human, and then had obtained her soul. The woman was pretty, nice, and weirdly enough, accepting of the silly monster who was trying his best.

She'd had no intention of interfering.

Magnar and Delora had Reia and Orpheus to guide them.

Except they're moving too fast to be guided! Things should have progressed at a slower, more normal pace. Not... not this!

"Oh well," Lindiwe murmured as she rose to her feet. "There's nothing that can be done now. I've told Magnar to take her to Spiral Haven. So long as they get prepared, all should be well."

"Does this mean you're staying in Austrális?"

"Of course. I can't leave now, not when they really need me the most."

"What about our current young offspring?"

"They will have to wait. I can't give them their skulls and horns yet."

She'd need to stay with them for a year or so after they became adults to help guide them and protect them from nasty Demons. She also needed to stop them from massacring the first town their curiosity led them to and help them get used to humankind. She needed to make sure Demonslayer organisations in that part of the world didn't harm them either while they were finding their feet. Not to mention stopping them from drowning or falling off a cliff.

Basically, she had to keep them from accidentally – temporarily – killing themselves. They had a habit of doing that in a long list of ways.

I like being near when they're just starting out.

She opened the front of her cloak and reached in to grab one and then the other, holding one in each hand. They both gave a cute squeal when she lifted them into the air and rubbed her nose with theirs, one at a time.

"Once I help Delora give birth and things are stable between them, I can head back to Mongulien."

It was just a few months. Lindiwe had held onto some of her children for over a year.

⚮

April 17th, 2023

Standing before Leonidas – or Kitty, as he preferred – Lindiwe put her hands up to block his path through the forest.

"You need to leave the Veil," she demanded, her tone firm to ensure she couldn't be ignored.

He snorted a huff through his feline nose hole, and on all fours, stepped around her. *"Why? I should be fine."*

"Because Jabez and his minions are on the move. They're hunting, and I'm worried he's hunting Duskwalkers." She quickly chased after him. "I've already warned the twins, since they've been lingering around the centre of the Veil lately."

A low chuckle slipped past his sharp fangs. *"Only an idiot would attack them."* His short-furred feline tail curled at the end. *"You need to stop worrying. I won't allow myself to be harmed again."*

"You say that, but his ability to teleport may render that argument moot."

He shrugged. *"I'll rip him to shreds if he tries. His ability to disappear isn't enough to save him from my claws. He's already tried, and failed, to capture me again."*

His muscled biceps flexed with each movement as he carefully traversed through the forest. The backs of his hands grazed over twisted tree roots and rocks, while he looked one way, sniffed the air, and then brought his feline skull forward.

"Please. For once, just listen to me," she pleaded, running in front of him and throwing her arms out. "He knows your skulls aren't indestructible. He's already tried to kill Orpheus."

Leonidas sighed, and his yellow orbs turned black when he hung back for a moment. They opened, and he shone them at her. *"You said his female companion is dead. Isn't she the one who wanted Mavka dead?"*

"It's more than that. Jabez has his own vendetta against your kind, and he's become... unhinged since she died."

It'd only been half a year, and his movements had been... different. He left his castle often, rather than remaining inside it. He was more aggressive, more violent, to the point that the moment she saw him in the Demon Village, she got out of there quickly. There was a dark, crazed edge to his eyes that was more apparent than ever before.

Something in him had snapped, and she didn't want to know what the result of it was.

"Even if it's just for a little while, I think it's best if you all leave the Veil for a few years. Let things die down. Especially you, since your home was taken from you because you left it for too long."

"I'll consider it," Leonidas stated, stepping around her again.

That's his way of saying he won't!

Unlike Orpheus, who had stopped hunting humans due to wanting to make them his companion, Leonidas hadn't. He was younger than his brother, but far more intelligent.

But it doesn't make him any smarter sometimes.

He also couldn't be told what to do, and he liked roaming the Veil as much as the surface. He was strong, formidable, and unimaginably quick – even compared to his brothers. He thought this made him safe.

He's able to befriend some of the Demons. Does he think that sets him apart from the others? It didn't matter if he'd made friends with some of them; Jabez didn't care about such things. He'd kill Leonidas and then those Demons under the guise that it progressed his war and vendetta. He'd destroy anything and everything, so long as it gave him what he wanted.

"They've entered the village," Weldir told her as she watched Leonidas walk off, unsure of how to change his mind.

"Ugh!" she bellowed, raising her hands with tense fingers because nothing was working out for her right now.

She was out of time. It'd taken Delora and Magnar days to get to the centre of the Veil, and during that time, she'd been hunting down her wandering children to get them to leave. She wanted them on the surface, where it was safer.

Talking to the twins was impossible, as they hadn't obtained enough humanity yet. Getting them to leave had proved futile;

they preferred to chase her through the forest like they were playing a game rather than listen.

At least I know Merikh is safe, she thought solemnly, watching Leonidas' tail swish before his backside disappeared into the blue-white mist. *He's travelling through human towns still.*

I can't help any of them if they won't fucking listen to me.

"Keep an eye on him," she bit out as she pulled her feathered hood tighter over her head.

"I always do. I'm watching them all, Lindiwe. I will tell you if something goes astray."

She nodded her thanks, growing more tired and irritable by the day. She shifted into her owl form and quickly lifted off to head towards Spiral Haven.

I was hoping to get rid of the haunted ones there before they arrived. There would likely be many souls waiting to be harvested, and she'd intended to rid the village of them before Delora and Magnar made it there. *But I had to warn my children first.*

The woman being given a fright from a few Ghosts was nothing in comparison to the danger Jabez presented to her children – even if she was pregnant and in a fragile state.

I feel bad for her. I know her mind isn't well. Despite the light beginning to return to her deadened eyes, she just didn't seem all that happy. *And being pregnant with one of their kind really heightens our emotions.* From what she'd witnessed, Delora was really struggling, just as Lindiwe had when she'd first started carrying them.

Nathair had been the hardest, as he'd been the first.

Hopefully Magnar is wise enough to not bring her to the meat market. She unfortunately doubted it. She knew her children, including how the level of their humanity could affect whether they made bad choices or not. *He probably doesn't even know she'll be able to see the Ghosts, unless Reia mentioned it.*

One of her infant babies accidentally unlatched from her feathers, and she dived to catch them in a taloned foot before they reached the treetops below.

That was close. Last thing I need is to chase after one through the forest... again. Thankfully it was a rare occurrence.

She flapped her wings faster to get to Spiral Haven as quickly as possible.

FORTY-SEVEN

A time unknown, but of misery

Situated on top of Nathair's lazing rock, while he was deep in a trance within his lake, Weldir had multiple viewing discs around him.

At the forefront was Magnar as he walked down the porch steps holding his small, newly born offspring. They sulked, screeching as they crawled over him in search of something before giving a wail. They only calmed when he spoke to them, constantly shoving their ear holes up against his fox skull.

"What do you *mean* she gave birth already?!" his mate yelled, half-awake as she scrambled to leave her bed.

The blanket twisted around her ankle, and Lindiwe fell face-first off the side of her bed and hit the ground. He winced on her behalf, especially when she groaned. One of their offspring crawled out from underneath her, gave her a bawk, and then proceeded to start climbing into her curls – to her annoyance.

"I've done this too many times in my life," she muttered, rotating her body to sit. She untangled her leg, placed her hands on the side of her head, and let their offspring do whatever they wanted as both climbed all over her. "Are you sure?"

"Yes, I'm quite sure," Weldir answered. "Magnar is currently holding them outside, and I believe she is inside. You know I cannot see too closely due to his ward."

"Why?" Lindiwe whined, throwing her head back. "Why did no one call for me?! I told them I was nearby should they need me."

Weldir couldn't help chuckling. *You know they are independent creatures. It is just the way they are.*

"I know that! But this is different." She slumped against the side of the bed while remaining seated on the ground. "I would've helped. I've done this plenty of times myself, and had I known they *wouldn't* call for my assistance, I would have informed her what would happen immediately after giving birth. I just... I didn't want to frighten her when I could simply use a scent cloak and help in the moment."

She speaks of the way Mavka will attack their mother, due to her smelling of blood during the birthing process. Even Weldir considered this a flaw in their design.

"Would you like me to transport you there now?" Weldir offered, seeing she was rather dispirited.

"What's the point?" She sighed and closed her eyes. "I can't help them if they won't let me. They think they have to do it all on their own when I'm right here."

Weldir grew quiet. *I don't know how to comfort her.* Especially when she was just like them – she thought she had to do it all on her own with a brave face when he, too, was right here.

Well, some of the time.

Due to her request for no more intimacy, he'd been focusing on spreading his mist. He spent what he gained, pushing it further and further until he now thought he'd covered half of the landmasses where there were portals. In some places, he'd even managed to cross the oceans and cover some small islands.

The last time she was in my realm for an extended period was when Leonidas was captured. He knew that was quite some decades ago. He'd thought of it fondly, despite her tears, simply because she'd permitted him to hold her for an extended period. She'd cried in his tendril arms and against his barrier, clinging so tightly it seemed like she didn't wish to let go.

Since then, and like before it, their face-to-face interactions had been minimal.

"Weldir?"

"Yes, owlet?" he asked, still rather smitten with the nickname he'd given to her long ago.

Her cheek twitched; she was always surprised by the endearment. Each time, something glinted in her pretty brown eyes, something tender that she quickly hid. That, or he was misinterpreting it because he wanted to.

"Maybe I should just leave them be," Lindiwe said, looking up at the ceiling of her small home. "Maybe... you shouldn't sleep for a while and watch them, while I move on. You can always bring me back here."

"That's unlike you." He lifted his gaze to the brightness of Tenebris, unsettled by her response. Enough so that his mist tightened against him. "When something important is happening, you like to be near."

"I know." She wrapped her hands around one of their offspring and brought them close to her belly. "But all I'm doing is sitting here, waiting for something to happen. I don't mind doing that, but it... it hurts that they shun my presence. I must move on and focus on those who *do* need and want me right now."

She speaks of these two. He watched one of their featureless offspring snuggle into her stomach, while the other made her wince when they tried to get out of the labyrinth of curls they'd gotten themselves lost in. She helped extricate them and brought them on top of the other so all three could cuddle.

It wasn't often that Lindiwe shared the truth of her thoughts. He'd known for a very long time that she was discontented with the way their offspring treated her, and there was little he could do to help. He sometimes spoke to their offspring when she wasn't around and they were walking through his mist across the world, but they often barked and snapped their maws at the unseen entity bothering them.

If I had a true form, I could ease her. She wouldn't have to be doing this all by herself, nor would she have to *be* alone.

As the years passed and she still rejected his realm, Weldir found himself wanting to join hers. He'd always had this yearning, but it was growing by the day, like something had always been missing and it was only found at her side.

He used to not let such things bother him; why yearn and hope for things that couldn't change? He couldn't seem to stop himself now, staring at her silently, wanting nothing more than to dive through his viewing disc and join her.

It'd even come to the point where he found himself walking by her side on Earth, his female none the wiser that he was right there with her as she traversed the world. That was until she exited his mist and unwittingly left him behind in it. Seeing her grow smaller as she took each step into the distance formed an ache in his mind he couldn't be rid of.

Even now, he'd like to go to her side and reach his hand out to help her to her feet, so she wasn't sprawled on the floor.

But he couldn't.

I have searched my mind endlessly, and there is no solution. He was ill-formed, a deity without the capabilities of true life, and nothing, no amount of knowledge, offered an answer. *So how else can I help her?*

He didn't like that she was often forlorn, reclusive, and withdrawn from life. That wasn't something he'd ever wanted for her. She hunted for souls, she took care of their offspring, but other than that, she did very little for herself anymore.

She'd become a shell of the spritely person she once was and detached in a way that bothered him. It felt wrong for her personality. Like the change was through suffering, and she didn't know how else to combat it but by turning her mind away from horrible things and the way they hurt her.

I miss her fire, he thought, placing his chin on his closed fist. *I also miss the way she reached for me, clawed at me.* In any and every sense.

He still didn't know why she no longer wanted to, despite many decades passing. *She doesn't seem unhappy with me.* Not like in the beginning, where she wore a hateful glare whenever he spoke to her. No, she always welcomed his voice these days, but there was an emotion reflecting in her gaze at the same time as the one that said it wanted him there – one that said it didn't.

My realm feels emptier without her presence in it. It made him realise just how uninhabited and desolate it was.

Giving up on his thoughts, considering he'd annoyed himself and there was nothing he could do to change her and her decision, he shifted his gaze to Nathair.

He has entirely ceased speaking to me. Weldir doubted it was his fault. His serpent offspring had lost the desire to live this stagnant life or learn about what happened in a world he couldn't go to.

The fragments still bothered him, only giving him moments of proper lucidity before stealing him away again. Weldir thought he might prefer it, as it stopped his mind from having to be present in Tenebris and its nothingness.

"If that's what you would like to do – return to the northern hemisphere – then I have no issue with remaining awake to assist," Weldir stated to Lindiwe.

It would be a good opportunity for him to build the reserves of his mana again. It was thickening faster than it used to.

The next time I rest, I should be able to reach much further if I have a store collected. Rather than doing it bit by bit and sleeping more frequently.

Hmm. Perhaps I'm becoming like Nathair. Letting himself be whisked away to refrain from being present in this lonely misery.

Not that he'd ever shared that hardship with Lindiwe – nor did he care to.

It's not like I can feel the true ache of it, he thought, leaning back nonchalantly to stare up at his false sky. *Not like her.*

FORTY-EIGHT

Lindiwe smiled as both her babies played in a flowery meadow. Purple pincushion flowers danced and swayed in the light wind, barring a few broken stems in the wake of the vigorous wrestling match. They gave squealing roars, so cute and unmenacing no matter how ferocious they tried to sound.

Sitting on a short boulder with her feet flat on the ground, she rested her chin on her hand. She inspected their featureless, blobby black forms.

"I can't decide what their skulls and horns should be."

Did she want them to look similar, like with Aleron and Ingram, or different so they had different strengths to help each other?

At the sound of her voice, they came running over to her with joyful trills and climbed her legs.

"Heya babies," she cooed, scratching both under the chin and completely incapacitating them.

"You could give them the same horns again," Weldir suggested. *"Although they aren't truly twins."*

"Mmm. But they're still siblings."

A warm chuckle vibrated in her mind. *"Their skulls will make them look like Mavka regardless."*

She answered back with her own laugh. "I guess that's true."

As she lifted one into the air, their hands opened and closed in her direction as they emitted a happy squawk. "Leopards are still common, and I've always wondered if their fur patterns would be present on them."

"Leopards are the spotty felines, aren't they?"

"Yeah. I guess I'm running out of ideas after twenty-three children." These two made twenty-five, and it was a lot of skull and horn variations to go through.

She remembered each one vividly. She knew their names, their faces, their special animal features, and where each one was located. She knew how old they were to the day, what colour their orbs were.

So many lives. So many deaths. So much work and effort.

Only one had ever willingly hugged her as an adult, and that was Leonidas after he was tortured. Lindiwe still held out hope that it was possible.

The twins are rather accepting. They liked playing with her and even let her rest against the outside of their cuddle when they were feeling generous. *I guess a part of me is hoping that if these two form a bond, they'll let me do the same thing.*

She'd love to know how warm and soft it was under Aleron's wing, or even Ookpik's – although he was a rather stern, quiet, and solitary Duskwalker. He didn't even like Demons and considered everything beneath him.

I think if I tried now, a few might be accepting.

It'd been years since she'd visited many of them, and most of them had changed. A few were like Orpheus and Magnar: seeking a companion, a bride. They'd even gone to lengths to befriend a few stray humans, although it never worked out.

But it's possible, she thought with a smile. *They can be happy, achieve love.* That was more than she'd ever asked for. *They're even having kids of their own.* It'd been around two weeks since Magnar and Delora's child, Fyodor, was born, and all things looked to be going well.

Delora seems so much happier too. Weldir even said her soul, although still plagued with the coal markings from her depression, looked brighter and healthier. *I'm so glad things are going well for–*

Lindiwe gasped when one minute she was sitting in bright light, and in the next, she was shrouded in shadows. Her hair and cloak lifted around her like she was thrown into water.

"Weldir?" she asked, surprised he'd brought her to his realm without warning.

She searched for him, and from what she could tell of his visible parts, he had his back turned to her. It was easy to find him from the bright viewing discs surrounding him like a ball.

She swam to his side, and he pulled his physical self to his shoulder so she could place her hand on it.

"You must go," he said sharply, as two discs moved from opposite directions to stop in front of him. "Both Orpheus and Leonidas are in danger." Then his face coalesced so they could meet each other's gazes, revealing his cheek, eye, brow, pointed ear, and tapered horn. "Pick one. Leonidas, or Orpheus and his bride. Both are within the Veil's forest."

Cold dread slipped down her spine, and she hugged their babies closer. "Who's in more danger?"

Lindiwe's heart raced with her indecisiveness. Why was this happening so suddenly and at the same time?

"Both are being chased by a group of Demons. Orpheus is encumbered by items from the village, and he hasn't been able to remove them. Leonidas doesn't carry anything – he is also quicker and closer to Magnar's ward and safety."

"Jabez?"

"I cannot see him just yet. I'll keep an eye out."

She nodded. "Take me to Orpheus and Reia then."

She was sure Reia was being smart and remaining incorporeal, but she was also likely to try to defend him with her sword. She was brave, maybe foolishly so. Orpheus might react to protect her and leave himself open to attack.

But most importantly... *If Jabez has instigated this to happen at the same time, then he'll go after them.* He'd go after the two who killed Katerina.

In a rush, Lindiwe was shoved into the early afternoon in Austrális. The Veil's forest offered little light, giving the impression night was almost upon them when it was truly hours away.

It made it difficult to know which way to go, especially since Orpheus' fur was black. A blur of white passed just up ahead, tailed by a whisk of colourless spirit. Even if she hadn't seen it, the sharp and heavy pants of a large creature running on all fours would have alerted her to their whereabouts, as well as the fast thumping of his hands and back paws.

And the many that followed.

Turning incorporeal, Lindiwe chased after them.

It was difficult. Orpheus was a Duskwalker sprinting at full speed and panicked. Her only advantage was that he had to navigate the terrain, whereas she ghosted through tree trunks without needing to evade or sidestep them.

In front of her, Orpheus ducked beneath a Demon as it leapt from the side. Another came from the other direction and managed to grab one of the straps of a satchel to cling to him.

"Orpheus!" Reia shouted, and he slowed down to look behind him with white orbs.

It gave the blonde-haired woman a chance to catch up, jump onto his back, turn physical, and pull her sword from its sheath. She stabbed the Demon in the back, deep enough that it sliced through the bag beneath it. Salt dribbled from it as she managed to stay on top of him while he continued to sprint. Her pale-blue dress, cinched by a brown girdle, flapped behind her as she yanked her sword out and kicked the vile creature away.

Her silver diadem glinted whenever a tiny streak of dappled light hit it.

Reia turned incorporeal again just as a Demon dived at her. It went through her ghostly body, smashed into another on the other side, and they both hurtled to the ground. She hopped off so Orpheus could move with ease, resuming to run behind him in her incorporeal form.

This gave Lindiwe a chance to catch up, and she managed to

fall in step with Reia.

"You're here?" she asked, her blonde brows furrowing in Lindiwe's direction. Her green eyes, narrowed with determination, had a worried edge to them. That anxiety seemed to double when she brought her stare back to Orpheus, who darted to the right to avoid a Demon trying to cut him off.

Lindiwe nodded. "Stay in your Phantom form. Orpheus will try to defend you otherwise."

Reia shook her head with her frown deepening. "But he knows I can't die."

"Do you think that matters to him?"

She opened her mouth to argue, only to promptly shut it. No, it wouldn't matter to Orpheus. If his bride was in danger, he'd lay his life down to defend her, even if that was pointless and a little silly. He was protective, he loved her, and he didn't care if he came to harm, so long as not a scratch landed on her pretty head.

"He just needs to keep running." Lindiwe nodded to him. "He can outrun the Demons if you don't distract him like before."

"But if he's hurt–"

"It doesn't matter."

The look she gave Lindiwe was deadly, likely thinking she was being callous.

"Jabez knows their weakness," she reminded Reia. "These Demons likely know it now too. What's a wound, so long as he lives?"

Reia threw her arms up with a grunted scream. "Can't you do something to help?!"

"No. I can hold off a few, but that will put me behind you both. I need to remain at your side."

"I thought you had all this power and shit!"

Orpheus gave a bellowing roar when a Demon, who had managed to get a hold of his bag straps again, bit into the side of his neck.

Lindiwe didn't interfere; she didn't need to.

He smashed his side into a tree trunk, squishing the Demon until it let go before sprinting at full speed again.

"I'm more worried about the danger that is likely to show himself at any moment. We must wait for that, rather than expending our energy and resources now."

Reia's lips thinned in understanding, and she nodded. That's when Lindiwe manoeuvred herself beside Orpheus, so she could be close enough and ready.

Jabez will show himself soon enough.

No matter how fast they ran, or the distance they covered, a horrible feeling came over Lindiwe the longer the chase went on and Jabez didn't appear. Even just an hour further into the afternoon made the Veil more shaded, setting her on edge.

It'll be harder for me to see in the dark.

That was likely what he was waiting for. That, and for Orpheus to tire out.

A time unknown, but one of danger

Weldir's head changed direction constantly.

One moment he was staring at the combined viewing discs of Orpheus and Lindiwe, the next at Leonidas. He also made sure none of their other offspring – no matter if they were in Austrális or not – needed assistance as well.

Despite the chaos, as he watched two of his offspring being hunted by a pack of Demons each, everything seemed relatively calm.

Both were fast and outrunning their assailants. They were often cut off, which slowed them down and put them in reach of striking claws, but they were easily able to escape.

So long as they keep running and don't stop, they should be fine.

That's what he thought. It was also likely what Lindiwe thought.

The truth was eventually revealed in the form of an

expressionless Jabez, who materialised from thin air in front of one of Weldir's offspring. Leonidas was unprepared and ran straight in his direction.

Jabez jumped, twisted in the air, and grabbed one of his backwards-curving ram horns to hold on when he landed on top of him. His long hair whipped behind him as he lowered himself for better balance, then grabbed Leonidas' other horn to make sure he couldn't be thrown off no matter how much the feline-skulled Mavka bucked.

In the span of those seconds, Weldir snapped his gaze to Lindiwe's disc.

"Jabez has appeared with Leonidas."

The determined, alert look in her eyes morphed to shock. "What? *Why?* I thought he'd come for Orpheus!"

The answer was obvious.

Jabez yanked Leonidas' skull to the right, making him bash into a tree. He roared, tripped, and Jabez was thrown from him before sliding across the ground on one knee and a hand. He was quick to dive for Leonidas before he could find his paws and wrapped his thick thighs around his snout to clamp his fangs shut. Then, while facing him, he grabbed his horns and pulled in two different directions.

"Orpheus was a diversion. Jabez knew you'd think he'd target him." It was a cunning trick, one that was obvious now that it was in play.

Jabez released him when trying to pull his skull apart didn't work and he needed to evade Leonidas' claws. He backed off and disappeared. Leonidas quickly rose to his feet, even when a pile of Demons attached themselves to his back and legs. He spun, bucking at the same time to dislodge most of them, then shot through the forest on all fours once more.

"Take me to him!" she exclaimed, pulling her hood over her head. She turned physical and then hastily turned into an owl.

"Where are you going?!" Reia yelled when Lindiwe not only let herself get left behind, but then lifted off with a flap of her wings to leave them. "What the fuck?!"

Rather than pull Lindiwe to his side, he said, "One moment. I will try to assist."

Her beak parted with an owlish shriek, likely in confused anger.

He calculated Leonidas' path and sent a soul there instead. Although his mana resources were already low, as he hadn't been awake long, he tore the soul in half. Immediately, his mana was depleted by a large amount as a portal opened right before Leonidas.

His offspring, quick and agile, fucking evaded it. Leonidas went around it at the last second and wasted time by going around a collection of trees rather than through the portal to safety.

Weldir shut it before it could do any more damage, but the initial opening of it was chaotic to his power reserves. It weakened him hard and fast, like a giant mouth taking a massive gulp of his shadows.

Jabez reappeared again, this time in motion as he flew sideways through the air to kick Leonidas' torso from the side. He was flung into the trunk of a thick tree and roared in pain when his body wrapped around it before dropping to the ground.

Jabez teleported above him, grabbed a horn to steady himself, and repeatedly punched the brow of his skull. There was no grin, nor laughter, just the cold, unfeeling gaze of a male determined on destruction. The bone was thick and required an unfathomable amount of strength to destroy – strength that, hopefully, Jabez didn't wield.

Leonidas rotated his feline snout a hundred and eighty degrees. He shoved it forward just as Jabez went to punch and missed biting around his fist by half a second when he disappeared once more.

Weldir pulled Lindiwe to his side. "I opened a portal to Magnar's ward, but he evaded it," he told her. "I will try again when the opportunity arises."

She tilted her feathery owl head questioningly. He offered her a meaningful glance before sending her back to Earth, this time to Leonidas' side. She flew above him, this form quicker than her human or Phantom forms.

What a waste of mana, Weldir grumbled with annoyance. *She probably questioned why I would attempt it.*

He yanked another soul from his stomach, from Tenebris, and waited to see if he needed to use it. He didn't want to, despite being ready and willing. His mana wasn't recuperated enough, and using a second would likely be too much for him.

If it assists Leonidas, then so be it.

This restlessness from within his shadows, where he was safe and impenetrable, was unbearable. He'd never felt more useless than being forced to *witness* his offspring and mate in danger, unable to do much about it.

Had I a physical form, I could have ended this easily, he thought, just as Jabez showed himself once more.

He stood no chance as she turned into a human, fell from the air to land on top of him before he could grab Leonidas again, and rolled them both backwards, ending with her on top of him. As if he was prepared for a random and sudden attack, he rolled forward and threw her off. As she was flying through the air, Lindiwe twisted and threw a dagger made of shadow in his direction.

He teleported away before it could land.

She chased after Leonidas, returning to her Phantom form to stay safe and be quicker. She was left behind this time, unable to catch up to one of the swiftest Mavka.

Weldir left his realm to put himself at Leonidas' side.

"Go through the portal," Weldir said, knowing that, even if he couldn't be seen, he could be heard. "It will take you to Magnar's ward."

Leonidas turned his feline skull and white orbs in his direction, following the sound of his voice. White condensation came from his nose hole when he gave a huff in answer.

Weldir threw the second soul in front of them, tore it apart, and conjured another portal. Leonidas' muscles bunched, his shoulders up and his head lowered in determination as he sprinted harder and headed straight for it.

He was choosing to trust the unseen voice.

Jabez materialised in front of it, and the comforting yellow of the portal suddenly glowed menacingly from behind him. His red eyes were alight with cold malice and bloodthirst. Wind gusted his hair and pants to the right, while his fingers were rigid and ready to strike with sharp claw-like nails.

Leonidas snapped out a snarl and stepped to the right, bypassing Jabez – and consequently, the portal. He was cut off by three Demons, who lunged and forced him to halt and back up.

"Fuck," Weldir bit out, closing the portal and retreating back to his realm.

Jabez won't let him go through them now. Their only opportune moment for that avenue was the first time. *I now lack the power to help.* In fact, he could feel his consciousness trying to fade, but he forced back the darkness closing in on his sight so he could at least be a set of eyes for Lindiwe.

She caught up just in time to create three tentacles and wrap them around the Demons, who darted at Leonidas one at a time to confuse him.

Lindiwe was like a beacon in the shade, her dress and cloak stark against the shadows. Her brown hair flicked behind her, and she was swift despite being a little female.

"Run!" she screamed, throwing one Demon to the side while yanking another from his leg.

He bolted, leaving her behind.

Jabez materialised behind her, grabbed her long hair, and went to slice open her neck. He missed, clawing across part of her face until she turned incorporeal to evade the end of the slash.

Every time she caught up to help, the moment she turned physical, she was forced to turn ghostly to evade Jabez. When she used shadowy tentacles or a blade, she took a little more of Weldir's power. His vision blurred before he forced it to sharpen again.

Then the Demons turned on her instead, managing to gouge their claws into her bit by bit. Her ability to time when to protect herself or to be human to attack was overshadowed by the chaos of the moment.

It put unwanted space between her and Leonidas.

He assisted by calling her back to his realm and then shoving her back to Earth without warning. She saved Leonidas once from Jabez before she was tackled by a Demon, who bit into the back of her neck.

But rather than lance her flesh, they *took* something instead.

"No!" she yelled, lunging forward with her hand out, when the attacker stole one of their infant offspring. She screamed when a Demon got its claws into her chest from behind and ripped back.

Weldir was unsure of why she was so frightened. Their offspring were indestructible when they weren't fully formed, and he experienced no worry when they were swallowed whole.

He just waited for the inevitable: the little feral Mavka would eat the Demon from the inside out.

As expected, they eventually burst through the roaring Demon's stomach in a spray of blood, intestines, and carnage. They began to eat it entirely as she fought to get to their side, then more Demons came to eat their own kind like cannibalistic nightmares.

Or perhaps she'd never been worried about this, and it was the aftermath. How, once its head was consumed, their offspring began to grow an odd skull – and then worse, roared at her and darted into the forest.

"Weldir! Grab them!"

Perhaps she should've left them with him to begin with, but he knew why she hadn't thought of it. They were with her all the time, and this had never happened before. There was also another reason, and it was why he couldn't take them now.

"I cannot," he answered quietly. "I'll trap them here."

"What?" she whispered while chasing after them.

"If I take them now, you won't get them back until I return."

That fear was likely why she'd never left them with him in the first place. It'd never been an unfounded worry. He'd disappeared suddenly many times over the course of their bond. Their children were indestructible when little, so why worry too much in battle when they weren't able to come to harm? The biggest issue was if they were temporarily lost, but she'd be able to find them eventually, or Weldir would.

In another viewing disc, he missed seeing the impact that caused Leonidas to roar, or when Jabez managed to crack his skull. He only witnessed the result, where Leonidas went berserk and turned feral. His movements became too erratic for even Weldir to follow, then he leapt and vaulted from a tree trunk to the ground, zig-zagging through the forest as he encroached on Magnar's ward.

He was getting closer to safety, but the purple blood dripping from the crack in his skull was stark against the whiteness of bone. In that moment, Weldir didn't know how to tell his mate that their offspring's death was imminent.

Maybe not now, or even soon, but his skull was no longer sturdy. Even if he escaped now, it would, in time, break.

He also didn't wish to distract her as she chased after their infant offspring, while his sight blurred from enfeeblement, pushing his mind under the waves of unconsciousness.

A useless god indeed.

FORTY-NINE

June 19ᵗʰ, 2023

I'm afraid to fall asleep, Lindiwe thought, staring into a small viewing disc of Leonidas.

The winds around her campfire were rough. Sitting in the dismal sunlight, her warming talisman did nothing to protect her from the way it cut across her skin, or how her hair kept passing over her face like it wanted her to breathe it in and choke on it. Her eyelashes bent in awkward directions, causing her to blink rapidly.

Winter had come, and a storm in the southlands made it colder than usual.

As much as she wanted to go inside and close her eyes, she found it difficult to pull her gaze from the crack in Leonidas' feline skull.

Since the night she'd desperately tried to heal him of the wound to no avail, her pulse had been racing. Her anxiety constantly set her on edge, just waiting for the moment when she tried to call his face to the surface in her scrying spell... only for it to never come.

Almost a month had passed since that day.

A part of her was already mourning the loss of him, and she'd break out in tears at random. A stray thought, a memory of the way he used to play by trying to catch her before she could turn incorporeal. She thought the world would suffer a great loss without his rather sassy attitude in it. Her heart was dying in her chest, and she often sought the sun just to feel anything other than cold, unyielding sadness.

It's why she'd made a temporary home within the mountains of the north to be closer to Leonidas, just in case. For what? She didn't know. She had this overwhelming desire for nearness, but it wouldn't matter. Maybe it was so she could collect the pieces of his skull so no one else could have them. So she could protect them before she inevitably gave them to Weldir for safekeeping.

Such thoughts always made her eyes brim with tears.

As much as she wanted to stare at her son with grief and loss already twisting her heart beyond repair, Lindiwe had to end the spell. She cast it briefly once a day, rotating between each child for just a few minutes, and then ended it once she knew none of them needed her.

But it was that gap, that stretch in time before tomorrow came and she could check them again, that worried her. The nagging desire to give in was like an itch that needed scratching, but doing so would only bloody an already gaping wound.

I can't use his magic right now. The more she used, the longer it would take for Weldir to return. So she used as little as possible, and relied on her mana stone that had its own source of magic, and her Phantom abilities which were all hers.

She returned to Spiral Haven once a week, taking all the souls she could from there while avoiding Jabez entirely. After the battles they'd endured, things had taken a turn. Although their truce within the village remained, it was rocky and uncertain.

Duskwalkers could no longer enter it, and he'd given her the warning personally when she'd returned to the village to collect souls. Her task was permitted, only because it benefited him and his people.

All that matters is everyone is safe.

Orpheus and Magnar no longer left their protections without each other, choosing to hunt as a pair. Merikh hadn't returned to the Veil in over a year, but even the surface world had grown more violent. The twins didn't care; they were together, and therefore, dangerous – not even idiotic, lower Demons would dare attack.

And Leonidas... well, he'd finally taken her advice and left the Veil.

So, he's gone back to that house, she thought, wrapping herself up in her cloak to escape the winds, unable to fly through such a storm.

Her hand itched to bring up his face again to see the quaint home in the background. He was hidden, watching over it silently from the trees or in the snow.

She didn't know why, only that he returned to that house, situated in the north's forest, every year or so. There had once been a young woman there, her hair as black as night and as straight as an arrow, but she'd stopped returning many years ago. Leonidas had watched over her father and his declining health before he, too, stopped being there.

Even when it was absent of life, Leonidas returned.

She's there now, though. Was that why he was constantly drawn to that house, just for the chance to see her? The windows had been lit up from within, and she'd left to go hunting that very morning, geared up in winter clothes, a sword, and a bow and quiver.

The woman was in her late twenties, and there was a sharpness in her brown eyes that Lindiwe only ever saw in those who had seen death and survived.

They were the eyes she saw in her own reflection.

A cold, unfeeling logic in the face of adversity or pain. Self-sacrifice in the name of betterment, even if it wasn't always good. Someone strong, unafraid, and resilient.

To know her child cared for someone deeply enough to want to spend his final moments watching over her was heartbreaking. Even more so that she didn't even know he existed, and the potential future they could've had was now... impossible.

How sad, she thought, wrapping her arms around her babies, and cuddling them close. Her heart throbbed for Leonidas, and she wished things didn't have to be this way. *And there's nothing I can do to fix it.*

A time unknown, but where hopelessness fractures

A tug yanked Weldir awake.

It was tight, like a string being pulled taut so it could retract towards his centre in a burst of kinetic energy. He'd felt it before. Only once, but it was strong enough to pull him from slumber sooner than he should have.

So, Leonidas' skull has broken, has it? he thought, as he lifted his hands to see what he'd managed to recuperate.

He was surprised to see there was so much of his physical self, considering he'd been held under the waves of mana exhaustion. *How long has it been?*

He brought up a viewing disc of Lindiwe, only to note which season it was, as it was unlikely she'd left Austrális during this time. *Winter?* Only a few months had passed then.

That was enough to give him strength, especially as his mana and power were quicker to return now that he'd covered much of the world. Sure, it was difficult to maintain, but he'd long figured out how to automatically consume souls even when asleep.

He could unconsciously heal and expel, consume and strengthen, and place them in their locations to rest.

Lindiwe wandered near and around a town in search of something. When she couldn't find what she sought, she transformed, left the town's location, and headed to another. *She only does this when she's searching for souls.* Could this be the reason he'd gained so much strength in such a short time? *She's been aiding me.*

He considered telling her about Leonidas, but decided against it for now. First, he needed to bring his offspring to his side, even if he wasn't in his mist and easily reachable.

Waving his hand, he summoned all his fate tethers to become visible. He found the one that was tighter than the others, as if it wanted to be returned to him, and its twisting yellow and black informed him it was Leonidas' – although another of his offspring had a similar colour.

Weldir gingerly wrapped it around his forefinger, locked onto it, and pulled to call his soul to him. Oddly enough, it held firm. He tried again, using only a small amount of force, as that was all he'd needed to obtain Nathair's.

It didn't relent.

I don't understand. If Leonidas was dead, his soul was no longer anchored to his skull. *It should come easily when called.*

Weldir waved a hand to conjure a viewing disc of his offspring, and all he saw was his yellow spectral soul moving around in a blurred, white environment. Weldir was unable to properly see the real world, when Faunus was a part of the afterlife.

With his finger still wrapped around his child's fate tether, he yanked again. Leonidas snapped out a snarl only he could hear and shoved himself forward to fight the tug that Weldir had on his spectral spirit.

I see, he mused, releasing the string. *He isn't ready to let go.* He was holding onto life, seeming to follow someone or something, and Weldir could *just* perceive the movement of life in the murk surrounding him.

Weldir would give him a little more time to process his own death before fate itself would take him anyway. He had a day on Earth before his soul would be yanked to Weldir, even if neither of them wished it.

He watched as Leonidas whimpered. He backed up and then whined while covering his chest as if someone had walked through him without seeing him.

Lindiwe, on the other hand, barely stopped moving. She continued her search, finding one soul along the way, and sucked it into the vial that contained a few already. Only when she couldn't seem to keep her eyes open any longer, did she find a tree to perch herself on in her owl form, and slept for a few short hours.

Weldir let her be for now. He took the quietness of Austrális' night to check on his other offspring.

All were well, so he visited Nathair.

"You will have a Mavka companion soon," Weldir informed him, since he was lucid.

Nathair's orbs shifted to dark yellow in curiosity, and he signed, "What do you mean?"

"The feline-skulled Mavka's skull is broken. He's being stubborn currently, so I'm giving him time to say goodbye to life. But soon he will have no choice, and neither will I." He turned his face up towards Tenebris' false blue sky and ever-constant sun. "He may need much of our assistance to adjust to his new life here."

"I'll do what I can." Nathair turned his serpent skull towards the meadow-filled horizon. "It's... lonely here. Another would be welcome, even if it's due to an unfortunate reason."

"Agreed. His life will end there, but start here."

Nathair lifted his hands to sign something, but they twitched with hesitancy. "Are you sure there is nothing you can do?"

"No," he answered immediately. "I can create life from nothing, but I cannot give back a life that is taken."

At least... he couldn't give back a life to a Mavka, who had an existence after death. He was unsure if he could bring back a human. To do so might mean he'd have to bond them to himself, in turn making them a mate. And, considering Lindiwe's rejection of such a notion, that was a possibility he'd never experiment with.

I wonder if it's different if I were to bond a human to one of my offspring, though. The question was: why would he ever do so?

When a day must have passed since Leonidas' unfortunate death, he felt another tug.

He left Nathair's side and materialised in his darkness to

wait. His soul would come eventually, even if Weldir didn't pull on his family fate tether.

His soul would be asleep, as that had been the case with Nathair's. When a soul was brought to him, it was always in a state of rest as it waited for him. That was no different for his offspring. It was only when they entered Tenebris, leaving the limbo in between, that they could be awakened.

The minutes passed. At least he thought it may have been minutes. Then an otherworldly yellow glowing spirit came to his void, except... it was only his head.

The string was still taut, yet now it vibrated, causing his mist to pulsate. He conjured a new viewing disc, and what he saw surprised him.

His offspring's soul was in two pieces. His physical body from the neck down was attached to his broken skull, which had also regained its headless, spiritual body – with the head missing. The world around it had sharpened, and he lay curled up in a ball asleep just outside a frozen forest. A strange rope, shimmering with an enchantment, had been tied around his neck and leashed him to a tree like a pet.

Weldir brought his spectral yellow skull closer and investigated the *filled* crack in it. It was evident that it'd once been broken, that there should be no true life in it, yet he couldn't pull the two pieces of his spirit skull apart with ease.

Although he didn't put too much force into it.

Someone has tried to fix it. Well, kind of. Enough to revive him in some sense, but not enough to make him whole. *He's in a state of half life.*

"Lindiwe," Weldir finally called.

Her owl head was quick to rotate forward, and she gave a hoot and lifted her wings to remove some of the snow that had fallen on her. Her black eyes darted around the forest she was in.

"Leonidas is..." He paused in thought. "Hmm... how to explain this? He's alive, but he's also dead. Someone has tried to fix his broken skull, and it's tethering him to life."

She lifted the arch of a wing to push back her hood, and she morphed into a human. Her backside fell onto the branch so she could sit.

"What does that even mean?" she whined, throwing her hands forward before having to catch herself on the branch so she didn't fall metres to the ground.

"It means there may be hope for Leonidas after all," he said, unable to keep the grin that was likely present on his face from his voice. "I cannot bring him back to life on my own, but if whoever has tried to save him is willing, *they* might be able to."

She raised a sceptical brow, but the panic in her gaze had softened. "Can you better explain it?" She lifted a hand to rest the side of her face in her palm, with her elbow on her knee when she brought it up. "You always make things so confusing."

"I will need to go to him."

Her lips pursed. "But you can't leave your mist."

"Not unless I use another soul," he pointed out, reminding her of how often he'd done so in the past for her.

"Can you do that?" She chewed on the inside of her cheek nervously. "You just woke up. Do you have enough power right now?"

"No. Not really. This will likely put me back to sleep for an exceptionally long time. Will you be okay with that?"

Lindiwe lowered her hands so she could pick at her fingers, and her fidgeting was a sign of her uncertainty. Her gaze dropped, forlorn and saddened. "If... if it brings him back to life, then yes. I've tried to use your magic sparingly. I'll continue to make sure I don't use much, and I'll keep hunting for souls like I have been."

"If any of our other offspring need us..."

"I know!" she said a little louder, half shouting as she clenched her eyes shut. "I know this means I'll be trapped here in Austrális, unable to help any of the others. So long as none of them are in danger of death, they can survive the rest. I can't... I don't want to lose him, Weldir. *Please.*"

"As you wish."

"Wait," she rasped, leaning forward before biting her lip. A glob of snow fell on her head from above as she rustled the tree more forcefully. She either didn't care or didn't notice as she looked to the forest with her eyes softening. "Thank you so much. I know you're trying, and I know this is all a lot on you. Thank you for going out of your way for him, for them."

"Lindiwe, I cannot do much from this side of life and death. If this is all I can do, then so be it." Then, wanting to end this temporary goodbye on a lighter note, he asked, "How are the little ones?"

Her lips curled upwards slightly. "They're good," she said, before her small, broken smile fell. "Except one has a Demon skull, and I'm not sure if that's a good thing or not."

"A Demon's skull? How odd." A light chuckle fell from Weldir. "I guess I'll have to investigate that when I return. Hopefully nothing more happens during my absence."

"If you could make that hope tangible, I'd appreciate it more than anything right now."

So would he.

When he tore apart a soul to make himself visible, then tugged on Leonidas' fate tether – not to bring him here but to go to him – he was thrown into a winter land. In the background, a small cabin with a smoking chimney lay before his offspring.

Weldir hadn't expected a short, black-haired woman to be kneeling in the snow sobbing. Nor to learn that Leonidas' new name was... Faunus, as she poured her heart out to his feline Mavka offspring.

He'd been half expecting a Demon to be the reason for Faunus' curse of a half life or perhaps an Anzúli. Just someone with magical capabilities.

"So this is where you are," he said, alerting the female to his presence, while greeting his offspring.

Alright, Leonidas. Let's see if we can save you.

"If it is so beautiful, I hope I never see it then," said the little fawny female – whose name Weldir forgot to ask for – after he explained what Tenebris was like.

"It appears you won't, for now." He turned his face away from Faunus to her, with pressure cutting across it – a smile, probably. "He has accepted your soul, and it has allowed the part of him that is here to strengthen through the bond so I could force the lost fragment back together in that powerful moment."

He'd bonded a human soul and a Mavka soul, threading them together by force, and thus answering a question he'd always wondered. If he were to manually tether a deceased human to a Mavka, he could indeed bring them back together.

Faunus' new bride's brows knitted together with concern as she stared down at his feline skull. "But his eyes are still gone."

"I'm sure they will appear – give it time," he said as his form hovered backwards in the desire to retreat. "Since I'm no longer needed here, I will leave while I still have power from the soul I have consumed. Spooking my mate in this realm tickles me rather deeply, especially since I can't do so very often."

And his mist shimmered with triumph. He was excited to see how Lindiwe would react upon learning he'd brought back their offspring. *She will be pleased.* But it was her expression he longed to see, cast *at* him.

Sensing where she was in the world by their bond, Weldir shifted himself through space to be at her side.

She was within a village and didn't appear to have been there long. She'd just finished asking someone if they'd heard any rumours about haunted ones – ghostly beings that may lurk in the town or the forest. It was rare for a human to see them, but it wasn't completely uncommon.

"Hello, Lindiwe," Weldir said right in her ear.

His female let out a squeak, like a hidden scream, and with wide eyes and covering her right ear, she turned. Then she waved her arms through him as if to dispel him. She ran in between the gap of two buildings nearby.

He followed with mirth vibrating through him.

"Are you insane?!" she whisper-yelled, peeking out from their hiding place to make sure no one saw them. "Why would you come here like this?"

He chuckled at her reaction. *It almost makes using a soul like this worth it.* She acted similarly every time he appeared when it had nothing to do with their offspring.

"I told you I would be using a soul," he said, crossing his arms and tilting his head at her.

His mist was thinning rapidly, but he had a few more minutes before it was disastrous.

"Yes, but not like this." She eyed him over, his visible fullness, and nibbled her lip. "How... how did things go?"

"Leonidas is now called Faunus." Her eyelashes didn't flicker, informing him she already knew his newly appointed name. "He is also alive." As soon as those words left him, all the stress, the pain, the fear, melted from her in the form of joyful tears. "He's also bonded to a female with black hair."

"Mayumi bonded with him?!" she asked, her pretty brown eyes brightening as a large smile curled her lips.

"Was that her name? She agreed to offer her soul in exchange for his life. We have her to thank."

"I guess I'll have to figure out how to do that," she stated with a laugh, her eyes darting this way and that, only to fall to the fading white soul partially hidden within his shadows and mist.

Lindiwe wrung her hands and stepped a little closer while staring up at him. She looked awkward and more out of place with him than usual – and that was saying a lot.

It looked like she wanted to *reach out* to him. Then again, Weldir could be mistaken, wanting that to be the truth. Or perhaps it was that *he* wanted to cup the side of her cheek affectionately.

Her smile right now is worth much. It was what he'd wanted to see, for it to be shone directly upon him for the first time in nearly fifty years since their unwanted distance began.

It was why he came here.

"I'll have to sleep for a while. I ask that you remain safe."

His mate laughed lightly, happier than he'd seen her in a long while – likely from the high of her relief. "You're forgetting what I am."

I am not. He worried for her regardless of the fact that she was a Phantom, as she could still suffer pain in her heart and soul.

FIFTY

February 11th, 2024

Opening and closing her hands, Lindiwe hissed through clenched teeth at the agony that radiated down to her bones.

Fissures had grown over the skin of her fingers and hands. They looked like cracks of lava as much as they felt like it. They were hot, constantly aching, and nothing Lindiwe did removed the pain. It hurt to touch anything, let alone move her hands. Every time she tried to make a fist, the skin pulled taut and tears threatened her eyes.

I wish Weldir was here. He'd likely know how to fix the pain, and this magical wound she'd given herself.

Her years with the Anzúli had taught her many things. Magic detection was one of them; another was how to sap excess magic from a person. However, due to the nature of how she healed, which was the same as her children, she had to bear the wound herself.

Merikh didn't even thank me for helping him.

Just once she'd like him to see all that she was doing – all the ways she was trying to make amends – and accept it. But, as usual, he wanted to see the worst in her, even when she healed a strange Elvish woman he was keeping in his cave.

She was healing her magic depletion on her own, yet he tried to give her some of his to help her. He said it was because she had a use to him, but Lindiwe wasn't an idiot, and she'd been watching closely. Well, as close as his ward would allow. *Why does he have an Elf anyway? How did she get to Earth?*

Her pointed ears and height were a dead giveaway, as was her white hair. From seeing such features in Jabez, Lindiwe had known straight away she wasn't human. And considering she lacked horns or fangs, she also surmised the woman wasn't part Demon.

Her eyes had been brown, with starburst pupils rather than black circles, and she had tight, coily, corkscrew hair. Her skin had been a deep brown, with a grey undertone that didn't match the depth seen in humans – but appeared beneath their skin. She'd also only ever seen this in Jabez, who was an Elf as well.

She was very pretty, Lindiwe mused, leaning her back against the wall on her bed. *He likes her, even though he lied about it.*

Merikh was gentle with Raewyn in ways Lindiwe never thought possible. He took care of her while allowing her to keep her independence, likely due to Merikh desiring that very same thing. With her teasing him, he often joked back in return, or covered his face to hide his reaction, and to quieten his chuckles.

A few days ago, she'd also accidentally witnessed them entangled sexually before she quickly shut her viewing disc. *I tire of witnessing my children partaking in acts a mother really should not be seeing.* Each time, she wanted to scratch her eyes out, even though it did make her hopeful for their potential future happiness. *Why do they keep doing it outside when they have beds?!*

Grabbing her pillow, she brought it to her lap and hugged it. She rested her chin on it and grumbled to herself. "He refuses to listen to me, no matter if I have his best interests at heart."

The Elven woman couldn't stay here; she needed to go home. She didn't belong on Earth, and Merikh *shouldn't* go with her. *What if it endangers all his brothers?* Not just the ones in Austrális, but the entire world. *I know Weldir wants to keep what he's been doing a secret.*

He worried they'd strip him of his ability to reach Earth, leaving all of them without his assistance. And with Jabez on the loose, crazed for bloodshed and war, they'd all – including her – need him more than ever.

And it's not just Jabez. There were other Demon factions across the world that had their own menacing leaders. Most considered Duskwalkers a threat, since they ate them, but they weren't planning an all-out war with them, from what information she'd gathered. *Things are shifting.* Much was happening.

Austrális felt like a catalyst. Soon enough, Lindiwe expected battles to break out between Duskwalkers and Demons across the world. Right now, all she could do was be here for those within Austrális. Eventually, she would have to help the others.

We need to be rid of Jabez now, before I'm forced to stretch myself across the world. She'd sincerely need Weldir's help then.

I also don't know if an Elf and a Duskwalker can bond. And Weldir wasn't available right now to answer that question; he'd been asleep since helping *Faunus* achieve full life by bonding him to his bride, Mayumi. *I'm worried Merikh is setting himself up for failure.*

I'm also human. I think the reason the other brides can have children with my sons is because they're human. What if it was different between Merikh and this Elven woman? Say they could bond, they may not be able to have children together, if that was what they wanted. *I tried to explain this to him, but he didn't want to listen.*

"He *never* wants to listen," Lindiwe grumbled to no one. "He always grunts, snaps, and snarls, thinking I'm trying to get in the way." She buried her face in her pillow. "I want him to find happiness."

She wanted all her children to be happy. To find brides and fall in love.

"What if he goes with her to the Elven realm and they try to destroy him?" She worried about this constantly. Lindiwe wasn't privy to what the Elvish people were like, but she knew they weren't above imprisoning people for years when they were young boys or Demons who sought sanctuary.

Sure, they'd imprisoned them for good reason – to protect the hundreds of thousands at the cost of a few – but it was still undeniably cruel. There were likely other avenues they could have tried first, but they'd obviously let fear get in the way of logic.

What if that same fear saw them trying to imprison Merikh, or kill him, or other horrible unknowns she couldn't even possibly imagine? Fear was a horrible emotion. It made people do stupid, cruel things. It could make people change or force an entire society to go against its own moral code.

That same fear pulsed in her veins for him.

He's suffered enough.

He didn't need to be tortured or attacked when he was just trying to find a place to exist without being hated.

If he goes there... then I'll never be able to help him. If he needed her aid, he'd be too far away. There would be nothing she or Weldir could do.

That was part of the reason she'd tried to beg him to stay. And it was likely that same reason that he hated her even more.

I just want to protect him. Physically, emotionally, mentally. *Why do I keep failing when it comes to him?* He was so hard to connect with. His anger and spite, even at himself, made it difficult to convince him to soften and see her side.

Maybe I should just leave him be.

He was an adult. He could make his own choices and mistakes, even if they weren't things she wanted.

"It's not like I've ever had a say in the matter."

If he wanted to throw all his hope at a strange Elvish woman and go with her to Nyl'theria, then so be it. *But if this brings harm to his brothers...* Lindiwe didn't think she'd ever be able to forgive him.

It'd taken her years to forgive him for killing her first child.

If he brought destruction to all the others due to his selfishness, then she'd find that irreparable.

"I miss Nathair," she said with a sniffle, rubbing her face against the pillow she hugged to rid herself of any tears. She hissed again at the pain in her hands, when tightening her grip made them ache even more. "Every time I see Merikh, it reminds me of him."

It was probably the same for Merikh.

I miss Weldir too. Constantly.

It'd been seven months since he'd gone back into a magic recuperative slumber, and that silence was getting harder and harder to bear. She missed his presence, his voice, his guidance, and his... distant care.

It'd also been the same amount of time since Faunus had bonded with Mayumi, who had given birth to a baby two and a half months later... only to immediately fall pregnant again.

At least he was happy, they were doing well, and they'd long built their home within the Veil with the help of Orpheus and Magnar. Well, mainly Orpheus, who enjoyed helping his siblings even if he grumbled about it – Lindiwe had a feeling he didn't know how to take compliments, so he liked to pretend everything bothered him to shy away from how it made him feel.

He often hid his bright-yellow orbs of joy whenever they were near, and only truly let Reia see the positives he felt. *He's not used to happiness or contentment after nearly two hundred years of pain.*

Delora was also much happier, and she followed Magnar around wherever he went like she was his shadow, clearly smitten with him. If she wasn't with him, she was with Reia or Mayumi – who had become fast friends and training buddies.

Whenever she saw Magnar's tail wag at his bride, or any of their orbs turning bright pink for their females, Lindiwe couldn't help the adoration that swelled in her chest like liquid fire. The burn hurt, but it felt nice at the same time.

It was a welcome change.

Which only made her more anxious for if, or when, things went horribly wrong. Luck had never been on her side, and she worried about how all this would come crashing down.

Please.

She didn't know what she was pleading for anymore.

She just needed some... *hope.*

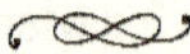

March 4th, 2024

"He's really gone," Lindiwe said as she entered Merikh's empty cave.

Then again, she'd known that by the murkiness she'd seen when she scried for him earlier that morning. He was under some kind of ward, and she figured it was the protection bubble that surrounded the Elven city. She'd seen it herself once, as she'd gone through one of the portals and flown over Nyl'theria in curiosity.

When she'd no longer been able to see him, she hadn't been able to help herself. She flew over the Veil westward to see for herself that his cave was vacant. There was no trace of him other than the lingering of his citrusy scent and all the things he'd left behind. It didn't look like anything had been packed, as if none of it mattered to him and he'd left it all behind.

His bed was unmade, his shelves the way he left them.

"I've been inside here so many times," she murmured aloud as she brushed her fingertips over his stone workbench. "It always feels lonely here."

Not once had it been filled with a warmth that was left behind in a loving home. Just once, she would have loved to sit inside it with him and have a pleasant conversation.

That was now entirely impossible.

He was gone, and any hope of mending their relationship was gone as well.

A part of Lindiwe grieved his absence – she always had –

but it was different now. He was completely out of reach, and to her, that was the same as being dead. Like Nathair, he was in another realm, one she couldn't go to, or be a part of.

She came here to absorb that, as she likely wouldn't ever return. *This cave and lake is where I lay the worst of my sorrows and regrets.* She needed to leave them behind or forever grieve those emotions with festering, worsening wounds.

Just as she turned to leave, something pulsed with a yellow glow in her periphery, dim against the shrouding shadows. She reached across the stone workbench and tentatively retrieved the blue mana stone she'd once given him. Except unlike before, yellow pulsed from within intermittently.

He's left behind his glamour? No, it was more than that; he'd... changed it somehow. Even she could tell the spell was different.

She curled her fingers around it, wincing at the pain from the cracks of lava forking across her skin and knuckles – the wounds from healing Raewyn yet to be healed even after months.

I'll give it to Weldir.

When he woke up, whenever that may be, he'd likely have an answer.

If Merikh has left Earth, then there's no problem with me taking it. If he left it behind, he wasn't coming back for it.

"I'm sorry for all we've done to hurt you," she said to Merikh's empty cave. "I hope you find the happiness you've been searching for, and a place to fit in and be welcomed."

She'd just prepare in case this brought ill winds for her other children. And for her and Weldir.

I hope... you found love and it heals you, Merikh, my little bear cub. She looked up at the ceiling of his cave. *I think you deserve it more than anyone.*

FIFTY-ONE

A time unknown, but of disconnection between ideals

When Weldir felt a tug, he was drawn from slumber. He knew what it meant; he'd felt its familiar pull only recently.

He opened his consciousness so the blackness of nothing met the blackness of his empty realm. The darknesses were different – one without thought, the other with it. One motionless and uneventful, the other controlled by the push and pull of his will.

Like before, he brought forth the fate tethers that connected him to his offspring and mate.

Only one was taut, the others drifting and swaying as loose, glowing strings that twined with his shadowy thread. *I thought it was Faunus again,* he mused, as he wrapped his finger around the one in a different state from the others.

He yanked the pink glowing string, and there was no resistance this time. The Mavka came to him easily, and within a second, Aleron's spectral, ghostly pink body was brought to him. He lay asleep in the darkness, one wing resting back as if he lay on something, while the other hugged the top of him.

His chest was unmoving, and no heartbeat throbbed. But even if it didn't seem like it, his offspring was alive, just not in the realm of life.

What of Ingram?

Weldir waited to see if his raven-skulled offspring would be joining his twin, the bat-skulled one, but he never came. Considering their special bond, and their inability to leave each other's side, what had felled one should have gotten its claws into both.

When he willed the viewing disc of Ingram to the surface, instead his mate appeared.

Hugging his large raven skull, which seemed to encompass the entire length of her torso, Lindiwe knelt on the ground, swaying back and forth as she screamed out hysterical sobs.

Half of her face was torn apart and bloodied, and only a few patches of her cloak remained white. Her hands glowed with strange streaks of lava, and if she experienced any pain from it, or any of her wounds, it was obvious she couldn't feel it under the waves of her grief.

She refused to let go of Ingram's skull, even when she buried her wounded face between his short ram horns and cried against it. Her shoulders shook as she heaved.

"I'm so sorry, Ingram," she sobbed against his skull. "I'm so fucking sorry. And Aleron..."

She couldn't get her next words out, instead screaming a breathless cry to the world. Thankfully she was protected under Merikh's glowing red ward, and the surly bear Mavka was nowhere in sight.

"Lindiwe?" Weldir called.

"Weldir!" she rasped loudly. "Aleron… Aleron is *gone*."

"I know. His death woke me."

"I had to choose! I had to choose which one to save." She buried her face against the top of Ingram's skull once more, smearing her own blood upon it. "I tried so hard to save them both, but there were too many of them. I couldn't... I tried... I had to watch him *die*. Why?! You weren't there. I had to do it all by myself. And then I had to *flee* just to protect the ones I carry because you weren't there to take them. It's not *fair.*"

"This was the risk we took to save Faunus," Weldir answered curtly, disliking the possibility she was insinuating he'd had a choice in the matter.

"I know!" she yelled, shaking her head. "I know it's not your fault, but I can't do this anymore. I can't watch them die, knowing there is nothing I can do to save them. I shouldn't have to bear witness to this!"

"Aleron is here with me, Lindiwe," Weldir reminded her, his tone softening, understanding now that she wasn't blaming him – just grieving. "In Tenebris, he'll be with me and Nathair. We will take care of him."

"It's not the same! *There* doesn't exist! It isn't real! It doesn't matter to me when I can never see or speak to him again, and it won't matter to Ingram when he comes back to realise his twin is truly gone!"

He was rendered silent. He didn't know how to respond.

He... could never feel the same as she did regarding this death. For him, it opened new possibilities, new avenues. In Aleron's death, his life with Weldir started. It may be a pointless life, but it was one Aleron could share with him and Nathair.

As opposed to the sadness she felt, Weldir experienced... joy. The loneliness of his realm would become less apparent. It would be filled by another of his offspring, one with whom he could truly interact, speak, and play. Someone who could touch him, and he would reciprocate, even if he couldn't feel it.

"Let me bring you to my realm so I can heal you."

"No!" she yelled, squeezing Ingram's skull tighter. "Just leave me alone. I want to stay with Ingram."

"Then bring Ingram with you. You can meet Aleron's soul before I consume him."

"I don't want to see it! I don't want to see my son's dead fucking soul." She shook her head frantically. "I want to be left alone. I don't want to see you, or it, or do anything but be here. Just... you don't understand. I know you don't, so *please*."

She's right – I don't. He never could.

To say he was disappointed was an understatement, as she was missing out on seeing the ethereal beauty of their offspring's soul. It looked just like him in form, only pink and transparent.

At the same time, Weldir could see how much this burdened her. He didn't know how to comfort her through this, what to say that would ease her weeping, or how to hold her when it was obvious she wanted nothing but to break down before she undoubtedly collected the shattered pieces of herself.

"Please don't ask me to collect his skull fragments," she whispered with a whimper. "They're everywhere. The Demons took all of them. I wouldn't even know where to start, and I... can't do it. It hurts too much to touch their skulls when they aren't whole."

"As you wish." Just before he turned from the viewing disc to tend to Aleron's soul, he paused. He watched her for a little while longer before he said, "Call out for me when you are ready, Lindiwe. I will heal you and do whatever it is you need from me."

"Okay," she croaked.

Weldir finally gave his attention to Aleron.

Her anguish had guilt shimmering through his mist at the elation he experienced from seeing the soul of his winged Mavka. The feeling deepened when he knew that consuming it would not only give him another offspring to meet, but that it would empower him immensely.

More than any untainted soul he'd ever eaten.

I'll never tell her so, though. He could only imagine how angry she'd become if she learned that eating his own children made him far stronger.

At least I'll have more mana to spare, should we need it.

He made Aleron's soul shrink, so he could place it in the centre of his palm, and quickly swallowed him down. Then he teleported to Tenebris to greet him in the afterworld with shadowy open arms.

March 14th, 2024

Lindiwe managed to swallow the barbed sorrow long

enough to speak with Ingram when he came back to life after *she* had beheaded him. It had been just as horrible an experience as the first time she'd ever done it, and it didn't get any easier – but she'd needed to stop him from fighting the Demons after Aleron's death.

It'd taken her hours to get the worst of her grief out. Hugging Ingram's skull had been unbearable, knowing her child wasn't going to be okay at the loss of his twin.

She knew he'd never accept it, that he wouldn't be able to handle it any better than her. He might even suffer more due to it. Their bond was special; they spent every waking and sleeping moment together. The absence of Aleron's constant presence would be sorely missed.

It was for that reason that she swallowed the heavy poison of her grief, so that she wouldn't burden Ingram with it. She needed to hold it in long enough to help him through something he didn't have the emotional maturity to handle on his own.

To be a rock for him, when she felt like fractured glass.

She hadn't known that she'd put him on a path of foolishness. *He plans to seek out humans to help him kill Jabez.* It was futile. The humans would never help, and even if they did, they wouldn't do so alongside a Duskwalker.

The only thing she could think to do was follow his snarling, whimpering form while she flew above him as an owl. *Maybe I can speak with whomever he goes to.* Whether it be the Demonslayer guild or a human town of soldiers.

She had no idea where he was leading them, only that violent determination and utter loss forged their path.

I can be a buffer. She'd explain the situation, so they didn't harm him and then take him away before chaos ensued when he was rejected.

No one would ever know how much his path took a toll on her. How she wasn't allowed to properly grieve because she had to watch over him instead. How it'd barely been two days since Aleron's death, and instead of wallowing in her pain, of absorbing the loss of another child, she was forced to grin and bear it.

She was struggling.

Her heart felt broken into jagged little pieces. How much more could she take before Lindiwe lost her mind to all this? How much more emotional anguish would she have to suffer before she just... *couldn't* anymore.

She could feel her mind fracturing.

Everything felt hopeless.

Her children were being targeted, and the threat of that constantly lingered over her head like a horrible storm cloud. The person she loved was unobtainable and out of reach, and she so desperately wanted to cave to him. To have him collect her in his non-existent arms and just... take this pain away, exist with her in a way where she didn't have to feel like she was doing this all on her own.

If only he could grieve with her, rather than be so detached from it he couldn't even properly support her.

Lindiwe knew Weldir saw no issue with their deaths because it meant they achieved new life with him. They eased his loneliness, even if it stopped them from truly living.

But she'd never feel that same relief.

They were gone, Nathair and Aleron. Their breaths had ceased, and they'd left behind those who cared about them deeply. Merikh, too, was beyond reach.

She was slowly losing them.

She feared for Ingram too. That she'd lose him one day if he continued on this path of vengeance. To kill the Demon King? It seemed impossible, even for Lindiwe to achieve.

She feared where he was going when their direction made itself apparent. Ingram was walking across the surface world towards one of the most dangerous Demonslayer guilds she knew of. *This will not end well.* Zagros Fortress had always been known to be rigid and harsh.

A training facility situated in the barren mountains made any person hard. The inhabitants destroyed anything that was a monster, and that included monstrous humans. Their leader was known for being cold and unfeeling – even more so than the one who recently died at Hawthorne Keep, killed by Mayumi, Faunus' bride.

Lindiwe landed in front of Ingram and thrust her wings out to block his path. *Go back. These people will not listen to you.* His growl, with his orbs shifting from the blue of loss to the red of rage, warned her to move.

She conceded, flying off before he could charge her.

I don't know what to do.

"*Lindiwe,*" Weldir called, and she answered with a hoot as she flew after Ingram. "*I know you wish to stay with Ingram, but we have a problem.*"

Oh god. What now?!

Lindiwe transformed into a human, landed on a branch, and balanced herself on her feet and a hand. "What is it?"

Her chest seemed to burn more at his voice. Her heart hadn't stopped sprinting since Aleron and Ingram first started running, and she worried nothing would ever be able to settle it again. That it would always ache in loss, the pain of it as scorching as it was cold.

Those few months of cheer, she'd known they'd come back to bite with horrible little fangs. This was worse than she'd imagined.

"*Sayrn has left Earth.*"

Dread gripped her around the throat as she jumped to a new branch to follow Ingram. "What do you mean he's left Earth?"

"*We knew this day would come. That one of our offspring would go through one of the portals.*"

Terror suffused her so tightly she struggled to get through her next panted breath. "No," she rasped, her widened gaze pulling away from Ingram to stare at the autumn leaves. "He went to the Elven realm?"

Sayrn, once known as Ari, was exceptionally intelligent. He was also a massive pain in the butt, and violent in a way that differed from Merikh. He wasn't angry; he was just ruthless. He liked to kill, liked to eat, and his diet consisted entirely of

Demons now that he'd grown enough humanity.

"I was checking on all our offspring and noticed his environment was different. It glowed, and only Nyl'theria does this."

Lindiwe's eyes bowed in anguish, and her breaths came out more rapidly. Her vision shook as panic clutched her so deep, she was frozen. Within seconds, her lips shook as she let out a sharp sob. "Why?! Why now?"

She was so close to giving up. For a moment, she considered just letting Weldir take her to his realm and forcibly put her to sleep if he could. To let her escape because she didn't know if she had the will to protect her children, who kept making stupid choices!

But she couldn't. No matter how much she wanted to escape responsibility, her heart, her burning, breaking heart, just *couldn't.*

Her stubbornness wouldn't let her. Her painful resilience refused it.

I have to choose – again.

Between Ingram, who was about to face off against thousands of humans, or Sayrn, who would be in a world filled with Demons. Both were in danger.

Only one was at risk of death.

Lindiwe managed to shove down the next sob, even if she couldn't cease her tears. "Do you know which portal he went through?"

"No. Only that he is there."

There were two portals in Zafrikaan. *He's usually southward, where there are more forests.* Where there were more Demons to prey upon.

Lindiwe's wounded hands gripped the bark of the tree. "Take me to the southern portal," she demanded.

I'm sorry, Ingram.

Sayrn needed her more, even if that came at a cost.

Within seconds, she was swallowed up by Weldir's darkness, and she turned transparent for him. She refrained from asking why his form was more solid than usual, considering one-third of him was currently visible when she'd expected it to be barely a fraction of that.

Looking upon him was hurtful. More than ever, she wanted to crawl into his arms and be hugged, even if it was truly just tendrils and barriers and not a real body.

Weldir healed her wounds the moment she arrived, and she was thankful for that. They hadn't hurt as much as what ached within, and part of her preferred them, as they were a distraction from her inner turmoil.

She hadn't wanted to admit that.

"Can you please take these two?" Lindiwe asked, pulling away the two babies attached to her, thankful they were asleep and didn't cry at the loss of her. "I don't want to take them somewhere so dangerous."

"Yes. I have more than enough power right now to risk taking them," Weldir said. "Be careful there."

Lindiwe nodded as their babies were taken from her person by shadowy tendrils and brought to his side.

"Okay. I'm ready," she stated firmly, waiting to be sent away.

"One moment. There is something pulsating from you." A tendril dug into one of her cloak pockets and pulled out the mana stone that had been on Merikh's table. "What is this?" Weldir asked as he held it in his hand.

"We don't have time for this!" Lindiwe exclaimed, wondering why he wasn't sending her away so she could go after Sayrn.

Weldir looked up from the stone, and half his revealed face showed nothing. No emotion, as per usual. "This is Elysian magic, Lindiwe. How did you obtain it?"

"I found it in Merikh's cave. He had an Elven woman there."

"I'll have to ask you for details about that later." He brought the blue stone closer to inspect the way the centre intermittently glowed a dull yellow. "I've never seen this kind of spell before."

His curious nature got the better of him.

Weldir activated it, and agony like she'd never known cut

through her. Lindiwe screamed just as her Phantom form tried to push out of her physical human body. A blinding light brightened his realm, swallowing up all the shadows until only white remained.

It seemed to sear her down to her very soul.

"Stop it, stop it!" she screamed, before everything went dark.

Lindiwe knew she'd passed out. She came to with her muscles twitching erratically, and Weldir holding her limp head from behind to steady it.

"Are you okay?" he asked, a frown marring his chalky forehead.

"No," she croaked, although she felt nothing, as if he'd healed her or the pain no longer existed anymore.

"It appears to be some kind of sun spell." He continued to hold her, and for a moment, Lindiwe basked in it – even though there was no warmth of true skin or life. She'd wanted to be held so badly by him that she kept her limbs loose just for a little while longer. "This stone is dangerous, but even I can see its potential. This might be the answer we have been seeking."

"In what way?" she asked softly.

Seeing as she was fine enough to respond, he let go, and she held back the urge to keep him to her.

"Let me experiment with it before I give you a proper answer." He put space between them while inspecting it inquisitively, his focus solely lost on it. "You'll have to take our offspring, though, as it had an effect on all three of you. The spirits of Tenebris seemed to be unaffected by it. Go to Sayrn."

"But what about them?" she asked when he handed the sleeping babies back to her.

"It's unwise for them to remain, as the stone is harmful to them," Weldir said. "And if it drains my mana, or I have to use a soul for any means..."

She considered telling him she didn't care if they were trapped here temporarily – no harm would come to them. Yet... the idea of being without them for an extended period, which could be upwards of many years, frightened her just as much.

Reluctantly, Lindiwe nodded and brought them closer to her torso again.

He wants to do it now. And telling him to sate his curiosity later was pointless. He was a fickle demi-god at times.

"Okay," Lindiwe answered.

There's no point in arguing with him.

She had a funny feeling her wants would get nowhere with Sayrn as well.

Whatever Weldir had discovered in the stone, she refused to have any hope. She was tired of hoping, only to see things fail.

FIFTY-TWO

March 19th, 2024

Locating Sayrn in an unfamiliar environment swarming with nightmarish monsters, some bigger and more intelligent than any other Demon she'd faced, had been difficult.

In her search, she'd been attacked from the air by flying Demons, her white feathers unusual to them and easy to spot even from a distance. The sun had been hot, baking her skin and feathers so quickly she had to remain in the shade or suffer burns. It was nothing like summer on Earth – even the air was scorching and difficult to breathe through.

In the days it'd taken to find Sayrn and confront him, she'd learned it had all been... pointless.

She'd left Ingram's side, essentially abandoning him when he needed her, for a child who utterly refused to listen. In the few days he'd been in Nyl'theria, Sayrn had battled many Demons and had been victorious. Vicious as always, and a hunter at heart, he wanted to stay – even at the cost of his own life.

"This is what I want," Sayrn said, leaning against the side of a stark, bleached trunk.

The tree itself was gigantic and measured a hundred metres tall, if not more, with a mixture of pink-and-purple leaves. With his arms crossed and his lion tail flicking to the side, he looked self-important.

"It's dangerous here." She gestured to the strange forest that glowed in the constant shade provided by the ancient and startlingly daunting forest. "There are no other Daesrin" – his word for Duskwalker – "here. I can't assist you easily like I do on Earth. You'll be entirely alone, and that means you could... *die.*"

Her translation amulet allowed her to understand him, even though he spoke Nyl'kira, like many Demons did, when he said smoothly, "I want to prey on the Daekura until they are gone, or I am. This is my purpose."

Lindiwe wanted to tell him it wasn't, but he was right, despite not knowing it. Other than Merikh, she'd never told another Duskwalker why they'd been born, worried they would react just as badly. The less they knew, the better – a blessing, in its own way.

Merikh had told Faunus, likely to upset him, although it didn't have the desired effect.

"I've lived a long time. It's all been the same, so I want to try somewhere new." He turned his lion skull to the side and stroked his fluffy mane absentmindedly with sharp claws. "I've been curious about where the Daekura come from. I've seen them enter my territory from the portal and have been wanting to see the other side for many years. If I want to return, I will."

"It's his choice, Lindiwe." She wanted to tell Weldir to shut up and deal with the stone she'd found in Merikh's cave, instead of eavesdropping. *"I'm not pleased either, as he'll no longer ferry souls to me, but if this is what he wants, then so be it."*

But this... scares me, she wanted to say, but knew expressing it was futile. *If I try to take him by force, he'll return to Nyl'theria now that he knows what's on the other side of the portal.*

Only Lindiwe cared and feared for them so fervently, more than even their concern for themselves. It left her wondering *why* she should, when it was obvious her wants and concerns mattered little. They died? They went to Weldir to live another life. They were harmed? They'd heal in due time and live to battle another day.

She hated the idea of them living such horrible, painful lives, yet this was their nature. To be bloodthirsty and violent when they saw fit, or protectors only for their chosen bride – and a destroyer to all others.

"Fine," Lindiwe bit out, averting her gaze, clenching her jaw, and curling her hands into tight fists. "I can't change your mind either way, but you must know this is stupid and suicide."

"Is it?" Sayrn mused with humour. "I'm a strong Daesrin. Nothing has bested me yet, not even when they try to break my skull."

Your luck can only run so far, she thought spitefully. And it wouldn't be him or Weldir who truly faced the consequences of that, but her.

Movement shifted underneath her cloak, and a baby Duskwalker licked across her rapidly fluttering jugular. They wanted to soothe her, to the point that they even nuzzled their strange skull against her.

"Hmm?" Sayrn leaned forward, his arms still half folded with the fingers of one hand pausing in his mane. "A youngling Daesrin? Its skull is strange."

She reared her head back so she could look down at them before pulling out one of the babies. "They have a Daekura skull. I didn't know that was possible until recently."

"They should become very strong then." He let go of his mane to hold his hand out, wiggling his clawed fingers at her. "Can I see?"

Lindiwe stared at his big paw hesitantly, then placed them inside it. They looked so tiny in comparison to him, even though she needed two hands to hold them comfortably. Despite having a Demon skull, they still weren't very aggressive. They sniffed his palm, gave the side of his thumb a nibble, then stomped around in a circle.

"Give them my horns. They will be even stronger if you do."

Lindiwe couldn't help but laugh at that. He was so proud of

himself.

In its own way, this felt like a... goodbye.

Her relationship with Sayrn had improved over the years since she first sat with him around that fire eighty-seven years ago. It was a quiet and distant relationship, as he was a solitary being, but he didn't outwardly reject her anymore either. However, she could only be a temporary intrusion in his life before her lingering annoyed him.

He was one of the few children who tolerated her. Although those who were older were growing to be similar, so long as they consumed many humans.

I wonder if he'll let me hug him, Lindiwe thought, when he went to hand back her baby. Just as her fingertips made contact with the baby Duskwalker being held out to her, there was a flash of colour, and they... disappeared.

Something fuzzy – a mixture of orange and green with fluffy wings – had darted between her and Sayrn. With what looked like many feet, it had snatched her baby from both their hands during the exchange.

Lindiwe and Sayrn shared a confused and surprised look, right before his orbs turned white and she gasped. At the same time, they darted after the Elven creature.

Sayrn shifted to his monstrous form to be on all fours and faster, while Lindiwe transformed into her owl form to go after the flying creature. Panic flooded her veins, and it made her wing flaps more frantic.

Sayrn was swifter than her, even as she flew through the air, but he was stuck on the ground. She was able to see the creature as she gained on it, and it looked to be a mixture of a moth, with fuzzy green antennae and eight legs, and a cat body and head with little antlers. Spots along its body glowed orange.

Just as she was almost upon it, her child held securely by its eight legs, she rotated her body to catch the creature in her talons. She didn't get the chance to grab it.

Something else intercepted from the side; something large, and far, far worse. Much bigger than Lindiwe and nearing

Sayrn's size, a winged Demon flew off with the fuzzy cat-moth thing and, incidentally, her baby.

And due to their size, they were much, much faster than Lindiwe, who used every ounce of her strength to go after them. Within seconds she was left behind, as they were able to navigate the unfamiliar forest much better than her.

Lindiwe shrieked *repeatedly.*

As if he knew she was calling out for help, Weldir said, *"I cannot grab them. They are not within my mist."*

Shit! What was she supposed to do then?!

"They are indestructible. If they are eaten, we know they will eat the Demon from the inside out. I can help you go in the right direction." Then, softening his tone, he added, *"We will find them again."*

I wanted to leave them with you in the first place! If he hadn't wanted to inspect the stone Merikh had, this wouldn't have happened.

It may have been due to an accident, and because she was *finally* sharing a fond moment with Sayrn, but she hadn't wanted to bring either of her babies to Nyl'theria for this very reason!

But he was right; she'd find them. The question was *when* and what was happening with Ingram in the meantime.

She didn't even have time to check, and Weldir's silence regarding it didn't make her feel any better.

All she knew was that he'd been captured.

Curses. Curses. CURSES. Fuck!

FIFTY-THREE

March 22nd, 2024

When Lindiwe finally managed to get her child back, all safe and sound – although a touch bigger – she immediately left Nyl'theria and its unknown dangers. She didn't even go back to find Sayrn to finish their proper goodbye. Finding the entire endeavour an egregious waste of her time, she returned to Weldir's realm. There, she learned that the child she shouldn't have abandoned wasn't just simply captured but was being tortured at the hands of merciless, cruel humans.

Weldir hadn't wanted to tell her in case it was a distraction.

Lindiwe was at her wit's end, being pulled in a hundred directions all at once. Orpheus, Magnar, and even Faunus, who now resided near them, had all been attacked – although they were fine now. Ingram was in the hands of Demonslayers, and even a few of her children across the world had been in danger, like in Englian, Unerica, and Eyropea. Pile on Sayrn going to Nyl'theria, and she was beginning to lose it.

Thankfully everyone but Ingram had managed to be victorious in their struggles, but that meant little to her. *I wish I had the ability to multiply myself so I could be in a dozen places at once.*

She exited Weldir's mist bordering the Veil to fly straight to Zagros Fortress with vengeance boiling in her blood, wishing he could have materialised her right at their gates. The day's flight felt long and gruelling.

For the first time in her long life, Lindiwe had the temptation to destroy an entire human settlement. To burn it to the ground with black flames until the walls melted and the people inside it were consumed in a fury-filled blaze.

All because they had harmed her sweet Ingram.

She could forgive a battle; her child had run headfirst into such foolishness.

But torturing him? Cracking open his chest?

Lindiwe found that unforgivable.

She didn't know how she could live with herself if she did such a thing, though. She'd spent the last three centuries preserving human life, and being a reaper of humankind felt unjust. Especially when such actions would have dire consequences for the villages, towns, and cities that relied on the Demonslayers' protection. Men, women, children, the sick, and the old would pay for her crime against humankind.

It was for *them* that she held back when she snuck into Zagros Fortress and came face-to-skull with her child strapped to some kind of contraption.

"*Free me,*" he whimpered. "*I should have listened to you. I am sorry. Please free me.*"

The best Lindiwe could come up with was an apology and a half truth, without having to explain the real reason for her delay: that Sayrn had left Earth.

But nothing I say will make either of us feel better, she thought, investigating the chains and rope trapping him there. *I feel so awful for going after Sayrn.* And she was very, *very* angry with Weldir for *not* telling her what was happening here.

Lindiwe used her nails to pick at the knot of his bindings to give him a bit of movement. "Curses!" she spat out, stepping back. "The knot is too tight."

And when she pushed detection magic into his trappings, there was nothing Lindiwe could do with her powers to assist him – they were enchanted with Anzúli magic. She would have to find the key to his chains and cut the rope with a blessed obsidian dagger.

"Cut off my head," he demanded.

She eyed him with a dark intensity. He had no idea that what *he* thought was a mercy was emotional torture for her. She understood he just wanted freedom, but even if it helped them, she truly struggled to harm her children, her precious babies – no matter that they were large, frightful, and *beautiful* monsters.

When Wren, a well-known Demonslayer Head Elder, entered the dark and dank dungeon, Lindiwe turned incorporeal and floated within Ingram to hide. Two others in their customary black uniforms filed in behind her. Unlike Wren, who had her hood back to reveal her scarred face and red hair, their hoods were up to hide their features.

"I will try to find the key to your chains," she whispered so only Ingram could hear her. "Please, just wait a little longer."

She felt awful about having to leave him again, especially with a doctor who wanted to do more horrible things to him, but she would remain nearby and Weldir was watching. If they tried to harm him again, she'd come to this dungeon and wreak havoc upon them, human deaths be damned.

First, she needed to find *where* the contraption keys were stored. In her ghostly form, she followed Wren until she revealed the location, which was within a safe, and where the keys to that were. She waited until the woman was unsuspecting before she pilfered them straight from her person.

Then she needed to be patient and wait for her to leave the room the safe was in. In the background, Weldir informed her of all he'd learned about the stone she'd found in Merikh's home – now that he was done investigating it.

"The spell is strong. Not of a deity's level, of course, but it's powerful. It's doubtful you'll be able to use it properly without Elysian mana."

"Does that mean we can't use it?" Lindiwe asked, rushing to the safe just as Wren exited her office.

She cycled through different keys on the metal keyring and quickly slid each one into the lock. *If only I could grab solid things while in my Phantom form.* She wouldn't have needed the keyring to begin with.

"The stone is volatile. A mere crack in it will cause it to explode, and the energy from it will mean death for anything in its proximity."

Finally one of the keys twisted in the lock and it clicked open. "Like some kind of sun explosive?"

"Exactly. Considering how your Phantom spirit tried to separate from your human body, you will be unable to use it."

Her brows drew together as she looked around the office. "Why not?"

"It will likely destroy you. I believe the vibration that radiates from the spell is what started to separate your forms, but it was also pulling apart your soul."

"What about a Duskwalker then?"

"You're more similar to them than you are to a human. Even the younglings we had here were impacted by it. Their bodies will separate from their physical selves if they try."

Looking down at the key that would lead to Ingram's freedom, she clenched her hand around it.

"Then I'm the only one who *can* do it," she answered.

Even if it means I have to die, I'd rather that than be the reason another one of them dies. She expected to feel saddened by that realisation, or even a little frightened. She felt none of those things. Determined resolve overtook her, and there was... *relief* in it.

She'd lived long enough, and Weldir had enough children to feed him souls. She wasn't needed anymore, and none of her children really wanted her interference.

"No." The word was curt and dark.

"No?" Lindiwe lifted her gaze to the window, and she was so high up in the fortress she was able to look over it entirely. "If neither a Duskwalker nor their bride can use it, then it has to be me."

"I understand. My answer remains the same. No."

"Why not?!" Lindiwe retorted, before quietening her voice when she realised she'd half shouted it.

"This stone won't just kill you; it'll completely eradicate your soul. I won't be able to bring you back. I will not see my mate perish. I refuse."

Lindiwe stamped her foot. "There is no other way!" She raised her arms to gesture at herself. "I won't be able to take it if another one of them dies, not when we have the answer! What does it matter if I die so long as they live?"

"Because it matters to me!" Weldir roared, making her flinch. *"You, little female, do not seem to realise how much I care for you. My answer is no. It will always be no. And I'll never give you the stone unless I know you won't use it for such a reason. My answer is definitive, and if you try to convince me otherwise, or state such a thing again, you will **deeply** regret doing so, **owlet**."*

Lips parted in shock, Lindiwe didn't know what to say, or how to feel.

It just reminded her that she didn't know how he truly felt about her. Because... she didn't want to know the depth of it and had been trying to hide from it for half a century, while running from her own love of him. Because it was too painful otherwise.

Sometimes he makes me feel like he is capable of love, she thought solemnly, as her face tingled, tears imminent if she didn't quickly distract herself.

"Okay." The word cracked from her lips. "I'll figure something else out. I... I need to go save Ingram."

She needed to turn away from her thoughts, and the way they made her heart ache.

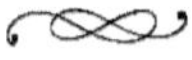

Lindiwe held back the army of Demonslayers that tried to go after Ingram and the human named Emerie, who had helped him escape. She was a guildmember who had surprisingly taken pity on him, distraught over what they were doing to him.

Admittedly, Lindiwe was thankful for her help.

Getting Ingram out had always been certain, but *how* had

been a worry. As much as she wanted to stab every guildmember in the heart for what they'd done, she truly didn't want to leave the civilians they protected without soldiers.

Their presence was needed – desperately.

With Emerie's help, there had been minimal casualties. Lindiwe even held back the army by using a shadowy shield to bar them from exiting their fortress gates. They attacked it with spears, arrows, and swords, but she refused to relent.

She barely saw them as her mind whirled.

Emerie is human. It was obvious that she didn't trust Ingram, nor he her, but could they learn to trust each other over time? *If Ingram truly wants to destroy Jabez, and we have a means to do so, then he'll need to go to his brothers.*

To the Duskwalkers and their brides living in proximity to each other.

If Ingram doesn't bond with her... Her chest swelled with guilt so deep, it cycloned down to her stomach with a sickly swirl. *Then could she use the stone?*

But asking a human to sacrifice themselves for us might be too much. Why would Emerie do such a selfless thing for creatures she likely considered monsters? *But we would need a human to do it.* Someone who had no spiritual tie to a Duskwalker.

Someone who would be willing to face the devil, and grin as they literally blew him up.

But what if Ingram does *want to bond with her if they spend an extended period of time together? He's already lost Aleron...*

"Weldir," she called, her throat thick with emotion. "Will a human's soul be destroyed by the sun stone?"

"I cannot answer that. The deceased souls are unaffected, as they have no physical body, but I cannot accurately tell you if a living soul will be destroyed or not."

"Say they're not, would you be able to bring them back to life if they were to bond with a Duskwalker?"

"I cannot answer that either. I may be able to, but I've also never tried. I know I can bond a living soul, but a deceased one

may be different."

So I can't even promise that she'd be returned if he did want to make her his bride. That's even *if* that was an option.

The question still remained: why would Emerie even agree to it in the first place?

She cared enough to free him, but would she give up her life for him? Lindiwe mused on that question as she effortlessly continued to hold back the Demonslayers.

Then a selfish, callous, and just downright despicable thought came to mind. She clenched her jaw so tightly she felt like she was pulverising her molars in penitence.

What if I make them journey to the Veil together in hopes that she falls in love with him, and the others? Her chest sawed in and out as anxiety clutched her. *Gosh. I truly have become a horrible person. I'm willing to use someone's love and kindness to manipulate them into saving my children.*

Tears welled in her eyes, and she released the shield when all her strength and determination sapped straight out of her. The Demonslayers crept forward in surprise. Then they paused, unsure of what to do with her standing there and no longer blocking their path.

Covering her face with a sob, she thought, *I've become so awful. I don't deserve to live with such selfishness in my heart.*

Worse still, she didn't think her guilt was enough to stop her if it preserved the lives of Duskwalkers – especially those with brides and children of their own.

If he makes her his bride before they reach the Veil... then the option is out of my hands. She'd find someone else to help them, a different human.

As she turned into an owl before the eyes of the Demonslayers, she lifted off to go after the escapees.

Hopefully they make that decision for me. If Ingram took Emerie's soul, then there was nothing she could do about it.

She had no intention of intervening to stop them from growing fond of each other, even if it meant things took longer.

I'll find someone.

Even if she had to force them to. If it couldn't be Emerie now, then someone, surely, would be desperate enough to trade their life for something. What she could offer in exchange, she didn't know.

A sacrifice, just like me, just like Orpheus' offerings.

Someone needed to end this cycle before it was too late and more precious lives were lost.

FIFTY-FOUR

A time unknown, but of mischief

Weldir feigned leaning left, just so he could bounce to the right and intercept his offspring darting around him.

He grabbed Aleron by the rear leg and dragged him backwards.

"Nooo! I do not want to fall!" Aleron yelled, gouging his claws into the ground.

Black goop bubbled from the marks he left behind, a flaw in Weldir's design of Tenebris; he'd forgotten to place dirt beneath the grass.

"You should learn how to fly," Weldir argued, as he approached the edge of a cliff he'd managed to trick Aleron into nearing.

In reality, he could've forced the issue by teleporting Aleron into the air, but Weldir found this *much* more fun. Teasing his rather playful offspring was quickly becoming a highlight of spending time within his own realm.

"I am sorry! I will not do it again!" Aleron whined, trying with all his might to win the battle against Weldir – to no avail. *"No more eat souls. Promise."*

"You're turning out to be a big liar, Aleron," Weldir said with a chuckle. "You've already eaten three, and you've said the same thing each time. This also isn't punishment."

Although Weldir had initially been annoyed his bat-skulled offspring had picked off a few souls, on purpose, when he wasn't around to stop him, he hadn't remained upset. Weldir wasn't using much of his mana right now, instead storing it in case Lindiwe had need of him.

Swallowing Aleron had increased his reserves to a little over one-third. Of course, since he'd eaten a few souls, it'd brought that down to one forth. That was more than enough to keep him useful, and his offspring was now a little more intelligent.

Most importantly, Weldir had managed to remove the shattered fragments of each soul from Aleron immediately, preventing him from being afflicted with the same curse as his serpent sibling.

His back muscles had also strengthened around the base of his wings. From what Weldir had been able to gauge, he *should* be able to fly now.

He didn't mind Aleron stealing a few souls if it improved his quality of life here. Especially as he'd struggled to adjust to Tenebris at first.

His initial reaction had been panic. Not at his death, but that his twin, Ingram, wasn't with him. Aleron didn't mind that he'd died; he'd just expected Ingram to be with him if he did.

He was slowly accepting it.

However, Weldir couldn't conjure his viewing discs near him, as Aleron would want to stare at Ingram for hours on end. It was unhealthy, and it made him even more stagnant than he should be. He'd also whimper as he did, and Weldir didn't want him to be sad within his realm if he could prevent it.

With regard to another sibling, Aleron couldn't figure out Nathair.

That was due to Nathair being a bully. He'd sign at Aleron, who had no idea what he was doing, and then the serpent Mavka would chortle and snicker when it bothered him. He was having fun teasing his sibling, and he'd personally asked Weldir not to reveal *why* he was silent until he was ready to have the conversation with him.

Nathair made up for it by not only allowing Aleron to lie next to him, but he would curl his tail around him so he could feel secure. Then, he'd pet his bat skull silently, so long as he wasn't deep within a trance – Nathair would always be a little grumpy afterwards otherwise. He'd often retreat into his lake to hide away his anguish.

It was also his way of hiding from Aleron when he found his playfulness too much.

Weldir's current attempt at a flying lesson was halted when Aleron managed to clamp his hands around the base of a tree. Weldir jerked back and turned. As soon as he let go, Aleron tried to sprint away. Weldir wrapped Aleron up in tendrils and forced his offspring to his side. He then proceeded to flip him onto his back, pick him up until he was in the air above his head, and walk to the cliff edge.

Aleron roared when he tossed him, and Weldir leaned over the edge to see how he fared. He kicked and shoved his hands downwards as he fell.

Weldir changed the pressure of the air so it was thicker, and his wings started to spread on their own. He tried to emulate wind, and after a few intermittent flaps, Aleron spread his wings. He began to glide, and his yelling ceased.

"Ha! I knew he'd get it this time."

He glided downwards, rushing with intense speed.

"Alright, Aleron. Flap," he whispered.

He didn't; he just kept his wings wide.

"Flap your wings," he whispered again, yet he still didn't, even as he rushed towards the tops of trees. "Shit."

Weldir teleported to the bottom of the cliff, at the start of the forest, and began to grow his size. It was too late. Rather than acting like a stone wall, he caught Aleron, and they went rolling back to soften his fall. Except Aleron, the uncoordinated goofball, didn't bring his wings in. He gave a sharp yelp when one snapped as it hit the trunk of a tree.

Weldir healed him when they stopped rolling, then sat on the ground with him as Aleron wheezed. After a moment, he bounced up onto all fours and jumped excitedly.

"I flew! I did it."

Weldir chuckled. "I wouldn't say you flew. More like glided down to the trees and crashed."

"No. I flew!" He ran in a circle and then continued to jump, his wings twitching. *"Again. Again!"*

Well, at least this is a start. And he no longer seemed to be afraid, despite getting hurt. Weldir placed his hand on his bat skull, rubbed it, and teleported them back to the top of the mountain. Aleron spun, sprinted for the edge himself, and leapt with his wings wide.

This time, Weldir formed his own wings from nothing, and teleported to his side. He fell with him, then glided when he did.

"Flap your wings. Like this." Weldir shot in front to demonstrate what he meant, and he turned his back to the ground to make sure Aleron followed his instructions.

When the process was about to fail again, he teleported them both back to the starting point where they'd begun to fall. He did it repeatedly, keeping his back to the ground while inverting his false wings to demonstrate, until Aleron eventually figured it out.

The moment he did, Aleron took off into the sky, and Weldir flew with him.

For the first time since his offspring arrived in Tenebris, he laughed while dipping to the side so he could bank left over his realm.

It was obvious he didn't know what to do with his legs and arms as they flapped around, so Weldir came closer to show him how he thought they'd be best tucked up and in. Aleron followed the silent instructions, and it looked more comfortable.

There, he has learned to fly.

Aleron was a winged being. This should be freeing for him and give him an independence that had no emotional tie to his twin. Something entirely new that he could do on his own.

Maybe now he'll stop being cheeky and picking off my souls one by one. Or maybe Weldir had just made the problem worse.

∽

A time unknown, but of unwanted burdens

"You don't seem pleased about this," Weldir stated, watching his mate *very* closely, who had the sun stone on her person.

He was ready to snatch her back to his realm if she so much as dared to go near Jabez's castle with it alone. Seated on a tree stump, she stared at the tent belonging to Mayumi, which had been set up under Faunus' ward. She was waiting to see if Emerie would leave the borrowed tent on her own so she could speak to her privately.

"I'm not," she grumbled. "I don't want to ask her to do this."

"Then why are you? Surely we could find another human to do it."

Lindiwe lowered her gaze to the stone in her nimble hands as she rested the backs of them in her lap. Her face shifted to appear downtrodden.

"Because I don't know where to start, or who to ask to do this for us. I'm worried that if we wait too much longer, another one of them will die."

"Then they die," he stated, unsure why she just couldn't seem to understand or accept this. "They will just come to me and start their life here. They would be safe."

"They've only just found brides, Weldir. They've only *just* achieved happiness." She thumbed the stone. "They all deserve to live a proper life. And what if it's Faunus? I think something in me would break if I'd have to look after my own grandchildren because their parents died. I... don't want to do that. I will, if I must – if it comes to that. But it shouldn't have to be that way."

Hmm. I never considered the impact on those who have younglings. Or hadn't yet had the chance to make their own. *I... also don't know what would happen to the bride, should their*

Mavka die. They would no longer be alive – that's all he knew.

Lindiwe lifted her gaze to the night sky and let out a defeated expire.

"How did things go so wrong? I feel so awful having to ask this of Emerie, but what if waiting ends in disaster? I know this will likely hurt Ingram, and I know he's already lost so much, but she isn't his bride. He *can* find someone else if we're unable to bring her back to life."

"You could always inform them of that potential."

"And give them false hope, only to find out we're wrong? That her soul is destroyed upon using it? That seems so much worse. I'd feel like a liar in the worst way. I'd rather not say anything at all and then present them with the hope when it's a real possibility."

"I'm unsure of how to ease you," he admitted, hoping she'd understand that he *wanted* to, he just didn't know how. He often said the wrong thing.

She pressed her fists to her forehead, just as a small, soft sob cracked from her.

"Help me feel better about this. That I'm making the right choice – because I don't know what I'm doing anymore, Weldir." A glittering droplet fell from her chin and landed upon the skirt of her dress, darkening the white of it. "I feel like I'm becoming a selfish, horrible monster. That something inside me is rotting. The fact that I'm even going to do this, knowing how much it will hurt them both, makes me feel so awful that I don't know how to swallow it. But I keep thinking about Faunus and Mayumi, and their babies. About Orpheus, who waited so, *so* long for someone to love him. About Magnar, who wants to greet Fyodor again one day. How desperately they are all trying to survive just another day. Ingram's future is undetermined; his bride isn't set in stone. He will live past this, and yet I can't help thinking how unfair this is on him too. I just... I feel so lost, Weldir."

"It cannot always be humans that make sacrifices. Our offspring must also help, even if it isn't always for their betterment."

He actually had a solution, but he knew it was morbid, and something she would never agree to. If Emerie was destroyed, then Lindiwe could destroy Ingram's skull herself and let him be with his twin. They could traverse Tenebris together, just as they did on Earth. There would be no difference for them, as all they'd done was adventure and play.

But she doesn't see Tenebris as a second life for them, like I do.

"I know," Lindiwe said, wiping the back of her wrists against her cheeks. "It just feels wrong. I wish you'd just let me do this instead."

The growl that snapped out of him was lethal.

"Oh, be quiet. I know you won't let me." She sniffled and lowered her hands to reveal how glossy and swollen her face had become. "I'm just expressing how I feel. But thank you for listening. For letting me get this out."

Emerie finally emerged from the tent, and his mate's expression grew cold as she stood.

"Always, Lindiwe." As she approached the woman from behind, he added, "I have enough mana right now to produce a portal, perhaps even two. All we can hope is that she agrees, and that her soul isn't disintegrated in the process."

"I know," she whispered.

Then, she grabbed the redheaded woman from behind while covering her mouth so she wouldn't scream and wake Ingram.

Weldir listened in on their conversation with a heaviness weighing down his mist. He sympathised with his mate, even if he couldn't relate nor truly understand her pain.

What's done, is done, and what may come, will come.

All they could do was try... and witness the results thereafter.

FIFTY-FIVE

A time unknown, but of uncertain change

"I'd say things went considerably well," Weldir mused, as he watched his mate land outside her little hut.

Her snowy owl form was like a bright beacon in the dark and haunted Veil. Folding away her wings, she pushed back her hood to reveal her tangled and unkempt curls – the evidence of being locked in battle and surviving it.

"That was anxiety inducing and horrible," she answered with her bottom lip pouting forward. "You weren't there when we fought Jabez, and having to watch each of my sons' brides be murdered while protecting Emerie was sickening. Poor Reia was targeted first."

"I did assist."

"Yeah, with a portal and letting me use your magic."

"There are challenges in being able to do nothing – I couldn't even watch." Weldir leaned back to gaze at Tenebris' blue sky while situated in the clearing on top of his favourite mountain – that led to his cave of memories. "But Emerie was able to be returned, and now Ingram has his own bride. Aleron liked her, from what I can tell."

Currently his bat-skulled offspring was getting to know Emerie's brother, Gideon. He'd decided to leave them be, hoping they'd find companionship within his realm.

He didn't inform Lindiwe about this new situation. *Even if they want to bond, they cannot do so here.* And he couldn't give them life; he had no such ability.

Why let her know of that sad news?

"I'm so overjoyed that things turned out the way they did," she said, right as little tears welled in her eyes. The smile present on her face had to be of relief. "It made everything worth it."

"Hmm. Maybe. I have yet to find Jabez's soul," Weldir stated absentmindedly as he felt a shift in energy.

It'd been happening for a while. Something was changing outside his prism, and he wasn't quite sure what. Only that there was movement, and Leyfr's vines weren't throbbing as much as they did before.

"Ugh. Really? You couldn't let me have just a moment of happiness over what we achieved?"

"My apologies. I was merely stating the truth. He could have teleported away at the last second."

"I know," she grumbled, as she pushed open the door to her home. Lindiwe immediately fell onto her bed on her front and sprawled out. "I feel like I could sleep for an eternity. I slept in your realm, but I'm still so emotionally worn out."

"Rest. For now, things are calm. Even if Jabez is still out there, he'll be injured at the very least. There is little he'll be able to do until he finishes licking his wounds."

He wasn't even finished speaking before he heard a soft snore, and humour shimmered through his mist. *She's fallen asleep.* Their young offspring climbed out from within her cloak, and one nestled up into the crook of her neck, while the other tucked themselves between her arm and side.

Weldir had held onto them when she went into battle, keeping them safe and entirely out of harm's way. He'd enjoyed their company, even if they'd been asleep the entire time.

Watching his mate rest peacefully for the first time in over a year, Weldir tried to gauge what was happening outside his prism.

The only thing that made sense was... *I think... my mother has finally woken.* Not just a peek open of her weary eyelids and then back to sleep, but fully awake. Power surrounded him, even if Leyfr's vines had softened in their pulses. The power was weak, but he wondered if it was hers he was sensing.

What else could it be? She must wake sooner or later. She must return to her station, especially after such a long time.

His mother had nearly died. Coming back from such a brink, where she teetered on the edge of everlasting death, was difficult for a deity. And the more power they had to start with, the longer it took. The more damage it did.

He'd spent half a century slumbering like her due to Nathair, but his mana resources were nothing like the Gilded Maiden's, who had such intense otherworldly strength it had literally leaked from her eyes as golden tears.

I've been feeling her stir for years. He lowered his gaze to look over the rolling meadows and beauty that was Tenebris. *I have done as I promised.*

He'd not taken life by his own mist, had not stolen souls from the living even though it would have benefited him and saved them much trouble. He guarded the many portals they'd placed, and he collected souls to take care of them within the realm of his stomach.

They must know all this.

They likely know of Lindiwe and my offspring by now as well, but technically I haven't broken any rules. He was still unsure how they'd taken it, as none had come to reprimand him for it. *Perhaps they are waiting for my patience to run out, or for Mother to be better restored.*

Yet, as he brought his gaze back to his snoozing mate, he realised his patience was running out.

There was also something he wanted to do, and it was entirely selfless.

She has done enough for me, Weldir thought, as he watched her grab the offspring at her side, rotate and bring them up, and then cuddle them properly. *She is discontent. I would like to provide her with a different option.*

Even if that meant... losing her.

With a sadness shimmering through him, he sighed and crossed his legs to ponder with his chin on his fist. *So, Mother, I'll give you a little more time, and then I want my reward for all I have done.*

A single tear shouldn't be much to ask for.

Weldir was deeply concerned, and perhaps a touch mortified, when he discovered his winged offspring in the connective tunnel between his statues of all the Mavka in Austrális and his cave of intimacy revolving around his mate. Even more so when he saw Aleron's purple tongue down the brown-haired male's throat.

"I considered not interrupting," Weldir stated behind them, "but I'd rather you didn't do this here."

Aleron's wings shot up as he pulled his tongue from Gideon and darted his skull in Weldir's direction with a rumble.

Vexation collected his mist tighter against him, and he folded his arms to show his displeasure. "Little one, did you just *snarl* at me?"

"Leave us," Aleron barked at him.

He considered teleporting him into the sky to punish him for his insolence. Or maybe he'd do it to the human, just to give him a fright.

"No, I don't think I will." He gestured towards the exit. "You both will quit trying to hump each other and leave this special place."

At least the human saw sense and obeyed.

Thankful he'd interrupted them, and hoping they had gone no further or seen his memories of Lindiwe, he led them outside his cave. *I would have hidden the entrance had I known Aleron would find it and grow curious.* He had all of Tenebris to discover, so why be here in the one place Weldir didn't want him?

Much time had passed – a month or so, Lindiwe had informed him. The twenty-ninth of May, in the year two thousand twenty-four. She always told him the date, as if he would have any idea how long it'd been when he asked so infrequently.

But this should be enough time for Almethrandra to have gained a little more strength. Enough that he didn't feel so bad about sending this Mavka on a quest for him.

He, too, had slept during this time to give himself that little bit more mana. Especially as he'd destroyed three souls to make portals recently: one to take Lindiwe to Jabez's castle, and the others to transport Ingram to and from his realm.

His mana had been low, and near the point of deep sleep. Luckily, he'd had just enough to do it all.

Now, he had to waste more, but at least it would solve this issue in the future. It'd be arduous, but so long as nothing happened in the interim, he should be able to handle it.

"What I need is for you to ask the Gilded Maiden for a single tear," Weldir stated. "I have not been back to Nyl'theria since the Demons were brought to Earth, but I will try my best to transport you to Lezekos, the Elven city."

He'd seen Nyl'theria once with the help of Leyfr. It had also been the last time he'd spoken to the Evergreen Servant after he'd crossed through Jabez's portal and laid his mist there. What the male deity didn't know was that Weldir had left behind just a tiny cloud of mist in Nyl'theria in case he ever wanted access to it – he'd just never nurtured it.

Wisely so, as it was a sneaky forethought that was useful for this.

Aleron agreed – after some annoying questioning. However, apparently Gideon, his new companion, had to accompany him, since Aleron wouldn't leave without him.

Seeing it was best just to give in, Weldir agreed.

What does it matter, so long as they achieve the goal?

FIFTY-SIX

A time unknown, but of golden opportunities

When Aleron and Gideon had left his realm, Weldir had been unsure about his decision. He hadn't been able to monitor them, as the viewing disc of Aleron brought up nothing.

He'd wanted to know what would transpire, as he wasn't fond of surprises.

I never thought it would be this, though, he mused, as he stared down at a fragment of the Gilded Maiden's halo crown.

It glowed bright gold in his darkness, even if it didn't illuminate far. Sitting cross-legged, with no viewing discs around him to disrupt his musings, he let himself dwell on it.

This is far more than I asked for, and more than I ever expected.

What Weldir could do with this... was limitless.

This wasn't just some pretty piece of a crown, but part of Almethrandra's life force. This was pure, unadulterated mana. Not just any kind, but one that could be manipulated in ways he normally couldn't do.

At least, not on his own.

I have proven I can restore life, so long as it has some kind of anchor. Emerie was an example of this. *I can create life.* Proven by his many offspring. *I can offer power through me.* As he had with his mate.

I am a being of death, of life, and in between.

He made the crown shard float between his hands and sent a jolt of mana through it to see how well it mingled with his own. *And since I'm her direct descendant, our magics mix well.*

Now to test it properly, without informing anyone.

Weldir called Lindiwe's soul to him. He broke off just the tiniest piece of the palm-sized fragment and pushed the grain of golden crown towards the citrine flame. Then he pushed in his own mana.

Immediately both began to vibrate, and threads began intertwining with each other. He immediately halted the spell, as it confirmed what he'd assumed without making it permanent. He would also need much more to successfully complete what he'd tested.

But it gave him his answer.

Next, he called the broken pieces of Nathair's skull. He removed a little more of the crown, made it collide with the other detached fragment, and then put it between the many pieces of his skull. It vibrated, as did the skull, which began to reassemble.

The pieces meshed together so seamlessly that they were barely noticeable except for a hair's width of gleaming gold.

Weldir held Nathair's serpent skull, whole and mended.

The question is, will I be able to attach his soul back to it? He rotated it one way, and then the other. *I don't see why not, as his anchor is whole once more.* If he could bond skull to soul, he could free him from death.

Uncertainty ruffled his mist, and he tapped a foreclaw against the skull's snout. *I would like to try.* It may allow Nathair to live on Earth again. *I know it would make Lindiwe happy if he is returned to her.*

If it was successful, how could he do the same for Aleron? *We don't have his skull pieces.* He tapped his foreclaw faster. *Perhaps if she obtains the same fruit-bat skull and similarly shaped goat horns, I can mould them to his soul.* He could at least attempt it while informing her not to get her hopes too high.

Firstly, I'll have to try with Nathair.

If this works... A rather foreign and unsettling emotion thickened the very space surrounding him. Sadness, perhaps? His own form of grief? *It means they will leave.*

He'd no longer be able to interact with his offspring and would once again be alone. Entirely.

I like my offspring nearby. He enjoyed conversing with them, playing with them, and teaching them. *Oh well. This is what we wanted all along.*

There was no point in being upset about it. He was used to the utter solitude, although he thought it might be more sorrowful now that he'd experienced companionship.

"Lindiwe," he called, before he even pulled up her viewing disc.

When he did, it made a ring around her deep in the mountains of Mongulien on a summer's day. *Good, she hasn't yet fully evolved our offspring.* He figured she was nervous about doing so just in case something went awry.

"Yes, spirit of the void?" Her lips curled a little in mild humour.

He chuckled. *I see she is back to being her perkier self.*

"I didn't inform you, but I sent Aleron to Nyl'theria to meet with the Gilded Maiden."

She halted in her travels across the base of a mountain, and pushed back her hair when a rather strong gust of wind slipped it all forward. Her cloak and dress swayed, following its direction. "What? Why?"

"I wanted a gift, and I have received a rather substantial one. She has given me part of her life force."

"Okay. So what does that mean?"

His answer was quiet and heavy as he said, "I may be able to bring Nathair, and possibly Aleron, back to life."

Her eyes widened as her lips parted. She said nothing, utterly speechless.

Which was fine with him.

"I make no promises, but I have mended Nathair's skull. I may be able to attach it back to his soul, and he should reform his body like all Mavka do when they are beheaded." Then he looked down at it in his lap. "Firstly, I ask that you obtain a skull and horn type similar to Aleron's before I do so, so that I can see if it's possible to do the same for him."

"Yes. Absolutely. I can do that now if you send me back to Austrális." There was a giddy spring in her movements, and she jumped up and down on the spot, so overjoyed she needed an outlet for it. Her smile was bright and larger than he'd ever seen. "I know exactly where I can find those pieces. I could probably get it done in just a few hours."

"Excellent. I'll bring you back there now."

Before he did, he brought the crown fragment closer, noting how little he'd needed to mend Nathair's skull. *I wonder what else I can do with this.*

If it could help him restore his offsprings' lives, could it... possibly... give him one?

He looked at his beautiful mate, who smiled as she fought the wind, her brown eyes sparkling with cheer and life.

Or do I gift her a different life? One away and completely detached from him.

Something to consider and weigh later, he figured, as he brought Lindiwe to his weightless darkness.

First, let's see if it's at all possible.

FIFTY-SEVEN

A time unknown, but of troubled offspring

When Weldir placed Nathair's serpent skull over the face of his soul, and it bound together with a little help from his own spiritual essence – a different kind of mana – a sense of triumph overcame him.

It was strong enough to overshadow the regretful sorrow and longing as Nathair's body grew in a flurry of black, glittering sand.

Saying goodbye was easy – Weldir avoided it entirely. He pulled Nathair out of Tenebris by his fate tether without a word.

Lindiwe was waiting for Nathair in the dark nothingness of his void, and her smile was bright and teary. He waved at her and then signed his greeting, which Weldir translated for him. He would try to assist in this regard in the future until she learned 'Nathair speak' so she could communicate with him.

He would've let them speak sooner, if being outside of Tenebris in the limbo realm didn't instantly put spirits to sleep. The same had happened to Aleron and his human companion, and they'd woken up again in Nyl'theria as a pair of Ghosts wandering the Elven realm.

The reintroduction between his mate and the serpent Mavka was short – he needed to send them back to Earth. Considering he had little mana, he'd taken a grain of his mother's crown to empower him enough to make a portal. He could bring Lindiwe back and forth, but not Nathair, who now had a physical form.

Before he moved through the portal, Nathair turned to Weldir and signed, "Thank you for all you have done. It is..." His fingers twitched as he tried to figure out the right words to say. His hands weren't often hesitant or unsteady. "...difficult to leave your side, but I do appreciate this opportunity."

He hadn't been able to avoid a goodbye, after all.

"You're welcome, Nathair. I've enjoyed your company within Tenebris. I'm still sorry that I have not been able to remove all the fragments from you, but hopefully returning to life will do what I could not."

Then, without another word from either – although Lindiwe shared with him a strange, tender smile – they left together. He placed them north of the Veil, just at the fringes of his mist on the surface, and watched to see how they fared.

Chaos immediately ensued.

Whether it be the sounds of life, the smell of it, perhaps even the way the wind felt brushing along his scales, Nathair went from calm to panicked. The fiery vortex of his orbs swirled with an array of colours, and he clutched the sides of his skull with a bellowing roar.

He started bashing his skull on the ground, then against the closest tree trunk, as if to break it once more. He clawed at his own neck to decapitate himself just to stop the fragments that came at him with a vengeance.

He'd done this many times in the beginning when he'd first awoken with the fragments.

"Weldir! Help!" she yelled.

Nathair lashed out at her voice and bit into her shoulder so swiftly not even Weldir saw it coming. She hadn't expected the strike, hadn't expected him to lash out when it was obvious he wasn't enraged. Although his squirming, self-mutilating hands were a clear warning, she'd allowed herself to be struck.

Lindiwe didn't seem to care about her wounds.

She backed up as her form flickered between physical and

Phantom. She winced each time she was human, but her eyes never strayed from a distressed Nathair.

"There is nothing I can do now for him," Weldir stated. "He is out of my reach, my magic, and my capabilities."

"H-how do I help him, then?" she asked, clutching her shoulder and putting space between them.

"Put him to sleep. That is how I assisted when it was this bad in the beginning." After Weldir had removed enough of the fragments to take him out of his permanent seizing.

Her complexion grew ashen as horror fell over her features. "The only way to do that is to behead him."

"Hmm." Weldir regarded Nathair and the way he tore into his own throat. "If you're unable to do it, he will surely do it himself."

"Ugh!" she screamed. "I hate this!"

She went to lift both hands to help him, to get it over with, rather than him clawing at himself slowly and painfully until he achieved unconsciousness. Only her left arm rose, as the other twitched and spasmed, but wouldn't lift more than partway.

Lindiwe placed her hand over the wound, then lifted it away to look at the blood coating her fingertips. "His venom. I forgot about it." Her right leg shook before her knee gave in. She caught herself with her left hand when falling nearly made her go face-first into the ground. "Uh, Weldir?"

Before he could answer, Nathair dived for her. Her scream cut short when he dug his claws into her neck and abdomen, and pulled in two different directions.

Weldir brought her to his realm before Nathair could do any more damage and likely eat her. Their two young offspring shrieked when they lifted off her, reaching for her with little kicking arms and legs. They'd arrived awake and in their physical state, intangible to him.

Their flailing spun them around, sending them further and further from her.

Weldir neared while grumbling in anger at the life draining from her. Blood trickled from her deep wounds, her lips, and nose, and each scarlet drop floated off her skin and surrounded her.

"I cannot heal you until your body disappears and you return to me."

He tsked, rather fucking angry about this, her pain, and the events. When her heart ceased, her body began to crack and break apart like chalk, and disintegrated bit by bit.

He looked at the viewing disc of Nathair, who had finished decapitating himself with a gush of purple blood streaming from his headless throat – before he exploded in a cloud of black sand.

Their young offspring continued to let out shrill cries as they blindly searched for her with grabby paws reaching in the direction of her scent.

"Well, this could have gone better." He moved towards his offspring. "Perhaps you two should stay with me until Nathair stabilises."

Although being eaten by a Demon ensured they'd birth themselves from its stomach, he had no idea what would happen if a Mavka ate them. *I'd rather not find out.*

Considering Nathair's current instability, it was a possibility that he could turn on her again and might do so when Weldir wasn't watching. Which meant... she would return to his realm after being eaten by her own son if he managed to get his venom into her.

"I imagine that will be quite horrifying for her."

He wished he could feel his palm as he rubbed his face. *She will be upset.* Not just about that, but about Nathair's mind in general. *I did warn her, but I had power in Tenebris that she cannot wield.*

If worst came to worst, and Nathair couldn't adjust to life due to his fragments, then it might be a mercy to bring him back to Tenebris.

Despite the circumstances, Weldir decided to revive Aleron without waiting for Nathair's body to return. There was no use in putting it off.

There was also little else for him to do between waiting for Nathair and Lindiwe to return.

So, he took himself back to Tenebris.

He found his winged offspring and the human locked in a naked cuddle, Aleron rumbling a purr as Gideon chuckled in answer.

"I leave for a few hours, and this is what my poor eyes are blessed with upon my return?" Weldir teased half-heartedly, rather surprised by these two.

I hadn't truly expected Aleron to find a companion within Tenebris. He actually thought his winged offspring would let this human male slip from his claws in some way, but they continued to persist and were now intimate.

Aleron squeezed his wings tighter around the tanned male. "Go away."

"Yeah, shoo, Mr Dusty Man! Or I'll sic my giant feather duster on you," Gideon chimed in. "We've had enough of your interruptions."

"He is rather dusty."

They both cackled within the shelter of Aleron's wings.

Weldir wished he could feel the power of his sigh. *Both are so insolent.* He cared little about what they did together, but now they were just being playfully irksome. After watching his mate perish and his offspring behead himself, he wasn't in a particularly grand mood.

"As much as I would prefer to leave you be, there is something I must discuss with Aleron. It is of great importance."

Once they unfurled themselves, Gideon covering his privates with a hand until he requested clothing once more, Weldir explained the possibility of revival for his offspring. There were some minor issues, mainly a miscommunication instigated by Weldir, but they were quickly resolved.

Thankfully. For he currently lacked any patience.

Then again, he didn't realise Aleron's infatuation with the human went beyond filling the loneliness of Tenebris. That it was, in fact, much deeper. Thus, when he fitted Aleron's skull to his soul once more – with a little manipulation, as it wasn't *truly* his but pieces Weldir had spliced together – he regarded the human differently.

A male bride. I never considered it an option, but I'm pleased my offspring are open to such avenues. The gender of their partners didn't matter, so long as their hearts were good to his Mavka and treated them well. *I want my offspring to be happy.*

Even if it meant Weldir was alone.

He hadn't foreseen Gideon losing all his memories of Tenebris, as that hadn't happened with Emerie.

She was only here for a day, though. Which was not much time to retain.

It brought on unforeseen complications and issues that Weldir had to battle while Lindiwe was preoccupied with a chaotic and erratic Nathair. He would have preferred her to take care of the relationship matters, as she could've done so in person.

Especially as Gideon – traumatised, lost, and very confused – wasn't handling his new life well. He'd completely forgotten his love of Aleron and was trapped with him, inadvertently torturing him as he repeatedly rejected the bat-skulled Mavka's advances.

The only thing he could assist with was manipulating the male's spirit by shoving his own memories of their final hours of Tenebris into him to *remind* him of his own words, and his promise. He'd also used yet another fucking soul in a way he'd never needed to – and hadn't been sure would work.

At this rate, I'll use Almethrandra's crown fragment entirely just to bring my offspring to life and settle their problems.

The only consolation was there were none of his offspring left for him to attend to, and he only needed to use a grain of it at a time. He'd barely removed a tenth of it.

After a few weeks, the world frosted with winter, and he watched Lindiwe finally leave Nathair's side. The serpent Mavka had forced the solitude by slipping inside of a pond and discovering a cave at the other end of it.

She could have followed, but there was little point, as it was obvious he wanted to adjust on his own now that he'd eased the worst of the fragments. As time had gone on, and he'd almost eaten her again, Nathair had grown more desperate to leave her side to protect her from himself. Lindiwe wasn't ignorant of that fact.

Nathair had apologised for hurting her repeatedly and thanked her for staying by his side when he needed her most, many times. Weldir had translated on his behalf, often eliciting a smile from Lindiwe.

But she continued to express her desire to stay, informing him that she didn't mind her wounds. She wanted to be near him, to be with him, after he'd been absent from her life for over three hundred years.

She relented when she could see it was distressing him more and more.

Her care and adoration of their offspring always made Weldir's mist shimmer with tenderness. Her beauty had not changed, and his appreciation for her had deepened over the centuries – to the point of utter obsession.

He still visited his cave of memories regularly, even if it made him sour and... lonely.

She has pulled away from me these last few decades, he thought, as he witnessed Lindiwe come to Aleron's side in her owl form.

He was flying from Merikh's ward towards the group of Mavka in the east: Orpheus, Magnar, and Faunus' empty home.

They will find Ingram. Hopefully *after* their relationship had finished repairing itself. *The human is softening towards Aleron again.* It's why he'd never told them where to go, as they needed the journey in order to repair Gideon's mind and heart.

At least they were finally on the correct path. *It shouldn't be too much longer. Which means I can finally act...*

He brought the crown fragment to him with a sense of uncertainty. He still didn't know what to do with the rest of it.

The longer he stared at the glowing concentration of mana, and perceived its unceasing power-filled throbs, the less... confident he felt about her answer. Weldir intended to present her with a choice, one that would greatly impact him.

I am... unsure if she will choose me.

It was making him hesitate. His mate was a mystery, even now, and her inner thoughts had always been unspoken.

Did Lindiwe care for him in the same way he did her, or had she been trying to make the best of her situation? *I still remember her hateful gaze.* He'd found it insignificant then, but not so much now. *We have a companionship, but it has always been shaky.*

And given that she no longer desired to be near him or intimate with him, even after many decades had passed, he wondered if perhaps she'd just grown bored. He'd offered her no future other than the one they currently had, and it had always been for Weldir's selfish gain.

Such things probably lingered over their bond like a dreary cloud. Perhaps any fondness from her was as false as she found his realm and his body.

Yet, he didn't want to believe that things had been so shallow and surface level. He wanted to believe there had been more, even if she hid it for whatever reason. Maybe it was a stretch, and he was being foolish, but he simply didn't want all the affection and intimacy to be a lie.

There is only one way to find out.

And once Aleron found Ingram, and Nathair settled into life fully within his cave, Weldir was ready to present the choices to her.

The crown fragment flashed with light when he shoved his own mana into it.

This will be my final gift to her.

FIFTY-EIGHT

July 8th, 2024

The spell sputtered out when Lindiwe once again tried to see Fyodor, Magnar and Delora's daughter. Not only did nothing show, but the scrying disc also wouldn't conjure at all.

Her worry deepened.

"Why can't I see her anymore?" she whispered, bringing her knees up while seated on her bed. "Did someone give her a new name?"

Without it, Lindiwe couldn't scry for her. It was the same when her children obtained new names, as picturing their faces while thinking of their names was what the spell required.

"But who would give her one? She doesn't have enough humanity to make a real companion." Her lips tightened in thought. "Unless she suddenly gained humanity. But *still*."

Lindiwe sighed and racked her brain about what to do. She'd already visited Fyodor's burrow to find it empty, and Weldir was unable to see her, as she wasn't his direct descendant.

She'd grown into a full adult when he'd been asleep right after Faunus' skull was first cracked, and she hadn't returned to the Veil since. Had she done so, he could have familiarised himself with her spirit to manually link their family threads.

Without that established connection, the only way he'd be able to find her now was if she were to walk into his mist.

Unless she does so when he's asleep again. She already could have right before Nathair and Aleron had been brought back to life, but Weldir had slept for a month during that time as well. *Ugh! This is so frustrating. I want to make sure she's okay!*

She scratched behind her ear in irritation. *I should have paid more attention, but I was dealing with Nathair.* She'd relied on Weldir during that time to make sure all the Duskwalkers were well, forgetting that only *she* could see Fyodor.

"If she doesn't turn up shortly, I'll have to go find her myself."

Right now, Lindiwe was taking a... break.

She was emotionally worn out and just wanted a period of ease before jumping back into her life. After the hellish past two years, where almost every day had been anxiety inducing as Lindiwe waited for Jabez to make a move, she thought she deserved a reprieve.

"Well, me-and-you-two time," she said with a small laugh, watching her babies wrestle on the bed. "Hopefully the dust has settled enough that I can give you both your skulls and horns."

One was a little bigger than the other and bore a skull kind of like a human's but with large canine fangs on the top and bottom jaws. The other still looked like a newborn Duskwalker.

She threw her foot out when they were close to tumbling off the side of the bed that wasn't up against the wall, and her leg stopped them both from falling. She placed them back in the centre so they could continue to play.

"Lindiwe," Weldir called softly.

"I swear, if you're about to tell me a Duskwalker is in danger, I will come to your mist and strangle you," Lindiwe answered playfully, although she wasn't entirely joking.

She really did just want everything to be fine for a little while.

His answering chuckle, although light, was like a balm to her spirit. *"No. All is well regarding them."*

She smiled softly. "That's a nice change."

"I was wondering if you would be available to have an

important discussion."

"Sure," she answered, as she scratched behind the skull of her baby. "I'm all ears."

"I would prefer to speak with you in person."

Hard to do that when you're not a real person. He was a shadowy entity.

She understood what he meant, though.

She considered denying him. Lindiwe didn't want to be in his realm, or near him. It still hurt, and that hadn't gone away even if the last two years had been a distraction of sorts from her heartache.

But it's not often he asks me to come to him anymore.

Considering how much he'd done to help over the past few years, denying him felt unfair. She had relied on him a lot – magically, physically, emotionally. He'd been there for her as much as he could and had gone beyond his usual capabilities to do so.

"Okay." She grabbed both her babies. "I'm ready."

She was brought to his comforting weightlessness, and she turned incorporeal for him. When she finally located his mist, Lindiwe squinted at him while leaning forward.

"There's so little of you," she stated quietly, noting that there was barely a sixth of him.

Streaks only a few centimetres long wrapped around his entire body sparsely. Enough for her to see him, so long as he didn't move suddenly.

Then he made what seemed a deliberate movement. Perhaps he looked at his own hands? It was impossible to tell. "Yes, I'm aware."

Guilt and gratitude swirled together in her chest. *I didn't know it was this bad.* Her eyes followed the patterns. *Does this mean he'll sleep for a long time again?*

Lindiwe didn't know if she was relieved or saddened by that. She always missed his presence when he was gone, even if he was distant in another realm. She liked being able to talk to him freely, despite how it made the ache in her heart worsen at times.

"You wanted to talk to me?" she asked, hugging their sleeping babies to her chest.

"Yes." From what she could tell, he lifted an arm and called a brightly glowing, golden *something* to it. The piece of weird, broken, glittering metal hovered above his clawed hand. "I wanted to show you what has allowed me to be so useful lately."

"Is that the gifted piece of the Gilded Maiden's crown?"

"It is." He drifted closer so she could see it properly. "I've used a small amount, but most of it remains."

She wanted to reach out and touch it, but hesitated. It looked... hot, like it was molten despite its solidness.

"This is pure mana. It's different from mine. I can manipulate it and pour essence into it. I can change it, create and destroy with it." He lowered his face to regard it closely. His expression remained unchanging, as usual, but his following silence made the moment seem heavy. Important, almost. "I... know you have become discontented with our bond. I want to present a different option to you, as you have done much for me over the past few human centuries. A person should only have to suffer the whims of a demi-god for so long before being rewarded."

Her brows drew together tightly as she flicked her gaze between it and his unchanging expression. Something about his deep voice, and the way it sounded solemn, twisted her belly with nervous unease.

She shrugged. "I guess."

"With this, I would be able to give you back your soul, and more. I would be able to give you power that isn't mine, and it would be totally your own to wield." He lifted his face to hers, and she wished she could see more than an eye and part of his nose. "You could even choose between continuing your immortality or becoming mortal."

"Weldir?" Lindiwe's confusion deepened her frown as she shook her head. "I don't understand where this is coming from."

Nor why he was saying it.

"I would only need half to do this for you, and the other half would give me enough power to cover the rest of Earth in my mist. I can take care of our offspring with that reach, especially as I think I can convince a few to assist me, like Nathair and Odie. You would be able to live a life I have robbed you of, or continue as you are but without any attachment to me. You would be able to form a bond with another, as I have no need to create more servants. We have made plenty, and they can act as my physical self in that world as you have. They are even making more themselves."

Squeezing her arms tighter around her babies, Lindiwe's pulse raced. She knew he could hear it, and so could she, as it thrummed frantically in her ears.

"I... have no more need of you," he stated quietly. "With this crown fragment, I can do the rest on my own."

She knew why it felt like her heart was bleeding through her chest. Lindiwe had thought the longing and yearning would go on forever. That her unrequited affection and love would eventually eat her whole and spit her out until she was a misshapen version of herself.

This was a solution to that. A way to move on and finally be... free.

It hurt more than she could bear.

For over three hundred years, she'd been tied to this person. This strange, mesmerising, beautiful being, and she didn't know how to live her life without him anymore.

Now that she had this option, she didn't actually know if she truly wanted it. *But I can't keep living like this.* Both options seemed impossible for her to accept, and she wondered if perhaps death was preferable.

She didn't think her love for Weldir would simply end. Even if she found someone else, they wouldn't be him, and she would always remember the person who owned her heart as much as her soul.

He said he doesn't need me anymore. Why did that make her feel so insignificant? That all the tenderness she felt for him meant nothing, and that she, all this time, had just been a tool.

A servant. Someone to be used rather than truly cared for.

She only realised she'd actually started crying when she licked her lips before parting them to speak and tasted the salt of tears. "Is that what you want?" she asked, her voice cracking as she tried, with all her might, to stop her lips and hands from trembling.

"No. Not particularly." Weldir looked down at the glowing gold fragment once more. "But I wanted to present you with the options clearly so you could make the most informed decision. What I truly want... is you. The added bonus is that I will also get something else I've sought from the moment I was born. But... I want you to be happy more, even if that means I cannot have either. That is my gift to you. Your happiness, freely given and well earned, even if it is to my detriment."

"I-I don't understand."

"As I said, I can manipulate this mana, and I can create with it." He lifted it higher so it was between them. "I will gain no power in doing so, but I can give myself a physical form. Not just temporarily, but one that will have life, where I can leave my realm... and live in yours."

"You'll have a real body?" she asked, her voice filling with hope. Her heart fluttered at the idea, and her trembling lips curled into a broken smile. "Y-you'll be able to feel?"

"Yes. *But*... I have no idea what it will look like, or to what extent." He tilted his head from side to side. "I'm certain it would be Elven formed, as that's what my soul is like, but other than that, I'm unsure. As you know, much of what I do is a guess."

"Why didn't you just start with that?!" Lindiwe shouted, wishing she could bash his stupid chalky shoulders because the intense stress and hurt he'd just put her under was near cruel! "The decision is easy, Weldir. I would rather you have a physical form."

"Really?" he asked, his head rearing back, mirroring the surprise in his voice. "But you would continue to be tied to me."

"All I've wanted for the longest time was for you to join me on Earth, to *feel* it with me. To be real, and not some half-tangible being shrouded in shadows and trapped in a world of dark void." Lindiwe looked down at her arms full of two Duskwalkers, and even in her Phantom form, she could feel their heat. Bashfulness lifted her shoulders at her next words, and she'd been waiting so long to utter them that subtle shyness made her cheeks warm. "I love you, Weldir. I have for a long time, but it hurt too much to be near you, knowing that any future with you was just... empty. That's why I had to pull away from you."

"Why didn't you tell me?"

She clenched her eyes shut. "What would it have mattered? It would have changed nothing." She opened her eyes to stare at their babies before lifting her gaze to him. "So, of course I'd rather be with you. I want that more than anything."

"You understand I will never let you go if I do this?" he asked, just as part of a large grin began to pull at his face. When Lindiwe nodded in answer with her own smile, he said, "As you wish, then."

He pulled back to give himself space, and she was thankful that she wouldn't have to be kept in suspense for too long.

The golden crown fragment hovered between his hands as he started to manipulate it. Shadowy essence swirled around it like chalky clouds of a tornado. A tendril pierced the middle, and it pushed inside and widened it until it became a cylindrical pole. Once it was in that hollow shape, he moulded it further until he made what she could only describe as a stick figure.

Honestly, she was surprised at how far such a tiny piece could be spread out.

Then Weldir grabbed it by its stick arms and shoved it into his torso. The limbs began to separate until they made arm and leg bones, while hands and feet bones morphed into shape. The torso changed, spiking apart to make a ribcage, pelvis, and spine. Then, finally, a skull began to form that looked an awful lot like the Demon skull of the baby in her arms.

Lastly, tapered horns formed at the edge of his hairline,

tucking closely to the top of his head, before the narrow ends pointed up at the back.

When it was done, Weldir was essentially just a skeleton with mist surrounding him, and the world around her began to wobble and vibrate. She perceived a change in the air, like pressure spiralling around and around, as it pulled towards a centre – him.

The darkness surrounding her sucked away like water, and brightness crawled closer as seconds passed. Within only a handful of moments, it all retreated into his form, and light ate at the utter darkness in a flash.

A world beyond came into view.

Upwards and around her was a room that was so large she felt like a tiny ant. The clear crystal container they were in had too many surfaces for her to count accurately to gauge its true shape, but it appeared to be sitting on a purple cushion on a table of some kind, which was situated up against an obsidian wall.

Weldir lifted his hand above his brow to shield himself from the light.

"Too bright," he hissed.

Mist expanded from him, and it shoved them back into a strange, grainy darkness. It wasn't as solid as before, making everything look dark grey.

The lightness of it allowed her to see what he looked like when they both stood and faced each other.

Her eyes widened because it absolutely wasn't what she'd been expecting. *Oh god. He looks like a Demon.*

His skin was... well... it was like a spectral void holding his insides in place, just like a Demon. It was glossy and inky, like the night sky reflecting off a pond.

Except it was transparent.

Most of his golden bones were visible. They were duller in places that were covered in thick skin and muscle, like his thighs, calves, biceps, and forearms. When he lowered his strange, ethereal face, that of a golden humanoid skull with large canine fangs, he wiggled his hands.

The skin and muscle of his palms was thicker than across the backs of his hands, making the bones harder to see.

Two brows of pitch-coloured hair came together before he lifted his head. He looked one way and then the next as two long and pointed ears, like those of an Elf, flicked rapidly.

"Is that what a heart sounds like? How noisy," he stated, and somehow his voice was unfairly richer than before, with a huskiness to it that instantly had her nipples pearling in delight.

Lindiwe hesitantly came closer while keeping one arm on their babies. She reached out while he was distracted and went to touch his abdomen with her fingertips, heart swelling with tender warmth.

Her stomach dropped when she passed right through him.

Seeing she'd neared him, Weldir looked down at her, and panic suffused her as she looked up to his onyx eyes – exactly the same as they'd been before. There was no sclera, no irises, just that glossy darkness like before that always felt all-consuming.

Honestly, the weirdest thing was that he actually *blinked*. "I'm no longer intangible."

Understanding instantly dawned, and she shifted to her physical form. She tried again, and her fingertips met solidness. And warmth. And a torso that expanded and contracted from breaths. She placed her whole palm against his void-like flesh, and muscles leapt to her touch, right before a clawed hand wrapped around the back of hers.

"I can feel that," he said quietly, as a soft exhale came from him. "I can feel you."

A quiet sigh left her, just as a small smile formed. Bringing her palm up, he placed it over his bare chest, and a real, beating heart resonated beneath. He lifted his own hand and cupped the side of her face, then brushed his thumb up and down her cheek before inching over to do it to her lips.

"Your skin is softer than I thought it was," he murmured, then he drifted his hand back and brushed the backs of his claws through the underside of her curls. "Is this what silky feels like?"

She didn't know what to say. Any words that tried to climb up her throat formed as a lump of emotion. She wanted to say he looked magnificent – in an otherworldly way. That she was so happy this was happening, and that she could sense his heartbeat while he felt her.

All she could do was stare, and when he cupped the side of her face again, she leaned into it and gave his palm a nuzzle.

His black eyelashes were long and fluttery as he peered down at her, and his gaze held an edge to it that hadn't existed before. Piercing, all-seeing, and intense. She felt herself being swallowed up by the pools of obsidian.

She thought his eyes might be moving across her features, but it was impossible to truly tell. His tongue darted out, dark grey and slightly pointed, and dabbed at the seam of his lips. Every time his lips parted ever so slightly, the gold of his teeth and fangs was bright.

When he didn't do anything, just stared while caressing her cheek, she leaned up. "Well, are you going to kiss me or not?"

A deep, body-tingling chuckle vibrated from his lips. "I thought you'd never ask."

Weldir met her halfway and slanted his mouth over hers. It was overly gentle, like he remembered their horrible first kiss and didn't wish to repeat it. Not only did she instantly melt into it, she deepened it.

Lindiwe let go of their babies, knowing they'd be caught in the weightlessness he was providing, and both squealed as they spun. She leaned up further, wrapped her arms around his neck, pulled him closer, and kissed him harder. He was quick to grip her in return, his arms catching her around her middle and pulling her in tighter.

Warmth radiated everywhere as a completely solid form pushed back against her own body. Muscles pressed into her everywhere they touched, not a single part of him missing, while a strong heartbeat thumped against her chest. Breaths shoved his torso against hers, and she felt them all the way to her middle.

She tilted her head to intensify the brush of her lips over his soft ones, and he eagerly followed her increasing speed. For the first time, he had his own saliva to share with her, and it helped to make their kiss messy. He tasted like a diluted version of his scent. She'd always imagined he'd smell smoky and of fire due to his other form, but he actually had an amber-and-geranium aroma to him.

The taste of him, the warmth of his mouth, the textured firmness of his tongue when it greeted her, made her moan.

The squealing in the background quietened. Shadowy tendrils retreated to him, like he'd made the two floating baby Duskwalkers go to sleep, just as her eyelids drooped and then slid shut.

When Lindiwe slipped her tongue forward, he grunted in surprise but quickly met it. It was obvious he didn't know how to move his own properly, as kissing like this in the past had been odd – it was only when she found out he couldn't feel her tongue that she understood why his had always been so domineering.

Now, it felt compromising, giving pressure while also taking hers.

A strange noise came from him, and one of his clawed hands darted down to her arse. It squeezed hard through her dress and cloak, just as firmness lengthened against her abdomen. The knowledge that it was likely his cock – a proper one that could actually *feel* – had her pussy clenching in response.

She grabbed the ties of her cloak to get it off her, and it floated away. Weldir adjusted his hand, and more of his palm encompassed her backside. Lifting her legs, she wrapped them around his narrow hips, and they both hummed into the kiss when the underside of his growing erection slipped over her clit through her underwear.

That was also when his movements became deliciously more aggressive.

A soft growl came from him as he ground his hips against

her, and he pulled away from her lips to kiss along her jaw, then down her neck. Weldir buried his nose in the crook of her shoulder. A *warm* exhalation fanned anywhere her skin was exposed, and goosebumps prickled beneath it, making her shiver in adoration of the sensation.

"So, this is what you smell like," he rumbled, his lips muffled against her.

"And what do I smell like?" she whispered with a laugh, utterly overjoyed by the weirdness of her question.

Someone once said she smelt of white roses and pear.

"You're asking the wrong person. I have no idea, but you smell tantalising."

He rubbed his nose up the side of her throat, with his firm and wet tongue following it. She panted out a moan when he nipped her skin, and his left ear flicked at the sound she made.

"This needs to go," he rasped, as he fisted the back of her dress and simply tore it off her.

It wasn't like in the past, where it unthreaded itself. Instead, the drag of the ripping fabric stung, but the burn was welcome against her heated flesh. When it was gone, her naked breasts moulded against the chiselled muscles of his lean chest, and the heat coming off him made her nipples harden further.

"You're starting to smell real fucking intoxicating," he practically growled, as his licking kisses against her throat quickened. They left behind a wetness that made each of his shallow pants tingle in their wake.

She couldn't begin to imagine what this all felt like for him, especially for the first time. How overwhelming it might be. But when she speared her fingers into his hair, and her nails scraped against his scalp, he offered her something she'd been waiting *forever* to hear.

Weldir thrust his cock against her hard, shuddering in reaction, just as a deep, shaken, almost pitiful *groan* fell from him.

Her breath hitched at the sound, and her insides clamped up, leaving behind a growing pool of wetness at her entrance. She did it again, raking her nails against his scalp, and the next groan sounded so desperate she moaned in answer.

She wanted to do it again, and again. The resulting masculine, blissful noise teased her to such pitiful lengths, she thought she might come from it.

"Fuck, Lindiwe," he muttered hoarsely, before snapping into action.

In one second, her underwear was torn from her, and in the next, his cock ground against her constantly. She bucked against it when it nestled between the lips of her pussy and grazed her clit repeatedly. Squeezing her legs around him, she pulled them tighter together to increase the pressure, and every time it was perfect, her pussy spasmed and started to ache.

She felt so empty, so needy, that each of his breaths and quiet groans set her on edge. His hands gripped her tighter, one arm crossed over her back to cup her side, while the other kneaded her cheek so hard she thought it might bruise. She wanted it to, wanted more.

More heat, more movement, more of those little noises.

She let out a small cry while tilting her hips back and forth, trying to find the end of his cock so she could mount it. So it could shove in deep and get rid of the tender ache that nibbled at her until she was shaking with need. Yet her clit was greedy, and every time the rim of his cockhead grazed over it, she pushed back madly.

She glanced down to see what it looked like, and bit her lip. Phallic in shape, it thankfully looked like a human dick except spectral black like the rest of him.

"Inside me, Weldir. Please," she rasped around little cries. "I need it. I need you."

With a grunt, he shuddered at her pleading, and his mouth paused at her throat. His fangs grazed over her as he let out a shaking pant. "I'm fucking *trying*."

He pulled his hips back, and just as the head tucked against her, she tilted her hips to get it to slip inside. Their different thrusts misaligned them, and his tip ground so hard against her clit her head fell back in bliss. As he prodded her again, she shoved down just as he shoved up, and they missed once more.

"Stop moving," he bit out huskily.

He grabbed her arse tighter to halt her, but she was now so close to climax that her movements were maddened with lust. She bucked, and thrust, and lowered her head to lather his cheek and ear in messy kisses.

"Lindiwe, please." His ears flickered wildly when she licked the tip of one as she ground against him. "Oh, *fuck...*"

Oh god. I'm about to—

Just as her body started to clamp up and her eyes rolled back, right there and ready to detonate, he fucking stopped moving! Quaking, Weldir shoved up, squeezed their bodies together so tightly that his cock was squished between them, and then moaned so loud that she froze.

Her breath hitched at the rich decadence of the sound, and she pulled back to see his eyes were shut, his mouth agape, and his brows were furrowed deeply, just as warm liquid began to spurt up her abdomen. At the first rope of semen, he chased his orgasm by rocking against her, while his entire body twitched and quivered. His claws cut into her skin, but she barely felt it as she took in that moment with awe.

It was hot, and sticky, and so erotic that she ground her hips into him just to deepen his pleasure.

When he stopped, shaken and panting in her arms as aftershocks riddled him, she realised she'd grown so wet that her arousal leaked from her. She ached even more than before, and she pulled back, loosening her legs from around him so she could look down the length of her body.

Eyes wide, she took in the pearlescent milky-grey liquid coating her belly. If his pulsating, throbbing cock hadn't been enough to tell her what just happened, those streaks were.

"You *came*," Lindiwe whispered in surprise.

It hadn't happened with measured control, but suddenly, unexpectedly, and because it felt *good.* And just from a little rubbing in a few minutes!

Why do I find that so sexy?! Like he hadn't been able to hold it in because he was just that excited by her.

With a half smile, her thighs squirming with her pussy saturated with arousal, she lifted her gaze to meet wide onyx eyes, as if he, too, couldn't believe it. Except it was obvious he didn't feel the same way. He looked rather... horrified as he stared down at her.

Then, in a puff of dark cloud, he was... gone.

FIFTY-NINE

A time unknown, but of sensation and intimacy

I can't believe I just did that, Weldir thought, pressing the pad of a thumb and two fingers against his closed eyes.

His new heart was sprinting, the lingering pleasure colliding with embarrassment so intense he found the organ wildly uncomfortable. If this was what mortification felt like, he thought he'd rather remain a bodiless mist entity forever.

I fucking came, and I wasn't even inside her. He'd ejaculated... prematurely. *I'm a god. A fucking god, for pity's sake, and my cock blew because it felt so good it was like my damn soul was being petted.*

He growled quietly, frustrated with himself and this new body.

As much as he knew evaporating like that wasn't the wisest nor proudest choice, he just couldn't face his mate in that moment. He was being bombarded by all these sensations, things he'd never felt before, alongside physiological reactions to his emotions. He was vibrating under the onslaught, to the point that even his muscles leapt at the weirdness.

Two warm and soft hands caressed the tops of his shoulders.

Weldir barked out a quiet yelp and startled forward, as he'd *never* been surprised before in his entire life.

"You didn't have to run away," Lindiwe said in a low,

comforting tone, as she wrapped her arms around his neck from behind. "You're also very easy to find now."

His immediate instinct was to flee again, but he shuddered when soft lips pressed against the side of his nape, just as fingertips *tickled* down the front of his chest. He arched into the touches, somehow mollified by them because they just felt so *nice*.

He also found the smell of her dizzying, and his muscles bunched with this primal urge to capture her, pin her down, and mount her fiercely until he utterly drowned in every inch of her. His drained cock swelled in reaction, and the only reason he didn't act on the impulse was because he was so powerless to her little kisses and hands, which soothed him and had his void skin cascading with intense prickles.

"You don't have to feel bad for being excited," she whispered, her melodic, feminine voice right in his ear, causing the point of it to draw back and flick rapidly. The intensity of it had an expire humming from him, followed by a shiver. "I liked it." As if she could tell he was having an enormous reaction to her, she brushed her lips back and forth over the length of his ear, with her hot breath fanning over it. "You can always make it up to me. Although... I think I have much more to make up for, many years to give back. Many *orgasms*."

Something in Weldir snapped – that tiny semblance of control gone. He spun around, pinned her arms down against a flat barrier he created beneath her, and placed himself above her with a looming, quiet warning rumble. The vibration of it was unfamiliar as it resonated deep within his chest.

Rather than being afraid, she bit down on her bottom lip and looked up at him with crinkling eyes. The softness in her gaze, mingled with tenderness and the desirous heat he knew all too well, did strange things to his mind. There was also trust, and in that moment, he didn't know what he wanted to do.

His erection demanded he bury himself to the base and pump his way to the ball-clutching, pelvis-tingling bliss he'd felt before. Yet he also had this yearning to kiss and nip every inch of her beautiful brown skin, or delve his tongue into every hollow and over every line of her body. His lips wanted to crush hers since they didn't look swollen enough from their earlier kissing. His hands itched to knead every swell of her curves, but also dive into her pretty curls until he made them messy from fisting them. His body needed to mesh up against every part of hers until they weren't only entangled but moulded into one aching being.

His heart seemed to thrum everywhere, and it was so heavy and so fucking *noisy* that it overshadowed his chaotic thoughts until just pure instinct thrummed to take over. His body was hot, his skin taut and on fire, and all of him tingled with violent arousal.

And her scent was driving him so mad that every breath in was laced with it, making him salivate to taste her. She also now smelt of him, and that satisfied a rather dark part of him that he didn't understand.

Weldir gave in to multiple desires at once.

He released her wrists so he could shove his fingers into her curls, fist them tightly, and cover her mouth with his. He kissed her hard enough that it pained his own lips, yet she didn't seem to mind as she cupped the sides of his face and pulled him in. When her tongue, rounder than his own, clashed with his, he produced a groan.

Now he understood why Lindiwe liked to kiss, why she'd often brought him in for one. It was easy to get lost in the act; the sharing of their breaths, the wetness, and even the warmth clawed at his heart.

But he was quick to move away as other parts of her called to him. Her pulsing throat had tickled his lips before, and he brushed them over it as he created a path downwards. Then further down still, since he had foolishly not appreciated her full and perky breasts earlier.

He tried to be gentle as he cupped her left breast, surprised that it was so soft and squishy, and that her nipple was remarkably firm. He cupped the underside of the other and brought it to his mouth, remembering fondly how much she enjoyed having her nipples teased.

She hummed with contentment and pressed her chest into his face and hand for more. Admittedly, touching her by feel was much easier and much more fun than by pure sight. He licked around her nipple before lashing across it, repeating this multiple times while he plucked the other. Then he switched sides, bringing much of her breast into his mouth so he could suck the hard peak tightly, while his left hand caressed and squeezed.

But somewhere else was beckoning him, and the longer he teased her, the worse his need to go there became. Her scent kept calling to him, and it made his cock twitch and pulsate constantly. He was so hungry for it that saliva gathered in his mouth and created a sticky string between her nipple and his lips when he pulled away.

Weldir didn't even tease a path to his destination.

He pushed up from her, grabbed the backs of her thighs, and spread her open as he shoved his slightly pointed tongue right into the source that was fucking annihilating his senses. She gasped in surprise at his tongue suddenly deep inside her cunt, while he produced a hopeless, guttural groan.

His eyes rolled back in rapture before he shut them at the taste of her, while his claws dug into the flesh of her thighs. His tongue swirled and drew back and forth so he could collect more, swallow, and then dip in for more.

He was immediately enamoured with doing this, tasting her, and he knew with absolute certainty that she was going to struggle to separate his mouth from her pussy in the future.

His mate tasted like a delicious reward, and Weldir was a rather selfish and self-gratifying god. A lucky male.

Lindiwe grabbed his horns. He couldn't feel her hands, but he felt the tug across the top of his skull as she spread her thighs wider and ground against his face. He nuzzled his nose and face against her clit and folds for her, and she gifted him with a cute moan, one that had his pointed ears drooping in contentment.

He pulled back just enough to lash her clit with his tongue one way and then the other before snarling as he buried his tongue into her tight, wet hole once more.

His cock ached desperately to the point that he considered fisting it just to get rid of it, so he could focus on this, on her. Yet he didn't have the strength right then to do anything more than shake with need as he tasted his mate for the first time. She felt so soft, the petals of her pussy a caress to his tongue, and he pulled out of her momentarily to trace along them. Her sweet cry every time he grazed over her clit was like a gift, and he nuzzled harder with his nose and face just so he could return to where he wanted to be.

Breathing was rather difficult, and he wished he no longer had the need again. Her pants grew shallower and higher pitched, echoing with little cries, ensuring he didn't actually mind that he was half suffocating.

Then her legs locked around his head, trapping him to her – not really, he was much stronger – as her back arched. Her pull on his horns strengthened as a loud, beautifully haunted cry sang from her, right as her little cunt tightened around his tongue. As she sweetly surrendered, her liquid coated his tongue, and Weldir nuzzled his face into her folds for every drop.

Lindiwe stretched back and arched repeatedly, helping to draw out her climax until she was done. As soon as she went all soft, he drew away while licking across his lips. He grabbed just above her knee and yanked her down hard, while this time fisting his cock so he could actually aim it.

His frenzied gaze darted all over her parted and exposed body, all of it beautiful, mesmerising, cock-throbbing. Her full breasts, her spread pussy, her heated eyes lazily looking up at him, even the line of her waist and her hip bones were given his appreciative appraisal.

Aggressive desire struck him deeper.

"I'm sorry about this," he whispered between erratic, frantic pants. "But I sincerely cannot wait anymore."

He shoved her down just as he thrust forward and forced her pussy to swallow him in one go. A crying gasp ripped from her, while his loud, quaking, grunted groan was so strong it was palpable. The fit was unbearably tight, but her orgasm had softened her against his long and hard girth, and he shoved in deep with a rabid snarl.

For a second, he didn't even need to move, the pressure wondrous. He gnashed his teeth and fangs at the utter bliss that greeted him, experiencing how snug, hot, and wet she was. How her pussy rippled and quivered around him, while her little heartbeat fluttered along every inch. How fucking tightly she cuddled him, so that it was comforting and torture at the same time.

Weldir placed his hands on the barrier, one on either side of her, and simply tried to adjust to the mind-bending, soul-altering sensation of them finally joined.

This was what he'd been fucking missing out on? *This* was what it fucking felt like? What she tasted like, smelt like, sounded like when he could truly absorb it?

He'd be angry if he wasn't so damn elated to finally experience it.

He was also trying not to release already, and she made it that much fucking harder when she finally pulled herself from her arch, softened beneath him, and then cracked half a smile that made his chest *hurt*. Panting beneath him, she spread her thighs for him, welcomed him in, and her pussy spasmed in a way that was like she was trying to suck him in deeper. He pulsated, and he *felt* a bubble of liquid crawl up his cock, and it was just enough to hold back his impending orgasm.

Until he was rushed that much closer to it on his slow retreat. It was like her body didn't want to let go, clutching him, and the tug of it around his cockhead electrified his groin. He only made it halfway before he surged forward, and they moaned in tandem.

"Does it feel good?" she whispered beneath him, just as he pulled back again.

He wished he could do more than groan in response, but each measured thrust was felling him. His skin felt too hot and tight – to an uncomfortable degree – and he was unused to the sweat that began to coat him. His muscles flexed, and twitched, and leapt when she rubbed her hands up his chest to cup the sides of his neck.

Apparently the uncontrollable noise he'd made was enough of an answer because she yanked him down for a kiss. His arms collapsed beneath him, Weldir weak to her, and he wrapped them behind her when he fell on top of her. He held the back of her head as he returned her kisses, his hips starting to go faster and his eyes nearly rolling back each time.

Good was an understatement. No, he felt like he was moments from disintegrating within her, his mind numbing with each thrust.

She threaded her arms beneath his to hold his back, and his spine arched when her nails softly bit into his sensitive skin. She broke the kiss so she could shift her face beside his, and her throaty, panting voice in his ear nearly felt cruel with the way it seemed to make even his soul shudder.

"I've waited so long for this. To feel your warmth, your breath, to hear your moans." Her pussy squeezed tight, and she sang a hum of pleasure before her next exhale was hot and fluttery against his ear. "Your cock feels wonderful inside me. So big, and hard, and *warm*. I can feel your heart, your skin. I love it, Weldir."

His hand on her hip shot down to her round, plump arse, so he could push her into each of his measured thrusts. It was all he could do to respond – that, and whatever strangled noise crawled up his throat when her teasing words made his balls clench so hard it bordered on pain.

"I'm so close." Her heels shoved against his backside, trying to get him to go faster. "Please, Weldir. I want to come around you."

Weldir whimpered, fucking *whimpered*, because she drove him so quickly to the edge that it was near unbearable.

Don't come, he mentally chanted with every ounce of will, despite his quaking shudders. *Don't come.*

Now that she'd put it in his mind, he wanted to feel what her orgasm was like. He knew what it tasted like, what it felt like around his tongue, and now he needed to know how it fluttered around his cock.

His groans were constant as he pumped harder, faster, deeper, anything to get this female to break apart. He gripped her arse harder to keep her nice and still for his fucking with mindless abandon.

And when she did, multiple sensations yanked him in different directions. Her cry was loud, tingling in his ears. Her breasts, so soft and full, rubbed against his chest when she arched. Her cunt tightened around him, crushing him to the point that every thrust was more intense and better, so he ramped up his speed.

"Oh, fuck..." he whispered against her hair.

But it was her nails, giving him the first true understanding of pain as they tore into his back, that made him dart his head forward. He bit her so hard blood instantly welled around his golden fangs and teeth.

As her insides rippled and clenched around him, Weldir gave in with a muffled roar as staggering bliss clutched his groin. His balls clamped up, and he emptied them with each spurt.

Then he wasn't quite sure what he did. How his hands moved, if he fisted her hair too tightly, or if he cut his claws against her backside as he pumped through body-tingling bliss. He was too hot, was choking on his breaths, yet it felt so good that he simply didn't care if he passed out afterwards.

His release was more powerful and intense than the first, while he was being comforted and nestled within her. Hugged tenderly.

He was also so enamoured with this, with her, utterly smitten, that when he did finish flooding her, Weldir didn't stop. His cock was still insufferably hard, nagging at him with need and desperation. His body didn't feel empty enough, or satisfied enough, and it called him to fuck and rut her until there was nothing left.

Her naughty scent still covered his face, spurring him headfirst into more, and her little cries continued to fire him up. And now that he'd experienced her coming, he wanted her to do it repeatedly around him.

He also wanted to take back a little of the control he usually had and stop this female from stealing it from him in an overload of sensation.

Slipping his cock from her, he flipped Lindiwe over, picked her up, and then guided himself back into her from behind. Her cunt easily accepted him, now moulded to his shape, and he found that rather satisfying.

His barrier disappeared, no longer needed in the weightlessness. He crossed his arm over her front to lock her against him as he grasped a breast to play with, while the fingers of his other hand dipped into her pussy lips so he could tease her clit.

He felt a little calmer, a little more rational, now that he'd released a second time. It didn't make him any less aggressive or primal as he lapped up a little of her blood when he licked across the bite mark he'd given her.

He'd take any drop of this female he could get.

His hips began a steady, quick thrusting rhythm, and he was pleased when she grabbed a horn so she could hold on to him, embracing it.

She shivered at his laboured and shallow pants against her with her eyes closed and her mouth open on cute cries. Her hips twitched every time he pressed a certain way on her clit, and he felt it resonate deep within when she momentarily strangled his cock in a lovely yet too-brief squeeze.

"I hope you don't mind if I take out my lust on you for a little while," he rumbled with a light but excited growl. "You have a god pumping inside this tight little cunt of yours, and I have many years to release." He nipped the nape of her neck. "*So many* years of being teased to take out on you."

And that didn't include the millennium before her. He had inhuman, godly stamina; he could already tell he could come over and over again until *he* was the one who was done. Which was lucky – or perhaps unfortunate for his little mate – since he could already tell he was rather obsessed.

"So, owlet, I'm going to fuck you until you pass out. Then I'm going to fuck you again, and again, until I'm satisfied."

He licked the side of her neck before burying his head against the crook of her shoulder to prepare himself for his next thrusts, which he intended to be much faster and harder than before.

"Don't expect to leave my realm for quite some time," he warned, as he pinched her nipple and greedy clit between his fingers. "I won't let you go until you're nice and full of me."

The final thing Weldir did before he fucked this female like a crazed male hellbent on pleasure was push a spell into her skin.

One that ensured he could have as much fun with this beautiful, supple body, without any breeding repercussions. So his passion could be ravenous, unyielding, and unimpeded.

You are all mine now. She had better be prepared for the repercussions of her choice.

SIXTY

Day unknown, July 2024

Nuzzling her face into the side of a firm chest, Lindiwe slowly eased out of sleep.

Their limbs were locked, his legs intertwined with hers while he had his arm around her back to hold her thigh. Her arm lay across his chest, which moved up and down with deep, rhythmic breaths, his hand on top of hers.

When she peeked open her eyes to look down the plane of his front, she froze when she saw his cock was hard. It was *always* hard. She was actually a little frightened of it, as every time Lindiwe had woken over the course of who knew how long, she'd get a few moments of lucidity before she was being pumped into.

So this is what it's like to be at the mercy of a horny god. It was like his body sought hers constantly to take out all his lust and need on.

She woke up in his arms each time she dozed off, only to be pulled under once more after he had his way with her. On more than one occasion, as if he could tell she was stirring, his damn head went between her thighs, and she woke up fully screaming from an orgasm. That, or it was his fingers petting her to alertness by her clit before he made her pussy swallow them deep.

At this point, she was ready to crawl away to salvation, where she wasn't being fucked into by a sex-crazed maniac.

Lindiwe... also wasn't all that beaten up about it. She loved every second of it, every touch and caress, every moan and quaking breath he shared with her.

The realness of it all was just so lovely that she didn't mind spending hours, or even days, screaming with abandon so long as he remained this way.

A real person, capable of experiencing sensation and proper emotion.

She didn't even feel guilty that they hadn't checked on their adult children the entire time – or maybe he did while he waited for her to wake once more. She wasn't sure. Nor did she feel awful that their babies were still asleep, floating in the ether somewhere unseen.

They deserved this tranquillity and unruly passion after three hundred years of having neither.

Honestly, she was waiting for him to realise she was awake and attack her once more, lathering her in tickling kisses and mean little nips of his teeth. For the solidness of his hips to slot between her sensitive thighs, or his lips to clamp around her nipples, clit, or the side of her neck.

None of those things happened when they definitely *should* have.

Sliding her face against him, she turned slightly so she could shift more on top of him. She expected a set of otherworldly onyx eyes to greet her and instantly narrow with violent desire.

Instead, he didn't even twitch in response.

His lips, thin and firm, were parted ever so slightly, and his eyelids, tipped with long lashes, were closed. Which didn't particularly coincide with the monster between his hips that was seemingly awake.

She looked down at his cock, admiring its strength. Long, phallic shaped, with a slightly bigger head and a slit in it at the top, just... slightly translucent in its void colouring, like a ghostly spectre. She could even make out the inside of her palm whenever she wrapped her hand around it.

She flicked the tip. *Still hard, even in sleep.*

When not even that stirred him, Lindiwe smiled and moved her hand up so she could place it over his beating heart. Staring up at him tenderly, she rested her chin on the backs of her knuckles.

His hair swayed around his tapered horns, the cracks in the segmented layers golden while the rest was pure darkness. Her eyes perused the golden bones she could see clearly, especially in places where the skin was thin, like his forehead, cheeks, and jaw. The rest of his body was similar, with places where there were muscles shadowy enough to mostly hide his visible bones.

She couldn't see his spine from the front of him, but she could clearly see it from behind. His knuckles, elbows, and even collarbones were bright.

He looks so strange, she thought as she wiggled her other arm underneath her and caressed the void shadows of his cheek.

None of his body looked matte – all of it rather shiny. There was no hair on his jaw, or really on his body. It was fully localised to his head and brows.

He's... gorgeous. In the most mystical, unearthly way.

She used the pad of her thumb to lift his lip and get a good peek at his golden fangs. He had a rather nasty bite when he didn't want to be sweet and gentle. He'd healed her, many times, but it often hurt and made her claw him in return.

Then, tired of waiting, considering she'd prodded him enough in curiosity, she poked his cheek. "Weldir."

He didn't move or even react.

Her smile fell, and her brow furrowed. She grabbed his chin and shook his head. "Helloooo, spirit of the void."

Nothing.

Panic settled in. Her eyes widened, and she sat up as best as she could in the floating nothingness and shook his torso.

"Wake up. Don't you dare leave me here in this realm while you sleep!"

It could be days, months, fucking years!

His face crinkled, pinched with a cringe, and he turned his head away. "So noisy," he croaked in a deep, sleep-laden voice.

His arms wrapped around her, pulled until she was lying on top of him, and his eyes cracked open to peer down at her with lazy lids.

She relaxed and buried her face against his sternum with relief. "Oh thank goodness."

"If you're going to wake me, at least do it around me," he said in a husky voice that was so delicious it should have been a sin.

Then he pushed her down, and she sputtered out a gasp when he made her mount his engorged cock. She pushed up and regretted it when it made him hit so deep inside that her knees buckled inwards. Lindiwe was till tender and swollen from the sex before she'd fallen asleep, and he felt bigger than before.

"Mmm. That's better."

Her fingertips dug into his chest, and her eyes squeezed shut as she winced – but her pussy betrayed her by clenching around him happily. She even grew wetter at the fullness, and she sunk onto him more, while her hips ached to rotate and tease him – and herself.

She *barely* managed to hold back.

"Don't you want to experience the real world?" she asked, wondering why they were still here even after so long.

"No. I just want to experience this for now."

His eyes opened a little more before he licked across the seam of his lips and lifted his hands to cup her breasts like he couldn't stay away from them. His cock swelled within her, pulsated, and grew thicker.

"Don't you want to leave here?"

If she'd been trapped here for as long as he had, she would've run so fast that she tripped through the portal's threshold.

"No. I just want more of you."

Her heart stuttered a little and swirled with warmth at his words. Okay, that was rather cute, but still...

"I don't understand."

His playful, teasing chuckle was more titillating than it really should have been. Weldir leaned up to press his lips to the underside of her jaw as his hands wrapped around her hips.

"I have plenty of time to greet Earth, or even Nyl'theria. What I want right now is to be deep inside my mate while she cries my name, as I call hers. To experience all my first sensations wrapped up entirely in all that I find mesmerising and thrilling in you, as you surrender to me."

A small rasp left her, and she leaned into his embrace for more.

Then the tip of his nose brushed over the edge of her jaw as he said, "The first thing I smelt was you." He pressed his lips to hers. "The first thing I tasted was your lips." His hands gripped her hips as he pushed himself impossibly deeper inside. "The first thing I felt was all of you. And right now, I'm rather obsessed with all of that. I want to tease you while I experience all of your little trembles, your heart beating rapidly for me, the way your body clings so tightly it wants to suck me in. What's a few months more of waiting, when I have you to discover?"

"A few months?!" she exclaimed.

He fell back with a boisterous laugh. "I was being generous. I spent hundreds upon hundreds of years without touch, and I'd prefer just as many taking all of it from your body."

Lindiwe whimpered in answer. She wanted to deny him for her own sanity, but he gazed up at her, all confidence, with a large grin and his face full of hungry excitement, and it was nearly impossible. He looked boyish, happy, and she just couldn't say no.

"But if it sways you, I'm happy to change my shape for you, so long as you stay right where you are." When she tilted her head in question, his face dipped in a way that made it obvious he was tracing his sight down her body. "I can reshape my new bones and make my form be any way you'd prefer, even serpent-like if you so wish it, or winged so we may fly. I can make my skin harder or softer, rougher or silkier." Then a rather malicious grin caused him to flash his fangs at her. "I can pleasure you with two cocks, or three, if you desire."

Just when she felt her insides *convulsing*, not her doing but his, she smacked him in the chest. "Don't you dare!"

He was perfectly fine as he was, and she didn't really need anything overly erotic or complicated. She just wanted *her* Weldir. It was all she'd ever yearned for.

He gave a low chuckle. "Teasing you is fun." Then he caressed his hands up her sides, his claws tickling her as he did. "Sleeping from physical exhaustion felt odd, but it was nice waking up to you," he admitted, while reaching up to cup her breasts again, and he thumbed both her nipples at the same time.

The more he touched them, the more wicked his eyes became as they zeroed in on her breasts and then where their bodies were joined, and his cock noticeably swelled in excitement. His nose crinkled, and a single fang nibbled on his bottom lip as his eyes glittered with obsessive heat.

"Lindiwe, if you don't start moving, I don't know how I'm going to react."

She could feel him throbbing within her, filling her to the brim while she was pinned on top of him.

She wanted to tease him, act all sultry and naughty on top of him, but she actually kind of worried about his threat. He'd pulled her legs in all sorts of directions or had pinned her between a barrier and himself as he'd pounded manically. He'd snarled and growled while he'd bitten her, clawed her, and had seemingly tried to consume her entirely.

She shunted her hips forward, and any tension in his body eased. *I haven't ridden him yet.* She would enjoy watching him lose his mind to pleasure as she took him nice and slow.

Oh, who cares?!

Life could wait. The world could wait.

She wasn't quite ready to stop either. She wanted to witness him experiencing pleasure, and she'd always been greedy about her own. She was happy to give back and make up for everything he'd missed out on, and more.

And I do really love the way he feels inside me now.
It was different, and so much better.

A time unknown, but of disappointing discoveries

Weldir felt a familiar disturbance, one that his mist had recognised for centuries.

He peeked open his eyes and considered ignoring it as he brought a beautiful woman tighter into his arms. He patted her curls from the outside, ensuring his claws didn't accidentally dive in and rip into the tangled strands from their constant intimate and rigorous entanglements.

Warm. So soft. He nuzzled his nose into the crook of her neck and took in a long, delicious breath. *She smells so nice.* As he had nothing else to compare it to, Weldir had no idea of her scent, but he wanted it tingling his nostrils always. He pressed his lips to her dancing pulse just so he could feel it.

His mate lay sleeping and languid in his embrace, her breaths light and lulling.

Like a persistent ache, his cock was hard, annoyingly throbbing, and he wondered if there would be an end to the torture of it. He never thought he'd feel lust not just between his thighs as a hot, pulsing rod, but boiling in his bloodstream, in his muscles.

It had taken over his mind, his wants, and desires so totally, he often mused on whether this was what Mavka experienced when enraged. An inability to stop or control themselves until they consumed their prey.

And Weldir had consumed her multiple times. She didn't seem to mind his head between her thighs constantly, though. It wouldn't be long before he was inside her once more, with her wonderful hands rubbing over his chest, his arms, his back, and sometimes gripping his arse to help guide him into whatever speed or depth she wanted.

I do like that her body is rather greedy. It hungered just as deeply as his did, and it meant he didn't feel bad at all that he'd essentially trapped this female in his realm for who knew how long. *She's the perfect mate for me.*

But that disturbance continued to radiate and call to him, and he knew he needed to check.

He lifted up slightly to make sure she remained asleep. Her eyelids flickered back and forth as she dreamt, completely out of it.

At some point he would feel bad that he was hiding this from her – what his mist had likely discovered – but he just wanted his mate to be his own for a little while longer. To selfishly have her and ignore all the things that would distract her from him.

Gingerly rolling away to leave her floating by herself, he moved to a safe distance. He brought up his viewing disc, and the face of his enemy, alive and well, came into view. Walking beside him through the Veil was a rabbit-skulled Mavka with teal orbs.

I knew I felt that soul wander into my mist, Weldir thought, watching Jabez and his new companion. *So, he wasn't destroyed.*

That was vexing – and concerning.

Even more so when he noted fully who was beside him. *I don't know her soul.* He brought himself into a cross-legged position, finding it even more comfortable than when he did it as a bodiless entity, and tapped his claws against one knee. *Is this perhaps Fyodor? I'll have to manually tie our threads, so that I can find her in the future.*

His brows narrowed in concern at their companionship, as they spoke closely as if they knew each other well. Too well.

Jabez climbed down the side of the Veil's canyon wall with Fyodor above him in a low-quality dress that flapped in the wind. When she slipped and fell, the strong male was quick to save her, and his enraged expression revealed the pain it caused him. Yet he didn't bark or snap at the Mavka, and just quietly assisted her – he even climbed behind her to secure her to the wall and soothe her with words.

Hmm. I didn't foresee this happening.

Which wasn't unusual for Weldir, who never saw anything coming. A godly flaw, but alas, something he definitely couldn't change. He also didn't know if he wanted to; divination was a horrible ability, as it took away the fun of the unknowns of life.

Then Jabez spoke her name, and it was different to the one Weldir knew. *Zyh'lah? Like the black-and-white poisonous Nyl'therian flower?* No, he pronounced it a little differently – more like *Zylah.*

So, this is why Lindiwe was no longer able to see her. Jabez had renamed her.

I should tell her. His mate would like to learn about these new events. *I don't want to, though.* He wanted to keep it his little secret for a while longer.

He is currently harmless, as his mana has been depleted. He could see the cracks of lava in Jabez's green-and-blue soul, the evidence of the ookmanik. *Which explains why he is climbing down the side of the Veil, rather than teleporting.*

A few days wasn't much, if it meant he kept Lindiwe all to himself. *I've grown selfish in my embodiment.*

Except... it took him too long to notice the breaths behind him, and how they grew more frantic with each second. Or the quickening heartbeat that mirrored them.

His pointed ears flattening and darting back, he turned slightly to find Lindiwe behind him. He'd considered ending the scrying spell but knew there was no point. The deeply crinkled expression of worry on her face as she bit her lips together revealed she'd already seen it.

"He survived," she rasped with fear. "He is also with Fyodor, which is why I couldn't see her."

She drifted a little closer, her troubled expression growing hopeless, and he snatched his naked female. He brought her sideways across his lap, ignoring the way his cock instantly grew erect again upon looking at her alluring body, and hugged her.

"Lindiwe, there is no point lingering on this. He is currently powerless without his mana, and she is safest at his side, like how Merikh was."

"But everything we went through, the horrible things I had to do, they were... *pointless.* " She wrapped her arms around his neck, while her sharp little nails dug into the backs of his shoulders. "I just wanted this to finally end." She glanced over at the disc, its edges swirling with black smoke and glitter. "If he's powerless, now is the time to go after him."

"And enrage his companion? We both know that if she's attached to him, she'll fight you, and he is still a dangerous force even without his abilities. If we intervene, he may turn on her instead in revenge."

She covered her face with her hands. He thought she was about to cry, but she drew them down while doing her best impression of a growl. "Ugh! So frustrating! I hope she eats him!"

"That would be humorous justice," Weldir said with genuine mirth.

Lindiwe reclined in his arms, her lovely backside resting in his lap, and gave a solemn sigh. Then she brought her hands to her middle and picked at the sides of her fingers nervously. Her eyelids lowered slightly as she looked up at him, her expression assessing.

"Did you try to hide this from me? Is that why you moved away?"

He winced, but he really would have preferred he hadn't. Controlling his expressions was more difficult than he'd ever imagined.

"Perhaps," he answered coyly. Then, trying to subdue her possible ire before she could lash it at him, he pulled his lips back into a fanged grin. "Can you blame me? I have an exquisite female trapped in my realm, and I'm not quite finished having my way with her."

Her bottom lip pouted forward, and she pointed up at his nose. "Compliments will get you nowhere, spirit of the void."

He hummed out a warm chuckle. "Not quite a spirit

anymore."

She rolled her spellbinding brown eyes flecked with amber. "Demi-god, then."

He leaned down to nibble at the side of her neck, a sensitive spot right below her ear. "Not quite that either," he stated while lowering his voice so it was huskier.

Elation thrummed through him when she shivered in reaction, her body easy to play with to get what he wanted. Then she wriggled on his lap, on top of his aching erection, and she was so fucking lucky he didn't retaliate by spreading her legs around his hips right there and then.

"What do you mean?"

"I may not be completely formed still, but I *do* have a physical form. I'm now a fully fledged god, even if my power is limited. That will only grow."

He wasn't stuck in some half-death; he was able to live. In that, his abilities would shift in some ways, and he was excited to discover how.

She cocked an eyebrow at him. "Does this mean you're going to get a big ego?"

"Only if yours dances with mine."

I doubt she understands that I'm at her mercy.

She had a god of shadows, of darkness and spirit, wrapped around her finger, and he was quite content to knot himself up further. She could be his puppeteer and guide him in this new life – he really didn't mind.

SIXTY-ONE

Day still unknown, probably early August 2024

The first time crossing from Weldir's realm to Earth *together* kind of felt odd. Convincing him to leave was a whole other story.

At least Lindiwe felt better after not only confronting Jabez on the ruined rubble of his castle after he and Zylah went to the village, but also discovering he'd since left Earth as well afterwards. She only knew that because their ability to scry for Zylah was murky and indecipherable, similarly to what happened with Merikh.

She didn't know how to tell Magnar and Delora the news, but figured in due time it would be revealed on its own, or it would work itself out.

She had her own issues to contend with, and they revolved around a strange entity that had never touched life. Right now, Weldir needed her more, even if he never stated so.

When they arrived above the edge of the Veil, the view of it before them went on forever into the horizon. The midafternoon sun was pleasant. Even in the forest of the surface, shielded by dappled light and much shade, it was bright enough that it was very pretty.

She hadn't expected to hear a hard thud the moment her feet touched the earth. Or to turn around and find Weldir with his butt on the ground and a pained cringe marring his face.

He placed his hand over his brow to shield his eyes. "Too bright."

He considers this dimness bright?

He blinked rapidly, trying to adjust to it with squinted eyes. "Perhaps it would have been best to come here at night."

"Are you okay?" she asked, bending over with a frown. "Why are you on the ground?"

A loud, boisterous laugh came from him, frightening off whatever birds dared to land this close to the Veil. Their departure was punctuated with squawks.

"I wasn't expecting my body to feel so heavy," he answered warmly, bringing his feet closer with his knees bent. He rested his forearms on his thighs and looked around with a grin. "I'm used to feeling nothing and being in weightlessness. *Gravity* isn't something I've ever experienced. Nor this light." He looked up at the canopy of intersecting branches as his pointed ears flicked wildly. "I'm not used to so much noise either. I... need a moment."

Lindiwe couldn't imagine what all this must be like for him, or how overwhelming it must be. She'd kind of expected that he'd just step onto Earth and be fine, like it mattered little to him and the changes would be absorbed in the manner of some arrogant, overly confident god.

His reaction is so... human, she thought fondly, as she knelt between his legs and rested her backside on her heels.

She watched as he lifted the back of a void-black hand to play with the light as it streaked across the back of his knuckles, then turned his face in the direction of a chilly wind. His flesh rose with goosebumps just as he shivered, but he didn't complain. The nostrils of his straight nose flared as he sniffed the air, and his gaze seemed to follow whatever scent caught his attention.

It was impossible to know exactly where his onyx eyes were looking, but the light wind made his long black eyelashes flutter, and he closed one eye in reaction. His hair, around two inches in length, wasn't as wispy as it was before, but it danced around his forehead, ears, and his long horns.

He reached sideways a little to pick up a twig and sniff it, then a leaf, and even, surprisingly, a rock.

His gaze was curious, although it didn't particularly appear awestruck. Just someone absorbing a maelstrom of sensations all at once and attempting to adjust while remaining overly calm.

She remained with him silently, having no need to insert herself into the moment. She'd placed herself in a way that he could lean on her, should he need it.

At the same time, she felt her heart growing... shy.

Seeing him in brightness was different. His golden bones seemed to hide from the light but also became more pronounced at the same time. The blackness of his spectral form was darker and more pronounced in shadows, yet in the light, the gold was brighter and seemed to almost glow.

It reminded her of how a set of eyes could appear so different when one was in the shade and the other in sunlight.

It also made his features more recognisable, and the man was gorgeous to the point that it was heart-stuttering. Honestly, she wanted to cover his face in a burlap sack and hide it so not even the forest critters could become lost to his magnificent allure.

His eyebrows were strong, twin arches of thick black hair. His straight, softly aquiline nose led to thin and firm lips. His jaw was broad, his chin round, and his cheeks high. The masculine lump at the front of his throat bobbed up and down as he swallowed, and it instantly called Lindiwe to lean under his chiselled jaw and lick across it.

His eyes had always been riveting, but the obsidian pools were more hypnotising than before.

And his body... Lindiwe wanted to groan while biting her lip.

He wasn't overly muscled. He had the evidence of them, but they were only pronounced by the fact that he had little fat — which would make sense, as he'd never eaten a damn thing in his life. Long limbs flexed, and the mixture of light and shadows danced all along the lines and dips of them.

The ends of his fingers were tipped with sharp, glossy black claws, while his hands had thick veins covering the backs of them. The kind that could make many women swoon.

She didn't even care that he was hairless, although she would have liked that too.

Her eyes drifted down to his limp dick and balls, haloed by golden hip bones, and it was nice to see it soft for once. She quickly darted her gaze away with her cheeks heating.

I'm not ogling him. She totally was. *He's trying to figure out life, and we literally spent however long having sex, and already I want to mount him.* Oh god, he'd turned her into a pervert.

Well... more than she'd been before.

He was just so damn pretty that her heart stammered in her chest, while her stomach flipped and knotted because he was *hers.* All hers, no one else's, and that brought on a deep sense of triumph.

No one else in the world had a partner like her, which made her feel rather special. She fidgeted nervously, bashfully even, as she peeked at him once more.

His eyes were already on her, his ears tipped back, and a lopsided grin curled his lips.

Worried that he'd be able to *smell* where her thoughts had gone, she rose and held her hand out to him. "Would you like to see more? There's a whole world for you to discover."

He regarded her open palm and placed his own in it. She narrowed her eyes on him, a silent warning not to pull her down into his lap, and he complied by letting her help him to his feet. She went to steady him, but there was no need.

He'd just needed a few minutes and was now able to walk seamlessly on his own. He brushed the backs of his knuckles underneath branches to gently lift them out of his way, his gaze upwards and drifting around.

He was taller than she expected, almost reaching seven feet, but it shortened with each step as if he wanted to match her a little better until he was just a head or so taller.

She looked at him, only to shy her gaze away with her cheeks heating. "Uhhh... are you able to conjure clothes, or should we procure some for you?"

In her periphery, he looked down at himself, and it was obvious the thought had never crossed his mind. He lifted his face in her direction and cocked a brow.

Shadows, so thick they looked like layers of material, surrounded his body to give him a dark-grey, nearly black robe that had flaps around his shoulders. If he'd created clothing underneath, she didn't know. She bet it was weightless, even if it looked heavy from afar.

"Is this better?"

She turned to him fully with a smile. "Much."

"I can even give it a hood, if you'd prefer," he said, as he made one form. The shade of it instantly hid the gold of his skull.

Lifting her hands, she waved them. "No. Just the robe is fine. It's not normal to walk around naked here."

"I'm pleased." The hood disappeared, and he gave her a relieved smile. "I thought perhaps my appearance was suddenly off-putting."

"Not at all! I, uh, actually find the new you rather beautiful."

She couldn't believe he'd think that, when she'd just spent days, maybe even weeks, riding him. Seeing his ethereal face between her thighs had turned her on so much she'd been a little embarrassed by how wet she'd gotten, especially when it was obvious he was looking up at her all heated and naughty-like.

"Is that so?" he asked with a hum of humour.

She backed up when he prowled towards her. When her back met a thick tree trunk, her spine went rigid. He placed a hand above her head and dipped his horned head lower as he lightly grasped her chin and forced her to look up at him.

"I'm finding this side of you rather cute, Lindiwe. I can still hear your heartbeat, so fast and nervous, but your body betrays you in a way I couldn't sense before."

His stupid, handsome voice sent a shiver cascading over her,

her nipples pearling so fast as her stomach flipped. Her eyes darted between his, and she licked her lips when they suddenly felt dry – although her pussy was the utter opposite.

His nostrils flared at her scent, and he released her chin to grab a lock of her curls, rubbing it between his fingers. His voice was husky as he rumbled, "You are being *very* distracting."

Lindiwe ducked underneath his arm and backed up, and he instantly frowned, bothered that she'd fled him. *It's like sex is all he thinks about.* And if she let him sweep her away, they wouldn't get very far on Earth at this rate. *Seems I'm going to need to have the control for both of us.*

His eyes narrowed into a glare. "Come back here, little mate."

"I-I was actually wondering..." she said, placing her hands behind her back while putting more unwanted space between them – for her own sanity. "Since I have a Phantom form, do you have one as well?"

A soft, disappointed growl huffed from him as he straightened and withdrew his hand from the tree. "Of course. That ability stems from me."

A bright smile curled her lips as giddy playfulness swirled in her chest. "Can I see it?"

"Sure. I don't see why not."

I imagine it will look like before. Like mist and cloud, except maybe denser.

She was half right.

When he turned incorporeal, his body – all of it visible – swirled like thick, matte-black smoke. What she hadn't expected was his eyes to shine entirely gold, or for golden streaks of mist and dust to rotate within the swirls of his cloud.

He stepped closer, despite the fact that he floated off the ground by a few centimetres, and stood over her rather magnificently. *Sigh. Even his Phantom form is too handsome.*

And if it was the same as when she touched any of the Duskwalkers' brides when they were in Phantom form, then she should be able to touch him. She doubted they'd be able to feel each other, though.

But she wouldn't be able to escape him now if she used it as a way to flee him and his touch.

"Now that you have seen it," he said, his lips pulling into a grin, "can we resume what you tried to run away from?"

Immediately knowing exactly what he meant, she couldn't help her eyes widening. But she had two reasons for asking if he had a Phantom form, and it was so she could be prepared for a little fun.

He turned physical, and she shifted to intangible. His smirk fell, and his eyes narrowed darkly on her as she backed up with a smile. When he shifted forms, she did the same, ensuring they were on opposite sides of life and death so neither could touch the other.

"Lindiwe," he warned.

"Weldir," she sang in answer.

His deep chuckle was a little more threatening than she expected it to be. "You do realise this will have consequences for you if I catch you."

For the first time in her long life, she laughed so hard she felt it in the pit of her soul. "I guess I'd better not let you catch me."

Weldir's expression gave new meaning to the description of one's gaze darkening. "Vexing female."

I have much to show you, and there is more to the world than this. There was a way to frolic in it, live it, play in it. Lindiwe hadn't done so in over three hundred years, and she'd like to do it with the being she'd waited so long for. *I want to show him how to live.*

She laughed, turned physical straight away, and waited for him to do so as well. She didn't really want to play a game of tag, or hide-and-seek, or whatever it was that two beings who could transcend life and death with their very bodies might do.

Instead, she held her palm out. "Can I hold your hand?"

He halted and stared down at it with a puzzled frown, his lips tightening.

When he pushed his hand into hers, his claws gingerly

tickling across her flesh, warmth radiated between them. It swelled in her chest, especially when he regarded her oddly with one side of his lips quirked up, while they walked together through the forest and the world he'd never touched before.

Hand in hand, together, alive and real.

SIXTY-TWO

A time unknown, but of silent oaths

Seated on the forest floor, Weldir had his side to the hot flames that reflected across his glossy flesh like rippling water. He saw it over the backs of his hands, while one of his offspring dangled from his claw tips with an adorable trill. The other, this one bearing a skull that looked rather similar to his own, slipped sideways on top of his head, rolled over his horn, and grabbed it to hold on.

The world was bright, the day early, and it was apparently spring. The middle of September or something – not that he truly cared, no matter how many times Lindiwe noted the date at the top of her journals or told him.

Time was still not a construct that interested him, not when he'd live forever. Days passed, all of them a blur, except for her. Never her.

Crouched behind him, Lindiwe stirred a pot over a small morning campfire. She'd gone to a nearby village, the name he didn't care to learn, and obtained a handful of ingredients. She was cooking for him, wanting him to experience all kinds of tastes and textures.

He didn't have the heart to tell her that food interrupted Tenebris, and he had to teleport it from him before it could enter his realm of souls. Her smile, overjoyed and soft, was just too lovely to dampen by refusing her offerings.

He peered at her silently, content that she was even there and wanted to stay by his side. Then he tipped his head so he could retrieve his falling offspring from his horn, as the sound of them thwacking against the ground was upsetting – even if they were never hurt.

He sat with them often, letting them crawl all over him as much as they wanted. He enjoyed feeling their warmth, their little paws stepping on his skin, and the way they nuzzled into him for more of his scent.

They lived underneath his robe of cloud dust, and he ferried them through the world as he explored it.

"They really like you," she said in an uplifted tone, her dark eyelashes fluttering.

"It is probably instinctual," he responded plainly. "I like them as well."

He'd taken over the parental duties entirely and secretly coveted the task. Lindiwe had been a mother to all their offspring, but this was the first time he'd truly been a father. He was soaking in as much of it as he could, even though they were often a nuisance.

Especially when he wanted her naked and up against him.

Weldir would throw them into the ether of his prism, where he'd left behind his mist so he could be trans-dimensional. At some point he'd reveal to the Elven deities that he'd left his prism. Then he'd request that they do not touch it. He liked having two realms, even if one was really just a prison he found comfort in because he and his mate could easily escape to it should they need to.

It was a safety net, even though he could transport them anywhere across the world his mist touched.

"How is everyone?" she asked, leaning back to observe the viewing discs he had before him.

It was annoying that he couldn't surround himself with scrying discs like he was within the centre of a ball, since he didn't float in this new form and the ground was in the way. He also limited it to what was in front of him, so that he wouldn't impact her view.

"They are fine. Nothing truly exciting to note, except for maybe Nathair."

Her dark, arching brows drew together. "Everything okay?"

A black tendril shot out from his knee so he could grab Astar, the Demon-skulled Mavka he'd named, when they wandered off too far.

"I'm not quite sure what is happening, if I'm being honest." He brought Nathair's viewing disc to the centre and waved all the others away. "It appears he's made friends with a human town, and they are currently putting him in some kind of dress."

Her wooden spoon clunked against the rim of her pot, and she rose to her feet, walked over, and knelt beside him. Her frown deepened as she tried to understand what was happening.

A smile curled her lips. "I didn't know he bonded with that human. Linh, right?"

"Yes, I believe that is her name."

Situated between Nathair's hooked ram horns, a reddish-orange soul flame glowed brightly. It looked like the little female he'd had in his keeping beneath the earth in the watery cave.

"It's custom for both the bride and groom to wear some kind of flower crown," a human male, whose face had a light sprinkle of facial hair, said.

Then he stepped on a wooden stool to place a tangled ring of white flowers over Nathair's horns. His orbs instantly reddened at the human being far, far too close to his bride's soul, and his sudden, bursting snarl frightened the male so much he fell off the stool and into a fence. The flower crown landed lopsided on the serpent Mavka's head, and he tore it off, petals cascading over him.

Weldir tsked. *I would have reacted the same.*

Which is why he'd hidden Lindiwe's precious soul deep within his chest – a place no one could see or touch it except for him. He didn't even want *her* near it, as it was his and he was never going to give it back, especially not after their recent heated intimacy.

"Oh my goodness!" Lindiwe exclaimed, patting his forearm repeatedly while bouncing on her knees. "Are they getting married? Like a real, human wedding?"

"Is that what's happening?" he asked, tilting his head. Now that she'd said it, the scene made a lot more sense, except... "Why? It seems rather redundant, considering they're already bonded on a spiritual level."

"Because it means a lot to a human and is our way of expressing how much we love someone." He wasn't sure if she was aware that she gripped the back of his hand and wrist. "Aww. That's so beautiful, and he looks so handsome in his suit. Can we go?"

She gazed at him beseechingly, her eyes sparkling with adoring hope. He wouldn't have denied her, even if she hadn't looked at him in such a way that his chest tightened uncomfortably – the sensation tender, painful, and warm.

As if she thought he'd deny her, she continued, "It wouldn't have to be long, and I know you can't really be seen, but I'd prefer to watch in person rather than through a scrying spell."

Weldir sneaked a look at the bubbling pot, thankful he didn't have irises or pupils to give away where he looked.

He offered her a grin. *Any excuse not to eat that.*

"Of course, owlet."

Hidden down a narrow alleyway between two buildings, Weldir and Lindiwe watched Linh walk silently, without even a single note of music playing, down an aisle of people. A long red dress swayed around her legs, and a golden tiara glinted in the sun above her black hair, which was wrapped into a neat bun. A small amount of make-up had been applied to her dark, fawny skin, making her brown eyes and full lips pop. The male who had upset Nathair earlier accompanied her down it while she held his arm, and both smiled – the human male a little teary-eyed.

Sighing, Lindiwe leaned into him while absentmindedly wrapping both her arms around his right wrist. "She looks so beautiful. I wish I could meet her."

"Why don't you?" he asked, unsure as to why she was hesitant.

He may not be able to leave the shadows, but she, who looked human, surely could.

"Because today isn't about me, or my wants. As much as I would like to congratulate them, I don't know how Nathair would feel about it." She met his stare, and the joy that had been in her eyes just seconds before was obscured by lingering pain and loneliness. "None of them ever react well to me. I just... I don't want to ruin their day. I can meet her another time. I'm just happy I get to watch, and I'm glad we didn't miss it."

He didn't know how to respond, or what words he could use to comfort her. *Now that I have a physical form, perhaps I can discipline my offspring to stop being so insolent regarding her.* He'd like to see them try to snap and snarl at him, when he had power he could now expend in the real, living world.

Since he had a physical form, his mana, too, was tangible.

He offered a distraction. "Is this something you once wanted? To be wed?"

"Once, but that was a very long time ago." Her smile returned, and it made her eyes crinkle. "I'm content with how things happened, as they were the beginning ripples to where we are now."

That was good – Weldir wasn't interested in partaking in such an event that was beneath him.

She seems... happy. He'd never seen his female this uplifted. Now that there was an absence of anxiety, he realised she'd been utterly strangled with it for centuries. She no longer felt as though she had to do it alone, now that he was present, and he could see how much that eased her.

It softened the way she spoke, the way she held herself, and even her gaze. She came across as more human, freer, but in a way that was a mystery for him to uncover. It was like she'd finally lowered her guard, or rather, had invited him to join her on her side of that invisible, hard barrier, while she kept it up against the rest of the world.

He liked it. He liked that there was little separating them.

Her white owl feathers swayed against her jaw and neck as a light gust of wind pushed from behind them in the alley. A handful of her cloak feathers were brown now. Austrális didn't have snowy owls, and there hadn't been any left within his prism realm. But it'd needed repairing, so they'd hunted for a masked owl local to these lands. Its plumage had brown and white in it.

She'd expressed that she didn't mind the change of colour and was thankful she could keep her preferred avian shape.

"Oh, curses!" Lindiwe bit out, gripping his wrist tighter. "We've been spotted. Let's go before we get into trouble."

His gaze snapped away from peering at his beautiful mate, lost in her as always, to look upon his serpent offspring. When his gaze met Linh's, a strange discomfort sliced through him. His first reaction was to shield his face, hiding its oddity from her and the world. He realised then that he wasn't used to having the eyes of others on him that weren't his mate or his offspring.

It was odd that the human had turned around to find them at all, since her back had been towards them during the wedding ceremony.

At his mate's request, he teleported them away from their location before the newest Phantom, or Nathair, could spot them again.

Until I'm used to this world, I think it's best if I keep my appearance hidden from all. At least, until he was used to existing in it and could bear the weight of their judgement or inquisitive curiosity.

SIXTY-THREE

A time unknown, but of woven threads

Curled up on a large enough bed to fit his height, with a soft and warm Lindiwe in his arms, Weldir had been sleeping peacefully. The magical barrier he'd placed against every wall of this human hotel, in some random Austrális city he cared little to remember the name of, kept out all noise and danger.

She'd paid for their stay with the gold she'd collected, which he'd manipulated into coins in the past at her request.

Admittedly, it was nicer than her tiny hut with a bed that could barely fit her, let alone him. He also didn't want to return to his prism realm; the longer he stayed away from it, the more hellish it felt. He'd never uttered this to Lindiwe, but he was now terrified of becoming trapped within it again.

Or of losing this form somehow.

Which was why he struggled to sleep soundly, even after five months of existing as he was. Having Lindiwe's sweet, feminine scent and warm, luscious body against him eased him. He often woke up, buried his face into her curls, let out a contented chuff, and was able to drift off again.

Except in this instance, a loud and spiteful offspring roared his name so loud, he was surprised she didn't wake up from the bellow that radiated within his mind. Not wishing to alert or worry her, he placed her under a minor sleep spell and pulled up a viewing disc.

Once he noted the surroundings of the violent male, he teleported.

I'll tell her afterwards. Or... maybe not at all. It really depended on what happened.

"You called, little one?" he asked, materialising on top of the ruined metal cage that surrounded Jabez's portal – something used to keep whatever came through confined until properly guided.

He was seated with his legs crossed, a position he favoured, and peered down at the five people below him.

Merikh lifted his bear skull topped with bull horns up at Weldir, his chest clad in a red singlet. At his side was a tall brown Elven female with long, white, coily hair, who wore a pale-pink dress with a black skintight bodysuit underneath. She carried a full-blooded demonling in an orange dress, whose hair had been tied back to show her little pointed ears. Zylah, the rabbit-skulled Mavka with antlers that had shrunk since her growth into adulthood, lifted her bony snout towards him as well. Her short and revealing teal dress swayed in the wind.

Lastly, and the most surprising, was Jabez. His outfit was different to what it'd once been, since he donned a dark-blue robe shirt similar to Merikh's and light-purple loose pants. Like the females, he also wore a black skintight suit.

Weldir couldn't take his gaze off Jabez, and more importantly, his green-and-blue swirling soul floating between Zylah's antlers. *I see... that's quite unexpected.*

His mate, passionate and hateful of Jabez, would begrudgingly accept this. Weldir, on the other hand, didn't quite care. This would be a peaceful way to appease their issues, preventing any further destruction or hindrance. He'd always disliked Jabez because they had suffered the same fate but had reacted differently to it, and always he knew the male would come sniffing at his mist for aid that he wouldn't give.

"So... it's true. You've obtained a physical form," Merikh commented.

Weldir slipped his unfeeling gaze to his offspring. "What is it you need, Merikh?"

"Where is the Witch Owl? She's usually the one who comes when I call you."

"You mean your mother?" he corrected with a slight sharpness to his words, disappointed in Merikh's constant wrath and general insolence.

At some point, his offspring needed to emotionally mature and settle his own anger, in the same way life had given Weldir much to reflect on.

"She is resting," he continued. "What is it you seek?"

As he spoke with Merikh, Jabez, who likely thought he was being sly, inched to the side to see within Weldir's shaded hood. He gave the male a teasing glimpse of his face, but not enough to help him decipher what he saw.

When Merikh asked to see all his offspring, Weldir considered overwhelming him with viewing discs of every single one of the many Mavka across the world. He wanted to prove to him that he knew nothing, that he was insignificant in the grand scheme of Weldir's plan, and that he tired of the way Merikh upset his mate.

But he didn't.

It was best he remained a shaded entity in the dark corner of Merikh's mind, rather than a deterrent that stood between him and Lindiwe. She wished to withhold this information for now, and so be it.

He did as requested, showing him his siblings in Austrális only. And thus, revealing that his brother, Nathair, was not only alive, but he was well. Merikh's orbs flashed with blue, and he was unable to hide how the information shook him, no matter how much he tried.

The whole situation was... unexpected, and curiosity nipped at Weldir *physically,* which was surprising but welcome – and fun. Except when he mentioned that, his offspring was a right fuckhead about it.

"What are you planning, Merikh?" Weldir asked, mildly concerned about his intentions. "You've brought your mate and someone we consider an enemy."

"You're no longer needed," the bear-skulled Mavka bit at him. "No doubt you'll watch regardless. Figure it out on your own, but stay the fuck away from me. Lindiwe too."

If he continues to annoy me, I'll trap him in my prism realm away from his bride and their demonling until we have settled our discourse.

He could interrupt their bond enough to keep his bride away, and he was sure Merikh would then understand that, although Weldir was his father, he was still a god who desired a modicum of respect. He could force it over the course of days, weeks, or even years without batting an eyelid, utterly unbothered about giving his insolent offspring some 'alone time.'

Merikh wasn't the only injured baby bird in the world, and at some point, he had to stop pecking everything that came along. He had to learn to regulate his emotions, in the same way that Weldir had to deregulate them from the unfeeling logic that persisted even after his embodiment.

Since he'd been dismissed, he faded back to Lindiwe's side, only to sigh as he stood over the bed in which she lay. He crossed one arm across his torso and tucked his hand into the crook of his elbow, then placed his other palm against his cheek.

I'm sure if I did that, though, she would think me inhuman and callous. She wouldn't approve of such dire methods as temporary isolation and imprisonment. She didn't like his morality – and often lack thereof. He only refrained from acting violently because he was uncertain of the consequences from the other Elven deities.

Tsk. How bothersome.

November 23rd, 2024

Seated on the apex of Magnar's wooden, slatted roof, Lindiwe kicked her feet back and forth, her heels going under the roof's edge. Beside her, Weldir sat cross-legged and controlled their two babies from crawling or rolling away by the use of his tendrils, placing them back on himself whenever they attempted to stray.

She didn't have the heart to take them from him when he just seemed so delighted to hold them. It was also why she hadn't given them their features yet, as she was waiting for him to decide when he was ready.

Especially when they had plenty of adult children to contend with, seven of whom – and multiple grandchildren – were congregating below them.

It was the end of spring, on the cusp of summer, and the day was so balmy it was as though the scorching temperatures had come early. It was enough to make anyone sweat, although Weldir seemed to be enjoying it comparatively to winter.

The forest within Magnar's ward thinned the closer it got to the log cabin home situated in the middle. The trees helped to keep the eeriness of the Veil out, acting as a barrier of sight and sound, while the open clearing directly around the house allowed bright sunlight in.

A small piece of haven had been created here within the otherwise nightmarish forest, and the two other houses not far from Magnar's, belonging to Orpheus and Faunus, were the same. She was aware the twins and their brides stayed at Sunnet Hill Springs within the border of the southlands, and Nathair, his bride, and their baby twins lived within the mountainside of the north.

Merikh and Zylah, and their families, resided in Lezekos, the last Elven city within Nyl'theria. She was happy for all of them, except for the pointy-eared jerk she wanted to throat punch. Although her conversation with him on top of the ruined rubble of his castle *had*, ever so slightly, softened her to him. Especially as he'd apologised for Aleron's death, and how he'd attempted to prevent it and undo his malicious mistake.

Lindiwe noticed Nathair's hands were still, and he'd long buried his serpent snout into the side of Linh's neck. He seemed to prefer being near Merikh and Jabez, perhaps because they weren't as talkative and were more stoic than the rest of her adult children, who were chattering away with each other.

Orpheus, Magnar, Faunus, Aleron, and Ingram had formed a murder of Duskwalkers. Their brides were off to the side on blankets rolled out like they were having a picnic, and eventually they were joined by their Duskwalkers. Then tails, wings, and long legs filled up much space and forced them to spread out as they cuddled.

"This is nice," she commented cheerfully, the corners of her lips curling up. "They're all getting along. This is what I always wanted."

"I'm displeased by the requirement of it," Weldir chimed in. "But I could have done all this, if any of them requested it. Now that I have a physical form, making temporal passageways is easy enough."

She muffled a small laugh behind her lips to hide it. "You sound a little jealous."

"Jealous? Unlikely. More annoyed that *he* was needed when I now have the capabilities to do much more."

She leaned forward so she could peek inside his hood. "You forget, none of them have met you like this yet." She pulled back and noticed the many dark-yellow orbs and snouts pointed in their direction. "They're curious about you. That's a good sign."

"I'm not quite sure if I want to be dissected by their gazes in blatant inquisitiveness. If they attempt to prod me, as they have done to each other, I will be angered."

"What? You mean like this?" She sneakily poked his thigh and then side multiple times, without hurting him.

He grunted. "Exactly, but I don't mind you doing it."

I think... he's afraid. Even though a little over three and a half months had passed since he first stepped onto Earth, and five since obtaining his new body, Weldir was still adjusting. He was uncertain of their children, as he'd never been spoken to in a swarm, and they both could foresee their reactions. *All I can do is support him.*

She was patient, and willing.

Out of the corner of her eye, Nathair finally unfurled himself from his rested position. He put his hand out, telling his bride, Linh, to wait as he approached Magnar's home on his own. He tilted his serpent skull up to them and then gestured with his hands in sign language.

"He wishes to speak with us," Weldir translated.

"Can we?" she asked, with a beseeching, hope-filled gaze.

His big warm hand slipped underneath her cloak to clasp the small of her back, and Lindiwe prepared herself to dematerialise. In the blink of an eye, she was before Nathair, who stood eight feet tall, if not more. He shuffled down to lower his own height for their comfort, although Weldir definitely could have matched it freely.

"For the sake of conversational ease, I'm going to relay your words directly into her mind. Do you have any objections to that?"

"No," Nathair signed, and unfortunately, the voice distinctly sounded like Weldir's. At least his lips didn't move. *"I actually like that. It would make things simpler if I could share in that ability."*

As Lindiwe pressed closer to Weldir's side, her heart fluttered a little faster with nervousness, and her hands shook in excitement. She couldn't believe she was having a proper conversation with him, or that he'd wanted to talk to her at all! He might be the first of her children ever to do so, without there being *meaning* or dire requirement behind it.

"Weldir is going to teach me in the future," she told him. "Now that I can actually see his hands, it'll be easier to learn."

She also just hadn't been prepared for his sudden return to life, and never thought she'd need it. A language was best learned when it was in repeated use.

"I would appreciate that." Nathair's orbs glowed a bright yellow before they quickly dulled back to his normal orange. He twisted to her a little more and even lowered his head. *"I wanted to thank you for all you did for me after I was brought*

back to life, and apologise for the many ways I hurt you — physically and emotionally. It was..." His hands paused, his fingers twitching in hesitancy. *"It wasn't an easy time for me. It would've been more unbearable without you at my side."*

Not expecting this, Lindiwe had to bite back the tingle of tears. None of her children had ever thanked her or apologised for all the hurt they'd put her through. She couldn't believe one even wanted to, from the bottom of their heart, and that it was Nathair, her first, and the one she'd felt as though she'd failed the most from the very beginning.

It was overwhelmingly emotional. All she could do to combat the way her heart ached in reaction was force a broken smile on her face.

"Of course, Nathair," she answered with a croak. "I would do it again in a heartbeat."

All the pain, the claw strikes, being envenomed and nearly eaten, Lindiwe would do it all again so long as it helped him.

Nathair then waved his claws in a beckoning motion, and a little female not much shorter than Lindiwe came over. Her eyes were such a dark brown they nearly looked black in the shade, but were molten in the sunlight. Her face was sweet, young, and heart shaped, and she smiled freely at Lindiwe as her set of long black braids swayed in the warm breeze.

"This is Linh. She has been wanting to say hello since she saw you at our wedding."

"Hello, Linh. It's a pleasure to meet you," Lindiwe greeted with a smile.

"Hi," she answered with a wave.

"And these are our younglings."

As if expecting him to mention them, Linh was already pulling their twins from her person to hand them to him. Nathair then, surprisingly, shoved them at Lindiwe so she could hold them.

Oh my gosh. I can't believe I'm holding two of my grandbabies! Her heart was bursting with affection. She never thought she'd be allowed!

She couldn't help laughing, especially when they both curled their serpent tails around her forearms.

"I can see you want to make them like you, Nathair," she stated warmly. They looked nearly identical, and very much like him when he was a baby. "Make sure to feed them fish until they gain their gills and fins."

"We'll definitely remember that," Linh answered with a giggle.

Then Nathair reached out to Weldir, who darted his shadowy hand upwards and blocked the serpent Duskwalker from grabbing his hood with the back of his wrist.

"Don't," he warned.

With a snorted huff, Nathair pulled his hand back to sign. *"Come now. I want to see your face."* He lowered to the side and flicked his forked tongue out in his direction. *"I should be the first to see it. Why hide it?"*

Weldir didn't like to be bested, nor did he want anyone – except maybe her – to know how he really felt. He grabbed the sides of his hood and flicked it back until it evaporated in smoking shadow.

Just as he'd feared, the other Duskwalkers came over like a stampede, except for Merikh and Zylah, who were, in general, wary of the others. Then again, the female Duskwalker just seemed a little awkward in general, even as she looked at him curiously.

She reminded Lindiwe of a wallflower.

Both of Weldir's hands were lifted so the golden bones in them could be inspected, all their adult Duskwalker children, for some reason, seeing him as harmless. Except when their brides also tried to approach, then they were quick to shuffle them back to a safe distance, warily.

He said little, just answered their questions in his usual indifferent, dull way, but she knew he was holding it in. So when Nathair, cheeky and quite used to Weldir, went to grab a horn, her overstimulated mate materialised them both back to the top of Magnar's home.

He shuddered next to her but didn't yank his hood back up. "I knew I would despise that."

She offered a comforting smile, then slipped her hand into his shadowy cloak as it opened to allow her in, and grasped his much bigger palm. "At least it's done."

When the afternoon began to truly creep in, Linh approached Mayumi to ask about the tent she'd offered to set up in Faunus' ward. They left temporarily to make sure that was done before night fell, with the intention of returning.

Now that there were fewer eyes on him temporarily, Jabez brazenly approached them. He climbed the side of Magnar's home with his bare hands and feet, as if he worried about startling them by transporting himself to their side.

Just as he neared, a shadowy tendril, rigid and sharp, pointed right in front of his face. Jabez halted, and his red eyes crossed as he inspected it before pulling back slightly. Then he leaned sideways to look at them while remaining crouched.

"Touch her, and I'll finally break my oath and kill you. You're lucky that Mavka is the only reason I have not turned my fury from the past on you."

Lindiwe expected him to grin or be a cocky little shit. Instead, his lips drew down, and he nodded. "Fair enough. Although, aren't I impervious to death? Unless you want to destroy your own granddaughter."

Weldir leaned back, and for the first time ever, greeted Jabez's gaze properly. "Your threads are woven, but I'm still a god of souls. I can surely unravel them with a little practise."

Jabez threw his hands up with a sigh. "I have no interest in this shit anymore. Trying to move on from the past, blah blah blah."

"Doesn't mean we have to forgive you," Lindiwe cut in.

Still crouching, Jabez placed his fingertips against the rooftop to balance himself. "I'm not particularly asking forgiveness, nor do I want it. I can be as sorry and regretful about the past as I want, but we all know it matters little to fix what I have done, how I have done it, and what harm I caused."

He lifted his free hand and shrugged. "However, obviously I have no interest in my war anymore, to my annoyed dismay. I come with a peace offering and a request."

"You have quite the hide to ask anything of us," Weldir stated coldly.

Jabez gave a low, dark chuckle. "I have always been arrogant and opportunistic. Merikh is unlikely to approach you soon, whereas I am impatient and would rather have my answer now. If I ask it, would you be willing to lower your ward?" He quickly put up his finger to pre-empt them interrupting him. "Not for war, but to end it. I want to replicate Spiral Haven within Nyl'theria, and having citizens who understand how to govern themselves would increase its potential for success. I've already spoken with the synedrus council, and they have agreed to it pending your answer."

Weldir was silent for a long while, perhaps too long. Jabez didn't move, no matter how the minutes passed by, awaiting an answer. The lack of one was surprising, and likely a good sign for him.

"For now, no," Weldir answered.

Disappointment deflated Jabez entirely, and he fell back from his crouched position to land on his arse. With one arm across his upright, bent knee, he threw his hand up. "Why the fuck not? Isn't that what you deities want? Peace and control, so the Elysians can eventually take back their realm?"

"Because it has never been about my wants, but my duty." Weldir interlocked his fingers in his lap and tapped his clawed thumbs together. "I'll have to speak with the others first. With their approval, then I can do so, although it would be in a controlled environment. I have yet to reveal that I have left my imprisonment, so I must speak with them personally about this."

Jabez perked his head up. "So that's technically a yes, pending the approval of the Gilded Maiden? She has awoken, you know."

"Of course I know," he stated curtly, snapping his gold fangs with a light growl. "I'm not so detached from them that I am unaware of what has happened."

That... might've been a small lie.

Jabez nodded and then teleported away, now that he had his answer. Merikh had long ago stood up, holding a sleeping Lehnenia against his chest with her face planted into his neck and shoulder. He spoke to Raewyn, who appeared to be attempting to drag him back to his family – he was obviously trying to avoid them – by wiggling her fingers to take back their adopted child.

Since Jabez had been absent from her side, Zylah had willingly approached Delora and Magnar alone. She tried to instigate a conversation herself, and her little bunny tail wiggled – as did Magnar's fluffy fox one, when he responded to her at all.

It was obvious she was becoming increasingly more comfortable with her parents as the many hours passed. *These things take time,* she thought, and it had only really been a day of true understanding of what a family was for Zylah. The fact that Delora had gotten a hug earlier, when Lindiwe still had never received one, made her a little jealous.

But not enough to quell the joy on her face.

"This is nice," she murmured. "I don't even care that we aren't really a part of it. It's just lovely to see them all together."

"You know Nathair will likely tell them of the other Mavka," he pointed out.

"*Duskwalkers,*" she corrected playfully. "But yes, eventually they must learn that the world is larger than they think it is. He's a little preoccupied, though. I doubt he's given it a second thought considering he only just came back to life six months ago and so much has happened for him – a bride, then a family."

"That's true. He likely wants to focus on those in front of him for the time being."

"They don't seem to realise how much they care for each other as siblings, and how much they've evolved that this was even at all possible. They love their brides so much and are loved in return – it just makes me so happy to witness it like this."

I wish this was possible everywhere. She lifted her eyes to the darkening sky. A whole day, from morning to dusk, had been filled with this reunion. *I wonder if we can wrangle all of them together in the years to come.*

She looked down to see Merikh being surprisingly docile as he spoke to Orpheus. Reia and Raewyn smiled brightly as their conversation deepened, then Gideon and Emerie joined in – both rather humorous and quick to stir laughter.

Emerie's light skin was covered by a simple blue dress – which was so different to the Demonslayer attire Lindiwe had met her in. The colour made her bright-orange hair brighter, and highlighted her blue eyes as she smiled at Gideon or Ingram, her partner. Gideon, wearing a white tunic and black trousers, often returned her smile with dimples forming and a softness in his green eyes. His hazelnut hair was longer on top than the sides, and even from a distance, Lindiwe could note the shadow of hair across his cheeks and jaw.

The silver rings both he and Aleron wore glinted in the sunlight.

Her eyes fell back to those from Nyl'theria.

I wonder how long they can stay here for. She had already overheard that those from the Elven realm only had a Nyl'therian day here, not that she knew how long that was.

Jabez had resumed his seat on the tree stump, but he didn't appear as stoic as before. Rather, he pensively tapped across his lips with his elbow resting on his knee, likely thinking over what Weldir had said.

"As much as I hate him... I can see that he has changed, and that he cares for Zylah deeply. Maybe there's something we can do to help bring them here more often? Maybe you could–"

Weldir gently grabbed her hand and held it within both of his own. It silenced her, as she wasn't expecting it, and she lifted her gaze to his face. He was peering out over the horizon, expression so relaxed that his long, pointed Elven ears were drooping.

A semi-clear bubble, likely a sound dampener, formed around them, giving them some privacy.

His tone was deep and quiet. "I love you too."

"What?" she rasped, surprised by the suddenness of it.

Why here? Why now, of all times?

She also hadn't said it more than once, and that had been months ago, when he'd first obtained his physical form.

"I wanted to understand this body, and what emotions truly felt like, before I answered you. I wanted to be able to say it, confident that you wouldn't disbelieve it due to my lack of experience."

He lowered his face and twisted it towards her, the sun glinting off his black horns while making the right side of his face a bright-golden skull. Her gaze bounced over his features, noting the intensity of his eyes as she soaked in the gravity of this moment.

She'd never expected him to say it back to her or feel something that sweet, innocent, and pure. At least not so readily, or so soon, considering he'd barely been truly alive for half a year.

She'd been willing to wait, even if it took another hundred years, to know just how deeply he felt. Or even for it to die out within him now that he *could* experience life and no longer had a singular Lindiwe to keep him entertained.

She didn't realise just how insecure she'd felt about it because he'd never answered her confession – until now... when it no longer seemed to matter.

Lindiwe, rendered completely silent, was unable to do more than stare at him wide-eyed and listen to his rich baritone speaking so quietly, so gently, and with solemnness.

"You were right when you said that my emotions were based on logic and thought. Now that I can truly feel them, they don't compare to the unyielding obsession I have with you, your beauty, your very soul. I've been trying to decipher it – the depth of what I've felt within my heart from the very moment I obtained one and looked upon you. But now I know, with utter certainty, it's that I love you madly." His expression grew darker, even more serious, as his hands tightened on the one of hers he held. "I've always admired your strength and have been proud of all you've done. It hasn't been easy, and I know I have much to make up for, but I'm thankful you chose me, chose this new life with me, even when I offered you an escape."

"You... love me *madly*?" was all she could croak out, since she *hadn't* been mistaken and had heard him correctly the first time. Her breaths were shaky and uneven, and her heart fluttered so shyly it made her stomach flip.

"Perhaps a little too much. It makes it... *difficult*... to refrain from touching you. I have a godly appetite for everything, and it appears it is rather bottomless when it comes to you." Then his eyelids drooped, highlighting that his gaze had lowered, and she wasn't sure if it was on her lips, her breasts, or further down. "Every time I look at you, my chest swells acutely. It makes me want to take it out on you in a frenzy." He gave a low, humming chuckle that crinkled his eyes. "I feel rather mortal when that happens."

He held her gaze, and hers bounced over his mesmerising features, while every word he spoke tended to the wounds over her heart. Those that had lingered for over three hundred years.

"You are the most beautiful creature I've seen, from this world or even my home realm. Your loyalty has never faltered, and has been as unbending as your strength and will, and I have long ago admired you for these things. I even appreciate your unfair teasing, and have become quite enthralled by it, now that I have a physical form I can punish you with. You are soft, kind, intelligent, and brave. You are... perfection."

A voice off to the side tried to steal her attention, someone laughing while a Duskwalker gave a curt growl in response.

The world had been falling away, and she wanted it to entirely. She wanted to tackle Weldir into a hug but refused to do it in front of everyone – as her intentions afterwards wouldn't be decent for their eyes and orbs.

Because now that he'd said it, Lindiwe wanted to show it with every inch of her body he so boldly admitted he hungered for. She wanted to love every inch of his new body, so he could *feel* how much she adored him, from his shadowy golden toes to the tips of his horns.

She leaned a little closer while licking at the seam of her lips.

Weldir answered her with a chuckle, and with tendrils attached to their middles, he threw their babies to the side. They squealed and then fell asleep as they disappeared into thin air – likely to Weldir's mist realm he often tossed them to for safety, or privacy.

"Come here, bewitching female," he coaxed, beckoning with a clawed hand. "Let me show you and surrender to you, as you do for me."

Heart excitedly thrumming, the moment Lindiwe's hand slipped into his soft, warm palm, they both vanished into thin air as well.

SIXTY-FOUR

A time unknown, but the end of the beginning

Weldir hadn't known where else to take them, as they had no permanent fixture that really suited both of them. He hadn't wanted to go back to the place of empty darkness he'd been trapped in for so long. So he could only think of one other location where he could ravish his mate in privacy, although the inside of it wasn't particularly big enough to fit him.

When they materialised into the clearing in front of Lindiwe's tiny home in the inner ring of the Veil, she jumped, wrapped her arms around his neck, and kissed him.

He was quick to catch her, one of his hands slapping down on one of his favourite spots – her soft, round backside – while the other crossed her back to hold her. He pulled her tighter against him, dipped his head to the side, and delved his slightly pointed tongue between her soft lips.

Lindiwe moaned into his mouth, and he responded with a soft, pleased growl.

She broke from their kiss to peck her lips over his jaw, lathering him in messy kisses. "S-say it again."

His chest cycloned with emotions, those he'd begun to understand for what they were. The painfully tender aches that hurt in a rather adoring and treasuring way. And how they were surrounded by dark, deadly flames of infatuation, obsession, and utter fixation. How he wanted to show reverence to this little female, from head to toe, until every inch knew it was cherished.

Seeing how much she adored learning his true feelings only deepened his affection for her in that moment. He'd held off, as he wanted to say the words with confidence and a certainty that not even *she* could deny.

"I love–" He didn't even get to finish.

She squealed, her legs kicking up behind her, and slammed her mouth over his once more, cutting off the words she apparently wanted to hear. She gifted him soft, warm, passionate kisses with her eyes closed, as if she wanted to just soak it in and savour the sentiment as she ravished his lips.

Had I known she'd react like this, I might have said it sooner. When he'd first started recognising it.

Knowing she was safe and that he wouldn't dare drop her, she brought her hands back to cup the sides of his face. Her kisses slowed, but they weren't any less hungry. Weldir nipped at her bottom lip, trying to stir her back into speed as he walked forward to pin his female against a tree.

"Not yet," she whispered against his lips, lowering her legs so they'd dangle. "I want to do something else first."

But Weldir didn't want to put her down. Now that his mind had locked onto the idea, he wanted to tear her cloak and clothing from her, pin her against something, anything, and slam his cock into wet bliss. He was rather single-minded about it, and he didn't give her much of a chance to combat it.

Even when her hand dived through the shadows of his robes – which he then made vanish – and grasped his cock, he still didn't release her. He did stop striding forward as a shallow exhale shuddered out of him when she drew her tongue across his neck.

"You never let me play with you," she whispered with a pout evident in her voice as she stroked up his growing erection.

Mollified for the moment, and resisting the urge to thrust into her hand, he buried his face against her ear and neck.

"I like to touch, taste, and fuck my mate." He nipped her neck to make her breath hitch as his own grew shakier just from her light touch. "I fail to see how this is a problem."

She had stroked him many times, but it was a very quick and certain way to make him crazed, ache, and turn rather feral – the feel of her pleasuring him was all it took to break his control. He'd much rather have it the other way around, drawing out their intimacy for as long as possible by teasing her before he could think of nothing else but being buried within her wet haven.

"What if I want to touch and taste my own god *before* he fucks me?"

His cock swelled, pulsating hard in her palm at her suggestion. But his chest tightened at the same time.

He was utterly conflicted.

If her sweet hand was enough to make his muscles leap and bunch with intense need, he knew he'd be fucked if she put her lips around him. The idea of watching her, as he'd done once before, while he *felt* it all, rotated in his mind dangerously. Desire clawed low in his groin until he was unbearably hard.

He yearned for it, rather immensely.

But he worried that he might lose the little control he had and hurt her. He had far more strength than her – something he'd already proven – and he didn't always know how to wield it carefully when distracted. He didn't like admitting that he was inexperienced in all this, considering their intimate past.

But... what happened then didn't stop all of this from feeling new or overwhelming now.

Even the world could often be too loud, too bright, too hard or soft. The only thing that brought him comfort was this female. He wanted her to see him as a safe place in return; he didn't wish to ruin that.

He considered not putting her down and taking over as he usually did. It would be easy to distract her with her own pleasure until she was a needy, trembling female that could barely conjure a coherent thought. Yet she looked up at him more expectantly than usual, and her mesmerising eyes – two pools of molten, rich brown – glittered up at him.

They were filled with such tender warmth and loveliness that Weldir became stuck between multiple wants.

As if sensing his hesitancy, even if she didn't know why, she cupped the sides of his face, lifted up to brush her lips over his, and then bit down on his bottom one. She brushed her hands down his jaw, his neck, and to the top of his chest until each of her fingers plucked his nipples.

"Don't gods like to be worshipped?" Her sultry voice was teasing and haughty, making his pesky ears flick in reaction. "Weldir, I want to worship you, my shadow god, with my mouth." Her lips trailed down his skin until she sucked on his throat. "I thought you might like to *witness* that."

Yes, Weldir was weak to this human, who definitely had an unfathomable power over one such as him – who also, at times, damningly seemed to know it.

He easily broke from only a little more teasing than usual, and he lowered her to her feet.

Just be gentle with her, he thought, as he watched her slowly dropping to her knees. He conjured a blanket of shadows to cushion her from the ground and placed a barrier around them so they wouldn't be disturbed. *Don't grab her hair and fuck her face.*

His fingers and hips already ached to do so.

He shuddered when she glanced heatedly at his cock and then fisted the base of his shaft. As he'd thought, having her pretty face this close to it as she licked her lips in preparation was already too much to bear. The pearlescent milky-grey precum that welled from the slit in his tip heightened the sensation of cool air mingling with her hot breath, which fanned more intensely when she leaned closer.

This had always been one of Weldir's favourite memories within his cave.

It absolutely couldn't compare to the anticipation he felt right before her full, plump lips pressed so lightly to the side of his shadowy head. The sensation was so minute, so minuscule, and his reaction was too much. With a mental curse, he wondered if caving to her was a terrible idea. Especially when she lifted her gaze up to meet his, wrapped her tongue around the bottom, and slipped it within the heat of her mouth.

Hot, damp softness enveloped him as she stretched her lips around his girth and then glided them down his length. Each inch further inside had him hissing through clenched fangs, while her lapping, soft, moulding tongue caused his knees to shake before he steadied them. Her teeth were a little sharp, but their texture was welcome, and he liked when they caught on the rim of his tip when she pulled back.

Lindiwe popped him out, as if she only wanted to satisfy him a little, show him what he *could* have, before she really teased him. She gave the entire surface of his cock little fluttering kisses, and their gentleness left tingles in their wake and felt so damn nice. Her tongue darted out occasionally, infrequent and always surprising, ensuring he never knew what was coming next.

He'd been resisting the urge to cup the back of her head, but it was impossible to deny himself when she licked down the underside of him and then over his sac to bring one ball into her mouth. He fisted her curls as a jolt shot up his cock and more precum dripped from him. She shifted to give the other one attention, and this time his lower back arched a little.

Each gentle caress of her lips, her tongue, and even her teeth when she bit into the side of his dick, was torturous bliss. Even when she wrapped her palm around the bulbous head and stroked just enough to temper the worst of his need, it was mind-numbing.

Panted huffs constantly escaped him as he refused to take his eyes off his mate pleasuring him on her knees. Watching her lips brush him and her tongue lash him that first time did little to prepare Weldir for the mind-melting way they would actually feel – not to mention how they drove his heart to beat just that little bit wilder, and his skin to become that much hotter.

He could feel need hammering in his gut, and the longer she didn't bring him back into the rapture of her mouth, the more aggressively his muscles bunched.

When she raked her little nails up the inside of his fucking thigh, the growl that burst from Weldir was more beastly than intended. His whole leg shook in reaction to that, and his cock swelled in her fist, while his fist tightened in her hair as an anchor.

Lindiwe pulled away just long enough to bite her lip up at him with her eyes crinkling in joy, only for her to dart forward and lash her tongue across the spilling droplet of his precum. She offered him a little moan, sucked the very tip, and then pulled away as her right hand descended along her body.

Torn between wanting her to hurry up, and not being able to do anything else in his stunned state but be overloaded by sensation, his expression pinched. He groaned, his cock tingling, pulsating, and throbbing in utter suffering, and Weldir knew he was moments from snapping.

The impending danger meant he had to pull his clawed fingers from her luscious curls. He almost slid them back in to anchor himself when she *finally* sunk her mouth around him again but *moaned* as she did. That sweet noise vibrated all the way down to his centre and then sparked across his groin.

"Owlet," he groaned, his fangs parting, his head thrown back, and his hips surging forward.

Then she slipped up and down him, going halfway, which was as far as she could reach before he butted against the back of her throat. She was slow at first, but she quickly sped up, her movements controlled and occasionally teasing as she constantly flicked her tongue around the rim of his head. There was a spot right beneath it that had an exhalation falling from him each time.

Don't grab her head, Weldir reminded himself, her slowness and depth spiralling him into swifter passion. *Her mouth is not as yielding as her pussy.* Although the limitations were minimal, breaching her throat, especially with his size, was likely to be unappreciated.

He'd rather just hump her in a way she'd enjoy.

He truly was revelling in this, but it was growing increasingly hard to hold back. His body twitched and flexed in restrained control, his legs shaking and moments from buckling, but it was also aggravating him. Any longer, and he was sure to lose it.

And when she answered his growly groan by moaning around him again – this time much deeper, as if *she* was enjoying it – he simply couldn't take it anymore.

He grabbed the back of her head and yanked her off.

"Hey! Wait! I was still playing with that."

She gasped when he picked her up with his tendrils and the shadowy blanket he'd placed underneath her until she was safely gripped in his large palms.

"I need inside you, *now*," he rumbled, wrapping her thighs around his waist as he shoved her up against the closest tree.

Her clothing barely lasted a second as more tendrils tore her dress and underwear from her in one go, leaving his lovely mate bare to him. Her cloak, still wrapped around her neck and shoulders, would be the perfect cushion, stopping her soft skin from scraping too badly.

"I was hoping to taste you, you know." Lindiwe looked down when she must have felt his cock sliding over her slit. She held onto him by the back of his neck and spread her thighs in welcome.

He gripped her arse to stop her from moving, nudged against her opening, and then shoved in, impaling her on his cock. He watched her spreading over him, how her pussy lips parted and stretched to accommodate him.

Damp heat gloved him so snugly that his eyes instantly rolled back when he was swallowed all the way to the base.

"Mmm, so wet," he groaned, leaning forward to be near her ear. She shivered at his voice, his breaths, how close he was to her. "Sucking me made you nice and prepared for me. Next time, I'll try to make sure I taste you in return first."

"Okay. Whatever you want," she whispered, thrusting her hips forward. "Just... hurry."

He chuckled at that, at his pleasure-greedy little mate, who was just as insatiable as he was. Then, considering how they got here, he wondered how she'd react if he said it again, now, while balls-deep inside her.

"I love you, my owlet," he stated, his voice low and deep in her ear.

Weldir bit his bottom lip with a cutting fang and grinned when her lovely little cunt squeezed him so fucking tight. *Ah. She likes it.* Her naughty scent deepened to a drool-worthy degree, and she grew much wetter. Now that he was able to feel, he was able to sense how her whole body seemed to reach out to him, and how his own called right back to give her his all.

He pulled back to gauge her face. Yes, there was need, passion, and desire, but there was also love, affection, and devotion. And... determined annoyance? Or was it a hint of playful mischief?

Her next words gave him his answer.

"I love you, too, spirit of the void," she whispered, looking up at him through long, dark lashes.

The snarl that burst out of him was lethal. He grabbed where her backside met her thighs, kept her nice and wide for him, and began to pump hard and fast into his misbehaving and wicked mate. He pinned her hard between his firm body and the tree, and she bounced from each thrust with her head falling back on sharp, happy cries.

Since she'd already teased him with her mouth to the point of madness, he knew this wasn't going to last long. He was likely to join her the moment she started orgasming.

He didn't mind.

Humour and tenderness, need and fire, created a swirling vortex within his chest. Instead of clawing into her skin when she clenched him, Weldir let go of one thigh, wrapped a tendril around it to keep it in place, and balanced himself against the tree. He rent it with his claws as violent aggression thumped within his chest and cock, but at least her sweet pussy could handle him attempting to destroy it.

There were plenty of trees in the Veil for him to claw, rather than his precious female. Perhaps they could spend their entangled foreverness leaving their lustful marks upon each one.

Regardless, there was one thing that was certain.

Her soul was his to keep, heal, touch, guide, revive, steal, protect, and embrace. It was his, her fate threads knitted to him by his very own hands, and she was adored and loved by every bit of his newly created form.

She was the flower that bloomed in his dark ether, and he could finally nurture her the way she deserved. She was his sanctuary, and he wanted to be hers. The world would have to fear him if it dared to try and harm his precious, delicate – yet thorny – flower ever again.

Because Weldir was no longer a spirit of the void.

His heart held the wrath of a *living* god inside it, and the only thing stopping him, calming him, was this beautiful little Phantom, who soothed him as much as she toyed with him.

Their foreverness, entwined in body and spirit, had truly just begun – and it had only taken three hundred human years to get here.

Not that Weldir had been counting.

The end.

Thank you so much for reading **To Free a Soul**, the second, and last, book in the **Duskwalker Beginnings** miniseries.

I hope you enjoyed Lindiwe and Weldir's story, and learning the truth as to why they were both kind of absent in the main series. There were a lot of babies to contend with, and most of our lovely Duskwalkers didn't know Lindiwe was right there if they called out to her.

Her loneliness was deep and echoing. In the future, in times I couldn't detail in this book, she'll eventually receive a hug and acceptance from all her children. I just had to end the story where Weldir and Lindiwe are happy and finally beginning their *true* romance.

They have gone through so much together. Both reaching out, but unable to grasp each other's hands. I've been so excited to write Weldir's physical form made of gold bones, and it was one of the reasons I kept writing even when I was feeling exceptionally low. That, and him prematurely ejaculating, because I really do love that in a story!

Weldir was, and always has been, so fun to write. I love his inhumanness, and his logical emotions rather than explosive impulses. He's calm, collected, but always a little confused about his pretty mate.

I'll be honest, I've found the process of the prequel disheartening. Readers aren't picking it up like the rest of the Duskwalker Brides, and many that did seemed to miss the point or were impatient. This was always going to be a slow burn – hell, it was even in the trigger warning! Yet that didn't stop people from negatively reviewing the slowness. This story was always going to be a balance of plot and world building with slow romance. Three hundred years is a long time, so to cheapen it for the impatient readers wanting a fast burn would have been disingenuous to the story. Not to mention unfair to me and to those who wanted the true depth.

I lost heart at about the halfway point of this book. With the encouragement of friends and readers, I managed to push through, but it has taken a massive toll on my mental health. Namely, my paranoia about my future now that the series is officially over. Will readers continue to read my other books, or will they shelf me as an author they read in the past once the hype of skull daddies is over? These thoughts haunt me, but they've also given me motivation to try something new, so I'm putting my hand in a certain cookie jar in hopes of a bright future.

I will be sharing some amazing and very special news soon.

Please stay with me, read my other books, and wait for more updates. I have projects in the works, one of which is happening by the end of the year, which includes a few other authors. And there will definitely be some personal happenings next year.

Lastly, I want to thank all the amazing readers who stuck with me until the very end. Thank you for keeping me going when my brain fog was so bad during my transition into motherhood, and for encouraging me when I struggled the most. I see you, and I've always appreciated you.

Thank you for coming on the Duskwalker Brides journey with me.

Also by Opal Reyne

WITCH BOUND
The WitchSlayer
The ShadowHunter
(More titles coming soon)

Completed Series

DUSKWALKER BRIDES
A Soul to Keep
A Soul to Heal
A Soul to Touch
A Soul to Guide
A Soul to Revive
A Soul to Steal
A Soul to Protect
A Soul to Embrace

DUSKWALKER BEGINNINGS
To Trap a Soul
To Free a Soul

AN MM FAIRYTALE REIMAGINING
Chased by the Fairy

A PIRATE ROMANCE DUOLOGY
Sea of Roses
Storms of Paine

If you would like to keep up to date with all the novels I will be publishing in the future, follow me on my social media platforms.

Facebook Page:
https://www.facebook.com/OpalReyne

Facebook Group:
https://www.facebook.com/groups/opals.nawty.book.realm

Instagram:
https://www.instagram.com/opalreyne

Twitter:
https://www.twitter.com/opalreyne

Discord:
https://discord.gg/opalites

TikTok:
@OpalReyneAuthor